THE DUNN FAMILY SERIES: BOOKS 1-3

THE DUNN FAMILY SERIES BOXSET

RICKY BLACK

A DUNN FAMILY PREQUEL

BLOOD
AND
BUSINESS

RICKY BLACK

CHAPTER ONE

JULY 2002

THE WINDOW of the cramped bedroom was thrown wide open, clothing strewn across the floor, a large bed taking up most of the room.

Tyrone Dunn sat in the bed, sweat beading his muscled chest, a slender woman pressed against him. He glared down at her, wriggling free and standing. Picking up his nearby watch, he checked the time, seeing it was just after 1 am.

Pulling on his trousers, Tyrone rubbed his eyes and headed downstairs. Rooting around the basic living room, he cursed as he stubbed his toe on a toy left on the floor. Scowling, he headed to the back door, grabbed a cigarette from his pocket, and lit it.

Tyrone opened the door and stood outside, staring out into the darkness. The summer seemed hotter; he put this down to the shootings and beef that had plagued Leeds for the better part of a year.

Tyrone was aware of his place in the street hierarchy. He and his brother ran a successful crew, but there were bigger ones out there, which didn't sit well with him. He wanted more, and as was common nowadays, this led to him overthinking the future, wondering how he could step up his game and ascend.

Finishing the cigarette in contemplative silence, Tyrone flicked the butt and closed the door, fixing himself a coffee.

A creaking from above caught his attention, and he rolled his eyes. Tyrone recognised the movements and took a seat, savouring the warm mug. Soon, Shardell appeared in the doorway, looking in on him.

'What are you doing up?'

Shardell was an attractive woman; tall and long-legged, with dark hair flecked with brown highlights, dark brown eyes and delicate facial features. At twenty-five, she was several years younger than Tyrone, but they looked the same age.

'Couldn't sleep,' Tyrone replied.

'Drinking coffee won't help.'

Tyrone tensed, but ignored Shardell, sipping his drink. Shardell moved towards him and held out her hand. Without a word, Tyrone passed her a cigarette, and she smiled at him. She stood by the door, lighting the cigarette, smoke wafting all around her.

'You look like you have something on your mind,' she said after a few moments.

'I don't.'

'Why else would you randomly wake up at this time? It's not like I didn't tire you out,' she said, shooting him a saucy smile. Again, he sipped his drink and paid her little attention.

'Don't worry about it.'

'Why won't you talk to me?'

Tyrone kept his steady gaze on her.

'You don't need to worry. I just told you.'

Snorting, Shardell shook her head, nostrils flaring.

'I don't know why I even bother.'

Silence lingered. Tyrone finished his drink and clambered to his feet. Despite her mood, Shardell's face softened, and she moved over, kissing him. Tyrone allowed it, but didn't prolong it any more than necessary, and she moved her lips from his, but remained pressed against him.

'Come back to bed, Ty. I'll tire you out again.'

'I need to go. I'll get a shower and let myself out.'

'Why do you have to go? You said you'd stay the night.'

'Just go back to sleep, Shardell. I don't have time to deal with this right now.'

Tyrone headed upstairs, turning on the shower, undressing and climbing straight in. He liked the water piping hot, and closed his eyes as the water beat down on him. When he was done, he towelled off, put his trousers back on, then headed back to the bedroom. Thankfully, Shardell was asleep by now. Tyrone grabbed the rest of his things and silently padded down the stairs, closing the door behind him.

As he approached his ride, Tyrone surveyed the quiet street, reflexes honed from years of street battles ready to act at a moment's notice. He climbed into the BMW 5-Series and drove away, eyes flicking to his mirrors, checking for potential tails. He flicked on his *Mobb Deep* CD, bopping his head to *Quiet Storm*, hoping it would calm the restlessness surging through his body.

Arriving at his destination, Tyrone parked, heading inside and locking the door. He didn't need to turn any lights on, able to navigate in the dark. He did this now, taking off his clothes and dumping them in the washing machine. Heading upstairs, he climbed into his bed. Tia sleepily shifted, but made no move toward him. Fatigue washed over Tyrone, and he closed his eyes, grateful that his body was allowing him the rest he needed.

As his mind drifted from the streets, to Shardell, to Tia, Tyrone's eyes opened briefly, softly closing again shortly after as his body relaxed.

CHAPTER TWO

THE SOUND of his Nokia mobile phone chirping forced Tyrone's eyes open. Grumbling, he sat up, groping for the stupid device, noting at the same time that Tia was already awake. He couldn't answer the call in time, but recognised the number as Cropper's, his right-hand-man.

Rather than call back, Tyrone threw on some clothes, stuffed the phone in his pocket, and headed downstairs. He smelled the fried breakfast long before he reached the kitchen. Tia Dunn pottered around, making herself a drink, allowing Tyrone to get his plate. He kissed her on the cheek, which she didn't return. The dirty look on her face told Tyrone that she knew exactly what he'd been doing the night before.

Tyrone ignored this, stifling a yawn.

'Can I get a cup of coffee, babe?'

Tia shot him another evil look. 'You can if you get it yourself.'

Tyrone's eyes narrowed. 'Why are you in such a bad mood?'

Tia didn't respond. Snorting, he stood and made his own drink. Sarcastically thanking her, he sat and devoured his food.

'Where's Nat?' He asked, his mouth full of eggs and plantain.

'Out. Probably getting into trouble,' she replied, her demeanour darkening. Tyrone smirked. Nathaniel was eleven and big for his age. He was lively, and Tyrone believed he was destined for big things.

'He's a good lad. I'll catch him later; maybe take him to play football or summat.'

'Nat doesn't want to hang out with his dad. He wants to do things with his friends,' Tia cuttingly said. Tyrone frowned, slighted by her comments.

'I'm more fun to hang out with than you. All you do is sulk and watch shit TV.'

Tia shot him a withering glare, shrugging. 'Believe what you like, Ty. You always do. The fact is, Nat didn't even ask about you today. I don't think he cares as much as you want him to.'

'Whatever. Why aren't you at work?'

'I have the week off. I told you yesterday, and I told you last week. I arranged it ages ago.'

Tyrone grinned.

'Must have forgotten. Doesn't matter. Why don't you go away with your friends? You could go London or summat?'

'Oh, you'd like that, wouldn't you?' She snorted.

'What do you mean by that?' Tyrone asked, affronted.

'Forget it. I wouldn't leave Nat with you, anyway. Nothing would get done, and you'd lose track of him like you always do.'

'Sorry, I forgot, you're the perfect parent who can do no wrong, and I'm the waste of space,' he snapped, irked by her attitude.

'I didn't say that, but we have different ideas about raising a child.'

Tyrone's phone rang before he could reply, which was probably for the best. He answered, keeping his eyes fixed on his wife.

'Yo,' he said.

'It's me. I tried you earlier. We need to talk.'

'I'm just getting ready. Pick me up in an hour. Got a few errands I can run at the same time.' Tyrone hung up once Cropper had confirmed, then he finished the coffee, and left the cup and plate on the table as he hurried from the room. After a quick shower, he threw on some clean clothes, picking a grey long-sleeved top, jeans and boots. Snapping on his watch and grabbing his phone, he thundered back downstairs.

Tia was still in the kitchen, now washing up.

'I'll be back later,' Tyrone said to her.

'Fine,' she replied.

'Tia, what the hell is going on? I don't know why you're in such a bad mood, but you need to fix up.'

'If you need to go, then just go.'

'Fine. I left some money for you next to the bed. I'll come and look for you and Nat later.'

———

CROPPER WAITED by the curb in a Blue Renault Clio. He was a stocky man, with big ears and wide nostrils. He wore a hooded top, tracksuit bottoms and all-black trainers. Cropper had been working for the Dunn's for five years. He kept to himself, and was a hard worker Tyrone had taken under his wing, keeping him close and schooling him.

'Where are we going?' Cropper asked, as Tyrone jumped into the car and grunted a greeting.

'I've got some pickups to do. Drive up to Beeston and I'll direct you.'

'Think there'll be trouble?'

Tyrone shook his head. 'People know not to play with my money.'

Satisfied, Cropper nodded and drove away.

'What did you want earlier?' Tyrone asked.

'Craig Hynes has been hanging around our people.'

'Hanging around how?' Tyrone felt his muscles tense.

'He's cornered a few of them around the Hood. Always while they're not working, making general chit-chat, seeing how they feel about things.'

'Has he made any threats?'

'Not yet.'

Craig was a dangerous goon, connected to Snypa, a well-respected Jamaican associated with a feared group of killers known as the *JK Posse*. Tyrone had known Craig for years, and they'd never gotten along, yet they'd never had issues. The timing of the conversations was telling, and they would need to do something about it.

'We're gonna need to get deep on this one,' he said.

'Definitely,' replied Cropper as they stopped at a traffic light. 'He's headstrong and independent. Plus, he's been grumbling about you and Mitch for ages.'

'Even so, the timing is weird,' said Tyrone. 'I'll speak with my bro and see what he thinks. When we're done here, I need you to get either Ban-Dan or Nathan to keep an eye on Craig's people. If Snypa or any of his people are around them, I wanna know immediately.'

'Got it, Ty. I'm on it.'

CHAPTER THREE

AFTER FINISHING his pickups and getting food, Tyrone met Mitch at his Moortown home. In 1994, the Dunn's had an issue with another gang that escalated. Out to make a name for themselves, this gang targeted Mitch, shooting up his house.

By chance, Mitch had been out when the attack occurred. He and Tyrone hunted down the crew, wiping them out. Soon after, Mitch was contacted by a down-on-his-luck associate, who had a house in Moortown and was looking for a quick sale. Mitch took the offer, and had been living there for the past eight years.

As Tyrone entered, Rudy was already with Mitch. He was a good friend of Tyrone's who had worked in the crew since its inception, moving up in the ranks until he worked alongside Mitch. He had no official title, but *Peacekeeper* seemed the best fit. He ensured the money was always right and handled business when it wasn't.

On paper, the Dunn brothers equally ran the crew, but to the streets, Mitch ran the show. He was seen as the smart one that made plans, and Tyrone — who enjoyed getting his hands dirty — was seen as a thug, who handled security and pickups, hitting hard against anyone who attempted to go against the crew.

They converged in the kitchen, the door behind them wide open.

Mitch had a beer in his hand, as did Rudy. He was well-built, shorter than Tyrone, and bald-headed with a tidy goatee and the same sharp features Tyrone possessed. Rudy was a few inches shorter than Tyrone and Mitch, and had a wiry build with corded muscle.

As both men smiled at him, Tyrone took a moment to look between the pair, hard-faced and unsmiling. He grabbed a bottle, opened the beer, and took a long pull before taking a seat. His phone rang, but when Tyrone realised Shardell was calling, he ignored it. Mitch noticed, smirking.

'Which of your women is trying to get to you?'

Tyrone glowered as Rudy chuckled.

'She's a pain. I swear, I'm gonna cut her off if she carries on.'

'You're not cutting off anyone, bro. You're as hooked on these women as they are on you. You can't quit them.'

'Bollocks. I can move on any time I like,' said Tyrone defensively, frowning at his brother. 'When are you settling down, anyway? Are you waiting for Rudy to declare his love or summat?'

Rudy flipped his middle finger at Tyrone, still smiling, happy to let the brothers go back-and-forth.

'Anyway, what were you talking about before I came over?' Tyrone asked. The pair had been hanging out before he arrived, and he was curious about the discussion.

'Nothing important. Just chit-chat,' said Mitch.

'If it's business, I wanna know what's going on,' Tyrone insisted, knowing how cagey his brother could be.

'Honestly, there's nothing to say, bruv. If there was, you'd be the first to know.'

Rudy nodded in agreement, and Tyrone again shot both men a look, before he changed the subject.

'I delivered a few late drop-offs to Cassim,' he started. 'He said he'd speak to you about it later, Rudy.'

'Yeah, he sent me a text. That's cool.'

'Any problems collecting?' Mitch asked. Tyrone shook his head.

'Everyone paid. A few are getting a bit too frequent with the late payments. We need to stamp that out.'

Mitch scratched his chin, putting his empty bottle on the kitchen sink.

'We'll cross that bridge when we come to it. For now, we'll keep an eye on them.'

Tyrone shook his head. He didn't think keeping an eye on late-payers was the answer. It was a sign of disrespect and would fester if it wasn't handled.

'That's not enough. We look soft, and that brings me onto the next thing. Craig's sniffing around our people.'

Rudy and Mitch shared a look. Tyrone picked up on it, eyes narrowing when they didn't immediately clarify.

'What's going on?'

Rudy sipped his beer before he spoke.

'Craig reached out to me personally.'

'Saying what? Why did no one tell me?' Tyrone's voice rose.

'We were waiting for the right time. It was a general chat, but he was fishing, seeing if I was happy working for you,' said Rudy.

'Is that all he said?'

'Pretty much. He warned me about keeping my mouth shut. Not directly, but, it was implied.'

Tyrone mulled this over, still annoyed that they hadn't spoken with him.

'Ty, I know what's going through your mind, but I wasn't trying to keep shit from you. We wanted to see if it became something,' said Rudy.

Mitch lit a cigarette and cut in. 'We're having our best year yet. We're low on the police radar, and we've done well to stay out of the mix.'

Again, Tyrone shook his head. 'You're missing the point. This isn't about Craig; it's about the people he works for. Snypa is probing, and if we don't act, we're gonna look weak.'

Mitch remained impassive. 'If Craig or Snypa dare make a move, we'll crush them. Until then, we need to avoid making waves — the streets are still tetchy after all the drama. People just wanna quietly make money.'

Smiling, Tyrone nodded. He knew how stubborn his brother could be. Mitch was set in his ways, and being older, always expected to get what he wanted. Despite the apparent subservience, Tyrone was already planning his moves. He didn't intend to wait around to be picked off by anyone.

———

TYRONE HUNG OUT A LITTLE LONGER, then left, looking at his phone as he climbed into his car, debating whether to go home. Starting the engine, he remained in place, his mind buzzing. Finally, he called Shardell.

'I'm on my way. Have a cuppa ready for me.'

CHAPTER FOUR

TWO DAYS LATER, Tyrone and Rudy went for drinks. He'd kept his moves to himself during that time, the streets as quiet as Mitch had mentioned. Other than posturing and people trying to show off in the hot weather, nothing had transpired.

It was early evening, and the pair sat outside a pub. Tyrone's eyes gleamed as he scoped various women in the multitude of people, holding eye contact with a few.

'Have you heard anything else from Craig?' He asked, sipping his beer. Rudy shook his head.

'Nope, nothing since the last time.'

Tyrone leaned forward, elbows on his knees, looking into the distance.

'Just thought I'd check, seeing as you lot don't tell me anything.'

Rudy sighed. 'C'mon, Ty. Don't be like that. We weren't keeping it from you.'

Tyrone straightened, eyes boring into his friend's, instantly snapping out of his reverie. 'It's done. If he reaches out, I want you to play along.'

'How far do you want me to take it?'

'Make it sound like you're receptive to switching teams, and take that as far as you need to. I'll let Mitch know what the skinny is.'

'You haven't spoken with him yet?' The worry on Rudy's face further annoyed Tyrone.

'Listen, we *both* run the crew. I'm running it by him as a courtesy. The same way you lot kept key info from me, works both ways. Get it?'

'Don't be like that, Tyrone. I'm just saying. It's a big move, and I don't want Mitch having me taken out because he thinks I'm snaking the crew.'

'I'll talk to him. It's fine.' Tyrone dismissively waved his hand. Rudy nodded, knowing that the matter was settled.

'What's the next step then? I know you're planning something big,' Rudy pressed.

Tyrone grinned.

'You'll have to wait and see. I'll bring you in when I need to.' Tyrone's eyes flitted toward a bottle blonde in a vest top and cut-off shorts. 'I'll be back in a minute.'

Rudy chuckled to himself as Tyrone approached the woman.

———

TYRONE WOKE EARLY the next day. He'd flirted with a few women at the pub and taken the number of one, but went no further. He traipsed downstairs, grinning when he saw his son, Nathaniel, eating in the kitchen. He tussled Nathaniel's hair, grabbing a cup and spooning coffee into it.

'Where's your mum?'

'She went out, but I didn't wanna go with her. Think she went shopping,' said Nathaniel. Tyrone nodded, still smiling.

'Look at you, Nat. Go on, stand up.'

Nathaniel rose to his feet, his head reaching his father's chest as he looked into Tyrone's eyes.

'You've grown,' Tyrone went on, 'and so have these!' He squeezed his son's bulging biceps, smile widening. Nathaniel chuckled, looking at the ground, hiding his own bashful grin. 'Go on, sit down, son. Eat.'

Nodding, Nathaniel returned to his breakfast.

'I'm sorry I haven't seen you much lately,' he said, reflecting on his conversation with Tia. 'Things have been mad out there lately, and I have to keep them in line.'

Nathaniel nodded, munching his toast. Tyrone noticed his shoulders slumping, though, and it tore away at him. At times, he wasn't sure he was doing the right thing with his son, but he had little to guide him. His father had left him, Mitch and their mum when they were kids, and they'd had to make their own way in the world, battling for everything they had. He didn't know what to think of a son that genuinely wanted him around, but he didn't like the thought of disappointing him.

'Just . . . make sure you keep training hard when I'm not around, Nat. And don't just be building show muscles to impress the girls. You can't slip up. The streets are waiting for that, and they'll tear you apart if you're not prepared. Get me?'

'I know, dad. I've been doing exercises every other day. I've even got Cam doing press-ups and sit-ups.' Nathaniel intentionally avoided responding about girls, but his flushed cheeks were telling.

Tyrone sipped his drink.

'Good. I'm gonna finish my coffee, then we'll get in a workout. Go let your food settle for a bit.'

———

WHEN TYRONE WAS READY, they headed to the garage, where he'd set up a makeshift gym, with weights, a heavy bag, a bench press, barbell and several exercise mats. Tyrone immediately noticed that several of the larger weights were askew. He glanced at Nathaniel, who froze.

'Have you been messing with the big weights?'

Sighing, Nathaniel nodded. Tyrone shot him a hard look.

'You're eleven, Nat. Give your body time to grow before you get on them. They're too big for you right now.'

'I could almost lift one,' Nathaniel protested.

'Did you hear what I said?'

'Yeah, dad.'

'Good.'

They began their workout, and Tyrone was pleased to see Nathaniel keeping up with the pace and intensity.

'Who are you chilling with at the moment? You mentioned Cam earlier.'

'Yeah, me and Cam are tight. There's a few other guys, but it's mostly me, Cam, and Darius.'

Tyrone scratched his head, taking a break from his latest exercise.

'Is that Two-G's son?'

Nathaniel nodded.

'Yeah. The one you told me to look out for at school.'

'Good. Two-G's alright,' said Tyrone. 'What else is going on? You after any girls? Bet that's why you're training so hard.'

Nathaniel shook his head.

'I'm not!'

'Why did you react so quickly? Who are you after?' teased Tyrone.

'No one! I swear down,' said Nathaniel.

'For now. Soon, you won't be able to stop thinking about them. When that happens, be careful not to go too far with them; otherwise, you'll get in trouble. Got it?'

'Got it, dad. I'll be alright.'

'Good. Grab those weights, then. We've rested long enough.'

Tyrone's phone rang a while later. He instructed Nathaniel to do some press-ups while he answered.

'Cropper, what's going on?'

'Just checking in. Did what you said, and spoke to a few people about Jamar, and he's apparently not happy.'

'For real?' After meeting with Rudy and Mitch, Tyrone had ordered his crew to dig into Craig's people. He knew Jamar was someone Craig kept close, meaning he would have access to him.

'He's feeling unloved and left out. A few people are saying the same thing, and they're not people prone to telling tales.'

Tyrone grinned, his eyes on his son, pleased to see he wasn't slouching with his form.

'That's our way in then. Find out where Jamar hangs out.'

'Will do. Get at you later.'

Tyrone hung up, grabbing some water before re-joining his son.

———

BY THE TIME Tia came back, Tyrone had seasoned some meat and was in the process of preparing dinner. He poured her some wine and, after they had eaten, sat to watch a football game with Nathaniel, who smiled widely throughout.

When Tia got up to go into the kitchen, Tyrone went with her, snuggling her from behind, kissing the back of her neck. Tia relaxed at first, then stepped away, breathing hard.

'Don't even start,' she warned. 'Go to one of your other women if you're after that.'

'You're being daft,' said Tyrone. Tia shook her head, not even looking at him as she added a teabag to a chipped blue cup.

'You're the daft one if you think I don't know what you're out there doing.'

Ignoring this, Tyrone moved closer, blocking her path.

'Tia, you're my wife, and I love you. That's the only thing you need to concern yourself with. You and Nat are the most important things in the world,' he softly said. This time when he kissed her, Tia didn't pull away.

CHAPTER FIVE

DAYS LATER, Tyrone sauntered toward the entrance of a club on Friday night. Two burly bouncers were in the middle of denying entry to a loud group of young men. One of them shot a dark look at Tyrone, barring his path.

'Where do you think you're going?'

Before Tyrone could respond, the other bouncer stepped in.

'He's good. Let him past.'

'Good looking out, Adam.' Tyrone grinned and slipped the man twenty pounds. He was a former bare-knuckled fighter who wore the scars from his previous profession, with his cauliflower ears and crooked nose. Adam smirked, pocketing the money with thanks.

Inside, a UK garage act was performing, but it wasn't one Tyrone was familiar with. The skinny white DJ accompanying him was more recognisable, but he still couldn't put a name to him. Tyrone wasn't the biggest music guy. He liked hip hop, but he could see why people in the vicinity were dancing and smiling to the energetic beat and lyrics.

Tyrone moved through the crowd, giving several women a once-over. Soon, he saw the person he'd come to see. Cropper's intel had proved correct. Jamar sat amongst a group of people, a morose expression on his thin face. The group was mixed, and the smattering of women hanging around weren't paying attention to Jamar, which surprised Tyrone. Jamar was slender and wore glasses, but he wasn't bad looking. He appeared to lack confidence, though, and they sensed this.

Tyrone grinned to himself. There was an easy way to play this, and he didn't need to rush it.

Heading to the bar, he ordered a beer, moving through the crowds again and approaching Jamar. When Jamar noticed Tyrone, he visibly tensed.

'You know who I am then?' Tyrone asked, his voice carrying over the music. A few of the group glanced over, but quickly lost interest.

Jamar nodded, his grip on his glass of brown liquor tightening. 'I don't want any trouble.'

'What is it you *do* want?'

The question stumped Jamar, as Tyrone had assumed it would. He sipped his beer.

'When you figure it out, or want to chat, come and see me. I'll hang about for an hour.' Tyrone moved away. He finished his beer and ordered another, making small talk with various people and having a dance, shimmying between two dark-haired white women in clinging leather outfits.

Jamar finally approached when Tyrone was getting a phone number from one of the giggling women.

'What's this all about?' He asked, eyes flitting between Tyrone and the women.

'I guess you're ready to talk then. Ladies, this is Jamar. He's a proper big deal in Leeds; can get you whatever you want. Jamar, talk to the women.'

Tyrone did his best to wingman Jamar, but his shyness quickly put off the women, and they moved away. Tyrone resisted the urge to laugh at the devastation on Jamar's face. He led the man outside, and they walked a little down the road.

They stood in a back alley. At the far end, a thoroughly drunk man urinated against the wall. He zipped up his trousers when he finished and tottered past the pair without shame.

Jamar still looked nervous, unable to meet Tyrone's eyes. Tyrone reached for a pack of cigarettes, the movement making Jamar jump. Tyrone didn't comment, offering him a cigarette, then lighting it for him. The gesture seemed to relax Jamar, and he took a deep breath.

'I'm glad you came to speak to me.'

'I still don't know why you wanted to,' said Jamar, closing his eyes and savouring the smoke.

'It's good that things in the streets are so quiet now. For a while, it got a bit mad.'

Mad was an understatement. Tyrone was in the know, but even he was unsure of the exact cause of the recent wars. There had been building tension between several gangs with West-Indian roots, and the local English-born gangs. Jealousy on both sides over money and market share, combined with loosely related scuffles involving various women, ratcheted this in a significant way, with deaths on both sides, the most high profile of which being a high-ranking Yardie known as *Leader*.

'It still is,' Jamar replied, his jitteriness returning. Tyrone smirked.

'You don't need to be so nervous.'

'I'm not really trying to get my head kicked in.'

'You wouldn't have come outside with me if you thought I was gonna do that,' said Tyrone.

'I didn't think you'd give me a choice if we're being honest.'

Tyrone didn't immediately respond, letting Jamar stew.

'I've heard good things about you. Heard you keep to yourself and that you work hard. Craig doesn't know how to reward that.'

Again, Jamar tensed.

'I've known Craig a long time.'

'So have I. He's greedy and out for himself.'

'I can't say anything about that,' said Jamar.

'I think you can. You're smart, and I think you, better than anyone, know exactly what I'm talking about.'

Jamar's eyes flitted from Tyrone's to the floor. Again, Tyrone waited, finishing his cigarette and flicking the butt to the floor. Spotting a woman he knew walking down the nearby road, Tyrone called her over. They spoke for a minute, before he told her he would come and look for her soon. Turning his attention back to Jamar, Tyrone noted how hungrily his eyes followed the woman.

'I think there's a way we can work together.'

'How?' Jamar dreamily responded, his imagination holding his attention.

'If you're interested, meet me tomorrow night. I'll give you the address.'

Jamar's eyes narrowed.

'How do I know you're not trying to set me up?'

'Because you're smart enough to know that if I was, I'd just break both of your legs right now.' Tyrone stepped towards Jamar, who instantly moved back. 'If I did, no one would stop me. They wouldn't even call you an ambulance.'

Jamar audibly swallowed, the threat doing its job. Tyrone patted him on the back, making him jump.

'C'mon, mate. Let's get you another drink.'

THEY HEADED BACK INSIDE. Tyrone had a few drinks, flirting with several more women around Jamar, noting the man watching with a forlorn expression on his face.

Tyrone was charming a mixed-raced girl, eyes drifting to her prominent chest as they spoke, when he was shoved from behind. Righting himself, he saw a stocky man with peanut butter-shaded skin and closely cropped hair.

'Are you taking the piss?' He snarled.

Tyrone glanced down at his designer top, eyes narrowing when he realised his beer had been spilt down it. Glancing back at the man, he repeated the question back to him.

'Are *you* taking the piss?' He dabbed the stain with his thumb.

'Do you think you can just flirt with my girl?' The man snapped.

'Baby, it wasn't like that. We were just talking,' she pleaded.

'It was definitely like that, mate,' taunted Tyrone. 'I wouldn't waste my time talking to a woman I wasn't going to fuck.'

Jamar hung back, tense from the exchange, not wanting to get involved and set off either man.

'You're not gonna disrespect me like that and get away with it. Step outside,' the man said.

Tyrone's nostrils flared. 'Why go outside?' He pushed the man, knocking him back. The man lunged forward with a right hand that Tyrone ducked under, swinging his beer bottle and crashing it into the man's temple.

Tyrone stood over him, the smashed bottle in his hand, dropping it beside him. He ignored the screams of the man's girlfriend as the bouncers swarmed. Calming down, Tyrone allowed Adam to lead him from the club without further issue, exchanging a final look with Jamar as he did so.

CHAPTER SIX

'WHAT THE HELL DO YOU WANT?'

Tyrone grinned at Shardell. She stood on her doorstep, arms folded, glaring out at him.

'I'm here to see you, obviously. Haven't you missed me?'

'You've been ignoring my calls for like a week. I can't believe you're just brazenly turning up like this,' said Shardell, her eyes hard.

'I wanted to see you. I didn't want to talk on the phone. You know how things get for me. I'm out there in the world, but I'm here for you whenever I can. Just like this.'

As always, Shardell visibly softened at his words.

'I just don't want you to take me for granted,' she said, her voice shaky.

'I won't, but like I said, it's deep out there. I don't work a nine-to-five, and you know that.'

Shardell nodded, hanging her head. Tyrone tilted her chin, so he was looking at her, gazing into her eyes.

'Are you going to let me in, or do you want me to go?'

Wordlessly, she stepped aside. Tyrone entered the living room, flopping down on the sofa, glancing at the action figures and other toys in the corner of the room.

'Do you want a drink?' Shardell asked.

'Yeah. Summat strong if you've got it,' replied Tyrone.

'I've got some brandy you left, if you want that.'

'Sounds good.'

After finishing his drink, Tyrone again gazed at Shardell. She sat in an armchair, rubbing her arms. Music played in the background. Tyrone didn't recognise the R&B singer.

'Who's this?' He asked, motioning to the hi-fi.

'*Tweet*,' Shardell replied.

'Never heard of her.'

'Seriously? She's amazing,' Shardell gushed. Tyrone tuned her out as she spoke about the singer.

'Tell me more about her later. Come and sit next to me. I don't know why you're sitting all the way over there.'

Soon, Shardell sat on his lap, allowing his hands to roam over her body as they passionately kissed. Amid the heated session, a knock on the door stilled them.

'Who the hell is that?' Shardell climbed from his lap, straightening her clothes and smoothing her hair. Tyrone followed, a small smile tugging the corners of his mouth. Positioning himself behind her, he watched as she opened the door to Jamar.

'Who are you?' She asked. Jamar struggled to meet her eyes, tongue-tied and tripping over his words. Tyrone took pity on him and gently moved Shardell, allowing him to come in.

'Make yourself comfortable. Shardell will get you a drink,' said Tyrone. 'Shardell, this is my mate, Jamar. Jamar, this beautiful woman is Shardell.'

'Nice to meet you,' said Jamar quietly. Shardell ignored him, glaring at Tyrone.

'What the hell is this?' She snapped. Tyrone signalled to Jamar.

'Go and sit. I'll be with you in a minute.'

'Are . . . erm . . . are you sure?' said Jamar.

'Yes, now go.'

Tyrone led Shardell upstairs to her bedroom, closing the door.

'What the fuck are you playing at? This is my house, Ty. My son is sleeping here, and you think it's acceptable to do business here and invite strangers over?'

'It's no big deal. Jamar is cool, and look at him. He's soft. I need to chat with him, and we're gonna hang out for a bit. That's it. Your kid's fast asleep, and we're not gonna wake him up, okay?' Before Shardell could answer, Tyrone gathered her in his arms, giving her another deep kiss. 'Can you do me this favour?'

It took a few more kisses, but Shardell sighed, pulling away from him.

'Guess I'd better introduce myself properly,' she said.

Shardell refreshed Tyrone's drink, pouring one for Jamar. She made conversation with him and seemed in a better mood, but Jamar still seemed uneasy. Despite his unease, he stared at Shardell every moment he could, trying and failing to be subtle.

After a while, Tyrone reached into his pocket, pulling out a baggie full of white powder.

'Who wants a bump?' He asked.

It took little effort to persuade the pair, who snorted a few lines off the coffee table. They quickly relaxed, starting to enjoy one another's company. The conversation nicely flowed, the pair laughing and joking like they were old friends. Tyrone watched with a smirk. It vanished when he glanced to the corner of the room again, noting Shardell's son's toys. He didn't say anything, but used some kitchen roll to clean the cocaine residue from the table.

'This thing you were saying the other night about Craig . . . what did you mean by it?' Jamar asked after a while, wiping his nose and sniffing. Tyrone wasn't sure if he was a regular drug taker, but the potent cocaine had done its job. Shardell danced nearby, hips popping as she shimmied to the beat. Jamar was managing to avert his eyes more successfully, Tyrone reasoned. Having been caught gawping a few times, he clearly didn't want to run the risk again.

'Chill for a bit, Jamar. We'll get back to that soon enough, but we're just relaxing for now,' said Tyrone. After a few minutes, he slid to his feet, taking Shardell by the hand and leading her into the kitchen. Once he did, she pushed him against the wall, pressing her body against his, biting his lip in her haste to stick her tongue down his throat. Tyrone held her close, then pulled her away by her hair, savouring her hiss of desire.

'We'll get to this later,' he said, his voice ragged with passion. 'I need you to do me another favour.'

'What is it?'

'Take Jamar upstairs.'

Shardell frowned. 'What for?'

'You know what for . . . he likes you. Just take him to your room and make him happy.'

Tyrone waited a beat, knowing the risk and how easily this could blow up in his face. The frown on Shardell's face flitted to stunned shock, then almost immediately to rage.

'Who the fuck do you think you are?' She thundered. 'More importantly, who the hell do you think I am? You think I'm some slag you can whore out to your mates?'

Tyrone expected the anger. This had been the plan since he'd spoken with Cropper, and he'd had plenty of time to formulate a counter-response to her fury.

'I need you,' he replied.

'Are you stupid? You *need* me to fuck another man?' Shardell stepped away, folding her arms and scowling.

'He doesn't look it, but Jamar has some big-time connections. You know what that means? We keep him sweet, and I make some big moves. More money, fewer problems.' He saw her weakening, continuing to talk. 'We can stop sneaking around in the shadows . . . look at getting a nice place together. Don't you want that? Don't you want me?'

The pair stared at one another, and Tyrone fought to keep his expression neutral. He had other women he could call on, but none would be any easier to convince than Shardell. There was also the risk that he would overplay his hand with Jamar if he had to try it with another woman.

The moment lingered, and just as Tyrone was ready to give up, Shardell sighed. She moved to make another drink, downing it.

'I need another line.'

Tyrone laid out another line of cocaine, which she snorted off the kitchen counter. Without a word, she sashayed into the living room and took Jamar by the hand.

'Come with me. I want to show you something upstairs.'

Stunned, Jamar made a barely decipherable noise, wide eyes flitting to Tyrone's in alarm. Tyrone grinned, and Jamar allowed himself to be pulled from the room. As Shardell led him away, she mouthed the words *I love you* to Tyrone. He returned a warm smile, but once she was out of sight, the smile turned cold and hard.

Tyrone made another drink, ringing Cropper to check-in. Cropper asked about Jamar, but Tyrone said he had it in hand before hanging up. A few more people tried to ring him, but he put his phone on silent, built and lit a spliff, turned on the television and, after trying and failing to find a football match, settled for MTV Base.

Soon, Shardell and Jamar came back downstairs. Jamar wore a goofy smile, looking more relaxed than Tyrone had ever seen him.

'Give us a few more minutes,' he said to Shardell, who was smoothing her hair. She hesitated for a second, then did as he asked.

'Ty . . . I . . .' Jamar started. Tyrone shook his head.

'I want us to work together. Craig treats you like shit, and you deserve better. You deserve more respect.'

Jamar looked terrified. 'Craig's a psycho. He'll kill me if I move against him.'

'Anyone can be taken out. If we do it right, nothing can go wrong. I just need you to trust me and do what I say.'

Jamar looked past Tyrone to the kitchen, brow furrowing as he considered the options. After a moment, he nodded.

'Fine. I'm in. You need to look after me, though. If anyone finds out I'm dealing with you, I'm finished.'

Tyrone grinned.

'You have my word. I'll take good care of you. Now, let's get this girl back in, and you can tell me what you know.'

CHAPTER SEVEN

JAMAR SHARED as much as he could about Craig and how he did business. Mostly, he taxed smaller dealers for protection money, along with all the bits he did for Snypa and Trevor. Tyrone's main point of interest was the side deals Craig was doing. He had dealings with a Polish man who lived and worked in Beeston.

According to Jamar, Craig confessed to this when the pair had been drinking. Tyrone knew of the polish man, who went by the name *Piotr*. Though he kept his plan from Jamar, he had something in play.

———————

PIOTR WAS HOME, relaxing on his plush blue sofa and watching a movie on his widescreen television, when his door was kicked open. He jumped to his feet and reached for a knife on the nearby coffee table, but he wasn't quick enough. Tyrone closed the distance and socked him in the face, sending the large man stumbling back. He then kicked his knee and dropped him with a vicious body shot and a hook to the jaw. Pulling his gun, he aimed it at Piotr.

'I've heard a lot about you,' he said, grinning at the man through the holes in his balaclava. 'Heard you're the man to know around here.'

Piotr sat up, grimacing, wiping his mouth and glaring up at Tyrone. 'What is this about?'

'This is about you paying up. I know you've got stuff in the house, and I want it.'

Piotr shook his head. 'Whoever told you this is lying. Only a fool keeps things in the house.'

'If you don't, I'm gonna have to trash the place and hurt you. If there's something here, I'll find it,' Tyrone warned. Piotr's glare remained in place, but he remained still.

'Who told you to come here?'

'Why does that matter?' Tyrone played along. 'Are you saying they gave me the wrong info?'

'Yes.'

'I don't think you're being honest. They told me all about you. You like boxing. You even took it up for a bit, but you gave up. That's probably why I dropped you so easily,' Tyrone taunted.

'Tell me who it was.'

'Maybe later. I've got a search to do.'

Using some cloth to gag Piotr, Tyrone taped his hands behind his back, then taped his ankles to ensure he couldn't move. He then systemically trashed the house. He wasn't bothered about finding anything. The goal was to create chaos. After some time, he returned to the room, breathing hard from the intensity of the search.

'Maybe what you're saying is true. Maybe I should shoot you now,' he said, yanking the gag from Piotr's mouth.

'If you do, your life will end. My people will never stop hunting for you, and if you're this loud when conducting business, it will only be a matter of time.'

'Don't be so sure. If your people are as slack as you, I'm not worried. You're just as soft as he made you out to be. I'm gonna have to go back to *Craig* and . . .' Tyrone broke off. 'Shit.'

Piotr's eyes gleamed.

'So, Craig sent you. That's good to know.'

Tyrone shrugged. 'Fuck it. I don't think he'll mind you knowing.

He doesn't think you're a threat, anyway. I'll let you go, but remember, I'm watching you. You better have eyes in the back of your head when you're doing deals, because I'll be there, waiting to take you out.'

Leaving Piotr tied up, Tyrone left.

———

IT DIDN'T TAKE LONG for the effects to be felt. Word spread about the issues Craig was having in Beeston. He had to appease Piotr and his people, who were spreading the word about how Craig betrayed them.

Tyrone gave it several days before he made his next move. Jamar provided Craig's address, and Tyrone watched the house, learning the best time to strike.

On the third night, he broke into Craig's house. He stood over him, gun pointed at the man's sleeping frame.

'Oi,' he hissed. Craig shifted, his eyes opening, then widening when he saw Tyrone standing over him.

'What the fuck?'

'You twat. Did you think you could come for me and my brother and that I wouldn't do anything?'

Before Craig could speak, Tyrone pulled the trigger, a loud ping echoing around the room. Craig's head flew back, blood covering the headboard, the bed and the pillows. Even knowing he was dead, Tyrone fired again to be sure, then left.

CHAPTER EIGHT

AS TYRONE EXPECTED, Craig's murder had everyone talking. Piotr was the immediate suspect, as word spread about their conflict. On the instructions of Tyrone, Jamar subtly played it that way, keeping Tyrone updated.

Tyrone went about his business as usual, pleased he'd removed a potential enemy with little effort. He liked Jamar's usefulness but considered whether to get rid of him. He knew a lot about the play Tyrone had concocted.

In the end, Tyrone decided to let him live; Jamar was clearly terrified of him, and had roots within Snypa's organisation.

TYRONE KNOCKED on Shardell's door, looking back at his car, the engine still running, scowling. He softened his features as Shardell opened the door and smiled out at him.

'Hey, Ty, come in.'

He shook his head.

'Can't stop. Just wanted to drop this on you.' He gave her a bundle of notes. 'I'm gonna pass back through later and see you.' He moved to turn away.

'Wait up. What's going on with the business?' She asked, still clutching the money.

'Don't worry about business, Shar. You're best off out of it.'

Shardell's hand went to her hip, glaring at Tyrone.

'I'm already involved. I helped you, because you said we were building towards something, remember?'

'I remember,' Tyrone quickly said. 'It's not an overnight thing, though. I need to think about my son, and you need to think about yours.' He smiled. 'Look, keep things to yourself for now, and I'll let you know when something changes.'

Shardell didn't respond, her glare only deepening. Tyrone tilted her chin, staring into her eyes.

'Do you understand?'

Shardell slowly nodded.

'Good. People are waiting on me, but I'll ring you.' Returning to his car, Tyrone drove away, not giving her a second thought.

———

THAT FRIDAY, Tyrone was in the Hood with Cropper and Ban-Dan. They were sharing a spliff, hanging around Tyrone's car. The warm weather had people out in droves. Tyrone was wary about collecting phone numbers in Chapeltown. Still, he discretely spoke with a few women — preparation for replacing Shardell, something he'd need to do if she kept overstepping the mark.

'Still can't believe you handled the Craig mess without us,' said Cropper. Other than the surveillance on Jamar, he and the crew hadn't been involved in what Tyrone had done.

'It needed to be done quietly, so I went in solo. It was easy,' said Tyrone. Before Cropper could respond, they saw Nathaniel, Cameron, and a third boy Tyrone assumed was Darius, walking along, talking in loud voices. Tyrone grinned, liking how natural his son seemed at the head of the group.

'Oi, Nat, c'mere.'

Nathaniel looked up, smirking when he saw his dad. He and the crew ambled over.

'Hey, dad. What are you lot doing around here?' Nathaniel asked. His friends nodded at Tyrone, but didn't hold his gaze for too long. Nathaniel touched fists with Cropper and Ban-Dan, and Tyrone liked his son's gesture and manners.

'I was gonna ask you the same question. Hope you lot aren't out here causing trouble.'

Nathaniel shook his head. 'We were playing footy earlier, and now we're just walking around.'

Tyrone nodded. 'Fair enough. Just remember where you are, and keep your eye out. Anything happens, come look for me. Make sure you don't stay out too late either.' He reached into his pocket, handing Nathaniel several twenty-pound notes. 'Split that with your friends.'

The boys all said thanks, hurrying away.

'Your son's got a nice little crew around him,' Cropper remarked as they watched the group vanish. 'He's gonna go far.'

Tyrone nodded, proud that people saw what he did. 'He is. I want him to be even better than I am, though. No matter what he decides to do.'

They spoke about family a little longer. They'd begun talking about food when a black Polo slowly pulled up. The window wound down, and a fleshy-faced man with brutal features and harrowing eyes, looked out at Tyrone.

'Can we talk?'

Tyrone nodded as Trevor stepped from the car. He'd come alone, which surprised Tyrone. He'd figured Snypa would be there. Trevor was built along the same lines as Tyrone, but was slightly taller.

The pair stepped away from the group, Cropper and Ban-Dan knowing to stay back without being told. Tyrone waited for him to speak first.

'Take it you heard about Craig?'

Tyrone nodded.

Trevor assessed him. 'I know that Craig was sniffing around you and your brother. Me and my guy are asking if you had anything to do with what happened.'

Tyrone didn't flinch. 'I thought the white dudes in Beeston did it?'

'We interrogated them. Thoroughly. They're swearing they had nothing to do with it.'

'Would they ever admit otherwise?' Tyrone had to hide his smile. He didn't like Trevor or Snypa, and getting one over on them felt good.

'Snypa knew about Craig's side deals, but they were small-time, so he didn't care. It would have been dumb for those Russian boys to burn that bridge, and Craig would be really stupid to skank people he's been working with for a while.'

'I think they're Polish, mate. Not Russian.'

Trevor didn't look pleased at being corrected. 'I think you're focusing on the wrong thing.'

'Maybe. I'll focus on summat else then. What did you and your boss think about Craig apparently moving against me and my brother?'

'We didn't think anything of it,' Trevor flatly replied, Tyrone noting that he'd not denied they'd had full knowledge.

Both men stared the other down, neither budging an inch. Finally, Trevor leaned forward, touching Tyrone's fist.

'Look after yourself.'

'What was that about?' Cropper asked, when Trevor drove away, and Tyrone returned to the group. The weight of Trevor's words had landed, and he had to fight to maintain his temper. Just as he'd suspected, both Snypa and Trevor had been fully aware of Craig's moves, and had likely endorsed them.

'They were backing Craig,' he said coldly. 'They're gonna die for that.'

CHAPTER NINE

TYRONE PUT the conversation with Trevor behind him that night. He spent time with Tia, and they drank wine and watched a film. They were curled up on the sofa when there was a knock at the door. Tyrone tensed

'Who's that?' Tia mumbled. Tyrone ignored her, eyes darting around the room, seeking something he could use as a weapon if needed.

'Ty? What's going on?'

Tyrone slid to his feet, then moved towards the door as the person knocked again.

'Ty?'

'Be quiet,' he hissed. Clenching his fist, he opened the door.

Mitch stood there, impassively staring back. Tyrone let him in. Tia shot him a mutinous look, and Tyrone pulled her close, hugging her.

'Sorry, love. I didn't want anyone creeping up on us. You know how the game gets sometimes.'

'Hey, Tia. Sorry for turning up without calling. How's everything? How's work?' Mitch asked, giving her a quick hug and a kiss on the cheek. They made small talk, then Mitch shot Tyrone a look. Without a word, they went out to the garage. Tyrone closed the door behind them.

'I haven't been in here in a while,' Mitch said, caressing the heavy bag. 'You must be putting a lot of time in here. You look bigger lately.'

Tyrone leant against the wall by the door, coiled and waiting.

'What happened to Craig?'

'He's dead, isn't he?' Tyrone replied, rolling his eyes. Mitch shook his head.

'Why would you do it?'

'Why wouldn't you tell me about Rudy?'

Mitch's eyes narrowed.

'What are you talking about?'

'Craig threatened Rudy. You both knew, and you didn't tell me. Even Trevor fucking knew.'

'So, because of that, you killed him?'

'I killed him because he was a threat to the team. If you want me to share my moves . . . share yours too. We're partners,' said Tyrone.

Mitch's jaw tensed.

'It was being handled, Ty. That's why we didn't say anything. We could have handled him if he had made a direct move. All you're doing is making business harder.'

'Business will be even harder if we get killed because people think we're weak and open to be challenged.'

Mitch's glare hadn't abated. The brothers stared one another down.

'Will you just fucking blink? My eyes are drying out,' said Mitch after a few seconds.

Unable to hold his reaction, Tyrone burst into laughter, both brothers shaking their heads, laughing ever louder.

'I love you, Ty . . . Even if you are a psycho.'

Finally moving, Tyrone slapped his brother on the back.

'Come on. Let's get a drink.'

––––––––

FOR THE NEXT WEEK, Tyrone remained focused on business. He spent time with Nathaniel, even taking him to a meeting and introducing him to some of his associates. He spoke with him about the streets, surprised at how much Nathaniel and his friends knew about the gangs and their politics. The beef with the Yardies had spilt over into the schools, and Nathaniel knew numerous kids who had been maimed in attacks. It was strange for Tyrone to consider. Nathaniel was only eleven, but sometimes he seemed older.

'You've got it good,' Tyrone said to his son. 'When I was young, we had nothing. My dad left us, and me and Mitch were out here from an early age, just doing what we could to survive, and provide for your nana.'

'Is that how you got started?' Nathaniel asked. The pair sat in the garage, having finished another workout. Tyrone nodded.

'Yeah. Things snowballed for us. We showed we were tough and didn't back down. The money started coming in, we got the right people, and just kept pushing.'

Nathaniel grinned as he always did when Tyrone told his stories.

'You don't have to do that, though. If you did, you've got a nice little crew around you, but you can do anything you want. What do you wanna do? Have you thought about it?'

'I want to be a footballer.' Nathaniel pushed out his chest, a smug expression on his face. Tyrone chuckled. Nathaniel shot him a look, likely wondering what he was laughing at, but Tyrone didn't elaborate.

'You think that'll be easy because you love football, but it won't be, Nat. You'll have to work harder than you could ever imagine,' Tyrone started. 'You don't even play for a team yet. It's fun running rings around your friends in the street, or at the park, but actually playing is different.' Tyrone smiled at Nathaniel. 'I'm not saying it's impossible . . . you're my son; anything is possible. But it'll be hard. Plus . . . and this is the big one: you'll need to stay out of the streets with your people.'

'Why can't I do both?' Nathaniel's eyes narrowed.

'Let's break it down: You get into it on the streets with someone, and that argument blows up. You're already known as a baller . . . *the next big thing; destined for the Premiership*. What's the first thing your enemy's gonna do to send a message? They'll take your kneecaps off.' Nathaniel went to speak, but Tyrone held up his hand. 'You're probably thinking that you wouldn't be out there to be found, but if you're playing footy once a week, and training a few times a week, you're accessible. Anyone wanting to do you harm will know exactly where you are. It's out in the open — makes it harder to investigate and pin down whoever is responsible.'

'I get what you're saying, dad, but—' Natty started, only for Tyrone to interject.

'I'm saying, just think about all this if it's what you really wanna do. Some kids in other cities were in the life, but they wised up and left it all behind when it was time to take football seriously. The flip side . . . we all know someone who couldn't leave the streets alone, and ended up wasting their talents.'

Nathaniel rubbed his forehead and didn't reply.

CHAPTER TEN

'WHAT DID HE SAY THEN?'

Trevor paced the room as Snypa watched. The pair were at one of Snypa's hangouts, a semi-detached spot near Chapel Allerton. One of his women lived here for appearances, but she had been trundled off so they could talk business.

Snypa had been out of town for almost a week, meaning this was the first chance the pair had to speak.

'He's cocky, Snypa. I can't wait to kill him. He didn't outright admit it, but it was obvious. He sussed out that we sent Craig to harass his people.'

Snypa considered this. It had been a miscalculation on his part. He saw the Dunn's as passive, ready to be squeezed. Snypa hadn't expected Tyrone Dunn to be more like himself than his brother, which shocked and impressed him.

'What did the Polish lot say?'

Trevor stopped pacing, rubbing his jaw.

'We gripped three of them. Smacked around two and made sure they were telling the truth. They didn't go after Craig. It was on the books, but they didn't act.'

'Are we sure?' Snypa pressed. Trevor nodded.

'They're not killers. Not like that, anyway. They wouldn't have gone straight to blowing off Craig's head while he slept.'

'Fine. Tyrone was the one who did it then. Okay.'

'He's brazen,' said Trevor. 'I should've killed him and his friends right there.'

'Chill. What's Mitch saying?'

Trevor shook his head. 'Forget that. How the fuck did Tyrone work out what we were up to?'

Snypa shrugged. 'Tyrone's clearly a hothead, but he's not stupid. He knows Craig worked for us. It's not much of a leap to work out that we might have a hand in what's been going on.'

Trevor stopped pacing. 'We need to wipe them all out right now. I'll get a crew together.'

Snypa shook his head. 'Just Tyrone. We go after him for now.'

Trevor looked incredulous. 'If you take out Tyrone, Mitch will come after us.'

'Mitch is sharp, but maybe he doesn't realise how much he needs his brother for rep. He's smart, but the money sucked him in. He's not deep like we are, and he's not willing to kill anymore to get what he wants. We are. So is Tyrone. If we get him, we can bully Mitch and Rudy into working with us.'

Trevor's nostrils flared. He didn't like letting the crew slide, but agreed that Tyrone was the major threat right now. Everyone knew Mitch was the wiser brother and the brains behind the crew, but that wasn't the worry right now. The concern was that Tyrone feared nothing, had murdered one of their men, and wouldn't hesitate to go after them.

'Fine. How are we gonna do it?'

CHAPTER ELEVEN

THE NIGHT after his talk with Nathaniel, Tyrone and Rudy went out for dinner. They were both fans of Indian food and headed to a restaurant in the city centre. Both men were in good spirits, laughing, drinking beers with their food as they spoke.

Near the end of the meal, they got down to business.

'What do you think of the move?' Tyrone asked.

Rudy wiped his mouth with his napkin, then sipped his beer.

'You handled it well. It was quite subtle for you too. I don't think Craig was ever a threat, though.'

'What's my brother said to you about it? I know you've been talking with him about this stuff,' said Tyrone.

'He thinks you're warmongering.' Rudy didn't meet his eyes.

'He said as much the other day. Gave me a *big brother* lecture about what I was doing. Maybe I am, but I'm the only one looking at the bigger picture. Everything is there for the taking, and we need to get our share, because everyone else is gonna go for it too.'

'This is what I don't understand.' Rudy started. 'What exactly is it that you want? We're respected, and we have our place on the streets. We're not the biggest team, but we're far from the smallest. Even Snypa's people are wary of directly going at us.'

Tyrone cut his eyes to Rudy. *'Wary?* They publicly threatened you. Doesn't seem like they're all that wary. We're not seen as untouchable. Little pricks like Snypa trying us, is a sign that we're not as big as we should be. If we keep placating and laying low, that's just gonna grow.

'I get all that, but sometimes just waiting is the best way. Let people commit, and get themselves tied up, and then strike . . . when they're vulnerable.'

Tyrone kissed his teeth. 'You sound too much like my brother. He's shitting it over enemies. He's shitting it over police. I can't even spend the money we're stacking. What's the point?' snapped Tyrone.

'Is Mitch wrong? I get what you mean, and there's things I wanna buy that I know I can't, but we both know dozens of people who flossed their money, got arrested and had everything taken. I'm not going out like that.'

'What are you trying to say?' Tyrone glared at Rudy.

'I'm just saying Mitch is right to be a bit paranoid about us getting hit by the feds.'

'If we do our jobs right, he doesn't need to be.'

Rudy grinned. 'You're too stubborn, Ty. Always have been. I'll back you, though. Outside of all this street shit, you're my brother, and I'll always support you.'

That brought a smile back to Tyrone's face. He understood the positions of Rudy and Mitch, but was determined to show them he was right.

'Whatever, you soft prick. Let's move on. How's the love life? You banging anyone?'

Rudy chuckled. 'There's just a woman I've been seeing lately. It's no big deal.'

'Course it's a big deal,' Tyrone exclaimed. Rudy kept his business internal and rarely let anyone know any personal details about him. Even Tyrone, who had known him the longest, knew little more than most. 'I know what you're like. If you're telling people about her, then you're already basically married.'

'Piss off. Like I said, it's no big deal. How are you doing with your situation? That girl still annoying you?'

Tyrone snorted. 'She's a pest, but lately, she's been kinda distant. I'm not sure why, and I haven't cared enough to investigate it.'

'Maybe she's got a man,' said Rudy. Again, Tyrone snorted.

'A man that can do the things to her that I can? I doubt it. She's my fluff, and she always will be. You wouldn't believe the things I've made her do.'

Rudy shook his head, his expression hardening for a moment. 'You're something else. I'll never understand the success that you have with women.'

Tyrone pondered this for a moment, rubbing his eyebrow. For all his success, he didn't feel he had a handle on the major women in his life. Tia was a constant pain, and Shardell's clinginess was irritating.

'What's there to understand?' He finally replied. 'I speak their language, and they know it.'

'Sure. You best hope Tia doesn't chop it off.'

'Tia knows her place,' said Tyrone dismissively. 'She knew what she married. Come, let's have one more drink and then get out of here.'

As Tyrone paid the bill, he thought about Shardell and her attitude. She was attractive, and he enjoyed the sex, but he didn't want to be thinking about her when he didn't need to. For her annoyances, Tia was his wife, and he was at least obligated to try with her. With Shardell, he wasn't. Despite the fun he'd had with her in the past, he would easily cut her off if she didn't shape up.

'I'll ring you tomorrow, and we'll have a chat,' said Rudy, patting Tyrone on the back and walking away. Tyrone yawned, moving toward his car, swaying slightly on his feet. He didn't think he'd drank much, but his legs were still shaky. When he got home, he planned to have one or two cups of coffee to wake up.

A movement out of the corner of his eye surprised him, and instinctively, Tyrone moved back.

The move saved his life.

A knife sliced into his chest, the glancing blow failing to deeply penetrate. Alert, Tyrone slammed his fist into his attacker's jaw, then pushed him against a nearby wall, the knife clattering from the man's grasp. The smaller man struggled, his features hidden by a balaclava. Tyrone hit him again, this time in the stomach.

'Who sent you? Huh?'

The man didn't answer, sagging under the power of the hits.

'Ty!'

Rudy hurried over, panting. Tyrone's eyes cut to him, the distraction allowing the would-be assailant to push free of Tyrone's grip and rush away.

'Are you okay?' Rudy asked. Tyrone ignored the knife on the floor, looking in the direction the man had run. His chest pounded, adrenaline surging as he realised how close he'd been to dying. He'd never seen it coming.

'Ty?'

Jerking from his reverie, Tyrone faced his friend. He touched his blooded top. The wound wasn't deep, but he would still need to get it cleaned, just in case.

'I'm fine.'

'What the fuck happened? I doubled back because I left my phone and saw you holding the man against the wall. Who was it?'

'They had a mask on. I didn't have time to unmask them. Doesn't matter, anyway. We know who sent them.'

Rudy sighed. He didn't need to say anything else.

CHAPTER TWELVE

MITCH CAME to see Tyrone the next day. Tyrone's wound had been cleaned and stitched by then, but he burned for revenge.

'How are you doing, bro?' Mitch asked. Like last time, they were in Tyrone's garage. Tyrone sat on the weight bench, Mitch remaining on his feet.

'They tried to kill me,' Tyrone replied.

'I think if they wanted you dead, they'd have sent someone more effective. Rudy said you smacked the guy up and had him against the wall when he came over.'

'You're wrong,' retorted Tyrone. 'They probably wanted to cause confusion with the method. The streets would have assumed it was a mugging gone wrong, and they could have carried on moving in the dark.'

Mitch frowned. 'Slow down, Ty. I know what you want to do, but—'

'But nothing. They made their move, and they failed. We know how this goes now.'

'Ty, wars cost money. Look at all the stuff that went down with the Yardies and our gangs. No one in Chapeltown is gonna be pleased if you kick off another war.'

Tyrone shot to his feet, wincing as the cut on his chest seared.

'Why can't you just fucking back me for once? Business aside, I'm your damn family. They tried to kill me.'

Mitch's nostrils flared, and he threw up his hands. 'If they did, it was a response to you killing Craig.'

'That was a response to Craig muscling in our business. We could go back-and-forth like this all day.' Tyrone folded his arms, scowling at his brother. Mitch shook his head.

'You're doing too much. You know what your problem is? You blunder around, making messes, just blasting straight ahead, not thinking of the consequences. For a guy that wants to be *untouchable*, you're determined to get in your own way.'

Tyrone waved off his words.

'If you're not supporting me, then I'll do this without you.'

Mitch sighed, his expression softening.

'Ty, you're family, and I love you. I wish you would listen to me. You don't need to rush in. We don't need to be the biggest crew on the scene. The money is consistent. Be happy with what we have.'

'We don't have shit. Not yet.'

Mitch held up his hands.

'What are you talking about? We're deep in Chapeltown. People rely on us, and we have teams that we deal with throughout Leeds. We've got people working for us, bringing in fifty grand a month, minimum. Even after overhead, we're killing it.'

'What the fuck are you trying to say?' Tyrone snapped, wanting his brother to get to the point. Mitch sighed.

'I'm saying that if what we have now isn't enough, then nothing ever will be.'

Without waiting for a response, Mitch left.

CHAPTER THIRTEEN

A FEW DAYS after sitting down with Mitch, Tyrone's gang gathered at Cropper's. Tyrone sat on an armchair, while the others squashed together on Cropper's ugly orange sofa.

'Ty, what the hell are you wearing?' Cropper asked. The other crew members smirked at the expression on Tyrone's face.

'Fucking Tia,' he mumbled, trying to rub the creases out of his crumpled black t-shirt. 'She's on my case after the attack. Thinks I'm not being careful enough. We argued, and now she's refusing to do my washing.'

'I'll lend you a tracksuit if you like,' Cropper continued, smirking. 'Either that, or you need to sweet-talk your way back in.'

'Don't worry about it,' said Tyrone, shaking his head. 'We've got business now.'

'What are we gonna do then?' Ban-Dan asked, leaning forward in his seat. 'We can't be letting people get away with trying to do you in.'

'Who's talking?' Tyrone asked, nostrils flaring. He was still annoyed with Mitch and his lack of support in dealing with the situation. He didn't care what Mitch said about him blundering in: he was dealing with a legitimate threat that Mitch didn't want to accept was real.

'I've heard a few people talking about it, but no one's chatting like they have insider information, and no one is claiming it either,' said Cropper.

'They'd be claiming it if I was dead. Cropper, keep quietly digging around, and see what you can pick up. I wanna know who the guy was that tried to knife me, so I can finish him myself.'

'What do you want us to do?' Nathan motioned to himself and Ban-Dan.

'Get us some clean straps. We'll need a place to lay low too, that no one outside of this group knows about.'

Silence ensued. The group exchanged looks. Tyrone felt his jaw tensing.

'Just fucking say it,' he snapped.

'Why are we hiding shit from your bro? Is he an enemy?' Cropper asked. It didn't surprise Tyrone that he was the one to speak up. He was closer to Tyrone than the others, and always spoke his mind.

Tyrone rubbed at his lower lip.

'Mitch has his own way he wants to do things. He thinks that if we move against Snypa, other gangs are gonna switch on us for disturbing the peace.'

Cropper frowned. 'No disrespect, but that's nonsense. The other side are making moves. Craig did it first. Does he think Snypa's just gonna pack up and go away?'

Tyrone grinned. 'I don't know. Right now, it doesn't matter. We know what we need to do, so we'll focus on that and leave the other shit behind. There's a problem, and we're gonna deal with it. That's what we do. It's what we've always done. If anyone else wants to step up after that, we'll drop them too.'

The team were all smiles, and their reaction buoyed Tyrone. Mitch was in the wrong. Tyrone wasn't blundering in. He had a plan. He was gathering his strength, making strategic moves, and it would pay off in the end.

He considered reaching out to Rudy, but something held him back. Rudy was different lately. He had always been pragmatic, but he and Tyrone never seemed to agree on anything anymore.

Once Snypa was taken out, Tyrone would get things back to how they used to be.

———

AFTER SETTING up his plans with his crew, Tyrone called Shardell from his car.

'Ty?' She answered, sounding wary. Tyrone put this to one side, smiling.

'What's happening, sexy? Where have you been?'

'Nowhere. I've been local, just chilling.'

'I haven't seen you in ages. You haven't reached out to see me,' said Tyrone. He'd expected Shardell to sound angry or annoyed, but instead she sounded neutral.

'Like I said, I've just been around, chilling. You haven't reached out either.'

'I've been dealing with some street shit, but I'm gonna come and see you soon.'

Shardell didn't reply. Tyrone's eyes narrowed. Like the last time they'd spoken, he didn't like the vibe.

'Oi, are you still there?'

'Sorry . . . must have lost connection for a second. Look, I'll ring back later when the line is better.'

When she hung up, Tyrone stared at the phone, thinking back to Rudy's words last time. If his gift with women was leaving him, it was something else to think about after he handled his business.

CHAPTER FOURTEEN

TYRONE WAS in bed the next day when loud voices awoke him. Grumbling, he tried to go back to sleep and ignore them, but the voices persisted. Finally, he climbed from bed and stumbled downstairs.

'Wait til your dad finds out—' Tia was screaming, as Nathaniel sullenly stared back.

'Finds out what?' Tyrone asked, stepping into the room. Tia faced him, eyes flashing.

'Go on, tell him, Nathaniel!'

Nathaniel didn't speak. He looked away, his face tense.

'Nat, what's going on?'

'I got in trouble,' said Nathaniel in a low voice.

'Trouble for what? What did you do?'

Nathaniel didn't immediately speak. He looked to his mum, who still looked furious, then back to his dad.

'I . . . we . . . did a robbery.'

Tyrone's eyes widened. He opened then closed his mouth, incredulous.

'You what?'

Before Nathaniel could speak again, Tia took over.

'He and his bloody little friends robbed a boy. They took his phone and money, then threatened him if he told anyone.'

Tyrone was stunned. He didn't know what to think. He knew Nathaniel could be a handful, but he didn't think he had it in him to rob someone. Tyrone had committed robberies from a young age, but his family were broke, and he and Mitch had done them out of necessity.

'What were you playing at?' He asked his son. Again, Nathaniel didn't reply. 'Hey! I'm fucking talking to you.'

Nathaniel jumped, clearly racked with fear now. Even Tia looked surprised at Tyrone's shouting.

'I want an answer, Nat. I want it now.'

'We thought it would be a laugh and that, I dunno . . . we could make some money out of it,' said Nathaniel.

'Whose idea was it?' Tyrone demanded. Nathaniel's mouth closed, and Tyrone knew he wouldn't sell out his friends. 'What happened to all that shit about you wanting to be a footballer? Do you not remember what I said about how footy and the life are incompatible? What were you thinking?'

Nathaniel sullenly looked back, but didn't reply.

'If you don't give me an answer, I'm going for my belt,' Tyrone warned.

'Ty, you're focusing on the wrong thing,' interjected Tia, shooting him a look of disgust. 'I don't care whose idea it was. I care about my son being a thief, and the boy's parents. They're planning on getting the police involved.'

'Do his parents know who your dad is?' Tyrone asked Nathaniel. Tia's eyes flashed again.

'It's not about you! It's about your son having a criminal record when he's barely reached high school. Aren't you bothered about that?'

Tyrone rubbed his head and closed his eyes. This was the last thing he wanted to deal with right now. War was approaching, whether he liked it or not. He didn't need the domestic distraction.

'Nat, get upstairs. I'll be up soon to deal with you.'

Nathaniel's lips trembled. He looked again from his dad to his mum, then hurried from the room.

'What the hell is wrong with you?' Tyrone asked Tia. 'Why are you getting in my damn way and trying to talk down to me in front of my son?'

'He's *our* son, not just yours,' Tia fiercely retorted.

'He's a boy. He's gonna be a man soon, and I deal with discipline, not you.'

'You're doing a great job there, aren't you?' Tia clapped her hands, rolling her eyes. 'We're supposed to be above petty theft. That's a bit low class for a man with your rep, don't you think?'

Tyrone felt his anger rising. 'Shut your mouth. You don't know what the hell you're talking about.'

Tia shook her head. 'You don't get it, do you?'

'Don't get what? Why don't you share what I'm missing, seeing as you're so much smarter than me.'

'He's never going to be a bloody footballer. He's going to do what you do, so teach him properly. Thieving is one step above being a crackhead. Sort out your son, instead of running around banging every woman you can.'

Tyrone's fists clenched, and he moved toward his wife without realising. Tia's face blanched, but she stood her ground, meeting his eyes every step of the way.

'I told you once to shut your mouth. I'll deal with my son, my way. Stay the hell out of it.'

Tyrone left the room, grabbing a bottle of brandy from the kitchen with shaking hands. He poured himself a drink, then headed upstairs to Nathaniel's room.

Nathaniel sat on his bed, staring straight ahead. He glanced up when the door opened, the fear almost palpable. Tyrone stepped into the room, closing the door behind him. Again, he noticed Nathaniel's lip trembling.

'Here.' He offered the drink to his son. Nathaniel didn't move, but Tyrone nodded, and he took the glass, taking a big sip.

'Take it easy,' cautioned Tyrone, as Nathaniel started coughing, the potent liquor burning his chest and throat. He sipped the drink as

Nathaniel wiped his mouth and grimaced. 'I thought you were a big man now? You should be able to handle a big man's drink.'

'I'm sorry, dad. I shouldn't have done what I did,' said Nathaniel, staring at the floor.

'Look me in the eyes if you're gonna apologise.'

Nathaniel did as he was told.

'I'm sorry, dad.'

'Why did you do it? And don't tell me it was just about the money. I've been out there too long to fall for that crap.'

'We just wanted to see if we could do it. Darius said that robberies are easy, so we went for it.'

Tyrone shook his head, but didn't comment.

'How did you get caught?'

'We covered our faces with some bally's, but the kid recognised Cam's voice.'

'Who's the kid?'

'Just a boy that goes to my school. He's a few years older. He's going into year ten when we go back to school.'

Tyrone took a moment to reply, gathering his words.

'Remember our little talk last time, when we were training? You said you were gonna take football more seriously, but now you're out there, making silly moves.' Tyrone sat on the bed next to his son, putting his hand on his shoulder. 'Nat, the streets are ruthless. Everyone is out for something, and people will try you because you're a Dunn. They'll try to get you in trouble and do you dirty.'

'I get it, dad.'

'If you get it, then you have to be sharper in future. Think for yourself, and make the decisions you can live with. Don't mess up your life before you've even started to live it. Understand?'

Nathaniel nodded, his face softening.

'I want the name of the boy's family so I can deal with this.' Tyrone downed his drink. 'Meet me in the garage.'

'How come?' Nathaniel asked, likely still fearing the belt.

'We're gonna train, and I'm gonna work you harder than ever until you know not to do something so stupid again.'

CHAPTER FIFTEEN

WHEN TYRONE WAS DONE training Nathaniel, he sent him back to his room. After washing his face and freshening up, he went to find Tia. She sat on the sofa, legs folded beneath her, reading a book. Tyrone went to sit next to her. She didn't move or acknowledge him. He cleared his throat.

'I've spoken with him. He knows not to mess up like that again.'

Tia cut her eyes to her husband.

'Is that your way of apologising?'

'Look, we both said some things. Now, we're gonna work past it.'

'Work past it how? How's it going to look to people that our son is a little thief? It's embarrassing. Makes us look poor.'

'It's gonna be cool. No one will care about what he did. If they do, it'll be for five minutes until the next thing comes along.'

'How can you be so sure that he won't do it again? Does he understand the risk? Does he know that it's going on his record if they press charges?'

'It's not gonna get that far.'

'He hasn't learned anything. This is the point, Ty. Is he actually never going to do it again, or is he just going to aim to be smarter next time?' Tia asked.

'You don't need to worry about it. I'll handle the parents and keep an eye on Nat. It'll be fine.' Tyrone kissed Tia on the cheek. 'Make me a cup of tea, please, love.'

———

PUTTING the issues with Nathaniel to one side, Tyrone left his house in the evening and called Jamar from the car.

'Hey, Ty, what's happening?'

Tyrone frowned at how confident Jamar sounded. He tried comparing it to the nervous man he'd accosted in the club, wondering if Craig's murder had positively affected him.

'What do you have for me?'

'Everything's quiet right now. I haven't heard anything,' replied Jamar. Tyrone was sure he heard a voice in the background, but when he strained to listen closer, it was gone.

'No one's said anything about what happened to me?'

'Nah, I heard about it, though. It's good you pulled through.'

'Forget that. You need to start speaking to Trevor and other people in Snypa's camp. I need information.'

'I'm not in the inner circle like that, Ty. I can't do it.'

'You need to get in the inner circle. Don't fucking call me *Ty* either. We're not friends. If you're not useful to me anymore, that's something we'll need to discuss face-to-face,' said Tyrone.

'I don't know . . .'

'I'm not asking what you know. I'm telling you what to do.'

'I'm just saying I don't think it can be done. Look, I need to go, but I'll get back in touch when I know something.'

Before Tyrone could speak, Jamar had hung up.

———

CROPPER, Nathan and Ban-Dan met at a house in Harehills. Ban-Dan locked the door behind them, and they sat in the living room. Over a dozen guns, including a semi-automatic machine gun, were on the table. There were bags of ammunition alongside them.

'Any issues with the pickup?' Cropper motioned to the guns. Ban-Dan shook his head.

'Nah, they know us, and they definitely know Ty. They weren't gonna piss around and have him after them.'

'That's good. This spot is gonna do for us. No one else knows about it, and everyone in this area minds their business. Anyone heard from Ty?'

Both men shook their heads.

'I think we're all on the same page, gameplan-wise. Trevor is the best way to get to Snypa. He's his right-hand. If we get him, it weakens Snypa. We can work him over, and learn more about Snypa's plans.'

'Trevor's not gonna be easy to get, though. He usually rolls with people, and he's not soft.'

'We'll deal with him. If he acts up, Ty is madder than he is. They messed up when they didn't kill him. We're not gonna make those same mistakes.'

CHAPTER SIXTEEN

TYRONE PULLED up outside a semi-detached house in Chapel Allerton, hoping he had the correct address. The house was larger than the houses Tyrone saw in the Hood, and his nostrils flared. It was a blend of white and red-bricked, with two cars in the driveway and a well-tended garden. Parking on the street, he approached the house and knocked on the door. A woman answered, eyes widening when she saw Tyrone. She was red-haired and fleshy, with curly hair and pale blue eyes.

'Who are you?' She spoke swiftly, her voice refined, yet grating.

'My name is Tyrone Dunn. My son had some problems with yours, and I wanted to speak to you and sort it out,' replied Tyrone.

'Michael,' the woman said. 'There's someone at the door for you.'

A man stepped into view. He was tall and thin, with greying brown hair, glasses and no facial hair. He glanced quizzically out at Tyrone.

'Pardon me, I'm sorry, I don't know who you are?'

'He's that child's father. The one who robbed Gareth.'

Michael nodded, his brow furrowing.

'What exactly is it you want to talk about?'

'If we're going to talk, can I come inside, or can you step out here? Talking on the doorstep always makes me leery.'

Minutes later, Tyrone sat on the sofa. While Michael pottered in the kitchen, Gareth's mum shot him a disdainful look. Michael returned a few minutes later with a cup of coffee.

'Are you sure I can't get you a drink?'

'I'm fine, thanks,' said Tyrone. His gaze flickered from the mum to Michael. Michael was intimidated, but hiding it well, which Tyrone appreciated.

'Do you want to start?' Michael asked.

'I think that would be best. I don't condone what my son did, but I've had a word with him, and it won't happen again. He's been going through a rough patch and handled it all wrong. I'll take care of him.'

Before Michael could speak, his wife intervened.

'That boy of yours is a bully. Gareth's told us all about how he picks on kids at school.'

Tyrone fought to control his anger. He managed to keep his temper, but shot Michael a quick, hard look.

'Dear, calm down. Let him talk, and we can get this sorted for good.'

The woman sniffed, but didn't open her mouth again. Tyrone waited a moment.

'What happened to your son shouldn't have happened, and I want to make it right. I want to pay five hundred quid to you now, and that's the end. Your son can buy something nice, and I'll deal with Nat, make sure he gives your boy his stuff back. What do you say?'

Michael nodded. 'I think that's more than fair. I don't condone what your son did either, but children are like that sometimes. Instruct him going forward, and we're square.'

Tyrone smiled, reaching for a stack of notes, peeling off five hundred pounds. He handed the bundle of fifty-pound notes to Michael, who thanked him.

'These weren't the best circumstances to meet under, but I'm glad we got it sorted,' said Tyrone. He climbed to his feet, nodding at the woman, who stared blankly back at him.

Michael walked Tyrone out, holding out his hand at the door.

'I'm pleased we got this mess sorted,' said Michael. Tyrone shook his hand, then pulled Michael forward, still gripping him.

'What—' Michael tried pulling his hand away, but Tyrone's grip was like steel.

'If this happens in future, I won't be paying you a penny. Speak about my family again, or go near the police, and I'll tear yours apart while you watch, then I'll kill you last. Get me?'

Michael trembled, jerkily nodding his head. Beaming, Tyrone let him go and left, pleased he'd made his point.

———

TYRONE DROVE HOME with a massive smile on his face. He'd learned over the years that it was necessary sometimes to be diplomatic, but to leave people under no illusions where they stood. Michael wouldn't trouble him again. Tyrone wouldn't hesitate to follow through with his threat if he did.

Tia was back from work when he returned, washing up in the kitchen. Tyrone came up behind her, holding her waist and kissing the back of her neck.

'I sorted it, love. Spoke with the parents of that boy. They're not taking it any further.'

'That's good, but I still think you need to speak with your son,' said Tia, still focusing on the task at hand.

'I did speak to him,' retorted Tyrone.

'You need to sort him out. He can't go around thinking you're gonna get him out of all his messes. You need to drill into him that he's putting our family name at risk when he messes up like that.'

'He made a mistake, and he's paid for it. Why do we need to keep digging into it?'

Tia sighed. 'I told you before; Nat isn't going to be a footballer. He's going to do what you do, so school him. I won't have a thief for a son, and I won't have one that gets locked up over foolishness either. Teach him.' She kissed her husband on the cheek and walked away, leaving him pondering her words.

CHAPTER SEVENTEEN

DESPITE TIA'S WORDS, Tyrone considered the situation with Nathaniel handled, and turned his attention back to Snypa. Jamar had yet to get in touch, and Tyrone was still smarting over how he'd spoken to him on the phone. Sooner or later, that would be handled, and he would pay.

For now, he had somewhere to be.

Tyrone headed to a gambling spot in the Mexborough's, an area of Chapeltown. The terraced house blended into those around it, with the same faded reddish colour, surrounded by unkempt hedges. Numerous people hung outside, mainly a younger crowd uninterested in playing cards or dominoes. The owner of the spot refused to get a pool table, despising the youths.

Despite this, his oldest son worked with them, and several of the assorted youths sold drugs for him.

A kid who couldn't have been older than fourteen got in Tyrone's path. He was mixed-raced, wearing a baby blue tracksuit with light brown hair cut low, freckles across his face, and light brown eyes.

'You want some weed?' He asked. Tyrone didn't reply, simply staring the kid down until one of his friends pulled him away, whispering in his ear. Tyrone headed inside, greeting a few people with nods, hiding his smile when several others avoided his eyes.

Tyrone approached the bar, the owner's son hurrying to serve him.

'How's it going, Ty?'

'Can't call it, blood. Get me a Red Stripe, please. Tall-Man been in tonight?'

'He's back in room two now.'

'Cool. Get me what he's drinking as well.'

Tyrone paid, collected his drinks, then headed for the second room.

Marcus Daniels, aka *Tall-Man*, lounged at the back, smoking a cigarette, a half-drunk glass of brown liquor on the table in front of him. He was far larger than Tyrone, with a heavily muscled frame and fathomless, obsidian eyes. Despite the busy establishment, the crowd gave the man a wide berth.

Tyrone grinned to himself. Tall-Man was in his twenties, yet was respected and widely feared. He looked up at Tyrone, and the pair exchanged a nod. Tyrone approached and touched his fist, placing the drink in front of him. Tall-Man grunted his thanks.

Tyrone slid into the seat opposite. He respected Tall-Man, but didn't fear him as others did. There was a mutual respect, and they had worked together in the past.

'It's been a while,' he said.

'I've been grafting out of town.'

'I heard you had problems with some Yardies.'

Tall-Man shrugged, not directly acknowledging it. Respecting this, Tyrone savoured his drink and let the silence go on for a while. Tall-Man was the first to break it, having downed his drink, reaching for the one Tyrone had bought him.

'Heard someone tried knifing you the other day.'

'They tried and failed. I'm gonna address it soon enough. That's part of the reason I came looking for you.'

'I'm listening.'

'I've got a five-figure-payday lined up if you're interested. There's some wet work involved, but it's right up your street.'

Tall-Man shook his head. 'I'm not working at present.'

Tyrone's eyebrows rose.

'Teflon must be taking good care of you if you can afford to stay on the bench.'

'Everyone is eating right now,' replied Tall-Man. 'Plenty of money.'

Tall-Man's response reminded Tyrone of Mitch, and his brother's dire warnings that Chapeltown wouldn't support another war.

'Some people are eating more than others,' said Tyrone. 'If you're not available, then what's Shorty saying?' Shorty was another young man with a deadly reputation, who garnered a lot of respect.

Tall-Man shook his head. 'He's not doing freelance right now either. It's quiet right now, and he's got his own things he's doing.'

Tyrone nodded. Tall-Man and Shorty would have bolstered his team nicely, but it was a last-minute thought. He was confident they could eliminate Snypa without either man.

'I'm gonna get off,' he said. 'I might see you in the gym sometime.'

'Cool.'

Tyrone slid to his feet.

'Ty.'

He paused, waiting for Tall-Man to speak again.

'Watch your back. I know who you're going after, and it's not gonna be easy for you.'

'Is that why you don't wanna help? You scared?'

Tall-Man's demeanour didn't change, but Tyrone knew he'd gone too far.

'You're an *older*, but you know better than to call me scared. Take the advice, or don't. You're not the only one tooling up, though. Remember that.'

———

TALL-MAN'S WORDS left Tyrone deep in thought as he left the gambling spot. He wondered if the other side had approached Tall-Man, and whether he would take the offer if he had. Tall-Man was formidable and well-connected. Tyrone would struggle against him without serious backup, even before Snypa and the others were considered.

Despite the risk, something told Tyrone he wasn't in any danger. Tall-Man was no friend of the Yardies, and there were rumours he had executed a Yardie Kingpin, Leader. Tyrone didn't know who had started the rumour, but it wouldn't surprise him if it was true.

Tyrone resolved to keep watching his back, and to keep an eye on everyone around him. It was time to get things back in line, and he was going to start now.

———

JAMAR FROWNED as he opened the door to Tyrone.

'How did you find out where I lived?'

'It wasn't hard,' replied Tyrone. 'Do you mind if I come in? We have some things to discuss, and I respect you too much to talk your business in public.'

Accepting this, Jamar nodded, letting Tyrone in. Once the door closed, Tyrone reacted, slamming his fist into Jamar's stomach. Jamar sank to his knees, gasping for air. Tyrone smiled, then kicked him in the head, savouring the yelp of pain.

'I think I need to remind you who the fuck I am,' he said calmly, allowing the anger he felt to imbue him as he listened to Jamar's whimpering. 'Or rather, who I'm not. I'm not some little prick you can talk to like shit on the phone. You don't make demands of me, and you don't argue.' Grabbing Jamar by the scruff of his top, Tyrone pulled him into the living room, then flung him into the coffee table. Being of cheap quality, it collapsed when he made contact, leaving Jamar groaning amongst the remains.

'Ty . . . I'm . . .'

Jamar's wheezes were cut off by Tyrone, again kicking him.

'This is what's gonna happen. You're gonna arrange to meet Trevor publicly. I don't care what you tell him to make it happen, but you're gonna do it. If you don't, I'll kill you. If you try snaking me and letting him know, the money's already on your head. I've got a green light on you, and you won't go quick.' Tyrone studied Jamar, his lip curling at the snivelling wreck in front of him. 'Nod if you understand me.'

Sniffling, Jamar nodded, his spirit broken. Tyrone grinned widely.

'Good. Make sure you contact me, or I'll be back, and next time I'm breaking bones.'

CHAPTER EIGHTEEN

TREVOR SMOOTHED HIS T-SHIRT, glaring as he pulled up at the meeting spot. Jamar had been acting funny lately, and he was determined to get some answers. The pair had never been close. Jamar was Craig's knock-around guy, but he was decent at making money and followed orders, so he'd steered clear of Trevor's radar.

Things had changed lately.

Craig's death had been suspicious, and Trevor immediately knew the Dunn's were behind it. He knew Tyrone had pulled the trigger, but didn't know how involved Mitch was, being cagier and harder to read. Jamar had seemed jittery ever since, and at first, Trevor believed this was shock at how Craig had died, but now he wondered if it was something more.

So, when Jamar called him, saying he had to go through some business with him and that it involved the Dunn's, Trevor vetoed his request to come to his house, instead insisting they meet in public. Unbeknownst to Jamar, he was also bringing along a soldier as backup, who would be armed.

'What do you think this is about?' The soldier asked.

'He's being extorted. He said as much. We just need to get him talking and see what's what.'

'What if he clams up?'

Trevor grinned at the soldier. 'We'll *un-clam* him if he does.'

The men laughed. They were waiting on Bellbrooke Avenue in Harehills. It was early evening, and other than people walking by, the only ones in the vicinity were a few nearby kids, smoking cigarettes and throwing moody looks at the vehicle.

'Want me to chase the kids away?'

Trevor shook his head. 'They're not harming anyone. They won't do anything.'

After a few minutes, Jamar pulled up alongside them, stopping his car in the middle of the road. His face was drawn, his eyes flitting around, fear radiating from him. Trevor's eyes narrowed.

'What's up with you?'

'Nothing. What do you mean?'

Trevor shook his head. 'Forget it. Park up and get in the car.'

'Can we talk outside? It's hot.' Jamar's eyes flicked to the soldier, then back to Trevor. Scowling, Trevor climbed from the car, rubbing his knuckles.

'What's been going on with you lately?' He barked.

'What do you mean?' Jamar flinched, not meeting Trevor's eyes.

'Get out of the car so we can talk.'

Jamar hesitated, then did as he was told. The pair stepped onto the curb, standing outside of a house. The only difference between it and the other houses was the Sky television dish dangling from the side.

Trevor's jaw tensed before he spoke.

'You've always been a little squirrel, but lately, even weirder than normal. Who are you working with, and what have they got on you?'

'No one's got anything on me. People are just pushing me, and that's why I wanted to meet up with you. If you don't want to, then fuck off, and I'll sort it myself.'

Quick as a flash, Trevor grabbed Jamar and pushed him against a nearby wall. Clenching his fist, he pressed it to Jamar's face.

'Watch how you speak to me. I'm not Craig. I'm not gonna put up with your shit. I've never liked you. Never understood why he kept you about, and right now, I don't need to. You better chill, before you end up missing. Permanently.'

'I'm . . . sorry,' Jamar choked. Trevor let him go, nostrils flaring.

'Tell me what's really going on. I know it involves the Dunn's. I just don't know how.'

When Jamar's eyes widened, he knew he was right.

By then, it was too late.

Trevor heard the screech, whirling around to see the white van bearing down on them. Tyrone was on top of him before he could react, and a single blow to the side of the face made his ears ring and his jaw rattle. Through the explosion of pain, he remained dimly aware of shouting and scuffling around, but his eyes were heavy.

Another blow, and he sunk into deep darkness.

———

BREATHING HARD, Tyrone grinned down at Trevor. He'd easily gone down for a man with such a feared reputation.

'Oi, help us, you prick,' he snapped at Jamar, who jerked out of the stupor he'd been in. With Jamar and Cropper's help, they dragged him into the back of the van they'd arrived in. Already on point with the equipment, Cropper zip-tied his arms and legs, laying him on his side. Slamming the van door closed, they regrouped with Ban-Dan and Nathan, both panting.

'We took out his backup,' said Nathan, once he'd recovered. 'He tried getting to his strap, but he couldn't reach it. People were coming, so we couldn't kill him.'

Tyrone nodded. They had on balaclavas, so he wasn't worried about the witnesses.

Other than one.

'Make sure this stays quiet,' he warned Jamar, as the others climbed into the van. 'If it gets out, I know who to come for.'

Jamar frenziedly nodded as Tyrone and the others motored away, tires screeching. Fumbling for the car keys in his pocket, he shuffled to his car. They'd made a lot of noise, piquing the curiosity of several neighbours on the street. Unable to face them, Jamar kept his head down, climbing into his car with shaking hands, pulling away as the crowd pooled closer around the scene, a man kneeling by Trevor's beaten soldier. Dimly, he wondered if the blame would be pinned on him.

He was the only one without a balaclava, after all.

CHAPTER NINETEEN

TYRONE LOOKED DOWN at Trevor with a smile on his face. They were in the cellar of the safe house, with Trevor's arms and legs still tied together. He glared at them, venom in his eyes as he spat on the cellar floor.

'That's not nice, Trev, mate. Spitting is a disgusting habit,' said Tyrone. Cropper and the others glared at Trevor.

'Fuck you,' replied Trevor, unafraid. Tyrone took a step forward, the floorboards creaking underneath his weight. He locked eyes with the man, noting the bruising around his face from his attempts to struggle. He had a gun by his side and made sure Trevor could see it.

'Can I get you anything to eat or drink in the meantime?'

Trevor didn't respond, still scowling. Tyrone shrugged.

'Fair enough. Let me tell you how this is going to run. Tell me what I wanna know, and you can piss off for all I care. You're a nobody. I'm not bothered about you. I want that little punk Snypa, and you're gonna help me get him.'

'You must be mad if you think I'm helping you. You're gonna have to kill me,' Trevor retorted. Tyrone's smirk widened.

'Don't be so quick to reply. We'll be down to see you again soon, so get cosy until then.' Signalling to the others, Tyrone traipsed back upstairs, locking the door behind them. He led them to the kitchen, collapsing into a chair and yawning.

'That went as well as expected,' Tyrone said, to chuckles from the group. 'Ban-Dan, make sure he's secured and that the door stays locked at all times. You and Nath can take turns watching him.' He peeled off some twenty-pound notes and handed them to Ban-Dan. 'Buy some supplies, but don't go crazy. I want you lot in your right minds; no drink or drugs.'

Both men muttered under their breaths. Tyrone banged on the table.

'Do we have a problem?' He asked, his voice low. Both men shook their heads.

'Good. We'll be back soon.'

Tyrone and Cropper left the house, heading to a nearby parked Toyota. Cropper got in the driver's seat, and Tyrone jumped in the passenger side.

'We'll give him twenty-four hours to spill his guts, then we'll start carving him up,' said Tyrone.

'Makes sense. I don't think we've got anything to worry about, witness-wise. We were masked up, and there's only his little shooter that could kick up a fuss, and we whacked him up.'

Tyrone nodded, taking out his phone and calling Jamar.

'Did you get clear away?' He asked.

'Yeah. What's going to happen now, though? What if someone knows he was meeting me?'

'Say you couldn't stop it. Say that you were all ambushed. It doesn't matter. I wanna know everything that's said from Snypa. Get it?'

'How am I supposed to do that?' Jamar protested.

'Do we need to have another chat?' Tyrone asked. There was a sharp intake of breath on the other end.

'No . . .'

'Good. We're almost done with everything, so do what I'm asking you to do, and everything will be okay.' Tyrone hung up, shaking his head.

'Are you sure you can trust Jamar?'

'No, but fear works well with him. He knows what'll happen if he messes up. He's the least of our concerns right now. Trevor and Snypa first, then we'll have to look into Donovan and the JK Posse.'

'You think Donovan's lot will back them up?' Cropper looked wary.

'We can't afford to take the risk and get caught off guard.'

Cropper rubbed his forehead.

'I'm with you all the way on this one, but Donovan and them lot don't play. Snypa's one thing . . . I mean, we easily grabbed Trevor. The Posse are gunners. They'll shoot first and ask questions after. Do you think we need your brother and everyone with us on that?'

Tyrone shook his head. 'Let's handle Trevor and Snypa first, like I said. We'll deal with the Posse after.'

———

TYRONE ENTERED his home with a spring in his step. Heading to the kitchen, he located the food Tia had made, sticking it in the microwave. Fixing a drink, he sat at the table when the food was ready and began eating, famished after the events of the past few hours. Catching Trevor was a major move, and he grinned, thinking things were finally looking up.

Tia entered the kitchen a few minutes later, determinedly not looking Tyrone's way.

'Hey, babe,' he said after swallowing and wiping his mouth. 'How's your day been?'

Tia glanced at Tyrone, her brow furrowing.

'What?'

'How has your day been?' Tyrone repeated, grinning. 'We should go somewhere soon. If you get time off work, we can go abroad or something. What do you think?'

'Why are you in such a good mood?' Tia's suspicion hadn't abated.

'I'm having a good day. Guess you could say things are absolutely flying at the minute,' replied Tyrone. Tia's lip curled as she looked him up and down, shaking her head.

'You've got another one then . . .'

Tyrone blinked, puzzled. 'Another what?'

'You're really going to make me say it. You've found another little bit on the side, and you have the nerve to be around me, happy and smiling about that?'

'I don't have another girl. What the hell would make you think that?' said Tyrone, his smile fading.

'Because it's you, Ty. That's the way you are. I guess you're getting smarter, because you haven't been stuffing your clothes straight in the washer anymore when you sneak back in on a night.'

'Tia, you've got it all wrong. Nothing like that is going on.'

Again, Tia shook her head.

'As I said, it's just who you are. I guess the worst part is that Nat will probably do the same thing you're doing . . . it's not like you've taught him any better.'

Tyrone wiped his mouth, eyes flashing.

'I'm sick of this. Know your role and stop bothering me. I'm dealing with real stuff here, Tia. I'm trying to get us away from this damn little house and into something bigger and better. I want to be able to spend my money without looking over my damn shoulder, and I want to be able to get you and my son anything you want,' he snarled.

'What does that have to do with anything?' Tia retorted.

'That's my focus! Not other women. That's why I'm in a good mood, because business is going well. That has nothing to do with anything else, and if you can't get that, I won't bother explaining it anymore.'

Tyrone stood and stormed away, abandoning his food, needing to cool off.

CHAPTER TWENTY

TYRONE HADN'T CALMED down by the time he reached the safe house. He didn't understand why Tia was always on his case, but he would sort out the issue once he'd fixed this business.

'Didn't expect to see you back so quickly,' said Ban-Dan, as he let in Tyrone.

'Don't worry about it,' replied Tyrone, heading to the cellar, the others following.

Trevor had fallen asleep sitting up, his head lolling to the side. Tyrone kicked the bottom of his shoe, shaking him awake.

'Pick him up.'

Ban-Dan and Nathan obliged. Still dazed and sleepy, Trevor didn't resist. When he was upright, Tyrone slammed his left fist into Trevor's liver, Trevor gasping and sinking to one knee.

'Lift him again.'

Again, they lifted Trevor, still coughing profusely. Tyrone took his time, carefully picking his shots, relishing Trevor's painful shouts. He kept his hits centred around Trevor's chest and stomach, the man unable to protect himself. Every time he fell, Tyrone had him picked back up.

'What the hell do you want?' Trevor finally uttered, coughing and wheezing. Confused, Tyrone stepped into his eye line.

'Right now? Nothing. I'm just letting off some steam. Since you brought it up . . . what do you have to tell me?'

Trevor hesitated. Turning away, Tyrone rooted around behind him, finding a hammer in a rusted metal drawer in the corner of the room. Testing the weight, he stalked back towards Trevor.

'Hold out his arm.'

Trevor again struggled, but couldn't overpower the pair. Ban-Dan punched him in the stomach, and Nathan held out his arm. Swinging back the hammer, Tyrone smashed it against Trevor's left hand. Trevor screamed in pain. Pausing, Tyrone this time hit him in his left kneecap, the subsequent scream even louder.

'Let him go.'

Trevor collapsed to the floor, weeping in agony. The trio stared down at him, their faces impassive.

'Now then; talk, or do I have to break every bone in your body?'

'You're gonna have to kill me. I ain't telling you shit,' Trevor gasped, tears streaming down his face. Tyrone chuckled, hiding his annoyance.

'I guess we've got some more work to do.'

For the next thirty minutes, the trio worked over Trevor, taking turns to beat him, striking his right forearm and right kneecap with the hammer.

Still, Trevor wouldn't give up.

'I'm surprised he's still conscious,' Nathan remarked, hands on his legs, sucking in air.

'He's tough, I've gotta give it to him,' said Tyrone, still twirling the hammer. 'He's said he's not going to talk, so we'll finish him off.'

'How do you want to do it?' Nathan asked, replying as if Trevor wasn't there.

'Let's electrocute him. One of you lot run a bath. We'll get him in it, then toss summat in. Maybe a toaster,' said Tyrone. 'It's a bit quick, but we've got work to do if we're gonna hunt down that tosser Snypa.'

Ban-Dan nodded and went to leave the room.

'Wait . . . wait,' Trevor choked out.

Tyrone paused, looking down at his beaten foe.

'Talk.'

'I'll give you an address . . . Just stop . . .'

Tyrone nodded to Ban-Dan.

'Get a pen and some paper.'

Tyrone and the others hurried from the cellar when Trevor gave them the address.

'Ban-Dan, take Cropper and go check out the address. I need to go home and handle something, but I'll be back if it's a live spot. Nathan, stay here and clean up. We're gonna take him out quickly, once we've got confirmation.'

Nathan nodded.

'Got it. I'm gonna wash my face. I'm sweating from that beating.'

'You need to come and train with me. I'll get you in shape,' teased Tyrone. Laughing, the group dispersed, Nathan and Ban-Dan returning to the living room. As Tyrone made for the front door, a piercing scream stopped him in his tracks.

'We're gonna have to get soundproofing if he keeps up that damn noise,' he said to a chorus of laughter. Stepping out onto the street, he swung the door closed behind him.

None of them noticed the door to the cellar hadn't been re-locked.

CHAPTER TWENTY-ONE

TYRONE SAT AT HOME, surfing through the television channels, having worked through his anger on Trevor. Tia had stormed upstairs when he came in. He'd almost gone after her, but didn't.

Tyrone had intended to talk with Tia — hence leaving the safe house, but now wondered why he should bother. They'd got married just before Nathaniel was born. Tia wanted it, insisting their family needed to be protected. Tyrone hadn't fought, and now wondered if he should have.

Tyrone was fond of Tia, and thought he loved her, but they barely got along, and only ever seemed to argue. As he mulled it over, Tyrone noted most of their arguments were about Nathaniel. He recalled his conversation a while back with his son, about him becoming a foot-baller. He'd warned him then that transitioning from the streets to the football pitch was difficult, but he'd miss-sold it.

The streets were always watching. Most people Tyrone knew who were born to the streets, stayed in them. He wanted the best for his son, but at the same time, he wanted to ensure he was prepared for the inevitable.

He just needed to figure out the best way to do it.

Tyrone's phone rang, and he stifled a yawn before answering.

'What have you got for me, Cropper?'

'You need to get to the spot. Sharpish.'

Tyrone sat up, sensing the hesitancy in Cropper's tone.

'What's happened?' he demanded.

'He's gone.'

———

TYRONE MADE it to Harehills in record time. Car screeching to a stop outside, he hurried through the door, seeing his team waiting for him. Nathan had a sheepish look on his face. Behind him, Tyrone spotted the wide-open cellar door.

'What the fuck happened?' His eyes bored into Nathan's. To his credit, the man didn't look away.

'We left the door open after we smacked him around.'

'*We?* You were the one watching him,' said Tyrone, nostrils flaring.

'I was upstairs. I fell asleep on the bed. We definitely broke some of his bones. I'm surprised he could even walk,' said Nathan. Behind him, Cropper shook his head. Tyrone took a deep breath. It wasn't the time to blow up at Nathan.

'Where does he live? Where does his brother live?'

'Donovan stays in the Hood. He lives on Leopold Street.'

'And Trevor?'

'I don't know.'

Mind whirring, Tyrone made a quick decision.

'Everyone take a strap. Nathan, you and Cropper go to Louis Street — that's the address Trevor gave us for Snypa. You see anyone funny at the spot, light it up.'

Cropper nodded.

'What are you gonna do?'

'I'm gonna find Trevor.'

———

AFTER CALLING Jamar and giving him ten minutes to find Trevor's home address, Tyrone and Ban-Dan hurried out to Tyrone's car. They drove to the Hood, parking on Cowper Street. A purple Ford Escort waited. They climbed in. Ban-Dan drove, and Tyrone called Jamar again.

'What do you have for me?'

'Do you know how much shit you're putting me in? I had to make up an excuse to get—'

'Address. Now.'

Grumbling under his breath, Jamar gave Tyrone the address, and he hung up.

They drove to the reported location, a house on Bayswater Avenue. The lower room lights were on as they approached.

'Trevor doesn't have kids, does he?' said Tyrone, a moment later.

'Not that I know of,' replied Ban-Dan.

'Keep the engine running.'

Climbing from the car and making sure his balaclava was secure, Tyrone opened fire, the Mac-11 jerking in his hand. His aim was true as he fired into the house. He heard yells amid the shots. Stepping into the house, he cautiously moved through the haze of gun smoke and dust, stunned at the damage he'd done to the living room.

Trevor was on the floor, wheezing, bleeding from multiple wounds. Another man was face-down in a pool of blood. Approaching Trevor, Tyrone gazed at him for a long moment, then unloaded another volley of bullets into him, until he was still. Turning his gun on the second man, he pulled the trigger, flinching when he heard the gun click.

'Shit.'

Tyrone stared at the downed man for another moment. He'd made more noise than he'd intended, and had taken longer than planned. The police were likely already on route.

Making a decision, Tyrone left. The man would hopefully bleed out, but if he didn't, it was a problem for another time.

Hurrying to the car, he commanded Ban-Dan to drive.

Several streets away, they abandoned the car and removed their gloves and balaclavas, knowing the area would be crawling with police before long. Heading down Bankside Road to the Hood, they walked up to Cowper Street, keeping an eye out for anything out of the ordinary. Reaching Tyrone's car, they drove back to the safe house.

When they arrived, Nathan and Cropper were there, sipping beers. They stood when Tyrone and Ban-Dan entered.

'Did you get them?' Cropper asked. Ignoring him, Tyrone went right for Nathan. The man had no time to resist as Tyrone caught him flush on the nose with a vicious headbutt. Shoving him to the floor, he stomped on his chest and stomach, glaring down at his worker.

'You ever mess up like that again, and I'll kill you.' He stepped over Nathan's moaning frame and headed for the kitchen, signalling for Cropper to follow. He made himself a glass of brandy, adrenaline still coursing through his body.

'Trevor's gone.'

Cropper nodded. 'Figured you'd get him. He was duping us, anyway. We sat on the spot for a bit. One or two guys came and went, leaving with bags. Looks like it's a stash spot rather than a war-time location. Didn't see Snypa or anyone I recognised.'

Tyrone sipped his drink, mulling everything over, pleased he'd removed an enemy, but wanting Snypa out of the way as soon as possible.

'We'll rob the spot. If we don't get Snypa, then Trevor's body and us hitting his place will get him moving. Take Ban-Dan and set it up.'

CHAPTER TWENTY-TWO

OVER THE NEXT TWO DAYS, Chapeltown buzzed with the story of Trevor's murder.

Cropper knocked at Tyrone's door the following day. Tyrone came storming out, and Cropper noticed the bulky outline of a bulletproof vest as they walked to the car.

'You heard about Donovan then?' Cropper asked as they climbed into the car.

'Yeah. He was with his brother when I shot up the spot, and he survived. Everyone needs to have eyes in the back of their heads now,' said Tyrone.

'You gonna do anything about your family?'

'It's on my to-do list,' said Tyrone, already thinking of the hassle this would cause.

———

AFTER SPENDING some time going over the plan for Snypa with the team, Tyrone ran some more errands, then headed back home. He was dozing off in his chair just over an hour later, when there was a knock at the door. A scowl came to Tyrone's face when he noticed the police standing there. An older officer with balding salt and pepper hair, piercing eyes, and an intense red-haired man glared back at him.

'What can I help you with?' He asked.

'Just wanted to ask you a few questions,' the older officer said. 'I'm Detective Rigby, and this is Detective Murphy.'

'I'm not answering anything.'

Rigby smiled, nodding. 'Guilty conscience? We know what you did to Trevor.'

'Don't know what you're talking about,' said Tyrone.

'So you say. Your name's still being banded around. You're going to have some very angry Jamaicans after you soon enough. We might be the only friends you have.'

Tyrone shrugged.

'Honestly, I'd love to help, really I would. I mean, who doesn't love shovelling shit for pigs? Problem is, I don't know what you're talking about, so unless you wanna charge me with something, I'd suggest fucking off.'

Murphy's eyes flashed. He stepped forward, but Rigby laid a hand on his chest.

'We're not here for that. You've tipped over a wasp's nest, Dunn. I hope you can deal with the fallout.'

The officers left. Tyrone stared after them, his scowl deepening. He'd expected to be a suspect, but he still didn't like the police coming to the door and troubling him. He would have to be extremely careful going forward.

'What did they want?'

Tyrone jumped, startled as he turned to face Nathaniel. The boy stood at the bottom of the stairs, a troubled expression on his face as he studied his dad.

'Nothing you need to worry about, Nat.'

Nathaniel frowned.

'Is it about those shootings?'

Tyrone quickly closed and locked the door, eyes widening.

'What do you know about any shootings?'

'People are talking all around the Hood, dad.' Nathaniel's frown deepened. 'Some are saying you're gonna be killed.'

Tyrone wondered where the stories were coming from, assuming Snypa's team were spinning the propaganda in their favour. He was surprised he hadn't heard from Mitch yet, but knew the lecture was coming. Seeing that his son still looked worried, Tyrone hugged him, pressing a kiss to the top of his head.

'Like I said, you don't need to worry. I'm not gonna lie and tell you it's not serious out there, but I know what I'm doing. Dunn's don't back down. You remember that?'

Nathaniel nodded.

'I'll be fine, Nat. I'm always fine.'

Finally, Nathaniel smiled.

'I know, dad.'

Nathaniel headed back upstairs. As Tyrone was about to go and sit in the living room, he heard a screech of tires, and his stomach plummeted. Heart racing, he crouched, but then he heard nothing. Quickly unlocking the door, he hurried outside, noticing a car driving up the road.

Tyrone took a deep breath. He needed to end the situation before Snypa or Donovan's people could strike.

——————

THAT EVENING, Tyrone left the house, armed and still wearing his bulletproof vest. It had been a tense day of making phone calls, pumping people for gossip, and trying to find a direct location for Snypa's team. Anyone that knew anything seemed to have gone to ground, and he was displeased.

Tyrone needed to blow off some steam. He and Tia still weren't on good terms, so he couldn't do anything with her. He didn't know where he was at with Shardell. They hadn't spoken in a while, and she'd been distant the last time.

He'd considered again whether he was generally losing his touch with women, and off the back of this, he made up his mind to surprise Shardell and make amends.

Not for her sake, but for his own, Tyrone mused, driving the new car he'd temporarily swapped with an associate. It was a grey Volkswagen that ran well, but he missed his Beemer.

Pulling onto Shardell's street, Tyrone's eyes narrowed when he saw an unfamiliar car parked outside her house. Muscles tensing, he rooted around his ride for the 9mm pistol he'd stashed there, and put on his leather gloves. Knocking hard at the door, he grit his teeth, already feeling his breathing intensifying. When Shardell answered, she gasped.

'Ty—'

Tyrone pushed past her, sending her flying into the stairs as he stormed into the living room, almost tripping over a pair of Nike Air Max trainers. Jamar jumped to his feet from the previously comfortable spot he'd held on the sofa, eyes widening when he saw Tyrone.

'Ty . . . Tyrone, it's not what it looks like,' he gibbered.

'Really? 'Cause it looks to me like you're stepping on toes.' Tyrone went for Jamar, who ran for the kitchen door. With ease, Tyrone cut him off.

'Please, Tyrone, I'm sorry!'

Tyrone responded by crashing his gun against Jamar's jaw, gripping him by his hair and hitting him repeatedly. The red mist had descended. He was aware of Shardell's screaming but didn't stop hitting Jamar. A thin arm wrapped around his throat as Shardell attempted to restrain him, but Tyrone easily shrugged her off, turning on her.

'You're next if you don't stay there and keep your mouth shut,' he warned. Kneeling over Jamar, he put his gun in the bloodied man's mouth. 'I should blow your damn brains out right now.' Again, his eyes found Shardell's. 'And you, you dirty slag. Who do you think you are?'

'What was I supposed to do?' Shardell shrieked, overcoming her fear. 'Wait around for a man who didn't want me? I care about Jamar. This isn't just a fling.'

'Are you fucking serious?' Tyrone's finger rested on the trigger, Jamar unresisting beneath him. 'I put you two together. You're nothing but a bang to him.'

'And what am I to you? You've never cared about me, and you

don't care now. You're just mad because I'm not interested in you anymore.'

Tyrone's finger tightened on the trigger, tempted to kill Jamar and then Shardell. Breathing hard, he composed himself, sliding to his feet. Instinctively, Shardell reared back.

'You made your choice. The both of you. Go near the Feds, and you're both dead, along with your families.'

Tyrone stormed from the room, leaving behind a badly beaten man and a hysterical woman. In the car, he wiped down the gun, still trying to control the rage that wanted to take over, still smarting over Shardell's words. Glancing back towards the house for a moment, Tyrone shook his head. Turning the keys in the ignition, he started the car and sped away.

His phone rang as he pulled off from her street.

'What's up, Rudy?'

'Where are you?' Rudy's tone was urgent, and Tyrone sat straighter in his seat.

'I'm out. Going home now.'

'Mitch wants to talk to you.'

'Tell him to come and see me tomorrow.'

Rudy paused.

'He's demanding you come now. He's furious, Ty.'

CHAPTER TWENTY-THREE

BEFORE LONG, Tyrone stood in Mitch's converted cellar. Similar to his garage, a few weights were in the corner, along with a rower and a battered exercise mat. The room had a musty odour. Rudy smoked a cigarette in the corner. He nodded at Tyrone, who slowly nodded back.

Mitch hadn't spoken since he'd arrived. His jaw jutted under the low light provided by the dusty room. He kept his eyes on his brother for a long moment before he finally spoke.

'What the fuck were you thinking? Craig was bad enough, but now you've killed Trevor and winged Donovan. He's still in hospital, but his people will come for you.'

'Trevor admitted Snypa was behind Craig's little takeover scheme, just like I said. He wanted us out of the way, so I acted for our crew — the way I always do when shit needs doing. You're pissed, and I get that, but we need to bury it, work together on this, and take out the whole crew.'

'What the hell is wrong with you?' roared Mitch, nearly making Rudy drop his cigarette in surprise. 'The streets are baking hot. Two of our spots have been hit. Police are all around, getting into people's business, and it's all down to the carnage you've started. What did I tell you? I said that Leeds didn't want another war, and now I'm getting calls from everyone about us making it harder to eat.'

Tyrone unflinchingly stared back at his brother. 'I don't give a fuck about any of that. I care about our team, and how we move. We finish this, people fall in line, and we step up and take our rightful place at the top of the streets. Like we should have years ago.'

Mitch folded his arms, still furious.

'We're not doing that.'

Tyrone's eyes narrowed.

'Excuse me?'

'You heard what I said.'

Tyrone stepped toward his brother. Rudy straightened, eyes darting between the pair.

'You seem to keep forgetting that you're not my boss. This is our crew. We started it together, and you don't control it, or me.'

'You're tapped, bro,' said Mitch, sneering. 'While you've been out on your little crusade, I've kept things going. Kept money in people's pockets and kept steering the ship. You got yourself into this shit. You wanna go after Snypa and his team, and rob little drug spots, you can do it on your own.'

Tyrone frowned, considering which of his team was leaking information. After a moment, he spoke, keeping his words level as he fought to avoid tearing into his brother.

'You're a disgrace, Mitch. If it wasn't for me, every two-bit gangster in Yorkshire would be violating you.'

Mitch's mouth tightened, eyes blazing with barely-repressed anger.

'Get out.'

'What are you gonna do if I don't? You're soft, Mitch, and everyone's gonna see what I do.'

Before anyone could react, Mitch's fist shot out, catching Tyrone with a vicious hit to the mouth. It sent his head reeling back, but he kept his feet. Rudy moved, then stopped, not knowing what to do.

Tyrone spat blood on the floor, then touched his mouth with his fingers. His glare intensified as he stared at Mitch, that dark side of his mind screaming at him to destroy his brother; to punish him for daring to touch him. Rudy wouldn't be able to stop him if he did.

It was his brother, though.

Despite their differences, Tyrone couldn't hurt his family. With a final scathing look, he walked away.

———

TYRONE WAS BACK at the safe house, alone. It had been a few hours since he'd left Mitch, and he'd dealt with the fallout by having several drinks, lamenting the messy situation.

The argument with Mitch had been brewing for some time. They had fundamental differences in leadership, and they likely should have parted ways years ago. Mitch was too passive for his liking, and the streets had ways of dealing with passive people. They had looked out for and protected one another all their lives, but those days seemed a distant memory now.

Whether Mitch wanted to admit it, he knew Tyrone had the crew's best interests at heart. Tyrone was sure of it.

He had to wonder about what he'd done, though.

He was on the outs with his brother, who seemed to have usurped control of the crew. Tyrone's moves had backed him further into a corner. Mitch had said to him a while back that he kept moving forward, hitting the wall, not thinking of the consequences.

As he sipped yet another drink, Tyrone wondered if there had been a better way to deal with the situation, pondering what Mitch might have done if Craig had directly attacked.

Ultimately, what was done, was done.

There was no going back. Tyrone had to kill Snypa, because he'd taken it too far for Snypa to back down. He wouldn't be appeased, and for the first time, it truly hit Tyrone that he didn't have the backing of his brother.

A chill descended over him as he realised he would need to make a move after he killed Snypa. He would either need to take the crew by force, or somehow make peace with Mitch.

CHAPTER TWENTY-FOUR

TYRONE TOOK A DEEP BREATH, steeling himself for the phone call he needed to make. There was no place for regrets at this stage. He had to handle his business, and then he could think about everything else.

Finally, he called Tia. She promptly answered.

'Ty, what do you want? Where are you? People have been calling the house, looking for you. I tried calling Mitch, but he wouldn't tell me anything. What's going on?'

'Tia, listen. Look, I'm going to be gone for a while. I need to sort some things.'

'What the hell does that mean?'

'Just listen,' he repeated, already gritting his teeth. 'There's money hidden in a compartment in the garage. It's in the corner of the room, behind the heavy bag. Should be more than enough, but reach out to Mitch if you need more.'

'Wait, slow down,' Tia interjected. 'I still don't understand what's going on. How long are you going to be away?'

'I don't know, okay? If I did, I'd tell you. I'm trying to look after you and Nat.'

Tia paused before she responded.

'How long do we have to keep doing this?'

Despite his resolve, the pain in Tia's voice nearly broke Tyrone. He closed his eyes. There was no way to make her feel better. It had simply gone too far.

'I can't talk now, Tia. I lo . . . I have to go.' He ended the call and left the room.

————

THE CREW HAD ASSEMBLED in the living room, ready for orders. Tyrone had made a few calls earlier trying to find support, but he'd had no luck — other than a few wild bandits that would be more hindrance than help.

There would be a lot to answer once Snypa was dead.

Tyrone assessed each man, the trio standing with him, just as they had many times in the past.

Even Rudy was on the other side.

For a moment, Tyrone recalled Mitch's words the last time they'd spoken. One of his team had given Mitch and Rudy information about their plan.

This wasn't the time for confrontation, though. His people needed him. They knew what they were up against, and they needed motivation.

Tyrone could do that.

'This is it,' he started. 'We know what we're doing. It's nothing we haven't done before. We do this job, make more money than we've ever seen, and then the rest of the crew comes crawling back. The four of us will get it done. We're a smaller force, so we can't wage an all-out war with Snypa's people. Instead, we're going to cut the head off the snake.' He looked into each man's eyes, trying to transfer the adrenaline pumping through his veins. 'The city is ours. It starts tonight. Don't fucking hold back.'

They all smiled. Ban-Dan emphatically nodded, and Nathan grinned. Cropper had a frown on his face, but Tyrone wasn't worried about him. Cropper had been with him the longest; they'd been around the block. Cropper had handled similar business multiple times, and he knew his job.

Tyrone's phone rang. His nostrils flared when he saw Shardell's number.

'What do you want?' He barked.

'I'm really sorry about everything that happened, Ty. I got carried away, and I regret that, but I need your help. I need to see you.'

'This ain't the time for—'

'Ty, it's important! It's Jamar.'

She had his attention now.

'What about him?'

'He made a phone call from the house—'

'You're still seeing him?'

'Ty, just listen. I'm cutting it off with him, I promise. He spoke to one of Snypa's men. About you.'

Tyrone was alert, eyes flitting to his team. Finally, he noticed she was whispering.

'Is he still there?'

'Yeah. He's in a really good mood, but I'm calling you from the bathroom. I didn't want him to hear me.'

'Keep him there. I'm on my way.'

Hanging up, Tyrone stowed his phone. His team stared at him with narrowed eyes and frowns.

'What's going on?' Cropper asked.

'There's been a change of plan. I think Snypa's people know we're coming.'

The trio looked uneasy now, exchanging looks.

'What are we going to do then?' Nathan asked.

'I'm gonna go to Shardell's and snatch Jamar. He's been making calls from her house, and I think he's trying to set us up. I'll find out what's waiting for us. You lot sit tight until then.'

'Ty, I know what you're saying, but we may not get a better chance than this,' said Cropper. 'While you're doing that, I can still survey the spot. Take these two with you, and then we can coordinate after. At least that way, we're covering all our bases.'

Tyrone mulled it over. It was a good plan. He nodded his approval.

'Cool. Ban-Dan, Nathan, you're with me. Cropper, I'll ring you when we're through.'

The men slapped hands and shuffled from the house.

———

NATHAN DROVE. Tyrone sat in the back, fully armed, with a bulletproof vest and two guns, ready for war. He was ready to end all of this for good, starting with Jamar. He would take him from Shardell's, and kill him in the woods somewhere, after he learned everything he needed to know. He thought about Cropper for a moment, but relaxed. Cropper knew how to keep himself hidden. He'd be okay.

No one spoke during the drive, each man lost in his own thoughts. Tyrone wondered what was going through their minds; whether they regretted riding with him, then he shook off the negativity. It wasn't the time for that. He needed to be confident. To keep pushing forward.

'Right, when we get there, you lot hang back. I'll smack him around and drag him out to the car. We'll take him somewhere and get what we need from him,' he said. Both men grunted their understanding. They pulled onto Shardell's street. Glancing out of the window, Tyrone's eyes widened as he spotted movement within a garden.

'Ban-Dan, pull out; it's a trap!'

The sounds of gunfire extinguished his words. Nathan's subsequent yells were punctuated by shots and the screech of tires as Ban-Dan tried to get away, only to find their car blocked by another that had pulled up behind them. Tyrone had one of his guns up, but a shot to the arm disabled him, and he slid down in his seat. Dizzy and in pain, he didn't even know which direction it had come from.

Scrambling, he tried to get to his second gun, his fingers finding the trigger just as a man appeared at the car window, gun raised. Tyrone was a shade faster, a bullet finding the man's head.

He needed to keep moving.

Opening the door, he crouched low as more bullets whined around him. Tyrone zig-zagged, staying on the move, just waiting to feel the fiery pain of another shot. His left arm was still throbbing, the warm blood pouring down his arm. Lack of movement from the car behind him suggested Nathan and Ban-Dan were dead, or close to it. They'd sat in the front of the car, and were likely the recipients of most of the bullets. Tyrone didn't know how many shooters were still out there, but he jumped into a garden, needing to catch his breath and get his bearings.

The men approached, heavy footsteps slapping against the pavement. Popping up, Tyrone again began firing, managing to hit one of the approaching men and dropping him. His partner returned fire, a bullet lodging into Tyrone's bicep. He screamed, but managed to keep hold of his gun, hitting the man in the stomach. The bullet had caught Tyrone in the same arm he'd been shot in earlier, and the pain was far more intense. Gritting his teeth, he approached the man, gun raised. The gunshots had stopped, the air filled with acrid gun smoke.

The man he'd shot in the stomach sobbed in pain, eyes wide, illuminated by a nearby streetlight. He looked up at Tyrone, opening his mouth to speak.

The bullet snapped his head back.

Tyrone gingerly touched his arm, seeing spots in front of his eyes. He blinked them away, needing more than ever to stay active. Approaching the car, he confirmed his earlier suspicions. Ban-Dan and Nathan were both dead. Both had been riddled with multiple bullets. Tyrone hung his head in sorrow for a moment, then he was back to business. They would be avenged, but people were converging, some screaming, others shouting about calling the police. He desperately wanted to go and get Shardell and Jamar, but he couldn't. He needed to survive.

'Sorry,' he mumbled to his dead team, dragging Nathan from the driver's seat, then Ban-Dan. He climbed in and started the engine, elated it still worked. It took a few moments to get around the car that had boxed them in, but he burned rubber after that, needing to get to safety.

CHAPTER TWENTY-FIVE

TYRONE TRUDGED into the safe house, still heavily bleeding. He'd taken off his vest, and needed to call someone to look at his wounds before he could get any further. He hoped Cropper had stayed out of sight, but he would need to contact him soon so they could go underground and devise a plan. Getting to money would be difficult, but they still had weapons, and could strike Snypa and his team from the shadows.

After he'd tortured Jamar and Shardell, anyway.

When Tyrone entered the living room, his eyes narrowed when he saw the light in the kitchen. Cautiously, he approached, and his heart nearly stopped at the sight in front of him.

Cropper, getting himself a drink, whistling to himself.

Cropper, who had insisted the trio go to Shardell's.

Tyrone saw red.

'Glad you made it back, mate,' he said, voice shaking.

Cropper seemed to jump a foot in the air, his glass smashing on the floor. His eyes were wide as he assessed Tyrone, taking in his condition.

'What happened, Ty? I . . . left Snypa's stash spot. They moved out of there, so I came back. I was gonna call you after I finished my drink.'

Trembling, he pointed to the glass on the floor, but Tyrone's eyes didn't leave Cropper's. He shook his head, floored at the fact that Cropper, of all people, would plot against him.

'Ty, it's not what you think. I promise.'

'I hope the payoff was worth it,' replied Tyrone. Gun raised, he fired twice, hitting Cropper in the chest, watching his former friend twitch on the ground, nestled amongst the glass, as the life left him. Tyrone remained still, numb to the fact that he'd just killed a once-loyal friend.

A noise from behind startled him, and he pivoted, gun raised. Rudy was quicker, his gun already pointed at Tyrone.

'You turned on me too?' Tyrone asked, his tone incredulous, gun limply resting by his side. Rudy shook his head.

'I know it's all gone to shit for you. Cropper called me earlier. Told me about this spot. You need to come with me before this goes any further.'

Tyrone was only half-listening.

'Everyone switched on me . . . the only two that were loyal got gunned down like rats. They didn't even get a shot off,' he mumbled.

'Put the gun down, Ty. Come with me, and we can get this sorted.'

'I can't trust anyone.' Tyrone shook his head. His arm felt like it was going to fall off. He'd lost a lot of blood and needed to get some help.

Rudy wasn't that help, though.

He'd shown his true colours. Just like Cropper. Just like Shardell.

'You're nothing but Mitch's bitch,' he spat. 'I'm not going anywhere with you. Difference between us . . . is that I'm free. I always make my own choices.'

Tyrone raised his gun, but Rudy didn't hesitate.

The bullets slammed into Tyrone, and he stumbled backwards, landing near Cropper's dead body. He stared up at his friend, noting the saddened expression on Rudy's face as his eyes dimmed, and everything went black.

EPILOGUE
AUGUST 2002

THE DEATH of Tyrone Dunn stunned the streets, especially those not in the know regarding his campaign against Snypa. Few people knew the whole story, but word had spread that his team had been wiped out. He'd been found in a house in Leeds, along with the body of Cropper, identified as a long-time friend and ally.

Knowing Tyrone's reputation and the respect he garnered, people — police included — expected an immediate retaliation, but nothing transpired, and before long, people moved on to newer gossip.

———

SEPTEMBER 2002

Snypa smiled broadly as he sipped a white rum and ginger beer combination. The smile had been present for the past month, happy at the death of a man who had been a major thorn in his side. Tyrone Dunn was dead, which meant he could finally move on from looking over his shoulder.

'How are you feeling?' He said to his companion. They sat outside

Snypa's house, and had been posted there for the past hour, enjoying the last vestiges of sun.

'Why are you asking me now?' Donovan replied.

'I finally noticed you weren't drinking. Figured you were still on medication or summat. I'm surprised you're out of the hospital already.'

Donovan scowled.

'I won't be running marathons anytime soon, but the bullets didn't hit anything important. When I could move, I checked myself out. I go for checkups and stuff, but as long as I'm resting, they don't say shit.'

Snypa grinned. 'That's good. No reason for you to rush back to it.'

'Just tell me what the next step of the plan is,' said Donovan. Snypa was cool, but he dithered around the point too much. Donovan knew he'd been invited over for a reason.

'I'm gonna give it a little longer, but everything is in place. We're wiping out Mitch and Rudy. We'll give the rest of the team the chance to get down with us, or they go too.'

'Mitch isn't his brother. He's not gonna blindly run into traps, or act how you think he will.'

Snypa's smile slipped from his face. 'Mitch is a Dunn, and Dunn's aren't the smartest. He's gotta avenge his brother somehow, or he loses face.'

'You're missing the main point, Snypa,' said Donovan slowly, as if speaking to a small child.

'What's that?'

'We didn't kill Tyrone. No one knows who did.'

'So what?'

Donovan rubbed his eyes. Snypa wasn't getting it.

'We don't know if Mitch knows.'

'It doesn't matter if he knows or not. It doesn't matter how smart he is. He can't win.'

As the pair spoke, a man walked down the street towards them, wearing all black, a scowl on his face. They noticed him immediately. Snypa's nearby bodyguard straightened, hand drifting to his side where his gun rested. With all eyes on the intruder, no one paid attention to the two men approaching from the other end of the street.

The pair opened fire, riddling Snypa's bodyguard with bullets. Snypa and Donavan didn't even get a chance to run before the *distraction* shot both of them in the head, coldly watching as they slid to the floor amid blood and the remnants of their drinks. They dispersed in the opposite directions they'd come, leaving three dead men in their wake.

———

'IT'S DONE.'

Rudy still held the phone in his hand, looking at Mitch, who sipped a drink, not immediately acknowledging his words. Since Tyrone's death, Mitch had been in a funk. He knew why his brother had to die, but he hadn't enjoyed giving the order.

'Good,' he finally replied. 'Another team is taking care of Ty's bit on the side, and Jamar the fool.'

'At least we can breathe again,' said Rudy. He'd made his peace with Tyrone's death, still regretting the fact he'd had to pull the trigger, but accepting it needed to be done. 'Cropper fed us info on Tyrone's moves so we could look after him, but he tried playing both sides when he did the deal with Snypa's lot. I'd have taken him out, even if Ty didn't.'

Mitch shrugged. 'It'll take a while, but we got Mitch and Donovan. If the JK Posse make a move, we'll deal with them too, but I've got connections over there. Ty would have realised that, if he'd worked with me, instead of against me.'

Rudy stayed quiet. Mitch rubbed his forehead.

'You take Tyrone's spot. You run security, and oversee the streets from now on. Any expansion will go ahead, but we'll do it slowly, working from the shadows. Let the idiots go out and get themselves killed. We work smarter.'

Rudy smiled.

'Thank you, Mitch.'

Mitch shook his head.

'You earned it. Neither of us enjoyed what we had to do, but we both know it needed to be done.'

RUDY DROVE to see Tia after he left Mitch, still thinking about his promotion. He was pleased he would have more influence and sway over the team's direction. Tyrone was his best friend, but he had a one-track mind with the streets, whereas Mitch was more realistic. There would be positive changes, and the team was in a solid position.

Tia let him in, barely meeting his eyes. She'd been the same since learning of Tyrone's death. He'd caught her crying a few times, but she'd mostly tried internalising it.

Rudy pulled her into a hug. She relaxed against his chest.

'How are you doing, Tia?' He asked once they'd let go. 'I know it's a stupid question.'

'We just have to keep going,' she listlessly replied. 'Nothing else to do.'

'Mitch and I have you covered with whatever you need,' he said, and Tia nodded.

'I know. Mitch has been over to see us a few times, but I appreciate it. Thank you.'

They spoke for a few more minutes, then they shared another hug. Rudy kissed her forehead, the hug lingering for far longer this time.

'Nathaniel upstairs?' He asked. Tia shook her head against his chest.

'He's in the garage. He's always in there nowadays.'

Rudy headed out to the garage, where Nathaniel was lifting dumb-bells, eyes staring straight ahead into the mirror as he breathed in and out.

Rudy hadn't seen him properly since the funeral, but he seemed to have shot up in size. He recognised the fury and determination in the boy's face, and he had to push aside the guilt he suddenly felt.

Despite Tyrone's flaws, Nathaniel had worshipped him, and it would be hard for him to move forward.

'You're doing well with those weights,' he said, announcing himself. Nathaniel finished his set and then lowered them to the floor. He wiped his face with a flannel, budding muscles straining under the tight vest top he wore.

'Thanks.'

Rudy nodded.

'I spoke with your mum. I'll tell you the same thing. If you need anything, we're here for you. You don't need to go through this all on your own. Your mum has my number, okay?'

'Okay.'

With that, Nathaniel grabbed the weights and began lifting again, as if Rudy wasn't even there.

'Nathaniel.'

Nathaniel ignored him. Rudy's eyes narrowed, smarting over the disrespect.

'Nathaniel, I'm talking to you.'

'I don't go by Nathaniel anymore,' he replied, not even looking at him. 'I go by *Natty D* now.'

DID YOU ENJOY THE READ?

Thank you for reading Blood & Business!

My manager and I came up with the concept for this novella during a hike, and we bounced ideas off of each other, then I went away and crafted the end product.

Please take a minute or two to help me by leaving a review – even if it's just a few lines. Reviews help massively with getting my books in front of new readers. I personally read every review and take all feedback on board.

To support me, please click the relevant link below:
    UK: http://www.amazon.co.uk/review/create-review?&asin= B0BK771Y5Q

US: http://www.amazon.com/review/create-review?&asin= B0BK771Y5Q

Make sure you're following me on Amazon to keep up to date with my releases, or that you're signed up to my email list, and I'll see you at the next book!

READ HUSTLER'S AMBITION

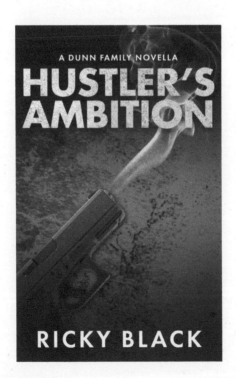

HUSTLER'S AMBITION SAMPLE

Read the latest novella in the gritty and gripping Dunn Family Series,
Hustler's Ambition Now.

CHAPTER ONE

MAY 2020

CAMERON GREENE STARED at his phone screen, ignoring the thumping rap music playing from a dock, the weed stench permeating the room. He hunched further over the phone, refreshing the page at regular intervals. After what seemed like an age, his bet disappeared from the screen. Heart racing, Cameron checked his settled bets, noting his horse had *placed*, but hadn't won.

'Fuck!'

Cameron slammed down his phone, breathing hard. He poured himself a drink from the brandy bottle on his coffee table, stewing over the missed opportunity.

Downing his drink, Cameron grabbed his phone and called a number.

'Yes, Cam. Everything good,' an airy voice answered.

'That tip you gave me was shit,' Cameron snarled. 'What the hell are you playing at?'

'Yo, you begged me for that tip,' the man replied, his tone instantly defensive.

'Whatever. You better come correct next time, or I'm gonna smack you up,' Cameron warned, before hanging up, still fuming over the situation. The winnings would have netted him eight thousand pounds, which would have enabled him to buy the watch he'd had his eye on for a while. Navigating back to the gambling app, he considered putting money on another bet, but hesitated.

Cameron didn't place bets at the same level as some of his associates. Every Friday, it seemed they were at the bookies, or making WhatsApp groups to trade bets. He'd had a few wins, though, and it always seemed like a viable way out. Cameron didn't think he was an addict — quite the contrary. He saw gambling as his answer to investing. Spence had mentioned it to him over the years, emphasising a long-term plan and being prepared for the future. Cameron disagreed. As far as he was concerned, investing and gambling were the same. The only difference was, gambling returned on his investment immediately.

Spence was one of his two best friends, both of whom he worked with. They primarily sold drugs, but had their hands in numerous nefarious ventures.

In their crew, everyone seemed to have a function. Natty Deeds was the ringleader. He ran their small sub-crew. Unquestionably talented, but highly connected, Natty was the nephew of the organisation's boss, Mitch Dunn. Cameron had been lucky to be hired, and was sure he wouldn't have a job if Natty wasn't Mitch's nephew.

It galled him at times. Cameron's friends always seemed to have money, yet he was living week to week, barely staying ahead. Despite their closeness, he couldn't help looking at his friends sceptically sometimes, wondering if he was being paid fairly and whether he could do anything about it if he wasn't.

Cameron's thoughts deepened. He didn't have the same connections as his friends, which left him feeling like he was playing catch up. Natty and Spence had been brought up around crime, moulded and shaped into useful parts of the machine. Natty had his uncle and his dad, and Spence's story was similar. All deep in the life, they could impart their knowledge and wisdom to those next in line.

Cameron didn't have that benefit. Beyond knowing his name, there was little he knew about his father. He'd left nothing to help Cameron learn and grow. Much of what he had learnt, he'd taken from his friends. Leaning on their expertise was uncomfortable for Cameron. He was behind in the game, and that frustrated him.

'Fuck it,' he mumbled, wiping his mouth. He would sleep on it, and sort out his problems tomorrow.

———

THE FOLLOWING DAY, Cameron woke up, still annoyed about the loss. He'd had to talk himself out of tracking down *Skinny Dave*, the man who had given him the tip. Cameron had won a few bets using his tips in the past, but mostly when backing the clear favourite.

Cameron wondered how connected *Skinny Dave* was. With each bet, Cameron got the increasing impression he was banking on a loser who was trying to get lucky.

Cameron checked the balance on his online banking app, scowling. He glanced around his living room as he ate breakfast, wondering if he had any money around the house. He scratched his chin as he cast his mind back. In his line of work, holding cash was a necessity. It avoided attracting suspicions and unwanted questions. But he doubted there was any he had forgotten about. He was regularly raiding his coffers for clothes and nights out. With a deep sigh, he realised he would have to find other ways to make his money back.

Hustling drugs on the side was a no-go. Their organisation was deep in the streets, and the consequences of getting caught weren't worth it.

Skills-wise, Cameron wasn't the sharpest, especially when he compared himself to his friends. What he did have was nerve. He was willing to do whatever it took to get to the top of the street crime pile.

After finishing his breakfast, he lit a spliff, still working out how to set things off. His initial instincts were to speak to Natty.

But was it worth involving him?

Natty was sharp and well-respected, with many of the same vices Cameron had. He brought a lot to the table, and Cameron could see the pair running the streets together.

Spence . . .

Spence was different. Cameron respected his dad, who he knew was a madman back in the day, but Spence wasn't the same. He was a thinker who read for fun. But worst of all was his natural charm. It had a way of pulling people in and rubbing off on people. Natty was an example of this. Being around Spence had changed him.

In Cameron's eyes, it had made him softer.

Robberies were another option to consider. They were a useful way to make money, but Natty always advised against them. In his eyes, it was a show of desperation. Cameron couldn't see how. He wondered whether these were more *words of wisdom* Natty had taken from Spence, but it was something he felt strongly about.

––––––

SOMETIME LATER, Cameron hit the streets, stopping by his crew's main hangout spot. Natty was already there, talking on the phone when Cameron entered. He nodded at Cameron, continuing his call.

'Yes, Cam,' said Carlton. 'You good?'

'What's happening, you little punk?' Cameron replied, grinning as he grabbed the younger man and put him in a headlock. 'What have I told you about staying ready? People aren't messing around on the roads,' he taunted, enjoying seeing Carlton struggle. He was a good kid, but Cameron remembered how he used to run around after Natty, begging to tag along. Natty had taken pity on him and given him a shot, but that didn't mean Cameron had to.

'Leave him alone, Cam,' said Natty. Evidently, he'd finished his call.

'Fine,' snorted Cameron, letting Carlton go. Carlton rubbed his neck, glaring. Cameron considered giving him a slap, but didn't want to hear Natty's shit. He took a seat near Natty, and Carlton left the room.

Their spot was a house that had once belonged to a punter. They'd hung around for years, giving drugs to the owner. They now resided at another place, and Natty and the others threw him a bit of money and product, and took care of the bills. The living room had light blue walls, the paint peeling in places. It had dark blue furniture, and an entertainment system, but not much else in the way of amenities.

'Why are you always defending that little shit?' Cameron asked, glaring at Natty. Natty was an imposing figure. He stood over 6 feet tall, with a muscular build. He had a look that made people take him seriously, but could be strangely charming. Cameron's glare deepened.

'He's a good dude, and he works hard. I don't know why you're always getting at him, but there's no need for it,' said Natty.

'Whatever. It's tough out there, fam. We both know it. I'm just trying to toughen him up.'

'Carlton's not soft. You don't need to worry about him.'

'Fine. Forget him,' said Cameron. 'What's going on?'

Natty shrugged, smoothing the creases in his grey designer sweater.

'Steady day. Spence is working later, but no issues so far. The packs are selling nicely. We've got a reload coming in later. You mind handling it if I'm not around?'

'Yeah, that's calm,' replied Cameron. 'I need to hit a lick or summat, though. My funds are low.'

Natty shot his friend a look. 'If you're broke, I can help you out.'

'I didn't say I was broke,' said Cameron, narrowing his eyes. 'I just want more money.'

'You should talk to Spence. You know he's doing well with his invest—'

'I don't have time to talk to him,' Cameron interjected. 'He's probably with that little slut of his, anyway.'

Natty shook his head, but didn't respond as Carlton re-entered. Cameron glared at his friend again, annoyed by his lack of response. Rising to his feet, Natty made his way to the door, stopping just before it. Turning around and surveying the room, his face contorted.

'This place is a shit-hole. Can you guys give it the once over?' he asked, opening the door and exiting.

Cameron snickered, pushing off from the seat with his hands and standing. After a long stretch, he made his way to the door.

'Yo Cam,' Carlton called out, 'Natty told us to tidy the place up.'

Cameron turned around and impaled Carlton with a glare.

'So fucking tidy it up then,' he replied, slamming the door as he left the room.

CAMERON PUT ASIDE his annoyance with his friends and focused on business. He held the main 'trap phone', directing sales to different places. It was easy enough for him to handle on autopilot, giving him plenty of time to consider his moneymaking options. What he needed were more connections. They would enable him to spread out and diversify his opportunities for earning.

But how he would make those connections, he wasn't sure.

Messing around on his personal phone, he made a few phone calls, trading gossip and little titbits with associates. He received nothing of value, but learnt of a party in the Hood.

———

CAMERON WAS INSPECTING the contents of his wardrobe later that day. Rifling through it, he selected his clothes, laying them on his bed. Picking up his phone, he navigated to his contacts and called Natty.

'Yes, Cam. What's happening, bro?'

'I've got a party for us later. Meant to be bare women there. Are you on it?'

Cameron heard Natty's yawn, and frowned, sure his friend would decline.

'Yeah, why not? If it's dead or there's no women around, I'm blaming you, though. Send me the details. I'll drag Spence along too. Cool?'

'Cool.' Cameron didn't think Spence would come, but it didn't matter either way. 'I'll send you a text with the details. Come to my yard tonight, and we can fly over there together.'

'Cool,' replied Natty, hanging up.

Cameron rubbed his hands together, grinning. He needed to cut loose, and the party sounded like the perfect way to do it.

CHAPTER TWO

CAMERON GRINNED as he entered the party, flanked by Natty and Spence. His grin faded when he saw people flock to Natty, touching his fist and engaging him in conversation, but he put it aside, determined to enjoy the night. He made a beeline for a table laden with drinks, fixing himself a brandy and coke. Spence followed, making his own drink as he surveyed the room in front of him.

Cameron didn't know how many people had initially been invited, but the house was packed. Though he'd recognised the address, he didn't know who the host was, but imagined they wouldn't be pleased with the number of people in the spot. As he thought this, he heard the sound of something smashing, followed by loud voices. Cameron grinned, knowing the owner would be pissed that things had been broken.

Spence nodded his head to the music, which surprised Cameron, as he'd never expressed an interest in any drill songs. Deciding it wasn't important, he finished his drink and made another, feeling Spence's eyes on him.

'What?' He said, cutting his eyes to his friend. 'It's a party.'

Spence shrugged, but Cameron noted the judgement in his eyes.

Before he could say anything else, Natty sauntered over with a smirk on his face.

'You definitely came through on the women front,' he told Cameron. 'Danny's been here an hour and has already got a gobble from some random girl.'

Spence made a face. 'Lucky guy.'

'Does your girl not give blowies?' Cameron snarked, knowing full well that she did. Unbeknownst to his friend, he had been involved with Spence's girlfriend Anika a few years ago, and knew precisely what she was and wasn't into.

Spence rolled his eyes. 'Here we go. Wouldn't be a night out without you finding some way to mention my girlfriend.'

'Nope.' Natty shook his head, making fresh drinks for everyone. 'We're not doing this tonight. We're here to have a good time. That's what we're going to do. Everyone drink up, and let's be happy.'

Spence and Cameron took the drinks, and the trio downed them. Natty thumped his chest, grinning.

'There we go! Let's get it popping in here.'

———

AND, so they did. Cameron lost track of the number of drinks he'd consumed. They did the rounds, drinking, partaking in smoking various joints that were going around. Cameron even did a few lines, then danced with fuzzy women that he struggled to recall. He didn't know when he left the party, or how he got home, but he awoke the next day in bed, to someone banging on his door.

Finally, he answered, letting Natty in.

'You look horrific,' said Natty, sounding spry, and much fresher than Cameron felt. Taking pity, Natty made them both cups of coffee, which they sat outside and drank. The hot drink made Cameron feel a little better, which he was thankful for. Despite feeling rough, he was glad he'd gone to the party. It had taken his mind off things, and he'd had a great time.

As the pair sat there, Cameron learned Natty had ended up at Lorraine's place. Their situation was a strange one. Natty had been on and off with her for years. In that time, she'd managed to have a child with another guy . . . Raider, a rival hustler and enemy of Natty's. Stranger still, Natty spent more time around Lorraine and her son than Raider did. Cameron didn't get it, but felt Natty was loved up, even if his friend would never admit it.

Cameron couldn't understand, and didn't think he ever would. Natty owed Lorraine nothing, yet remained a presence in her life. He grew angry at Cameron when he teased him about the relationship, but he'd put himself in that position.

Cameron put it to one side, and after finishing their drinks, his mind skipped back to Spence.

'I still feel rough,' he moaned, yawning as he put on a pair of trainers. 'Seriously, how long are we gonna let him get away with that?'

'What are you talking about?' Natty asked, frowning.

'Anika. You said in the beginning that she wouldn't change him, and I told you he was pussy whipped. Now look at him . . . leaving parties early when we're having a good time so he can run back to her.'

'They live together now. Spence does what he thinks is right. You don't know that she's having that kind of effect,' said Natty.

'I know her, remember? We both do.'

Natty shook his head.

'C'mon, let's just go and see the old man.'

That wasn't good enough, Cameron thought, as they headed for Natty's car. What Spence was doing wasn't right. He'd come out with the crew, and unless he hooked up with a girl at the party, he should have left with them. Instead, he'd ducked out early. The most annoying part was that Natty didn't seem to care. He constantly gave Spence a pass over everything, and once Cameron had noticed this, he couldn't stop noticing it. Whenever he opened his mouth, he was perceived as the bad guy.

He knew Anika, though. He knew her better than both Natty and Spence. She was a happy, good-time girl, who he'd pursued with ease, then cut off when she became too clingy. Somehow, she had ended up with Spence. Cameron wasn't sure if she had done it to get back at him, but wouldn't put it past her.

———

Natty drove to Rudy's office on Francis Street, the pair making conversation and listening to music. Cameron's head was pounding, and Natty was handling it in his usual manner, being louder and making his head hurt more.

Soon, they pulled up outside Rudy's. He worked out of a house belonging to an older woman, Delores. Cameron didn't know why, and had never been interested enough to see if Natty knew. They spoke with the guards milling around outside, then headed into the house.

Rudy sat in the kitchen, sipping a drink. Delores was pottering around. As always, she had a smile and words for Natty, yet ignored Cameron. He glanced at Rudy, hoping the older man would look up and take notice of him, but he didn't.

Rudy Campbell was the number two guy in the Dunn organisation. He had short hair, and wore a pristine white shirt, finally glancing up at the pair with his piercing eyes, which, to no surprise, lingered on Natty.

Cameron didn't pay much attention to the conversation. Instead, he studied the way the pair spoke to one another. Even with Natty's last name, and his status as Mitch Dunn's nephew, Rudy still outranked him by a considerable margin. The fact he was sleeping with Natty's mum also played into their relationship, which always seemed laced with tension.

Cameron spaced out for a moment, sure he wouldn't be involved in the conversation. His attention returned sharply when Natty mentioned *Elijah*. Cameron focused on the back of his friend's head as he spoke.

Elijah was a rival dealer who they didn't get along with. There had been tension between the crews for a while, and Natty was one of the most outspoken against them. But Natty lacked the objectivity to make a sound assessment. Lorraine's ex-boyfriend, Raider, worked for Elijah. It made it difficult to separate Natty's true concerns from his personal agenda.

Still exhausted from his late night, Cameron yawned, just as Rudy looked in his direction. Cameron froze, but Rudy had already focused on Natty again, making Cameron feel like he'd missed an opportunity to establish himself.

They didn't stay much longer, and Cameron's annoyance only grew as they headed back to Natty's car. Rudy had paid him little attention, and hadn't said a word to him. If he was ever going to ascend to the level he wanted, that needed to change.

'No point in me even going,' Cameron grumbled when Natty drove away. 'Rudy didn't even speak to me. Old prick.'

Natty didn't respond, lost in thought as he drove. Cameron scowled.

'Natty? What are you thinking about?'

'Elijah,' said Natty.

'What about him?'

'I don't trust him,' replied Natty. Cameron almost rolled his eyes. *Here we go again,* he thought.

'Him or Raider? You sure the fact your fuckpiece's ex rolls with him isn't clouding your judgement?'

'I'm sure. This is business,' snapped Natty. The conversation continued, but Cameron wasn't sure he believed him. Natty seemed different lately. Even when they went out, it felt like he was going through the motions at times, and Cameron was sure it was due to Lorraine.

If it wasn't him, it was Spence, loved up with his girlfriend. He didn't understand what was happening to his crew, making him wonder if he was the one with the problem.

Anika had fallen hard for him, he'd recognised that. She'd wanted a commitment, and he'd just wanted to sleep with her, and see her when it was convenient.

So, he broke it off.

And then one night, at a club, he'd watched from afar as she and Spence began talking — Natty stepping in and stopping him from intervening.

Now, a year later, they were still together, and Cameron hated it. It wasn't that he regretted his actions with Anika, or that he thought he'd missed his chance. He didn't want Anika, but he didn't want his friend to have her either.

'Don't overthink it, bro,' Cameron responded to a comment Natty had made about Rudy's judgement in potentially working with Elijah. 'Have the meeting, get shit organised, and keep it moving. We can get put on in a major way, and trust me, I need that.' He thought about the money he'd lost betting, and the money he'd blown on other things.

He needed to make it back, and then some.

READ GOOD DEED, BAD DEEDS

CHAPTER ONE

FRIDAY 1 MAY, 2020

FRIDAY NIGHT PLAYED host to another party in Chapeltown, Leeds; known fondly as *the Hood*. People milled around, some drinking, others building and smoking spliffs, talking easily over the thumping drill beats. Most present weren't aware whose house it was, the owner currently visiting her ill sister in Macclesfield. Her granddaughter foolishly decided to have a party, not expecting half the Hood to show. Unable to control the situation, she now stood in the kitchen, getting ever drunker and waiting for it to be over.

Outside, Nathaniel — aka Natty Deeds — grinned, a spliff between his lips, surrounded by his Day-One boys, Cameron and Spence. The trio were in their late twenties and had been close for years. His eyes were on Cameron, bleary-eyed and stumbling around.

'Go on, it's your turn,' he urged, hitting the joint and passing it to another man. Struggling to stay upright, Cameron chugged from the bottle of Hennessy. Finishing, he blinked and shook his head, thrusting the half-drunk bottle at Natty, some of the contents splashing on the ground.

'Your turn. Finish that, or I win.'

Natty snatched the bottle, buoyed by the surrounding eyes. He stood straighter, enhancing his powerful 6-foot frame, knowing he cut an impressive figure; hair neatly shaped up, gold chain bouncing against his designer sweater.

'Go on. Hurry up,' urged Cameron, a bead of sweat dripping down his forehead. Waiting a second longer to annoy him, Natty downed the remaining brandy, ignoring the burning in his throat and chest. After finishing, he held the bottle aloft as people cheered.

'Grab another bottle,' he said, blinking. 'Spence, play too.'

'I'm okay, thanks,' said Spence. He'd calmly watched from the side, nursing the same bottle of Red Stripe he'd had since they arrived. Shorter than Natty, he had hazel eyes, high cheekbones, and soft facial features to go with his slender build.

'He needs his woman's permission,' Cameron sneered. Spence had been in a relationship for a year, but to hear Cameron talk, you'd think they'd started going out yesterday.

'Cam, no woman in their right mind would even go near you.'

People nearby chuckled at Spence's response. Cameron frowned. He had a stocky build, sharp features, and a tapered fade. His dark brown eyes surveyed Spence.

'Laugh all you want, but I get it when I want it. Relationships are for mugs.'

'That's true,' agreed Natty, wiping his eyes as the combination of weed and liquor hit him.

'See? Natty kn—' Cameron stopped mid-sentence and hurried to a nearby bush, where he promptly threw up. Spence shook his head, and Natty laughed.

'I win, lightweight.'

Natty's phone vibrated. Squinting to see the screen clearly, he saw the name *Rudy*. Looking up from his phone, he snorted and stowed it back in his pocket. He had no desire to speak with his boss tonight.

Heading inside, a woman dancing in the corner of the room caught his attention, his eyes locking onto her swaying hips. He made his way toward her, sauntering through the crowd, aware of the hungry stares from other women. In Natty's drunken state, he didn't care.

'Hey sexy,' he said to the woman. 'You look beautiful.'

'Thank you,' she replied, looking away, her dark brown hair

obscuring her temptingly curved mouth for a moment. Natty inched closer, missing the look of alarm on her face.

'How come I've never seen you before?' Natty continued before she could reply. 'People call me Natty Deeds. Let me get you a drink.'

'No thank you.' She shook her head. 'I'm not thirsty, and I have a boyfriend.'

Natty's smirk widened as he swayed on the spot.

'We can just be friends, babe. Doesn't have to affect your relationship.'

Again, she shook her head, her lip curling.

'I'm not interested.'

Even in his drunken state, Natty finally realised she didn't want to be around him. Shrugging, he said, 'your loss.'

Before she could respond, a man draped his arm around her. He had broad shoulders and a muscular build beneath his pocket logo CP Company t-shirt. His eyes surveyed Natty, eyebrows creeping together.

'Do I know you?'

Natty returned the look. 'I don't know. Do you?'

'You're over here bothering my girl.'

Natty could have walked away, but a crowd had gathered. He had a reputation to maintain and couldn't be seen backing down.

'I was talking to her, not *bothering* her. Stop being insecure.'

The woman bit her lip, eyes darting between the pair. Natty stepped toward the man.

'If you really have a problem, we can step outside and deal with it.'

No one spoke. Natty waited for him to move. He glanced at Natty, then lowered his head.

'If you weren't bothering her, then we can leave it.'

Natty smirked, amused at his change of heart. As built as the man was, Natty was bigger. He looked the woman up and down as her man backed up.

'You're too sexy to be with a cowardly man that can't defend you.'

The man's eyes flashed at Natty's insults, but he swallowed and again looked away.

'You need to take a long look at yourself. You're pathetic,' the woman spat, eyes full of loathing.

'Take your pussy boyfriend and fuck off then. Anytime he wants to go, I'll put him on his arse.'

Spence came over after the couple had hurried away.

'Chill out and get some water,' he said, trying to calm him. Natty shrugged him off.

'I'm fine. You know I can handle my drink.'

Spence sighed. Getting through to Natty was impossible at times.

'I'm getting off, anyway,' he said.

Natty rolled his eyes.

'Seriously? We're just starting, and you're running off to your woman?'

'I'm not running.'

'Course you are.'

Spence patted him on the back. 'Be careful, bro. I'll get with you tomorrow.'

Blearily watching him go, Natty stumbled outside. Cameron was still doubled over by the bush he'd thrown up in, moaning. Natty chuckled at his friend's condition.

'You look terrible, bro. Let's get you another drink. That'll sort you right out.'

———

THE SOUNDS of someone shuffling around Natty moved him before he was truly ready. Light spilt through multiple slits in the blinds, making him groan, head pounding. Coughing to clear his dry throat, he sat gingerly looking around. The room wasn't his, but he recognised it, along with the woman tidying. His clothing had been carefully laid on a chair instead of the haphazard pile he'd left them in. The woman emptied an ashtray into a white carrier bag.

'Keep the noise down.'

'This is my house, in case you've forgotten,' she replied, hand on her hip as she impaled him with a ferocious glare.

'Calm down, Lorraine.' Natty winced, wiping his eyes. 'Got any painkillers?'

'Downstairs,' Lorraine replied. 'Before you ask, I'm not getting them for you.'

'C'mon, babe. I'm hurting.'

'Stop drinking so much then.'

Natty rubbed his head. 'Wasn't my fault. Cam got me into it.'

'You're always blaming other people, Nat. Take some responsibility.'

Natty waved an arm at her, not listening to her usual spiel. Lorraine glared back, unimpressed. A blue bandana obscured her silky black hair, and she wore an oversized plain black t-shirt and shorts. She was twenty-nine-years old, with light brown eyes, full lips, smooth features, and nutmeg-shaded skin.

'Seriously, Natty. We're not a couple. You can't keep turning up drunk, expecting to sleep in my bed.'

Natty leered, eyes locked onto her silken brown legs.

'I always make up for it in the end.'

Lorraine shook her head.

'I'm not interested in the leftovers from whatever girl you had last night.'

'You've got me all wrong. I was good,' replied Natty, thinking of the girl whose boyfriend he had nearly beaten up. Despite herself, Lorraine's expression softened.

'Get ready. I'll make you some food for when you're done.'

Agreeing with the plan, Natty headed to take a shower. Soaping himself with shower gel leftover from previous visits, he went over the day in his head. He needed to check in with his crew, and then find out what Rudy wanted.

For most of his life, Natty had sold drugs on the streets. He loved the money and the respect he garnered from people for doing it. He worked as a crew chief, one of many who reported to Rudy Campbell. He had seen him a few days ago, and there were no problems at the time, but he knew how quickly things could switch in the Hood.

Once washed and dressed, Natty headed downstairs, still ropey after his night. He saw a small boy playing on the carpet in the living room. Despite the widescreen TV displaying cartoons, he remained in his own world. When he looked up and saw Natty, his face immediately brightened. Natty grinned.

'What's happening, little man? What are you watching?' He bumped fists with the child, listening for a few minutes as he babbled about the show.

'Can we play on the PlayStation?' Jaden eagerly asked.

'Let me get some food in my belly; then we can play for a bit.'

In the kitchen doorway, Lorraine watched Natty and her son, overwhelmed by a surge of affection. For all Natty's faults, he doted on Jaden and spent more quality time with him than his dad. At the same time, she worried about Jaden being so enamoured with a man actively involved in the street life; one that had never truly committed to her and probably never would. She lowered her head, and then headed back to the kitchen.

Natty entered a few minutes later, making a drink and swallowing two paracetamols.

'Have you seen my phone?' He asked, inhaling the fried food scent in the air.

'On the table. I put it on charge for you.'

Thanking her, Natty sat down and tucked into his breakfast, checking his phone. Rudy had called several times, finally sending him a text saying to stop by. Reading several other random messages, Natty put his phone aside and finished his breakfast. Lorraine took away his empty plate, placing a cup of milky coffee in front of him.

'Feeling better?'

Natty nodded, rubbing his stomach. 'That was amazing. Thank you.'

'Whose party were you at? I didn't know anything was on.'

'People based out Rhona's nana's yard. Cam dragged me along last minute. Spence too, before he ran off to see his girl.'

'Leave Spence alone. He's maturing. You should think about doing the same.'

Natty scoffed at Lorraine's usual line of nonsense.

'I'm my own person. I don't need some woman telling me what to do,' he said.

Lorraine folded her arms, leaning against the kitchen sink as she surveyed him.

'That isn't what a relationship is. Relationships are about compromise; supporting one another.'

'Is that what you and *Raider* do?' He snarked, referring to Jaden's dad.

Lorraine's eyes flashed.

'No. You know it isn't. I still know what a relationship is. Do you? Or is this it for you?'

'What are you talking about?'

'I'm talking about life, Natty. What does life mean for you?'

Sliding to his feet, Natty took his coffee, shaking his head.

'I don't want to listen to this shit.'

Without a word, he headed into the living room. A few moments later, she heard him playing with Jaden, just as he'd promised. Lorraine remained by the sink, wishing Natty got it. He meant well, but it was so easy to dislike him. At times, he reminded her of Jaden's dad, but he had a softer side — a contrast to the rougher, darker side the other man routinely showed. It didn't help that Raider knew of her previous involvement with Natty, and suspected there was still something between them.

Raider was easy enough to handle, though. Despite the implosion of their relationship, he typically kept his distance. He tried his luck now and then, but was never successful.

Natty was a different story. Her closeness to him had pushed out Raider for good. Lorraine didn't understand why he had such an issue with relationships, but couldn't see it changing anytime soon.

CHAPTER TWO

NATTY HAMMERED on Cameron's door. After a few moments, he heard several bangs as the door opened.

'You didn't need to knock so loud,' Cameron muttered. Natty followed him to the kitchen, watching him shuffle around.

'You look horrific,' he finally said. Cameron glared back, shirtless, his pyjama bottoms rumpled and livid bags under his eyes. Natty took over and made them drinks. They carried them outside, Natty remaining on his feet, Cameron slumping on the front step.

Cameron lived in a terraced house on Gathorne Avenue. He'd lived with his mum, taking over the house when she remarried and moved in with her partner. An older lady shuffled past, smiling at them both. The house had a patch of dirt masquerading as a garden. Any plants formerly growing had since died with Cameron's disinterest in gardening. It had a black door, mid-sized walls, and an old-fashioned exterior and interior.

As they looked on, the sounds of a crying child punctuated the quiet, his mother dragging him along by the hand, threatening to beat him. It reminded Natty of how his mum had acted when he was younger.

'I'm not drinking with you again,' he finally said, rubbing his eye with his free hand.

Natty grinned. 'It's not my fault you can't handle it.'

'Whatever. You got lucky. Where did you end up, anyway?'

Natty sipped his drink, the coffee scalding his lips, causing him to grit his teeth. Cameron's coffee was horrendous. Natty had complained in the past, even leaving his own coffee at the house, which tasted better.

'Forget that. What happened to the coffee I brought around last time.'

'I used it. So what?'

'So, couldn't you replace it? Your stuff is terrible,' said Natty.

'I'm not paying stupid money for that expensive stuff you buy. Stop avoiding the question: where did you end up?'

'Lorraine's,' replied Natty.

Cameron's eyes gleamed. He rubbed his hands together.

'I'd love to run up in that.'

Natty impaled him with a glare. 'Watch your mouth.'

Cameron grinned.

'If you have a problem with me talking like that, step up and claim her.'

Natty shook his head. It wasn't the first time they'd had the conversation.

'It's not that simple,' he said.

'How come?'

'She's Raider's baby mum.'

Cameron snorted.

'Raider? C'mon, Nat. He's a mug.' He shot Natty a crafty look. 'Plus, it didn't stop you going over there to bang her.'

'We didn't have sex. I just crashed there.'

It was Cameron's turn to shake his head.

'You're turning into Spence, fam.'

Natty chuckled. 'Have you heard from him? He left before me.'

'He rang me an hour ago. He's handling the crew. No hiccups so far.'

Natty nodded. He could always trust Spence to keep things

moving. Spence had always shown a high level of managerial talent, and Natty believed he would make a good boss. Thinking of bosses made him think of Rudy, whom he needed to see. Inwardly, he cursed himself for taking his eye off the ball.

'Cool. Get ready, anyway. Rudy wants a meet.'

Groaning, Cameron clambered to his feet, draining his coffee, making a satisfied sound. Natty looked at him in disgust.

'You need help, Cam.' He poured his own coffee into the dirt.

'Speak for yourself. Hope Rudy's got some work for us. My funds are low.'

'You shouldn't have loaned that silly Rolex off Damanjeet. You got ripped off paying that deposit. I'm sure it's fake.'

Cameron waved that off. 'You're just jealous you didn't get it.'

'Jealous of what? You *need* that fake watch. It's the only way women will go near you.'

'Don't talk shit. I get as many women as you do.'

'You wish.'

While Cameron got ready, Natty messed around on his phone, replying to a few text messages. He thought about what Lorraine had said earlier. Natty felt he was being held to a higher standard based on Spence's willingness to have a relationship, and his reluctance to do so.

Spence had been more reserved than he and Cameron even before getting together with Anika. He often kept them from doing stupid things, always remaining calm, which helped calm Natty — and Cameron — down when needed. Yet, last night, Natty had almost gotten into a fight over a girl, and couldn't even recall what she looked like.

Maybe he needed to cool it with the drinking and partying.

'Seriously, I'm still rough.' Cameron yawned as he stuffed his feet into a pair of trainers. 'Should have done a Spence and left early. How long are we gonna let him keep getting away with that?'

'What are you talking about?'

'Anika. You said in the beginning that she wouldn't change him, and I told you he was pussy whipped. Now look at him . . . leaving parties early when we're having a good time so he can run back to her.'

'They live together now. Spence does what he thinks is right. You don't know that she's having that kind of effect.'

'I know her, remember? We both do.'

Natty shook his head.

'C'mon, let's just go and see the old man.'

Once Cameron was ready, they drove to Rudy's.

'We're out next weekend,' said Cameron, once they'd set off. 'There's an event near Albion Street that's gonna be jumping.'

Natty grinned. 'I thought you weren't coming out with me again after last night?'

'Whatever, man. We're going. I'll take it easy this time,' said Cameron.

'We'll see. What's the event?'

'I mentioned it ages ago. It's been in the works for a while. That DJ from London is performing. The fat one.'

Natty kept his eyes on the road, vaguely remembering Cameron mentioning it. Pushing his earlier epiphany about partying to the side, he nodded and said, 'cool. I'm up for that.'

'Yes! Knew you would be.' Cameron winced. 'We need to stop for paracetamol after this. My head's killing.'

'Sure, sweetheart!' said Natty, as loudly as he could, laughing as Cameron again winced.

———

Parking on Francis Street in the Hood, both men strode to Rudy's office, a red-bricked terraced house with a plain white door. It didn't have a garden, with only some messy bushes and a small pathway. Several guys hung around outside, talking in loud voices. They looked up when they saw Natty and Cameron, greeting them with grins and handshakes.

'Rudy in?' Natty asked. They nodded. 'Is he in a good mood? Anyone said anything?' He pressed.

'Same as ever, really,' one of them replied.

Natty left it there. They weren't bodyguards, but Rudy kept them close, using them for different jobs. Walking inside, they went to the kitchen, overwhelmed by the fried food stench. A heavyset woman hunched over the stove, muttering to herself. She glanced at the pair, her eyes lingering on Natty.

'Hey, Delores,' he said, beaming at her. Her stern face softened.

'Nathaniel. How are you? I never see you anymore.'

'I'm out here working,' replied Natty. 'I'll come and see you again soon.'

'Make sure you do. Stay out of trouble.'

'Yes, ma'am.' Natty kissed her on the cheek, turning his attention to Rudy. The older man sat at the kitchen table, sipping a pale concoction. He wore a white shirt and a thin chain, his greying hair trimmed short to disguise his accelerating baldness. Despite his advanced years, he'd maintained his looks. A sharp goatee framed his fame, his piercing coffee-coloured eyes surveying the pair.

He glanced from Natty to Cameron, signalling for the former to sit. Neither spoke at first; Natty used to the older man's theatrics. He looked around the comfortable, worn kitchen, as always unable to understand why Rudy was based there.

'How's it going, Rudy?' He finally asked.

Rudy straightened in his seat, not taking his eyes from Natty.

'Why didn't you answer the phone last night?'

'I was enjoying my night off.'

'We don't have nights off in our business. What if there was trouble, or a raid?'

Natty scratched his chin. 'I'd trust exemplary men like you to have things in order.'

Rudy's nostrils flared.

'Not good enough. You're representing the team, Nathaniel. You're always being watched, so getting drunk and throwing up at parties—'

Natty raised a hand, stopping Rudy mid-flow. Rudy's eyes narrowed.

'What do you think you're doing?'

'It was actually Cam that threw up . . . not me.'

Rudy looked from Natty to Cameron — whose eyes were currently burning into the back of Natty's head — then continued.

'Getting drunk and throwing up at parties, and trying to fight

people, is not what's expected.' Rudy's expression remained unyield-
ing. 'You know all this. We've spoken about it in the past.'

Natty resisted the urge to roll his eyes. Humour wouldn't cut it
right now. The realisation that someone was reporting his movements
suddenly struck him, and he frowned.

'The guy started with me. I wasn't gonna back down.'

'I didn't call you here to listen to your excuses. I need you to
arrange a meeting with Elijah.'

Natty's hands clenched before he could even think about it.

'I thought we weren't dealing with him anymore?' He asked, voice
thick with anger. Elijah had his own organisation, though there were
persistent rumours that he was a front for another gang seeking more
power. Natty and Elijah had a strained relationship; one Rudy was
familiar with.

'We weren't,' replied Rudy. He glanced to Delores, still muttering to
herself, and Cameron, who stifled a yawn. 'It's time we brought things
back in line between our organisations. Bad blood isn't good for
anyone. We've calmed things down lately, but none of us wants things
back to how they were a few years ago, right?'

Natty didn't speak, but knew Rudy was right. The wars that had
taken place had changed the landscape throughout Yorkshire, with
multiple crews involved and scores of murders and arrests. It had
stunted profits in all areas, with only their team remaining strong.

'Nathaniel, can you handle this?'

'I can,' replied Natty, nibbling on his bottom lip. Rudy kept his eye
on him a moment longer.

'Elijah is looking to make a move into a new area. Could be something for you to sink your teeth into if you play it right.'

Natty continued weighing up everything in his head. Elijah had
caused trouble for their organisation in the past, and the teams had
almost gone to war several times. Natty loathed him and the people he
kept close. He hoped Rudy had given the idea some thought.

'When do you want me to sort this meeting?'

'I'll let you know. People will be watching. Like I said, it's a great
opportunity. Use it to step up.'

Again, Natty almost rolled his eyes. Shaking Rudy's hand, he said goodbye to Delores and went to leave.

'Nathaniel.'

He turned. Rudy surveyed him for several seconds.

'Watch that temper of yours. It'll get you in trouble.' His face softened. 'You're a good man; a good soldier.'

That was the problem, Natty thought to himself as they walked out. He didn't want to be just another soldier.

'No point in me even going,' Cameron grumbled when Natty drove away. 'Rudy didn't even speak to me. Old prick.'

Natty didn't reply, deep in thought about Elijah, considering all the ways the situation could go wrong. He didn't trust him, wondering if Rudy had given him the whole story.

'Natty? What are you thinking about?'

'Elijah,' admitted Natty. Cameron scratched his head.

'What about him?'

'I don't trust him.'

'Him or Raider? You sure the fact your fuckpiece's ex rolls with him isn't clouding your judgement?'

'I'm sure. This is business,' snapped Natty.

'Rudy wouldn't get you involved if there was a chance something could go wrong. You're like a son to him.'

Natty almost reminded Cameron he'd just cursed out Rudy for ignoring him, but didn't bother.

'It's not that simple,' he finally replied. 'Summat's up with Rudy . . . his judgement might be a little off.'

'How?'

'He's got people following me around, reporting back to him. That's a waste of money and time. He's focused on the wrong things, so how do we know he's scoped the situation with Elijah properly?' said Natty.

'Don't overthink it, bro. Have the meeting, get shit organised, and keep it moving. We can get put on in a major way, and trust me, I need that,' Cameron replied, forgetting that he'd recently blown money on renting a snide watch.

———————

LATER, Natty left the gym after a tough weights session, his gym bag slung over his shoulder. It was often his escape; he went to mull things over, to kill time between shifts and sometimes, to forget.

The combined nagging of Lorraine and Rudy had affected his mood. That, combined with the prospect of doing business with Elijah, caused him to seek out a distraction.

After showering and changing clothes, Natty headed to the city centre, finding himself in a bar. He sunk three drinks quickly, not bothering to take stock of his surroundings. Not wanting the profile, he'd deliberately picked a more low-key spot near Briggate. As he sipped Southern Comfort and lemonade, he spotted a woman standing with a group of friends. She kept looking his way. Natty signalled for her to come over, and after a while, she did, allowing him to get a better look. She had chestnut brown hair, deep blue eyes, and a giggly, flighty demeanour. She looked delicious in her little red dress, and he reasoned she would make a good distraction.

'What's your name?'

'Jeanette,' she replied softly, her eyes shining.

'People call me Natty Deeds.'

'Why?'

'Because I'm generous, and I get things done,' he replied, enjoying the smile on her face. 'I'm glad you came over. You're the most beautiful woman in here.'

'Really?' Her eyes widened. Natty maintained eye contact, holding and stroking the top of her hand. He felt her shudder and lean closer.

'Trust me, it's not even a contest. Let me buy you a drink.'

After several expensive drinks and a few highly charged dances, they headed back to Natty's. Jeanette pounced the moment they closed the door, forcing her mouth against his. Responding with equal enthusiasm, Natty easily lifted her from the ground, nibbling on her lips and drawing her further in. Hiking up her dress, he tugged down his trousers and slid her underwear to the side before entering her.

They panted against one another when they were done, catching their breath. Disentangling, Natty straightened his clothes and showed

Jeanette to the bathroom so she could clean up. She tottered down-stairs a few moments later, back to her giggly self, playing with her hair.

'You were so good,' she gushed. 'Shall we get a drink and go again?'

'No thanks. You can go now.'

'What?' Jeanette's mouth fell open.

'I've got things to do. I'll call you an Uber,' said Natty flatly.

Jeanette's eyes flashed.

'You serious? You're kicking me out?'

Natty didn't bother replying. Lip curling, she stalked past him.

'You're scum, Natty Deeds. Don't contact me again.'

'Get home safely,' he mocked. Closing the door on her insults, his smirk faded, shoulders slumping as he sat on the bottom step. Despite his best efforts, he couldn't switch off. Thoughts of Elijah and Lorraine flitted away, replaced by Cameron's words about Rudy being a father figure.

Often, Natty thought about his dad. He'd been in the life too, a big, powerful man with a deadly reputation. He'd been murdered when Natty was 11, and things hadn't been the same since. Even knowing how scared people had been of his dad, all Natty saw was the man who bought him what he wanted, but also taught him how to fight, and never to back down.

Natty had kept that same mindset as he grew older, no matter how much trouble it caused. He'd not truly understood why his dad was murdered, but even at a young age, he vividly recalled wanting revenge.

Sighing, Natty closed his eyes, wondering what the world wanted from him, and how he could get what he needed.

––––––––

TWO DAYS after speaking to Rudy, Elijah still hadn't contacted Natty. Putting the meeting aside, he went to see Lorraine and Jaden, a new video game in hand.

'I've told you about buying him things before, Natty,' said Lorraine at the door, hands on hips. 'You spoil him.'

'That's my little soldier. I'm just looking out for him,' replied Natty, trying to make his voice as innocent as possible. It was a harmless, throwaway statement. Natty had love for Jaden and wanted to make him happy, but he was aware of Lorraine pausing, and gave her his attention.

He didn't know what had changed, but she was glaring at him, hands on her hips.

'What's wrong with you?' He said.

'My son is not your *little soldier*, Natty.' Lorraine's nostrils flared.

'What are you on about?'

'He's a young boy, and he's going to grow up to do great things. He won't do the stuff you do.'

Natty held up his hands.

'C'mon, you know I didn't mean it like that. I know he is. You know that.'

Lorraine visibly calmed down, nodding.

'Okay. I'm glad you feel that way.'

Natty's face tightened, head lowered, as Lorraine let him in. Jaden greeted him with his usual enthusiasm, which took the sting out of Lorraine's admonishment. After thanking Natty for the new game, they picked their favourite *Fifa* football teams and were off. Natty took the early lead, but Jaden brought it back with a lucky headed goal. With the final whistle imminent, Natty *accidentally* passed the ball back toward his keeper, allowing Jaden to get the ball and score.

'Yes! I won! Natty, I beat you!'

Natty took a moment to watch Jaden celebrate his winning goal like he'd just won the World Cup, an involuntary smile coming to his face at the sight.

After a while, he left Jaden playing and went to see what Lorraine was doing. She was hunched over a laptop at the kitchen table, tapping keys. She pushed the laptop away as he stood there, shaking her head. Natty watched silently for a few seconds until she noticed him, blushing.

'How long have you been there?' She asked.

'Not long. What's all this?' He motioned to the laptop.

'Studying. It's important I keep practising.'

'How long have you been studying? I didn't even know.'

'No one does. I want to have everything finished before I start telling people. My mum knows, because she helps with Jaden, and Rosie does, but that's it.'

'How are you finding it?'

Lorraine ran a hand through her hair, blowing out a breath. 'It's difficult, but I'm not giving up.'

Nodding, Natty went to make drinks for himself, Jaden, and Lorraine, missing the look of disappointment on Lorraine's face at his lack of reaction.

'I'll leave you to it,' he said, placing her tea beside her, then leaving the room.

Natty and Jaden played for a bit longer, then he returned to the kitchen.

'I'm gonna get off now,' he told Lorraine. She didn't react. 'Did you hear me?'

'Yes, you said you were leaving.'

Natty's eyes narrowed. 'What's up with you?'

'Nothing. I thought you were going?'

He stepped into the kitchen and gently lifted her chin to face him.

'What's your problem? Why are you going on dumb?'

'I'm not. I'm trying to work, and you said you were going.'

Natty didn't know why she had switched on him, but he didn't have the time or patience to deal with it.

'That's your problem; you're too moody,' he said, leaving before he ended up starting an argument. He couldn't deal with her weirdness right now.

GOOD DEED, BAD DEEDS

RICKY BLACK

CHAPTER ONE

FRIDAY 1 MAY, 2020

FRIDAY NIGHT PLAYED host to another party in Chapeltown, Leeds; known fondly as *the Hood*. People milled around, some drinking, others building and smoking spliffs, talking easily over the thumping drill beats. Most present weren't aware whose house it was, the owner currently visiting her ill sister in Macclesfield. Her granddaughter foolishly decided to have a party, not expecting half the Hood to show. Unable to control the situation, she now stood in the kitchen, getting ever drunker and waiting for it to be over.

Outside, Nathaniel — aka Natty Deeds — grinned, a spliff between his lips, surrounded by his Day-One boys, Cameron and Spence. The trio were in their late twenties and had been close for years. His eyes were on Cameron, bleary-eyed and stumbling around.

'Go on, it's your turn,' he urged, hitting the joint and passing it to another man. Struggling to stay upright, Cameron chugged from the bottle of Hennessy. Finishing, he blinked and shook his head, thrusting the half-drunk bottle at Natty, some of the contents splashing on the ground.

'Your turn. Finish that, or I win.'

Natty snatched the bottle, buoyed by the surrounding eyes. He stood straighter, enhancing his powerful 6-foot frame, knowing he cut an impressive figure; hair neatly shaped up, gold chain bouncing against his designer sweater.

'Go on. Hurry up,' urged Cameron, a bead of sweat dripping down his forehead. Waiting a second longer to annoy him, Natty downed the remaining brandy, ignoring the burning in his throat and chest. After finishing, he held the bottle aloft as people cheered.

'Grab another bottle,' he said, blinking. 'Spence, play too.'

'I'm okay, thanks,' said Spence. He'd calmly watched from the side, nursing the same bottle of Red Stripe he'd had since they arrived. Shorter than Natty, he had hazel eyes, high cheekbones, and soft facial features to go with his slender build.

'He needs his woman's permission,' Cameron sneered. Spence had been in a relationship for a year, but to hear Cameron talk, you'd think they'd started going out yesterday.

'Cam, no woman in their right mind would even go near you.'

People nearby chuckled at Spence's response. Cameron frowned. He had a stocky build, sharp features, and a tapered fade. His dark brown eyes surveyed Spence.

'Laugh all you want, but I get it when I want it. Relationships are for mugs.'

'That's true,' agreed Natty, wiping his eyes as the combination of weed and liquor hit him.

'See? Natty kn—' Cameron stopped mid-sentence and hurried to a nearby bush, where he promptly threw up. Spence shook his head, and Natty laughed.

'I win, lightweight.'

Natty's phone vibrated. Squinting to see the screen clearly, he saw the name *Rudy*. Looking up from his phone, he snorted and stowed it back in his pocket. He had no desire to speak with his boss tonight.

Heading inside, a woman dancing in the corner of the room caught his attention, his eyes locking onto her swaying hips. He made his way toward her, sauntering through the crowd, aware of the hungry stares from other women. In Natty's drunken state, he didn't care.

'Hey sexy,' he said to the woman. 'You look beautiful.'

'Thank you,' she replied, looking away, her dark brown hair

obscuring her temptingly curved mouth for a moment. Natty inched closer, missing the look of alarm on her face.

'How come I've never seen you before?' Natty continued before she could reply. 'People call me Natty Deeds. Let me get you a drink.'

'No thank you.' She shook her head. 'I'm not thirsty, and I have a boyfriend.'

Natty's smirk widened as he swayed on the spot.

'We can just be friends, babe. Doesn't have to affect your relationship.'

Again, she shook her head, her lip curling.

'I'm not interested.'

Even in his drunken state, Natty finally realised she didn't want to be around him. Shrugging, he said, 'your loss.'

Before she could respond, a man draped his arm around her. He had broad shoulders and a muscular build beneath his pocket logo CP Company t-shirt. His eyes surveyed Natty, eyebrows creeping together.

'Do I know you?'

Natty returned the look. 'I don't know. Do you?'

'You're over here bothering my girl.'

Natty could have walked away, but a crowd had gathered. He had a reputation to maintain and couldn't be seen backing down.

'I was talking to her, not *bothering* her. Stop being insecure.'

The woman bit her lip, eyes darting between the pair. Natty stepped toward the man.

'If you really have a problem, we can step outside and deal with it.'

No one spoke. Natty waited for him to move. He glanced at Natty, then lowered his head.

'If you weren't bothering her, then we can leave it.'

Natty smirked, amused at his change of heart. As built as the man was, Natty was bigger. He looked the woman up and down as her man backed up.

'You're too sexy to be with a cowardly man that can't defend you.'

The man's eyes flashed at Natty's insults, but he swallowed and again looked away.

'You need to take a long look at yourself. You're pathetic,' the woman spat, eyes full of loathing.

'Take your pussy boyfriend and fuck off then. Anytime he wants to go, I'll put him on his arse.'

Spence came over after the couple had hurried away.

'Chill out and get some water,' he said, trying to calm him. Natty shrugged him off.

'I'm fine. You know I can handle my drink.'

Spence sighed. Getting through to Natty was impossible at times.

'I'm getting off, anyway,' he said.

Natty rolled his eyes.

'Seriously? We're just starting, and you're running off to your woman?'

'I'm not running.'

'Course you are.'

Spence patted him on the back. 'Be careful, bro. I'll get with you tomorrow.'

Blearily watching him go, Natty stumbled outside. Cameron was still doubled over by the bush he'd thrown up in, moaning. Natty chuckled at his friend's condition.

'You look terrible, bro. Let's get you another drink. That'll sort you right out.'

———

THE SOUNDS of someone shuffling around Natty moved him before he was truly ready. Light spilt through multiple slits in the blinds, making him groan, head pounding. Coughing to clear his dry throat, he sat gingerly looking around. The room wasn't his, but he recognised it, along with the woman tidying. His clothing had been carefully laid on a chair instead of the haphazard pile he'd left them in. The woman emptied an ashtray into a white carrier bag.

'Keep the noise down.'

'This is my house, in case you've forgotten,' she replied, hand on her hip as she impaled him with a ferocious glare.

'Calm down, Lorraine.' Natty winced, wiping his eyes. 'Got any painkillers?'

'Downstairs,' Lorraine replied. 'Before you ask, I'm not getting them for you.'

'C'mon, babe. I'm hurting.'

'Stop drinking so much then.'

Natty rubbed his head. 'Wasn't my fault. Cam got me into it.'

'You're always blaming other people, Nat. Take some responsibility.'

Natty waved an arm at her, not listening to her usual spiel. Lorraine glared back, unimpressed. A blue bandana obscured her silky black hair, and she wore an oversized plain black t-shirt and shorts. She was twenty-nine-years old, with light brown eyes, full lips, smooth features, and nutmeg-shaded skin.

'Seriously, Natty. We're not a couple. You can't keep turning up drunk, expecting to sleep in my bed.'

Natty leered, eyes locked onto her silken brown legs.

'I always make up for it in the end.'

Lorraine shook her head.

'I'm not interested in the leftovers from whatever girl you had last night.'

'You've got me all wrong. I was good,' replied Natty, thinking of the girl whose boyfriend he had nearly beaten up. Despite herself, Lorraine's expression softened.

'Get ready. I'll make you some food for when you're done.'

Agreeing with the plan, Natty headed to take a shower. Soaping himself with shower gel leftover from previous visits, he went over the day in his head. He needed to check in with his crew, and then find out what Rudy wanted.

For most of his life, Natty had sold drugs on the streets. He loved the money and the respect he garnered from people for doing it. He worked as a crew chief, one of many who reported to Rudy Campbell. He had seen him a few days ago, and there were no problems at the time, but he knew how quickly things could switch in the Hood.

Once washed and dressed, Natty headed downstairs, still ropey after his night. He saw a small boy playing on the carpet in the living room. Despite the widescreen TV displaying cartoons, he remained in his own world. When he looked up and saw Natty, his face immediately brightened. Natty grinned.

'What's happening, little man? What are you watching?' He bumped fists with the child, listening for a few minutes as he babbled about the show.

'Can we play on the PlayStation?' Jaden eagerly asked.

'Let me get some food in my belly; then we can play for a bit.'

In the kitchen doorway, Lorraine watched Natty and her son, overwhelmed by a surge of affection. For all Natty's faults, he doted on Jaden and spent more quality time with him than his dad. At the same time, she worried about Jaden being so enamoured with a man actively involved in the street life; one that had never truly committed to her and probably never would. She lowered her head, and then headed back to the kitchen.

Natty entered a few minutes later, making a drink and swallowing two paracetamols.

'Have you seen my phone?' He asked, inhaling the fried food scent in the air.

'On the table. I put it on charge for you.'

Thanking her, Natty sat down and tucked into his breakfast, checking his phone. Rudy had called several times, finally sending him a text saying to stop by. Reading several other random messages, Natty put his phone aside and finished his breakfast. Lorraine took away his empty plate, placing a cup of milky coffee in front of him.

'Feeling better?'

Natty nodded, rubbing his stomach. 'That was amazing. Thank you.'

'Whose party were you at? I didn't know anything was on.'

'People based out Rhona's nana's yard. Cam dragged me along last minute. Spence too, before he ran off to see his girl.'

'Leave Spence alone. He's maturing. You should think about doing the same.'

Natty scoffed at Lorraine's usual line of nonsense.

'I'm my own person. I don't need some woman telling me what to do,' he said.

Lorraine folded her arms, leaning against the kitchen sink as she surveyed him.

'That isn't what a relationship is. Relationships are about compromise; supporting one another.'

'Is that what you and *Raider* do?' He snarked, referring to Jaden's dad.

Lorraine's eyes flashed.

'No. You know it isn't. I still know what a relationship is. Do you? Or is this it for you?'

'What are you talking about?'

'I'm talking about life, Natty. What does life mean for you?'

Sliding to his feet, Natty took his coffee, shaking his head.

'I don't want to listen to this shit.'

Without a word, he headed into the living room. A few moments later, she heard him playing with Jaden, just as he'd promised. Lorraine remained by the sink, wishing Natty got it. He meant well, but it was so easy to dislike him. At times, he reminded her of Jaden's dad, but he had a softer side — a contrast to the rougher, darker side the other man routinely showed. It didn't help that Raider knew of her previous involvement with Natty, and suspected there was still something between them.

Raider was easy enough to handle, though. Despite the implosion of their relationship, he typically kept his distance. He tried his luck now and then, but was never successful.

Natty was a different story. Her closeness to him had pushed out Raider for good. Lorraine didn't understand why he had such an issue with relationships, but couldn't see it changing anytime soon.

CHAPTER TWO

NATTY HAMMERED on Cameron's door. After a few moments, he heard several bangs as the door opened.

'You didn't need to knock so loud,' Cameron muttered. Natty followed him to the kitchen, watching him shuffle around.

'You look horrific,' he finally said. Cameron glared back, shirtless, his pyjama bottoms rumpled and livid bags under his eyes. Natty took over and made them drinks. They carried them outside, Natty remaining on his feet, Cameron slumping on the front step.

Cameron lived in a terraced house on Gathorne Avenue. He'd lived with his mum, taking over the house when she remarried and moved in with her partner. An older lady shuffled past, smiling at them both. The house had a patch of dirt masquerading as a garden. Any plants formerly growing had since died with Cameron's disinterest in gardening. It had a black door, mid-sized walls, and an old-fashioned exterior and interior.

As they looked on, the sounds of a crying child punctuated the quiet, his mother dragging him along by the hand, threatening to beat him. It reminded Natty of how his mum had acted when he was younger.

'I'm not drinking with you again,' he finally said, rubbing his eye with his free hand.

Natty grinned. 'It's not my fault you can't handle it.'

'Whatever. You got lucky. Where did you end up, anyway?'

Natty sipped his drink, the coffee scalding his lips, causing him to grit his teeth. Cameron's coffee was horrendous. Natty had complained in the past, even leaving his own coffee at the house, which tasted better.

'Forget that. What happened to the coffee I brought around last time.'

'I used it. So what?'

'So, couldn't you replace it? Your stuff is terrible,' said Natty.

'I'm not paying stupid money for that expensive stuff you buy. Stop avoiding the question: where did you end up?'

'Lorraine's,' replied Natty.

Cameron's eyes gleamed. He rubbed his hands together.

'I'd love to run up in that.'

Natty impaled him with a glare. 'Watch your mouth.'

Cameron grinned.

'If you have a problem with me talking like that, step up and claim her.'

Natty shook his head. It wasn't the first time they'd had the conversation.

'It's not that simple,' he said.

'How come?'

'She's Raider's baby mum.'

Cameron snorted.

'Raider? C'mon, Nat. He's a mug.' He shot Natty a crafty look. 'Plus, it didn't stop you going over there to bang her.'

'We didn't have sex. I just crashed there.'

It was Cameron's turn to shake his head.

'You're turning into Spence, fam.'

Natty chuckled. 'Have you heard from him? He left before me.'

'He rang me an hour ago. He's handling the crew. No hiccups so far.'

Natty nodded. He could always trust Spence to keep things

moving. Spence had always shown a high level of managerial talent, and Natty believed he would make a good boss. Thinking of bosses made him think of Rudy, whom he needed to see. Inwardly, he cursed himself for taking his eye off the ball.

'Cool. Get ready, anyway. Rudy wants a meet.'

Groaning, Cameron clambered to his feet, draining his coffee, making a satisfied sound. Natty looked at him in disgust.

'You need help, Cam.' He poured his own coffee into the dirt.

'Speak for yourself. Hope Rudy's got some work for us. My funds are low.'

'You shouldn't have loaned that silly Rolex off Damanjeet. You got ripped off paying that deposit. I'm sure it's fake.'

Cameron waved that off. 'You're just jealous you didn't get it.'

'Jealous of what? You *need* that fake watch. It's the only way women will go near you.'

'Don't talk shit. I get as many women as you do.'

'You wish.'

While Cameron got ready, Natty messed around on his phone, replying to a few text messages. He thought about what Lorraine had said earlier. Natty felt he was being held to a higher standard based on Spence's willingness to have a relationship, and his reluctance to do so.

Spence had been more reserved than he and Cameron even before getting together with Anika. He often kept them from doing stupid things, always remaining calm, which helped calm Natty — and Cameron — down when needed. Yet, last night, Natty had almost gotten into a fight over a girl, and couldn't even recall what she looked like.

Maybe he needed to cool it with the drinking and partying.

'Seriously, I'm still rough.' Cameron yawned as he stuffed his feet into a pair of trainers. 'Should have done a Spence and left early. How long are we gonna let him keep getting away with that?'

'What are you talking about?'

'Anika. You said in the beginning that she wouldn't change him, and I told you he was pussy whipped. Now look at him . . . leaving parties early when we're having a good time so he can run back to her.'

'They live together now. Spence does what he thinks is right. You don't know that she's having that kind of effect.'

'I know her, remember? We both do.'

Natty shook his head.

'C'mon, let's just go and see the old man.'

Once Cameron was ready, they drove to Rudy's.

'We're out next weekend,' said Cameron, once they'd set off. 'There's an event near Albion Street that's gonna be jumping.'

Natty grinned. 'I thought you weren't coming out with me again after last night?'

'Whatever, man. We're going. I'll take it easy this time,' said Cameron.

'We'll see. What's the event?'

'I mentioned it ages ago. It's been in the works for a while. That DJ from London is performing. The fat one.'

Natty kept his eyes on the road, vaguely remembering Cameron mentioning it. Pushing his earlier epiphany about partying to the side, he nodded and said, 'cool. I'm up for that.'

'Yes! Knew you would be.' Cameron winced. 'We need to stop for paracetamol after this. My head's killing.'

'Sure, sweetheart!' said Natty, as loudly as he could, laughing as Cameron again winced.

———

PARKING ON FRANCIS Street in the Hood, both men strode to Rudy's office, a red-bricked terraced house with a plain white door. It didn't have a garden, with only some messy bushes and a small pathway. Several guys hung around outside, talking in loud voices. They looked up when they saw Natty and Cameron, greeting them with grins and handshakes.

'Rudy in?' Natty asked. They nodded. 'Is he in a good mood? Anyone said anything?' He pressed.

'Same as ever, really,' one of them replied.

Natty left it there. They weren't bodyguards, but Rudy kept them close, using them for different jobs. Walking inside, they went to the kitchen, overwhelmed by the fried food stench. A heavyset woman hunched over the stove, muttering to herself. She glanced at the pair, her eyes lingering on Natty.

'Hey, Delores,' he said, beaming at her. Her stern face softened.

'Nathaniel. How are you? I never see you anymore.'

'I'm out here working,' replied Natty. 'I'll come and see you again soon.'

'Make sure you do. Stay out of trouble.'

'Yes, ma'am.' Natty kissed her on the cheek, turning his attention to Rudy. The older man sat at the kitchen table, sipping a pale concoction. He wore a white shirt and a thin chain, his greying hair trimmed short to disguise his accelerating baldness. Despite his advanced years, he'd maintained his looks. A sharp goatee framed his fame, his piercing coffee-coloured eyes surveying the pair.

He glanced from Natty to Cameron, signalling for the former to sit. Neither spoke at first; Natty used to the older man's theatrics. He looked around the comfortable, worn kitchen, as always unable to understand why Rudy was based there.

'How's it going, Rudy?' He finally asked.

Rudy straightened in his seat, not taking his eyes from Natty.

'Why didn't you answer the phone last night?'

'I was enjoying my night off.'

'We don't have nights off in our business. What if there was trouble, or a raid?'

Natty scratched his chin. 'I'd trust exemplary men like you to have things in order.'

Rudy's nostrils flared.

'Not good enough. You're representing the team, Nathaniel. You're always being watched, so getting drunk and throwing up at parties—'

Natty raised a hand, stopping Rudy mid-flow. Rudy's eyes narrowed.

'What do you think you're doing?'

'It was actually Cam that threw up . . . not me.'

Rudy looked from Natty to Cameron — whose eyes were currently burning into the back of Natty's head — then continued.

'Getting drunk and throwing up at parties, and trying to fight people, is not what's expected.' Rudy's expression remained unyield-ing. 'You know all this. We've spoken about it in the past.'

Natty resisted the urge to roll his eyes. Humour wouldn't cut it right now. The realisation that someone was reporting his movements suddenly struck him, and he frowned.

'The guy started with me. I wasn't gonna back down.'

'I didn't call you here to listen to your excuses. I need you to arrange a meeting with Elijah.'

Natty's hands clenched before he could even think about it.

'I thought we weren't dealing with him anymore?' He asked, voice thick with anger. Elijah had his own organisation, though there were persistent rumours that he was a front for another gang seeking more power. Natty and Elijah had a strained relationship; one Rudy was familiar with.

'We weren't,' replied Rudy. He glanced to Delores, still muttering to herself, and Cameron, who stifled a yawn. 'It's time we brought things back in line between our organisations. Bad blood isn't good for anyone. We've calmed things down lately, but none of us wants things back to how they were a few years ago, right?'

Natty didn't speak, but knew Rudy was right. The wars that had taken place had changed the landscape throughout Yorkshire, with multiple crews involved and scores of murders and arrests. It had stunted profits in all areas, with only their team remaining strong.

'Nathaniel, can you handle this?'

'I can,' replied Natty, nibbling on his bottom lip. Rudy kept his eye on him a moment longer.

'Elijah is looking to make a move into a new area. Could be some-thing for you to sink your teeth into if you play it right.'

Natty continued weighing up everything in his head. Elijah had caused trouble for their organisation in the past, and the teams had almost gone to war several times. Natty loathed him and the people he kept close. He hoped Rudy had given the idea some thought.

'When do you want me to sort this meeting?'

'I'll let you know. People will be watching. Like I said, it's a great opportunity. Use it to step up.'

Again, Natty almost rolled his eyes. Shaking Rudy's hand, he said goodbye to Delores and went to leave.

'Nathaniel.'

He turned. Rudy surveyed him for several seconds.

'Watch that temper of yours. It'll get you in trouble.' His face softened. 'You're a good man; a good soldier.'

That was the problem, Natty thought to himself as they walked out. He didn't want to be just another soldier.

'No point in me even going,' Cameron grumbled when Natty drove away. 'Rudy didn't even speak to me. Old prick.'

Natty didn't reply, deep in thought about Elijah, considering all the ways the situation could go wrong. He didn't trust him, wondering if Rudy had given him the whole story.

'Natty? What are you thinking about?'

'Elijah,' admitted Natty. Cameron scratched his head.

'What about him?'

'I don't trust him.'

'Him or Raider? You sure the fact your fuckpiece's ex rolls with him isn't clouding your judgement?'

'I'm sure. This is business,' snapped Natty.

'Rudy wouldn't get you involved if there was a chance something could go wrong. You're like a son to him.'

Natty almost reminded Cameron he'd just cursed out Rudy for ignoring him, but didn't bother.

'It's not that simple,' he finally replied. 'Summat's up with Rudy . . . his judgement might be a little off.'

'How?'

'He's got people following me around, reporting back to him. That's a waste of money and time. He's focused on the wrong things, so how do we know he's scoped the situation with Elijah properly?' said Natty.

'Don't overthink it, bro. Have the meeting, get shit organised, and keep it moving. We can get put on in a major way, and trust me, I need that,' Cameron replied, forgetting that he'd recently blown money on renting a snide watch.

———

LATER, Natty left the gym after a tough weights session, his gym bag slung over his shoulder. It was often his escape; he went to mull things over, to kill time between shifts and sometimes, to forget.

The combined nagging of Lorraine and Rudy had affected his mood. That, combined with the prospect of doing business with Elijah, caused him to seek out a distraction.

After showering and changing clothes, Natty headed to the city centre, finding himself in a bar. He sunk three drinks quickly, not bothering to take stock of his surroundings. Not wanting the profile, he'd deliberately picked a more low-key spot near Briggate. As he sipped Southern Comfort and lemonade, he spotted a woman standing with a group of friends. She kept looking his way. Natty signalled for her to come over, and after a while, she did, allowing him to get a better look. She had chestnut brown hair, deep blue eyes, and a giggly, flighty demeanour. She looked delicious in her little red dress, and he reasoned she would make a good distraction.

'What's your name?'

'Jeanette,' she replied softly, her eyes shining.

'People call me Natty Deeds.'

'Why?'

'Because I'm generous, and I get things done,' he replied, enjoying the smile on her face. 'I'm glad you came over. You're the most beautiful woman in here.'

'Really?' Her eyes widened. Natty maintained eye contact, holding and stroking the top of her hand. He felt her shudder and lean closer.

'Trust me, it's not even a contest. Let me buy you a drink.'

After several expensive drinks and a few highly charged dances, they headed back to Natty's. Jeanette pounced the moment they closed the door, forcing her mouth against his. Responding with equal enthusiasm, Natty easily lifted her from the ground, nibbling on her lips and drawing her further in. Hiking up her dress, he tugged down his trousers and slid her underwear to the side before entering her.

They panted against one another when they were done, catching their breath. Disentangling, Natty straightened his clothes and showed

Jeanette to the bathroom so she could clean up. She tottered down-stairs a few moments later, back to her giggly self, playing with her hair.

'You were so good,' she gushed. 'Shall we get a drink and go again?'

'No thanks. You can go now.'

'What?' Jeanette's mouth fell open.

'I've got things to do. I'll call you an Uber,' said Natty flatly.

Jeanette's eyes flashed.

'You serious? You're kicking me out?'

Natty didn't bother replying. Lip curling, she stalked past him.

'You're scum, Natty Deeds. Don't contact me again.'

'Get home safely,' he mocked. Closing the door on her insults, his smirk faded, shoulders slumping as he sat on the bottom step. Despite his best efforts, he couldn't switch off. Thoughts of Elijah and Lorraine flitted away, replaced by Cameron's words about Rudy being a father figure.

Often, Natty thought about his dad. He'd been in the life too, a big, powerful man with a deadly reputation. He'd been murdered when Natty was 11, and things hadn't been the same since. Even knowing how scared people had been of his dad, all Natty saw was the man who bought him what he wanted, but also taught him how to fight, and never to back down.

Natty had kept that same mindset as he grew older, no matter how much trouble it caused. He'd not truly understood why his dad was murdered, but even at a young age, he vividly recalled wanting revenge.

Sighing, Natty closed his eyes, wondering what the world wanted from him, and how he could get what he needed.

———

TWO DAYS after speaking to Rudy, Elijah still hadn't contacted Natty. Putting the meeting aside, he went to see Lorraine and Jaden, a new video game in hand.

'I've told you about buying him things before, Natty,' said Lorraine at the door, hands on hips. 'You spoil him.'

'That's my little soldier. I'm just looking out for him,' replied Natty, trying to make his voice as innocent as possible. It was a harmless, throwaway statement. Natty had love for Jaden and wanted to make him happy, but he was aware of Lorraine pausing, and gave her his attention.

He didn't know what had changed, but she was glaring at him, hands on her hips.

'What's wrong with you?' He said.

'My son is not your *little soldier*, Natty.' Lorraine's nostrils flared.

'What are you on about?'

'He's a young boy, and he's going to grow up to do great things. He won't do the stuff you do.'

Natty held up his hands.

'C'mon, you know I didn't mean it like that. I know he is. You know that.'

Lorraine visibly calmed down, nodding.

'Okay. I'm glad you feel that way.'

Natty's face tightened, head lowered, as Lorraine let him in. Jaden greeted him with his usual enthusiasm, which took the sting out of Lorraine's admonishment. After thanking Natty for the new game, they picked their favourite *Fifa* football teams and were off. Natty took the early lead, but Jaden brought it back with a lucky headed goal. With the final whistle imminent, Natty *accidentally* passed the ball back toward his keeper, allowing Jaden to get the ball and score.

'Yes! I won! Natty, I beat you!'

Natty took a moment to watch Jaden celebrate his winning goal like he'd just won the World Cup, an involuntary smile coming to his face at the sight.

After a while, he left Jaden playing and went to see what Lorraine was doing. She was hunched over a laptop at the kitchen table, tapping keys. She pushed the laptop away as he stood there, shaking her head. Natty watched silently for a few seconds until she noticed him, blushing.

'How long have you been there?' She asked.

'Not long. What's all this?' He motioned to the laptop.

'Studying. It's important I keep practising.'

'How long have you been studying? I didn't even know.'

'No one does. I want to have everything finished before I start telling people. My mum knows, because she helps with Jaden, and Rosie does, but that's it.'

'How are you finding it?'

Lorraine ran a hand through her hair, blowing out a breath. 'It's difficult, but I'm not giving up.'

Nodding, Natty went to make drinks for himself, Jaden, and Lorraine, missing the look of disappointment on Lorraine's face at his lack of reaction.

'I'll leave you to it,' he said, placing her tea beside her, then leaving the room.

Natty and Jaden played for a bit longer, then he returned to the kitchen.

'I'm gonna get off now,' he told Lorraine. She didn't react. 'Did you hear me?'

'Yes, you said you were leaving.'

Natty's eyes narrowed. 'What's up with you?'

'Nothing. I thought you were going?'

He stepped into the kitchen and gently lifted her chin to face him.

'What's your problem? Why are you going on dumb?'

'I'm not. I'm trying to work, and you said you were going.'

Natty didn't know why she had switched on him, but he didn't have the time or patience to deal with it.

'That's your problem; you're too moody,' he said, leaving before he ended up starting an argument. He couldn't deal with her weirdness right now.

CHAPTER THREE

LATER, Natty hung with his crew, watching a football match at Cameron's. The remnants of a Chinese takeaway littered the coffee table, along with a bottle of Hennessy and an empty cola bottle.

'Are we ready for tomorrow night then?' Natty asked.

Cameron rubbed his hands together.

'Damn right. Already got my outfit sorted. Spence, you on it?'

'I'll go for a bit. Can we talk about Elijah now?' Spence looked at both men. He'd only joined them because they'd planned to discuss business. Instead, they wanted to watch football and talk about nonsense.

'In a minute,' replied Cameron. 'What do you mean you'll go for a bit? Do you want us to talk to your missus?'

'Why do you always assume Anika's talking for me? I don't want to stay out all night, then be looking after the youngers on the early shift,' said Spence.

'Whatever,' Cameron scoffed. 'You could easily get that squashed. Why else would you not wanna chill with your people?'

'Chill with you . . . like I'm doing right now?' Spence's jaw clenched.

'It's not the same thing.'

'Forget this,' Natty interjected, tired of the back and forth. Silence ensued, both Cameron and Spence shooting the other dirty looks.

'We need to be careful about dealing with Elijah. He's sneaky, and if he approached Rudy, you know there's a reason behind it,' said Spence, his voice level.

'Course there's a reason behind it. It's called money,' said Cameron, rolling his eyes. 'I swear, you lot just like being broke.'

'There's good money and bad money, and bad money has all kinds of strings attached. I like to know what I'm getting into.'

'Look, we can discuss this more after I meet with Elijah. We're here to chill, so let's chill,' Natty interjected. He agreed with both of them. Natty believed he deserved a more significant role, and the money that came with it. He'd seen less worthy people being promoted over him, and knew he had more to offer the organisation.

'What's happened?' Spence asked, sipping his drink.

'With what?' Natty frowned.

'With you. You've been even moodier than normal. We've barely heard from you for the past few days when you're not working.'

Natty rubbed his forehead. He needed to replenish his painkillers; he'd used his stock trying to shift a persistent headache.

'Lorraine's going on dumb again,' he admitted.

Cameron grinned. 'You're mad over her? You're starting to sound like him.' He waved his hand at Spence. Rolling his eyes, Spence surprisingly didn't take the bait, instead focusing on Natty.

'What happened?'

'Don't have a clue. I was chilling with Jaden, and she was in the kitchen. Came to chat to her for a minute when I was making Jaden a drink—'

'Spending quality time with your kid. You're a good dad, Nat,' Cameron teased. Natty shot him a hard look.

'Kill the jokes. I'm not in the mood.'

'What was she doing in the kitchen?' Spence continued.

'Studying. Doing something on the laptop.'

'What was she studying?' Spence straightened, looking more interested. Natty shrugged.

'Was I supposed to ask?'

Spence shook his head. 'Nat, she's your girl.'

'No, she isn't.'

'Even if you're not in a relationship, you spend time with her and Jaden. You trust her.'

'So?'

'So, at the very least, she's a friend, and you could have at least asked about what she was doing.'

'It had nothing to do with me, so I left her to it. If anything, I helped by keeping Jaden out of her hair.'

'Studying ain't easy at any age, Nat. That's why she didn't want to talk to you; you didn't even show interest or ask about what she was doing.'

'Forget it,' said Cameron, clearly bored of the topic. 'Lorraine's not important. The new women at the spot tomorrow *will be*, so let's focus on them. They don't have silly complications and moods. They're just waiting for us to approach.'

Natty smiled at how simple life seemed to be for Cameron. Cameron didn't get it; he didn't understand why Natty was so bothered about Lorraine, and Natty supposed he didn't have to.

'I know we put a pin in the Elijah talk, but make sure the deal makes sense when you meet him,' said Spence, moving the conversation along. Natty cut his eyes to him.

'I thought you didn't trust him?'

'I think he's sneaky, but he's a businessman, and he's successful. He'll have told Rudy . . . or even your uncle, something good to get our team to the table. Focus on that part instead of trying to get laid.'

Natty didn't reply straight away. He didn't show it, but Spence's words had affected him. Spence was a more logical thinker, which always came across in his words. He was always looking at the big picture. Spence's dad had been in the crime game years ago and worked for a kingpin. Like Natty, Spence had been raised to study the streets, and all the major players.

'Back in your pop's day, what do you think he would have done? What was he saying when Delroy wanted to meet with Teflon and make peace?'

Spence rubbed his chin.

'He didn't like the idea of peace, and thought Delroy should be putting Teflon out of business. A few people thought that.'

No one spoke for a moment. Natty weighed up Spence's response, noting that he hadn't said whether he agreed with his dad's opinion.

'Did you tell Lorraine that you could be working with her baby father?' Spence's words jolted Natty from his thoughts.

'It doesn't have anything to do with her,' he snapped.

'She might not see it that way. You should talk to her.'

'Fucking hell, Spence. Are you still trying to pretend Anika hasn't changed you? You never used to talk all this nonsense before.' Cameron stared at him with disdain.

Spence glared at Cameron.

'It's okay to have different opinions, Cam. We don't always have to agree on everything. You think I talk to her about street shit? *Our shit?*'

'Anika got in your head with some nonsense, and now you're trying to do the same with Natty,' said Cameron, sneering.

'You need to grow up,' Spence snapped. 'Anika hasn't changed me, but if women *do* have that effect, you should try harder to get one.'

Cameron's mouth formed a hard line, not liking Spence's words. 'Make sure you ask for permission tomorrow. Wouldn't want her to cry if you go out otherwise.'

'For fucks sake, Cam—'

'Enough!' Natty roared. 'Both of you shut the fuck up, because you're getting on my nerves. I don't know what is going on with you two, but you need to fix it, because this back-and-forth crap is annoying.' Finishing his drink, he shot to his feet and stormed out, leaving his now silent friends behind.

———

NATTY LEFT the crew and headed for the spot where the underlings hung out. It was a house just off Spencer Place, with rooms reserved upstairs for the team to chill. Entering, Natty greeted a few faces, glancing at the screen, where people were gathered around watching two runners play *Fortnite*. The person Natty was looking for sat in the corner drinking a Lucozade, a battered Nokia on his lap. Carlton was one of the more reliable youngsters. Natty had schooled him, slowly giving him more responsibility.

'How's it going?' He asked. Carlton nodded.

'All good, boss. Almost sold out.'

'Bolki aware?' Bolki was in charge of delivering product, ensuring each team had what they needed.

'We're on his list. He's stopping by later with the reload.'

Natty patted him on the shoulder. 'Let me know if anything pops off. I'll be nearby.'

'Got you.'

Leaving the spot after hanging around for a few more minutes, Natty drove to his mum's house. She lived in the middle of Hares Avenue. Natty always felt weird being in the area; as if he was under surveillance. He'd heard rumours of a former distributor having an office in the area, protected from police presence by the nearby mosque, and all the political ramifications that came with it.

His mum lived in a red-bricked spot with a brown door, blended nicely with the other terraced houses around it. He'd never understood why she stayed there. She had the money to live in a better home, but she refused anytime Natty brought it up.

His mum sat on the sofa, smoking a cigarette and watching television. She gave him a sharp look when he entered. People often told Natty he had his dad's build, but his mum's facial features, which was never more evident than when he was with her. He had her nose and cheekbones, and she was currently giving him the same hard look he often gave others. The room stank of cigarettes, with various family photos dotted around, namely of Natty's dad in his younger days. Two cups rested on the coffee table.

Natty kissed his mum on the cheek.

'Do you want a drink, mum?'

'No.'

Natty took both cups from the coffee table and placed them in the kitchen sink. After making a coffee, Natty sat next to his mum.

'Got a cig for me?'

'This is my last one.' She handed it to him, and he took two long drags, passing it back.

'How are you?'

'Life doesn't change.' She shrugged, eyes back on the screen.

'It changes if you want it to. Do you?'

She scowled.

'Do I what?'

'Do you want things to change?'

'I don't have time for this,' she snapped. 'How many times have I told you not to bring that smart mouth around me?'

Natty didn't respond, already regretting visiting. He loved his mum, but she was challenging to be around.

'Spoken to Unc lately?'

Finishing the cigarette, his mum flicked the remains into a nearby ashtray.

'He had dinner with Rudy and me the other night.'

'You should have invited me. I'd have liked to see him.' Natty wondered why Rudy hadn't said anything.

Rudy and his mum had started seeing one another after Natty's dad had died, shortly before Natty began working with Rudy. He'd grown used to their relationship, but that didn't stop it from aggravating him from time to time.

Rudy was in a perfect position to put in a good word to Natty's uncle, but hadn't. It was galling.

'Suck up to your uncle in your own time. I won't be used so you can do it,' his mum said.

Natty glared at her. '*Used*? I come and see you all the time. You're the one who never has anything to say.'

'Maybe if you were genuine, I would.'

Natty swallowed down his anger.

'I'll stay for dinner, and we can watch a film or something. What are you having?'

'You're only offering to try to prove me wrong,' his mum replied.

'You're fucking impossible.' Natty rubbed his forehead.

'Don't swear at me. I won't have you in my home if you're going to disrespect me.' His mum's eyes narrowed.

'I'll leave then.' Natty drained his coffee and shot to his feet.

'See? You're selfish. You don't care about me. Just like your dad. That's why you're walking out now.'

Without a word, Natty slammed the door behind him.

CHAPTER FOUR

BY THE TIME the event rolled around, Natty's lousy mood hadn't abated. He hated that Lorraine and his mum were taking out their issues on him. Spence was right when he'd said Natty should have paid more attention, but Natty was sick of the games. He wanted women to be straight up, the way he was. He entered Cameron's, psyching himself up.

'Was starting to think you weren't gonna show,' said Cameron. He sat on the sofa, building a spliff, a bottle of E&J by his side. 'You wanna hit this? I've got some coke too, if you want some.'

Despite being tempted to say no, Natty nodded, snorting a line, before pouring a drink.

'That a new outfit?' He said, wiping his nose and sniffing. Cameron wore a tight navy blue t-shirt with a pocket logo, jeans and cream Balenciaga's. He topped it off with his thickest chain, and the snide Rolex.

'Yeah. Cost me two bags, but worth it.'

'You spent two grand on the clothes?' Natty's eyebrow rose.

Cameron shrugged. 'So what? That outfit you're wearing doesn't look cheap, either.'

Natty had foregone wearing a chain. He had a black shirt he'd recently bought, ripped jeans, and shoes.

'Whatever. Where's Spence?'

'Probably on his knees begging to go out,' snarked Cameron. Natty gave a short laugh, which appeared to please Cameron.

As Cameron called Spence, Natty wondered why he had such an issue with Spence and Anika. Unbeknown to Spence, Anika and Cameron had been a thing once upon a time, before Cameron ended it. Neither Natty nor Cameron ever mentioned it, and despite not entering into relationships, Cameron remained partial to casual affairs.

As far as Natty was concerned, if Spence was happy and kept working hard, it didn't matter. Seemingly, Cameron disagreed.

Spence arrived a while later, outfitted in a crewneck sweater and jeans.

'Looking sharp, gents,' he said, grabbing a glass and pouring his drink.

'Didn't think you were gonna turn up,' said Cameron, eyeballing him.

'I almost didn't.'

Cameron's eyes narrowed. He shot Natty a look, and then glared at Spence.

'I definitely need to have a word with your missus. You're fucking whipped, and it's sickening.'

Spence sighed.

'Once again, I'm capable of thinking for myself. Not everything revolves around my girl.'

'Seems like it does,' Cameron retorted.

'Are you jealous? You talk about Anika more than I do.'

Cameron laughed darkly. 'Jealous of you? She's been around the block. Only you would want *that*.'

Tossing his glass to the floor, Spence lunged for Cameron.

'Stop!' Natty broke them up before they could start swinging. He shoved Cameron away as the pair shot daggers, breathing hard. 'You two need to calm the hell down, fighting over this nonsense. Cam, go outside and cool off.'

'What about him? He's the one who can't handle the truth.' Cameron's nostrils flared.

'What?' Spence struggled against Natty, but Natty easily kept him in place.

'Just go, Cam. Don't make things worse.'

Cameron stomped from the room. Natty let Spence go a few moments later.

'I'm not gonna stand for the repeated disrespect,' Spence warned, eyes hard.

'Spence, ignore him. You know what he's like.'

'That's not the point.' Spence jerked away, continuing to take deep breaths, trying to calm down. Natty couldn't argue, but didn't know what to say. They had been cool for the longest, but things seemed strained with Spence and Cameron, and he didn't know how to get around it.

If they fought, would he have to take a side? If he did, which side would he pick?

———

LATER, Natty was at an apartment in the city centre. Despite all the hype, the event had been a bust. When a woman he'd clicked with suggested an after-party, he'd seized the potential distraction. He'd lost the woman in the shuffle of people, but wasn't bothered.

The two-bedroomed apartment had a spacious living room with a connecting kitchen. It had light cream walls, immaculate flooring, and a black and white rug taking up most of the space. A large sofa and several smaller chairs and tables were dotted around the room. The party was full of people dressed in tight, flashy clothing. Drugs freely flowed, a bevy of people lining up to partake.

Cameron and Spence had made up after multiple shots. They were talking to some women in the corner, Spence nodding along and backing up Cameron. Natty felt entirely out of place. He didn't like the crowd, and his bad mood hadn't shifted. He kept thinking about his issues with Lorraine, plus the Spence and Cameron drama. This was a night he'd have preferred being by himself.

Spotting an attractive brown-skinned woman conversing with some people, he wandered over, enjoying how her eyes widened when she saw him.

'Natty,' he said, introducing himself by taking her free hand and kissing it. Her face flushed, and he knew he'd had an effect.

'Alana,' she replied in a soft voice. The other women shared glances, then excused themselves with polite nods.

'How did you do that?' She asked. Natty grinned, maintaining eye contact.

'Guess they realised we were destined to talk.'

Alana rolled her eyes, but couldn't stop her lips twitching. She still held his hand and, upon noticing, flushed further and let him go.

'You're sweet.'

'That's one word to describe me.'

Alana arched a perfectly shaped eyebrow. 'Give me another.'

'*Determined.*' He kept up the eye contact, knowing it was crucial. A moment later, she looked away, blowing out a breath.

'I . . . need to speak with someone. Nice meeting you, Natty.'

'You too.' He could have stopped her from leaving, but didn't. Based on her body language, he assumed she had a boyfriend and didn't want to get carried away. Getting another drink, he made his way to Cameron and Spence.

'Having fun?'

'It's live in here,' Cameron slurred, his arm around Spence. 'Could have banged those little cokeheads if I'd tried harder.' He squinted at Natty. 'See you're finally smiling. You got over your shit?'

'I guess so,' said Natty. Even a few seconds of flirting had been enough for him, his worries abating for the moment. Scanning the room, his gaze rested again on Alana. She was sipping wine and speaking to a group of women. His eyes widened when he recognised one of them. Without a word, he moved in their direction, ignoring Cameron calling after him.

Alana's mouth opened as he neared, but ignoring her, he focused on another woman. She wore a fitted blue dress accentuating every delicious curve, and her hair was styled in neat box braids. Natty blinked, unused to seeing Lorraine looking so dressed up. He wondered for a foolish moment if he had manifested her presence.

'What are you doing here?' He asked before he could stop himself.

Lorraine blinked, surprised to see Natty. There was a moment where they continued staring at one another, each taking in the other's appearance. Behind them, the other women exchanged looks, Alana included. Lorraine's mouth opened and closed before she finally composed herself.

'I could ask you the same question.'

Natty frowned, caught off guard by the response. He wasn't pleased with just how sexy Lorraine looked. He thought about their last conversation and how cold she had been. The earlier feelings of annoyance returned.

'Where's Jaden?' He looked into her eyes, not wanting to get caught checking her out.

Lorraine folded her arms, drawing Natty's attention to her impressive chest for a moment. 'He's with my mum for the night. You know she loves to see him.'

Natty couldn't argue. He'd met Lorraine's mum dozens of times, and she was besotted with her grandson and enjoyed looking after him.

'You have a free yard then?' He wasn't sure why he said it, or where he was going with the question. Lorraine's eyes narrowed.

'Please don't think you'll be drunkenly crashing at my place, Natty. If you show up, I won't let you in.'

'What's your problem?' He snapped, tired of the attitude.

'Even if I told you, you wouldn't care. Have a nice night.' Lorraine stalked off, Natty glaring after her, his mood worsening when he saw several guys eyeing her up. Alana shot him an incredulous look, rolling her eyes. Cameron and Spence were talking to some more girls, so Natty went back over and joined in the conversation.

The women were younger and currently attending university. He quickly grew bored and couldn't help looking over to where Lorraine was. She was laughing with the same group of girls, and the guys from earlier surrounded them. Alana looked back at him, but Natty turned away.

As the party continued, people left, with more faces showing up. Some faces Natty recognised appeared; men he knew were connected to Elijah. He wondered if it was a coincidence. One of them noticed Natty and wandered over. He was a slim, light-skinned man with a neatly trimmed fade and a diamond stud in his ear. He slapped hands with Natty, a large chain around his neck jingling.

'What's happening, Nat? Didn't think I'd find you here.'

'I was at some event in town, and someone mentioned this spot.'

Wonder nodded. 'They have these parties every once in a while. Ellie's cool, and it's a good little breeding ground for making connections.'

'I'll have to come again in future,' said Natty.

Wonder sized up Natty, looking around before he spoke again.

'I heard we're gonna be doing some business together.'

'I heard the same,' replied Natty, wondering what Elijah had told his team. He glanced past Wonder, his eyes again resting on Lorraine. Wonder noticed, his eyes flitting between them before he spoke.

'Is that Raider's baby mum?' He asked, already knowing the answer.

'Yeah.'

Wonder raised an eyebrow. 'I heard you two were close. Raider's mentioned it before.'

Natty shrugged.

'We're friends.' For some reason, the words felt bitter as they left his lips. He wasn't sure what they were, but relegating it to friendship felt wrong. It was made worse because he couldn't seem to get anything right where she was concerned. Even the way she had walked off earlier riled him. His paranoid brain was working overtime. Elijah was up to something; he was sure of it. It was too coincidental that his people happened to show up when Natty and Lorraine were talking.

'That's cool, bro. Just be careful, because you know Raider sees her as his.'

At another time, Natty might have shrugged off Wonder's words as general advice. He couldn't stop him from hanging around Lorraine, and whether Raider had an issue, he'd continued to see her and Jaden.

In the mood he was in, he saw the words as a challenge.

'Why doesn't he see his son as *his* too?' Wonder opened his mouth to respond, but Natty talked over him. 'Raider needs to recognise when something, or someone, isn't *his* anymore.'

Wonder's eyes narrowed.

'Don't forget, Raider is on my team, Natty. We're cool, but play nice, and don't talk reckless.'

Natty took a step toward Wonder, closing any space between them. Wonder stood his ground. They both knew Natty would wipe the floor with him in a fight, but he didn't back up.

'Save all that tough talk for someone else.' Natty noticed the men Wonder had come with, inching closer, and defiantly met the eyes of each. Several of the partygoers picked up something was wrong, backing up and whispering amongst themselves.

Ignoring it, Natty focused on Wonder and his crew, piecing together a plan of action. There was little space in the cramped room, but he would have to deal with that if they rushed him.

'I don't want to start any shit, Nat. I just need you to be respectful.'

'You already started something when you approached me trying to give warnings,' replied Natty.

'You're always on one.' Wonder shook his head. 'I'm just giving you some friendly advice about *Raider's* baby mum. Chill.'

Natty continued to size up the crew, ready to throw the first hit.

'Nah, it's not happening like this,' said a voice from behind Natty. Cameron and Spence appeared on either side of him. The stench of liquor was overpowering, but they seemed to have quickly sobered, ready for whatever happened next. With the odds a little fairer, Wonder and his people lost their spirit.

'We were just talking,' said Wonder. 'No drama.'

Natty didn't say a word as Wonder and his men backed away. Cameron turned to him, still scowling.

'What was all that about?'

'They were talking about Lorraine and Raider. Wonder thought he could warn me off.'

'She's here, isn't she?' Cameron had a lewd look on his face.

'Thought I saw her earlier, looking super sexy. You're a fool for not claiming her.'

'I don't have time for this shit. I'm off to get another drink.' Natty walked away, still struggling to calm down after what had transpired. As he poured himself some brandy, his hands shook. It wasn't from fear. He wasn't scared of Wonder or anyone he had with him. He'd wanted the fight so badly, and it was something he could control. He could handle violence. Violence didn't play games and try to mess with his head. It was easy and had a resolution he could handle.

Natty took several deep breaths. He'd just downed the brandy and poured another when Spence made his way over, Cameron again trailing.

'Nat, I'm gonna bounce,' said Spence.

'Because of Elijah's people? Don't worry about them,' said Natty, waving his free hand.

Spence shook his head. 'I'm not scared of them. If you want me to stay and back it, I will.'

'You need to stay, anyway,' interjected Cameron. 'If they see we're a man down, they might try to rush us.'

Spence looked to Natty, waiting for his response.

'You're cool, Spence. Those pussies aren't gonna do anything whether you're here or not.'

'Are you sure?'

Natty sipped his drink, struggling to get a handle on his feelings. His frustrations bubbled to the surface, and he struggled to keep them tethered. Wonder was talking on the phone, his eyes on Natty. People furtively watched both groups, having seen the earlier exchange.

Out of the corner of his eye, Natty saw Alana and the other women leaving, the men that had crowded them, helping with their jackets, shooting nervous glances back at Natty.

Wonder kept his eyes on Natty. Natty's eyes narrowed; Wonder staring had his blood boiling. The anger had returned. He needed the drama; Wonder was the physical representation of his problems, one he wanted to smash through.

'These lot are getting too big,' growled Cameron. 'They really think they're running things out here. Spence, if it kicks off, go for Wonder. Natty and me can handle the others.'

'You need to get some water and chill, Cam. We don't need things getting any worse at a public party,' said Spence. Despite his earlier words, he'd stayed, too loyal to leave his friends, a resigned expression on his face.

Natty's fists clenched. He knew there would be consequences for the fight and that Rudy would undoubtedly find out, but right now, he didn't care. Wonder had tried talking down to him. He grabbed the brandy bottle, ready to smash it over Wonder's head.

Before he could take another step, Lorraine stepped in his path. Eyes remaining on Natty's, she took the bottle from his hand, then led him from the apartment. In the elevator, he snatched away his hand.

'What the hell are you doing?' He snapped, when they reached the ground floor and headed outside.

'What are *you* doing, you mean?' Lorraine replied with a question of her own. 'Are you *really* trying to fight Wonder and his boys? Were you *really* going to smash a bottle over his head? In public?'

'You shouldn't have taken me out,' Natty said, ignoring her questions. 'I won't have those little twats thinking I'm soft.'

'Natty, who cares what they think? What is going on with you? Why are you so determined to cause carnage?'

'What I'm doing has nothing to do with you. I'll tell you one thing: Wonder was ringing someone up there, and my guess is it's Raider. So, when your wastrel baby father shows up, I'm gonna deal with him, and you don't wanna be around to see that happen.'

'Don't be silly, Natty. You're going to end up getting arrested if you carry on. It's Ellie's party, and she's already threatening to call the police on all of you.'

'I can handle prison.'

Lorraine's eyes flashed, her nostrils flaring as she shook her head.

'Nat . . . I care about you and know how you are, but this isn't the way to go about things. I want to help you, so please tell me what is going on?'

'I'll tell you what's going on, seeing as you wanna know so badly. I'm tired of the women in my life taking out their moods on me. I'm tired of the bullshit games, and I'm tired of people not fucking respecting me!'

'Respect? What are you talking about? Who doesn't respect you? Wonder and his crew, who you don't even like?' Lorraine sighed, resting her hand on Natty's shoulder. He wanted to move it, but found he was powerless to do so. 'You're a great guy, and I have a lot of time for you. Everyone does. You walk around with a chip on your shoulder, though, and you think the world owes you something.'

'What the hell do you know about it?' He roared, stung by her words. 'What does any of this have to do with you?'

'Fine!' Lorraine snapped, fiercely meeting his eyes. 'Do what you want. I don't even care anymore. You and Raider are as bad as each other.'

Lorraine stormed off down the road. Natty closed his eyes, sighing deeply. He wanted to go after her, but knew he would only worsen things. He let the cold air sober him up, trying to get his bearings.

A few minutes later, a midnight blue BMW pulled up. Elijah slid from the car in a yellow and green Brazil football training kit. Natty straightened, knowing that despite his negative feelings toward Elijah and his team, he was a man who he needed to give his due to. Noticing him, Elijah nodded. Natty's hands clenched as he approached, unwilling to let his guard down.

'Where's Raider?' He asked, glancing at Elijah's ride, unable to see inside.

'At this time, probably drunk in a strip club somewhere,' Elijah replied. 'Wonder called. Mentioned there might be a potential issue.'

'He was talking reckless, acting like he wanted to go.' Natty was unnerved by Elijah's calm demeanour. There was barely an inch in height between them, and Elijah's powerful build was on a par with Natty's.

'I will handle Wonder. I want good relationships between our firms. I've spoken with Rudy. There's plenty of money we can make together.'

'What's your angle here?' Natty asked. 'Rudy trusts you, but you've done some slick shit in the past, and I don't know if I can just forget that.'

Elijah glanced around and signalled for Natty to sit in the car. He took in the fancy leather interior for a moment, then focused on Elijah.

'There was dirt on both sides,' Elijah finally replied. 'When all that stuff happened years ago, we were both there. Afterwards, our teams wanted to benefit from the power vacuum, and we bumped heads. It went away, though. It didn't linger. I've made money on my own, and you lot are absolutely killing it.'

'So, why bother working together if we're doing well separately?'

Elijah maintained eye contact. It was unsettling for Natty to see his strategies being used against him, but he persevered.

'Because the streets are ready for a change. Other little gangs are banding together, wanting more power and prestige. It's only a matter of time before people start looking at our teams and wanting to get some of what we're getting. If we work together, they won't try us. It won't be worth the risk.'

The idea had a lot of merits, and it was easy for Natty to see how Elijah might have been able to sell the concept to Rudy. He'd also noticed subtle changes in how the crew was perceived. There were a lot of compliments masking envy; passive aggressive remarks about the team taking a more significant piece of the pie than other smaller firms. Natty hadn't paid too much attention, but Elijah clearly had.

'I don't fully trust you, and I don't fuck with Raider. He's a piece of shit.'

Elijah held the stare a moment longer.

'I understand it's personal with you two, and I won't get in the middle of that. At the same time, Raider is my brother, and I can't have you disrespecting him in front of me.'

Natty could have made an issue out of it and forced a fight. Part of him wanted to. In the grand scheme of things, it would be pointless. It wouldn't get him what he wanted, and despite not trusting Elijah, he knew he was right with some of the things he had said.

The streets were ready for a change, and they had to make sure they changed with them. The old days were done with. The way things were set up, it was hard for one person to rule anymore. Maybe that would change in the future, but for now, this was how things were, and Natty had to deal with that like everyone else.

'Fine,' he finally said. Elijah nodded.

'Let's go inside and get a drink.'

Neither man spoke as they took the lift back up to the party. Several more people had left since Natty had gone outside. When he entered with Elijah, he saw Cameron's eyes widen. Spence had gone by now. Elijah and Natty headed for the table. They poured drinks of brandy, and Elijah held out his glass. Natty clinked it, and they both nodded. Elijah turned and headed over to Wonder.

Placing his glass back on the table, Natty walked away to find Cameron.

'What the hell was that about? Who invited him?' Cameron frowned at Natty.

'Wonder called him,' replied Natty. 'He thought things might get bad between us.'

'Where's Lorraine? I figured you two went back to hers, the way she dragged you out of here. Wouldn't have blamed you either.' Cameron smirked.

'We had another fight, and she stormed off.'

'A fight over what?'

Natty shrugged. 'Nothing. She just didn't want me to fight, that's all.'

Cameron sniggered. 'Gotta say, I was shocked when you picked up the bottle. You were gonna smash it over Wonder's head, weren't you?'

'If I had to.' Now that he'd calmed down, Natty felt foolish at the idea of bottling someone in the middle of a busy party.

As annoyed as he was with Lorraine, Natty was glad she'd stopped him from making a huge mistake.

'What did Elijah say to you?'

'He wants our teams to align, because other little teams are starting to band together. He doesn't think they'll come for us if we're united.'

'He's making sense. I know bare little teams that are working together, and not many of them like us.'

Natty agreed. Their team was in a strange predicament. They were successful and made big money, but they didn't have much say in how things were governed in the streets.

After the fall of the last big crews, the police and the streets, in general, seemed to have a vested interest in preventing any team from getting too big. The only reason their crew had prospered was that they were well-positioned before the change. It gave them a head start that others didn't benefit from. Their supply was mainly unaffected by the storms, and by the time the other teams got their acts together, they sat pretty.

'What else did he say? I know where one or two of those little crews hang. We can tool up and go sort them out.'

'Later, bro. Let's chill on the business now.'

Cameron sneered at Natty.

'Okay . . . let's focus on you moving to Lorraine's friend in front of her and kissing her hand like you're Prince Charming!'

Laughing, Natty took his ribbing for a while, then the pair headed to speak to some of the remaining women. The mood slowly started to pick back up after the tension, and Wonder even came over to apologise after a while. It was clear he had been prompted to do so by Elijah, but it was a nice gesture.

As the party continued, Natty noted how people were positioning themselves around Elijah and sucking up to him. Regardless of Natty's feelings, the man had presence and knew how to use it. He felt a little less unnerved about having to work with him, but resolved to keep an eye on him and his team, just in case. He continued drinking, even having a few shots with Wonder, and the night became a blur.

THE FOLLOWING DAY, Natty woke in an unfamiliar bed, with a strange woman draped over him. His head pounding, he extricated himself from her grip, gathered his clothes, and walked out without waking her. The place was an absolute mess, and he had no intention of helping her tidy up.

CHAPTER FIVE

ELIJAH'S WORDS stayed with Natty over the next day. He grudgingly found himself agreeing with what he'd said, and was warming toward the idea of working with him.

It remained to be seen just how much money they would make together.

Natty wondered which teams Elijah was concerned about that would make him seek out Rudy for support.

Ripples in the underworld were always met warily. Everyone recalled the dangerous, bullet-riddled years. Afterwards, the streets were wide open, and people took advantage, making quick alliances to survive the complex world.

Things had calmed since, but people remained cautious.

From complicated street politics, Natty's thoughts strayed to another complication . . . Lorraine; the argument they'd had outside the hotel. Whenever complications arose, he always fell into battle mode with Lorraine. He didn't like that she'd snapped at him, or that she had accused him of having a problem. Natty knew he was confident, but he didn't believe he had a chip on his shoulder, and didn't know why she was so mad with him. He decided to let her cool down before he spoke with her again.

The other thing Natty didn't want to admit was how good she looked. Natty knew Lorraine was attractive. There had been a vibe between them from day one, and he was no stranger to her body, but he was used to seeing her in sweatpants and hooded tops, or worn out from looking after Jaden.

The reminder of how she could look when she was trying was a gut punch, and he wasn't sure what to do next. He cared for Jaden and wasn't intimidated by Raider the way others were, but thinking about a commitment was another story altogether. He wasn't sure how to handle that.

There was also the issue of Cameron and Spence.

The pair had got along at the end of the night, but they had almost come to blows, and it wasn't something he could afford to let happen again. The issue of Anika seemed to be driving a wedge between them, and Natty couldn't understand why. He decided it was a bridge he would have to cross and that speaking to Cameron might help him understand what was happening.

———

'I WAS WONDERING when you were gonna show up,' said Cameron a short while later. They were in his kitchen while he made breakfast. Natty stood at the back door, smoking a spliff. Cameron didn't have a problem with him smoking inside, but Natty wanted fresh air at the same time.

'What do you mean?'

'You were absolutely gone last night. I thought you and Ellie were gonna start banging in front of us,' said Cameron.

'I might have gotten a bit carried away with the liquor,' Natty admitted, smiling.

Cameron sniggered.

'A bit? You were out of it. One minute Ellie's yelling at you about bringing drama to the spot; the next, she's grinding and kissing you in front of the whole room. I dunno what you have, but they like it.'

Natty sighed. He remembered flashes of having sex with Ellie, but a lot of the build-up was foggy.

'What are you doing here, anyway? You've got the day off.'

'I wanted to talk to you.'

Cameron nodded. 'The Elijah thing? I've been thinking about that myself since I woke up.'

'It's not about that, but go on.'

Cameron frowned, but finished making his breakfast and took a seat.

'I think it's a good move to be working with him,' he started, tucking into his food. 'As snakey as Elijah is, he's got connections, and he's right about one thing; teams are circling. I give it a few months before one of them gets their shit together and tries to take us out.'

Natty's eyebrow rose at Cameron's words, but he saw their merit.

'After last night, I'm guessing we'll set up a meet. There's no use waiting around,' he said.

Cameron nodded. 'What did you wanna talk about, anyway?'

Natty sipped a coffee he'd made before Cameron started cooking, again silently reminding himself to bring his own next time he came.

'This thing with you and Spence.'

'What about it?' Cameron's brow furrowed.

'I want to know why his relationship is such a big deal.'

'It isn't.' Cameron's voice rose.

'It clearly is. You bring it up at every opportunity, and you sound bitter. I need to know what's happening, and I want the truth.'

Cameron shrugged. 'I dunno what you want me to say.'

'Tell me what the problem is. Am I gonna have to worry about you two falling out?'

'That's up to him,' replied Cameron. 'I'm not the one selling out my boys for pussy. I'm right here with you.'

'So is Spence. You may not like what he's doing, but he still chills with us, and he works as hard as anyone, so kill it and dead the silly remarks.'

Cameron's nostrils flared. 'You're telling me that you're happy about them? She's basically living off him since they moved in together.'

Natty made a face. 'I don't care. If he was pillow talking and putting us at risk or her ahead of business, I'd have a problem. My main problem with her is that she was with you, but never told Spence. I think that's foul.'

'Why don't you say something to Spence then?' Cameron demanded.

'It's too late. We have to live with it, but you need to get over your shit.'

Cameron scowled. Natty let the words sink in before he spoke again.

'Leave Spence be. Focus on helping me make our team even stronger. If he ever becomes a problem, we'll deal with it.'

'What about Lorraine?'

'What about her? Didn't we already speak about Lorraine?' Natty's left eye twitched.

'I saw your face last night. You're into her, and it's not just about banging her.'

'No, I'm not.'

'Yeah, you are, and the fact you're lying about it only makes it worse.'

'The only one lying is you,' said Natty, annoyed at Cameron's repeated comments.

'You and Spence are changing and growing pussy whipped over women, but you both wanna act like I'm the problem.'

'You *are* the problem. Who the fuck is pussy whipped, you silly prick?' Natty's muscles tensed. He glowered at Cameron, who stood his ground.

'You are. Don't be getting all hostile with me. I'm out there repping the crew, making sure people fear us, while you're almost scrapping and getting in fights all over the place. Did you forget you were ready to take on Elijah's whole crew over that girl you claim you don't like?'

'Are you silly? I was ready to fight because they thought they could disrespect me. The same way you're trying to disrespect me now.' A vein in Natty's neck pulsed, his eyes flashing.

'You wanna fight me now? Is that it?' Cameron glared at Natty, who returned it. The look between the men grew more intense until, finally, Cameron took a deep breath.

'I'm sorry, okay? You're my brother, and I'm not gonna fight with you over some nonsense. You want me to leave Spence alone, then I will. When he fucks up because he's too busy thinking about Anika, I'm gonna be the first one saying *I told you so*.'

Natty grinned, knowing Cameron would do just that.

'Fine. Now, let's drop it and talk about something else.'

LATER, Natty drove to Lorraine's and parked across the road, not wanting to go home. He'd hoped to hear from her by now, but evidently, she was still angry.

Staring at the house, he thought about what she could be doing with Jaden, wondering if he should make the first move and knock on the door. He sat there for several minutes, then his phone buzzed. He looked down, seeing a text message from Ellie, speaking about their night. Glancing from his phone to the house, he took a deep breath, then replied to Ellie's message as he drove away.

Rudy had also sent several messages, wanting to speak to him, but Natty kept putting it off. He had no desire to listen to another lecture and was still annoyed at him for meeting with Natty's uncle without including him.

Natty had a contentious relationship with his father's brother. Mitch Dunn was a menace from day one, and one of few people to be in the same league as other respected Hood legends that had passed on. After Natty's father's death, Mitch continued to go from strength to strength, slowly removing himself from the public eye. Like Delroy Williams, he worked through his network and right now, Rudy was the man he spoke with.

Thinking of Rudy made Natty recall the argument with his mum. He hadn't spoken to her since and felt guilty, but she didn't make things easy. Rudy didn't either.

They had access to his Uncle Mitch. Natty hadn't spoken to him since he'd come to Natty's mum's for Christmas dinner, and even then, they hadn't talked business.

Maybe he needed to arrange a meeting?

He didn't know what he would say, however. He wanted to make money and more responsibility, but he also didn't want to be an idiot on the string, seduced by promises of a better life that would ultimately lead to nothing. Natty knew people like that, both in and out of the crew; the down-for-whatever types, who would kill, maim, or anything they could to get clout. To get put on; to get that reputation that would lead to the money and power they always wanted.

The cemetery was littered with the type.

One way or another, Natty needed to work out what he wanted. Until he did that, he was stuck in a rut.

It was well after eleven when he finally entered his house. Heading upstairs, he turned on the bath and stripped out of his clothes, doing press-ups while the water ran. His gym schedule was shot, and that reflected in his general mood. He'd not pushed, grunted, and sweated his problems out for a few days, and it showed. When Natty finished, his arms ached, but he felt slightly better. He glanced at his phone, seeing a text notification, which he ignored. He climbed into the bath when it was ready, playing a hip-hop album on his music dock. Closing his eyes, he let the heat take over, trying to bury his problems for good.

The talk with Cameron had been interesting. They'd been close to blows, but had been friends a long time. Neither held back, and that sometimes boiled over, but rarely lingered. Cameron had agreed to cease his comments about Spence and Anika, which Natty saw as a win.

He planned on having a similar conversation with Spence, and then from there, he would deal with Rudy.

———

'WHAT DID he say when you spoke to him then?'

Spence and Natty were in Natty's front garden the next day. Natty had a spliff in his hand, a beer bottle resting between his legs. Spence remained stood, holding a bottle of his own.

'He said he would leave things alone with you. Dunno how much stock I'd put in that if I was you, though.'

Spence nodded, sipping his beer.

'Have you thought about why he acts like he does?'

Natty shook his head. He was distracted for a moment by the flashing light and vibrating of his phone, but ignored it when he saw who it was.

'Cam is always gonna be Cam. He doesn't know any better, and I don't think he even wants to.'

'Do you think I'm doing something wrong with Anika?'

Natty weighed up his words carefully. As he'd said to Cameron, Spence's relationship hadn't affected his business, and they still hung out — as they were now. The pros outweighed the cons.

'No. Your girl is your girl. I don't think you'd be telling her things you weren't supposed to, so she can't hurt the team. Personally, I don't get why anyone would be in a relationship, but it doesn't threaten me that you are.'

Spence grinned.

'I appreciate that, fam. It's been a while now, though. We kept things low at first, but we're living together, and it hasn't changed me. I still take my job seriously. Now, I have more to focus on.'

'I can't promise things will be any easier, so just stay calm. That's all I'm asking,' said Natty.

'I will. Other than that, how are you?'

'I'm fine. Why wouldn't I be?'

'You nearly got into a fight with Elijah's people, for one. Then I heard you came back in with him a while later and seemed cool. That's on top of the whole Ellie and Lorraine situation.'

Natty scowled.

'There is no *Ellie and Lorraine situation*. It's handled.'

Spence stared ahead, his fingers gently tapping his bottle.

'I'm not trying to interfere, but I'm here if you need to talk. Are you gonna keep things going with Ellie?'

Natty grimaced. 'Definitely not.'

'Didn't you enjoy it?' Spence cut his eyes to him. Natty shrugged.

'Honestly, I don't remember much of it. I woke up, and I was just in bed with her. Cam said we were all over each other.'

'She's friends with Lorraine.'

'So?'

'So, you and Lorraine are cool, despite whatever nonsense comes out of your mouth. I saw how angry you were that night, but you still went outside with her.'

'So what? What does that mean?' Natty's eyes narrowed.

'I'm not saying it means anything. Your life is your life. I just think you need to accept the possibility that there might be something more between you.'

Natty didn't respond, even if he knew his friend was right. Things with Lorraine were at an all-time low, and when she found out he'd slept with Ellie, he guessed they would get worse. He would need to bite the bullet and deal with it. Mentally, he added the issue to his to-do list. He would eventually need to speak with Rudy and deal with his lecture, and then he was onto other business.

CHAPTER SIX

LORRAINE WAS HOME, watching Jaden play his game. Her mum had looked after Jaden earlier so she could study, but she'd spent most of her time stewing over Ellie's party and her argument with Natty.

'Are you hungry?'

Jaden shook his head, not taking his eyes from the flashing screen.

'Did you have a good time at Nana's?'

He nodded. 'She let me watch football.'

'That's nice. We can do something fun next week if you like.'

'Okay, Mummy. Can we bring Natty too?'

Lorraine blew out a breath. She didn't know what the thing was between them, but it was never easy. She had known Natty a long time; they had been on and off more times than she could count. Natty was a great guy; he was funny, smarter than he acted, and cared more than he wanted to admit. He had charisma and a way of pulling people toward him. He was loyal to his friends and often generous — hence the *Deeds* nickname. At the same time, he had a temper that he seemed unable and unwilling to control. He had never put his hands on her, but they'd had several screaming arguments where she thought he was going to.

During an off period with Natty, she and Raider had become closer. He was a few years older and seemed to represent everything Natty didn't. He was polite to her, considerate, and she was young and dumb enough to fall for his slick talk. She didn't see the flaws until it was too late. By contrast, Natty had never hidden his flaws.

Before long, she was pregnant, and Raider faded into the woodwork, claiming she had intended to trap him. She'd seen the real side of Raider at this point; a nasty, abusive side. All the false niceties and politeness immediately vanished once she'd refused to get an abortion. Lorraine buckled down, ready to be a single mother.

To her surprise, Natty stepped up during this period, often driving her to appointments and looking after her. She never asked him why, and he never explained himself. She'd often wondered if he'd felt guilty for letting her fall into Raider's clutches, but she was scared of the answer.

After Jaden was born, Natty remained around. He helped with feeds from time to time, and even took Jaden out with him. They would watch television, and go to the park. As Jaden grew older, he became used to seeing Natty. He knew Natty wasn't his father, and seemed to look at him as an older brother, which Lorraine was conflicted about. She didn't think Natty would willingly corrupt her son, but she had misgivings about his lifestyle. There were enough temptations around to lure young boys toward the street life, and she didn't want her son to be another statistic.

Lorraine's phone rang. Reading the screen, she saw it was Rosie, her best friend. Walking to the kitchen and taking a seat, she answered.'

'Hey, girl.'

'Hey, Lo. You okay?'

'Yeah, just having a lazy day. You?'

'I'm good. Have you spoken with Ellie?'

Lorraine frowned. 'Not since I left her place after the party. Me and Natty got into it, and I ended up leaving early. I don't even think I said bye.'

'She called me a bit ago. I've just got off the phone with her.'

'Why do you sound so weird?' Lorraine asked, not liking her friend's tone. She sounded like she had grave news.

'She and Natty got close after the party.'

Lorraine's stomach lurched before she could adequately comprehend those words.

'I heard that they were flirting,' she admitted, resisting the urge to be sick.

'They slept together, Lo. What happened with you and Natty? You said you got into it?'

Lorraine explained about Natty's standoff with Raider's friends, and how she had led him from the party before he could get into trouble.

'Are you okay?' Rosie asked.

Lorraine sighed.

'I can't *not* be okay, babe. Me and Natty aren't like that. I don't quite know what we are, but I don't think it gives me the right to get upset.'

'Course you do. Natty was drunk as hell, but he should have known better, and Ellie definitely should have. She said she's sorry, by the way.'

'Nothing to be sorry about. Natty is single. He doesn't belong to me.'

'Girl, this is me you're talking to,' said Rosie.

Lorraine's eyes narrowed. 'What does that mean?'

'It means I know you, and you and Natty are not *just* friends. He's basically a dad to Jaden, and you two are closer than you want people to think. He went off and got drunk after his argument with you because he needed a distraction. After arguing with him, you stormed off home and left a party early.'

'So what? We're not together. He's not Jaden's dad. He can do what he wants.'

'So, you two have some weird holding pattern that I don't understand, but everyone knows there's something there.'

They spoke for a while longer before ending the call.

Lorraine made herself a drink, thinking about Natty and Ellie. She was in two minds about what to think. She knew Natty was furious that night, and based on what Rosie had said, he was completely out of it. There were feelings that she didn't quite understand between her and Natty, but she didn't know if it was worth the long-term potential heartbreak. She had a perennial worry about him abandoning Jaden, as Raider had.

Tired of thinking about it, Lorraine resolved to focus on her son, rather than putting her energy into Natty.

———

THE NEXT DAY, Natty sat on the wall outside his house. Spence stood nearby, whilst Cameron leant on his car. The sun was out, yet grey clouds loomed above, and there was a chill in the air. Not that this bothered Cameron, who wore a grey vest.

'I'm telling you, I've found a tough new workout,' he said, flexing his bicep. 'Gimme a couple months, and I'm putting everybody to shame!' He exclaimed.

'Are you forgetting what happened last time you went gym with me?' Said Natty. 'You tried lifting 80 kg, showing off for those girls, and you nearly killed yourself.'

Spence sniggered, having heard the story before. Cameron pursed his lips.

'Bullshit. You dragged me to the gym, even though you knew I was feeling under the weather, and you tried to make me lift heavy. Fact of the matter is, I'm on it now. Bought some creatine earlier too.'

'What's with the sudden urge to get back into shape?' Spence asked, chuckling. Cameron's eyes narrowed.

'Get back into shape? I'm already in shape. Look at me.' Again, he flexed. Natty shook his head.

'You're gonna end up getting pneumonia before you make any gains. It's not warm enough for that little vest,' he said.

'Nat, you need to stop hating. I'm fine, this weather is nothing.' Cameron beat his chest with his free hand, still holding the joint. 'You've got bigger worries, anyway; let's not forget about your *Prince Charming* shit; kissing hands and searching for glass slippers.'

'What are you talking about?' Spence barely held back his laughter.

Natty took the joint from Cameron and inhaled, savouring the potent weed.

'Didn't you see it?' Cameron started. 'He moved to a woman at that party, kissing her hand like he was in a play! Funniest thing I've seen in ages.'

Spence burst into laughter.

'That's such a Natty thing to do. I've seen it before. He transforms when there's women around.'

Laughing, Cameron approached to take the spliff from Natty just as a blacked-out car pulled up next to them. Rudy stepped onto the pavement. Cameron froze with his hand out. Spence gawped at Rudy as the laughter vanished. The eyes of the trio lingered on Rudy, but he only had eyes for Natty.

'Seventeen phone calls. Eight text messages. No response,' said Rudy in a low, calm voice that fooled no one. Natty locked eyes with him, getting the measure of the man. He knew he was in for it. As the moment stretched with neither man speaking, he finally rubbed his forehead.

'I've been busy. I was gonna get back to you today.'

'Not too busy to be sitting outside, getting high and joking around, when you could be working, though?' Rudy shook his head. 'Get in the car.'

Natty's eyes narrowed.

'You don't need to come at me like that, Rudy,' he snarled, irritated at the way he was being spoken to. Rudy didn't respond, simply keeping his eyes on him.

With a huff, Natty took a hit of the joint, then slapped hands with Cameron and Spence. As he climbed into the car, he heard Cameron laughing. He shot his friend a hard look, and Cameron's laughter evaporated.

Natty closed the door, and the car pulled away. One of Rudy's men was driving, and he kept his eyes on the road. Rudy looked out the window in the passenger seat next to him, paying Natty no attention.

'Where are we going?' He quickly grew tired of the silence.

'Figured we'd go to the pub, seeing as you're so fond of drinking recently,' said Rudy.

Natty tried to swallow down his mounting anger.

'I barely drink,' he responded, but Rudy ignored him, and the driver pretended not to hear. Eventually, they pulled outside a pub in Middleton. As Natty climbed from the car, he noticed the clouds had thickened and turned darker.

Natty followed Rudy into the pub, wondering why they weren't going to Delores's place. It had an old-fashioned layout, with an old wooden partition and several tables, chairs and stools that had seen better days. The burgundy decor wasn't much better, but it was cleaner than Natty expected. The stench of beer hung heavily in the air. Someone jostled against Natty as they moved through the busy crowd. He shot the person a hard look and nearly pushed them back, but restrained himself. Rudy nodded to a fleshy, grey-haired landlady, and after a minute, they had a table. A football match played in the background, capturing the bar's attention.

The landlady took their orders. Rudy ordered a coke, and Natty had a lemonade he didn't want. He glanced around the pub, looking for women he could focus on. There were none.

'Talk me through it,' said Rudy, sipping his coke.

Natty resisted the urge to roll his eyes. The atmosphere in the pub heightened every time Leeds United touched the ball. As a player came close to scoring, the yells of encouragement gave Natty an extra few seconds.

'What do we need to talk through?' He finally replied.

Rudy's nostrils flared. Putting his glass down, he rubbed his temples. Noticing his mounting frustration, Natty spoke again.

'Wonder ran his mouth.'

'So?'

Natty shrugged. Rudy shook his head.

'What am I supposed to do with you . . .?'

'You tell me. I don't get any real sense of direction nowadays,' Natty flippantly replied. Rudy's eyes widened, shocked at Natty's audacity.

'If you're ever going to make anything of yourself, you need to start working out when it's the time to close your mouth and do what's best for the people above you.'

'Wonder ran his mouth. Not me.' Natty didn't respond to Rudy's words, though they'd cut him deeply.

'Nathaniel, we're trying to do business here. Make money. Is this the time for your little gangster shit?'

'There's no gangster shit here.'

'You're just fighting over a girl you're not even involved with. Where's the sense in that?'

Natty's jaw tightened.

'I wasn't fighting over her. It's not about her. It's about them.'

'Elijah's people are harmless, so I need you to ignore them and stop making the wrong moves.'

Natty sipped his drink, eyes blazing. Rudy sighed.

'Nathaniel, the streets are always watching. I don't need to tell you that. Your Unc is watching too, and this dumb shit always gets back to him. I know you're unhappy with how things are, but you need to see this as an opportunity to prove yourself.'

Natty levelled Rudy with a look.

'What more can I do?'

'What is it you think you *have* done? You have a problem with authority, Nathaniel, and you're too quick to flip out at the wrong times.'

Natty's eyes narrowed, but he didn't have an answer. He liked being part of the organisation, yet knew he deserved more. Putting that into words was difficult.

Realising an answer wasn't coming, Rudy continued.

'You have everything you need to get to the top. To lead. Lose that chip off your shoulder and go after what you want, but do it for you, not for what you think people want you to do.'

Natty shook his head. 'I don't care what people think of me.'

'Yes, you do. People know it, and if you let them, they will use it.'

Swallowing his frustration, Natty kept his voice level, scowling as the crowd noise increased again.

'You could have spoken to my uncle at any time and told him to elevate me, but you haven't. Save the preaching.'

Rudy's eyes bore into Natty's younger pair.

'First, watch your mouth. Second, I don't tell your Unc anything.

Outside of your mum, nobody does.' Rudy's nostrils flared. 'You've been in the game long enough to understand that one wrong move can have disastrous effects. It can even cost you your life.'

Natty wanted to keep arguing but decided against it.

'If Raider even looks at me wrong, I'll finish him.'

Rudy again shook his head, eyes tinged with sadness and disappointment.

'Is that all you are?' He asked, voice almost a whisper. 'You wanna be like your old man, is that it?'

'Don't talk about my dad.' Natty's fists clenched.

'I knew him, remember? Roughest of the rough, putting bodies in the ground. Where did it get him? It got him de—'

'I said, don't talk about my fucking dad.' Natty leapt to his feet, their drinks clattering to the floor. 'He was more of a man than you could ever be. Keep his damn name out of your mouth.'

Before Rudy could reply, Natty stomped from the pub, leaving a shocked, silent crowd in his wake.

Outside, Natty trembled with rage, glaring at Rudy's driver. He needed to get away before he did something he regretted. Whilst in the pub, it had finally started raining. Nostrils flaring, Natty put his hands in his pockets and began walking, cursing his lack of a jacket as he stomped on.

———

RUDY WATCHED NATTY LEAVE. Bringing up his father had been foolish, but he needed him to slow down and look at the situation. All eyes would be on him, and Rudy wanted him to succeed.

Sliding to his feet, he approached the bar. Dropping several notes on the bar top, he nodded and left.

CHAPTER SEVEN

ON THE NIGHT of the meeting, Natty prepared for Elijah. Spence and Cameron offered to go with him, but Natty decided to go alone.

He thought about Rudy and what he was expecting from this meeting. Natty hadn't spoken to him since their altercation at the pub. He regretted what was said, but he admired his dad and the toughness he brought to the streets. The thought of his memory being used to make a point evoked a wave of enduring anger.

Still, Rudy had done a lot for him and his mum, and as Natty picked up a pack of cigarettes from the coffee table, he knew he owed him an apology.

Unravelling the plastic from the packet, Natty pulled out a cigarette and lit it. Taking a long drag, he zoned out, thinking about his dad and his life. He wondered how he could have killed people. What it felt like. Who they were. There were rumours, but he didn't indulge them. It was one of the many unwritten rules of the streets.

Natty was terrified at the idea of dying. He knew people who had died — even his dad died violently, but the idea of life ending worried him, especially now. He hadn't done enough for people to remember him. He recalled the tepid response to his dad's murder. It was quickly forgotten, no one speaking about it other than contemporaries of his dad, waxing poetic about what a *real* guy he was.

Natty shook off the thoughts. He didn't want them clouding his mind right now.

Natty and Elijah met at Jukie's. Though it was his name on the building, Jukie was semi-retired and rarely moved around in the public eye anymore. There were rumours about him receiving a large amount of money in 2015. A few trusted family members now ran the business.

Natty had been in the gambling spot before, but it wasn't his scene. The crowd was a bit older, and he wasn't into cards or dominoes.

He greeted a few people when he entered, and ordered a beer. Scanning the room, he saw Elijah sitting in the far corner. The place was packed, so Natty was surprised he'd procured such a spot. It spoke to the clout the man had around Chapeltown these days. They shook hands, and Natty plopped into the seat opposite Elijah, glancing over his shoulder. He felt exposed, facing away from the rest of the room.

'I'm not going to off you in public,' said Elijah. 'I'm serious about wanting to work together.'

'Rudy mentioned that but was a bit vague,' admitted Natty.

'Vague in what way?' Elijah leaned in.

'I don't know why it had to be me in the chair.'

Elijah smirked. 'Plenty will step into your shoes if you don't want to do it.'

'Raider one of those guys?'

Elijah's smirk widened. 'Raider has a different type of skillset, but one that's equally useful.'

Natty didn't reply, thinking about Lorraine. They had yet to clear the air, but he missed her and Jaden. Natty didn't understand why he couldn't just walk away from them, and that confusion frustrated him.

'Raider will toe the line, if that's a worry of yours,' Elijah continued, wrongly believing Natty was mulling his words.

'I don't study Raider.'

'You study him far more than you should. That's part of the problem.'

Natty frowned, rubbing his forehead. He considered this the main reason why he and Elijah didn't vibe. Elijah thought he knew every-thing about everyone. Taking a moment to compose himself, he thought about Rudy's pep talk. There was a lot of subtext he was miss-ing, but he didn't want to miss an opportunity to elevate his game to a new level. He breathed deeply before he replied.

'I'm here and want to make this work, Elijah. I can put shit aside if I need to.'

Elijah blinked, clearly surprised.

'Well, that's good to hear. Is the only issue you have with me because of Raider?'

'Is that important?'

'If we're going to work together, then we should clear the air and get it all out in the open. I'll go first: I always thought you were a waste of space.'

Natty immediately went to jump to his feet, but Elijah held up a hand.

'That right there, is exactly what I mean. You dive in head-first, then you think afterwards. You're much sharper than everyone gives you credit for, but your temper gets in the way.'

'I don't let anyone treat me like a little man, and I never will. You might let people disrespect you, but I don't go for that shit.'

'Neither do I, but there's a time and place for anger, and the time isn't every time someone does or says something you don't like.' His eyes bored into Natty's. 'Pick your battles.'

Natty rubbed his nose, not enjoying Elijah talking to him like this. They were around the same age, both growing up in Chapeltown, knowing many of the same people. At the same time, Elijah seemed sharper than Natty, which was unsettling. His words seemed to hold more weight. He carried himself like a boss; unruffled, always meeting Natty's eyes, dressing the part in shirts, trousers, and shoes — other than when he'd shown up to Ellie's party in a tracksuit. Natty didn't like how insightful Elijah seemed, wondering where he'd learned to dissect people as he had.

Ultimately, Natty acknowledged that Elijah was being respectful with what he was saying, and realised it matched what Rudy had said last time — before he brought up Natty's father. He sighed, knowing more than ever that there was another deep conversation with Rudy in his future.

'It's your turn,' Elijah finally continued. 'Don't hold back.'

Natty didn't.

'I think you're sneaky. I also don't like the company you keep around you — Wonder runs his mouth too much, and Raider's a piece of shit.'

Elijah's eyebrows rose, but apart from that, he remained unruffled by Natty's words.

'Is the Raider problem to do with the woman you both like? His baby mother?'

Natty's nostrils flared. 'It's not about liking her.' He stewed, wondering why people kept saying it to him. Everyone seemed to think they knew him better than he did, which was galling.

Raider was a fool, and Natty didn't like his neglect of Jaden. That was it.

'What's it about then?' Elijah steepled his fingers, looking genuinely interested.

'We have history and I look out for her.'

'Raider also has a history with her.'

Natty gritted his teeth. 'I know he does, but he also ducked out on his responsibilities when he abandoned his child.'

Elijah bowed his head for a moment, then sighed.

'I'm not saying I agree with every decision he makes, but he's loyal, and I respect loyalty.'

'How can he be loyal to you if he's not even loyal to his son?'

Elijah rubbed his eyes, not hastening to reply. It was clear to Natty that he had stumped Elijah, and he allowed himself a small moment of triumph.

'I try not to involve myself in the personal lives of my team, but I can admit you've made some good points.' He grinned. 'Now there's a bit more understanding on both sides, we can get down to business.'

Natty straightened, ready to listen. Elijah glanced around again.

'I've scoped out some fresh territory in Little London.'

Natty's eyebrow rose, and he was immediately intrigued. To his knowledge, there were several little crews based in Little London, operating in a scattered but successful fashion. Alongside this, the council had renovated a lot of the area, building new apartments and catering to a younger, student demographic.

'There are several streets near Oatland Close that the gangs appear to have overlooked.'

'They might be overlooking it now, but when we bustle in and set up shop, we'll be on their radar, and we both know what that means.'

Again, Elijah nodded.

'That's where the resources of your team come in. We take over the blocks as a joint effort and see what sorts of moves the locals make. If anything goes down, we handle it.'

'Do you think anything will go down? Things have been relatively calm in Leeds since the big shootings.'

Elijah acknowledged this with a small smile.

'Of the players down there, only Warren will be a problem. He's one of those . . . hotheads too stupid to listen to reason.'

Natty acknowledged the pause, considering if it was a snipe from Elijah. He chose not to react, filing away Warren's name for future reference.

'The area is fertile. Plenty of students and sales around, and they love to get high. All they want is to do so safely, and if we can provide that, they'll do our marketing for us and spread the word on our product and discretion.'

Natty agreed with that. He had a few students and young workers that bought from him, and it was all they thought about, other than getting laid.

'What split are you thinking?'

Elijah didn't hesitate. '60-40 sounds fair.'

Natty agreed, but decided to push.

'60-40 our way works better.'

Elijah frowned. 'Our team did the due diligence. We saw the potential in the area.'

'True, but you came to us, and you need the muscle of our team. You've already admitted it might come down to war; even if it doesn't, the reputation of my crew trumps yours.'

Elijah rubbed his chin, mulling this over. Natty watched, his heart racing at his effective negotiating. He hadn't gotten aggressive. He'd stayed in control, using what he had just learned, to make his point calmly. He sipped his drink and waited.

'Fine. 60-40 your way. We'll see what the money is like when we get down there. I think there's more than enough to go around once we start.'

They shared another drink, talking about football and a bit of Hood news, before Natty shook his hand and left. He felt he had a greater understanding of Elijah. He didn't deny much of what Natty had said to him, and placed great emphasis on believing in loyalty. Natty wondered how much of his dislike toward Elijah had been perpetuated by what other people had said to him.

Hours later, Natty was home when he received a call from Rudy.

'We need to talk.'

THEY MET AT DELORES'S. She had already gone to bed, but Rudy had a key. He led Natty to the kitchen and poured him a glass of white rum. Under the flickering kitchen light, his face appeared more lined than usual, and there were bags under his eyes.

'You look tired,' said Natty. He sipped his white rum, the liquor burning his chest.

'I've been in and out of town all week. Haven't had more than a few hours sleep at a time. Not important, though. Spoke with Elijah earlier, and he said you got the deal done. I want to hear your side.'

Natty gave a quick overview of the conversation.

Rudy beamed.

'That is great work, Nat. I purposefully didn't give any instructions about the split, because I wanted to see how you handled it. Sixty percent is well beyond what I expected.' He gave Natty an approving look. 'I'll be telling your uncle about this, and he'll see it the same way I did. This is exactly what I was talking about last time, when I spoke of your potential. You're one of the best guys we have when you're locked on and focused.'

Natty's shoulders straightened, and he couldn't keep the smile off his face, happy Rudy was showering him with so much praise. The joy he'd felt earlier when doing the deal, came back tenfold. In the past, only fighting and successfully seducing women had given him the same rush. Now, he realised it was possible to get the same feeling when doing business the right way.

Rudy gave him a small smile in return before continuing.

'I want you working directly with Elijah, getting everything in order. Keep relatively hands off, but I don't need to micro-manage you on it. Get one of your people to cover your current day-to-day duties. I'm sure you have people in mind. Who are you going with?'

Natty took a few moments to consider. Cameron was more forceful and would likely crack the whip to ensure things got done. Despite that, Spence was the right person for the job, and the fact he was more confident overall, shone through.

'Spence is the right choice.'

Rudy nodded.

'Good. Cameron has skills, but he's not the most subtle person. Spence comes from good stock. His dad was a handful for Delroy back in the day. Anyway, I've spoken with Elijah about some of the particulars. Raider is to be kept away from the project. Wonder might be marginally involved. Keep doing what you're doing, and good things will happen.'

'Thank you, Rudy. About what happened last time. I'm sorry for how I acted. It's tough talking about my dad.'

Rudy laid a hand on his shoulder.

'I know, Nathaniel. I shouldn't have baited you, but I'm glad we're cool now. Spoken with your mum lately?'

Natty shook his head. They hadn't spoken since their argument the last time he'd seen her. Rudy sighed.

'She loves you, but she just worries sometimes. Doesn't always know how to say what she's thinking.'

'I don't think she's ever held back in her life.'

Rudy chuckled.

'I know it's not my place to get involved, but I care about you both. Talk to her.'

'I will,' said Natty. After finishing his drink, he left, Rudy following shortly afterwards.

———

NATTY MULLED over the conversations he'd had with Rudy and Elijah. He remained pleased with how he'd handled the situation even a day later. He called Spence and Cameron, arranging to meet in the afternoon at Cameron's.

Unable to muster the energy to go to the gym, Natty settled for continuous press-ups until his arms ached. Afterwards, he went to check on the main spot, speaking with the youngster, Carlton.

'Any issues?'

'Nah, Natty. Everything's calm. Police have been asking questions and driving around, but everyone is being careful.'

'How come the police are around?' Natty was suspicious.

'Someone got stabbed a few streets away. Teenager.'

'Fuck's sake.' Natty scowled. He didn't like kids stabbing one another in general, but he hated it when it happened near his spots. It made everything hot, making it harder for people to make money.

'Do we know who was behind it?'

Carlton shook his head. 'Some beef that started on the internet. You know what some kids are like.'

'If you find anything out, let me know. If it's over some nonsense, then the people involved need dealing with. Can't be having people think that sort of shit is cool.'

'Okay, boss. I'll keep my ear to the ground and see what I learn.'

After slapping hands, Natty left and went to see Cameron and Spence. They were there when he arrived. He'd stopped to get food beforehand, and they tucked into some chicken and rice. When they finished, Natty spoke.

'The meeting went well. We're in business.'

Both men grinned, thinking of the financial implications.

'How was Elijah?'

'He was cool. We had a decent chat.'

'Do you trust him?' Spence had his eyes on Natty.

'I do.' Natty wasn't exaggerating. He didn't think Elijah had an ulterior motive in wanting to work with the team, and his reasons made a lot of sense. Cameron snorted.

'Couple' meetings and you're sold on the guy,' he said.

'I'm willing to give him the benefit of the doubt,' replied Natty.

'It's in his best interests to play it safe. If not, it's war. I don't think any of us want that,' said Spence.

'I don't give a fuck about a war. I stay ready,' replied Cameron. 'Every now and then, it has to happen. Look at the last one. It changed the game.'

Natty frowned. 'The last *war* was between Roc and D-Mo.' They were two youngsters who'd run around shooting one another, recording it online for clout. The police had swiftly arrested both crews, hitting them with huge sentences and crippling both gangs.

Cameron shook his head. 'I'm talking about Teflon's wars. Those guys are legends.'

'The game is bigger than that, Cam. I want a career and the money that goes with it. I don't want pointless clout.'

'Behave, Nat. As long as I've known you, you've wanted a name on the streets. Look at the shit you used to get into, trying to build a rep,' Cameron finished with a sneer.

'It's okay to change. I still think Elijah is sneaky, but the plan is a good one and makes a lot of sense. We can do our legwork and drive around the area, check things out.'

Cameron's nose wrinkled. 'It's a shithole. There's no point.'

Natty glanced at Spence, who didn't say anything.

'With all the extra work I'm gonna be doing to get this off the ground, someone needs to step up and run the crew day-to-day.' Natty saw Cameron's eyes gleam, but pressed on. 'Spence, you're up.'

Spence nodded, giving Natty a small smile. Cameron's eyes bulged. His nostrils flared as he looked at both men, incredulous.

'Are you serious? Did you forget I've been down since day one and always had your back?'

'Course not. You've never shown any interest in running things. I don't see what the big deal is.'

'Spence hasn't either,' Cameron pointed out, but Natty shook his head.

'Not true. We've had conversations in the time about how things run, and what to look out for. He's contributed strong ideas.'

'Why haven't you had the same conversations with me?'

'Because you never asked, and Spence sought me out to learn. That's the difference.'

Cameron frowned, scowling at Natty.

'Well, I want the information too.'

'Good. You can learn it from Spence.' Natty stared into his friend's eyes. 'This is a big move for all of us. We can use it to really put ourselves on the map.'

Cameron's scowl didn't shift.

'It's a big move for you lot more than me. I've been repping this crew since day one, putting myself on the line when we needed it, and I'm being left behind.'

'Cam, it's not like that,' added Spence, but Cameron shook his head.

'Yeah, it is like that. You didn't speak to me about any of this. You just expected me to fall in line. That's fucked up.' Cameron jerked his hand at Spence. 'How can you depend on this guy to lead? He can't even drag himself away from his girl.'

'Are we going on about that again?' retorted Spence. Cameron shot him a scornful look, shaking his head.

'You need some time to chill and get your head around things,' said Natty. Cameron responded by lighting a spliff and flicking on the television. Natty held up his hand, the same way Elijah had with him during their meeting.

'This is exactly why you're not ready to lead, bro,' he said. 'You lose your temper, and then nothing else matters. You just switch off.'

Cameron took a long drag of the spliff, shrugged, then continued watching the television.

———

SPENCE AND NATTY didn't stay long. Cameron's mood had soured the night. They sat outside Spence's, Natty on the wall, and Spence sitting on his step. Anika had come out to check on Spence, then left the pair to it.

'Maybe you should have him run it instead of me,' said Spence.

Natty shook his head.

'You're the best man for the job. I can't change that for the sake of his ego. We'll give him time to cool off and get used to the idea. If the money is good, that's all Cameron will care about. We both know that.'

Spence nodded, a look of approval adorning his features.

'You seem to be in a better place,' he said softly.

'What are you talking about?'

'You seem calmer; like you're thinking more clearly.'

Natty thought about that. He hadn't noticed, but now that Spence had mentioned it, his mindset had undoubtedly changed. His talk with Elijah had helped establish some common ground, and there was even some merit in the things Rudy had said about his father, and how that had affected Natty.

'Maybe I am,' he finally said. 'It's like, sometimes I just feel angry at the world, and I don't even know why.'

'I think we all get like that sometimes.'

'When I do, it's like all I have to offer is violence, and that's when I want to start fighting people, and get rid of some of the emotion.'

Spence mulled that over before he spoke again.

'Have you spent any more time with Lorraine?'

Natty shrugged. 'Not yet. We didn't leave things in a good place after Ellie's party.'

Spence grinned. 'Talk to her. See where her head is at now.'

'For what?'

'For anything,' replied Spence. 'Fun, love, comfort . . . whatever. You don't need a specific reason.'

Natty let Spence's words resonate, blowing out a breath as he placed his hands in his pockets.

CHAPTER EIGHT

THAT NIGHT, Spence relaxed on his sofa, Anika snuggled against him as they watched the end of a Netflix documentary. The meeting with Cameron and Natty was on his mind. Spence liked the idea of stepping up, pleased Natty had chosen him. He had ideas to help grow the business and make them all more money. Natty had made an intelligent decision and seemed to be carrying himself differently. Because of this, they had an opportunity to step up, meaning everyone had to play their role.

Including Cameron . . . He thought.

'Are you okay?' Anika murmured as the show came to an end. She was mixed race, short and curvy, with curly black hair and brown eyes so dark they were almost black.

'Yeah,' Spence replied. 'Just work stuff. I'm gonna be busier going forward.'

Anika reached for the remote and paused the television.

'How come?'

Spence stifled a yawn. 'Natty's gonna be busy, so I'm stepping up. Money goes up too, which is good.'

Anika didn't say anything. Spence glanced at her.

'Are you okay? I probably should have discussed this with you earlier, but it all happened so quickly,' he said.

'Your business is your business, Spence. You know that.' Anika's tone was strangely cold.

Spence shook his head.

'We're partners, babe. Do you remember what we recently spoke about?'

Anika's stomach plummeted.

'Refresh my memory,' she replied.

'The future. We have this place, but it would be nice to start pooling money and aiming for something bigger. We could even rent this place out.'

'I'm still thinking about it,' Anika said. 'You have to admit, it's a big commitment.'

'No bigger than this commitment.' Spence pointed around the room. 'You wanted us to move in together.'

'Are you saying you didn't?' Anika narrowed her eyes. Spence chuckled.

'Course I did. Don't flip out on me. I'm just saying, saving our money to get another place isn't a bigger commitment.'

'It's a much bigger financial commitment. What if we didn't stay together?' she said, interested in how Spence would respond.

'I see no reason that we wouldn't,' he replied. 'We're compatible, and I like to think we compromise and talk about things when they're on our mind, like we're doing now. Still, I don't want to pressure you. Tell me about work.'

Anika frowned. 'What do you want to know?'

'How is it going? Do you still enjoy it?'

'Better than going into an office every day,' Anika replied. She was a self-employed beautician and enjoyed it, for the most part. She could pick her hours and had loyal clients. She didn't contribute as much monthly as Spence did, but made a decent living. Anika was content where she was at and had no great desire to push things. At the same time, she liked being challenged, so she kept an open mind.

It was hard explaining that to Spence sometimes.

'Yeah, I wouldn't want to work in an office either. I wouldn't mind

owning one or two, though,' he said. Moving away from Anika, he
picked up his laptop, booting it up and going online.

Anika glanced over his shoulder, seeing he was on his investment
portfolio portal, looking over the numbers. He did this often, having
taken to investing with a level of zeal that Anika hadn't expected. He
would read books on investments and financial strategy, and his
internet search history was littered with bookmarks from articles and
financial tips.

For the most part, she was proud of Spence and the fact he used
everything to make himself stronger. He was constantly pushing
ahead, with a desire and thirst to learn and do more. It was inspiring,
but it was also cloying and caused her insecurity to flare.

She often felt that she couldn't keep up with him, and that eventually, he would realise, and things would become harder for her.

Trying to push the negative thoughts to one side, she snuggled
back up to Spence, resting her head on his shoulder and closing her
eyes.

———

THE NEXT DAY, Natty decided to see Lorraine and clear the air between
them.

Before going, Natty cleaned himself up, going for a haircut and
trimming his beard. He didn't know why he was making an effort, but
instinct told him it was the smart thing to do.

Lorraine answered the door, her face blank. Natty wondered what
she thought about him and Ellie. He wouldn't bring it up unless she
did, though.

'Hey,' he finally said.

'Hello,' Lorraine replied, her tone as neutral as her face. He hoped
it was just down to their argument, but it was telling that she hadn't
yet invited him inside. He couldn't remember the last time they had
stood at the door to talk, which wasn't a good sign.

'How are you?' Natty inwardly cringed when Lorraine scowled,
hand on her hip, blocking any attempted entry. She was casually
dressed in an oversized t-shirt and jogging bottoms, but Natty recalled

how she had looked on the night of the party. No matter how much he tried, he couldn't get the image out of his head. He wondered how things might have gone, had things not got so heated between them. Whether he would have ended up in her bed instead of Ellie's. His stomach clenched, but he fought to remain neutral.

'What do you want, Natty?'

Natty almost flared up, ready to snap back at her, but inwardly calmed himself.

'I'm sorry for flipping out on you the other night,' he said. Lorraine remained silent, her expression unchanged. Realising it wouldn't be that easy, Natty blew out a breath. 'I was going through some stuff, but that's no excuse for my behaviour. You were right about some of the things you said, and I know I need to fix up. I guess I just needed you to know that, and that I really am sorry. You've always been real with me, and taking out my issues on you isn't the way to go.'

Before he could know if his words had any effect, they were interrupted by Jaden bounding to the door, beaming when he saw Natty.

'Natty! Have you come to play *Call Of Duty*? Where have you been?'

'I've been working, little man.' Natty couldn't hide his smile. He was genuinely happy to see Jaden, but he also knew that now that he'd seen Natty, Lorraine would let him in.

Grinning, Jaden tugged on his mum's sleeve.

'Mummy, can Natty stay and play *COD* with me?'

'Natty's busy, baby, so he can't come in.'

Smile widening, Natty replied.

'Actually, my plans have changed. I can stay.'

Jaden's eyes lit up.

'Please, Mummy. I'll be good. Promise.'

Lorraine cut her eyes to Natty, who maintained his grin. She sighed and stepped aside to let him in as Jaden cheered.

Jaden led Natty into the living room, talking a mile a minute about school.

'How's Anton doing?' Natty knew Anton was Jaden's best friend at school.

'He's good. We're not talking to Robert, though. He said he's a better footballer, and he told Ms Rainer that we were talking in class.'

Distracted, Natty observed Lorraine leaving the room.

'You been playing football?' He asked, not hearing the reply about Robert. Jaden nodded.

'I've been using some of the things you taught me. I scored two goals in the last game,' he said proudly. Natty ruffled his hair.

'That's my boy. Keep it up, and you'll only get better. I was a sick footballer when I was younger.'

'How come you never played in the Premiership?' asked Jaden.

'I went in another direction,' replied Natty. He'd been nowhere near the standard, and didn't want to disappoint Jaden by admitting it, nor did he add that he'd started selling drugs instead.

After a while, he left Jaden playing and headed into the kitchen. Lorraine was at the counter, her phone playing *Jorja Smith*. Natty knew she was a fan of the singer, but she was too soft for his liking. He was a rap fan, preferring *Skrapz* and *Nines*.

An awkward silence ensued, Lorraine continuing to add seasoning to some lamb chops near the kitchen sink, working around Natty. He jammed his hands in his pockets, wondering when things had become so complicated.

'How's the studying going?' He finally asked, unable to cope with the tense silence.

'Just stop, Natty,' she replied.

'Stop what?' He frowned.

'You're not interested, and you don't have to pretend to be,' she said icily. Once again, Natty almost lost his temper and stormed out, but somehow maintained his composure.

'Look at me,' he said. Sighing, Lorraine paused her music and faced him, eyes flashing.

'If you're interested, then I am too,' he said. 'I'll make us some drinks, and you can tell me all about it.'

Lorraine's mouth hung half open as Natty made her some green tea, and himself a black coffee. He sat at the kitchen table, giving her an expectant look. She shook her head.

'You're the most annoying man I've ever met,' she said softly.

'I always aim for the top.'

Lorraine giggled.

'Idiot.'

Natty waved her words aside.

'Right then; studying. How long have you wanted to do it?'

'I thought about it a few years ago, but I didn't think I could do it.'

Remembering what Spence had said about taking an interest, Natty had his next question primed.

'Why did you think that?'

Lorraine shrugged.

'It seemed hard, and I didn't think I was good enough to do it.' She lowered her head a moment. 'Eventually, mum and Rosie talked me into it.'

'For what it's worth, I think you can do it too. You're the smartest person I know.'

Lorraine rolled her eyes, but it was evident by the slight smile on her face that his words had touched her.

'What is it that you're studying, anyway?'

'I want to get into software engineering.'

Natty's eyebrows rose. It was the last thing he had expected her to say.

'What? With cars?'

Lorraine giggled.

'Not with cars. At the moment, I'm learning how to code,' she replied.

'What made you want to do that?'

'It's hard to describe, but it's like magic . . . close as you can get in reality, anyway. The opportunities are endless. I mean, if you can imagine it, you can pretty much do it. The limit is your imagination. Where we are . . . how we grew up . . . I felt trapped; like I'd been dealt my hand and that this was it for the rest of my life. Learning to do this; it lets me express myself, and kinda break away from that.'

Natty sat in stunned silence, in awe of Lorraine's passion. He'd never heard her speak like this before, and he felt terrible that he hadn't had a clue, when she was clearly so invested in it. Still, this wasn't about him right now. It was about Lorraine. As she reached for the drink he'd made her, he intercepted and squeezed her hand.

'You'll be great, Lorraine. Don't ever think any different. I'll help you in any way that I can.'

They held hands, the moment lingering for several seconds. Lorraine pulled her hand away, and straightened herself.

———

CAMERON LAY IN BED, staring at the ceiling with a small smile on his face. A woman was pressed against him. He'd met her at a party, and it hadn't taken long for his charm to work. They'd left the party to go back to his place. The sex had been good, and they'd finished, rested, and gone at it again.

'You need to go,' he said.

'What do you mean?' She said sleepily.

'I've got some things I need to do. I'll get you an Uber.'

'You're really kicking me out like that?' She sat up.

'Don't start,' said Cameron. 'I just told you I had things to do.'

'How can you just use me and kick me out?'

'We both had fun, and now it's done. If I wasn't busy, I wouldn't be making you go.'

She scowled. 'Whatever, Cameron. Fuck you. I'll get my own Uber.'

'Suits me.'

Cameron lit a spliff when she'd gone, having already forgotten about the woman. He found his thoughts drifting to Spence, and the argument they'd had. He liked Spence, and thought he was sharp. He differed from Cameron and Natty, which meant they balanced one another. Cameron didn't like the effect Anika had on him; the way Spence had changed since getting with her. He believed she'd softened him, which wasn't suitable for any of them.

He wanted Spence to return to what he considered *normal*, which was how he and Natty acted.

Deep down, he didn't want Spence anywhere near Anika, and he knew it.

Cameron had his dreams, the same as anyone. His plan had been consistent since he was young. He wanted to be a major player, and constantly recalled the older days; the things he had seen, and the stories he'd heard.

The level of power that former Leeds kingpins' had was intoxicating. Cameron wanted that. He wanted the juice, and the money that went with it. He wanted a mansion, a fleet of cars, and for people to show respect whenever he entered the room. Natty understood that dream to a degree, but his family were practically royalty.

Cameron didn't understand why they hadn't taken a firmer hold of the streets. They had everything in place, but had focused more on maintaining.

If Cameron had the opportunity, he would be ruling Leeds with an iron fist, making all the little teams pay a street tax, and bribing the police to keep them in line. Instead, he was down at the bottom with Natty and Spence.

Cameron was fully aware that the trio complemented one another. Natty was charismatic, and people gravitated toward him. Spence was structured and subtle, often providing a diplomatic voice of reason.

As for Cameron, he was the forceful one, always willing to go out and make something happen. With their combined efforts, Cameron felt they could truly run the streets. Unlike the others, he recognised they needed to keep Rudy sweet to do that.

Shaking the thoughts, he read a text message on his phone, pulled on a hoody, and left the house, hitting the streets.

CHAPTER NINE

OVER THE NEXT FEW DAYS, Natty and Elijah got to work in Little London. They procured numerous spots in the area, making deals with the people renting the houses to ensure they stayed out of the way. Natty had surmised that the locals wouldn't be a problem, as long as they played ball and kept things low-key.

Elijah put the crew together, everyone handpicked by him and Rudy, a mix of the two teams. On the first night, they gathered in the neatest of the spots. Elijah and Natty stood before them as they crammed into the living room. Natty briefly glanced around, hoping he'd made the right decision by choosing to trust his rival. Brushing aside these worries, he stood straight, meeting the eyes of those assembled.

'We wanted to link up and run you through what we have going on here,' said Elijah, his eyes sweeping the room. 'This is opportunity in its purest form, and we need you guys to remember that and represent yourself accordingly.'

Natty was impressed by Elijah's speech. His cadence was smooth, and his words were carefully chosen. It was evident by the straightening of backs and the emphatic nods, that they'd also had an effect on the team.

'We're not here to cause trouble. There's more than enough money around here for everyone, and we're definitely going to take our piece of it. This is a chance to take things to the next level. We're gonna move the usual stuff; white, dark, spice, weed, and pills. All the shifts and teams have been organised, so don't mess around, and you'll be treated well.'

There were more nods now, and even a few smiles. Natty, too, bought into the speech. If Elijah wasn't selling drugs, he'd be cleaning up making money as a salesman. He had it down to a T. His consistent narrative left no doubt as to what his intentions were.

'That said, I want to hand the floor to Natty, who has something to say.'

Natty hid his surprise as all eyes were suddenly on him. He hadn't thought of anything to say, and it hadn't been discussed that he would speak. Elijah had thrown him under the bus, though; it was sink or swim time. Swallowing down his moment of nervousness, he immediately composed himself and spoke.

'. . . Elijah said most of what I think needs to be said, but remember, it's possible to beat the game we're all playing. One of the most important commodities is teamwork; having one another's back. Two crews that haven't always gotten along, are now working together. Toward a common goal. A goal that will improve all of our lives. The only way we can do this is by leaving old grievances in the past, and moving forward.'

When he finished speaking, there were even wider smiles and some firm nods, and Natty felt good, even as his heart raced.

Later, Elijah caught up with him.

'You did well.'

'Is that what you wanted to happen?' Natty hadn't forgotten Elijah throwing him the ball without warning.

'I was curious,' Elijah admitted. 'Everyone knows how good you can be. You're not gonna get a better chance than this to show everyone. Remember, *you* gave a speech about unity. We can do a lot of good here, and we can get super rich at the same time.'

Natty touched his fist, committing to giving it a try.

AFTER THE MEETING ENDED, Elijah stayed with the team, who planned to order some food and have a small party. Natty walked the area, wanting to get a feel for things. He was walking down a street when he saw a woman openly watching him from the window. She jumped when she saw him, but he gave her a small smile, an idea forming. He knocked at her door, and she answered after a few moments, suspicion etched onto her face.

'Yeah?' She said. Natty's smile widened. She was on the heavier side, with lank brown hair and tired blue eyes. Behind her, Natty heard kids running around, making noise.

'Good evening. My name is Natty,' he said smoothly. The woman looked around him, clearly still startled.

'Julie,' she finally replied.

'Nice to meet you, Julie. Listen, I'm new to the area, and I figured you were someone I could speak with about what goes on around here.'

'Why me?'

'You were watching out of the window, for one. I'm guessing you have a good idea of who's who. That could be useful.'

Julie licked her dry lips, eyes dancing. Natty saw he was losing her and took out a twenty-pound note, which her eyes locked onto. He held it up.

'This is yours; there's more where that came from.'

Julie visibly relaxed and invited him inside. Before closing the door, she peered out onto the street, looking each way before closing the door behind her.

'Sorry about the mess,' she said.

'Don't worry about it,' replied Natty, the thundering of footsteps and commotion amplified now he was through the door.

'Oi, shut up! I'm sick of all the bloody racket!' Julie screeched. 'Take the noise upstairs!'

The kids — three unruly young boys — promptly ignored her, until she grabbed and smacked one of them. After two more hits, he ran upstairs crying, and his brothers followed.

'I'll crack you all if you break anything,' she called after them. Natty wasn't phased by her threats to her kids; he'd grown up around similar threats, and had seen it all of his life. He followed her into the living room, stepping over various toys. Despite not being particularly dirty, the room was undoubtedly untidy. Natty plopped on the sofa, which creaked beneath his weight. A large television was mounted on the wall, and Natty imagined that was the main reason it was unscathed.

Julie sat next to him, biting her lip, eyes darting all around the room. She gnawed at her nails, waiting for him to speak. Natty winced. He'd always hated the sound people made when biting their nails.

'Why don't you go and make yourself a drink?' He said, wanting to relax her. Julie leapt to her feet like she worked for him, hurrying to the kitchen.

Natty glanced at the television, distracted by the yells coming from upstairs. There was a loud bang, then the sound of someone crying. He thought of Jaden then, and the fact he had no brothers or sisters to roughhouse with. It made him wonder if Lorraine had ever wanted more kids.

Julie returned with a cup of tea and sat back down.

'I guess I won't have a tea then,' Natty joked. Julie laughed, and it cut through the tension.

'I can make you one if you like?'

Natty shook his head, still smiling. 'It's fine. Seriously.'

'Sorry about the kids,' she said. 'They're an absolute nightmare when they're cooped up like this. Run around doing what they want.'

'Don't worry about it,' replied Natty, taking control of the conversation. He took out a wad of money, watching her eyes lock onto it, then laid another twenty-pound note on the chipped coffee table. 'What can you tell me about the local area?'

'Are you police?' She asked, eyes narrowing. Natty shook his head. 'You know what I am.'

Julie sipped her tea, visibly more relaxed.

'It's bedlam. I don't want any trouble, and I don't know much. There's a lot of gangs in the area. Warren's crew are the worst, but I'm guessing you already knew that.'

Natty didn't immediately respond. Warren was the main threat in Little London, and his name was linked to numerous murders. He was definitely going to be a problem, and he had everyone in the area terrified of him. They would need to devise a way to handle him if they were to establish themselves.

'Why's Warren so bad?'

'He's horrible. Likes to hurt people. A lot of the kids around here are just following his lead. I can't even let my lot play out. They'll be running for him by the end of the week.'

Natty didn't dispute that. Julie was right. The lure of the money always got to most youths, making patterning them a breeze.

'Other than Warren, who else should I be looking out for?' This time, Natty laid a ten-pound note on the table. Julie nearly spilt her drink to gather up the money.

'Harry and Rodney,' she finally said. 'They're young, keep themselves to themselves. Got a few kids working for them, and they study. I don't know what, though. They seem to stay out of people's way. Guess they're only bothered about the money.'

'Personality-wise, what are they like?'

Julie shrugged. 'They're nice to me, if that's what you mean. They've never given me money before, though.'

A plan was unfolding in Natty's head as Julie spoke. One of the main ways to take over in any area, was to understand the terrain. Julie was going to be a major cog in that information bracket. He slapped five more twenties on the table, thinking how lucky it was he'd happened to carry more money than usual. This time, Julie didn't go for them immediately.

'What do I need to do for it?' she asked.

'Nothing that will get you in any trouble. I just want you to keep an eye on things for me. I want to know who is doing what and where. There's more money in it for others who want to earn.'

Julie tensed back up. Natty smiled, again looking to disarm her with his charm.

'Listen, I just want the area to thrive. I want to make money, but I want you to be able to let your kids play footy outside like they should be. We can do a lot around here, and with my people in charge, I promise you nothing but positive vibes.'

Julie nodded, successfully mollified. Natty stood and walked to the door.

'Right, I'm gonna head off. Let's see if I make it where I need to go without dehydration taking me down.' He grinned, and Julie again laughed. 'I'll check on you soon.'

The smile vanished when the door closed behind Natty, and his face tightened, back in business mode. Leaving Julie's garden, he spotted a young fiend — a *sale* — limping down the street. His clothes were worn, and his face drawn, but he didn't have the battered look of a fully developed addict, and quickly stopped to talk when Natty called him.

A deal was quickly struck. Natty offered to buy him a cheap camera phone, in exchange for the sale discreetly taking photos of the various dealers around Little London, offering to pay for each name and face. He wanted to know precisely who everyone was, and who they worked for.

'You can earn a few hundred for helping,' he told the sale, 'and get a little discount for yourself.'

Needless to say, the man was tripping over himself to sign up, and Natty inwardly beamed, knowing he'd made significant steps.

———

THE NEXT DAY, Cameron headed out. He had a job to do. Christian Price was one of Rudy's clients. He lived in a dreary house at the top of Beck Hill Grove, and had taken the piss paying for drugs. Cameron had been contacted by one of Rudy's men and offered the job, with instructions on handling it.

Cameron had previously dealt with the client, so he hadn't questioned the task. He took a taxi down the street from Christian's address, then headed up the road, keeping his head down just in case anyone was watching.

He knocked at Christian's door, watching the man pale when he saw him. Christian was slightly taller than Cameron, with a ponytail and designer stubble, his t-shirt stretched tight around a gut accrued from excessive takeaways.

Cameron smiled.

'Hi mate. Are you going to invite me in?'

Christian glanced around the room, looking like he would rather be anywhere but there. Cameron chuckled.

'C'mon, bro. We're good, and I know you don't want to talk business on the doorstep where everyone can hear us.'

Christian's shoulders slumped, and he allowed Cameron to enter. They went to the living room. Cameron slumped into a seat on the sofa, then put his feet up on the coffee table. Christian's jaw tensed.

'Look, Cam. I'm sorry I've fallen behind. Some of the lads I work with have given me the runaround.'

'And that made you think you could give *us* the runaround too? You know that's not how the game works.'

'I know, but there was nothing I could do, and I didn't think you would be understanding if I approached you about it.'

'We'll never know, I guess.' Cameron shrugged. 'Do you have it now?'

Christian nodded. He left the room and returned with a plastic bag. Cameron looked inside at the contents, seeing the notes hastily banded together. He took them from the bag and began counting. His eyes narrowed as he neared the end of the count. Christian cleared his throat.

'Erm, look, I have most of it, but—'

'Why did you tell me you had it?'

'Because I didn't want you to think I was playing games.'

'You *are* playing games,' Cameron snapped. 'Rudy isn't a patient guy, and neither am I. First, you don't get in touch and keep ducking when we're trying to speak to you. Then, you say you've got the full eight grand, when you only have six. What the fuck is going on?'

'I'm sorry . . .'

'I don't wanna hear how sorry you are. Doesn't mean fuck all to me. Tell me what the hell is going on?' Cameron's feet slid from the table.

'I told you. I've got people slipping me, messing with my drugs, trying to put me out of business. Why do you think I'm so far behind?'

'I think you're a greedy little prick. You should have gotten in touch and didn't, so now we're gonna get deep.'

Christian stepped back as Cameron rose to his feet.

'C'mon, Cam, other than this I've been loyal. You don't need to go on like that.'

Cameron sprang forward, covering the doorway so Christian couldn't escape. Christian put his hands up in surrender, but Cameron slammed his fist into his flabby stomach, then kicked him backwards, laughing when Christian toppled to the ground. He kicked him in the ribs when he tried to stand, then did the same thing again.

'You've been warned before about playing with us, you little prick.' Cameron kicked him after every word. 'You'll think twice about doing it again in future.'

Before he could hit Christian again, he heard a scream of rage and turned. At the last second, he was able to get his hand up, instinctively deflecting the knife that hurtled towards his face. It cut deeply into his wrist, the snarling woman raising her hand to strike again.

'Bitch!' Cameron snarled, backhanding the woman and sending her flying across the room, the knife clattering to the ground. Groaning, she crawled towards it, slowly stretching out, feeling for the blade. As the tips of her fingers touched it, Cameron's boot came crashing down on her hand. Screaming in pain, she cradled her hand as Cameron moved closer, breathing hard.

'Shouldn't have involved yourself,' he said, drawing his foot back and kicking her in the ribs. She let out a groan of pain, holding her hand, rolling into the foetal position. He kicked her again.

'Stop it!' Christian yelled. 'I'm sorry, that shouldn't have happened. Please, just leave her alone.'

Cameron whirled toward Christian, his eyes blazing.

'I'm coming back tonight. You need to have the rest of the money, plus an extra five bills, or else.'

CAMERON PULLED up outside Delores's, locking up the car and heading inside. He'd wrapped his wrist, the cut not as deep as he'd first thought. He and one of Rudy's men had stopped by Christian's as planned after he'd sorted his wrist. Cameron didn't know what Christian had done to get the money, but he'd taken the threat seriously, and had the rest of Rudy's money, along with the penalty fee.

Cameron hadn't seen Christian's girlfriend, and he assumed she was upstairs resting after the beating he had given her. He didn't feel bad. For the most part, he didn't believe in hitting women. The girl had tried to kill him, though. If he hadn't turned, the knife would have caught his head.

Pushing the thoughts away, he knocked on the door, smiling when Delores answered. She glared at him, even as his grin widened.

'Hello, Delores. You're looking well tonight.'

'He's through there,' she replied, kissing her teeth at him and turning away. He closed the door, his smile vanishing. He had no idea why the old bitch always looked down her nose at him. Anytime Natty was around, she was smiling and grinning, offering to make him food and drinks, treating him like her son, whereas Cameron was routinely treated like something on the bottom of her shoe.

Rudy sat in the kitchen as always, a folded newspaper on the table in front of him, next to a beer. He looked up when Cameron entered, putting the paperback he'd been reading to one side. Cameron handed him the money without a word, his heart hammering against his chest. He rarely saw Rudy without Natty there, and he didn't have the same dynamic Natty had.

'You take a piece?' Rudy enquired, counting the money. Cameron shook his head.

'Nah, I'd never do that. He gave me extra too, because of the runaround.'

Rudy smiled tightly. His eyes flicked to Cameron's injured hand.

'I figured you'd have kept the extra.'

'It's not my money,' replied Cameron. Rudy continued to survey him.

'You're not that bad, are you . . . we definitely picked the right person for the job. You're loyal.' Rudy peeled off some notes. He held them out to Cameron, then pulled back and added more to the pile.

Cameron thumbed through the money. His eyebrows rose.

'You didn't need to give so much. You said five.'

'Don't you want the extra?'

Cameron grinned. 'I didn't say that.'

'Good. Don't worry about it then. How did it go? Did Christian learn not to fuck around going forward?'

Cameron nodded. 'I gave him a beating he won't forget. His girl got involved, so I had to smack her around too.'

Rudy shrugged. 'I'm sure she deserved it. How is Nathaniel doing?'

'Natty's the same as ever.' Cameron almost rolled his eyes. He swore Rudy thought he was Natty's protector sometimes.

'I know about the party in town you all went to a while back,' said Rudy.

'What did you hear?' It wasn't a shock to Cameron that Rudy had heard. There were a lot of people at the apartment that night, and any of them could have passed word on.

'I heard he squared up to several of Elijah's men. You were there with him, right?'

'I was, so was Spence. That was Natty's thing, though. I backed my boy.'

'Like I said, you're loyal.' Rudy wasn't smiling anymore. His eyes were hard. Cameron instinctively straightened, noticing Rudy hadn't asked him to sit.

'Look, Natty is mad about a lot of things, but mostly that you've taken so long to give him more to do. He's here grinding, we all are, and we all want more.'

'Is that Nathaniel talking, or you?'

'Natty's the leader. I watch his back, same as always.'

'We have a lot riding on this, as you know. Nathaniel and I have cleared the air and he's getting on board, but we both know how he can get. I need you to keep him safe.'

'Natty can look after himself,' said Cameron.

'He doesn't always think. The day we left you and Spence, he threatened me in the middle of a pub.'

'What?' Cameron's eyes widened.

'I pushed him too far. Mentioned his dad.'

Cameron nodded his understanding now. Natty could be rough at the best of times, but he drew a line where his father was concerned, and speaking ill of him was a dangerous move.

Cameron recalled seeing Natty stomp people out for disrespecting his dad on more than one occasion. He wondered if Natty would have hit Rudy if he had continued.

'That'll do it. Natty doesn't take that shit laying down.'

'Regardless, keep an eye on him. You know how we do it. This will benefit everyone, and in the long run, everyone will make more. You're a good kid. That Spence is too. He's a student of the game. I spent time with dudes like *Teflon* and learned how they think. The game is the game. The money . . . the money can be absolutely everything. If we do it right. Are you with me?'

Cameron nodded, swallowing down a response to the comment about Spence. 'I'll keep you posted on Natty. Cheers for the bonus.'

———

AT HOME THAT NIGHT, Cameron sipped a brandy, ignoring a few calls and text messages. When he couldn't get hold of Natty or Spence, he had a few others he liked to hit the clubs in town and spend money with.

Lately, he wanted to be alone. He had a lot to think about.

Rudy's words about Spence being a *student of the game* had irked Cameron. Cameron had been in the crime life most of his life. He'd known Natty longer, and had proved himself numerous times. Spence had skills but was too passive; he didn't go and take what he wanted. His dad had been a menace in his day, but Spence wasn't like that.

Then there was Anika. Spence had fallen in love with her, and he didn't even know her.

Not like Cameron did.

Soon, Cameron found himself on Anika's social media profile page.

Checking her Instagram, he scrolled through her photos. He lingered on a few images, but when he saw a picture of Anika and Spence, his fists automatically clenched, and his nostrils flared.

A wave of anger cascaded through his body, and he struggled to get it under control. He read the comments praising their looks and closeness with gritted teeth. The longer he stared at the photo, the more his eyes started to water from the intensity.

Seeing she had recently updated her Instagram story, he noticed that she'd posted about going to a club in town for her friend's party — there was a countdown, which ended on a night Cameron knew Spence would be working. That meant he wouldn't be with her or be scheduled to turn up.

Cameron decided right then that he would go, even if he didn't have a plan, or know what he would say.

CHAPTER TEN

ANIKA BEAMED. She'd been planning her friend Carmen's birthday for some time, and was pleased it was all going off without a hitch.

They had met at Anika's for pre-drinks, then headed to several clubs. They had the full treatment in their current club. It was near Call Lane, and had a warm, inviting interior, with comfortable seating areas, a fancy bar, and a spacious dance floor. They'd done their dancing earlier, and now sat in a VIP section, drinking champagne, having taken photographs when the gold buckets and sparklers came earlier.

Carmen's face was flushed as she spoke with their friends, giggling and animated. Anika found herself studying her. Carmen was so different to her that she found it intriguing. She was engaged to her boyfriend; they lived together and wanted to be married.

Anika didn't understand why. Anika's parents had separated when she was younger, and her dad hadn't given her the time of day. He had a whole new family now — one she had never met.

She was happy for her friend, but couldn't relate. Anika had her dreams, and often fantasised about travelling, going off the grid and not having people relying on her. It was the opposite of what she had going on with Spence.

Deep down, Anika worried that Spence was a rebound guy. Somebody she had become fond of, but didn't properly love. Like a lot of people, she was scared of being hurt. It had happened before and she was determined it wouldn't happen again.

She closed her eyes. She didn't want these thoughts, but couldn't help it. At times she felt trapped in her own life, too scared to make the decisions she knew would drastically change her surroundings.

'Nika?'

Anika's eyes flew open, unaware she had zoned out. The group of girls were all watching her with various levels of curiosity.

'Sorry, I got a bit distracted. Are you okay?'

'Yes, babe. We were just wondering when you and Spence will get married?'

'Yeah, you guys have been together forever. You must be getting those thoughts now, right?'

Anika wanted to tell them that it had only been a year, but didn't.

'We need to sit and properly talk about it, I guess.' She dipped her head as she laughed for a moment. 'I'm just going to walk around for a bit, see if I can see anyone else.'

'We can see everyone from here,' said Carmen, awkwardly pointing around the club.

'I just want to stretch my legs. I'll be back soon.'

Anika hurried away from her friends without looking like she was doing it. She wished she had stayed home now, feeling she was ruining the vibe. Her friends deserved to be able to enjoy themselves without her overreacting and making things about herself.

Making her way through the crowds of people, she queued for the bathroom, checking her face in the mirror, and taking deep breaths that had the women at the next sink giving her strange looks. She forced the thoughts out of her mind and exited the bathroom.

Deciding she would go back to her friends and be in a better mood, her thoughts were scuppered when someone appeared in front of her. She glanced at them, then froze when she realised who it was.

'Hey, Nika.'

'Cam?'

Anika's stomach lurched, her chest tightening. It couldn't be a coincidence that Cameron happened to be here tonight. He was as good-looking as ever. He dressed nicely and liked fancy jewellery, but she had never cared about that. She always dug Cameron's passion for her, and the fact he did his own thing and took no shit. It was intoxicating.

The old flames stared one another down for a long moment, and then Anika sighed and tried to step past him. Cameron gripped her wrist, stopping her in place.

'What's your hurry?'

'I don't want to get into it. Least of all with you.'

'You don't have to hide. Spence is working, so you don't have to worry,' said Cameron.

'I know where my boyfriend is, thanks. Just like he knows I'm out with my friends.' She glanced around Cameron, realising he appeared to be alone. 'Why are you here?'

'Why aren't you with your friends?' Cameron avoided the question.

'I wanted a moment away from them,' Anika admitted. Cameron nodded.

'You look good.'

Anika shook her head.

'I'm not doing this with you.' She pushed past him and was ready to leave when he said a single word.

'*Fiji.*'

Again, she froze. Turning to face him, her eyes met his.

'You always wanted to live in Fiji for a year. You told me about it, way back when. Does Spence know?'

Anika gritted her teeth. 'Stop it.'

Cameron's expression remained the same.

'No matter what happened with us, I still remember what you said.'

Anger flared in her.

'You mean the bits you want to remember. You tend to ignore the rest.' She sighed, feeling tears prickle in her eyes. 'I don't want to do this with you.'

She expected Cameron to argue or counter, but instead, he tilted his head, shooting her an almost sad look.

'I hope you get what you want; what *you* want . . . not you trying to live up to *their* expectations at the expense of your own.'

Anika's mouth opened and closed, her heart hammering. She wasn't going to do this. She wouldn't get caught up in this again. Without a word, she walked away, and he didn't stop her this time.

She sat with her friends and tried to involve herself in the night again, but she was distracted. Her mind wandered, thinking of distant beaches and tranquillity. She wondered if Cameron being in the club was a sign, and was shocked that he'd remembered about Fiji. It wasn't like him, and he'd shown no reaction when she'd mentioned it all those years ago.

Anika had a few more drinks, wanting a distraction from her swirling thoughts. Her friends sensed something was wrong, but she lied and said she was okay.

Eventually, her phone buzzed when she was finishing her latest drink. It was from Cameron, and though her instincts told her to delete it without reading, she quickly opened it.

> Do you ever wish things had turned out differently?

A few seconds later, another message came:

> You don't need to reply. I really do hope you have a good night.

Anika put her phone down, holding her empty glass, feeling overly emotional, hoping she didn't break down and start crying in front of her friends.

Her phone vibrated again, and she steadied herself. This time it was Spence:

> Hey beautiful. I hope you're enjoying your night. Let me know if you want me to bring anything in for you. Speak to you later.
> Love you.

Anika stowed her phone away, unable to respond to the message. She had a few more drinks and a few dances before she replied with some generic mess. She couldn't shake her introspective thoughts despite her attempts to distract herself. Finally, she took out her phone and sent a message:

> I think about how things could have been, every single day.

———

CAMERON LOOKED DOWN at Anika's message and smirked. He'd gotten his point across. It didn't matter how much Spence wined and dined her. Her heart still belonged to him; he'd proved it. He'd discretely watched Anika try to pretend to herself that she hadn't spoken to him, trying to distract herself with drinks and dancing and her friends, but nothing had worked.

They had unfinished business, and now she realised that point too. He was living in her head, completely rent-free.

Taking stock of his surroundings, he finished the drink he'd ordered, making small talk with a bartender for a while. After a few more drinks, he decided to leave.

Going to the club to confront Anika had been a brainwave and as he strolled up Call Lane to book a taxi, he was pleased he'd planted a seed.

CHAPTER ELEVEN

TWO WEEKS PASSED. Natty met with Julie several times, getting the lay of the land. He learned more about Warren and his reputation. He didn't seem particularly smart, but had heart and aggression in spades. Natty wondered if he would be a problem to work alongside, concluding he would be.

The young drug addict Natty hired had taken to his task well, identifying numerous smaller players, enabling Natty to learn more about them. Most were on the younger side, just playing at the life. Several were supporting growing habits by dealing. Natty had spoken with Elijah and believed they could relieve the burden on these types by supplying them, getting them to take care of the distribution on their behalf.

Elijah was on board with the plan, and today, they were meeting Harry and Rodney, the dealers Julie had mentioned.

They met in the middle of a nearby park. Natty glanced around, feeling exposed out in the open. The youths, barely old enough to have facial hair, looked twitchy, dressed in similar black and grey tracksuits. One of them, a lanky, big-nosed kid with wavy brown hair, stepped forward to do the talking, his eyes warily straying from Natty to Elijah.

'What are you lot saying then?' He asked.

'Which one are you?' replied Natty.

'Harry.'

'You know why we're here,' said Natty. 'We're moving in, and we want to work with the natives rather than the alternative. We know you guys are decent little hustlers, and we want you to get down with us.'

'Get down how?' Harry glanced at Rodney, who didn't respond.

'Take our supply. You'll get our protection on top of that.'

Again, Harry looked to Rodney, then back at the pair.

'What if we don't want to work with you?'

Natty had expected a little resistance, and was ready to objection handle.

'Why wouldn't you?'

The question threw Harry, his eyes widening. He opened and closed his mouth. Natty continued.

'We have the infrastructure to make big things happen for you. There's even a little signing fee for working with us.' Natty was laying it on thick, but it would be worth it in the end.

'Oh yeah, what sort of fee?'

'Couple grand, at least. Enough to have a nice treat and then get on board with a winning team. If you're interested, we'll give you the full details.'

Harry rubbed his face, giving no sign of the direction he would pick, despite his jittery movements.

'We're interested, but there's one big problem, mate.'

'What's the problem?' Natty kept his eyes on him.

'Warren.'

Rodney nodded, showing more emotion than he had thus far.

'What about him?' Natty pressed.

'He's a fucking madman. He won't even like us meeting with you. He leaves us alone, but that'll change if we start taking sides,' said Harry.

'We'll talk with Warren; make him see sense.'

Harry scoffed.

'Good luck with that. Warren'll kill you. He's done it before.' His eyes furtively swept around the park. 'Nice to meet you lot, but we can't work with you. Warren's the man.'

'Looks like we have some work to do,' Elijah remarked when the youths had scurried away.

Natty rubbed his forehead, trying to hide his annoyance. The way the dealers sounded, they weren't going to make much headway in the area until they'd spoken with the local psycho.

'Yep,' said Natty with a sigh.

———————

SPENCE TOOK Anika out for dinner. She liked Italian food, and he had been meaning to try out a place on Park Row.

As they ate, he spoke to her about Natty and Lorraine.

'I don't get what's happening with them,' he admitted between mouthfuls of his food. 'Lorraine has always had a thing for him, and Natty can't admit he feels the same for her.'

'Do you really think he does?' Anika asked. She was interested in the back and forth between the pair. She had seen Lorraine around and knew Natty through her involvement with Spence and Cameron.

A wave of nausea hit her. Natty had been around back in the day when she and Cameron had their fling. If he remembered or told Spence, it would get awkward, and she couldn't face that.

She hadn't told any of her friends. She and Cameron happened so fast, and they got in too deep, too quickly. It hadn't lasted long, and she had tried to mask the pain, not wanting to face up to the depths of her feelings.

Even now, Anika was playing a dangerous game. Cameron could tell Natty what she had done. He could even tell Spence. She was risking it all, but couldn't help it. The day after she sent Cameron the message, she'd spent the whole day in a panic, thinking Spence would find out.

Cameron hadn't replied, which didn't surprise her. Deep down, she was hurt that he hadn't texted her, and wondered again what his game was, and if he just wanted the attention.

'Babe?'

She blinked, glancing at Spence, who looked at her in concern.

'Are you okay?'

She nodded.

'I'm just a bit tired. It's been a long day.' She toyed with the rim of her wine glass, worrying her bottom lip. 'What does Cameron think of Natty and Lorraine?'

Spence snorted.

'He thinks she's fit. Typical Cam way of looking at mature situations. He wants Natty to fuck her and to beat up her baby father. That's Cam all over. I think sometimes he comes across as bitter.'

'Really?' Anika had never heard Spence talk like that about Cameron before. Then again, he'd not said much about him in general besides grumblings about Cameron calling him whipped. It seemed a lot more visceral right now.

'I think he has some real issues where women are concerned.'

Anika sipped her wine, listening to the words, her stomach in knots hearing about Cameron. She tried to cobble together what she remembered about the old days, but they were mainly superficial thoughts. Cameron had turned so cold on her when she'd thought they had something, and trying to sift through those memories was painful.

'You know, it doesn't seem like you even like Cam sometimes.'

Spence pursed his lips, a sour expression on his face. He sighed.

'Cam's a cool guy most of the time, but he has a lot of dickhead traits, and he's constantly on my back.'

'Why?' Anika asked, her heart hammering.

'I've told you about it before,' huffed Spence. 'He's constantly bringing up our relationship, like it's some kind of bad thing.'

'Relationships aren't for everyone,' Anika replied, wondering if this applied to her. Spence made a lot of sense on paper, but she didn't feel the way she thought she should, and had no one she could speak to about it.

No one but Cameron, who was currently ignoring her text.

'I agree they're not for everyone. That's why it's important to find the right person, and to build together.' Spence squeezed her hand. 'Cam doesn't have that, and I don't think he ever will.'

When they finished eating, they headed home. Spence went to

shower, leaving his phone on the sofa. Anika looked at it for a minute, and then picked it up. He'd previously shared his pin with her, and she scanned his social media messages, her stomach turning when she saw conversations with other women.

She read the messages, unsure what she was searching for, but wanting a reason to be angry. She was in for a shock; the conversations were brief. Either short, friendly dialogues with no sexual undertones, or Spence shutting down other exchanges when they got flirtatious, openly saying he wasn't interested and had a girlfriend.

She put the phone away, and fixed herself a drink, mulling her dilemma, sure now that she was the problem, not Spence.

What kind of woman hoped her boyfriend had done wrong, so she had the excuse to be angry with him?

By all measurements, Spence was a good guy. He adored her, and he showed it every day. It made her wonder why, because she couldn't see what he saw in her. Her self-esteem was in the dirt and had been for some time. Anika didn't know how to take the necessary steps to heal, and doubted she even had the strength to do so.

Her phone vibrated as she sipped her drink, and she opened the message, her heart soaring when she read it:

I haven't forgotten about you. We have a lot to talk about.

Anika hated how hot and alive the simple message made her feel. She immediately replied, saying she was looking forward to getting some closure.

By the time Spence returned, wearing a pair of shorts and a plain t-shirt, she had a smile on her face.

'You seem in a better mood. What cheered you up?'

'I just got a text message that made me happy, that's all.'

'From who? Your mum?' Spence plopped onto the sofa next to her.

'No, it was from Carmen. She's always got something to say,' Anika lied.

Spence hugged her tightly, smiling, kissing the top of her head as he turned the television on. She was a horrible person, she mused, as she sat and thought about Cameron whilst his best friend hugged and kissed her, but she couldn't help it. She felt something she had been searching for when she thought about Cameron.

She remembered Spence's words about relationships, and she believed that she could be the reason why he was how he was.

Why had he stopped to talk to her? What had he hoped to gain by doing it? She couldn't tell.

––––––

THE NIGHT after their meeting with Harry and Rodney, Natty met Elijah in a club in the city centre. He'd been there a few times before, and always liked the vibe. It was on Briggate, near the top end of the city centre, and it catered to a more hood crowd. Consequently, Natty saw many faces that he recognised, and some he knew would be surprised he was meeting Elijah.

As always, Elijah was already there, and had procured seats that allowed him to see all the comings and goings. He wore a simple black shirt and jeans, not trying to stand out. Despite this, he still had a few ladies making eyes at him.

Natty stopped to hug a female he hadn't seen in a while, then kept it moving, sliding into the seat opposite Elijah. They shook hands.

'Ordered you a brandy. Figured you'd want something strong,' said Elijah by way of greeting. Natty thanked him and sipped the liquor. It was Courvoisier, which was second to Hennessy on his favourite brandies list. Nonetheless, he enjoyed the taste, taking in the overall vibe of the spot. He was surprised Elijah had come alone. Almost every time he saw Elijah, he was by himself.

Natty wondered why.

'So, let me just say I'm impressed,' said Elijah. 'I wasn't sure how you would do when Rudy put you forward, but you're solid. It's surprising you haven't been moved up already. You have the right instincts, and you're a moneymaking machine. Have you ever considered that maybe you're on the wrong side?'

Natty had, on more than one occasion. He'd wondered in the past if he was being held back because of who he was related to, but there was nothing to prove it. It was surprising that Elijah had picked up on it.

'Are you trying to recruit me?'

'You'd never work for me. Maybe working for yourself is something to consider.'

'My people don't like competition.' Natty knew enough about how his uncle operated to know that.

'They've allowed me and others to ply our trade. I'm not stupid, Nat. Everyone knows that your people were the strongest after Teflon and his people were done with Leeds. The police came down hard, but you lot could have pushed to control the Hood, but you didn't, which suggests that the people you're working for, want to do things quietly. That means allowing others to do their thing, as long as they play the game right.'

Natty said nothing, listening to Elijah talk. He liked what he was saying, though.

'The police pretty much leave us alone when we're not shooting and stabbing one another in the Hood. They're cool as long as we keep the dealing quiet in the catchment areas. They'll bust a few of us to hit their quotas, but they like order and hate boredom. A couple of us in the Hood, quietly going about our business, it drives them crazy.'

'Where are you going with this?' Natty frowned, surprised when Elijah smiled.

'All I'm saying is that you have serious talent, Natty. You could do your own thing, just like me. You don't have to be reliant on anyone, family or not. You've proved that to me, so give it some thought.'

'I will,' replied Natty, secretly buoyed by the compliments. He wondered if Elijah was trying to butter him up for something, but dismissed it. Elijah had nothing to gain from encouraging Natty to go out alone. Natty found himself considering how it could work. He could take Spence, Carlton and Cameron, and get a few youngsters. He wouldn't be making millions, but he would be his own boss, and could dictate more of what he did.

'You do that. For now, back to Little London. What's the next step?'

'The locals are ready for change, and the whole area is open. The money is good, but there is much more to be made if we can completely sew it up.'

Elijah grinned. 'I must say, I expected it to be a cash cow, but the money we're already making is what I'd projected after six to eight months of solid grinding. Getting some of the locals on board has been excellent for us. I thought it might just be a drain when you first tried it.'

'Speaking of drains, Warren's the damn *Deebo* of the area, and as positive as we are for people, he's still the one that the masses defer to. Everyone is scared of him, and he's got people shaking in their trainers. Look how Harry and his mate reacted.'

Elijah scratched his chin, savouring his red wine.

'Sounds like we should put him to work.'

'If we want things to continue, we need to do something. The early takings are creeping up, as you said. What we're putting out there is solid, and we're building a stable line that people want to get behind.'

'The money will be divided in two days. I'm planning on using mine to pay out some bonuses.'

Despite what he knew about Elijah's generosity, Natty frowned, surprised at the action.

'Why?'

'We're paying for the illusion of honesty, Nat. Do you understand what I mean by that?'

Natty shook his head.

'It means that loyalty is rarely earned anymore. It comes from perception, and money. We pay out bigger bonuses, people work harder, and they feel like they are part of something far bigger than what we actually have.'

'I'm not sure about that,' Natty admitted. 'We might build a workforce of entitled soldiers if we move like that. That's your thing, though. I'm interested to see how it turns out, but for now, Warren's the problem.'

'Warren won't be a problem.' Elijah pushed out his chest. 'We'll make him an offer.'

They spoke some more about the streets. Mindful that Elijah had ordered his last drink, Natty hit the bar to get the next round. He was almost there when he bumped into a more petite woman, steadying her to ensure she didn't fall. He grinned when he recognised her.

'Rosie. Fancy seeing you here.'

Rosie's eyes sparkled as she recognised Natty.

'Nat! What are you doing in here?' Rosie continued to take in Natty's appearance, and he grinned. 'You look good.'

'So do you. You look stunning.' Natty returned the compliment. Rosie wore a shimmery grey top and some jeans, her toned arms on display. Natty had never noticed how good her posture was before, but it was arrow straight. 'I'm meeting someone. What about you?'

'I'm chilling with some friends. It's my girl's birthday,' she replied. 'Who are you meeting? Spence?' Her eyes glittered. Natty chuckled.

'When did you start taking an interest in Spence?'

Rosie smirked. 'Spence has always been fit.'

Natty chuckled again. He remembered Spence having a thing for Rosie back in the day. At the time, she was in a long-term relationship, so nothing transpired.

'You're trouble, Rosie. Leave my boy alone. He has a girl,' he teased. Privately, Natty believed Spence and Rosie had better chemistry. He preferred Rosie in general between Rosie and Anika, but things hadn't turned out that way.

'I just asked if you were meeting him. It's been a while, but I remember how sharp he is. He knows his stuff.'

Natty nodded. 'He does. His head is definitely in the right place.'

'What about your head?' Rosie looked Natty in the eyes. He shrugged.

'I'm getting where I need to be,' he replied. 'How's Lorraine doing with her studying? Have you spoken to her lately?'

'Earlier today. She's stressed. You know how she gets with it. She told me you've seen her working in the kitchen when you're over. You should go back and make her feel better.'

'Feel better how?' Natty's eyebrow rose.

'In any way you feel would help her. I think she would definitely appreciate it.'

'Has she said something to you to make you think that?' said Natty.

'No, this is just someone who knows her friend and understands her needs well,' replied Rosie.

'Why?'

'You know why.' Rosie moved aside to allow someone to pass. 'Lorraine talks about you a lot, and I think you're a good influence on her.'

Natty was thoughtful as Rosie spoke, and he wondered how true that was. He didn't think he had ever been a good influence on anyone, especially a woman. He was usually the guy trying to tempt them to do silly things with him, at the expense of whatever else was going on.

Lorraine wasn't like that. He wanted her to succeed.

'Whatever, Rosie. Maybe I will. I'm gonna get these drinks and head back, anyway. Don't be getting my boy in any trouble.'

After hugging Rosie, Natty ordered and paid for his drinks, then headed back to Elijah, who stowed away his phone just as Natty returned.

'I'll arrange a meeting with Warren. I know a few of his people,' he said.

'Do you think he'll go for the meeting?' Natty asked.

'People will be looking at him sideways if he turns it down cold. In terms of a resolution, I'm not sure he would benefit from working with us, but he's not the sharpest guy. Some people are too stubborn to work with others. I used to think you were like that.'

'Fuck you,' replied Natty, his eyes narrowing. Elijah laughed, picking up his drink.

'I said *used to*. I'm happy to say I was wrong.'

Natty chuckled, not really angry with Elijah.

'In terms of a deal for Warren, what are you thinking?'

Elijah sipped his drink, then scratched his chin.

'I'm not sure. It's gotta be something that lets him see the benefits of working with us.'

'What about a discount?'

'What sort of discount?' Elijah frowned.

'Well, we want him to buy from us, so what if we give him a break on buying boxes?'

'What sort of break?'

'Two grand discount per kilo.'

Elijah's eyes widened. 'You're serious?'

'We want him to play ball, right? Like you said, it's gotta be something that benefits him.'

'I know, but that could get costly in the long run. It's not something I would want to do long-term.'

'So, we'll sort something out temporarily. He'll see the benefits by then, and we can move things along. Once Little London is fully set up, we'll be laughing. We can step it up to other areas.'

'That won't be easy. People are squirrelly nowadays about working together.'

'If they see us doing it, and getting big money, that might shift a lot of that reluctance,' said Natty. Elijah nodded.

'All right, I'm on board. You've clearly given this all a lot of thought.'

'I want us to succeed,' replied Natty, smiling.

The pair raised their glasses and clinked them together.

CHAPTER TWELVE

THE FOLLOWING DAY, Anika was home, lazing on the sofa. She had no early bookings, deciding to pass the time by reading. So engrossed was she in the book, a bang at the door jolted her out of the zone. Her heart hammered against her chest, more in hope than fear. She didn't know who was on the other side of the door, but she knew who she wanted it to be.

Surely, he wouldn't risk coming to Spence's house unannounced?

'Natty?' She said after finally opening the door. Natty smiled, towering over her, his build prominent under his simple white t-shirt. A few of Anika's friends had gone after Natty in the past, and she couldn't blame them. She wasn't interested but could certainly see what they saw. He had a nice smile, broad shoulders, and an appealing ruggedness. His smile widened.

'Easy, Nika. Spence around? I was meant to meet him, but he's not picking up. Figured he might still be asleep.'

Anika chuckled. 'Spence gets up early every day, no matter when he gets in. Refuses to *waste a day*.' Although harmless on the surface, her tone betrayed her feelings. In truth, a lot about Spence's character irked her. 'You missed him, though. He left a while back.'

Natty snorted. 'I've been dragged on a few early runs with him, before I put a stop to it. I didn't even notice the car wasn't there. Thanks, I'll catch him at one of the spots. Take care of yourself, love.' He turned to walk away, but Anika spoke again.

'Natty?'

Natty span around, a confused look on his face.

'Yeah?'

Anika's muscles twitched. She cleared her throat, trying to decide what she wanted to say. Natty's brow furrowed as he waited. The moment lingered for several more awkward seconds, before she finally spoke to cut the tension.

'. . . How are you and Lorraine getting on?'

Natty's expression was unchanged.

'Getting on how?'

'I just mean . . . you two are close, right?' Anika didn't know where she was going with this.

'We're friends. I'm sure she's fine.'

'Are you happy?'

Still puzzled, Natty watched her for a long moment. Anika's heart hammered against her chest, wondering if he could sense her inner conflict.

'What . . . Why would you ask me that? Everything okay with you and Spence?'

Hurriedly, Anika nodded. Natty tilted his head to the right, then rubbed his chin.

'Yeah, I'm happy. A big part of me wants more, though, and I'm trying to work out how to make that happen.'

It wasn't the answer she expected, and she was surprised he'd even given her one.

'If you had a way to get closer to those answers, would you take it?'

Natty didn't hesitate to nod. 'Of course. Why punish yourself by wondering when you can find out for sure? Are you sure you're okay?'

'I'm fine. I just wondered what you would say. Thanks for being honest.'

'Anytime, love. Look after yourself.' Natty bounded away. Anika remained by the door, unmoving. Although Natty didn't realise it, his words were a green light to Anika. A sign to press forward and get the answers she needed.

———

IT TOOK Anika a day to gather herself. Knowing Spence was working, she left their house the next night and took an Uber to Cameron's, taking the time beforehand to do her makeup and style her hair.

When Cameron opened the door, he had a hungry expression on his face, eyes gleaming as he took her in. When she'd sat down, he fixed her a drink, then sipped his own.

'Do you want anything else? I've got pills, coke, or some weed.'

They shared a spliff. After a while, Anika relaxed. She was half finished with her second drink when she finally spoke.

'A big part of me knows I shouldn't be here.'

'Is that why it took you like two weeks to reach out to me?'

Anika cleared her throat.

'I wasn't sure. Like I said . . . I shouldn't be here.'

'You think too much.' Cameron laughed, glancing at her legs. 'You're here for a reason.'

Anika's eyes narrowed.

'Does everything boil down to sex?'

Cameron swirled his drink around his glass before taking a long sip. Smacking his lips, his eyes fixed on the glass. Eventually, his eyes met hers.

'Why did you finally come to see me?'

'I want closure.'

Cameron shook his head. 'You want freedom, not closure.'

'That probably means getting bent over in your world.'

Smirking, Cameron didn't reply.

'I spoke with Natty,' Anika said.

Cameron jerked, spilling his drink.

'Shit.' He dabbed at his clothes, scowling. 'Does he know we're talking again?'

'Course not.' Anika shook her head.

Cameron took a deep breath, visibly relieved. He wiped at the stain on his top one last time, then left it.

'Good. Natty wouldn't understand.'

'How do you know that? He's a gyalist. He'd probably support you.' Anika knew Natty had been through his fair share of women, and hadn't displayed feelings for any of them, save for Lorraine. She recalled his reaction to her cringing questioning yesterday, inwardly shuddering.

Cameron shook his head. 'He and Spence are tight. He'd see anything I did as a violation.'

This reminded Anika of something she'd wondered for a while.

'Does Natty know how deep things were with us?'

Cameron studied her for so long that Anika started to think he wouldn't answer. Eventually, he shook his head.

'That's in the past. He knew we had a little thing, but it doesn't matter anymore.'

Anika's stomach plummeted when Cameron described what they had that way. Despite her best efforts, it was apparent they had vastly different ideas about what they'd shared back then. She drained her drink and poured another.

'Why did you never love me?'

Cameron rubbed his forehead, eyes narrowing.

'How do you know I didn't?'

'If you had, we would have been together.'

'If that's how you felt, you wouldn't have got with my friend.' Cameron's tone was like ice, and Anika blanched, before taking a deep breath.

'Spence cares about me.'

Cameron snorted.

'He's soft.'

'You two don't seem to like one another. Why do you still think you're friends?'

Cameron shrugged.

'We're just different.' He again looked Anika in her eyes. 'Doesn't mean you should have gone for him, though.'

Anika rubbed her eyes, growing steadily more frustrated with

Cameron's responses. 'I never had to guess how Spence feels about me. He tells me and shows me, and he wants to build something with me—'

'Why the hell are you here then?' Cameron snapped. 'Why sit with me when you can be at home with your perfect fucking boyfriend?'

'Because I don't love him!' Anika screamed, silencing Cameron. They both stared at one another, breathing hard. Anika continued.

'I wish I did. It would be so much easier, but I don't.'

'Who do you love?' Cameron's voice was softer now. Anika shook her head. She meant what she said. She wished her feelings were more straightforward, but they weren't. When Cameron moved closer, she didn't back away, and when his lips met hers, she kissed him back with fervour.

The kiss quickly intensified, any feelings of guilt extinguished as Cameron climbed on top of her on the sofa, pulling up her skirt and kissing her neck. When he slid inside her, she dug her nails into his back, wrapping her legs around his waist as he drove into her. As the pleasure intensified, she closed her eyes, savouring the ferocious climax that Cameron gifted her.

A little while later, the pair climbed into bed. Cameron wrapped his arm around Anika, a smile on his face. She traced patterns across his chest, her guilt beginning to return in the aftermath of what she had done. Spence didn't deserve this, yet a major part of her believed what she had done was right. The only thing she remained unsure about was what would happen going forward. She thought she had come to see Cameron for closure, yet she'd quickly fallen into bed with him.

'Cam?' She asked.

'You should jet soon. Spence is working, but he might drop in on you. See what you're doing.'

'Spence isn't like that. He trusts me.' Anika felt almost sick saying it. He did trust her. Not once did he ever question what she was doing, or who she was around. She had betrayed that trust in the worst way possible.

'Still, you don't wanna make him suspicious. Might make it harder to get away next time.'

'Next time?' She glanced up at him, irked by the smirk on his face.

'Yes, next time. Save all the hard-to-get shit. You loved what we did. You came like four times,' said Cameron.

'Just because I enjoyed having sex with you, doesn't mean anything has been resolved between us. What is it that you want from me, Cam? Do you want me to stay with Spence?'

'Do you want to?'

Anika didn't reply immediately. She didn't know what to say. She'd wanted closure, and now that the sex had finished, she felt used. Cameron wasn't giving her anything, and his deflections only worsened things. He hadn't even given her an honest answer about whether he loved her.

'Spence cares about me,' she repeated. She felt Cameron shift, but he didn't snort this time.

'Is caring enough?'

'Can you offer me something more?'

Cameron shrugged.

'I don't know. I guess I'd like to, but that doesn't mean I can.'

Anika appreciated the honesty, but wasn't sure that was enough. Without a word, she slid from the bed and began getting her things together.

'Nika?'

She glanced at Cameron. He had his arms behind his head, gazing at her.

'I'm glad you took a chance with me.'

CHAPTER THIRTEEN

DAYS LATER, Natty and Elijah arranged a meeting with Warren. Even with Elijah having connections in Warren's circle, it still took a while to set up.

Making concessions, they agreed to meet on Warren's turf, at a terraced house on Carlton Carr in Little London. Natty and Elijah climbed from their ride, glancing around and noting a pub at the top of the street. The pair were attending the meeting without backup, not wanting to send the wrong message.

A slim, pale woman with mousy hair and jittery features answered the door, her eyes darting between Natty and Elijah. Without a word, she led them to a small kitchen. It reeked of takeaways, but was relatively tidy, mostly taken up by a circular brown table and spindly chairs. Elijah took a seat, but Natty remained on his feet, glancing around, frowning.

'You good?' Elijah asked.

'If this isn't a massive setup, at least we can go to the pub afterwards and get drunk,' joked Natty. Elijah grinned.

Minutes passed. They heard random shuffles and noises, but no sign of Warren.

Natty ignored the growing anxiety he felt. They were in enemy territory, unarmed with no ready backup. Rubbing his jaw, he was about to tell Elijah they were leaving, when he heard heavy footsteps approaching.

A powerfully built man stomped into the room. He wore a black t-shirt, a hooded zip top, and some bottoms. He had a weapon in plain sight, jammed down the front of his trousers. Glaring at the pair, he subtly adjusted his waistband to draw their attention to it.

Natty kept his face neutral, but he already had a bad feeling.

'You must be Warren. Take a seat,' said Elijah, motioning to several seats at the other side of the table. Warren shook his head, his eyes hard.

'This is my meeting. I'm good standing.'

Sitting next to Elijah, Natty kept his eyes on Warren, not liking the hostile vibe he brought to the room. Before the meeting, Natty gave it 50/50 that they would come to an agreement. After this opening, he revised it to 20/80. Elijah took a deep breath, ready to speak.

'Who the hell are you, and what do you want?' Warren got right to the point. His eyes seared into Elijah's, his interruption working perfectly.

Elijah's eyes flashed, but he swallowed down the anger, seeing the disrespect as a cost of doing business. He filed it away, vowing to revisit it at a later time.

'We've been doing business in Little London for a while, and we think there's a way we can do some together,' he said, keeping his words soft.

'Who the hell are you, though? You didn't answer my question.'

Elijah didn't respond. Natty leant forward.

'You wouldn't be meeting us if you didn't know who we were. Let's cut the shit.'

Warren kept his eyes on Elijah for a lingering moment, before switching to look at Natty.

'Just because I know your names, doesn't mean shit. You lot reached out to me. Recognise that.'

'Despite that, we can all do good business.' Elijah paused, catching Natty's eye, willing him to keep his cool.

'What can you lot do for me that I can't do for myself?' Warren demanded.

'Your supplier is ripping you off. Our product is stronger. It's a big part of why we're doing well here. If you come on board with us, it only benefits everyone,' said Elijah.

'Come on board with you how?' Warren snorted.

'Start taking our product. We can get you what you need. You keep putting it out, and we all get paid together. You pay us two grand less than you're paying now, per box.'

Warren's eyes flitted between the pair of them. He folded his arms, his eyes lingering on Natty a second longer, his jaw tightening. Natty returned the look, not backing down. He'd seen this look all too often before; fists clenching, muscles tensing, eyes locked. It appeared Warren was preparing to fight. Natty shifted his weight slightly in his chair, clenching his fist, but concealing it out of sight. His eyes flicked to the weapon hidden in Warren's waistband. It was a problem, but it wouldn't be a factor if he jumped him before he could get to it.

'You lot look like dickheads. I don't trust you, or like the look of you, so why would I work with you?' said Warren.

'Well . . .' Elijah started.

'Nah, I'm not done talking. You could have spoken to me before you moved into my ends, but you didn't. So, here's how we're gonna do it. Pack up your people and move out. If you don't, we're gonna get down to it.'

'Get down to what?' Elijah's voice had cooled, and Natty could tell even he knew the meeting was over.

Warren pulled the gun but didn't aim it. His finger caressed the trigger, both men's eyes glued to the motion.

'I could take you both out right now. Carry on the way you're going on, and it'll happen. Get the fuck out of here, and take your runners with you.'

Natty held Warren's glare. Warren was stupid enough to shoot them in cold blood, with no provocation. Elijah stood, but Natty remained seated, still looking at Warren. Elijah tugged Natty's top, breaking the stare and prompting him to stand. Elijah left the room, his eyes on the door, but Natty's eyes followed Warren until he was past him.

'That's right. Don't even come around my ends talking shit, you pair of pussies. Little London is mine, and I ain't sharing with anyone, let alone you lot.'

Natty's eyes flicked to Elijah's. Subtly, Elijah shook his head, and they both looked forward, continuing toward the door. Natty loathed that Warren was talking to them like they were idiots, but now wasn't the time.

'I'm surprised you kept your cool,' Elijah said to Natty as they climbed in Elijah's car and drove away.

Natty took a deep breath, closing his eyes and trying to calm down.

Despite his outward showing, his blood boiled. He wanted to smash Warren's face in. There was no deal to be made from the start. Warren had no intention of dealing with them. He had wanted to try to make an example of them. Natty guessed he would spread the story of how he had punked them, and wondered how much traction it would get.

'He had a gun.'

Elijah glanced at Natty as they turned a corner onto another street.

'Do you think he really would have used it?'

'I wasn't going to risk my life finding out.'

Neither man spoke after that. The meeting had gone badly, and they had a problem on their hands with Warren. Threats had been made, and Warren had proved himself unwilling to do business.

They would have to get deep, deal with him, and prevent an all-out war in Little London.

————

CAMERON WAS at the spot with the youngsters, taking calls on the trap line and directing runners to meet with sales. He'd had some food earlier — chicken and dumplings from Dutch Pot — and was content. When he heard Spence enter, he attempted and failed to swallow down the wave of nervousness that spread through his body.

He couldn't let Spence find out what had happened with Anika.

Spence appeared unruffled in that calm, understated manner of his. The youths flocked towards him, greeting him and slapping his hand as he checked how they all were.

Cameron remained seated until Spence came to greet him.

'*Boss*, how's it going?' He said, noticing Spence's face tighten.

'You tell me. How are things?'

'C'mon, Spence,' Cameron waved his hand, 'we all know the play here. Things are going well.'

Spence looked to the youths, who had returned to what they were doing, then sat alongside Cameron.

'I've noticed takings in the middle shift have been consistently down for the past two weeks.'

'That happens sometimes. Things can be hit or miss, plus sometimes we don't clip the same level of fiends. You know that,' he said to Spence.

'I think someone is stealing.'

'That's nonsense. Our team doesn't get down like that,' said Cameron, his expression darkening.

'I want to set a trap and prove that.'

Cameron shook his head. 'Seems like a lot of trouble for nothing. Just give everyone a warning and see what happens.'

'It won't help us get to the root of the issue. We can use it to send a message and show people that we're on top of things.'

Cameron shrugged. 'If you wanna waste your time over pennies, go for it.'

Spence scowled at Cameron, tired of his friend's attitude. Spence was running the show, and the fact Cameron didn't respect that, was frustrating. His blasé attitude when it came to somebody skimming the profits stood out more than anything. Spence quickly came to a decision.

'Good. We'll go for it. Not only that, you're going to contribute.' He locked eyes with his friend, expecting resistance. Cameron swallowed down his annoyance at Spence, and nodded.

'Cool, bro. No problem.'

Cameron felt the guilt from earlier leaving him. He would let Spence go on his power trip, and focus elsewhere.

_____

NATTY AND ELIJAH knew they would have to deal with Warren sooner than later, but they were wary about how to do it. The last thing they wanted was an all-out battle that would draw more eyes and attention to what they were doing in the area.

Elijah reached out to his contacts for more information about Warren, and spoke of organising safe-houses and putting a shooter on standby near the area, just in case.

As far as Natty was concerned, Julie and the other locals he had spoken to had given him a solid understanding of what Warren was about. The meeting had validated that understanding. He'd come armed, and Natty knew it wouldn't have taken much for him to pull out his gun and start shooting.

_____

GAVIN THOMAS WAS an ex-baller who'd suffered a severe injury shortly after going pro. He'd tried to go legitimate after several comeback attempts, working some security jobs; but ultimately hated the 9-5 life. The lure of easy money drew him back to the streets. Gavin had charisma in spades, and had plenty of old tales about his football days, and the players he'd hung out with, that the youths around them ate up. Most of it was bullshit, but it sounded good.

He'd hit upon his scheme shortly after Natty ceded control to Spence. Cameron was in charge of the shifts most times and wasn't the most diligent of people. Gavin had started holding back his total profit and even taking drugs directly to sell on the side. Cameron and Spence were Natty's stooges. When Natty was around, he was on point, but he didn't believe he would have any trouble with his friends. He plied Cameron with spliffs and bottles of liquor, massaging his ego, keeping him distracted.

Gavin repeated his tricks until it was almost muscle memory. Time erased the nerves, providing reassurance. When more resources became accessible, his instincts abandoned him. Hungry for more, he feasted.

On the Friday of that week, he was on an early shift with Cameron and a few youths, when Spence entered, looking oddly serious.

'Gavin, how's it going?' He asked.

'Hey, Spence. It's going good, fam. Just telling these lot about the time I met Beckham and he bought me champagne.'

Spence nodded. 'That's cool. Everything good, though? How's your mum?'

Gavin's eyes narrowed. 'Why are you asking about my mum?'

'She was ill, wasn't she? I heard she had flu or something last week,' replied Spence.

Gavin relaxed. He'd fed this story to Cameron last week, giving him ample time to quietly sell his drugs on the side.

'She's fine. On the mend, but she's getting there.'

Spence smiled. 'That's good to hear. Turn out your pockets, please.'

The room fell silent, everyone facing Spence.

'What?' stammered Gavin, eyes flickering towards the door. Spence gave one of the larger youths a look, and he went to block the door, cutting off a potential escape route. Cameron looked around, noticing that a circle had been formed around Gavin, not enough to crowd him, but enough to let him know escape was futile.

'You heard what I said.'

'Cam . . .' Gavin turned to Cameron, who cleared his throat.

'Yo, Spence —'

'This is the last time I'm going to ask you,' said Spence, ignoring Cameron.

Gavin swallowed, seeing Spence was serious. Heart pounding, he did as he was told, several shots and bundles of cash tumbling onto the nearby coffee table. He heard the angry mumbles of the crew, and knew he'd messed up big time. Spence's face showed no reaction, though, and Gavin wasn't sure if this was better or worse.

'Yo, Spence, look, I know it looks bad, but I forgot I had it on me. I was gonna check it with everything else later. Same with the drugs. It's not what it looks like,' he tried. Spence held a hand up.

Cameron's fists clenched. Gavin had played him for an idiot. He knew it would look bad that all of this had happened on his watch. Before Gavin could say anything else, he drew back his fist, crashing it into the side of Gavin's face. For all Gavin's big talk, he wasn't a fighter, and the first blow folded him. He stumbled from the sofa to the floor, and Cameron continued to hit him.

'Fucking punk. Think you can steal from me and get away with it? Huh?' He signalled to the rest of the crew to get involved, but only two of them did, the rest taking their cues from Spence and remaining where they were. When the two that joined in realised this, they too stopped.

'Cam, that's enough,' said Spence after a few moments. Cameron cocked his arm back, but faltered. Leering down at the whimpering mess beneath him for a moment, he whirled around, turning his attention to Spence.

'What? After what he did? We need to send a message on this,' he snarled, breathing hard.

'He needs to make back what he stole. He can't do that if you break all his bones and kill him.'

'He fucked up good and proper. He needs to do more than just pay it back. What if someone else tries it?'

'Look around you, Cam. None of them are going to try it. They know we're on top of it, and that they will be caught just like Gavin was.' Spence motioned to the beaten man.

'That's not good enough. He made me look like a right dickhead, and I'm not standing for it.'

Spence's expression hardened.

'I'm in charge. This is the direction we're going in, and it's non-negotiable.'

Silence ensued, the two friends staring one another down. The entire crew held their breath, wondering how this would play out. They had noticed the growing tension between Cameron and Spence, and were ready for blows to get thrown. Gavin's cries of pain occasionally punctuated the silence. He crawled toward the door, but it was still blocked.

Cameron glared at Spence, furious that he was being belittled in front of people. Disagreeing with him was one thing. Ordering him around in front of everyone like he was disposable was another. He looked at each man in the room, then back to Spence, his nostrils flaring. Taking a moment, he smiled.

'Fine,' he said with a nod. 'You're in charge.'

When Gavin had been dragged to his feet, and led away by some of the team, Spence turned to Cameron.

'Thank you, Cam,' he started. 'I appreciate you listening to me, and going along with me on this. I know you had your doubts, but we're better when we work together, bro. Always have been.'

Cameron nodded, smiling. 'No problem at all, mate.' When Spence left the room, Cameron took out his phone and texted Anika.

Where are you at?

————

AFTER LEAVING Spence and the crew behind, Cameron headed home, pouring himself a straight glass of white rum and downing it.

He couldn't believe how things had turned out. Spence had been down with him and Natty for years, but Cameron had always seen himself as a step above the younger man. Now, Spence was showing he was a natural leader, and his treatment of Gavin exemplified that. Gavin had played Cameron, stealing money whilst smiling in his face and complimenting him, and he was furious that not only had he fallen for it, but that Spence's hunch was correct.

When Natty, Rudy and the others heard about this, they would look down on Cameron, and he couldn't accept that.

He was amid his brooding when there was a knock at his door. He went to let Anika in, not even offering her a drink as he stormed back to the sofa and sat down.

'You're in a good mood, I see,' she said, entering the room, watching Cameron slump onto the sofa. 'How come you invited me if you're angry?'

'What the hell do you care? You came, didn't you?'

'I can leave just as quickly if you don't change your attitude.' Anika's nostrils flared.

'Go then. See if I care.'

Anika stomped for the door, then turned at the last second to scowl at Cameron. He wasn't looking at her, but she noticed his shoulders shaking, awkwardly wondering if he would cry.

'I thought you were leaving?' Cameron said a second later.

'I'm still wondering why you invited me over here. What if I was with Spence?'

'Spence is working. He's got his little fucking promotion, remember?'

'Is that why you're angry?' Anika's eyebrow rose.

'It doesn't matter.' Cameron stood and approached Anika, backing her into the wall. Her chest heaved, breathing intensifying as she looked up at him. With no more words, he kissed her hard, instantly feeling her responding, a feeling of power returning. Cameron decided that Spence could take all the nonsense plaudits he wanted as the kissing intensified. In return, he would keep taking the love of his life.

———

THE NIGHT after his meeting with Warren, Natty went to Lorraine's, seeking a distraction.

She answered the door, her face drawn, her hair wrapped. She gave him a brief hug and let him in.

'Jaden's already in bed,' she said, collapsing onto the sofa with a sigh and getting her phone.

'How's your practising going?' He asked. He'd stayed away to allow her to concentrate, telling her to contact him if she needed him to look after Jaden. Despite that, Lorraine's eyes widened.

'You remembered?'

'Course I did.'

Lorraine sighed again, closing her eyes.

'Up and down, but mostly up,' she admitted. 'I've found some great resources online that are helping.

'That's great. I'm glad to hear it,' Natty replied. 'I've no doubt you'll do whatever you want.'

Lorraine's eyes flitted open, and she beamed at Natty.

'I appreciate the faith you have in me, Nat. Where have you been lately, by the way?'

'I told you to contact me if you needed me. I've been doing some work in Little London.' He scratched his chin. 'What do you think of Elijah?'

Lorraine blinked, clearly surprised.

'Why do you ask?'

'I'm doing some work with him.'

'Really?'

Natty nodded.

'Does that work involve Raider?' Her tone lowered.

'No. I made sure of that.'

Lorraine looked visibly relieved at his words.

'Elijah's nice,' she said. 'Polite, and seems to mean it. Doesn't really seem to fit in, though. I always wondered if he had a dark side.'

'Why?' Natty was intrigued.

'He just seems too kind. Figured there had to be a reason he had guys like Raider working for him.' She assessed Natty, staring intensely into his eyes. 'Be careful in Little London, Nat.'

Natty sat next to Lorraine, holding her close enough to feel her pounding heart. He swallowed, inhaling her scent.

'I'm always careful,' he replied softly. 'I appreciate you caring, still.' He remembered his previous thoughts from Julie's. 'Have you ever wanted more kids?'

'Are you offering?' Lorraine teased. Natty poked her in the side, and she giggled.

'I used to,' she admitted, once she'd calmed down. 'I wish Jaden had brothers and sisters to play with. What about you? Ever thought of having any?'

'Sometimes,' Natty replied, his thoughts on Jaden. Neither spoke after that, enjoying the tranquil vibe.

CHAPTER FOURTEEN

BIRDY and his friend Jack walked along Well Close Rise in Little London. Having finished serving some customers, they were strolling back to their base.

'When we clock off, there's a party we can hit,' said Jack. He was nineteen, dark-skinned with pale brown eyes and pockmarked skin. 'There's gonna be loads of girls there.'

Birdy stared at his phone, half-listening to Jack. He was a fair-skinned twenty-year-old with lank brown hair cut low around the sides, and dark eyes. He had a small amount of stubble around his jaw. Both were dressed similarly in bomber jackets over t-shirts and jeans.

They had been working the Little London patch for a few weeks, and so far, it had been easy money. They had the locals mostly sewn up, and both believed things would only improve.

'I'm tired,' Birdy finally replied. 'I can't be arsed with a big party.'

'Suck it up, bro. Have a line, or a Red Bull if you need to sharpen up. We can get some pussy.'

Before Birdy could reply, a tinted blue Audi sharply pulled to a stop next to them. Without communication, both men instantly began running. Jack was faster, charging up Carlton Hill, past several graffiti-ridden buildings. He didn't know the area too well but figured they could lose them nearby. This idea quickly evaporated as Birdy lost his balance and tumbled to the ground. Jack stopped to haul him to his feet as they again began pounding the concrete. The engine revving and yells of those inside the car grew ever closer.

At the end of the road was a locked gate leading to a building. They were about to take a left, when the click of a gun froze them.

Panting, they turned around, watching as four men approached, one of them still holding the gun. He was dressed in black, with a thin, ratty face and slim build. By contrast, his compatriots loomed, also dressed in black, but far more muscular.

Jack swallowed, hearing Birdy squirming next to him.

'Give it up,' the gunman said. The men behind him watched with angry expressions, breathing hard. Jack and Birdy handed over the money they had on them, their drugs, and their phones. One of the men moved forward and began patting them down, relieving Jack of a butterfly knife he hadn't time to pull earlier. Fear glissaded through his body. He was too scared to even look at Birdy.

'You little shits,' the gunman continued. 'I should blow both your heads off right here. Your bosses were warned, and you lot still thought you could do what you wanted.'

'We didn't—' Panicking, Jack tried to speak, but the gunman aimed the gun at him, and he fell silent, still trembling. He heard Birdy sniffing next to him.

'Don't try to explain it now. You're gonna have to pay the cost for their mistakes. This is Warren's turf, and he ain't giving it up.' He signalled for the others, and they swarmed the duo, beating them down. Jack and Birdy landed one hit apiece before being overwhelmed, falling unconscious after several punches and kicks to the chest and face.

———

NATTY SMOKED A CIGARETTE, staring at his phone. It had never been one of his vices, but that had changed recently. What started as a means to take the edge off the stress of the streets was quickly becoming a habit.

The kids that had been beaten up were okay, just bruised and a little shaken up. Tapping his phone screen, he took a deep breath, furious at the situation. He finished his cigarette and disposed of the remains. They needed to sort out the situation quickly, or people would be scared to work in Little London. The streets were watching.

He called Elijah.

'Is this important? I'm in the thick of it here.' Elijah's voice was harried, but Natty pushed past it.

'We need to regroup and get something going. If we let him get too much momentum, we're done,' said Natty, avoiding using names.

Elijah sighed. Natty sensed his exhaustion through the phone.

'I'll pick you up from Jukie's in an hour. We can talk on the move.'

Natty agreed, ending the call just as a text message came through. Scanning it, his eyes widened.

Another of their dealers had been attacked. He'd attempted to fight back, ended up getting stabbed, and bled out on the streets.

———

FOR THE THIRD time in three days, Natty and Elijah met. Neither was taking any chances. The Chapeltown safe house they were in was heavily protected, with several men around the perimeter, and another sitting in a car up the street, just in case.

The safe house had the basics: a small television and Kodi stick, cheap coffee table, and two hideous brown sofas in the surprisingly spacious living room.

Natty paced the living room, floorboards creaking under his heavy feet. He needed to keep moving, to work off the excess energy this situation was causing. Usually, he would work it out in the gym, but he'd found little time for it recently. He was running low on cigarettes, and though he hated himself for the smoking, he couldn't turn it off right now.

Elijah was seated, eyes glued to his mobile phone.

'These news stories are getting worse,' he said, eyes narrowing. 'They've got an interview with the police. They're promising to *crack down on a growing gang presence in the local Leeds area.*'

Natty snorted, still pacing. It was the last thing on his mind right now. One of their people had been killed, and they had yet to do anything to combat that.

'Things are going to get even harder now, Natty. Everyone has eyes on us.'

Natty stopped, assessing Elijah.

'We need to show them something then, don't we? We have people in place, so we need to hit back. Hard.'

Elijah blew out a breath, the bags under his eyes suddenly noticeable.

'There are multiple angles to consider.'

Natty shook his head.

'Warren's made it clear that he will not work with us. Either we fight back, or we leave Little London for good, and then how do we look?'

Elijah rubbed his eyebrow.

'We need to think about the politics of the situation,' he replied.

Natty smirked, letting out a harsh bark of laughter.

'Did you consider these politics *before* deciding to move into Little London?'

Elijah shot him a dirty look, but didn't reply.

'Look,' continued Natty, 'we have to do something. You wanted this alliance for a reason, right? We need to clap back. Like you said . . . *people are watching.*'

Before Elijah could respond, Natty's phone rang. He squinted at the screen. It was Junior, one of their people in Little London.

'Yeah?' He answered.

'One of the spots just got licked.'

'For real?' Natty's nostrils flared. A police raid was the last thing they needed. 'What did they get?'

'I can't get close enough to get a proper look, but they arrested two people.'

'Fuck. Right, don't say anything else. I'll ring you later, and we'll talk in person.'

'Cool.'

Natty hung up, stowing his phone. He rubbed his eyes, aware of an impending headache. From Natty's tone and demeanour, Elijah looked up, knowing it wasn't good.

'Police raided one of the spots. Make some calls, and get them to temporarily clear out of the other ones. I'm gonna speak with Rudy, and then we need to collaborate and properly sort our next move.'

Elijah nodded, knowing he couldn't argue.

———

NATTY MET with Rudy at Delores's. She was out, but Rudy made them cups of coffee, and they lit cigarettes, enjoying the quiet.

'You look like you need that.' Rudy motioned to the cigarette.

'I need more than that, boss. Shit is out of control. Warren needs dealing with.'

'What's Elijah said about it?'

'He's too busy trying to be the fucking UN. We've done decent work until now, but this isn't negotiation time. We already tried that shit, and he punked us. He's still punking us.' Natty's frustration from the past few days spilt out.

Rudy let him finish, sipping his drink and watching the younger man's reactions.

Eventually, Natty deeply exhaled.

'What do I do?' He asked.

'What do you think you should do?'

'Rudy, I know you mean well, but why can't you just tell me the answer? It's obvious there's something you want me to do.'

'I want you to think. You're the point man, so I want to know what you think is the best course of action.'

'Warren needs to go. That's the only way things go back to normal. He's not playing ball and is out there trying to kill my people. There's no going back from that.'

Rudy surveyed Natty, inhaling the smoke from his cigarette, savouring the nicotine.

'Are you the person to finish him?'

Natty looked away for a moment. He had considered this, and in the middle of the night, after several glasses of Hennessy, had considered going out and tracking Warren down himself.

'I'm the point man over there. Like you said.'

'You are, but that doesn't mean *you* need to rush out and get yourself in trouble. That's how your father did things.'

Natty glared at Rudy, remembering their argument in the pub a while back. Rudy shook his head.

'We're not going to have a repeat of last time, but I knew him well, Nathaniel. He was a good man, and like I said before, If I made you feel I thought otherwise, then I apologise. Your old man was a friend of mine, and he was one hell of a soldier. The last thing we want are special task forces and drug squads camped out in our backyards. Whatever happens, you need to distance yourself from the conflict.'

'That's weak.' Despite the words, Natty's tone was solemn. He knew Rudy was right, and it stung.

'It's smart. You're not a little runner anymore. You're not some crew chief either. For all intents and purposes, what happens in Little London is down to you. You're responsible for the area, but you need to think about the best ways to do things.'

Natty was conflicted. He understood what Rudy was saying, and liked the respect he'd shown his dad, but his father had truly lived the life. He had put people in the ground, and his reputation was top tier.

Natty thought about all the times his mum had brought up his dad. Sometimes, she sounded proud of his accomplishments, telling Natty his father had been a man among men, and someone that always handled his business.

At other times, she admonished him, saying he'd left her with nothing but a son, and that he was hot-headed and bloodthirsty, yet Natty was compared to him at every opportunity.

For a man trying to find his place in the world, that was confusing.

He put those thoughts to the side, stubbing out his cigarette in the ashtray in the middle of the coffee table.

'Warren started this,' he reminded Rudy. 'Not retaliating is a bad move.'

Rudy smiled. 'I'm not saying that you shouldn't retaliate. I'm saying there are numerous ways to handle the situation, and that you don't have to get your hands dirty.'

———

NATTY RETURNED HOME after his conversation with Rudy. He'd smoked several cigarettes, still on edge, waiting for any further news about Little London.

The talk with Rudy remained at the forefront of his mind. He'd absorbed what Rudy said, yet still felt the team needed to be more forceful in retaliating. That was the only thing Warren understood, and they needed to stop him before he gained too much momentum.

The longer the situation went on, the worse it would get for them.

Natty lit another cigarette, tempted to make a phone call, get some guns, and do the job himself. He sighed, cycling through numbers in his contacts, deciding who would be the best fit. Rather than call, Natty stubbed out the cigarette and stood, stretching. Rudy had more experience than he did — along with his uncle's ear. Natty would give him a chance, and not jump the gun.

With another sigh, he hoped this choice wouldn't lead to more bloodshed in Little London.

CHAPTER FIFTEEN

SPENCE SAT in a spot on Bankside Street near Roundhay Road. It was a quiet little area tucked away in a cul-de-sac. Around him, people came and went. Spence barely noticed, half-staring at an iPad, looking over his investment portfolio online.

In the corner of the room, a *younger* counted and banded money. Despite the turnover of people, no one made much noise. It was well known that Spence liked a quiet atmosphere.

Rubbing his stomach, Spence inwardly regretted the Caribbean takeaway he'd had earlier. As penance, he planned to go on an intense morning run to burn it off. Natty had contacted him earlier, but they hadn't spoken for long.

The situation in Little London was heating up, and Natty was right in the middle. Spence had heard through the grapevine about the kid dying from being stabbed. He wasn't happy that a young life had been snuffed out over something trivial. He'd popped in to see his dad earlier, who had tried pumping him for information about the conflict. He wanted Spence to get involved, stating it was an opportunity to grow.

Spence respected his dad's opinion, but had no intention of getting involved unless Natty dictated. It hadn't gone down well. Despite being a legal worker now, his dad had been heavily involved in the streets when Spence was younger, and had taught him numerous skills, including how to cut drugs and cook crack.

Still, despite his dad's experience, it didn't make him right, and Spence trusted Natty to get the right outcome.

Seeking a distraction, Spence closed the page he'd been perusing, checking Anika's Instagram page. He stopped at a photo of them from a new year's party, smiling and happy. He stared at it for a long moment. Anika had seemed distracted lately. Spence knew he had been working more, but wasn't sure if that was the cause of her moodiness. They hadn't argued, but she had given him the silent treatment multiple times. It never lasted long, but he'd considered addressing it with her, not wanting things to fester.

On the business front, Cameron had stayed out of his way, manning another spot near Markham Avenue, still embarrassed at Gavin's exposure. By all accounts, he seemed to now be taking things seriously. Spence hoped it lasted.

His phone beeped as he looked through more Instagram pages. He glanced at the screen, eyes widening when he saw it was from Rosie. He gawped at the message for a long moment, strangely giddy despite the platonic tones. Spence had known Rosie for a long time through Lorraine and her association with Natty. He'd had a massive crush on her back in the day, but she was always unavailable, having an ongoing relationship with an amateur boxer named Kyle. Kyle was currently locked up, having gotten caught up in an extortion scam.

Reading the message twice, Spence politely responded, wondering why Rosie had started texting him out of the blue. She'd had his number for years, and they had always been polite. The silly part of his brain wondered if she was after something more between them, then he immediately felt guilty when he thought about Anika.

Despite any issues they might have, he still loved her, and wanted the best for them.

Standing, he decided to go for a walk to clear his head, nodding at the diligent youngster still counting. After a moment's hesitation, he rooted around a nearby cupboard, taking out a small knife to carry, recognising they were going through tense times.

DESPITE THE DRAMA, Little London was still surprisingly quiet just after 11 pm. On Fieldhead Terrace, there were a selection of newer model flats, with very few lights on at this time. A car drove down the road, stopping in front of a house on the street. After a moment, the windows wound down, and multiple shots were fired, finding homes in the brickwork, windows, and gardens.

Immediately, the car screeched away, leaving screams and panic in its wake.

———

THE NEXT DAY, police were on the scene canvassing, neighbours hanging as close to the scene as they dared. The bullet holes in the flat could clearly be seen, and the area was taped off whilst the investigation was ongoing.

Nearby, Natty sat in the passenger seat of a BMW, glaring at the scene. His nostrils flared, showcasing his anger. They weren't doing enough, and the fact Warren could shoot at one of their spots with impunity, was a telling sign.

'Our people already cleared out, right?' He said to the driver, who nodded.

'The day before yesterday. Warren's people must not have up-to-date info.'

'They're not gonna stop either way. They've already killed someone, and we look weak just sitting here,' snapped Natty, eyes narrowing. 'We're gonna need to pull people out if things continue to escalate.'

The driver didn't respond, likely not wanting to piss off Natty further. Natty considered some of the basic information Elijah had provided about Warren, namely about his personality, and the fact he was a loose cannon. A lot of the info Elijah collated was information Natty already had, just by doing the rounds and speaking to people in the area. It was a sign that Elijah was too far removed from the situation, and that needed to change.

To Natty, it seemed Elijah and Rudy were too passive to do what needed to be done.

Yet, they ranked him. They seemed to be on the same page and had a similar rapport, whereas Natty felt he came across as an aggressive outlier, which wasn't true. Either way, he wanted the situation handled.

'C'mon, let's go,' he finally ordered the driver, who pulled away from the scene.

———

ANIKA WAS HOME AFTER WORK, watching television while Spence cooked in the kitchen. She could hear him singing along to the rap songs he was playing, and despite her ever-switching mood, it still made her smile. Picking up her phone, she scrolled through her social media sites when she saw something that made her pause.

Cameron had been tagged in some photos. In several of them, he was all over a trashy-looking brunette in a short, tight dress with a truckload of makeup on her pointed face. Anika's eyes blurred as she glared at the picture. She didn't recognise the woman, but her blood boiled at the sight of Cameron kissing her neck.

Locking her phone, she wiped her eyes as Spence came into the room smiling. When he saw the expression on Anika's face, he paused.

'Are you okay?'

Anika nodded.

'It looks like you've been crying. Are you sure?'

'I said I'm fine. Just leave it,' snapped Anika. Spence stared her down, his jaw tightening.

'Don't speak to me like that. I was checking if you were okay, because you looked sad, and you've been moody lately. I won't bother next time.' He returned to the kitchen, leaving a guilty Anika staring after him. It wasn't his fault she felt this way. The last thing she needed to do was take out her anger with Cameron on her boyfriend.

After a moment, she followed Spence, putting her arms around him as he stood over the kitchen sink, his back and shoulders tense.

'I'm sorry, babe. I didn't mean to snap at you. It's just silly social media stuff, that's all. Nothing worth worrying over.'

Visibly relaxing, Spence turned, taking Anika in his arms and hugging her closely.

'You can talk to me anytime, Nika. Don't feel you have to hold things in.'

Anika gave him a watery smile, and then buried her head against his firm chest.

'I'll bear that in mind,' she murmured, her thoughts back on Cameron and his mystery woman.

———

SPENCE WASN'T WORKING the next day, nipping into the city centre to do some shopping. As he browsed running shoes in a sports store, he remembered the altercation he and Anika had the night before. He'd slept on it, but still didn't like the fact she had snapped at him, especially over something so trivial as social media drama. Something didn't sit right, but he wasn't sure what it was.

As he chose and paid for a pair of shoes, he headed to an outlet store, looking for some new shirts. Whatever stresses Anika was going through, he hoped she would eventually let him in. He wondered for a moment if it was work-related, but dismissed this, knowing she wouldn't lie if that was the case.

Spence was lost in his thoughts, sifting through shirts, when someone called his name. He turned, recognising the voice, his stomach immediately fluttering when he saw Rosie heading towards him, a broad smile on her face that he returned.

'Hey, Spence. What are you doing around here?' She asked, trailed by two women Spence didn't recognise. He nodded, trying not to focus on how good Rosie looked. She wore a light blue sundress that hugged her body nicely, her toned arms on full display. Her brown eyes were bright and intense, and she had a chiselled bone structure. He audibly swallowed, knowing he couldn't get caught up. Clutching his shopping bag ever tighter, he responded.

'Just doing some quick shopping.' He gestured to his bag. 'What are you doing around here?'

'Same thing. We needed some things, and this place has a great selection. How's Natty? I ran into him in a club a while back.'

'Natty's good. He's just doing his thing,' replied Spence, wondering why Natty hadn't mentioned running into Rosie. Deciding it wasn't important, he focused on Rosie as she took a step closer. He froze as she sniffed him, at the same time inhaling her powerful wildflowers scent.

'You smell good. What aftershave is that?'

'Just some Zara stuff,' Spence replied, his mouth dry. Rosie was gorgeous and had a presence. She had to know what she was doing to him, he mused, resisting the urge to step even closer to her.

'It suits you.' Her eyes roved over his frame. Behind her, one of her friends coughed, the pair having watched the exchange with amused grins. 'Looks like I need to go, but it was good running into you.' She put her arms around him, clutching him for a long moment before pulling away. 'We should hang out sometime. We can talk about investments or whatever.' She held his stare for a second, then gave him a wave and left with her friends.

Spence remained in the same spot staring after her, his cheeks hot and his heart pounding.

He wasn't quite sure what had just transpired. He'd known Rosie for a long time, but had never seen her so flirtatious. He blew out a breath, returning to his shopping, dropping Natty a quick text message. He knew his friend was busy, but this was Natty's domain, and he needed his advice.

———

NATTY WALKED into the Bankside hangout spot with a smile on his face. It wasn't often Spence reached out for help, and he figured this would be a good distraction from the mounting problems in Little London.

Several workers were dotted around, and they greeted Natty with hand slaps and grins. He made small talk, then sought out Spence, who was in the kitchen, pottering around the kettle. He motioned to the kettle, and Natty nodded. Spence fixed him a coffee, and Natty took it with thanks, remaining on his feet as Spence collapsed into a chair, sipping his own.

'You probably need that with everything going on,' said Spence, referring to Little London.

'We can talk about that later. What's on your mind.'

Spence simply said, 'Rosie.'

Natty chuckled.

'I need more than that to go on, bro.' Inwardly, he recalled Rosie asking about Spence, when he'd seen her in the club. It still tickled him.

Women were interesting, he mused.

'I don't even know what to say. She sent me a few text messages recently, then earlier today I ran into her in town, and she was just . . .'

'Just what . . .' Natty prompted.

'*On.* I dunno. She was really flirty, and she said we should chill sometime.' Spence sighed, taking another sip of his hot drink. Natty followed suit, surveying Spence with amusement. He was the last person Natty thought would ever go through woman drama.

'What exactly do you want to happen?' Natty asked.

'What do you mean?'

'Do you want something to happen with Rosie?'

Spence shot Natty a look, warming his hands on the coffee mug. 'I have a girl.'

'I'm aware of that. We both know if it was that simple, you wouldn't have reached out to me.'

'I love Anika,' Spence replied. Natty didn't respond. There was no need. After a long moment, Spence sighed.

'I used to like Rosie. A lot. You know that. I guess the problem is that I'm not sure of her intentions, and I get the impression pursuing a friendship would be dangerous.'

Natty nodded, finishing his coffee, enjoying the burn in his throat and chest. He placed the cup in the sink before he responded.

'Rosie's fine as hell. I get it. I bumped into her a while back, and she asked about you. She definitely has you on her mind.'

Spence rubbed his eyes, then finished his coffee. Natty surveyed him, again liking that this situation kept him from overthinking his own issues.

'Bro, I don't know what you want me to say,' he went on. 'You're a good guy, and you'll do the right thing. If you don't want anything to happen, then it won't.'

Spence nodded.

'I appreciate you listening, Nat. Keep this to yourself, please. I don't need Cam to jump on this and start his shit again.'

'I won't say anything,' Natty assured him. Both men mulled the situation in silence for a few minutes.

'What would you do if you were me?' Spence finally asked.

'I'd sleep with Rosie.'

Spence's eyebrow rose.

'Just like that?'

Natty nodded again.

'What if it was Lorraine instead of Anika? Would you do the same thing then?'

Natty flinched.

'What's that got to do with anything?'

'You already know.'

'Me and Lorraine are just cool. There's nothing like that going on.' Natty looked away.

'I don't believe you, and you know that. There are feelings there, and I don't think you would want to hurt her by cheating,' said Spence.

'I've cheated before,' Natty reminded him.

'Yes, when you were young and dumb. You've changed, even if you don't want to see it. Lorraine is different.'

'Whatever,' said Natty, waving him off. The last thing he needed was to get caught up thinking about Lorraine.

'Fine. We can leave that for now. Guess I've got some thinking to do. In the meantime, what's going on with your situation?'

Natty rubbed his forehead.

'I don't even know what to tell you. We're losing face in Little London, and it seems like no one else wants to do anything about it.'

'Who are we talking about? Rudy? Elijah?'

'Both of them. They're happy to sit around and do nothing while Warren shoots at and stabs my people. I don't think it's the right move.'

'What are you going to?'

Natty didn't immediately respond. He still wanted to get a gun and do the job himself. At the same time, he wasn't a killer. He'd never shot anyone before, and the murder of a known criminal would catapult him into the police spotlight.

'There's nothing to do for now. I'm gonna listen to Rudy and maintain my position.'

Spence smiled.

'I wasn't expecting that. I thought you'd wanna charge in and do damage.'

Natty chuckled, despite his thoughts.

'I'm trying my hardest not to.'

———

TWO DAYS LATER, Anika flounced into Cameron's place, plopping on the sofa and crossing her legs, arms folded as she glared at him. Cameron chuckled.

'You look happy.'

'How am I supposed to look?' She snapped.

'What's happened? Spence pissed you off?'

'It's not about Spence,' she replied. 'It's about you.'

'What about me?' Cameron mockingly covered his mouth in shock.

'What the hell were you doing in town with that little slut?'

Cameron frowned. 'Have you been spying on me?'

'What? Course I haven't. You were tagged in a picture, and it popped up on my feed. Stop avoiding the question.'

'I don't need to avoid the question. You know exactly what I was doing.'

Anika shook her head. 'I can't believe you.'

'Why not?'

'We're supposed to have something. Why else would you stalk me in the club, mentioning *Fiji*, seeking me out?'

Cameron chuckled, the fact he wasn't taking her seriously only making her angrier. She didn't know what it would take to get him to understand how she was feeling.

She was sharply reminded of how things had been back in the day for them. Cameron had a wandering eye and would often flirt with girls around her and either play dumb, or downplay it later. She wondered what she expected from him, and why she was so surprised that he couldn't change.

'Don't laugh. It's not funny.' Anika threw up her hands.

'Depends where you're sitting, I guess. I think it's hilarious.'

Anika scowled. 'Did you sleep with her?'

'Does it matter if I did or not?'

'That's a *yes* then,' scoffed Anika.

'It doesn't matter to you if I did or not. You have a man. You're living with one of my best friends. Are you really going to pretend nothing is going on with you? Are you going to lie and say you're not grinding Spence?'

Anika's mouth fell open at the sight of Cameron's outburst. She wondered just how affected he was at the fact she was in a relationship with Spence. She started to think he had been hiding his feelings for a long time, and that the truth was slipping out.

'You approached me, Cam. Not the other way around. I didn't tell you to come up to me in the club and try sweet-talking me, did I?'

'You were fucking eager for it, though. You have been all along, because you knew we had unfinished business. That unfinished business had you coming all over my dick, didn't it?'

'Is that all it was about? Sex?'

'No, but we *did* have sex. You *did* cheat on your man, and now you're acting all confused and mad, but if you're really serious . . . if you're really about it, then break up with him.'

'What?' Anika gasped.

'Don't act like you didn't hear me. Dump him. Tell him you don't love him, move out of the spot, because I know it's all in his name, and move on.'

'Move on with you?'

Cameron shook his head. 'This ain't about me. This is about you.

There's a connection with us. Fucking lights up every time we're around one another, but I can't be your excuse to do what it is you wanna do in life. Have you ever actually been single?'

'What does that have to do with anything?'

'It has everything to do with everything. You just don't see it. We're not a couple, so you can't get mad at me for being around other women, especially ones that I *may* or *may not* fuck. That's none of your business, so figure your shit out and don't try to take it out on me.'

Anika's mouth opened and closed, unable to believe the way Cameron had sounded off on her. The worst thing was that he was right about everything.

Anika was confused about many things she wanted from life, but she was sure about one thing: she didn't want to be alone. Spence loved her and provided, and he was the ideal partner. She wished she felt the same way about him, but she didn't, and that hurt. She had allowed her emotions to override her logic. She couldn't demand anything of Cameron.

The smart thing to do would be to simply leave; to walk away from the good sex and the mind games, and the lack of respect, and go home to the relationship, and the arms of a man that she never had to doubt loved her.

Shooting to her feet, she headed for the door. Cameron watched. As she grasped the handle, he spoke.

'Fine. Walk out on me. I knew you didn't care.'

Anika whirled round, eyes blazing.

'Can you stop? You don't give a fuck about anything but yourself. How dare you try and guilt trip me after the way you've acted?'

Cameron sighed.

'Just go, Anika. I won't try to stop you.'

The pair stared at one another, Anika's heart crashing against her chest. She knew the sensible thing to do was to walk away from Cameron, but that didn't make it any easier.

She didn't know much about Cameron's life or upbringing and wanted to learn more.

What made him tick? What caused his issues with women, and why had he never been able to give himself to her?

Her head and heart once again battled for supremacy, and once again, her heart won. She sat back down, and Cameron sat next to her. He reached out to put his arm around her, but she resisted, shifting out of reach. Cameron nudged himself closer to her once more. He looked her in the eyes and kissed her on the cheek, heating the area. She melted into his arms, and he kissed her, working her neck as the intensity grew.

Before long, Anika was naked. Placing her hand on Cameron's chest, she pushed him down onto the sofa, climbing on top of him, slowly moving her hips backwards and forwards. Cameron reared up, digging his fingers into her back and placing his mouth around her nipple, biting so hard that Anika hissed. As her climax neared, her pace quickened. Cameron reciprocated, driving into her, urging her to finish. When it came, she threw her head back as she let everything go, the climax washing over her body, leaving her shuddering and twitching against him as he held her tightly.

'You'll never forget what I can do to you,' he mumbled against her ear. He gave her a few seconds of recovery, then chased his own finish.

Anika panted afterwards, trying to catch her breath. She met Cameron's eyes and shook her head, feeling like shit, but not immediately regretting what they had done.

Cameron had controlled her body. He'd given her an intense climax and taken what he wanted in return.

A wave of overwhelming guilt cascaded through her. Spence didn't deserve this. He deserved something better, and she thought about what Cameron had said; the possibility of breaking up with Spence.

She couldn't imagine being on her own, though.

Anika wondered if Cameron would even want her if she broke up with Spence, and it disgusted her that she didn't know the answer. Cameron had a friendship with Spence, and they were all in business together. She couldn't imagine him doing anything that would piss off Natty — knowing Natty was the glue that held their clique together. She recalled the suspicion in his eyes when she'd stupidly asked him if he was happy.

If Natty spoke up, would either of them even keep her around?

It was a terrifying thought, and she hated herself a little more for being so selfish.

Cameron stood and left the room, still naked. He didn't seem particularly bothered or chastened by what had happened. She looked down, realising she needed to clean herself up, deciding she would get a shower, whether Cameron said it was okay or not.

CHAPTER SIXTEEN

WARREN SAT UP IN BED, smoking a spliff, content and mellow. His woman of the hour lay next to him, rolled on her side, hair splayed over the pillow. He looked at her with a little smirk, satisfied with his surroundings. He was in a shithole spot, but it had three of his most trusted people watching downstairs, all armed.

Warren was ready to escalate things further. He knew of Natty and Elijah's plans to carve up Little London. Even before they reached out for a meeting, he'd heard all about their people sniffing around the area. He was pleased with how he'd handled them, and had no intention of working with them. It was a simple situation, and he had absolutely nothing to lose.

Warren knew Natty and Elijah's reputations were solid, but they tended to keep themselves out of the limelight. Knowing he had solidified his reputation, he hoped that meant theirs had taken a hit in the process.

The woman climbed from the bed, sashaying toward the bathroom. Warren watched her as she walked. She was better than his usual sort, with a slim build, dark hair, and Mediterranean features. Fuelled by drugs and drink, she'd given him the best sex of his life. He'd even ignored some of his regulars, making more time for the one woman who could give him what the others couldn't. If needed, he could get them back later.

If you had enough cash and reputation, women were easy.

Killing the spliff, he messed around on his phone. When she came out of the bathroom, he glared at her.

'What the hell were you doing in there?' His voice was low, and his eyes searching. He expected her to shy away as his women often did when they saw him flip the switch, but instead, she shrugged, fixing her hair, which she'd put into a simple ponytail.

'I wanted to look nice.'

Grumbling, Warren pushed past her and left the room to go to the bathroom. He washed his hands when he was done, looking at his face in the mirror with distaste. He needed to get a few good nights' sleep. He was slacking and didn't want to get caught unprepared.

Maybe he needed to take this girl away; leave the streets in the hands of his people. It wasn't like Natty or Elijah were making any moves against him.

After a few minutes, he re-entered the bedroom, ready for another round. His girl was gone, though. Frowning, Warren glanced around the bedroom, but saw no sign of her things. Collapsing back on the bed, he closed his eyes, choosing to push the sight out of his mind. She was pretty, but high maintenance. If she wanted to cut out, he wouldn't chase her.

He messed around on his phone and took a call from one of his youngsters. They were all armed with knives, just in case Natty and Elijah got cute and retaliated.

'What's going on out there?' He asked.

'It's quiet. Few fiends around, but no one from the other side.'

'Make sure you keep your eyes peeled. They might come for you at any time.'

'Can't I get any backup?'

'You don't need backup. Those lot are soft. Give it a few more days and they'll be out of here.'

The youth didn't speak. Warren's eyes narrowed. He could sense fear, and he hated it. Fear was weakness. Worse than fear, though, was insubordination.

'You wanna come and speak to me face-to-face?'

His voice was as low and dangerous as it had been with his girl. The youth folded.

'Nah, Warren. I've got it covered. You don't need to worry about me.'

'I better not have to. I'm gonna send someone out later to check on you, and you better be where you're supposed to, or we'll have that face-to-face. Understand?'

'Yeah, boss. I understand.'

Warren ended the call. Clambering to his feet, he went to go and see what his crew was doing. They would have seen her go, and he wanted to know if she had said anything first.

'Oi,' he said, traipsing down the creaky stairs, 'where did that girl go?' No one responded. He'd spoken clearly enough for them to hear him over the television, and they'd ignored him. 'Oi, don't fucking ignore me,' he snapped, storming into the room. 'Yo—'

Warren froze. His team slumped in their seats, bullet holes in their heads. They had been shot and left where they were.

Warren's eyes widened, his pulse racing. His mouth fell open, unable to comprehend what had happened. Coming to his senses he turned on his heel and rushed upstairs, adrenaline surging. He dove under the bed and pulled up with his gun in his hand. He made sure it was loaded, then ran back downstairs, gun at the ready, willing to shoot whoever had invaded his spot. He hadn't heard a thing.

How had this happened?

The television was loud, but this kind of commotion should have cut through.

He checked the remaining downstairs rooms, glancing around the kitchen, but nothing was out of the ordinary. He was amped. It had to be Natty and Elijah. They hadn't had the guts to come for him, instead cowardly taking out his people.

Deep in his thoughts, he heard a creak from behind. Instincts kicking in, he whirled around, but he wasn't quick enough. He saw a movement and felt immense pain as something sliced into his throat. Instinctively, he pulled the trigger, missing the woman. She rubbed her ears as he slid to the floor. He tried to lift the gun, but he was fading.

The last thing he saw before the end, was her calmly watching him bleed out.

The killer waited over a minute, watching Warren twitch. Her ears still rang from the sound of the blast, but that was her fault for being sloppy. She'd had the drop on him all night, and had played with him rather than finishing him straight away. Clarke would be annoyed, but she could deal with that.

Putting the knife away, she stepped over Warren and left the house, keeping her head down to prevent identification. Not that she was worried. Warren and his people hadn't known much about her, and she wouldn't get a pull from the authorities. She was two streets away before she made the call to get picked up.

———

NEWS OF WARREN'S murder spread through Little London and the Hood, sending a message to everyone, his crew included. The viciousness of the murder gripped the streets, and everyone had a theory about who was responsible.

Natty's name seemed to be brought up regularly. People were aware of the beef they'd had, and it didn't surprise him when police picked him up within a couple of days of the murder.

After having his belongings taken, he was sent to a cell after the custody sergeant was made aware of the charge. He stewed there, with his own theories over what had transpired.

The level of destruction involved and the lack of physical evidence suggested it was one of his uncle's killers. Natty recalled the expression Rudy had worn when speaking of Natty not getting his hands dirty. He had arranged this and used it to send the message. It was spectacular work, but Natty only hoped it wasn't the catalyst for him going to jail.

After a few hours, he was taken to an interview room. His solicitor was with him by now, and had been made aware of the facts of the case. As Natty entered the room, he thought about the last time he had been in one. Years ago, he and Cameron had been arrested on suspicion of assault. They were guilty, but the charges had been dropped, and they'd left without issue.

The room had beige walls, with a sturdy dark brown table, a recording device on said table, and metal chairs in the middle of the room. It reeked of cleaning solution and a lingering cigarette smell that made Natty's eyes narrow. He didn't understand how it could still smell of cigarettes, as smoking indoors hadn't been permitted in years. Despite the stale odour, he wished he had one.

Two officers entered the room — a man and a woman. Natty kept his eyes on the man — on the slight side, with receding, strawberry blond hair, and pockmarked skin. He maintained his cool, knowing he couldn't flinch or show weakness. Glancing at his solicitor, his gaze flitted back to the officers.

'Interview commencing at four twelve pm, present are myself, DS Lowther, DS Calrick, the suspect, Nathaniel Dunn, and his legal counsel,' said the woman — DS Lowther, after turning on the tape recorder. She had a slight hunch, dark brown hair, and visible crow's feet, wearing a blue blouse and dark trousers. Calrick sat in the corner, keeping his eyes on Natty.

'Nathaniel, you have already been informed that you are being held in connection with the murder of Warren Bull, which took place on Friday, 10 April 2020.'

Natty didn't react. He focused on Calrick, whose eyes bore into his, probably hoping to intimidate him.

'We are aware of the problems between yourself and Warren Bull. There was known bad blood, and we also know threats were made on both sides.'

'I'd suggest you ask a question, rather than speculating,' Natty's solicitor interjected.

'Did you know Mr Bull, Nathaniel?' Lowther didn't miss a beat.

'No comment,' replied Natty.

'Where were you on the night of Friday, 10 April 2020?'

'No comment.'

Lowther and Calrick shared a look. Lowther wiped a lock of hair from her face.

'Can anyone confirm your whereabouts on the night in question?'

'Which night again?' Asked Natty.

'The night of Friday 10 April 2020,' repeated Lowther.

Natty paused, eyes again flitting between the pair. He opened his mouth, then closed it. Lowther leant forward in her seat.

'Mr Dunn?'

Natty's eyes locked on hers, and he replied, 'no comment.'

Lowther slammed down her notebook and shot to her feet. Natty's solicitor leaned back in his chair, eyes glittering.

'Is that all, officers?'

Without directly responding, Lowther turned off the recorder.

'Interview terminated at four-twenty pm.'

'Thank you for your time and patience, officers,' said Natty's solicitor, his tone smug. 'Ensure that any further contact or questions are directed to my office. Please and thank you.'

———

NATTY GAVE it a day for things to cool off before he reached out to Rudy, who predictably already knew about his arrest. They met in public this time, returning to the pub Rudy had previously taken him to. It was midday, and they forwent pints, Rudy settling for a coke, Natty a lemonade.

'How are you?' Rudy got to the point after a cursory glance around the pub. Several regulars were in, making a lot of noise with their loud conversations.

'I'm good. Got a bit worried for a minute after what happened.'

Rudy's eyebrow rose. 'Why were you worried? You didn't do anything.'

'Wouldn't be the first time the feds have locked up the wrong person. Can't believe you handled it like that, though.'

'How did you expect it to be handled?'

Natty shrugged, sipping his drink. 'Guess I just thought you'd be more subtle about it, not be dropping bodies and knifing people.'

'The message is important.'

Natty met his eyes. 'Do you think I could have sent the same message?'

'Did you want to?'

Making a noise, Natty looked away. Rudy had a knack for getting under his skin, and he swore he did it on purpose.

'Nathaniel, I wanted you removed from the situation. I made that clear. And now, you've been picked up, and they know you had nothing to do with it. You were protected from the outcome.'

'Was it always the plan to deal with him like that?'

Rudy nodded.

'Did Elijah know?'

Rudy again nodded. As much as Natty wanted to flip out, he kept his composure. He wasn't going to storm out like he had the last time.

'What is the point in me being the guy over in Little London if I'm left out of the decisions? You could have asked me for my opinion.'

'If I had, you would have insisted that you do it.'

'So what if I had? Do you not think I'm capable?'

'I don't *want* you to be capable.' Rudy's voice remained level, but his eyes blazed. 'Don't you get that? I don't want you to do that sort of stuff. You don't need to.'

'What does my Unc think?'

Rudy picked up his drink, avoiding the question. Natty sighed. Rudy was hard work.

'What did Elijah think?' Natty tried again.

'He knew we could get it done.'

'Is that it?' Natty's brow furrowed. Elijah was a boss and, outside of Little London, had a solid reputation and a lot of weight. He couldn't imagine him simply going along with the plan.

Rudy shook his head.

'Son, you need to learn to see beyond the obvious. Elijah is successful because he knows when to be involved and delegate. Why piss all over the territory if you know someone you're in business with can do something better? He doesn't want the attention. He wants the business.'

'So, you want me to be thinking like Elijah?' Natty took a sip of his drink.

'I want you to go far beyond Elijah, and beyond me. Learn to use your reputation to work for you, instead of feeling you have to do things for the sake of it. You're doing great work, and I'm seeing the moves you're making. Just take it easy.'

Natty nodded, still annoyed, but at least understanding Rudy's position.

'Who did it?'

'We have people to handle wet work. Heed my words, Nathaniel . . . you don't need to do that.'

Both men silently mulled over the conversation. Natty considered the situation. He'd wanted to go right at Warren, but struggled to piece a plan together because he couldn't get to him — he was too well guarded. The murder was methodical; within days, someone had managed to infiltrate and systematically eliminate everyone in the spot. It showed how a professional truly worked.

Natty wondered about that. Initially, he felt inadequate that he couldn't get the job done. Despite that, it wasn't his skill set. Rudy wanted him to distance himself, and he could accept that was the right decision.

Natty rubbed his eyebrow, deciding to move past it. It had happened; a major pain had been removed. The police would move on, and Little London would now be theirs with little issue.

Natty wondered what was next for the coalition, and what plans the bigwigs were cooking up. He decided not to ask Rudy directly, instead wondering why he seemed so determined to protect him. Rudy was involved with his mum, but it wasn't like he needed Natty's approval. He'd schooled him from an early age, and even when Natty's dad had been alive, Rudy would see him on the streets, give him money, and tell him to stay in school.

Amid his musings, he thought about his uncle, and his lack of involvement in proceedings. Despite Rudy avoiding the question, Natty knew his uncle had given the order, and that he'd likely dictated how he wanted the murders to go down. Rudy had indicated his uncle knew of his movements, but Natty didn't know if that was a good or a bad thing, nor what his uncle's intentions for him were, other than to bring in as much money as possible.

Natty took a deep breath, inwardly calming himself. His job was to make money and elevate his people, so he would focus on that. He had work to do, and decided he would speak with Elijah later, then get started in Little London again.

With a plan in place, Natty found he felt much better, and he and Rudy eventually went for lunch, business talk finished for the time being.

———

NATTY WAS home after his conversation with Rudy, staring aimlessly at the television. He'd received a few text messages from acquaintances, trying to pump him for information about the Warren murder. Natty had ignored the majority, and downplayed it with the few he responded to. He wasn't going to fuel any gossip, or attempts at gaining clout from his name.

Warren was gone, and Natty needed to think about his next move.

Dozing off, he was awoken by a loud banging at the front door. Tensing, he hurried to his feet, moving swiftly to the door. Cameron stood there with a big smile on his face. They touched fists, and Natty stepped aside.

'Heard you've had a busy time,' he said.

Natty chuckled.

'That's one way to describe it.'

'What happened? You should have reached out.'

'Wasn't time. Whatever happened to Warren, I wasn't involved,' explained Natty.

Cameron's eyes narrowed.

'Little London is your thing, though. You're the guy down there. How could you not be involved?'

As Cameron was talking, it struck Natty just how long it had been since he'd chilled with his friend. A lot had happened, and they hadn't hung out as much since Natty had become the point man. He sat on the sofa, rubbing his eyes. Cameron sat on a nearby chair, hands behind his head, waiting for Natty to talk.

'Rudy wanted me to stay out of it, probably so that if I was picked up, I wouldn't know anything, which is exactly what happened.'

'And you don't know who dropped Warren?'

Natty shook his head. He wasn't on first-name terms with any of the killers his uncle had on the payroll, and figured it was best that way.

'It could have been you, though. Your name would have been ringing out if you'd done it.'

'My name was already ringing out,' Natty dryly responded. 'The Feds picked me up, remember? They thought I was the one who did it.'

'You should have called me, bro. I would have done it for you.'

'Just like that?' Natty raised an eyebrow, watching Cameron emphatically nod and puff out his chest.

'Course.'

Natty again thought to when he'd wanted to directly attack Warren. Ultimately, he was glad he hadn't.

'I don't think it would be as easy as you think. Warren had like six people guarding him, and they all got killed too. I don't know anyone that could get in and out like that unharmed.'

Cameron scratched his chin. 'Maybe . . . still, would have been a great way to prove myself.'

'Prove yourself to who? Rudy?' Natty asked. 'The bosses like things quiet. That's what I've learnt.'

'How can you say that? You just said they dropped Warren and all his people. What's quiet about that?'

'Warren had his chances to back away, and he didn't. I guess a message needed to be sent.'

'Exactly. And I could have been the one to send it.' Cameron's nostrils flared. Natty finally realised just how annoyed Cameron was about the situation. He didn't understand.

'You have enough to think about, without trying to become a shooter,' he said.

'What do you mean by that?' Cameron visibly flinched, eyes widening for a moment. Natty noticed, but didn't comment.

'I heard about the situation with Gavin.'

Cameron scowled.

'Spence been telling tales, has he?'

'No. There was a room full of people when you confronted him, Cam. Spence doesn't have to run and tell me anything.'

'It doesn't matter.' Cameron waved a hand. 'He violated and got dealt with.'

'He violated on *your* watch, You wanted to step up. You sulked because I picked Spence, and then you're letting people rob the team right in front of you?'

'It wasn't like that. He was sneaky.' Cameron's jaw jutted.

'Doesn't matter. The fact is, it makes us look bad. You're talking about the message, and how people see us . . . how they see you. You can't let things like that happen again.'

Cameron looked away, breathing hard. Natty assessed him, wondering if Cameron could have pulled the trigger, the way he seemed to think. He wasn't sure. Cameron had heart, but he was often led by emotion. Natty couldn't see him executing a plan to take out a room full of people by himself, nor did he think that was bad.

Natty rubbed his cheek, thinking of the difference that had cropped up between them. He hadn't wanted to take out Warren for the name. He'd seen it as the only viable way to resolve the situation.

'Let's just forget it. It's done. Warren is gone, and you lot sorted Gav.' He climbed to his feet. 'Let's get a drink. We haven't chilled in time.'

———

WITH WARREN and most of his team out of the way, business went on. The police continued half-heartedly searching for the killers, widening their list of suspects, with several dumb outfits claiming credit for the job.

After laying low for a few days, Natty put it behind him and visited Julie in Little London again, holding a football. She noticed, but didn't comment. The interior was unchanged from his last visit, just as untidy, with the kids making as much noise as ever. He declined Julie offering him a drink.

'See! When I offer you a drink, you don't take one. Don't talk to me about *dehydration* this time.' Julie's eyes twinkled as she grinned. Natty laughed.

'What's the word on what happened to Warren?'

Julie smiled.

'Apparently, he got too big for his boots and tried it on with the wrong people. No one's crying about what happened, let's put it that way.'

Natty nodded.

'He messed with a lot of people, but we move on. Are you ready to go to work?'

'Yeah, I've got some others interested now too.' She handed Natty a piece of paper with several addresses hastily written down. Natty pocketed it, leaving two twenty-pound notes on the table. Julie raised an eyebrow.

'Business drying up or something?' She said.

Smirking, Natty put a couple more twenties down. He liked the fact she had come out of her shell.

'Someone will visit you every week with your wages. I'm gonna give you the number of your contact. You see or hear anything, contact them,' he told her.

Julie ran a hand through her hair.

'Won't you be coming around anymore?'

Natty hid his distaste. Julie sounded almost sad, and he hoped she didn't imagine something would happen between them. Nonetheless, he gave her a little smile. If it kept her motivated, he was all for it.

'I'm sure I'll be stopping by now and then, but I want to make us all as much money as possible. The team does better, then we all do better. Stack some money, and then maybe you can see about moving into a better spot. For now, keep working and let your kids play out. Give them this.' He handed her the football.

CHAPTER SEVENTEEN

THE DAY after hanging out with Cameron, Natty's mind was back on Spence and his dilemma with Rosie. Warren's murder had taken precedence, but with normality restored, he wondered what his friend would do. As Natty had said, the fact Spence needed Natty's advice, despite being in a relationship, was a sign he was conflicted about how to move.

If Natty was honest, he wanted it to happen. His instincts told him there was something wrong with Spence's relationship with Anika. He wasn't against it for the same reasons as Cameron. He didn't think it had changed Spence or made him soft, but he didn't think his friend was being honest about his feelings.

Natty wasn't a fan of Anika. He could get along with her for Spence's sake, but he'd never forgiven her for hopping from Cameron to Spence. At the same time, he was equally as bad because he'd never told Spence, and now, over a year later, he had to live with the same lie.

Rosie was cool. He knew her well through Lorraine, and the pair had a solid friendship. She was refreshing, spoke her mind, and seemed to have more energy than Anika, who seemed disengaged most of the time.

As he made himself a drink, he considered how complex the situation was. Spence had liked Rosie for the longest, then he'd got a girlfriend, and now she was chasing after him. If it was another woman, he'd think they were messing around just to disrupt the situation, but Natty didn't think Rosie was like that and was prepared to listen to his instincts.

He wondered what Spence would do about Rosie, if anything.

After finishing his drink and making a few phone calls, Natty called Lorraine. He would need to go down and sort a few loose ends in Little London now that things were dying down, but he wanted to talk to her.

'Hey Natty,' she said, upon picking up. 'How are you?'

'I'm good,' he replied, gratified that she seemed happy to hear from him. 'This is gonna sound weird, but has Rosie said anything to you about Spence?'

When Lorraine started giggling, Natty had his answer.

'Next time you stop by, we can talk about it.'

'What are you doing now?'

———

BEFORE LONG, Natty was camped on Lorraine's sofa. Jaden was staying at a friend's house, and consequently, Lorraine seemed more relaxed. She was casually dressed in a vest top and leggings. Whilst Natty built a spliff, she went to make drinks.

Soon, *Maxwell* played in the background. Lorraine had lit some incense, the vibe extremely mellow. They took turns with the joint, Natty laughing as Lorraine coughed when she first inhaled. He leant back on the sofa after a while, realising that just being in the house and being around Lorraine, had drastically improved his mood. For the time being, his troubles had vanished.

'How have you been?' He asked. 'I know I haven't checked you in a while, but it's been hectic.'

Lorraine smiled, nodding. 'I get that. I've been good, but I've missed you. Guess sometimes I forget just how used I am to you being around.'

Natty grinned at her words.

'I'll be around a lot more. Things were going on that have mostly been sorted out now.'

'I heard you got arrested.'

Natty wasn't shocked. The tale had done the rounds, especially immediately after Warren's murder.

'I got questioned about something that happened, but they let me go.'

Lorraine didn't delve any deeper, which Natty was thankful for.

'Jaden will be happy you're going to be around more,' she remarked.

Natty felt a rush of warm energy seeping through his body, happy that Jaden and Lorraine wanted him around, and privately resolving to do something nice for the kid.

'What are you saying about Rosie, though?'

Lorraine coyly smiled, then sipped her drink. Natty followed suit. He didn't enjoy the taste of green tea, but wouldn't make a fuss.

'She didn't see what was right in front of her.'

'Meaning Spence?' Natty pressed. Lorraine nodded.

'You know about her situation back then. Kyle made it hard for her to be around anyone, even me.'

Natty tensed. He'd never liked Rosie's ex. Kyle had a woman-beating reputation for years that no one ever called him out on. Natty had fought him at a party over ten years ago. He didn't remember why, but recalled it getting broken up before he could hurt him too badly.

'Do you think she's only interested because Spence has a girl?'

Instantly, Lorraine shook her head, adjusting her position on the sofa. Natty fought to remain looking at her face, not wanting to be distracted by her cleavage peeking out of her top.

'Rosie isn't like that. She's had a thing for Spence for a while. I don't think him getting with his partner has anything to do with that. They just click, and she thought it would go away, but I guess her feelings have only grown stronger. She mentioned running into him in town recently and said there was chemistry between them.'

Natty mulled over what Lorraine had said. They killed the spliff and sipped their drinks, the silence comforting.

'He's loyal to Anika. I can't see him straying, even for someone as fine as Rosie,' Natty finally replied.

Lorraine elbowed him, rolling her eyes.

'You're shameless.'

'Don't get me wrong, I'd still rather have you,' said Natty. Lorraine couldn't hide the smile that appeared on her face. With all their ups and downs, there was no denying the good times she and Natty had shared. Especially in the older, pre-Jaden days.

Natty always had a presence about him, and the chemistry between the pair was palpable. They were more like friends nowadays, but the feelings were still there.

Lorraine wasn't sure they would ever go away.

'Can I ask you something?' Lorraine finally said.

'Of course.'

'Do you like Spence's girl? I know you've mentioned Cam seems to have a problem with her in the past, but you've never said how you feel.'

Natty didn't hesitate to respond.

'I don't like her,' he said, thinking back to his earlier thoughts, and the effect he felt she had on Spence. Lorraine's eyes widened.

'Just like that?'

'I don't trust her, and I'm not sure she has Spence's best interests at heart.'

'Why don't you tell him that?'

'It's not a conversation you can have with your boy. Not without being able to back it up with anything.' Natty blew out a breath. 'What do you think Rosie is going to do? I heard she was talking about them wanting to chill.'

Lorraine smirked.

'Rosie's not going to back down. I don't know her plan, but I'm sure about that. Spence needs to watch himself around her if the chemistry is there like she says it is.'

294

THAT NIGHT, Spence cooked for Anika. When they'd finished eating, he gathered the plates and cutlery to wash up. Anika went to take a shower.

Spence took his time, enjoying the mundane act. It allowed him time to think, and he liked the solitude. He was almost finished when his phone buzzed. Anika entered the kitchen as he was reading the message. Her hair was wrapped in a towel, and she wore a red dressing gown. She grabbed a teabag and plopped it into a cup.

'Who's texting you?'

Spence didn't lie.

'Rosie.'

Anika's eyes narrowed, forgetting about her drink.

'*Rosie* who?'

'She's a friend of Lorraine's. I knew her from back in the day,' said Spence.

'Back in the day before me?'

Spence nodded.

'I'm not sure why that matters, but yeah.'

Anika folded her arms, her cup abandoned on the table.

'Why is she texting you?'

'She was seeing what I was doing. I ran into her in town, and she mentioned we should chill sometime.'

'*She wants you to chill with her . . .*' Anika's voice was cool. Too cool.

'We have things in common. Like investments,' Spence said, knowing from Anika's demeanour that she was close to exploding. Though he didn't say it out loud, he realised it was the most emotion he had seen from her in a while.

Anika shook her head. 'You can't be serious. You're standing there telling me about some woman you used to know texting you, wanting to chill with you, and that's all you have to say?'

'You asked, and I answered, Nika. I don't get why you're reacting like this, but you know me. I'm not like that.'

'Does she know you have a girlfriend?' Anika ignored Spence's comments.

'Yes. Of course she does. Would you like to read the messages?'

Even in her rapidly angered state, Anika recognised how petty it would be to say *yes*.

'Just do what you want, Spence. If you want to hang out with some random girl, just do it. See if I care.'

'What is your problem? I didn't say I was going to hang out with her. I was just telling you what she said.'

'Like I said. Do what you want,' said Anika venomously. She went to leave.

'Get back in here.'

Something in Spence's tone stalled Anika. She turned to look at him, taken aback by the fury lining Spence's face. Anika had never seen him like this before, and was unprepared.

'I . . .'

'It's my turn to speak —' Spence cut her off. 'You asked who texted me. I told you. I was honest about the conversation, so don't you dare try to turn this on me and invent a scenario where there isn't one. Have I ever given you any reason not to trust me? Am I the one that doesn't want to have certain conversations, or is that you?'

Anika's mouth fell open, still unable to deal with Spence's anger. The fact he was still speaking in a quiet tone somehow made his words even more effective.

'I'm sorry,' she said after a moment, moving towards him, taking his hands in hers. 'I didn't mean to overreact. I just got jealous at the thought of some other woman being around you.'

Spence sighed, his anger dissipating. He hadn't meant to lose his temper with Anika, and now that he had, he wondered why, and if this was brought on by the fact he felt something for Rosie and liked talking to her. Not wanting to think about it anymore, he brought Anika in for a hug, clutching her tightly in the middle of the kitchen.

———

PUTTING his conversation with Lorraine about Spence and Rosie aside for now, Natty sewed up the business in Little London. The police presence had dissipated, and Natty took full advantage, reaching out to several smaller gangs, who came under the umbrella of Natty and Elijah in exchange for a discount on product.

With the streets working in tandem, the money quickly shot up for Natty, and within a month, he was earning far more than he'd ever made in his previous role.

———

SPENCE PULLED to a stop outside Cameron's house, yawning as he killed the engine. The last month had been interesting. When the tension died down, and the dust settled, Spence and Anika spoke openly about his friendship with Rosie.

Since then, he'd hung out with Rosie several times. Though there was evident sexual tension, nothing untoward had happened with them. Rosie was well learned and funny, and they always seemed to have something new to talk about. The conversation never felt forced, and they had history they could fall back on.

Spence had considered introducing her to Anika, but had decided against it.

Cameron let him in, and they touched fists. Spence entered Cameron's living room. It had been a while since he'd visited, but the large new television encompassing most of the wall caught his eye. He glanced at Cameron, taking in what looked like a brand-new black Gucci sweatsuit. Spence didn't comment. What Cameron did with his money was his business.

'Here you go,' Cameron handed Spence a packet of money. 'I was gonna have one of the youngers drop it off tomorrow.'

'It's fine,' replied Spence. Cameron disappeared into the kitchen, returning with a bottle of Courvoisier, motioning to Spence.

'Fancy a drink? We haven't chilled in a while.'

'Sounds good,' said Spence, privately unable to remember the last time the pair had hung out without Natty being present. Cameron poured them glasses of brandy, and they clinked glasses and drank, Spence savouring his, whilst Cameron downed his own. The brandy burnt his throat, but he enjoyed the feeling, allowing Cameron to top his glass up before he'd even finished.

'That's my lot. I'm driving.'

'We'll see,' replied Cameron, smirking. 'How've you been?'

'Everything is golden right now. Business is booming, and we're all making more money. The other gangs don't want any static, so there's no major drama.'

Cameron nodded. 'You're right. The other spots are clicking. What about your missus? Everything good?' Usually, he wouldn't bring up Anika around Spence unless he was teasing him, but he hadn't seen much of Anika since she had confronted him about the girl he'd been caught in the picture with.

Cameron had seen the girl multiple times since, but in the past month, he had only hooked up with Anika twice, wondering if Spence had something to do with it.

As Cameron sat there, he felt a trickle of guilt. Spence was his closest friend other than Natty, and he'd willingly sought out and slept with a woman he knew Spence was in love with. He swallowed his conflicting feelings, pouring himself a small glass of vodka from a nearby bottle.

'How's Anika doing with your promotion?'

Spence surveyed Cameron for a long moment, trying to work out if he was being funny. He shrugged.

'She's up and down about it. One minute she seems happy, and the next, she's miserable. I'm not sure what else I can do, but sometimes things just feel wrong.'

'Wrong how?'

'It doesn't always feel like she's invested in the relationship.'

Cameron was surprised to find his heart beating faster at these words.

'Have you considered ending it?'

Spence's eyes narrowed.

'Why would I?'

It was Cameron's turn to shrug.

'If you think she's not feeling it, and this is your life, then I dunno . . .' he trailed off.

Spence rubbed his chin.

'We've both sacrificed for the relationship. If I can fix it, I will.'

Spence hesitated, debating whether to share what had happened with Anika last month. He regretted speaking to her about Rosie. They'd gone back to normal, but there was a barrier in place, and Spence wasn't sure who'd erected it.

'We argued a while back,' he finally said.

'Who did?'

'Me and Anika.'

Cameron fought down his glee. Anika hadn't said anything to him.

Other than sex and a little pillow talk, they hadn't delved into the parameters of their situation, which Cameron was glad for.

'What did you argue about?'

Spence rubbed his forehead. 'I told her that I was thinking of chilling with Rosie.'

'Which Rosie? Lorraine's Rosie?'

Spence nodded.

Cameron sniggered. 'Bet that went down well.'

'She flipped out, then I got annoyed and snapped back at her.'

'Then what happened?' Cameron leant forward. He couldn't imagine Spence standing up to Anika.

'We just kinda squashed it.'

Cameron scratched his chin. 'Can't say I blame you. Rosie's fucking sexy. I've moved to her a few times, and she wasn't having any of it.'

Spence didn't let on, but he knew all about this. Rosie had mentioned during a recent conversation that Cameron had come onto her multiple times, at one time getting quite aggressive when she'd said no. Spence offered to force him to apologise, but Rosie hadn't wanted to make a big deal of it.

'Tell you what . . . I'd move to Lorraine if Natty wasn't all over her,' Cameron went on.

'That definitely wouldn't be a good idea,' said Spence. No matter how vehemently Natty insisted nothing was going on between him and Lorraine, Spence knew it would start a war if Cameron made a play for her.

'I know. Natty's funny like that. Think they'll ever get together?'

'I'm not sure,' admitted Spence. He thought they were a good match, but wasn't sure Natty would ever take the risk.

'He's doing well in Little London. He's raking it in down there. Think he'll bring us in on it?'

Spence shrugged. 'It's not really up to him. Guessing Rudy would have the final decision. Or Nat's uncle.'

'Mitch won't care,' grumbled Cameron. 'Neither will Rudy. Natty's running shit. Both of you are. It's only me that's still doing the same stuff.' His face darkened.

'Do you want me to talk to Natty for you?'

'He's my boy too. I can talk to him myself,' snapped Cameron. He took a deep breath. 'Sorry. Just stresses me out. You lot are stepping up. Guess I just want the chance to do the same.' He glared down at his drink.

Not knowing what to say, Spence finished his drink in silence, lost in his thoughts.

CHAPTER EIGHTEEN

NATTY DROVE INTO LITTLE LONDON, window wound down, allowing him to feel the heat of the warm summer day. To combat this, he wore a white t-shirt, grey shorts, and pristine designer trainers.

Driving up Meanwood Road, he turned onto Oatland Road, taking in the various terraced houses, a mix of red and pale-bricked spots, some newer looking than others. Kids rode around on bikes, a few children kicking a football to one another, mindful of the busy road. Natty grinned, reminded of Jaden.

'Are you staying in the car?' Carlton asked. Natty nodded.

'No need for me to go in there.'

Shortly afterwards, they parked on Carlton Place, a few streets away from where Julie lived. Natty wondered if she had been letting her kids play out after their last talk. His people knew to leave her children alone, even when they were patterning youths to come and work for them. Again, Natty thought of Jaden, remembering Lorraine's passion about her son never being like him.

Shaking off the thoughts, Natty glanced at the black Vauxhall Corsa parked next to him as Carlton climbed from the car and headed into a nearby house. Despite things being relatively peaceful, Natty kept his eyes on his mirrors, not wanting to be caught slipping in what had formerly been enemy territory.

After a few minutes, Carlton strolled out. He climbed back in, showing Natty the stack of money he held.

'They had four grand,' he said.

Nodding, Natty pulled away. A group of students walked by, outfitted with backpacks and strategically ripped clothing, talking over one another in loud voices.

The pair drove to various areas, collecting large amounts of money.

'Gotta say, boss; I thought the money would have slowed down by now,' Carlton admitted, a grin on his face as he looked at the stacks bundled into a black sports bag.

'Just make sure everyone remains on point,' replied Natty. 'No one should be slipping up.'

Carlton nodded. 'Got it.'

Natty eventually dropped off Carlton, driving through the Hood, ensuring he wasn't being followed. Gathering the sports bag, he took it into a house on Francis Street. A group of men sat in the living, which reeked of cigarette smoke. The whirring of money-counting machines permeated the room. Noticing Natty, one of them grinned and offered him a cigarette, but Natty shook his head.

'Latest takings,' he announced, dropping the bag on the floor. 'Just under forty bags, give or take. Wonder will probably do some more drops later.'

'We know the drill, Bossman,' the same man that had offered the cigarette, replied. Natty hung around for a few more minutes, then left. Approaching his car, he stifled a yawn, deciding to take a break to go and see Lorraine and Jaden, hoping she would cook for him. It had been a long day, and he hadn't eaten.

When he arrived, she gave him a quick hug and let him in, a harried expression on her face.

'Hey Nat, where are you coming from?'

'All over, handling business. What's up with you?'

'Trying to study, but Jaden is doing my head in. I might have to move it to when he's asleep, but I concentrate more during the day,' she said. 'Plus, it's kicking my arse.'

'How so?' Natty braced himself for more complex computer talk.

'I need to apply what I'm studying, and use it. That involves trawling different sites, watching videos, and searching forums to learn how to solve certain problems.'

'Sounds tough,' replied Natty. Lorraine nodded, rubbing her eyes.

'It is. My laptop's a piece of shit too. It's not powerful enough to run the programs I use, so it takes me twice as long. I keep meaning to buy a new one.' She shook her head. 'Forget it. Jaden will be happy to see you.'

Jaden leapt to his feet when Natty entered the living room. Natty hugged him and rubbed the top of his messy head.

'Yes, little man. You need a haircut,' he said, his heart warm at the sight of the kid. He beamed down at him, missing the smile on Lorraine's face.

'No, I don't. *You* need a haircut,' retorted Jaden, though he was grinning too. 'Will you play my game with me? We can play Fifa.'

'Jaden, darling, Natty is busy,' said Lorraine.

The sight of Jaden's head lowering broke Natty. He had love for Jaden, and didn't ever want to be responsible for seeing such a look on his face. He didn't have any plans, and made a split-second decision.

'Course I will, little man. Get the game ready, and I'll make a drink and talk to your mum for a minute.'

'Okay.' Jaden beamed and went to change the game. Shaking her head, Lorraine followed Natty into the kitchen.

'You don't have to stay with him, Nat. He'll sulk for a bit, but he'll get over it.'

'I want to spend time with him. Don't worry about it. Use this time to get your studying done, and I'll look after him. I might take him for a walk or something.'

Lorraine tilted her head, eyes slightly widening.

'Are you sure?'

Natty grinned.

'Wouldn't say it if I wasn't. Get set up, and I'll make you some of that green tea crap you like.'

'Oi, don't knock it. It's good for you.'

'Everything horrible is good for you.' Natty winked and busied himself with the kettle. When he'd made Lorraine's drink, he smiled at her, slapped his hands together, and walked into the living room.

'Right, I hope you're ready to get beat!'

Lorraine's eyes lingered on the spot Natty had disappeared from, a slight smile on her face. She shook her head, smiled a little wider, then returned to her laptop.

———

NATTY AND JADEN had three games on *Fifa*, with Natty winning one of the three. Jaden was putting in the time and was getting a lot better at the game, meaning Natty could play properly and didn't have to let him win anymore.

After playing, they got ready and headed to the park on Reginald Terrace. It always amazed Natty just how much the local area had changed. When he was younger, the park was far more haphazard, containing a rough concrete square where kids would play football. It was a battleground of broken glass, with the odd syringe. That had been scrubbed away, though. Now, there was a neat and well-kept park. It made Natty wonder what his life could have been like if he'd had a well-kept park when he was growing up. He glanced at Jaden, vowing to make sure Jaden's future was more positive than his.

Natty looked around the park some more. He'd heard rumours of several Chapeltown heavyweights banding together to pay for some of the development, but didn't know how true that was.

As Jaden ran around and exhausted himself, Natty watched from a bench, wishing he'd taken the cigarette he'd been offered earlier. He didn't like smoking around Jaden, and had warned him not to do it when he was older. It didn't stop him from wanting one now, though.

He thought about the moves he was making, and how things were going. With Warren out of the way, Little London was easy pickings, and the money they were making was a sign of that. That being said, he didn't feel he was moving quickly enough.

Thinking of the heavyweights of old made him anxious. Chapeltown had numerous legends that had the world at their feet; some had even reigned when they were younger than Natty. What made him more nervous was how few of those heavyweights lived to enjoy the life they'd forged. A couple had, but they were the exception to the rule. Only the truly elite had managed to cut and run at the right time.

Natty had a long way to go.

Eventually, Jaden wanted Natty to play with him, so they had to run around the park. It knackered Natty, and he was now happy he hadn't smoked earlier, meaning his lungs were clear for the unexpected exercise. Still, he liked seeing Jaden happy.

After a while, Jaden was ready to go, and Natty was ready to sleep forever. It struck him that he couldn't remember the last time he'd been to the gym. As they returned to the house, he placed his hand on Jaden's shoulder.

'Natty, can I ask you something?' Jaden looked uncharacteristically serious, and that drew his attention.

'Course, little man. What's up?'

'Do you know my dad?'

Natty glanced at him, tensing.

'I do.'

Jaden nodded.

'I don't know much about him, other than when he's come to the house, and that's mostly to see mummy. What's he like?'

Natty was tempted to let Jaden know the truth. He was an eight-year-old kid, though. He had all the time in the world to grow up and see how life really worked. Natty wanted to protect him, and also keep it real.

He settled for a safe response.

'I don't really know him that well.'

'Why doesn't he live with mummy and me?' Jaden kept up the questions. Natty stepped aside so a couple could walk by, the move giving him critical seconds to formulate his answers.

'It's just like that sometimes,' he finally mumbled. Jaden didn't respond, and Natty felt terrible. He was out of his depth and didn't know how to relate to the kid when he started asking about Raider.

'Look, J,' he continued, 'I get it. My dad died when I was young — not much older than you, actually. I'll always miss him, and it's tough even now with him not being here.'

'How did he die?' Jaden asked.

Natty had a flashback to his younger days, standing in a cemetery, staring at his father's headstone. His fists instinctively clenched, and he felt a wave of anger that he had to force away. Luckily, Jaden didn't notice.

'Let's play another game of *Fifa* when we get back. Bagsy PSG!' He said, and Jaden immediately forgot about the conversation in protest.

BACK HOME, Lorraine was still in the kitchen, poring over her laptop. Jaden kissed her on the cheek and then bounded back into the living room. Lorraine surveyed Natty.

'You look wiped out,' she said.

'Your son is better than any exercise bike,' he admitted. 'He's killing me.'

Lorraine laughed, closing the laptop.

'How's it going?' He asked.

Lorraine nodded. 'I've managed to focus, which is good. Still got a lot of work to do, so I hope I'm taking it all in.'

'You're the sharpest person I know,' said Natty. 'I know I've said it before, but I do think what you're doing is great. You're amazing.'

Eyes widening, Lorraine opened her mouth to speak, but they were interrupted by Jaden.

'C'mon, Nat! The teams are ready. You said we'd play!' He whined, pulling Natty toward the room.

'Duty calls,' said Natty. He made a crying face. 'If you're making coffee . . . mine is three sugars.'

When he left the room, Lorraine chuckled. She stood and added some water to the kettle. Switching it on, she stared straight ahead with a smile.

'Three sugars . . .' she repeated a moment later, realising how ridiculous the request was.

After playing, Natty made food for the three of them. Lorraine had finished her studying by now, and looked exhausted. Lorraine thanked him for cooking, and after eating, she went to make Jaden take a bath and get him ready for bed.

Natty made a few phone calls, checking in. Wonder had indeed done his drop-offs. Natty would need to speak with Elijah later and see if there were any further steps to take in the streets. On the other side, Spence was still handling the old crew. Natty didn't tell him he was with Lorraine, but was sure that Spence knew.

Lorraine collapsed on the sofa next to him, blowing out a breath. Despite her bedraggled state, she still looked gorgeous, and Natty felt the familiar stirrings. He tried his hardest not to put Lorraine in the category of a woman he just wanted to have sex with, but she made it incredibly difficult at times.

They sat quietly for a while, and the vibe was nice. He liked that she was comfortable enough just having him in the house around her son, and felt like he had earned it.

Natty cared about her and Jaden. It didn't make his feelings — if that's what they were — any less confusing.

'Tell me some more about your studying,' he said.

Lorraine smiled. 'What do you want to know?'

'You were saying last time that you were learning how to *code*. What does that mean?'

Lorraine gazed at him for a moment.

'It's software engineering.' Natty's face remained blank. 'Computer programming; the thing that makes that phone in your hand work.'

Natty looked slowly from the phone back to Lorraine, his mouth wide open. She continued.

'I like computers, and I want to learn to understand them, and parlay that into a job.'

'That's amazing.' Natty meant it. He had a laptop and tech devices like everyone else he knew, but he didn't know of anyone with a genuine interest in computers. He blinked, amazed at how her face had come alive when she talked about it.

'It really is. To most people, a laptop or a phone is just a thing to use, to do what they want with. With coding, the machine becomes a partner, working together on whatever venture they choose.'

Natty did his best to keep up, but when she started using words like *SQL* and *Python*, they turned his head to mush. He loved her passion, though; despite supporting her, it made him feel almost insecure. He'd never felt that passion for anything of substance, mainly just women and trying to look good. He did not doubt that Lorraine would achieve her dreams, but he had to wonder what his own were.

Natty recalled some time back, when Lorraine had asked him what he wanted from life. He'd been unable to answer then, and he wasn't sure that he had the answer even now.

'Thank you for looking after Jaden,' Lorraine said, pulling him from his thoughts. 'And for cooking. You didn't have to.'

'Jaden's my little guy,' he replied, not using the word *soldier* anymore. 'I love spending time with him.' Remembering their trip to the park, he asked her, 'does Jaden ever mention Raider?'

Lorraine sat up.

'Why?'

'He was asking me about him today. Wanted to know if I knew him, and what he was like.'

'What did you say?'

'I said I didn't know him so well.'

Lorraine seemed satisfied with that. She sighed, wiping her hair from her eyes.

'He used to ask about him when he was younger, but not so much anymore. I try to avoid it. When he's older, it's going to be so awkward if he wants to know where things went wrong.'

Natty shook his head. 'You've raised him properly. When he's older, he's only going to remember just who was there for him.'

Lorraine gave Natty a sad smile, snuggling close to him.

'You're there for him too, Nat, and I really do appreciate it.'

The pair shared a light, almost chaste kiss, then watched television in comfortable silence, with no more conversation needed.

CHAPTER NINETEEN

A FEW DAYS after spending time with Jaden, Natty was drawn back to the park. He sat on a bench, smoking a cigarette, thinking about life and what his future might hold. He didn't know what it was about the park that made him so introspective, but he enjoyed the insight it helped to unlock.

Natty was making more money, essentially running Little London, but it wasn't his. He didn't have anything of his own, feeling chafed under the rule of others. Natty saw how seriously Spence took his investing, Lorraine's passion for software development. He wanted something of his own.

The major problem was that all Natty knew was crime. Even as a child, being a gangster on the streets was his biggest dream and outside of hustling, he didn't know how to define himself.

Natty was tempted to approach Rudy, but wasn't sure what he would say to him. Instead, he contacted Elijah and arranged for the two to talk.

———

'WHAT'S UP THEN?' Elijah asked, shaking hands with Natty as he climbed into Elijah's BMW. 'Do you wanna go somewhere?'

'Here is cool,' replied Natty, formulating his words. 'I've been thinking lately that I want more, and I thought you'd be a good person to speak to. You mentioned before that I should go out on my own.'

'More what? Money?'

'I want something of my own. Guess I'm wondering how you managed to establish yourself. You're with me in Little London, but you have your own thing too.'

Elijah nodded, scratching his chin.

'It wasn't easy. I saw how the people that came before us did it, and I tried to learn from their mistakes. What is it that you actually want?'

'More,' replied Natty.

———

A FEW DAYS LATER, Natty went shopping with Cameron, watching as his friend went from shop to shop, burning money.

'Where'd you get so much money from?' Natty asked. He knew what Cameron earned selling drugs, but he'd spent thousands without batting an eyelid.

'Don't worry about that. I've been saving.' Cameron gripped a shopping bag containing the new designer trainers he'd just bought, along with several other bags.

'Saving?' Natty frowned.

'Yes. Saving. Why aren't you buying anything? You're paid now. Treat yourself.'

Natty shook his head. 'I don't need anything.'

Cameron sniggered.

'Bro, you're a boss, and you're not even stepping your game up. Buy a watch or something. Look at what you're wearing; my clothes and trainers are more expensive than yours.'

Natty took the taunting in his stride. Once upon a time, he'd have bitten, and bought something expensive just to shut Cameron up, but he didn't need to.

They went to a Japanese restaurant for lunch. After they placed their orders, Natty turned to Cameron.

'I'll pay,' he said. Cameron smirked.

'Oh, so you actually bought your bank card then?' He joked.

Cameron devoured the food like he was dying, likely because Natty was paying. When they finished eating, Natty paid for the meal. The pair stood.

'I've gotta shoot off,' said Cameron. 'Are you gonna look for anything?'

Natty looked past him, noting someone with a laptop bag being shown to a seat.

'Yeah. There's one more place I need to go.'

After saying his goodbyes, he headed off in the direction of the nearest Apple shop.

———

ANIKA STEPPED OUT OF AN UBER, looking behind her before she entered Cameron's garden. He let her in and made them both drinks, just like last time. He popped a pill and washed it down, but didn't offer her one.

'I was chilling with your hubby the other day,' he said.

Anika shrugged.

'You're friends. Of course you were chilling,' she said. She didn't want to talk about Spence when she was with Cameron. Their argument about the girl he wanted to hang out with still irritated her, but she'd done her best to let it go.

'We don't really chill one-on-one anymore,' said Cameron. 'I heard about your little talk.'

'I don't want to talk about it,' said Anika.

Cameron sipped his drink. 'Fine. Rosie's harmless, anyway.'

'How do you know?' Anika's eyes narrowed.

'I've been around them before. Lorraine and Natty are always eyefucking and sliding around each other. Rosie is always sniffing after Spence, but he never did anything.'

'Seriously?' Anika didn't like the sound of this, and it added credence to her initial response. Spence wanted to spend time with a woman who clearly wanted him, but she didn't know how he felt about her. 'Do you think she'd try something?'

'Fuck knows. Look.' Cameron took out his phone and loaded Rosie's page on Instagram.

Anika's stomach twisted when she looked at the woman. She was beautiful and clearly energetic. Her page was full of affirmations, and numerous photos of her out with friends, even a few of Lorraine, who Anika had always thought was stunning. She didn't understand why Natty wouldn't date her, but admitted there were bits about the situation that she wasn't privy to.

'She's pretty,' she said through clenched teeth. Cameron slyly smiled.

'I can't believe you're jealous, even though you've been banging me . . .'

'Fuck you, Cam.'

'Fuck you right back. Don't get mad because I'm right. Is that why you're here now? Revenge?'

'I'm here because . . .' Anika trailed off.

'It doesn't even matter. I'm proud of Spence, though. We don't always click, but I'm glad he stood up to you.'

Anika cut her eyes to Cameron. 'You don't think it's a little fucked up that this girl wants to hang out with him?'

'I think it's a little fucked up that he thought he had to tell you. He has his own life, and shouldn't need to check in with you all the time. I'm always telling him this, so deep down, maybe he's listening.'

Anika didn't like what she was hearing, and disliked that Cameron wasn't taking her seriously. He seemed to find the whole thing a joke, which she supposed was because he was getting what he wanted from the situation. He had co-opted her and seduced her. Now, he had her here, and he hadn't even had to try. She wondered if she could even trust the things he was saying, or if he was trying to manipulate her and keep her divided.

'You're a piece of shit. I don't even know why I'm here.'

'You're here because you like getting fucked, and you want to do it again. Stop trying to front and overthink it.' Cameron smirked.

Anika scoffed. 'You're so cocky.'

'Cockiness has nothing to do with it, Nika. We have a connection, and we're both here. Doesn't matter what Spence does in the end, if you're here with me. You must see that.'

Anika turned away, sipping her drink. She tensed when she felt Cameron standing behind her. He squeezed her shoulders, rubbing at the nape of her neck, and though she didn't want to do it, Anika leaned into his touch, feeling the security she craved.

'Nika, I know that things are fucked, and I know you're confused, but I'm glad you're here with me. Even if we don't do anything else and hang out like this, I'm good.'

'You mean that?' Anika looked up at him, shocked at what he was saying.

Cameron nodded.

'I do what I do, but there aren't many girls I know that I can just chill with like this.'

'You say that, but things never worked out with us,' said Anika, trying to believe in what Cameron was saying, despite what her gut screamed at her.

'People change. We were young, and you remember what it was like back then. Everyone and everything was wild. I was a kid on a money mission, and then I had this girl I didn't know what to do with.'

'You let me go.'

'Yeah. And you went, so don't act like it was all some one-way shit. We had something, and then we didn't, and we moved on, but that doesn't mean there aren't still feelings involved.' Cameron kept up his massaging. Anika closed her eyes.

'And for you, those feelings go beyond sex?'

'Where do they go for you? Don't forget, you're the one that's fucking my boy.'

'I'm in a relationship with Spence.'

'Yes, you are, but you're with me. Like I said, this thing between us, it's 50-50. Maybe you need to believe otherwise to alleviate that guilt you're probably feeling, but that's on you.' Giving her one last rub, Cameron sat down.

Anika didn't respond. The truth was that Cameron was right. She was here with him despite knowing she shouldn't be. Despite how awful she felt, being with Cameron was the only time she felt at least a little whole. They had never gotten over one another, and those feelings had influenced her relationship with Spence. She figured that was why she couldn't settle into the relationship, and why his attempts to get closer to her only seemed to make her more distant.

She went to sit with Cameron, and gripped his face, kissing him tightly. Cameron made no attempt to resist. He deepened the kiss, and before long, she was trailing behind Cameron, holding his hand as he led her up the stairs.

———

SPENCE SAT in Rosie's place, surveying the room as always. She lived in Oakwood, having grown up in Moor Allerton, despite having connections in the Hood.

Spence was especially fond of Rosie's living room. Her home, in general, had a comfortable feel, reeking of independence. She had a walnut Bornholm coffee table, various bookshelves, and a yoga mat in the corner of the room. Fresh white oriental lilies rested on the table, and the smoke grey sofas were adorned with throw pillows.

Sipping his drink, Spence delved into his thoughts. He and Anika remained up and down. After their argument, things had picked up for a few weeks, and Anika had seemed more engaged. Gradually, she became withdrawn again, and his attempts to discuss it with her had been rebuffed.

As Spence had left to go to Rosie's, Anika had been dressed to go out, wearing a short grey dress and high heels, her face heavily made up. She was meeting her friend Carmen and going somewhere, but Spence hadn't asked questions.

Rosie crossed her legs on the sofa nearby, sipping a glass of white wine.

'Even now, you always seem nervous around me,' she remarked.

Spence smiled, shaking his head.

'I have a few things I'm mentally trying to work out.'

'Anika?' Rosie asked.

'Sort of. We argued a while back about me wanting to spend time with you.'

'You spoke to her about it?'

'She came in the room when you messaged me, and I didn't have anything to hide, so I told her then. It didn't go too well at first,' said Spence.

'Why? You and I are just friends, right?' Rosie met his eyes. Spence fought to maintain his composure under her intense gaze. It was a habit of hers.

'I used to like you, so I guess that came across when I was talking to her.'

Rosie's eyes widened.

'When did you like me?'

'I liked you for years,' he admitted.

'Why didn't you say anything?'

Spence shrugged. 'You were never available, and after a while, I just stopped watching. After that, I fell for Anika.' Even after the brief conversation, he felt much better. Talking about what was on his mind was good for clearing his headspace, and Rosie was a good listener.

Rosie sighed. 'I guess I can understand that. I want to be friends, but sometimes I wonder if we're more than that.' Again, her eyes surveyed him. 'I think if we're being honest, there's something more here.'

The pair locked eyes. Without breaking eye contact, Rosie shifted closer to Spence. His heart pounded, and he fought to keep his expression neutral.

'It's not fair that we missed one another,' Rosie whispered. Spence's heart felt like it would burst from his chest, temptation surging throughout his body. Rosie smelled as wonderful as always, seeming even sexier and more alluring in her space. Spence's mouth was dry, and he yearned for her in a way he knew was wrong. With a deep breath, he pulled back.

'It's not fair, but it's the way it is,' he said, thankful that his words sounded firm. Rosie nodded, giving him a small smile.

'Let me get you another drink,' she said, grabbing his glass and sashaying to the kitchen as Spence let out a deep sigh of relief.

CHAPTER TWENTY

NATTY DROVE into Little London to get an update on the latest figures, reflecting on the brief conversation he'd shared with Elijah. Elijah hadn't given him much, other than stating he'd just gone for it, something Natty was thinking about more and more in his free time.

He didn't know how his uncle would take it, nor Rudy, but the idea of having something of his own fuelled him, and he felt it would be worth making less money short term, to properly benefit long term.

Natty knew what he wanted and knew who he'd take with him.

At the same time, there was always the possibility that his uncle wouldn't allow him to walk away, and if he did, that he wouldn't let people go with him. If he did that, Natty wouldn't be able to fight it. He didn't have the power to go up against the whole organisation, and the murder of Warren and his associates was a gruesome reminder that his uncle played for keeps.

Pulling up outside the main spot, he tensed when he saw Raider standing outside, talking with one of Elijah's people.

Immediately, they exchanged hard glares as Natty climbed from the car. He felt his fists clench and saw Raider's jaw reciprocate. The man he'd been talking to looked between them in alarm, giving Natty a tentative nod. Raider was physically imposing, and as much as Natty disliked him, he couldn't doubt this. Despite being an inch or two shorter than Natty, he was broader, with sharp features and a thick neck and shoulders. He wore a black coat, jeans, and high-top trainers.

'Elijah's doing well around here,' he said as Natty grew closer. Natty ignored the slight.

'I didn't know he'd given you permission to come around here,' he replied, watching Raider's face contort and twist with anger.

'You're lucky you're useful, Dunn. Keep running your mouth, though, and we'll see what happens. How's my girl? People tell me you're still sniffing around her, even after all these years.'

It was Natty's turn to react. He had expected it, but he still didn't like Raider bringing up Lorraine.

'Are *people* also telling you about the son you abandoned?'

The man Raider had been talking to, shook his head, walking away. He headed indoors as quickly as possible, away from the storm. Raider took a step towards Natty, his features hardening. Natty held his ground.

'You shouldn't talk about things you don't understand. Lorraine talks shit, and whatever you've heard, doesn't make it your business. Understand?'

'I understand that you're a deadbeat. Do you even know when your son's birthday is?' He interjected as Raider opened his mouth. 'You can come with all the big talk you want, but at the end of the day, you're a joke, and you always will be.'

Raider grabbed for Natty, and the pair tussled. Before they could get into it, several workers hurried outside to separate them. Not resisting, Natty headed inside with a smile as a fuming Raider left, feeling he'd won the exchange. He'd wanted to fight, but getting under his skin was the next best thing.

'Are you okay?' One of the workers asked, having followed Natty inside. They heard the distant sounds of tire screeches as a car drove away.

Natty headed to the fridge to get a bottle of Ribena. He turned, looking out to the room, noting that all eyes were on him. Opening the drink, he took a long swig.

'Ahhhh . . . refreshing.' He wiped his mouth on his sleeve and smiled, before finally replying to the worker, 'I couldn't be better. Now, tell me how much money we're making.'

LATER THAT NIGHT, Spence came to Natty's house. He handed him an envelope with the latest takings, and accepted the drink Natty gave him.

'Any issues?' Natty asked, as they sat outside.

'Not on my end. I was going to ask you the same thing.'

'What do you mean?'

'Everyone's talking about you and Raider getting into it. Was that smart?'

Natty snorted.

'He sought me out, not the other way around. I'm not gonna let him punk me out.'

'Is that what it's about?' Spence asked. Natty frowned.

'What do you mean?'

'I mean that you both have Lorraine and Jaden in common, and it's clear that's the problem. You said there's nothing between you and Lorraine, though, so you need to avoid becoming entangled. Fighting over a woman that isn't yours . . . that's not practical, fam.'

Natty stared down Spence.

'The shit with Raider is deeper than that. We've never gotten along, and he's not even supposed to be down with our thing.'

Spence nodded. 'I understand it's personal, but you need to rise above that, and you know it. You're killing it with everything you're doing now, and that should be your focus.'

Natty grinned, his mood improving. Spence loved to lecture him, but Natty never doubted it was coming from a place of love. The pair touched fists, finishing their drinks in silence. Natty appreciated the warning, but the streets were torrid at the best of times. The success simply didn't mean much if people didn't respect him. He was making more money, but was still seen as a little guy to people. No matter what, he would change that perception.

'What's on your mind?' Spence asked. 'You've been quiet lately.'

'I've been thinking about my future. Lately, I've kinda wanted to branch out and do my own thing.'

Spence's eyes widened in surprise.

'I wasn't expecting that. What's brought that on?'

'Everyone keeps telling me that I'm killing it in Little London. I got myself out there, built alliances, and got people working together, but ultimately, it hasn't got me anywhere. I figured my unc would do something else with me, maybe bump me up to a new position, but he hasn't. Seems he's happy to keep me at this level, but I'm not happy being here.'

'You've definitely been giving it some thought then,' said Spence, nodding his head in approval. After hearing about the exchange with Raider, he'd been worried, but Natty was definitely in a different place. When Natty was locked onto something, he found a way to make it happen.

'I have. I'd want you there alongside me. Me, you and Cam, working this thing by ourselves, with more money and responsibility in the long term.'

'Do you think that could work?'

Natty nodded. 'We clash, but we balance one another out. We always have.'

Spence patted him on the shoulder.

'I'm with you, Nat.'

Natty grinned, shocked at his friend putting it out like that.

'Really?'

'Course. I think you can do it, and if there's a proper plan in place, then I'm in. I can't speak for Cam, but I can't see him saying no either.'

Natty's grin widened. Spence's endorsement meant a lot. He was a serious thinker, and the fact he'd committed so quickly was a sign to Natty that his plan was fruitful.

'I'm glad to hear that. I'll keep you updated. There's a lot I still need to consider. Other than business, how are things with you?'

Spence scratched his eyelid, blowing out a breath.

'Rosie,' was all he said in reply. Natty chuckled.

'What happened?'

'We were chilling together, and there was a moment.'

'What did you do?'

'Nothing,' Spence quickly said, running through the situation, and the talk they'd had on her sofa. When he finished, Natty again chuckled.

'It's a messy situation, but you didn't do anything wrong. Sounds like you resisted her basically laying out for you what she wanted to happen.'

Spence nodded, his shoulders sagging. 'It was one of the hardest things I've ever done, Nat. Things with Rosie are easy. We clicked, and it seemed like she was saying she liked me too.'

'And Anika? Are things easy with her?'

Spence lowered his head. 'We're like strangers sometimes. She goes out a lot nowadays. Says she doesn't like being home by herself.'

Natty's eyes narrowed, not liking what he was hearing.

'Where does she go?'

'I don't know,' said Spence. 'I'm guessing she goes to Carmen's, as she's always getting dressed up. Carmen is her usual partner for going clubbing.'

Natty didn't respond, mulling over what Spence had said, his uneasy feeling growing. He didn't know much about Carmen, but knew she was engaged and lived with her fiancé. He didn't understand why Anika would get dolled up to hang out with them, but he intended to find out.

———

AFTER HIS CONVERSATION WITH SPENCE, Natty found himself mulling over Spence's relationship with Anika. He wasn't surprised Spence had told her about Rosie, but something about her reaction, and the behaviour Spence described, worried him. The more he thought about it, the more he reached a horrible conclusion. She seemed to be judging him by a standard that wasn't appropriate for Spence. He loved Anika and had been nothing but loyal.

Maybe she was judging him by her own standard.

Natty didn't think this lightly, but Spence had commented on her growing distance. He remembered her strange words to him when he'd gone looking for Spence; she'd enquired whether he was happy, and even now, he still thought it was a random question to ask.

It was apparent to Natty that she had checked out of the relationship. The only thing to consider now was what to do about it.

Natty had several options. He could speak with Spence, share his feelings, and allow his friend to talk it out with his partner. Or, he could confront Anika himself.

Natty knew which option he would pick. He felt he and Anika were long overdue a conversation. Even though her past with Cameron hadn't gone anywhere, it had somewhat sullied her in his eyes, especially when she'd never mentioned to Spence that she had been involved with one of his closest friends. He'd given her the benefit of the doubt in the past because Spence seemed happy, but now that was no longer the case, and all bets were off.

With this in mind, Natty grabbed his keys and left the house. He drove to Spence's place, knowing his friend was working, wanting to catch Anika alone.

The area was relatively quiet, with a few of Spence's neighbours pottering around. They recognised Natty, greeting him with warm smiles that he returned. Spence was good to his neighbours, especially the older ones. He'd help them with shopping and take in parcels on their behalf if he was home. He always had a kind word for them, and they loved him. Natty wasn't sure Anika inspired such loyalty.

Knocking hard on the door, Natty waited for her to answer. When he received no response, he waited almost a minute before trying again. Still no response.

'She's not in.'

Natty almost jumped at the sound of the voice. Spence's neighbour directly opposite was a middle-aged woman. She was on the heavy side, and had a kind, moon-shaped face.

'Excuse me?'

'Anika isn't in. Neither is Spence, but Anika left a short while ago,' said the neighbour.

'Do you know where she went?'

'I don't, I'm sorry. Looked dressed up, though. I assumed she was going to see some friends.'

Or she was going to see someone else, Natty thought darkly, his desire to confront Anika growing.

'Thanks.' He gave the woman a slight smile that he knew hadn't reached his eyes.

'Do you want me to tell them you stopped by?'

Natty thought for a moment longer than he needed to.

'No,' he replied. 'It's not important.'

———

WHEN NATTY RETURNED HOME, he trawled over Anika's social media accounts, but couldn't find any clue where she was. He knew a few of her friends, but their online profiles were equally bereft of information.

Slumping back on the sofa, he rubbed his forehead, wondering again if he should try speaking to Spence. He dismissed this. There was the possibility Spence would react badly if he accused Anika of cheating on him, especially without tangible proof. Despite her supposed faults, Spence loved her and wanted to build a life with her. That counted for a lot.

He called Cameron, wondering if he could share some insight, but his phone was off.

Closing his eyes, Natty soon dozed off, exhausted from the day.

———

PUSHING his worries about Spence and Anika to one side, Natty drove to see his mum the next day, already wary about how the conversation would go. Since their argument a while back, he'd stopped in on her sparingly, mainly at the behest of Rudy, who constantly insisted that his mum loved him and looked forward to his visits. She never showed that to Natty, though. Things between them had never been as straightforward as Rudy would have liked.

When Natty entered, his mum was sat in the living room, *Judge Judy* on the television. She glanced up when she saw Natty, her face noncommittal. Approaching, he gave her a light kiss on the cheek and sat next to her.

'How are you doing?'

'My hip hurts,' she responded.

'Is there anything I can do?' He asked. Rudy hadn't said anything about her hip the last time they'd spoken.

'No. I probably just slept on it funny. Don't need a big fuss made. How are you doing?'

'I'm doing well,' replied Natty. His mum scrutinised his appearance.

'You look well,' she agreed, the words bereft of joy. She almost sounded annoyed.

'Yep, things are good right now,' replied Natty, skipping past her demeanour. She folded her arms, staring at the screen. Natty didn't doubt she'd likely seen the same episode dozens of times. After all, she'd been watching the show since Natty was a child.

'That's good. Rudy still treating you well?'

'He is,' replied Natty.

'Do you want some tea?'

'Sure.'

Soon, he sipped the steaming tea. It was slightly watery, but he didn't comment.

'Make sure Rudy treats you right,' his mum said, as if they were mid-conversation. Natty wasn't sure how to take the comment, seeing as his mum was in a relationship with Rudy.

'I will.'

His mum sipped her tea, still eyeing him.

'He mentioned you had a girlfriend.'

Natty's stomach lurched, and he sipped the weak tea to distract himself.

'She's not my girlfriend,' he finally said. His mum nodded.

'Good. You shouldn't be raising some other man's kid.'

Natty felt the words needling away at him, which he was sure was his mum's intent. Pushing away his irritation, he responded.

'Is that how Rudy feels about me? You two are together, after all.'

The words had the effect he wanted. His mum gave a start, spilling some of her drink and cursing, hastening to clear the mess. Her eyes bore into Natty's, her demeanour unfriendly.

'You're a grown man,' she snapped. 'Rudy respects that, and our relationship is none of your business.'

'That goes both ways.'

Her mouth pursed.

'Watch how you speak to me.'

Shrugging, Natty again sipped his drink, eyes now on the television. The judge was laying into some poor fool, and he watched with a smile, appreciating the fact he'd survived a tongue lashing from his mum without snapping.

'Are you hungry?' His mum eventually asked. 'I'll make you something.'

'I could eat. Are you sure you can manage with your hip and all?'

'I'll be fine,' she responded, though Natty was sure that her limp on the way to the kitchen was for his benefit. He placed his empty cup on the coffee table, grinning as he hummed a tune.

———

THAT EVENING, Anika was in her living room, sipping wine and staring at her phone, ignoring the television playing in the background. A sharp knock at the door startled her, and she hastened to answer, her eyebrows raised when she saw Natty standing there.

'Hey Nat, are you looking for Spence? He's not here.' She smiled at him, startled when he didn't return it.

'Oh. I must have missed him,' he said. 'Sorry for disturbing you.'

'It's fine. I wasn't up to much. How have you been?'

'I'm good. What about you? Are you *happy?*'

The way Natty phrased his second question made Anika's insides turn to ice. Something was going on here, and she wasn't sure what it was. She wondered if Cameron had spoken to Natty about them, but couldn't think why he would.

'Why are you asking me that?'

'I'm just taking an interest,' said Natty blandly. 'After all, you're with one of my best friends. I want to make sure everything is good between you.'

Anika flinched. Natty zeroed in on this, surer than ever that something was going down.

'I'm fine, Nat. You just surprised me, that's all. Spence and I are busy all the time, and I guess that leads to stress. I am happy, though,' she insisted, heart hammering as Natty continued to survey her. Finally, he smiled, and she felt herself relaxing.

'Good to hear, love. I'll catch Spence later. Run a bath or something; keep those stress levels down.'

Anika returned his smile, though she still felt uneasy.

'I think I'll do that.'

———

CAMERON HESITATED. He stood on a street, looking at a house, taking deep breaths, trying to psych himself up. Rudy had again reached out, offering Cameron the chance to improve his standing by eliminating a problem. It was a clear test, and he felt the nerves settling in despite being eager to take it at the time.

After a minute, Cameron glanced around, checking no one was watching. He'd dressed in all black to blend in with the night. Finally, he entered the garden and knocked on the door.

Christian answered, warily staring out at Cameron. Cameron gave him a small smile. After the beating he'd given Christian and his girl, he'd collected from him again afterwards with no problems.

That was then, and this was now. Christian had messed up big time.

'Are you gonna let me in? You don't want your neighbours to hear our chat, right?' said Cameron. Christian swallowed, then nodded. The living room was unchanged from the last time Cameron had visited. An Xbox One controller rested on the sofa — the video game Christian had been playing currently paused.

Christian remained on his feet, surveying Cameron.

'Do you want a drink?'

Cameron shook his head. He felt calmer than he had outside. Something about Christian's nervousness relaxed him.

'I'm good. How have you been?'

Christian's eyebrow rose.

'Why are you asking me that?'

'We used to be cool before that bullshit you pulled. You paid for it, so no reason for me to hold a grudge,' he replied.

'I'm fine.'

'How's your girl?'

Christian scowled, folding his arms.

'We're on a break. She cheated on me.'

Cameron couldn't hide his smirk. Christian noticed.

'It's not funny, mate. I did everything for her, and she violated.'

'It happens. You can't trust women. Next time, you'll know to pick better.' Cameron's thoughts shifted to Anika for a moment. He didn't know what was happening with them, or what he wanted to happen. 'Anyway, how's business?'

'It's picking up. I've kept my head down, staying out of the mix.'

Cameron scratched his chin.

'Yeah?'

'Yeah,' replied Christian. 'I've just been stacking my money. I wanna get out of Leeds as soon as I can.'

Cameron didn't speak for a moment. He cleared his throat.

'You know what, I will have a drink after all.'

'What do you want?'

'Cup of tea. Milk and four sugars.'

Christian headed to the kitchen. Cameron could hear him pottering around, grabbing a cup. He took another deep breath, pulling out a gun, keeping it by his side. Christian had his back to Cameron, humming a tune. Cameron stepped towards him.

He must have been noisier than he thought, because Christian turned, eyes widening when he saw Cameron. He flung the cup at him, and despite Cameron avoiding the object, it allowed Christian to charge, slapping the gun from his hand. Christian dove for it, but Cameron kicked him in the side, then punched him twice, his fist crashing against the side of Christian's head. Despite clearly being stunned, Christian let out a roar and charged Cameron, slamming him into a nearby table. They fell to the floor, Christian mounting Cameron, hitting him twice. Cameron rolled over, overpowering Christian, hands wrapping around his throat. His teeth gritted, watching him attempt to break free. Tighter, he squeezed, wanting it to end.

Christian attempted to claw Cameron's face, trying to break free, but he held on tightly, feeling Christian's strength fade. After a few more seconds, he let go, crawling for the gun. Clambering to his feet, he pointed the gun at Christian's head, hesitating for only a moment before pulling the trigger three times.

Glancing at the dead body for only a moment, Cameron hurried from the house, gun by his side. He kept his head down, striding down the road, taking a left onto the street where he'd parked a stolen getaway car. Climbing in, he drove away at moderate speed.

After five minutes, he stopped the car, opened the door, and threw up.

When he was finished, he carried on driving.

———

CAMERON DIDN'T REPORT for work the next day. He told Spence he didn't feel well, and spent the day drinking alone, thinking about what he'd done.

Cameron was a career criminal and had sold drugs for longer than he could remember. He'd beaten people up, threatened them, and committed numerous robberies.

He'd never killed anyone. Until now.

In the past, he'd talked with Natty, bragging that he would have the guts to pull the trigger and feel nothing, but he'd lied to himself, because he'd struggled to sleep last night, seeing Christian's lifeless body. He wondered how Christian's ex would react to the killing; whether she would care, or regret cheating on him.

Snorting a line of cocaine, Cameron tried centring his thoughts. He'd stepped up and done the job, and Rudy had paid him well for it. No one else would know what he had done, and he had shown the higher-ups that he could be trusted to do the job. It didn't matter that he'd failed to sneak up on Christian, nor did it matter he had lost his weapon. The job was done, and he would eventually get over the feeling of wrongness permeating his body.

Pulling out his phone, Cameron debated trying Anika. After a few seconds, he scrolled further down his contacts list, calling another woman instead.

CHAPTER TWENTY-ONE

ON THE DAY of Jaden's tenth birthday, Natty straightened himself and knocked at the door, before walking in, ready to join the after-party — if a child ever needed such a thing. Natty had skipped the first part of Jaden's birthday, not fancying being surrounded by screaming kids in public.

When Natty entered the living room, he saw people milled around, before something slammed into his legs, making him stumble.

'Natty! You're here.' Jaden's eyes shone as he looked up at Natty. Natty lifted him off the ground with one arm, feigning a groan.

'I can barely lift you. You're gonna be bigger than me soon,' he joked.

'Really?' said Jaden, continuing before Natty could speak. 'What did you get me for my birthday?'

'Jaden!' Lorraine scolded him, having approached.

'Here. This is for you.' Natty set him down and handed him a carrier bag. As Jaden thanked him and fawned over the trainers and tracksuit, Natty said his hellos to the others in the room. Lorraine grinned at him, shaking her head.

'You spoil him,' she said, giving Natty a brief hug. Natty clutched her tightly, happy to see her smiling.

'He deserves it. He's the best kid in the world,' said Natty, watching Jaden showing off his new clothes to several of his cousins in attendance.

'What else did you get him?' Lorraine noticed Natty still held a bag. 'You've already given him enough.'

Natty smiled, his stomach fluttering.

'This is for you. Come with me.'

Natty led Lorraine to the kitchen. It looked like a bomb site, with children's coats strewn over the kitchen table and surrounding chairs. Numerous half-full juice glasses were on the kitchen counter, along with several unfinished packets of crisps.

Lorraine faced Natty, her eyes on the bag. Steeling himself against his nerves, Natty handed it to her. Keeping eye contact with him now, Lorraine opened it, eyebrow raised. When she saw what was within, her mouth fell open.

'You . . .' She shook her head, looking down at the brand new MacBook Pro, then back to Natty.

'The dude in the Apple shop said it was the best model,' Natty mumbled, pleased his voice hadn't cracked. 'Said you can easily install coding software, and that it's got some chip that makes it super-fast.'

'I can't believe you did this . . . why?' Lorraine remained at a loss for words. Natty rubbed the back of his head.

'You said a while back that yours was slow . . . I wanted to help so you could study,' he said, his face warm.

'I can't believe you,' Lorraine replied, hugging him. Natty again held her tightly.

'Are you sure? They're so expensive . . . I shouldn't take it,' she said weakly. Natty waved off the protests, noting a tear in Lorraine's eye. He glanced away.

'You're gonna take it, and you're gonna keep working hard, because it's going to pay off,' he said.

Lorraine nodded. Wiping her eyes, she composed herself, then took the MacBook and left the kitchen.

Natty waited another minute, buoyed that she'd liked his gift. By the time he left the kitchen, the MacBook had vanished, and Lorraine was talking to another woman. She was smiling widely and gesturing in the direction of the kitchen. Natty leant against the doorframe, grinning. Lorraine and her friend glanced over, Lorraine and Natty sharing another moment, the friend looking between them.

Natty spoke with a few more people, his eyes never straying far from Jaden and Lorraine.

His thoughts were interrupted by Lorraine's mum approaching. She wore a small smile, but her eyes were hard as she surveyed him.

'It's good to see you, Nathaniel. Jaden was worried you wouldn't show,' she said.

'I'd never let Jaden down like that,' Natty replied. The woman nodded, glancing in her grandson's direction a moment.

'I hope not.'

Natty didn't respond, used to her blunt ways after the years he'd known her. When he first started hanging around Lorraine, she'd hated him, thinking he was a bad influence. He couldn't say for sure what she thought of him now, but figured it was more positive. Natty had nothing but respect for her. She was tough, rarely minced words, and despite several hardships, had eventually carved out a successful catering business.

'It's good you came with presents too. He seems to like your taste.'

'We've been shopping before,' said Natty. 'He's not shy about telling me what he likes.'

'My daughter trusts you.'

Natty waited for her to continue, but she didn't. Without another word, she left. Lorraine glanced from her retreating mother to him, likely wondering what they'd been talking about. Natty gave her a small smile and kept it moving. After they cut the cake, he hugged a corner, happy to watch the proceedings as he scarfed down the chocolate sponge.

'Nat, good to see you, bro.' Lorraine's older brother Tommy approached. The pair slapped hands. He'd known Tommy longer than he had known Lorraine. At one point, Tommy had been knee-deep in the streets, but after a few prison sentences, he'd slowed down and seen the writing on the wall. Nowadays, he co-owned a local gym, and also held workout sessions for all groups in Potternewton Park.

'You too. Your kids are getting big,' said Natty, nodding to Tommy's children, running around after Jaden.

'Can I have a chat?'

Natty's eyebrow arched. Tommy's tone was oddly serious. Nonetheless, he nodded, and they went to stand outside.

They stood in silence for almost a minute. Natty surveyed Tommy. His jaw was tight, but he had his hands in the pockets of his jeans. Taking a pack of cigarettes from his pocket, he offered one to Tommy, who shook his head.

Tommy was old school and a proponent of the old school dress code. He refused to wear skinny or slim jeans, and tended to wear baggier clothing. Nonetheless, he had the build of a man who took his weight training seriously, similar to how Natty used to. He and Lorraine didn't look alike other than their colouring. Tommy's features were harsher, his nose and lips broader.

'I'll get right to it. What's going on with you and my sister?'

'We're cool,' Natty replied, confused by the question. He and Tommy had been friends back in the day, and other than threatening to kill him if he ever hurt his sister, they'd never discussed his and Lorraine's involvement. Tommy shook his head.

'I'm not an idiot, Natty. I was in the room before. You two are closer than cool. I've seen the way you look at each other.'

'What are you trying to say, Tom? Whatever it is, talk your talk.'

'Fine. Jaden's getting big now. You've seen him in there, running around with his family. Soon, he's gonna be grown, and he needs some structure. That means you and my sister need to be honest about what you both want.'

'What if I just wanted to screw your sis? Would that be okay?' Natty replied, annoyed by the conversation. Whatever was going on with him and Lorraine — and he still didn't know what that was — it wasn't any of Tommy's business. Tommy sized him up for a long moment, and Natty wondered if he was going to swing. Despite Tommy's reputation back in the day, he was sure he could take him if it came to it.

Silently, Tommy continued to stare him down. He held out his hand, and after a moment, Natty offered him the cigarette he'd turned down earlier. Lighting it, Tommy took a long drag, exhaling before he responded.

'Jaden looks up to you. He talks about you all the time. He wants to be just like you, and I don't think you'd be putting in the hours playing with him and taking him places, if all you wanted was to grind my sister. Fact is, Jaden needs a father figure he can look up to.'

Natty respected Tommy's approach, but the whole conversation made him nervous. He wasn't sure he was ready to tackle it, but it kept surfacing in his mind.

He knew he couldn't avoid it forever.

'It's not that simple,' he replied, his stomach lurching.

'Make it simple.'

The air around the pair seemed to cool, and Natty's eyes narrowed, not liking Tommy's tone.

'Don't threaten me.'

Tommy shook his head, taking another deep burn of the cigarette.

'I walked that same path you're on, Nat. Never forget that. The world is bigger than these streets, though, and I'm speaking to you as a man — one I think is good enough for my sister.'

Another silence ensued, but it differed from the others. There was a newfound respect between the pair, who shared a long look, clearly understanding where the other was coming from.

'Am I too late for the party?'

Both men whirled around, and Natty's hands immediately balled into fists. Raider stood there, a bag in his hand. His eyes locked onto Natty, who awaited Raider making the first move. Instead, Raider greeted Tommy, then walked by without acknowledging Natty. As he entered the house, Natty and Tommy glanced at one another again.

'Did you know he was coming?'

'I knew he was invited. I don't think he replied to Lorraine, though,' said Tommy, staring at the door Raider had just walked through. They headed inside, expecting to hear some shouting, or an argument. Instead, Jaden was talking with Raider, smiling as he stared at the present his dad had bought him.

'Thank you,' he said, holding up another pair of trainers — expensive Jordan 4's.

'You're welcome, J. Sorry I couldn't get here earlier, but look how big you're getting! You're almost a proper man.'

Natty grit his teeth, Raider's words almost echoing his own from earlier. The longer he watched them spending time together, the more jealous he grew. Raider could turn up out of the blue and get all of the plaudits, despite being absent for years. Natty didn't get it. Lorraine approached the pair with a wide smile, gushing over the trainers and handing Raider a beer. He took it with a smile, his eyes roving over her curvy frame.

Natty turned away, Tommy still watching him, as was Lorraine's mum. Not knowing what to say to either, he stayed silent, getting a drink of his own, watching the proceedings from the corner. The thought of Raider picking up right where he left off made him want to hit something — namely Raider. He hadn't forgotten the last time they had spoken; his words to Raider about not looking after his child. Clearly, they had been taken to heart.

Not everyone was as enamoured as Lorraine and Jaden. Lorraine's mum was guardedly polite when she addressed Raider, and Tommy found his way over to Natty's corner after a while.

'I can tell by your face you feel the same way as me,' he said.

'It's nothing to do with me,' replied Natty.

'Don't give me that shit. I saw the look in your eyes outside. You were ready to fight when you saw him.'

Natty said nothing.

'I don't blame you, but I'm glad you held it down. As nice as it would be to beat some manners into him, Jaden's the one that would be hurt. As it is, he's gonna be hurt anyway, because we both know Raider ain't sticking around.'

Natty didn't respond, but agreed with Tommy. He had wanted to fight Raider. He still did. Turning away before he hit him with a bottle, he sipped his drink as a distraction. Tommy patted him on the shoulder, then went to stand with his kids. Lorraine had stepped back, her eyes on Raider and Jaden, who were still talking at length. Steeling himself, Natty went to stand next to her.

'Hey, Nat. Are you having a good time? I know we haven't spoken much,' she said, wiping a stray lock of hair from her face.

'It's cool. This is Jaden's day. This is a nice turnout.'

'It is. I still think he got too much stuff, but I can't blame people for wanting to spoil him.' Lorraine's eyes hadn't left her son and baby father. Natty took a deep breath.

'Lorraine?'

'Don't, Natty.'

'Don't what?' He replied, frowning.

'Whatever you're about to say about Raider, just don't. Please.'

Natty didn't know how she knew, but he pushed ahead anyway.

'Look, I know you don't want to hear it, but you need to be careful around him.'

Lorraine shook her head.

'Natty, it's Jaden's day. I don't want to do this right now, so leave it.'

'I'm only looking out for you both,' Natty said thickly, stung by her response.

'Look, he's happy to see his dad. So please, for Jaden, don't start anything. Okay?'

Natty scowled. Sighing, Lorraine moved away. Again, Natty felt Tommy's eyes on him. Whether he agreed with Lorraine, she was right about it being Jaden's day. As much as he wanted to, he wasn't going to do anything to ruin it for him. He finished his drink, and then said his goodbyes. Still busy with his dad, Jaden barely gave him a wave, and Lorraine's goodbye was perfunctory. Raider smirked his way, then winked.

As Natty left, Raider shifted closer to Lorraine, his arm already around his son.

CHAPTER TWENTY-TWO

NEEDING a distraction from thinking about his plans, or overthinking about Lorraine and Raider, Natty stepped up his investigation into Anika. He'd wondered if he would hear from Spence about turning up at his house, but either Anika hadn't said anything, or Spence was keeping it to himself.

Either way, Natty had someone else to speak to.

Carmen was Anika's closest friend. Natty followed her on Instagram through a burner account, and it was easy to find her in town after checking her story. She was walking out of a nail salon when Natty accidentally crossed her path.

'Natty?' She said, recognising him immediately. Natty stopped short, smiling at her.

'Carmen. How are you doing, babe? You look good as hell.'

Carmen preened, a flush appearing across her pretty face. She had curly blonde hair, pale green eyes, thin lips, and a slender figure.

'Don't start, Natty. You know that I'm taken,' she said, giggling. Natty held up his hands in mock surrender.

'I'm just telling you the truth. Your fella is truly a lucky guy.' Natty surveyed the gleam in Carmen's eyes. If he pursued her, he was sure he could make it pay off, but he had work to do, and the last thing he needed was more female drama. 'Seriously . . . how's everything going? I saw Anika the other day. Her and Spence seem well.' He watched Carmen closely for any sort of reaction.

'I assume she's doing well. I mean, we text every now and then, but I haven't properly hung out with her since my birthday. She's always busy with work, but we're definitely due a messy night out.'

Natty smiled at Carmen's words, more convinced than ever Anika was cheating. Spence had mentioned her getting dressed up to go to Carmen's, meaning she'd lied.

'You should definitely ring her and sort something out. She's her own boss, so she should be able to make the time for her best friend.' Natty glanced around. 'I'm gonna let you get back to your man, anyway. You can show him how pretty your nails look.'

Natty was ready to leave, but Carmen surprised him by hugging him. He held her tightly for a moment and went to move away, but she held on a second longer, biting her lip and looking up at him, her face flushed.

'It was nice running into you, Natty. Maybe I'll see you again soon,' she said, walking away. Natty watched her leave, amused at her antics. Turning away, he forced Carmen from his mind, already coming up with a plan for dealing with Anika. He considered going to Spence with what he knew, but he wanted more proof. It was the least his friend deserved.

———

NATTY'S DETERMINATION TO expose Anika led to him waiting on Spence's street the same night. Spence was working, and he wanted to see where Anika went, or if anyone suspicious came to the house. He parked across the road, no music playing, staring at the house, hoping nothing untoward happened, yet preparing for the worst.

The lights were on, but there was no movement so far.

As Natty stifled a yawn a while later, a taxi pulled up. Natty straightened in his seat as the Uber stopped outside Spence's. After a few minutes, Anika sauntered from the house, looking in far better spirits than the last time Natty had spoken to her. She wore a red vest top and tight white trousers with heels. Her hair was elaborately teased into curls, dark red lipstick adorning her mouth. She climbed into the back of the taxi, which drove away.

Natty pulled out after a few seconds, following at a distance, keeping a car between them. His heart raced as he gripped the steering wheel. Carmen had said they weren't spending much time together, and she was Anika's closest friend.

They drove toward the Hood, Natty's suspicion ever increasing. Whoever Anika was creeping with was going to get a beating. There was no way around it. He continued the steady pursuit, driving past the Northern Dance School and further up Chapeltown Road. He slowed at some traffic lights, mimicking the car in front, but cursed when Anika's taxi zoomed through the amber light. Natty turned onto Cowper Street and pulled up after the light's turned green, unsure where the taxi had gone.

Natty pulled out his phone and called Cameron, hoping he was home and could do a search for the taxi. It rang through to voicemail. Kissing his teeth, Natty tried again, still receiving no answer. He tossed the phone onto the passenger seat and drove home, his mind buzzing.

———

NATTY MULLED over the situation with Spence and Anika for the rest of the night, irritated that he still didn't have adequate proof about Anika. His gut told him she was up to no good, but that wasn't enough. He wondered if he could discreetly put the word out. If she was messing around with a guy in the Hood, someone had to know about it.

Natty called Carlton. He worked with Natty in Little London, but moved between their teams. He could do the rounds on Natty's behalf and get more information on Anika's Hood link.

'Yes, boss. What's good?' said Carlton.

In an instant, Natty changed his mind, not wanting to involve more people than necessary in Spence's business.

'Just checking in. Everything good?'

'Better than good, bro. The numbers are high.'

'That's what I like to hear. Listen, I'll check in on you soon. Shout me if you need anything.'

Natty hung up, still holding his phone. Lately, he had dedicated a lot of time to this task. Things in Little London were running smoothly, but Natty needed to be able to handle both.

Again, his plans were at the forefront of his mind. He called another person.

'Rudy,' he said when the man answered. 'Fancy a drink tomorrow?'

———

THE NEXT NIGHT, Natty and Rudy went for drinks at another pub — this time in Headingley. After paying for their drinks, they sat outside. Natty surveyed the woman arrayed around the spot. The weather hadn't cooled yet, and his eyes lingered on the shapely ones wearing sundresses and floaty skirts. He felt young and carefree for a moment, but wondered when life had grown so tough.

'How are you getting on?' Rudy asked after a moment. He sipped his beer, his eyes on Natty.

'I'm not sure.'

Rudy frowned.

'I don't understand. You're doing extremely well in Little London. You've made a name for yourself out there. You're making more money . . .'

'True. I want more.'

'More money will come, Nathaniel. You're making the right moves, and your name is in the right circles. What you need to do is stop wasting the money you have. Keep hold of it, because you never know when you might need it.'

Natty scowled, annoyed at Rudy's assumptions. The fact was, he'd saved up a decent amount of money. He wasn't going out as much, nor was he spending silly money on clothes and jewellery he didn't need.

Until now, he hadn't considered why.

'Money isn't a problem, Rudy. I want more responsibility.'

Rudy took another sip.

'I'll relay this back to your uncle, but I'm not promising anything.'

'Why can't I speak to him myself?' Natty's drink remained untouched.

'I can't stop you speaking to your family, Nathaniel. You have his number, but we both know your uncle respects structure. He won't appreciate you calling about business. I think you know that.'

Natty rubbed his forehead with his free hand. He hated that he had to go through so many hoops, comparing this talk to the time he and Rudy had gone to the pub after his argument with Elijah's team. He'd asked what he had to do to step up, and had been annoyed by Rudy's answers then. Still, he'd kept his head down and did what he needed to do.

Now, he was in the same position.

'Are you still getting along with Elijah?' Rudy asked after a long moment. Natty simply nodded. 'What about that girl you like? Anything going on there?'

Startled, Natty glowered at Rudy, surprised he would bring up Lorraine.

'We're friends,' he said, not mentioning that he hadn't seen her in a while. Finishing his drink, Rudy said no more.

———

AFTER LEAVING RUDY, Natty stewed at home, unsatisfied by the meeting. He'd kept his temper and avoided saying something he couldn't take back, but he wasn't sure how much longer he could carry on at his level. The money in Little London was good, and for what he needed to do there, extremely easy. It wasn't enough, though. Not anymore. He was thinking deeply about his future, and the logical next steps he could take.

Natty's thoughts slipped to Anika and Spence, irritated he hadn't gotten anywhere. He considered reaching out to Cameron. He hadn't seen his friend much lately, and Cameron knew about Anika — he could give some insight into what was going on, or who she could be hooking up with. His phone buzzed, drawing his attention.

Natty's stomach fluttered when he saw a message from Lorraine, asking how he was.

Staring down at the message, Natty locked his phone, clambering to his feet and shuffling off to bed. He wasn't tired, but wanted to try to get some sleep regardless.

———

LORRAINE SAT in her living room, her hair wrapped, legs curled under her as she typed on her MacBook. She'd been working steadily for over an hour, and when she grabbed her cup of tea, she frowned when she realised it had gone cold. Taking a short break, she poured the remains down the sink and made a new one.

As she waited for the kettle to boil, she glanced at the kitchen table, recalling Natty approaching the first time he'd seen her working. He hadn't cared then, but he'd since shown more of an interest. Lorraine wondered what he was doing. She hadn't heard from him since Jaden's birthday party. It had been nice seeing him there, and she liked that he got along well with her family. Her mum liked him, and so did Tommy — who didn't like many people. Raider included.

Lorraine smiled, thinking of Jaden and his attempts to sleep in the tracksuit Natty had bought him. He wanted to wear it everywhere, and she'd caught him in the mirror, flexing his muscles and trying to smirk and stand like Natty. It warmed her heart.

With a sinking feeling, she realised that the last time she'd spoken with Natty, he'd tried talking to her about Raider, and she'd silenced him, not wanting to have an awkward conversation during the party. Recalling he'd bought her the laptop that she loved, her stomach fluttered, remembering the moment he'd given it to her in the kitchen.

Before she could change her mind, she sent him a text message, to see how he was doing.

Lorraine was unsure of the implications of Raider being back around. Since the party, he'd come over a few times, chilling with Jaden for a while before leaving. There had been no drama, and he hadn't tried it on with her, or asked about Natty.

As the kettle boiled, Lorraine wondered about Raider and whether he wanted to be in Jaden's life full-time. She hoped he did. Whilst she had no desire for any relationship with her son's father, she wanted her son to still have one. After a while, she was back working when there was a loud banging at the door, startling her. She opened the door, and Raider stumbled inside, grinning, eyes red and bloodshot.

'What are you up to?' He slurred, pulling her in for a hug, hands roving over her curves. Lorraine tried to pull away.

'Get off me. Keep the noise down too. Jaden is sleeping.'

'What are you doing? You still ain't answered me.' Ignoring her, Raider pulled her into the living room and flopped on the sofa. 'What do you have to drink?'

Lorraine's lip curled. 'It looks like you've had enough.'

Raider scoffed.

'You're not my mum.' His eyes gleamed as he checked her out. 'I've never gotten over you, Lorraine. We should try again. Things will be different this time.'

Lorraine blinked, unsure where the words were coming from. She folded her arms, thinking of the older days, when her weaker self would have fallen for his shtick.

'I don't think that would be a good idea.'

Raider's eyes narrowed, his drunken grin finally dissipating.

'We could be a family: me, you, Jaden. We could even have another one. You always wanted a little girl, didn't you?'

Lorraine wiped away an angry tear, furious at his attempted emotional manipulation.

'You don't care, do you? You'd really use your son as an excuse to get your leg over?'

'It's not like that, babe. You know how I feel about you,' said Raider.

Lorraine tensed.

'Do *not* call me babe. I know exactly how you feel: entitled; like I belong to you, but I don't, and I never will.'

'What are you trying to say?' Raider's voice was dangerously low, but Lorraine didn't let it affect her.

'I've already told you before. I don't mind if you want to spend time with Jaden, but beyond that, there is nothing further between us.'

Raider gawped at Lorraine, startled she was speaking to him like this. Attempting to swallow down his anger, he spoke again.

'Is this about that prick Natty?'

Lorraine shook her head.

'Natty has nothing to do with this.'

Raider sat up, nostrils flaring.

'Bullshit! You've always been all over him. Even back in the day. When I first wanted to check you, everyone said you were taken, but I was dumb enough to believe you when you said you weren't. Tell me the fucking truth!'

'Keep your voice down,' Lorraine hissed. 'Your son is trying to sleep, or do you no longer care because I won't fuck you?'

'Don't change the subject, Lorraine. You're supposed to be my girl. What was the point in even making a baby if I can't have you?'

'Have me?' Lorraine laughed incredulously. 'It takes two to make a baby, Michael, but you did it because you could. From day one, you've done your best to stay uninvolved, thinking you can pop up for a bit, then disappear again. Also, let's not forget the fact you tried to make me get an abortion.'

Not wanting to admit she was right, Raider pressed on, eyes blazing.

'Fuck that. This isn't even about us. It's about Natty, trying to take something that's mine.'

'No, it isn't about Natty. This is about you and your responsibilities as a father. Responsibilities you've never taken seriously.' Lorraine took a deep breath, feeling a tightness in her chest. 'I want you to leave, Michael. I'm tired of having this conversation. Come back another time if you want to see Jaden.'

'Why are you trying to get rid of me? Who do you have coming round?'

'No one. Please, just leave. Don't wake up your son and let him see you like this,' said Lorraine.

Raider rubbed his forehead.

'I'm sorry, babe. I do care. About you and about Jaden.'

'I said, *don't* call me babe, Michael. Please, just go.' Lorraine had heard all of this before, and it was draining.

Raider ignored her, continuing to stare her down. She could see his muscles trembling, realising he was furious at her defiance. When she didn't see him move, she made a decision.

'Fine, you can deal with Tommy.'

Snarling, Raider leapt to his feet and grabbed her when she went for her phone. Lorraine lashed out, attempting to defend herself. She caught Raider in the face, and he snarled. Slapping her twice in retaliation, he shoved her into the coffee table. Lorraine shrieked when her back slammed into it, pain shooting through her. Raider didn't hesitate, drawing his foot back and kicking her in the ribs. She curled into a ball, gasping for breath.

Raider glared down at her trembling form, breathing hard.

'I'll knock out your brother if he talks shit. He's not in the life anymore, and he's washed up.' He yanked Lorraine by her hair and pulled her up. 'I breeded you, not Natty. Remember your place, or else.' He stormed out, letting her drop to the floor, leaving Lorraine weeping in pain, her ribs almost certainly broken.

CHAPTER TWENTY-THREE

CAMERON SIPPED A GLASS OF BRANDY, staring at his phone. Lately, he found himself staring off into space from time to time.

He was a killer.

The knowledge weighed heavily on him, yet lately, he felt more like his old self.

The word on Christian's death had flittered around the Hood, but he was such a small player that it didn't linger for long. Rudy had hinted at more jobs for him in the future, and despite his mixed thoughts, Cameron liked the idea of being considered important; there was a particular reputation that came with being a shooter, and he was ready to grasp it, no matter who he had to take out.

Cameron's ringing phone took him out of his thoughts. He glanced down at Natty's name, wondering what he could want. Though still close, they hadn't hung out much. Natty was focused on growing the Little London market, and Spence was taking his responsibilities running their crew seriously. They didn't have as much time for Cameron, and he wiped his mouth, unsure whether he was still bitter about this fact. Finally, he answered.

'Yes, Nat. You good?'

'I am, bro. You home? I need to speak to you.'

'Yeah, I'll leave the door unlocked,' said Cameron, a sliver of fear glissading down his spine. 'Everything okay?'

Natty didn't speak for a moment.

'I'll tell you when I get there. I'm on route.'

Natty hung up. Cameron drained his drink, then went to wash his face and sharpen up. He didn't know if Natty had heard about Christian, but he didn't think he could link it to him, regardless.

When he returned downstairs, the door opened, and Natty walked in, nodding at him. He seemed the same as ever, his solid build and height imposing. His eyes seemed different. Sharper somehow, but with small bags underneath, suggesting late nights on little sleep. Cameron knew the feeling.

'You look tired,' he said. Natty grinned his agreement.

'I'll be alright. Pity your shit coffee won't do anything for me.'

Cameron laughed. They went to the living room. Natty glanced at the huge television Cameron had bought, his eyebrows raising.

'When did you get that?' He asked.

'I can't remember. A few weeks ago, I think.'

'You have a family member die or something? You're spending money like you own Amazon.'

Cameron chuckled. 'I'm just being better with my money,' he said easily. 'Maybe Spence is having more of an influence on me than we thought.'

That got a smile out of Natty.

'Maybe. I've noticed I'm not spending as much lately,' he admitted. 'Spence is the reason I'm here, anyway.'

'What's happened?' Cameron asked. He'd finally gotten over the humiliation he felt after Gavin played him. Since then, he'd remained vigilant and was sure that nothing else had got past him.

'Anika.'

Cameron froze, fighting to stay neutral. There was no way Natty could know.

'What about her?' He was pleased his voice sounded normal.

'I think she's creeping.'

The bad feeling in the pit of Cameron's stomach grew. He coughed into his fist.

'I'm thirsty. Do you want a drink?' He asked, motioning to the empty glass on the table.

'I'm good,' Natty replied. Cameron topped up his drink, taking advantage of the moment to formulate his responses. He was prepared to blame it all on Anika if it came up. Natty would be angry, but if Cameron focused his ire on Anika, he could get through it.

'Right,' he started, sipping his brandy to fortify his nerves, 'what were you saying about whatshername?'

Natty kept his eyes on Cameron, arms folded across his chest. His expression was grim, and that made Cameron as nervous as his words.

'Back in the day, you lot had your thing . . .'

'. . . That's old news. What about it?'

'You know her better than I do. What was she like back then?'

Cameron's mind whirred as he formulated a response. Natty knew something. He didn't realise it was Cameron, but he knew Anika was messing around with someone. He could still get out of this if he said the right things.

'What have I missed?' He asked after a moment. Natty continued to stare him down. Cameron fought to stay calm, but with every passing second, his panic grew.

'Back in the day, you lot had your thing. Do you remember her checking for any other guys in the ends?' Natty finally spoke.

Cameron scratched his chin, needing the extra seconds. The time back then was a blur. He remembered randomly meeting Anika in a club, the vibe between them heated from the beginning. She liked to go out and party, occasionally partaking in drugs. Cameron couldn't remember her sniffing around other guys, nor could he think of a patsy he could use to potentially divert suspicion from himself.

'Nah. She liked to go out, and I'm guessing she had connections in the Hood, even back then.'

'What makes you say that?'

'She just seemed comfy,' replied Cameron. 'You know the rep Chapeltown has sometimes. Seems scary to people outside of the bubble, but she was always calm.'

Natty didn't respond, still deep in thought.

'Why do you think she's creeping?' Cameron pressed.

'She's been acting funny for a while. Saying she's going to see friends, but going somewhere else. I caught her leaving the other night. She took a taxi to the Hood, but I lost track of her at some lights.'

'For real? That's mad.' Panic warred with fury in Cameron's mind. He couldn't believe Anika had been so stupid with her excuses and attitude.

Now, Natty and probably Spence were onto her.

'I'm gonna find out who she's dealing with, then I'm gonna deal with them. No one fucks with my people.'

'I get it, Nat,' said Cameron, unease growing at Natty's words. He didn't doubt he meant them. 'What do you need from me?'

'Just keep an eye on things. If anyone says anything about Anika or Spence, I wanna hear about it. If anyone is bragging about a new ting they're banging, I wanna hear about it. Cool?'

'Cool, Nat. Spence is my brother too. We'll deal with this.'

Natty slapped Cameron's hand. They hung for a while longer, talking about general things, before Natty's phone rang, and he left.

Cameron locked the door behind him, remaining standing, breathing deep after the revelation. Natty was relentless when it came to investigating matters like this. He wouldn't stop until he found something, and if he interrogated Anika, it would end badly for both of them. Cameron stomped back to the living room and grabbed his phone, needing to have words with her.

———

ANIKA'S MIND whirred as she leaned back in the taxi. Cameron had been contacting her all day, insisting on meeting. It was so against how they usually did things, that she found herself suspicious.

Was he trying to set her up?

Anika dismissed the idea as quickly as it came to her mind. Not because she fully trusted Cameron, but because she knew that he would also be at risk if anyone found out about them. She thought about Natty turning up to see Spence again, flipping her question on her by asking if she was happy. It had baffled her; she'd wondered if he had meant something by it, but couldn't work out what.

Finally, Anika had put it to the back of her mind, not needing more things to worry over.

Anika worried something was broken between her and Spence. She wished she could say it was due to his desire to have a friendship with Rosie, a woman she knew was beautiful. More than this, Anika and Spence seemed to be on opposite sides, like passing ships shuffling around each other. They rarely spent time together, nor did they seem to actively pursue it. Occasionally, one of them would offer to cook, or suggest going out to eat, but these times were few and far between. Further, since their last argument.

Anika had backed down, unwilling to impose her own cheating ways and assumptions on Spence. He had told her of Rosie. He hadn't lied.

He wasn't sleeping with her best friend.

Wiping her cheek, Anika blew out a breath, an action caught by the taxi driver. He shot her a look.

'Everything okay?'

Anika nodded.

When she arrived, she glanced around her, not wanting any of Cameron's neighbours to see her. He'd assured her they were cool, but she wasn't sure what that meant. Luckily, Cameron was quick to answer, all-but dragging her inside and locking the door behind them. She jerked her arm away, glaring.

'What the hell are you doing?'

'I could ask you the same damn question,' Cameron snapped.

'What do you mean?' Anika's brow furrowed. Cameron looked furious, his eyes flashing, mouth set in a hard line. She didn't know what could have caused it.

'Natty came to see me.'

Anika's insides twisted. Natty randomly showing at the house again flashing behind her eyes.

'Why?'

'Because he thinks you're cheating on Spence.'

Anika's knees weakened, nausea swimming around her throat. She took several deep breaths, forcing the bile back down.

'Why does he think that?'

'Because you have no fucking chill,' Cameron snarled. 'What the hell is going on between you and Spence?'

'What do you mean?' Anika repeated.

'Natty says Spence thinks you've changed. He's seen you getting all dressed up, and Natty knows you're not going to your stupid friend's house. He even followed you to the Hood . . . the last time you came here.'

'What?' The words struck Anika like blows. At first, she struggled to comprehend what Cameron was saying. 'How does he know all of that?'

'Because he's smart,' Cameron roared. 'He put it together, and now he's asking me questions about you; about dudes you might know in the Hood.'

'What did you say to him?' Anika's heart leapt in her throat. She couldn't believe this was happening. Natty hadn't come to the house looking for Spence. He'd come to see her, wanting the measure of her, to see how she responded to his riddle of a question.

'What the fuck do you think I said? What was I supposed to say? I said I would ask around.'

Neither spoke for a moment, gathering their thoughts.

'Well?' Cameron finally demanded.

'Well, what?'

'What is going on with you and Spence?'

'Nothing,' she snapped. 'We're barely communicating, but that doesn't mean —'

'What? Doesn't mean he should speak to his friend and tell him you're different? Use your damn brain. Spence is too smart for his own good, and Natty is sharp. He sees the things Spence doesn't.'

Anika took a deep breath, wanting to retort, yet not seeing the point.

'What do we do now?'

Cameron rubbed his forehead, sighing.

'We keep it calm. You need to fix your relationship and stop Spence suspecting anything. Doesn't matter how you do it . . . listen to Spence talk about his day, or sit and watch Netflix. It just needs containing. If that happens, he'll tell Natty it's calm, and things will return to normal.'

'Okay. What happens after that?'

Cameron didn't know what to say. He wondered why he was fighting so hard to keep this going with Anika. He'd gotten her back, even when she was in a serious relationship with his friend. She'd succumbed to him multiple times.

So, why was he continuing it?

———

LORRAINE LAY IN A HOSPITAL BED, staring up at the ceiling, unable to speak. When she'd recovered some of her strength, she'd called Rosie. Rosie had called Lorraine's mum, who'd stayed with Jaden while she went to get checked out.

Lorraine felt overwhelming emotions over what had happened. Despite how things had been with her and Raider over the years, she never thought he would attack her. He hadn't even cared his son was in the house.

In the afternoon, Rosie entered the room, eyes glistening when she saw her friend's state.

'Raider?' She asked, already knowing the answer. Lorraine nodded. 'Have you called the police yet?'

'I don't want to do that . . . I just want to forget it happened. The doctors said I can go home later. I just want to focus on that.' Lorraine rubbed her arms. She shifted, unable to get comfortable, wincing as she stared straight ahead.

Rosie hated how broken her friend seemed. When Lorraine called, all she'd said was that she'd been hurt, refusing to give any details about the attack to either Rosie or her family. Rosie's veins thrummed with rage at the thought of Raider putting his hands on her best friend.

'You can't let him get away with this. He could have killed you. You're lucky your ribs aren't broken,' she said.

'Trust me, badly bruised ribs aren't that much better,' said Lorraine, wincing as she moved.

'Lorraine . . .'

'It's my life, Rosie. This is my decision to make.'

'Do you remember what I went through with Kyle? How I buried my head in the sand every time he kicked the shit out of me?'

'Do you remember when you wanted to be left alone to deal with it?' Lorraine retorted.

Rosie sighed, trying to calm down.

'I spent more time than I ever wanted in this place. I hate it.' She looked around the boxy, white-walled room, cleaning solution mixed with a putrid *hospital* stench, filling her nostrils. A tear spilt down her face. 'I'm going to have a cig, and when I come back, we can talk about anything you want.'

Lorraine gave Rosie a grateful smile and closed her eyes. When Rosie headed out, Lorraine succumbed to tears, tired of holding it together; reliving the fear she had felt when Raider loomed over her.

His child's mother.

As Rosie headed away, she heard Lorraine's tears, which wrenched her heart. Tears ran freely now, hurting over the pain her friend had suffered. When Rosie reached the exit, She called a number, steeling herself for the person answering.

'Spence? It's Rosie.'

———

NATTY AND SPENCE were in the middle of a lazy day. Natty had been running himself ragged in so many different circles that he just wanted to relax. He still felt like he was at the precipice of an important decision, but for once, he didn't want to overwhelm himself with thoughts about his issues.

The pair had eaten lunch in the Hood earlier, now sitting in Spence's garden with cans of ginger beer, and containers of cake and custard. Natty sat on the wall, his snack resting on his lap, enjoying the feel of a gentle breeze on his arms. Times like this, he felt he could stay this way forever.

Spence's garden had a small patch of well-tended grass, surrounded by a concrete square. He wasn't much of a gardener, but they had enough room to sit comfortably. Natty knew Anika was at work — at least, that's what Spence believed. He'd yet to hear anything back from Cameron about men from Anika's past, and his subtle inquiries about recent high-profile hook-ups had gotten him nowhere.

'Feels like we haven't done this in a while,' Natty said after a while.

Spence, resting peacefully against a small brown fence separating his garden from the next, cleared his throat.

'We're busy men these days. I can't remember the last time all three of us kicked it.'

Natty considered this. It had been a while. Since he began overseeing Little London, he couldn't think of a time they had all hung out, hoping it wasn't a sign they were growing apart.

'How has Cam been with you lately?'

'He's doing better, it seems. He's not getting on my back about Nika anymore, and he does his job without issue. That shit with Gavin and the missing product knocked him back.'

'I can see that. Cam's not a guy that likes making those kinds of mistakes.'

'He's learned from it and chilled out by the looks of things. He's not causing drama. In fact, he's not really around.'

'What do you mean?' Natty's ears pricked up.

'Nothing really. He just works and bails. Doesn't hang around like he used to.'

'Why do you think that is?'

Spence shrugged. 'Couldn't tell you. It's not something I've thought about. Do you think something is going on?'

Natty wasn't sure how to answer. It was a change of character for Cameron. He thrived on being seen, and when Natty was previously around the base, Cameron was always around, whether he was working on not.

'He might be freelancing. That, or he's got a girlfriend.'

Spence chuckled.

'Wouldn't that be something? Cam all loved up, after all the shit he gave me?'

Natty too laughed, nearly choking on his drink. He wiped his mouth, deciding to give the matter more thought later.

'How are things with you and Anika lately?'

Spence's jaw tightened, Natty immediately noticing.

'We're fine, I guess.'

'You guess?'

'We argued over Rosie, but that was ages ago. Thought we got past it, but I dunno. Doesn't feel like she's all in.'

Natty mulled the words, combining these with the lack of emotion in his friend's voice. He desperately wanted to mention what he suspected about Anika, but couldn't. Not yet.

'How are you doing with Rosie?' He smirked, noting how flustered Spence was.

'We're fine. Nothing since the last time I thought she was gonna try something.'

Despite Spence's nonchalance about the time he spent with Rosie, Natty knew there was chemistry between them, and couldn't see that changing any time soon.

Before he could question this any further, Spence's phone rang. Spence glanced at the screen, eyes widening before he answered, pressing the phone to his ear.

Natty tuned out while he was talking, thinking about Spence and Rosie. He wished he could speak to Lorraine about it, but he hadn't responded to her last text message, and felt weird trying to start another conversation. The longer it went on, the harder it seemed. They'd worked hard to get past all the nonsense before, and he missed her. And Jaden.

Despite that, he didn't like how she'd responded to Raider at Jaden's party. Draining his drink, he put the can on the wall beside him. Turning to Spence, he frowned when he saw the worried expression on his friend's face.

'Spence? What's up?' Natty's immediate thought was that something had happened with Anika.

Spence took a deep breath.

'Nat, I need you to stay calm. That was Rosie. Something happened to Lorraine.'

'What happened?' Natty felt a weight on his chest, lifting his shoulders, bracing himself.

'Raider attacked her. She's in hospital.'

A great chill overwhelmed Natty as he absorbed what Spence had said. He felt his hands clench and unclench, an edgy, twitchy feeling surging through his body.

'Is she okay?' His voice sounded foreign and far away. He hadn't realised he'd climbed from the wall, the can and container tumbling to the ground. Ignoring them, Natty focused on Spence.

'She's bruised and a bit shook up, but she's fine. I know what you're feeling, Natty, but you need—'

'Is Jaden okay? Did he see anything?'

'Rosie didn't mention him, so I'm guessing he is. He's probably with Lorraine's mum. Nat—'

'Don't, Spence. Don't even try.'

Spence's shoulders slumped. He'd watched Natty's reaction, startled when his friend had leapt from the wall. For a moment, Spence had thought Natty would attack him. He knew exactly how things were going to play out. Natty wouldn't be stopped.

He tried anyway.

'Nat, stay calm. Speak to Elijah; get him to sort it with Raider. Think about the business.'

'Fuck the business,' Natty replied, his voice calm. Spence closed his eyes, acknowledging his friend's words. An angry Natty was hard enough to get through to. It rarely surfaced, but when it did, logical and calculated Natty was terrifying. His mind was made up, and there would be no telling him otherwise.

'Speak to Lorraine, because I guarantee she won't want you getting into trouble over her.'

'She should have come to me. I would have protected her,' replied Natty, pacing on the spot, voice trembling.

'She probably didn't want you to get yourself in trouble, like I said.' Spence tried again.

'Spence, it's already done. You're not gonna talk me out of it.' Natty didn't even look at him.

'Lorraine wouldn't want you to get involved.'

Natty faced him, his eyes locked onto Spence's.

'Not Lorraine. You. *You* don't want me to spoil the flow of money into your fucking pocket, so don't pretend this is about her feelings.'

Spence took a step back, realising he needed to back off. Natty took a deep breath, seemingly calming down.

'Are you at least ready to admit it then?' Spence asked.

'Admit what?'

'That you have serious feelings for Lorraine.'

Natty shook his head.

'It isn't the time for that conversation, Spence.'

'Fine, let's get real. Raider is super-tough. He's a throwback to one of those crazy street dudes from the early two-thousands. Remember the beef he got into with Drakey? He almost killed him.'

'Whatever happens, happens. I'll get with you later, Spence.' Natty left, ignoring the calls of his friend.

———

AT HOME, Natty stared at his phone. It had been nearly an hour, and his anger hadn't abated. He wanted to contact Lorraine, but he wasn't supposed to know what happened.

Spence was right about one thing; Lorraine had tried to keep him out of it, but he wasn't going to listen. He was going to handle this, once and for all. He would do it for Jaden and Lorraine. The thought that Jaden might have seen his mum get attacked was too much for Natty to cope with, as was the thought of Jaden potentially receiving the same treatment.

He made a few calls, trying to get Raider's number, his anger growing every time another contact let him down, either unknowing or unwilling to share Raider's number. He tossed his phone aside after trying Rudy and Elijah, nostrils flaring. He needed to find Raider. An alternative was to spin the streets in the Hood, looking for him. Rubbing his knuckles, he pondered the dilemma until an idea came to him. Grabbing the phone, he found a contact a pressed the call button, jamming the phone to his ear.

'Yo,' the person answered.

'It's Natty. You good?'

'Yeah, fam. What's going on? Not like you to reach out,' said Wonder. They'd buried the hatchet a while back, and the few times they'd hung around each other since Ellie's party had been amicable.

'I need Raider's number. Figured you'd have it.'

'What do you need it for?' Wonder's tone had changed, becoming more guarded. Natty couldn't blame him. Everyone knew their issues.

'I wanted to speak to him about burying the beef.'

'Why?'

'Our teams are working well together. Everyone's making more money, so why hold a grudge?'

Wonder didn't respond. Natty's heart thudded as he waited, worried he'd overplayed his hand. If this didn't work, he'd hit the streets, vowing not to rest until he'd found Raider.

'Look,' Wonder finally said, 'I'll give you the number, but don't tell him you got it from me. Raider is funny about people chatting his business.'

Relief flooded Natty.

'I won't say a word, bro. Next time we're out, the drinks are on me.'

Laughing, Wonder relayed the number and hung up. Natty immediately inputted Raider's number and called him, trying to control his roiling emotions. The effort to stay calm during the call with Wonder had tested his resolve, but it was worth it.

'Who's this?' Raider's tone was dismissive, full of malice, and only made Natty angrier.

'You know who this is.'

Raider snorted.

'Guess she told you what happened. Figured she'd go running to her little sideman.'

Natty didn't respond, letting Raider talk.

'What do you want, Dunn? Did you ring me just to hear me breathing? How the fuck did you get my number, anyway?'

'We need to talk.'

Again, Raider snorted.

'Are you sure you wanna do that?'

'We're going to do it. If you're the man you're claiming, you'll do it one-on-one.'

Raider chuckled.

'Okay, fam. You wanna die so badly, you can. I'll be waiting at my spot.'

Raider gave Natty the address, then hung up without waiting for confirmation.

———

NATTY DROVE to Raider's place, parking across the road and wondering if he should have brought a weapon. There was always the possibility Raider was setting him up, but Natty decided it wasn't in his nature. Raider wanted this as much as Natty did. This thing between them had festered, reaching its breaking point. There was only one way to resolve it, and Natty recognised that.

Raider stayed on Hamilton Avenue, the terraced spot blending in with the houses around it. It had a black door and a matching black gate with chipped paint. Natty climbed from the car and strode across the road, walking into the living room with his hands down. Raider wasn't going to jump him. He didn't know how he knew, but he did.

Sure enough, Raider stood in the cramped living room. He'd already moved a cheap coffee table to the corner of the room, giving them space. His eyes glittered as he stared down Natty, a smirk gracing his brutal features.

'Should have known she'd go running to you. Where's Tommy? Was he too pussy to come after me himself?'

Natty just watched, heart thudding against his chest. He tried to stay in control. Raider was tough, and this fight was going to take a lot out of him, but there was no way around it. Business or not, this needed to happen. Realising Natty wasn't going to reply, Raider spoke again.

'I dunno what any of them see in you.'

'You shouldn't have put your hands on her.'

Raider shook his head.

'You should have put a baby in her. She'd always have been yours then. Instead, you're fucking hanging around, anyway. Confusing shit.' Raider took a step forward. 'You're the reason she took a beating.'

Both men cautiously moved toward the other. Natty's eyes widened as a fist shot towards his face quicker than expected. He dodged, but it still glanced against his cheek, smarting. Raider chuckled.

'Everyone says you're a badman. Thought you were rougher than this.'

Enraged, Natty lunged in, missing the smirk on Raider's face as he played right into his hands. Grabbing him, Raider slammed his fist several times into Natty's stomach, each blow more punishing than the last. Natty spluttered from the hits, finally managing to get his knee up, breaking the hold. He caught Raider with an elbow. Raider backed away, no longer smiling. He wiped his mouth.

'They all think you're so fucking special, but you're not. Without Rudy and your uncle, you'd be nothing.'

Breathing hard, Natty began circling, putting his hands up. Rushing in before was silly, and he needed to avoid making a similar mistake. Raider was much stronger than he'd expected, but there was no going back now. They were here, and this had to happen. Raider was strong, but emotional. Natty wondered if that was his way in. Either way, he needed to fight carefully. Raider's eyes narrowed.

'What are you waiting for? Fight!'

The fight continued, both men trading blows. Natty got in too close, taking more damage from Raider's solid hits. He was still working out how to defeat Raider; the retaliatory hits his price to pay. He'd realised that when Raider's guard was high, it caused the punches Natty threw to deflect away from his face. After one such barrage, he again backed away.

Raider wiped his mouth, breathing hard.

'You shouldn't have come, Natty. You're a pussy. I don't even need to try against you.'

Losing his composure, Natty again charged, forgetting what had worked for him, taking a vicious knee to the stomach, which drove all the air from him. Raider drilled him in the face with a sharp right, and Natty tumbled to the ground, body screaming in pain. Raider mounted him, punching Natty several times in the face.

'Lorraine is mine,' he hissed. 'I'm gonna pay her a visit, and she's gonna know you died because of her.'

Natty's eyes dimmed, his energy slipping. He was in a precarious position, and knew he wouldn't survive too many more blows. Raider had played it perfectly, using his anger against him, and it surprised Natty. With all the stories he'd heard, he'd assumed Raider was a mindless brute, but he was far more intelligent than expected. As Raider raised his fist to hit him again, Natty thought of Jaden, imagining him scared and worried about his mum. Before Raider could hit him, Natty laughed. Raider's eyes narrowed, startled at the action.

'Y'know,' Natty croaked, 'Lorraine always said I fucked her better.' Raider stilled, and Natty knew he had him. 'She had your son, but her heart and pussy will always belong to me.'

'Fuck you!'

Raider was distracted enough for Natty to push him off. Both men scrambled to their feet. Natty's eyes flickered. He was unsteady on his feet, fighting to keep his guard up. By contrast, Raider was barely scratched. It took only a moment for Natty to work out what he needed to do. He launched forward. Raider's eyes lit up, thinking Natty was making the same mistake he'd made earlier. Raider raised his guard to deflect the blow, but Natty dropped, delivering a shuddering punch to Raider's rib, bending the brute over double. Gripping him, Natty kneed Raider in the face. Forcing him to the floor, Natty climbed on top of him, pounding into his lifeless face.

Natty drew his fist back one more time, but hesitated, staring at Raider's battered face. He dropped his hand, leaning back and sucking in air, adrenaline beginning to ebb as he realised how much trouble he was in.

CHAPTER TWENTY-FOUR

NATTY STEWED AT HOME, going over everything that had transpired. His hand ached, and as he'd calmed down, he considered his next move. There were several ways he could have handled the situation, and now he would have to deal with the politics stemming from his decision.

Spence came over the next day. Natty had called him after leaving Raider. His tense face told the story.

'They found him. Everyone's talking. With Raider's reputation, people are querying who could have beaten him up like that; what they might gain from doing it.'

Natty didn't respond, and after a moment, Spence pressed on.

'How are you feeling?'

'I don't regret it, if that's what you mean. I was reckless, but there was only one way that situation was gonna end.' Natty's vibrating phone stole his attention. He looked at the screen, then dropped it on the sofa.

'They're not going to stop calling, Nat. Rudy and Elijah are gonna wanna speak to you. The streets may be speculating, but it'll be obvious to the higher-ups who did this.'

Again, Natty didn't speak, rubbing his head. Spence was right, and he knew it. The beating Raider had taken, suggested it was a personal attack. Elijah, in particular, knew of the hatred between Natty and Raider.

Spence blew out a breath.

'Do you need anything?'

Natty shook his head.

'Have you spoken to Lorraine yet?'

Natty froze. He'd forgotten to speak to Lorraine in his haste to get back at Raider. The rage had taken over.

'No, I haven't.'

'Maybe you should, bro. Listen, I need to go away for a couple of days. One of my cousins down in Portsmouth died, and me and my pops are gonna go down for the funeral.'

Natty glanced at his friend. 'Sorry to hear that, bro. Do you want me to come with you?'

Spence shook his head.

'I'll be fine, fam. Stay here, and get your shit sorted out. Ring me if you need to talk some more.'

Spence gripped Natty's shoulder, then left him to his musings.

———

LATER THAT NIGHT, Natty was in an Uber on the way back from the hospital. When the pain in his hand had grown worse, he'd gone to get it checked out. Several hours later, he'd received some strong painkillers after an examination. His hand was simply sprained and would need a short while to heal. Nothing was broken, which he took as a relief. Hopefully, he wouldn't have to punch anyone soon.

Before going to sleep, Natty sent Lorraine a text message, asking if he could see her the next day. When Lorraine confirmed he could, he read the message several more times, before finally putting his phone away.

After a restless sleep, Natty showered, dressed, then left the house.

———

LORRAINE GREETED him at the door with a short hug, wincing, which refuelled Natty's rage. She had bruising on her face and was still moving gingerly. Inwardly, he felt satisfaction over the beating he'd given Raider in her honour.

'Are you okay?' She asked, watching his changing emotions. Natty nodded. Lorraine traced the bruising on his face, eyes widening. 'What happened?'

'Nothing.' Inwardly, he tensed, wishing he'd thought of an explanation for his face. Lorraine didn't respond, but glanced at him a moment longer, before they headed inside.

Jaden beamed when he saw Natty. He was on the sofa, a gaming device in his hands.

'Hey, Natty. Where have you been?'

'Just been busy, little man. How are you doing?' Despite his current problems, Natty smiled at Jaden, his heart lifting at seeing him.

'Fine. Mummy's not well. She fell over and hurt herself.'

Natty looked from Jaden to Lorraine. A long moment passed between them, before Natty cut the conversation with Jaden short, heading into the kitchen to make a drink, trying to keep it together.

'Natty.'

Natty's eyebrow rose when Tommy entered the kitchen. They bumped fists. Tommy grinned.

'Heard what happened to Raider. Glad you handled your business for my sister.' He glanced at the door, then back to Natty. 'Surprised you let him live.'

'I almost didn't,' admitted Natty, making a face. The painkillers he'd taken last night were wearing off, and he hadn't taken any more since waking up. Rooting in Lorraine's drawers, he found some ibuprofen and dry swallowed two tablets.

'What's going on now? The streets are talking. Elijah's gonna be out for blood.'

'What do you want me to say, Tom? I smacked him up, and I'll deal with whatever happens.'

Tommy hung his head. 'She's my little sis. I should have dealt with Raider. Deep down . . . I don't know if I'd have won.'

Natty shrugged, understanding how hard it was for Tommy to admit that.

'It is what it is. You don't need to worry about it now.'

'Nat?'

Lorraine appeared in the doorway, and both men froze, wondering how much she'd heard.

'How are you feeling?' Natty found his voice first, struggling to stay neutral. Lorraine kept her eyes on his.

'I'm fine.' She noticed the pack of painkillers. 'Why do you need those?'

'I had a headache,' said Natty. Lorraine frowned.

'Are you sure you're okay? What are you two talking about?'

'Just street stuff,' Natty replied. He pulled out his phone. 'I need to go.'

'You just got here. I need to talk to you,' protested Lorraine. Natty fought the urge to stay with her, slapping hands with Tommy, then giving Lorraine a short hug.

'I'll come back and see you later.'

Lorraine held her stomach and said, 'Natty, I really need to talk to you.'

Natty's hand rested on the door handle. He locked eyes with Lorraine, both recognising the sadness in the other. After a moment, he turned the handle.

'I know, Lorraine. I'll be back soon. I promise.'

———

AFTER LEAVING LORRAINE'S, Natty sat in his car, taking a deep breath. Lorraine didn't know about Raider yet, but it would only be a matter of time, especially if word was out about what had happened to him. Ignoring another call from Rudy, his stomach lurched, wondering how much longer he could get away with it.

Pulling up at Cameron's, he banged on the door, figuring he would need to rouse his friend. Seconds later, Cameron answered with a scowl.

'Couldn't you have called before you turned up?' He said.

'What's the big deal? Are you busy?'

'Nah, nothing like that. You just knock like you're fucking police.'

'Whatever. Move out the way and let me in.'

Chuckling, Cameron did as he was told. Both men headed for the kitchen, and Cameron fixed himself a coffee. He offered to make one for Natty, but he declined.

'Figured I'd hear from you. Streets are saying some shit about Raider. Was that you?'

Natty nodded. Cameron shook his head, laughing.

'You nearly killed him. What made you go off like that on him?'

Natty filled Cameron in. Cameron stopped chuckling, his brow furrowing.

'You're playing a dangerous game, Nat. Raider's a prick, but he's Elijah's boy. He can't lose face on this one. What if he snitches on you?'

'I don't know, Cam.' Natty rubbed his eyes. 'I tried calling Elijah beforehand to get Raider's details, but he didn't answer. I wasn't gonna wait.'

Cameron sipped his drink, his expression surprisingly unreadable.

'I always knew you were whipped over her.'

Both men shared a look, laughing for a moment.

'This isn't about that. He beat her up for no reason, and I wasn't gonna take that.'

'Big difference between smacking someone around and nearly killing them.' The image of Christian slumped on the floor flashed into Cameron's mind. He felt himself flinch.

Again, Natty shrugged. He didn't have the words for Cameron.

'At least you didn't kill him. I'm surprised you didn't.'

Natty frowned at Cameron's words. They weren't killers, but then again, he recognised that he had been angry enough to do it.

If he hadn't pulled his fist back at the last second, he might be sitting there having murdered someone.

'It doesn't matter now. Did you handle that thing?'

'What thing?' Cameron's brow furrowed.

'Anika. Did you learn anything?'

'Oh . . . Nah. If she's creeping with someone in the Hood, she's keeping it lowkey.'

'Spence is out of town, so I figured this would be the time for her to link her dude on the side. If I didn't have all this going on, I'd watch the house to see where she went.'

'Leave it with me, bro,' said Cameron after a moment. 'I'll look into it some more. You've got enough on your plate.'

'Okay. I appreciate it. Ring me if you hear anything.' Natty touched fists with Cameron, then left.

———

CAMERON LOCKED the door behind Natty, glad he hadn't stayed longer. With Spence having gone to a funeral, Anika hadn't wanted to stay home alone.

Staring into space for a moment, he gathered himself and headed back upstairs. Anika sat on the edge of the bed, pulling on her clothes. She glanced up at Cameron.

'Who was that?'

'Natty.' Cameron paced the bedroom. 'He was asking about you.'

'He knows I'm here?' Anika jumped to her feet, panicking.

'Course not. If he knew, he'd have dragged you out of the house.'

'And you'd let him do that?'

The pair locked eyes. Cameron weighed up his words, deciding to give it to her straight.

'We need to stop this.'

Anika's mouth fell open. Cameron could see her struggling to compose herself.

'What?'

'It's getting on top now. Natty ain't gonna stop until he finds something, and we're getting sloppy. You should have never stayed the night. We should have done this after he first came to me.'

'You . . . you can't be serious. What about everything we have? Everything you said to me?'

'We got sloppy,' Cameron repeated. 'You have a man, and I'm not waiting around for things to come out. We need to end it now.'

'I can't . . .'

Cameron held up a hand, losing patience with her. Anika wasn't seeing what was right in front of her. She was cheating on her man, and now they were at risk of being discovered.

'It's over. And let me tell you right now, don't let me hear about you saying anything to anyone.'

Anika's eyes widened.

'You're threatening me?'

'Only if you're dumb enough to call my name. Don't put me to the test. Even if anyone says anything, you'd better make something up. Got it?'

Anika stared at him.

'I said, *got it*?' Cameron took a step forward, and Anika flinched, the fear palpable. She nodded. Gathering her things, she hurried from the house without a word. Cameron sighed, knowing he'd done the right thing deep down. He'd allowed himself to get too close, but he had fixed it in the end.

Collapsing onto his sofa, he built a spliff, needing to relax.

———

ANIKA KEPT her composure until she reached her car. Before she could start the engine, she burst into tears. There was no going back for her now. Cameron had callously cast her aside, and the worst part was that she should have seen it coming. She had dealt with him when she was younger and stupider, but had learned nothing.

Her shoulders shook as she let go of her emotions. After a few minutes, the tears subsided, but the desolation and awful feelings swirling around her stomach went nowhere.

After several deeper breaths, she came to a decision, one she knew there was no coming back from.

———

ANOTHER DAY PASSED, and Natty knew he couldn't avoid Elijah any longer. He finally answered his call as he sat home, ignoring the football highlights on the TV.

'Elijah,' he said by way of greeting.

'Oh, good. That hand's not too injured to answer the phone. I was beginning to worry. Natty, we need to talk.'

Natty didn't hesitate. 'I'll come to you.'

They met at the house of one of Elijah's women. Natty had been there before, both with and without Elijah. The woman was one of his past contacts, a pretty brown-skinned girl called Charlene. She let him in, keeping her face neutral as she led him to Elijah.

'Give us some space, baby.' Elijah stood in the living room, ignoring the television, a cigarette in his hand. Charlene left them alone. Natty, too remained standing. Elijah's posture and demeanour were hard to work out, but that wasn't a surprise. Elijah went to great lengths to stay in control of his emotions. An empty cup rested on the coffee table, alongside two mobile phones. After a moment, Elijah faced Natty, eyes boring into him.

'What the hell were you thinking?'

Natty stayed quiet.

'Raider's in critical condition.' Elijah's eyes narrowed. He looked angrier than Natty had ever seen him. 'Was this your plan all along?'

Natty shook his head.

'He went too far when he beat up Lorraine.'

'That's what this is about? Raider's baby mother? Again?'

Anger flared up in Natty.

'I told you I would keep Raider under control—' Elijah started.

'You didn't, did you? He smacked her around despite your *control*,' snapped Natty.

'Did I know that? Did you speak to me before you went off and nearly killed him? Did you even check if I knew about the situation?'

'I called you. You didn't answer.'

Elijah's eyes widened.

'Once, Natty. Why didn't you try again? Or wait for me to get back to you? It's almost like you didn't want me to answer . . . so you could take it upon yourself to react in the way you wanted to.' Elijah continued to smoke his cigarette, the tension in the room ebbing.

Natty's mind raced. He wondered what Elijah's next move would be. His eyes darted around in anticipation, exploring Elijah's demeanour. Seeing his fist clench, Natty's jaw tightened, and he adjusted his feet slightly.

Finally, Elijah spoke.

'I'll speak with Rudy directly. For now, any business between our crews is on hold. Stay away from Little London for the foreseeable.'

'Excuse me?' Natty gawped. Elijah continued to meet his furious gaze with his own colder one.

'See yourself out.'

Natty stepped forward.

'You need to watch how you talk to me,' he snarled.

Elijah didn't back down. Their eyes locked, neither saying a word. After a few seconds, Natty picked up the pack of cigarettes from the coffee table. Lighting one, he blew the smoke in Elijah's face, then turned and left.

———

LORRAINE'S THOUGHTS kept slipping to Natty, and the injuries he was trying to hide when he came to visit. She had finally gone online and had learned about Raider's injuries. People spoke of him being in a bad way, asking for prayers and hope, which made her feel ill. Raider was undeserving of anyone's support. He didn't deserve her sympathy, but she found he had it anyway for a reason she could not work out.

She'd tried speaking with Tommy, but he remained as evasive as ever, retreating when she began probing. Natty's face was bruised, not to mention his damaged hand. Lorraine had seen the ibuprofen he had taken, and all signs pointed towards him being involved in what happened to Raider. She pondered how he could have found out about the assault so quickly, and as Jaden cheered the goal he'd scored on his football game, the answer came to her.

'I'll be back in a minute, baby. I'm just going upstairs,' she said to Jaden.

'Okay, mummy.'

Hurrying up the stairs as fast as her injuries would allow, Lorraine closed her bedroom door behind her and called Rosie.

'Hey, Lo. How are you feeling?'

'Who did you tell about what happened to me?' Lorraine got to the point.

'There was a moment of silence, then a sigh.'

'I told Spence.'

A sharp knocking at the door cut across Lorraine's response. She curtly told her friend she would speak with her later, then shuffled downstairs to answer. Her stomach lurched when she saw the two police officers standing there. One male, one female.

'Lorraine Richards?'

'That's me,' she replied, eyeing the officers, her head flinching slightly.

'Can we come in? We just want to ask you a few questions.'

Lorraine couldn't avoid it. She led them to the kitchen and told Jaden — who looked at the officers with wide eyes — that she wouldn't be long. She sat in the kitchen, waiting for the officers to speak.

'I'll keep this brief,' said the male officer. He was taller than his counterpart, with short hair and a scruffy beard. 'We're investigating a recent attack on Michael Parsons. We understand he is well known to you.'

Lorraine nodded. It wasn't often anyone used Raider's real name.

'He is the father to your son, is that correct?'

'If you want to call him that. He's not the most active participant in his son's life,' replied Lorraine, praying that Jaden didn't walk in on them.

'Mr Parsons suffered serious injuries. He's currently in intensive care, and his condition is touch and go. If there is anything you can tell us about the circumstances, we'd appreciate it.'

Lorraine thought she was going to be sick. She'd read about Raider's injuries, but the police being there made it ever more real.

'I'm sorry, but I don't know anything. Michael and I are not that close.'

'When did you last see him?'

'Several nights ago. He came to the house, and we had a conversation, then he left,' lied Lorraine, jumbling the facts. She wasn't about to tell them about the assault. That would only make things worse and drag her further into the situation. She had Jaden to think about.

'I can't help but notice you're sporting a few injuries,' said the female officer, who'd silently assessed Lorraine as she spoke with her colleague.

'What's your point?' replied Lorraine, clearly rattled.

'Did Mr Parsons cause those injuries?'

Lorraine grit her teeth, her attention flitting to the female officer, who'd hit the nail on the head.

'As I said, we had a conversation, then he left. Now, if you don't mind, I need to return to my son.'

The officers shared a look, and Lorraine's heart raced, wondering if they would arrest her, or interrogate her further. Her shoulders visibly relaxed when the male officer handed her his card.

'Please get in touch if you think of anything else. Any little detail could help us.'

Lorraine saw the police out, locking the door behind them. Her heart hadn't stopped racing as she shuffled back into the living room. Jaden paused his game and looked up at her.

'Are you okay, mummy?'

'I'm fine,' she responded, her mind on Natty, and the conversation they needed to have.

CHAPTER TWENTY-FIVE

NATTY LEFT ELIJAH, still furious with how the conversation had transpired. All the good work they'd done had seemingly vanished, all over someone like Raider. It made him feel sick. When the decision was made, he'd struggled to control himself. Natty felt hurt and disrespected, and, in the life, those feelings almost always led to confrontation.

Pulling up outside his house, he noticed a blacked-out Nissan 4X4 parked nearby. Sighing, he didn't bother going inside, instead walking towards the vehicle and climbing in the back. As soon as the door slammed shut, the car drove off.

Natty recognised the driver as one of Rudy's men and nodded. The man didn't return the gesture, focusing on the road. To Natty's surprise, they didn't drive toward Delores's as he expected, but to another spot.

Anxiety gnawed at him as they eventually reached the destination. There were numerous men posted in and around the spot. It didn't look good, and he started to fear his uncle was behind this. Stories of Warren's murder flashed in his mind. He took a deep breath, trying to calm himself, focusing on what he could say; how he should look. The

372

minor details were necessary, and he needed to ensure he got them right.

Natty followed his escort inside. They headed down to the cellar, and Natty's worry only grew. He glanced around, looking for potential escapes, quickly realising all his possible exits were covered.

Rudy waited in the cellar, which was larger than Natty expected. It was the same size as his living room at home. Rudy smoked a cigarette, face twisted in anger as he scowled at Natty. The men left the cellar without a word, leaving the pair alone. For several minutes, Rudy finished his cigarette, each moment growing more agonisingly tense for Natty. He wanted Rudy to speak, to say something. Anything. Finally, he did.

'What the hell were you thinking?' Rudy started. Natty opened his mouth, but Rudy raised his hand, and Natty immediately fell silent. 'You've jeopardised an alliance, undone months of hard work with your stupid stunt.'

'That wasn't the intention, Rudy. Raider beat up his baby mum, knowing full well what I would do.'

'I don't care about that,' said Rudy, his scowl deepening. 'This is real life. Not television. You involved yourself in a situation you didn't need to be in. You didn't think about the bigger picture; the effects your actions would have on the wider scheme. Now, you've fucked everything up. If Raider doesn't recover, we'll need to make it right with Elijah. He's out for blood.'

Natty listened to Rudy's words, and rather than feel chastened, his annoyance grew.

'You may not care about the situation, and Elijah may not, but I do. Raider overstepped the mark, and you lot weren't going to deal with him. So, I did.'

Both men stared at the other, Natty's gaze defiant. Rudy was almost impressed with his demeanour, but shook his head. He stepped closer to Natty, almost nose-to-nose with him, looking him dead in the eye.

'You were doing so well, Nathaniel. For a while, we thought you could do it. We thought you could ascend to that next level, but you've undone all that hard work. You're out.'

Natty frowned.

'Out of what?'

'You're gone from the crew. Effective immediately. We don't want to see you at any of the spots. You'll be paid up to date, and that's it.'

Natty froze, unable to believe what had just happened. He knew he'd messed up, but he had done it for the right reasons. Never did he imagine it would go like this. He cleared his dry throat, thinking of the words to save this.

'I . . . let me talk to my uncle. I can fix this.'

'There's nothing to say, and nothing to fix. The man you came with will escort you out. Goodbye, Nathaniel.'

———

AT HOME, Natty sat in stunned shock, still reeling from the meeting and realising it was all over for him. Despite his words at the end, he knew his uncle wouldn't change his mind. Wiping his eyes, he looked down at his phone, seeing missed calls from Lorraine, Tommy, and Spence. He had a quick conversation with Spence, trying to sound calm, telling him he would speak to him when he was back in Leeds.

Next, he spoke to Tommy.

'Tom. What's happening?'

'Just giving you a heads up, fam. Lorraine knows what happened. She's on the warpath.'

Natty closed his eyes. This was the last thing he needed, but there was no way around it.

'Thanks for the warning. I'll handle it.' After a little more conversation, he ended the call.

Looking at his missed calls after hanging up, he saw three of them were from Lorraine. He stared at her name for a few seconds, his finger hovering over her name, considering calling her back rather than facing her. After a few moments, he put his phone away, deciding to speak to her face-to-face. Walking to the door, Natty again took out his phone, checking the temperature, deciding to grab a hooded top. Slowly, he pulled the basic grey hoody over his head and returned to the door. His hand rested on the key, but didn't turn to open the lock. Natty stared at the key, his mind racing. After a few more moments, he shook his head, annoyed. Turning the key, he swung the door open and walked through it, locking it behind him.

Taking a deep breath, he set off.

———

SPENCE ARRIVED home after dropping off his dad, his mind whirring with the news about Natty.

Word had spread swiftly about his dismissal from the organisation. Despite the severity of what Natty had done, Spence was still shocked that it had happened. He had always seen Natty as untouchable while he was working for his uncle, and it seemed crazy that anything could have gotten him the sack.

Spence wondered if it was a sign that the alliance between Elijah's crew and their team had grown ever stronger.

Regardless, he wanted to speak with Natty. They would need to discuss a plan. He hoped Natty had money saved. If not, Spence would help him out, knowing Natty wouldn't hesitate to do the same if the situation was reversed.

Spence hummed a tune as he unlocked the door. He hadn't heard from Anika while he'd been away. Locking the front door behind him, he called out for her, leaving his travel bag in the hallway, but heard nothing. Frowning, he went to check upstairs, assuming she had gone to bed early. Entering their room, he froze.

Anika's wardrobes were opened, all her clothing missing. Stomach lurching, Spence noticed her perfumes and jewellery were gone. He swayed on the spot, barely avoiding throwing up. As he systematically searched the house, he tried convincing himself it was a mistake, but by the end, he collapsed onto the sofa in the living room, tears prickling his eyes. If he was being honest, he'd known before the frantic search that he wasn't going to find Anika. The moment he'd seen her clothes were missing, he knew.

The tears streamed down Spence's face, and he angrily wiped them away, not knowing what could have caused this, but blaming himself. He should have probed more, listened to her and got her to admit what was on her mind. Instead, he had let it fester. Frantically, he called her friend Carmen, heart racing as he waited for her to pick up.

'Hey, Spence.'

By Carmen's solemn tone, he knew she was aware of what had transpired.

'Where is she, Carm? Please, don't mess me around.'

'Spence . . .'

'Carm. Please.' Spence's tone hardened.

'I don't know. That's the truth. She said she was sorry, but she couldn't stay. I couldn't get her to tell me where she was going, but she's got family down south. She might have gone there.'

Spence's stomach sank.

'She must have mentioned something when she stopped with you the other night.'

'Spence . . . she never stopped with me. She hasn't for a while now.'

'Is there someone else?' Spence's heart broke anew even uttering the words, but he had to know.

'I don't know. It would explain a lot, but Anika loves you, Spence. This could just be temporary. Hang in there.'

'Hang in there?'

'Spence—'

Spence swallowed the harsh words he'd wanted to unleash on Carmen.

'Yes?'

'She . . . left you a letter. She didn't tell me what was in it. She just said it would be where she stacks all the rest of the post. She said you always hated it when she did that. That you never did manage to tame her messy side.'

Spence stood, arm falling by his side. He noticed a letter atop the stack of post near the door, just where Carmen said it was. He heard Carmen's faint mumblings in the background as he slowly moved toward the letter. When he reached it, he placed his right hand on the note, ending his call with the left.

Opening the letter, he began to read, a tear escaping his eye, tracing down the page.

Entering Lorraine's, it was clear from the outset that this wouldn't be easy. Jaden was already in bed, unable to distract Lorraine. She glared at Natty as he walked in, and he swallowed down the lump in his throat. Lorraine's eyes flitted to his injured hand.

'How is it?'

Natty's eyebrow rose.

'I'll be fine.'

'What the hell were you thinking?' Lorraine snapped, her manner eerily similar to Rudy's earlier. Natty rubbed his eyes, but met her stare.

'Raider hurt you.'

'Raider is my problem, Nat. I didn't ask for your help. You put yourself at risk with what you did, not to mention that you nearly killed him. How would you have explained it to Jaden if you had?'

'He's never been a dad to Jaden,' Natty snapped, watching Lorraine's eyes flash with anger.

'That doesn't involve you. I . . . appreciate everything you've done for my son and me, but you could have killed Raider, and that's unacceptable.'

'I did it for you.'

Lorraine shook her head.

'Don't even try that shit. You did it for ego. It's always about ego with you. You and Raider, you always want to be the big dicks. You may have convinced yourself that it's about me, but it isn't. Me and Jaden are in the middle, and I won't put up with it anymore.'

With a sinking feeling, Natty again met her eyes.

'What are you saying?'

Lorraine lowered her head for just a moment, eyes glistening with tears.

'I don't want you around my son, Nathaniel. I want you to leave, and I don't want you to wait for me to cool down, or to try to sweet talk your way around me in future. Leave, and don't bother coming back.'

Lorraine's words twisted Natty's stomach in a way he had never experienced. His legs felt heavy, and maintaining his composure was the hardest thing under the weight of her words.

'I *did* do it for you,' he said, knowing that the words would have no effect. 'No matter what you say, this isn't about me.'

Lorraine shook her head, tears streaming down her face.

'If that was the case, you would have spoken to me first. I had you all wrong, and that's something I will need to deal with. You don't respect me, and you didn't consider my feelings.' She took a deep, shuddering breath, pointing to a bag on the sofa. 'I want you to take the laptop back. It wouldn't be right to keep it.'

Natty stared at Lorraine, sadness in his eyes.

'No. It's yours,' he finally replied, heading for the door.

———

AFTER LEAVING LORRAINE, Natty once again stewed at home, the pain he felt quickly turning to anger. He'd spoken with Elijah, Rudy, and Lorraine, but none of them truly believed Natty had done what he did for Lorraine. Instead, they thought it was an excuse to get back at Raider, which Natty knew wasn't true. Only Spence seemed to believe him.

Upon entering the house, Natty had tossed his phone on the sofa, grabbed a bottle of brandy from the kitchen, then commenced drinking. Rudy had left him in the lurch, kicking him from the crew and claiming the decision was made by his uncle. As Natty sipped his brandy, he wondered how integral Uncle Mitch was in making the decision, and if Rudy had tried speaking up for him. He imagined he hadn't. Rudy knew better than to speak up against his uncle, especially when it came to protecting someone else.

Through a blurry haze a while later, Natty became aware of a knocking at the door. Stumbling to his feet, he still clutched the bottle, ready to use it as a weapon. When he saw Spence standing there, he let him in, missing the devastated look on his friend's face.

'Have you heard?' Natty said, when they were both in the living room. He collapsed back onto the sofa and took another sip. Spence remained standing, not responding. After a moment, Natty glanced over. His eyes widened as he noticed how unkempt Spence looked. His eyes were swollen and drawn, and his clothing was rumpled. 'What happened?'

'Anika left me.' Spence gnawed his upper lip, cheeks quivering. Natty blew out a breath. He wished he could say it was surprising, but it had been building for a while.

Spence swallowed down a lump in his throat, his voice hoarse.

'She took all her things and left. I tried speaking with Carmen and her friends, but they're not telling me anything. I don't know what to do.'

Natty sat up on the sofa, wiping his mouth. This was the worst time for Spence to be unloading on him. He'd lost a lot in a short time with his demotion and rejection. He had his own issues to deal with. Blinking tightly, Natty tried his best to sober up. Spence needed him.

Spence waited for Natty to respond. After a moment, he spoke again.

'Bro, what am I supposed to do now?'

'Nothing you can do but move on,' said Natty, eyes fixed ahead, thinking of Lorraine, their moment by the door, when he'd walked away.

'How?'

'Don't think about her. Don't let her have that power over you.'

Neither man spoke for a moment.

'I loved her, bro. We were building something, and now she's gone. Just like that. What did I do?'

Natty shook his head. 'You didn't do anything, fam. You were there for her. This isn't on you.'

Spence leant against the wall, sighing. 'Then why do I feel like it is? Why do I think I should have done more?'

'What more could you have done?' Natty thought about his reaction to Lorraine's assault.

He hadn't even checked on her. He'd charged after Raider instead.

'I could have listened more. Could have asked what she wanted, rather than going about by myself; my goals and aspirations.'

Natty took another deep pull of the liquor, wincing as it burned his throat. He wiped his eyes with his free hand.

'Look on the bright side, bro. You're free. We're both single, and ready to move on.' He forced a chuckle, finally glancing at Spence. Spence's laugh was equally forced, and silence ensued again, both men considering their situations. Natty took another sip, then offered the bottle to Spence, who shook his head. Shrugging, Natty took another.

'Bro, you're better off without her. Think about it. You know Rosie likes you, so see what she's saying. She'll be good for you.' Rosie made him think of Lorraine, and his stomach clenched. He took another deep swig. Realising Spence hadn't responded, he glanced at him again, taken aback by the disgust on Spence's face.

'It's that fucking easy for you, isn't it?' he snarled, his lip curling.

Natty's body tensed, his muscles quivering.

'Wait a fucking minute. You've no idea what it's like for me.'

'Don't I? You've told me to move on, and you're already suggesting women I can move on with.'

'That has nothing to do with me. I'm doing it for you; so you can get over that stupid bitch.'

'She's not a stupid bitch,' roared Spence. 'I love her.'

Natty's eyes flashed with anger. Staggering from the sofa, he scowled at Spence.

'Are you really this stupid?'

'What?' Spence was stunned at Natty's change of demeanour.

'I'm saying . . . how could you not see it? All those times you were out working, and she's getting dressed up to chill with her friend, who has a fiancé she's loved up with . . . you can't see it? Where were the photos of the nights out if she was out all the time? Why did she get so fucking camera-shy all of a sudden? She was cheating, and you were too fucking whipped to see it. She was getting fucked in the Hood. I followed her.' Natty's scowl intensified. 'She fucked Cam, you know . . . back in the day. Did she ever tell you that, when you were talking shit about building a future with her?'

Silence ensued. Spence's eyes opened, staring at Natty in horror. Natty breathed hard, hand tightening around the bottle. The moment lingered. Shaking his head, Spence made his way to the door, leaving without saying a word.

CHAPTER TWENTY-SIX

'I'M SORRY ABOUT ANIKA.'

Rosie had never seen Spence looking so dishevelled. They were sat in his living room. Rosie had never been to the house before, and had been surprised when he'd reached out, wondering if he was ready to get something going with them.

Upon arriving, she realised Anika wasn't there, and Spence had quickly told her what happened. Rosie's surprise at being invited turned promptly to shock when she learned the whole story. Anika had apparently been cheating on Spence, and he and Natty had fallen out most explosively.

Spence's demeanour was alarming. His shoulders were slumped, and he looked tired and drawn.

'Are you really?' He replied after a few moments.

'Am I really what?' Rosie blinked, confused.

'Sorry.'

'Yes. It's no secret that I like you, but I wouldn't want you to get hurt so I could get what I wanted.'

Spence sighed, lowering his head.

'I feel like such a fool. I was so focused on bettering myself that I couldn't see what Natty could.'

Rosie cleared her throat. 'Do you know how Natty is doing? Lorraine has fallen out with him. Big time.'

Spence looked at her sharply. 'Because of Raider?'

Rosie nodded. 'She doesn't want him around her and Jaden anymore. I feel bad. If I hadn't told you, then it wouldn't have happened.'

'It would have got out either way, and Natty wasn't going to hold back. You know how he feels about her. About both of them. Still, I haven't spoken to him since the fallout.'

Rosie sat closer to Spence, resting a hand on top of his.

'Spence, I know you're hurting, but Natty needs you.'

Spence shook his head.

'I'm not sure he does. He seemed pretty mad when I saw him. I still can't believe he would snap on me like that, or that he wouldn't tell me about Cam and Anika.'

'The only way you'll get those answers is to speak with him,' said Rosie. 'Despite everything, he's your best friend.'

Taking a risk, Rosie rested her head on Spence's shoulder, gratified when he didn't pull away.

SEVERAL DAYS after his fight with Spence, Natty was in a club. He'd had several drinks, trying not to think about his problems. Cameron had been unable to meet him, and Natty hadn't had a proper conversation with his friend about the current state of affairs. He didn't know how to initiate the conversation, and he had no plan in place.

Nothing but getting drunk and distracting himself.

With that in mind, he headed towards a group of women, shocked at how shaky his legs were. Zeroing in on a curly-haired mixed-race woman, he smiled at her.

'What's your name?' He asked, noticing her eyes slightly widen. She gave him a coy smile, obviously surprised he'd approached her in such a way. Natty waited her out. Despite his mounting issues, he knew how to approach and deal with women. *Most women*, he corrected, Lorraine flitting across his mind before he ruthlessly pushed her out.

'Gaby,' she replied, her soft voice barely heard over the music. Natty gave her his name, gave her friends a cursory greeting, then took Gaby to get a drink. It took her a second to warm up to him, but soon she'd given him her life story. She'd broken up with her boyfriend a few weeks ago, and though she claimed it was for good, Natty had dealt with enough of these women to be able to read between the lines. He predicted she would be back with him by the end of the month.

'What about you?' She asked, twirling her hair with her free hand, eyes glistening. 'Are you seeing anyone?'

Natty shook his head.

'It's been a while since I've done the relationship thing,' he said.

'That's too bad. How come?'

'Guess I've been waiting for the right woman,' he replied, keeping eye contact. It was a corny line, but Gaby still giggled.

'I guess you have. What happens when you find her?'

'I'd have to shoot my shot and see what happens.' Natty stepped closer to Gaby, watching as she instinctively moistened her lips. He could see in his mind how this would all play out. They'd go back to her place and undoubtedly have sex; after that, it would be up to him. Maybe this was what he needed. It was easier than the complexities of dealing with feelings, and actually *liking* people.

Try as he might, he couldn't shake the memories of sitting on Lorraine's sofa, with her head on his shoulder, content and happy in a way he'd never felt with another woman. Internally he groaned, feeling his stomach tighten.

'Natty?'

He blinked, now back in the sweaty, dark club. It had lost its splendour. Even the drink didn't taste the same anymore. He didn't want to be here.

'Natty? Are you okay?'

Gaby was trying to talk to him, a look of concern quickly giving way to annoyance when she realised he was ignoring her.

'Yeah. I'm fine.'

'Are you sure?'

He nodded. Gaby placed her hand on his, but he pulled away.

'I can't do this. Gotta go,' he said, disposing of his drink and leaving the club.

By the time he made it home, it was almost midnight. He'd been off the radar for the past few days, trying to avoid thinking about his problems. It was becoming clear that approach wasn't going to work. He knew his feelings for Lorraine were the real deal. He'd been hiding from himself, and his attitude had led to this isolation. Most of his world was alienating him, and he couldn't blame them.

Natty slumped on his sofa and stared into space, thinking of his dad. He knew of his dad's killer reputation, but he wondered if he'd ever gone through issues like this. He wondered if he'd ever had feelings for a woman like Natty did. He wondered if his dad had ever felt such a way for his mum, but he wasn't sure.

His whole life, Natty had fought his way out of any problems. He'd developed a reputation, refusing to back down, doing things his way, always ready to take it to the next level, but that wasn't what he wanted to be, and the high of battling always left him feeling hollow afterwards. Fighting always led to more problems, and in the end, none of it was worth it.

Natty didn't regret his decision with Raider, but knew it could have been handled better. He could have shown more maturity, but the rage had taken over. It had taken over his conversation with Spence too. Spence had always dared to be himself; to show his feelings even at the risk of being mercilessly teased by his friends, and now he was hurting. He had come to Natty for support. Natty had shattered his world further, and he hadn't heard from Spence since.

The longer he sat there, the longer Natty knew he couldn't go on like this. He couldn't hide from the world and pretend things weren't going on. He had to show some of the maturity Lorraine and Rudy had previously lambasted him about. Even if he didn't get the resolutions he wanted, he still needed to try. With that in mind, he left the house.

———

SPENCE'S STREET was empty as Natty hesitated outside his place, some of his newfound courage dissipating. He rubbed his hands, feeling the early morning chill. He'd said some horrific things to Spence, and now he was terrified that he might have gone too far to be able to fix the friendship. That desire to show maturity emanated through, though, and he knocked on the door. Spence opened it almost a minute later, his expression hardening when he saw Natty standing there. He rubbed his eyes, adjusting the dressing gown he'd clearly thrown on before answering the door.

'Hey,' said Natty.

'Nat,' Spence's tone was icy, but Natty wouldn't let that bother him.

'I wanted to talk to you.'

'Are you sure you didn't say everything you needed to say last time? You were pretty thorough.'

Natty sighed, lowering his head.

'I shouldn't have thrown Anika and Cam in your face like that,' he said. 'I'm sorry, Spence. You're one of my best friends, and you deserved better.'

Spence blinked, but maintained his stiff demeanour. Natty blew into his hands, rubbing them together. Noticing, Spence stepped aside so Natty could enter. Heading into the living room, Spence switched on the light, both men remaining standing.

Natty glanced around the room, thinking of the last time he'd been to Spence's. Life had gotten so hectic for him lately, that he couldn't recall. The living room remained the same; various books splayed across the dark brown coffee table. Several plants dotted around, along with a bookshelf, a sofa, and several smaller chairs. The walls were a caramel colour that gave the room some nice character.

'Why did you never tell me?' Spence spoke after a long moment.

Natty searched for the words.

'Those two were in the past, and I guess I thought it wasn't such a big deal. Besides, you were happy. You both were. I didn't wanna say something that caused issues.'

'It was obviously a big deal. Cam had a thing about my relationship for the longest time. Anika was distant and awkward about our future, and all of that was probably because the pair of them had a history, one

I was too stupid to see.' Spence sighed, a tear leaving his eye. 'I . . . don't know how I'm supposed to feel.'

Stepping forward, Natty gripped his friend's shoulder.

'Spence, you can feel any way you like, fam. You have the right to be hurt, and I had no right to speak to you like I did. Deep down, I always respected you for owning your feelings and being honest, even when I was teasing you for the same thing. Avoiding my own problems has landed me in my current pile of shit.'

Nodding, Spence bowed his head for a moment.

'How are you doing with not working? Must be tough to get used to.'

Natty blew out a breath.

'I deserved it. My life is in complete shambles right now. Lorraine won't speak with me. Fuck knows what Elijah is gonna do. Tonight, I hit a club by myself, so I could get a woman, but when it came time to close the deal, I flinched. Should have listened to you instead of getting caught up.'

Spence shook his head.

'Your heart was in the right place. Right now, you seem like you're thinking clearly. You should speak with Lorraine and Rudy, and tell them how you really feel about things.'

'Speaking with Rudy won't get me my role back.'

Spence met Natty's eyes.

'Is the role what you really want?'

'What do you mean?'

'The life . . . hustling. Is that what you really want? You have an opportunity to truly reinvent yourself. Not many people get that.'

Natty felt a smile coming to his face, overwhelmed by positive emotions towards Spence.

'You're a little genius, Spence, you know that?'

'Less of the *little*,' chuckled Spence. 'Don't forget, I still couldn't solve my own problems. My girl still left me.' Some of the light left his voice then.

'You had the balls to try. It'll take time, but you will come out of this stronger. Onto bigger and better things. Speaking of which . . .

have you spoken to Rosie lately?' Natty smiled warmly at his friend, who returned it.

'It's just that easy for you, isn't it?' he replied. Both men laughed, feeling truly better for the first time in days.

LORRAINE SAT AT HOME, watching television. She was still recovering from her injuries. Rosie had kept her company, but left a short while ago. Lorraine had appreciated the distraction, and with Rosie around, hadn't had much time to think about her issues. At first, she'd been annoyed at her friend for going against her wishes and telling Spence about what Raider had done, but Rosie's heart had been in the right place.

Jaden had already gone to bed with little fuss. She still hadn't told him what had happened to Raider, but he'd asked several times about Natty, and whether he would be coming around to play with him. Lorraine did her best to avoid giving a definitive answer.

Truthfully, she didn't know what to say to him. Deep down, Lorraine accepted that Natty had been protecting her, but she still wished the situation had been handled differently. Things with Natty had never been simple, though; it was just another thing she had learned to accept.

Despite all of Natty's flaws, his heart had always been in the right place. Lorraine only wished that was the same where she was concerned. Looks and demeanour aside, she had always wanted more from Natty, and for a while, it seemed things were trending in that direction. Their recent interactions before their fight had evolved, going from arguing at parties and drunken sleepovers, to conversations about careers, Natty letting her confide in him, and most importantly, being there for her son in a way his dad had never been.

He'd even bought her a new laptop so that she could keep studying. The gesture had meant so much to her. It was a sign Natty was no longer just invested in what he could get out of the situation; he was invested in Lorraine; her success.

Lorraine blinked, emotions ablaze, realising she had delved far further into her feelings than anticipated. When her phone beeped, she gratefully seized the distraction. Her heart clenched when she read the message from Natty:

Come outside.

After reading the message twice, Lorraine sat still, weighing up whether to do it. They'd had harsh words last time they'd seen one another, and she didn't see how things would be better this time. Still, Natty had sent a text, rather than knocking at the door, or shouting for her to come out, and she was curious enough to wonder what he would say. Clambering to her feet, she slipped on a pair of sliders and unlocked the door.

Natty stood in the garden, hands in his pockets. The first thing Lorraine noticed was that he didn't seem as cocksure as he usually did. He appeared to be standing straighter, and was meeting her eyes. Lorraine kept her eyes on him, waiting for him to speak.

'How are you?'

Lorraine blinked. She hadn't expected that. Instinctively, her hand went to her ribs.

'I'm getting there. Is that all you came to say?'

'I came to apologise. Seems to be a running theme of mine. I've been saying it a lot lately.' Natty rubbed the back of his neck. 'I've fucked up a fair few things.'

Lorraine stayed quiet, not knowing what to say. Natty cleared his throat.

'I . . . have feelings for you. Proper ones. I hid from them for a long time because I didn't think we could work out, and I *knew* you were too good for me. I knew it then just as I know it now. Doing that, though, it led me here, with everything around me turned to shit.'

Lorraine opened and closed her mouth before she realised she'd done it. Her heart raced, unable to believe it was Natty speaking.

'I grew up wanting to be just like my dad. Then, he died, and I was just there, pushing forward in a life that didn't love me. The only one that I knew.' Again, Natty cleared his throat. 'I wish I'd spoken to you before I went after Raider, but I'll never feel bad about protecting you, Lorraine, because I love you.'

Lorraine gasped, the first noise she'd made since Natty started speaking, unable to believe what she had heard. Natty's eyes blazed as he stared at her.

'Anyway, look after yourself. You have my number if you need anything — anything at all.' He left, swallowed by the darkness before Lorraine could unstick her throat enough to speak actual words. Helplessly, she stared at the spot he'd vacated, a storm of emotions swirling inside her.

'Natty . . .' she whispered to the night.

———

As NATTY HEADED TO DELORES', he expected to feel bashful at baring his soul to Lorraine. He hadn't expected to use the *L word* during his speech, but didn't regret it. Once he said it, he knew it to be true. It had been true for a long time, and he was done hiding from it.

When he reached Delores' place, he knocked at the door, but no one answered. The light was on, though, so Rudy was likely inside. Delores never stayed up late. He tried the door, which was unlocked. Natty entered, going over the words he planned to say to Rudy, intending to keep it short and sweet as he had with Lorraine and Spence.

'Did you handle the pickup?'

Rudy's voice made Natty pause. He hadn't realised he would be interrupting a meeting. He almost turned to leave.

'Course I did,' replied a familiar voice. Natty's eyes widened. He hadn't realised Wonder and Rudy were on speaking terms. 'The Money is low. Second week running.'

'That's the *Natty effect*,' said Elijah. 'Say what you want about him . . . He knew how to keep that team humming.'

Natty stepped closer. Despite the harsh words last time they were face-to-face, Elijah sounded impressed. It was a reminder to Natty of how well he had done to establish a base in Little London.

Before he messed it all up.

'I'll get them in line. Don't worry about that,' said Wonder, snorting. 'Natty's not the only money-maker.'

'Forget that.' Rudy's voice cut through the conversation, and the others fell silent. 'Little London served its purpose, but we have other things to consider. Who should we use for the hit?'

'I'd have used Raider, if your stepson hadn't nearly killed him,' replied Elijah.

'I could do it,' said Wonder.

Natty's heart pounded, wondering if they were talking about killing him. Warren had been the last major casualty, and that was due to his refusal to fall in line. In his time running Little London, Natty hadn't heard of anyone kicking up a fuss, and didn't see what could have changed in a few weeks.

'Clearly, we need to think on this some more,' said Rudy. 'Mitch won't be easy to get.'

Natty's brow furrowed. He couldn't think of any *Mitch* involved with Little London, and certainly not one that warranted such a discussion.

'Anyone can be taken out,' said Elijah. 'We've already gone over this. Our people won't wait forever.'

Natty was half-listening, going over the name *Mitch* in his head. Stomach jolting, he thought of his uncle.

Was it possible they were talking about him?

Rudy grunted. Natty had never heard him sound so tired.

'We won't get a second chance. I've worked with him for decades. I know how he thinks.'

'You mean you've worked *for him*,' retorted Elijah.

Natty froze. Blood pounded in his ears. They *were* talking about killing his uncle.

The men continued talking, but Natty wasn't listening. He needed to let his uncle know what had happened.

Moving back slowly to escape, a floorboard creaked beneath his feet. Heart thumping, Natty stopped, wondering if they'd heard. When the sounds of their voices continued, he breathed a sigh of relief.

He turned to leave, only to find himself face-to-face with another man.

For a second, neither moved, and then the man charged. Natty forced him into the coffee table, then to the floor. Taking in the man's face as he groaned in pain, Natty realised he didn't recognise him. As he coughed and spluttered, the air driven out of him, footsteps ensued. Elijah and Rudy stumbled from the kitchen, Rudy's eyes widening when he saw Natty.

'He heard everything. Kill him.'

Natty didn't hesitate. He turned and ran as a flurry of bullets were fired his way.

CHAPTER TWENTY-SEVEN

NATTY SURGED DOWN THE STREET, ducking low when he heard the crack of another nearby bullet. His heart raced, stunned over what had transpired. *Rudy was working against the crew.* Elijah's men were after him, and he needed to get away before they killed him. Once he'd done that, he could make sense of what was happening. He didn't know who was involved, but he needed to get to people he could trust.

Right now, that meant Spence and Cameron.

Increasing his speed, he hurried down an alleyway, his long legs helping him accelerate from his pursuers. Hearing their shouts, he ducked into a garden, crouching down, stilling his breathing. He knew he was on Markham Avenue. He was close to his mum's house, but he couldn't involve her in this mess. It was his problem to sort out. He pulled out his phone, but the heavy breathing of his pursuers caused him to pause.

'Where's he gone?' One of them asked.

'He must have run ahead,' a voice Natty recognised as Wonder's, replied. 'He's one of those fitness freaks. We should have popped him in the room, the little pussy.'

'Can't believe he outran us, still. I used to win awards for running in school.'

'No, you didn't. You barely went, and you were never a runner. Remember, I knew you back then.'

'Whatever, Wonder. You don't know everything. You just think you do.'

Natty listened. They weren't directly outside the garden he'd hidden in, but were close by, and were taking little care to keep their voices down. Their sloppiness worked to his favour.

Natty was tempted to jump out and attack the men. He knew he could take Wonder, but didn't recognise the voice of the second man, and the fact they were both armed stopped him. He just needed to wait a while longer.

'Fuck it, let's go back to Elijah. He'll know what to do next. We'll get Natty next time. Better still, Rudy can do it. This is his problem.'

After the pair stomped away, Natty waited another five minutes, stunned by his good luck. In their shoes, he'd have searched every garden on the road, but the fact they hadn't suited him. He tried his uncle, but the number wouldn't connect. Chest heaving, Natty dialled a special number he'd left for him years ago. After he told his uncle what was going on, he would meet with Spence and Cameron and devise a plan.

'Yeah,' a voice answered, not one Natty recognised.

'I need to talk to my Uncle Mitch.'

'No *Mitch* here. Think you've got the wrong number.'

'Don't take the piss. I was given this number, and told to call if there was an emergency.' Natty's voice rose. He'd have torn this man's head off in person, but he needed to keep his wits, now more than ever.

'Was the number the only thing you were given?'

'Yeah . . .' Something went off in Natty's head. 'Wait! *Loyalty1212*,' he said, remembering the code phrase he had been given. The person on the other end paused.

'Okay. Leave your message, Natty.'

He blinked, surprised the person knew his name. He assumed it was tied to the word he had been given, and that each person had a different one. It was a clever bit of skill, but he didn't have the time to admire it.

'Listen, Rudy's dirty. He's working with Elijah, and the plan is to take out my uncle and take over. I don't know how many people they have, or who is involved, but they tried to kill me.'

'I'll relay the message. For now, you need to stay out of sight.'

'Did you hear what I said? Rudy's a snake!'

'Like I said, I will relay this, but now is the time for you to listen. Do you have a spot you can lie low in?'

'Yeah, I'll—'

The line went dead. Eyes widening, Natty glanced at the phone, his stomach lurching as he realised the battery had died. Stupidly, he'd forgotten to charge it in the morning, and now it had cost him.

Clambering to his feet, he left the garden, running down the road. He needed to get to Cameron's as quickly as he could. Once there, he could regroup and ring Spence. Natty thought about the man who had answered the phone, annoyed that he didn't know more about the inner workings of his uncle's organisation.

For all he knew, they were in league with Rudy, and he had just tipped him off.

Taking another deep breath, he forced down the negative thoughts. They wouldn't help him in this situation. Cameron didn't live far away, and he would have weapons. Natty didn't want to kill anyone, but if it came to his life or theirs, he wouldn't hesitate.

Through sheer luck, he didn't run into any of Elijah's or Rudy's men on the streets. By the time he reached Cameron's, he was panting, his t-shirt sticking to him. Sucking in air, he knocked twice then tried Cameron's handle, pleased to find it was unlocked.

Cameron sat in the living room, sipping a glass of brandy. When he glanced up and saw Natty, he gave a start, spilling the drink on himself.

'Shit,' he cursed, leaping to his feet and wiping away the mess. Natty looked from the glass, to the bottle on the table, then to his friend.

'Why do you look so shook?'

'I didn't expect you to just burst in my door like the police,' said Cameron. 'I'm a little drunk; plus, I had a few lines earlier.'

'Why?' Natty asked. He knew Cameron liked to dabble, but indulging in drink and drugs when he was alone, with no events or parties on, seemed strange.

'This chick was meant to roll through, but she cancelled.'

'Fine,' replied Natty. 'My phone died. I need to make a call.'

'What's going on?' Cameron asked. Natty was tempted to have a drink, but needed to keep a clear head.

'Rudy's working with Elijah.' Natty gave it to him straight. Cameron's eyes narrowed.

'Course he is. We all are.'

'No, not like that. They're in an alliance,' said Natty. Cameron still looked confused, so Natty broke it down, telling him of the meeting he had interrupted.

Cameron shook his head.

'I can't believe that . . .'

'It's happening, so you'd better believe it,' replied Natty. 'They're gonna take out anyone who doesn't go along with the plan.' He watched Cameron, expecting him to start panicking and overreacting. Instead, Cameron refilled his drink and took a sip, his brow furrowed.

'What are you going to do?'

Cameron's reaction pleased Natty. He hadn't wanted to talk his friend around, and he'd simply reacted how Natty had wanted. No dramatics; keeping things simple, wanting to know the plan.

'They had me trapped, and my phone died as I was calling for backup,' Natty replied.

'Who were you trying to call?'

'Do you have a charger? I need to use it.'

Cameron pointed to a corner of the room. Natty located a frayed charger. It had seen better days, but would do.

'Ring Spence. Get him over here ASAP.'

'I can ring some other people too. Get more bodies.'

'We don't know who we can trust, bro. Rudy is talking about a takeover. It only works if he has pieces on the inside. Until we know who we can trust, it needs to be me, you, and Spence.'

'Spence is probably holed up with his bitch.'

Natty's nostrils flared.

'Anika left him. But that doesn't matter now. Just do it.'

Cameron smirked, but didn't say anything. Natty headed to the kitchen and downed a glass of water. He refilled it and downed the second, then let the water run, washing his face, feeling refreshed afterwards.

'Spence ain't answering.' Cameron stood in the doorway. Natty wiped his face with a paper towel, then disposed of the rubbish.

'Shit. They could have sent people there already. They know he's down with us. Rudy knows everything about us.'

'What are we gonna do? Wanna go to his house?' Suggested Cameron.

'Nah, we need to stay holed up here for now. I need a strap.'

'I've got one hidden upstairs.' Cameron hurried from the room, and Natty took a deep breath. It worried him that Spence was off the radar. He thought about how logical his friend was. Spence not answering his phone was serious. There could be multiple reasons he wasn't responding, and Natty hated that his paranoia had set in. He hated himself for questioning Spence's loyalty, but based on everything that had happened tonight, it was justified.

Panic rising, Natty hurried to his phone. It had only been charging a few minutes, but he turned it on, and saw a text message from Spence:

> Heard there was a shooting near your mums.
> You good?

Natty's heart stilled. Cameron had said he couldn't get through to Spence, yet Spence was active. Before Natty could consider this, he pushed the call button. It rang twice.

'Nat?'

'Spence?'

'Who else would it be? Glad you're alright. What's the deal with the gunshots?'

'Look, there's no time. I'm at Cam's, and—'

'Hang up.'

Natty turned, unsurprised to see Cameron aiming a gun at him. Without a word, he ended the call and dropped the phone.

CHAPTER TWENTY-EIGHT

'WHY, CAM?' Natty asked, trying to maintain control.

'You're not the only one who has plans,' replied Cameron, the gun aimed at his chest. 'Big things are happening. I was smart enough to get in on the ground floor.'

Natty shook his head, his stomach dropping. Cameron was one of his oldest friends, someone he had known since childhood. He couldn't believe he had betrayed him.

'I may have had plans, but you were always with me, fam. I'd have taken you wherever I went, and you know that,' Natty replied.

'Don't give me that crap!' Cameron exploded. 'All you care about is yourself. You didn't bring me into Little London to get money with you. You put Spence in charge over me, and just expected me to take it. When did you ever do anything for me?'

Natty kept his eyes on Cameron, knowing now more than ever, he needed to remain calm. He would deal with Cameron's betrayal if he ever got out of his predicament. Right now, he needed to keep him talking.

'Who turned you? Elijah? Rudy? One of the flunkies?'

'Does it matter? You're finished either way. Your uncle can't survive what's going on. He'd never have gotten as far as he did without Rudy.'

Natty tried putting the pieces together, his chest jolting from all the possible implications.

'Is Spence involved?'

Cameron scoffed.

'Spence is as soft as you. You're both pussy whipped, especially you. You should have died for the beating you gave Raider.' Cameron smirked. 'Truthfully, Elijah pushed for that, but Rudy talked him out of it.'

That fact surprised Natty, and he struggled not to show it. *If Rudy was out for his blood, why wouldn't he let Elijah kill him?* He wanted to ask, but knew he wouldn't get the answers.

'How long have you hated me?' Natty decided to go in another direction. He needed to keep Cameron off balance. By any means necessary. He couldn't rush him. Smartly, he kept himself out of reach, his hands unwavering.

'I don't hate you.' Cameron's mouth fell open a moment, then he smiled. 'You're just weak. The moves you've made have been trash. You're a little bitch for your uncle, and he's a damn coward. Too scared to even show his face in public.'

Natty was intrigued, but didn't know where Cameron was taking it. When Cameron didn't add anything else, he spoke.

'What happens next?'

'I called Rudy. Men are on their way to take care of you.'

Natty smirked. Cameron's grin vanished.

'Why are you smiling? Did you hear what I said?'

'No matter what team you're on, you end up as the bitch, don't you? Whether it's me, or Elijah, or Rudy, no one respects you. We use you for the little things,' said Natty.

Cameron stepped forward, fury lining his face.

'I'm a big part of the plan. For once, you're not the main guy, and you can't deal with it.'

Natty laughed.

'I'll die knowing I'm not a boot licker like you, Cam. People only respect you because of me, and deep down, you know that. I bet that's how they got to you. I'll tell you this, though: first chance they get, you'll be out, because without me, you're nothing.'

Cameron's finger tightened on the trigger. Natty's heart slammed against his chest. He needed to play it carefully here. He didn't want Cameron to shoot him, but he also didn't want him thinking clearly. He needed to keep him distracted.

'Are you even *allowed* to kill me?' He laughed. 'We keep our instructions simple with you, so you don't fuck them up. It's part of your programming.' Natty resisted the urge to tremble, breathing slightly deeper to steady himself.

'You lost, Natty. I could take you if I wanted to. I don't take orders from anyone.'

Natty grinned. His attempts to distract Cameron by preying on his obvious insecurities was working.

'You still need to wait for backup, right? You ran to call as soon as I got here. Didn't have the guts to take me on without a gun, right? And you have the nerve to call me and Spence pussies?'

That was the clincher. Cameron's jaw jutted, putting down the gun and kicking it away. With a yell, he charged Natty, who didn't move, allowing himself to be taken to the floor. They wrestled around, Natty quickly getting the momentum.

Cameron was no slouch, but Natty was bigger and more scientific. Landing several solid punches to his chest and stomach, he wrapped his arm around Cameron's throat and squeezed. Cameron began kicking, trying to break the grip, but he had the move locked in, feeling his movements growing weaker.

Heavy footsteps distracted him, causing him to loosen the hold. Cameron took advantage, elbowing Natty several times and breaking free just as Spence burst in, aiming a gun at Cameron. Before he could act, Wonder and the other man came through the front. Cameron grinned.

'I was wondering when you guys—'

The rest of his words were cut off when Wonder shot him in the shoulder. Cameron toppled to the ground with a yelp, cradling his bleeding arm. Once Spence entered, Natty had grabbed the gun, now aiming it at Wonder. Spence trained his gun on the second man, and no one moved.

'Drop the guns. We've got people on the way,' drawled Wonder. 'If you hurry, we can get some help for your friend there.'

'He stopped being my friend when he held a gun on me and took your boss's money,' replied Natty.

'You can't win. You already ran from us once. Make it easy on yourself and come quietly.'

'I'm not going anywhere with a little pawn like you,' said Natty. Wonder grinned.

'*Pawn*? You're calling me the pawn? That's rich.'

'Let's be honest: if I hadn't beaten Raider within an inch of his life, he'd be the one stood there, not you.'

'You think?' Wonder's brow furrowed.

'I know. We all know. You're a little punk, and you always have been. If you had any brains, you'd have gone for Spence, not that idiot.' Natty jerked his thumb at Cameron, still whimpering on the floor.

Before Wonder could speak again, more people entered, their weapons far larger than any of the others in the room. There were six in total. Natty's stomach plummeted. He hadn't done enough, and now he and Spence were dead.

Before he could put his hands in the air, the group aimed their guns at Wonder and the other man. Natty's mouth fell open.

'One time only: drop them or die.'

Wonder and the other man didn't hesitate. They placed the guns on the floor and were quickly overpowered by four of the men. Their arms were zip-tied behind their backs.

The leader stepped forward, lowering his gun.

'I'm Clarke. We spoke on the phone. You need to come with me.'

Natty nodded, not bothering to argue. Clarke gave more instructions to his men. Spence stood stupidly, gun by his side, watching everything with his mouth wide open. Without a word, Clarke swept from the room and Natty followed, stunned by everything that had transpired.

'You're lucky, Natty. After the phone cut out, we sent men to Spence's. We figured you would be at Cameron's when he wasn't in.'

Natty didn't respond. They climbed into a car, and the driver immediately pulled away.

'What are you going to do with Cameron?' Now that his adrenaline ebbed, Natty couldn't believe what his friend had done, and how quickly it had bounced back on him.

'He will be taken care of.'

It wasn't much of an answer, and Clarke added nothing further. Natty stayed silent as they drove to an area he recognised as Harehills. They walked into a house, and down to a cellar. Natty's stomach lurched when he recognised the two men tied to wooden chairs.

'You lot are going to pay for this. You know who I am and what I can have done to you, so you'd better let me go.' Rudy's eyes were alight, nostrils flaring in fury as he struggled against his binds. By contrast, Elijah sat calmly, not attempting to fight. He was resigned to his fate. Rudy's eyes narrowed when he saw Clarke.

'You work for me. Stand down, and get me out of here. Now.'

Paying him no attention, Clarke handed Natty a gun. Natty glanced at the heavy weapon, then to Clarke, whose expression remained placid.

'As you can see, we were able to get these guys too. Your warning helped . . . but it was always in hand. Your uncle wants you to kill them both.'

Natty didn't respond, nausea bubbling in his stomach. Rudy faced Natty.

'Nat, this is me. You know me. You're better than this. The stuff that is going on is business. You're like a son to me, and you wouldn't have been harmed. You know that. The bullets were just to scare you.'

Natty let him speak, trying to control his fluctuating emotions. He had history with Rudy, and the idea of killing him filled him with dread.

'Think about your mum. She loves me. If you do this, she will never forgive you.'

Natty ignored Rudy, taking a minute to weigh up his options.

Regardless, the men would die. He didn't have to know everything about his uncle's business to realise that.

But, could he do it?

Natty thought about his dad; imagining all the times he'd been in similar situations. It didn't make him feel any better about his current predicament.

'If I don't do it, what happens?' He finally asked Clarke.

'Nothing will happen to you.'

Even in the middle of the situation, Natty understood the double meaning. If he didn't do it, he would never ascend. Taking a deep breath, he stepped in front of Rudy, raising the gun to his head. Rudy's face was ashen, his lips and chin trembling.

'Nathaniel,' he said.

Natty's finger tightened on the trigger, and Rudy sighed, his hope evaporating. Natty squeezed the trigger, blood spraying the wall behind Rudy, his head falling limp.

Without consideration, Natty moved to the side, standing directly in front of Elijah. They shared a look. Elijah smiled.

'So, this is it then?'

Natty raised the gun, pointing it at his head, just as he had with Rudy.

'This is it.'

Elijah's smile faded, giving way to a defiant look of anger. Through gritted teeth, he said, 'get it over with then.'

Obliging, Natty pulled the trigger, spraying the wall with identical splatter.

He held the gun in place for a moment, his eyes exploring the scene. Giving way to the gun's weight in his hand, he felt it slip to the side. As it did, Clarke reached out and took it from his hand.

'Breathe,' he said.

Natty didn't respond, eyes still studying the men. Unlike Rudy, Elijah's head had shot backwards, allowing Natty to see the bullet wound in his head. Worst of all, he could see the look of terror in Elijah's eyes as the light was extinguished from them. In a way, Rudy's head slumping after he shot him was fortunate, because if Natty had seen the same look on Rudy's face, he probably wouldn't have been able to shoot Elijah.

Falling to his knees, Natty emptied his stomach. When he'd finished, he remained on his knees.

'You did well,' said Clarke. 'Your friend has already been taken home. Ant will take you. People will be in touch.'

Natty said nothing as he was led out. In the car, he remained in a daze. He had killed two men. Cameron's betrayal had rocked him, and he wondered how much of their friendship had been a lie.

When the men dropped him home, Natty crawled into bed, the numbness growing, realising he could easily have died tonight.

He probably should have, he thought.

Instead, people were dead because of him.

Clutching the covers tightly and pulling them closer, he considered which option would have been worse.

Squeezing his eyes shut before he could decide, Natty's body gave into his exhaustion, falling asleep, cheeks still wet.

EPILOGUE

FRIDAY NIGHT PLAYED host to yet another gathering in the Hood. Music played, people congregating, dancing, and having fun.

Natty stood in a corner, his face solemn as he sipped his only drink of the night, doing nothing to stand out. There had been so many spots like this one where he'd sought to be the centre of attention, and he felt ill thinking back on that fact.

Everything had changed.

The bodies of Rudy and Elijah were found, with people immediately pointing to an attempted gang war between their respective crews. Wonder had sworn revenge, but did nothing, left in place to sell the lie. Elijah's crew now worked for Mitch, paying large percentages to remain in business.

Cameron had disappeared, with Natty unsure if his former friend was still alive.

Even now, the killings continued to take their toll. He lived in fear of being arrested, or never getting over what he had done. He and Rudy had been close, and to learn he'd attempted to engineer his downfall was hard to swallow. His mum was worse than ever, refusing to admit her heartbreak over Rudy's death. Consequently, he spent less time around her.

Natty nodded at a man he knew, ignoring the hungry eyes of several females. When another man approached him, he was relieved.

'It's time.'

Natty was led to a backroom, where his uncle waited, sat in a leather office chair. He remained as wiry as ever, but looked worn and far older, other than his eyes, which were as intelligent as ever.

'You've grown, Nathaniel.'

Natty didn't reply, trying to remember the last time he'd talked business with his uncle. For so long, word had come down through Rudy, and to be here in his presence was almost surreal.

'How's your mum doing?'

'She won't accept what happened.'

'I doubt she will,' said Mitch. 'We can discuss her another time. I want you to take Rudy's position. Money goes up, of course.'

Natty froze, unable to believe what was happening. He had dreamed of the moment he would get a promotion more times than he could count, and now that it had happened, he was astonished.

'Are you serious?'

'I don't joke about business.'

'Why?'

'Because you finally showed me something. You've been a star from day one. Rudy saw it. It was just that temper of yours getting you in trouble. You've gotten over that. You showed real character keeping your little friend calm until Clarke arrived. You put down our enemies, and you kept your mouth shut afterwards. You've learned what you needed to learn. This is the result.'

Natty weighed over those words, part of him thinking this must be a dream. After a moment, he opened his mouth to reply.

'I can't take it, Unc.'

Mitch didn't react. His eyes remained locked on Natty.

'What if I offered you half a million pounds up front?'

Natty's stomach fluttered at the amount offered, but it didn't change his answer.

'It's still a no.'

'Why?'

Natty blew out a breath.

'For the longest, this was all I wanted. I was so mad at you and Rudy for holding me back, but lately, I've realised how right you were. I jeopardised so much with my attitude, and I held myself back. Even now, I've still got a lot of growing up to do. One thing I've realised is that I'm not a leader.'

Mitch smiled, his eyes twinkling.

'Yes, you are. The fact you don't see it, only enhances that fact. I won't force you, however. I'll promote someone else for now.' His smile vanished, all business once again. 'Rudy and Elijah are not the only ones clamouring for the throne. Leeds has been quiet for too long, and the little crews aren't gonna stay subservient forever.'

Natty nodded his understanding, shocked to see his uncle's face soften.

'I'm proud of you, Nathaniel. Your dad would be too. Gangster stuff aside, you stepped up for the family, when you could have said no to taking care of Rudy and the other one. We will talk soon. Feel free to stick around for the party.'

With those words ringing in his head, Natty walked out, almost in a trance. As he left the building, he wondered if he had done the right thing in turning down the promotion. There was no guarantee it would be offered again.

Putting that to one side. He climbed in his car and drove away.

———

NATTY STOOD OUTSIDE LORRAINE'S. He'd been there for nearly five minutes, his heart racing. He had been here more times than he could count, routinely walking in. Things were different now. Everything had changed, and he was trying to find himself amid that.

With a deep breath, Natty finally knocked, his heart leaping into his throat when the door opened.

Lorraine gazed out at him. He looked right back, and for a few seconds, neither moved. Without a word, Lorraine stepped to the side and let him in as Jaden came running to tackle him. Natty felt weightless as he embraced Jaden, his heart racing. He looked up from the hug to Lorraine, and they smiled.

DID YOU ENJOY THE READ?

Thank you for reading Good Deed, Bad Deeds!

This was the first book I planned after finishing the Target series, and it took a while for the pieces to align, but I love the end result, and hope you did too.

Please take a minute or two to help me by leaving a review – even if it's just a few lines. Reviews help massively with getting my books in front of new readers. I personally read every review and take all feedback on board.

To support me, please click the relevant link below:

UK: http://www.amazon.co.uk/review/create-review?&asin=B0B7JZXF2J

US: http://www.amazon.com/review/create-review?&asin=B0B7JZXF2J

Make sure you're following me on Amazon to keep up to date with my releases, or that you're signed up to my email list, and I'll see you at the next book!

READ HUSTLER'S AMBITION

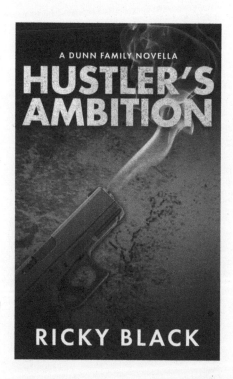

HUSTLER'S AMBITION SAMPLE

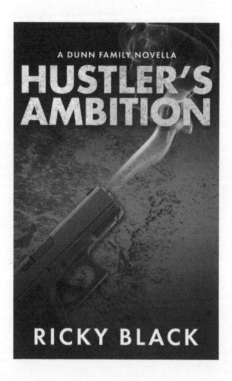

Read the latest novella in the gritty and gripping Dunn Family Series,
Hustler's Ambition Now.

CHAPTER ONE

MAY 2020

CAMERON GREENE STARED at his phone screen, ignoring the thumping rap music playing from a dock, the weed stench permeating the room. He hunched further over the phone, refreshing the page at regular intervals. After what seemed like an age, his bet disappeared from the screen. Heart racing, Cameron checked his settled bets, noting his horse had *placed*, but hadn't won.

'Fuck!'

Cameron slammed down his phone, breathing hard. He poured himself a drink from the brandy bottle on his coffee table, stewing over the missed opportunity.

Downing his drink, Cameron grabbed his phone and called a number.

'Yes, Cam. Everything good,' an airy voice answered.

'That tip you gave me was shit,' Cameron snarled. 'What the hell are you playing at?'

'Yo, you begged me for that tip,' the man replied, his tone instantly defensive.

'Whatever. You better come correct next time, or I'm gonna smack you up,' Cameron warned, before hanging up, still fuming over the situation. The winnings would have netted him eight thousand pounds, which would have enabled him to buy the watch he'd had his eye on for a while. Navigating back to the gambling app, he considered putting money on another bet, but hesitated.

Cameron didn't place bets at the same level as some of his associates. Every Friday, it seemed they were at the bookies, or making WhatsApp groups to trade bets. He'd had a few wins, though, and it always seemed like a viable way out. Cameron didn't think he was an addict — quite the contrary. He saw gambling as his answer to investing. Spence had mentioned it to him over the years, emphasising a long-term plan and being prepared for the future. Cameron disagreed. As far as he was concerned, investing and gambling were the same. The only difference was, gambling returned on his investment immediately.

Spence was one of his two best friends, both of whom he worked with. They primarily sold drugs, but had their hands in numerous nefarious ventures.

In their crew, everyone seemed to have a function. Natty Deeds was the ringleader. He ran their small sub-crew. Unquestionably talented, but highly connected, Natty was the nephew of the organisation's boss, Mitch Dunn. Cameron had been lucky to be hired, and was sure he wouldn't have a job if Natty wasn't Mitch's nephew.

It galled him at times. Cameron's friends always seemed to have money, yet he was living week to week, barely staying ahead. Despite their closeness, he couldn't help looking at his friends sceptically sometimes, wondering if he was being paid fairly and whether he could do anything about it if he wasn't.

Cameron's thoughts deepened. He didn't have the same connections as his friends, which left him feeling like he was playing catch up. Natty and Spence had been brought up around crime, moulded and shaped into useful parts of the machine. Natty had his uncle and his dad, and Spence's story was similar. All deep in the life, they could impart their knowledge and wisdom to those next in line.

Cameron didn't have that benefit. Beyond knowing his name, there was little he knew about his father. He'd left nothing to help Cameron learn and grow. Much of what he had learnt, he'd taken from his friends. Leaning on their expertise was uncomfortable for Cameron. He was behind in the game, and that frustrated him.

'Fuck it,' he mumbled, wiping his mouth. He would sleep on it, and sort out his problems tomorrow.

———

THE FOLLOWING DAY, Cameron woke up, still annoyed about the loss. He'd had to talk himself out of tracking down *Skinny Dave*, the man who had given him the tip. Cameron had won a few bets using his tips in the past, but mostly when backing the clear favourite.

Cameron wondered how connected *Skinny Dave* was. With each bet, Cameron got the increasing impression he was banking on a loser who was trying to get lucky.

Cameron checked the balance on his online banking app, scowling. He glanced around his living room as he ate breakfast, wondering if he had any money around the house. He scratched his chin as he cast his mind back. In his line of work, holding cash was a necessity. It avoided attracting suspicions and unwanted questions. But he doubted there was any he had forgotten about. He was regularly raiding his coffers for clothes and nights out. With a deep sigh, he realised he would have to find other ways to make his money back.

Hustling drugs on the side was a no-go. Their organisation was deep in the streets, and the consequences of getting caught weren't worth it.

Skills-wise, Cameron wasn't the sharpest, especially when he compared himself to his friends. What he did have was nerve. He was willing to do whatever it took to get to the top of the street crime pile.

After finishing his breakfast, he lit a spliff, still working out how to set things off. His initial instincts were to speak to Natty.

But was it worth involving him?

Natty was sharp and well-respected, with many of the same vices Cameron had. He brought a lot to the table, and Cameron could see the pair running the streets together.

Spence . . .

Spence was different. Cameron respected his dad, who he knew was a madman back in the day, but Spence wasn't the same. He was a thinker who read for fun. But worst of all was his natural charm. It had a way of pulling people in and rubbing off on people. Natty was an example of this. Being around Spence had changed him.

In Cameron's eyes, it had made him softer.

Robberies were another option to consider. They were a useful way to make money, but Natty always advised against them. In his eyes, it was a show of desperation. Cameron couldn't see how. He wondered whether these were more *words of wisdom* Natty had taken from Spence, but it was something he felt strongly about.

————

SOMETIME LATER, Cameron hit the streets, stopping by his crew's main hangout spot. Natty was already there, talking on the phone when Cameron entered. He nodded at Cameron, continuing his call.

'Yes, Cam,' said Carlton. 'You good?'

'What's happening, you little punk?' Cameron replied, grinning as he grabbed the younger man and put him in a headlock. 'What have I told you about staying ready? People aren't messing around on the roads,' he taunted, enjoying seeing Carlton struggle. He was a good kid, but Cameron remembered how he used to run around after Natty, begging to tag along. Natty had taken pity on him and given him a shot, but that didn't mean Cameron had to.

'Leave him alone, Cam,' said Natty. Evidently, he'd finished his call.

'Fine,' snorted Cameron, letting Carlton go. Carlton rubbed his neck, glaring. Cameron considered giving him a slap, but didn't want to hear Natty's shit. He took a seat near Natty, and Carlton left the room.

Their spot was a house that had once belonged to a punter. They'd hung around for years, giving drugs to the owner. They now resided at another place, and Natty and the others threw him a bit of money and product, and took care of the bills. The living room had light blue walls, the paint peeling in places. It had dark blue furniture, and an entertainment system, but not much else in the way of amenities.

'Why are you always defending that little shit?' Cameron asked, glaring at Natty. Natty was an imposing figure. He stood over 6 feet tall, with a muscular build. He had a look that made people take him seriously, but could be strangely charming. Cameron's glare deepened.

'He's a good dude, and he works hard. I don't know why you're always getting at him, but there's no need for it,' said Natty.

'Whatever. It's tough out there, fam. We both know it. I'm just trying to toughen him up.'

'Carlton's not soft. You don't need to worry about him.'

'Fine. Forget him,' said Cameron. 'What's going on?'

Natty shrugged, smoothing the creases in his grey designer sweater.

'Steady day. Spence is working later, but no issues so far. The packs are selling nicely. We've got a reload coming in later. You mind handling it if I'm not around?'

'Yeah, that's calm,' replied Cameron. 'I need to hit a lick or summat, though. My funds are low.'

Natty shot his friend a look. 'If you're broke, I can help you out.'

'I didn't say I was broke,' said Cameron, narrowing his eyes. 'I just want more money.'

'You should talk to Spence. You know he's doing well with his invest—'

'I don't have time to talk to him,' Cameron interjected. 'He's probably with that little slut of his, anyway.'

Natty shook his head, but didn't respond as Carlton re-entered. Cameron glared at his friend again, annoyed by his lack of response. Rising to his feet, Natty made his way to the door, stopping just before it. Turning around and surveying the room, his face contorted.

'This place is a shit-hole. Can you guys give it the once over?' he asked, opening the door and exiting.

Cameron snickered, pushing off from the seat with his hands and standing. After a long stretch, he made his way to the door.

'Yo Cam,' Carlton called out, 'Natty told us to tidy the place up.'

Cameron turned around and impaled Carlton with a glare.

'So fucking tidy it up then,' he replied, slamming the door as he left the room.

CAMERON PUT ASIDE his annoyance with his friends and focused on business. He held the main 'trap phone', directing sales to different places. It was easy enough for him to handle on autopilot, giving him plenty of time to consider his moneymaking options. What he needed were more connections. They would enable him to spread out and diversify his opportunities for earning.

But how he would make those connections, he wasn't sure.

Messing around on his personal phone, he made a few phone calls, trading gossip and little titbits with associates. He received nothing of value, but learnt of a party in the Hood.

———

CAMERON WAS INSPECTING the contents of his wardrobe later that day. Rifling through it, he selected his clothes, laying them on his bed. Picking up his phone, he navigated to his contacts and called Natty.

'Yes, Cam. What's happening, bro?'

'I've got a party for us later. Meant to be bare women there. Are you on it?'

Cameron heard Natty's yawn, and frowned, sure his friend would decline.

'Yeah, why not? If it's dead or there's no women around, I'm blaming you, though. Send me the details. I'll drag Spence along too. Cool?'

'Cool.' Cameron didn't think Spence would come, but it didn't matter either way. 'I'll send you a text with the details. Come to my yard tonight, and we can fly over there together.'

'Cool,' replied Natty, hanging up.

Cameron rubbed his hands together, grinning. He needed to cut loose, and the party sounded like the perfect way to do it.

CHAPTER TWO

CAMERON GRINNED as he entered the party, flanked by Natty and Spence. His grin faded when he saw people flock to Natty, touching his fist and engaging him in conversation, but he put it aside, determined to enjoy the night. He made a beeline for a table laden with drinks, fixing himself a brandy and coke. Spence followed, making his own drink as he surveyed the room in front of him.

Cameron didn't know how many people had initially been invited, but the house was packed. Though he'd recognised the address, he didn't know who the host was, but imagined they wouldn't be pleased with the number of people in the spot. As he thought this, he heard the sound of something smashing, followed by loud voices. Cameron grinned, knowing the owner would be pissed that things had been broken.

Spence nodded his head to the music, which surprised Cameron, as he'd never expressed an interest in any drill songs. Deciding it wasn't important, he finished his drink and made another, feeling Spence's eyes on him.

'What?' He said, cutting his eyes to his friend. 'It's a party.'

Spence shrugged, but Cameron noted the judgement in his eyes.

Before he could say anything else, Natty sauntered over with a smirk on his face.

'You definitely came through on the women front,' he told Cameron. 'Danny's been here an hour and has already got a gobble from some random girl.'

Spence made a face. 'Lucky guy.'

'Does your girl not give blowies?' Cameron snarked, knowing full well that she did. Unbeknownst to his friend, he had been involved with Spence's girlfriend Anika a few years ago, and knew precisely what she was and wasn't into.

Spence rolled his eyes. 'Here we go. Wouldn't be a night out without you finding some way to mention my girlfriend.'

'Nope.' Natty shook his head, making fresh drinks for everyone. 'We're not doing this tonight. We're here to have a good time. That's what we're going to do. Everyone drink up, and let's be happy.'

Spence and Cameron took the drinks, and the trio downed them. Natty thumped his chest, grinning.

'There we go! Let's get it popping in here.'

———

AND, so they did. Cameron lost track of the number of drinks he'd consumed. They did the rounds, drinking, partaking in smoking various joints that were going around. Cameron even did a few lines, then danced with fuzzy women that he struggled to recall. He didn't know when he left the party, or how he got home, but he awoke the next day in bed, to someone banging on his door.

Finally, he answered, letting Natty in.

'You look horrific,' said Natty, sounding spry, and much fresher than Cameron felt. Taking pity, Natty made them both cups of coffee, which they sat outside and drank. The hot drink made Cameron feel a little better, which he was thankful for. Despite feeling rough, he was glad he'd gone to the party. It had taken his mind off things, and he'd had a great time.

As the pair sat there, Cameron learned Natty had ended up at Lorraine's place. Their situation was a strange one. Natty had been on and off with her for years. In that time, she'd managed to have a child with another guy . . . Raider, a rival hustler and enemy of Natty's. Stranger still, Natty spent more time around Lorraine and her son than Raider did. Cameron didn't get it, but felt Natty was loved up, even if his friend would never admit it.

Cameron couldn't understand, and didn't think he ever would. Natty owed Lorraine nothing, yet remained a presence in her life. He grew angry at Cameron when he teased him about the relationship, but he'd put himself in that position.

Cameron put it to one side, and after finishing their drinks, his mind skipped back to Spence.

'I still feel rough,' he moaned, yawning as he put on a pair of trainers. 'Seriously, how long are we gonna let him get away with that?'

'What are you talking about?' Natty asked, frowning.

'Anika. You said in the beginning that she wouldn't change him, and I told you he was pussy whipped. Now look at him . . . leaving parties early when we're having a good time so he can run back to her.'

'They live together now. Spence does what he thinks is right. You don't know that she's having that kind of effect,' said Natty.

'I know her, remember? We both do.'

Natty shook his head.

'C'mon, let's just go and see the old man.'

That wasn't good enough, Cameron thought, as they headed for Natty's car. What Spence was doing wasn't right. He'd come out with the crew, and unless he hooked up with a girl at the party, he should have left with them. Instead, he'd ducked out early. The most annoying part was that Natty didn't seem to care. He constantly gave Spence a pass over everything, and once Cameron had noticed this, he couldn't stop noticing it. Whenever he opened his mouth, he was perceived as the bad guy.

He knew Anika, though. He knew her better than both Natty and Spence. She was a happy, good-time girl, who he'd pursued with ease, then cut off when she became too clingy. Somehow, she had ended up with Spence. Cameron wasn't sure if she had done it to get back at him, but wouldn't put it past her.

NATTY DROVE to Rudy's office on Francis Street, the pair making conversation and listening to music. Cameron's head was pounding, and Natty was handling it in his usual manner, being louder and making his head hurt more.

Soon, they pulled up outside Rudy's. He worked out of a house belonging to an older woman, Delores. Cameron didn't know why, and had never been interested enough to see if Natty knew. They spoke with the guards milling around outside, then headed into the house.

Rudy sat in the kitchen, sipping a drink. Delores was pottering around. As always, she had a smile and words for Natty, yet ignored Cameron. He glanced at Rudy, hoping the older man would look up and take notice of him, but he didn't.

Rudy Campbell was the number two guy in the Dunn organisation. He had short hair, and wore a pristine white shirt, finally glancing up at the pair with his piercing eyes, which, to no surprise, lingered on Natty.

Cameron didn't pay much attention to the conversation. Instead, he studied the way the pair spoke to one another. Even with Natty's last name, and his status as Mitch Dunn's nephew, Rudy still outranked him by a considerable margin. The fact he was sleeping with Natty's mum also played into their relationship, which always seemed laced with tension.

Cameron spaced out for a moment, sure he wouldn't be involved in the conversation. His attention returned sharply when Natty mentioned *Elijah*. Cameron focused on the back of his friend's head as he spoke.

Elijah was a rival dealer who they didn't get along with. There had been tension between the crews for a while, and Natty was one of the most outspoken against them. But Natty lacked the objectivity to make a sound assessment. Lorraine's ex-boyfriend, Raider, worked for Elijah. It made it difficult to separate Natty's true concerns from his personal agenda.

Still exhausted from his late night, Cameron yawned, just as Rudy looked in his direction. Cameron froze, but Rudy had already focused on Natty again, making Cameron feel like he'd missed an opportunity to establish himself.

They didn't stay much longer, and Cameron's annoyance only grew as they headed back to Natty's car. Rudy had paid him little attention, and hadn't said a word to him. If he was ever going to ascend to the level he wanted, that needed to change.

'No point in me even going,' Cameron grumbled when Natty drove away. 'Rudy didn't even speak to me. Old prick.'

Natty didn't respond, lost in thought as he drove. Cameron scowled.

'Natty? What are you thinking about?'

'Elijah,' said Natty.

'What about him?'

'I don't trust him,' replied Natty. Cameron almost rolled his eyes.

Here we go again, he thought.

'Him or Raider? You sure the fact your fuckpiece's ex rolls with him isn't clouding your judgement?'

'I'm sure. This is business,' snapped Natty. The conversation continued, but Cameron wasn't sure he believed him. Natty seemed different lately. Even when they went out, it felt like he was going through the motions at times, and Cameron was sure it was due to Lorraine.

If it wasn't him, it was Spence, loved up with his girlfriend. He didn't understand what was happening to his crew, making him wonder if he was the one with the problem.

Anika had fallen hard for him, he'd recognised that. She'd wanted a commitment, and he'd just wanted to sleep with her, and see her when it was convenient.

So, he broke it off.

And then one night, at a club, he'd watched from afar as she and Spence began talking — Natty stepping in and stopping him from intervening.

Now, a year later, they were still together, and Cameron hated it. It wasn't that he regretted his actions with Anika, or that he thought he'd missed his chance. He didn't want Anika, but he didn't want his friend to have her either.

'Don't overthink it, bro,' Cameron responded to a comment Natty had made about Rudy's judgement in potentially working with Elijah. 'Have the meeting, get shit organised, and keep it moving. We can get put on in a major way, and trust me, I need that.' He thought about the money he'd lost betting, and the money he'd blown on other things.

He needed to make it back, and then some.

READ DEEDS TO THE CITY

CHAPTER ONE
FEBRUARY 2021

NATHANIEL 'NATTY DEEDS' Dunn stood in front of his dad's grave. It had been a while since he had visited, the area around the headstone unkempt, bereft of flowers or care.

Tyrone Dunn
June 10, 1965 - August 2, 2002
Loving Father and Husband

Around Natty, the chilly wind rippled his coat, and he jammed his hands deeper into his pockets, unable to tear his eyes away.

Looking around, he noted the cemetery was empty, and cleared his throat.

'Sorry I haven't been to see you in a while, dad,' he mumbled. Again, he cleared his throat and continued, 'don't really have an excuse, but I've missed you more lately. I always do, but shit's different now, and I wish you were here to tell me what to do. Nowadays, I feel like I understand what you went through when you were alive, but I don't know how you coped. You were loved and respected. I'm not even sure what I am now. I'm a little lost, dad. I wish I could speak to you. I wish you could put your hand on my shoulder like you used to and set me straight. You'd know what to do . . . I know you would.'

Natty continued to stare at the headstone, not knowing what he had expected to happen. He shook off his embarrassment, needing to say more.

'I guess I've been wondering lately how you felt about the things you had to do. For the game we're all playing in the Hood. Whether you enjoyed it or did it because you had to. I'm at a point where I don't know whether I'm coming or going. It feels like I'm looking for a sign . . . something to tell me what to do next. I guess that's why I'm here.'

Natty stopped speaking, wiping his eyes. His dad was thirty-seven when he died. Natty was almost as old as he was, yet life had been different. He'd worked for his uncle, Mitch Dunn, his entire adult life. Starting as a runner, he became a crew chief, languishing in that position for years. A few months ago, circumstances changed when Natty unearthed a plot to bring down his uncle.

The memories overwhelmed Natty as he stood there. What he needed above all else was to talk to somebody. To make sense of what had happened, and why things had turned out as they did.

But who?

With those closest to him central to the plot against his uncle, Natty didn't know who to trust anymore. Spence and Lorraine were probably sick of listening to him, he reasoned, as he scratched his chin.

Natty's phone rang. He glanced at the screen, noting Lorraine was calling.

'Hey,' he said.

'Hey, Nat. Where are you?'

'I'm just out,' he replied. 'Is everything okay?'

'Jaden was asking if you're stopping by. I'm about to start dinner, so I thought I would check.'

'Yeah, I'll be there in twenty minutes,' said Natty.

'Okay. See you then.'

Natty hung up, again staring at the headstone. He frowned, noting some cobwebs at the top of the stone, which he crouched down to wipe away, vowing to come more often. It was clear nobody else visited. *His mum certainly didn't.* Natty couldn't recall the last time they had been together. He tensed. His mum was yet another situation he needed to resolve.

Straightening, he wiped his hands on his trousers. Finally, he whispered goodbye to his dad, leaving the cemetery.

———

'NATTY!'

Jaden ran at Natty as soon as he entered the house. Natty hugged him, ruffling his head.

'Yes, J! Have you been looking after your mum?'

Jaden nodded, and Natty grinned at him. Jaden was ten-years-old and favoured his mum, looks-wise. He had her eyes and colouring, but his nose was similar to his dad's. Natty and Jaden had always got along, but Natty wondered how things would change once Jaden realised Natty was in a relationship with his mum. So far, Jaden hadn't commented on the fact Natty seemed to be spending more time at the house, instead revelling in the extra attention.

'Come on, Natty. Let's play on the computer.' Jaden took Natty's hand, leading him into the living room.

'Get everything set up, little man. Let me speak to your mum for a few minutes.'

Jaden nodded, and Natty headed to the kitchen, where Lorraine sipped a cup of tea, her eyes lighting up when she saw him. The pair shared a hug and a kiss.

'Wow, you brought the cold in with you,' said Lorraine, shivering.

'Sorry about that. I'm glad it's warm in here, though,' Natty said. He released her, and made himself a drink, the mug warming his hands.

'Are you helping me with dinner?' Lorraine asked. 'Or has my son monopolised your time again?'

'I don't mind helping,' said Natty. Lorraine shook her head.

'I was just teasing. Go and play with Jaden. I'll call you if I need you.'

'Make sure you do,' said Natty. He again kissed her, this one lasting longer than the first. They broke away only when Jaden called for Natty, stating he had everything ready.

'Duty calls,' Natty said with a wink. Still holding his cup, he went to Jaden, Lorraine smiling after him.

———

THAT EVENING, Lorraine and Natty snuggled on the sofa. Jaden had gone to bed an hour ago, and the pair were watching an action film they'd stumbled across on TV.

'Where were you earlier?' Lorraine asked, pressed firmly against him.

'I went to visit my dad,' he said, keeping his voice neutral, hoping a big deal wouldn't be made. This was dashed when Lorraine immediately muted the TV.

'You did?'

Natty nodded, his cheeks warming slightly as his embarrassment at the cemetery returned to him.

'You should have told me. I would have gone with you,' she said, pouting.

'It's fine,' he replied, appreciating the fact she'd offered.

'What made you go?'

Natty sighed.

'I really don't know. I just feel . . . lost. I needed some guidance, and lately, I've been thinking about some things my dad taught me when I was younger, and how much I enjoyed being able to turn to him when I needed help.'

'Can I ask you something?' Lorraine said.

'Course you can.'

'Are you happy?'

'Yes,' Natty instantly replied. 'This thing, whatever it is . . . it's not about being sad. I feel adrift, like I want to do more, but I don't know how.'

Lorraine didn't immediately respond, but Natty didn't rush her. He had been guilty of doing it in the past, but he was learning to read the signs, and knew Lorraine liked to mull things before she spoke. It was why he wasn't surprised she'd waited so long to ask where he had been earlier.

'You were doing what you did on the streets for a long time. It's bound to take some time to switch off.'

'If I ever can,' Natty murmured.

'Have you spoken to Spence about any of this?' Lorraine asked.

'No. Haven't had the chance.'

'He's your friend, Nat. If you tell him what's going on, he could help you.'

'He's dealing with his promotion. That and whatever is going on with Rosie. I don't wanna overwhelm him with my shit too.'

'Don't be silly. That's what friends are for.'

Lorraine snuggled closer against him. Natty closed his eyes, enjoying the feeling, hoping he could get things in line.

'Mich—Raider's auntie contacted me today. She's been reaching out for a while,' Lorraine said, after a few minutes.

Natty went still. 'What does she want?'

'She wants me to bring Jaden to see Raider.'

A wave of annoyance rose in Natty. Raider was Jaden's dad, and the pair had never got on. This was taken to a new level last year when Raider severely beat Lorraine in a drunken rage. Natty retaliated, fracturing Raider's skull and landing him in hospital. He'd heard through the grapevine that Raider was out of the hospital, now recovering at home.

'Do his family know what he did to you?' He said.

'No. I never told them.'

'Why not?'

'Because I didn't want them to know,' said Lorraine. She shifted away from Natty, playing with her fingers.

'They should know what sort of man he is, and what he did,' said Natty.

'I just want to forget about it, Nat. I don't want to think about Raider or any of that. I'd rather focus on us,' she said, smiling softly. 'Are you spending the night?'

Natty nodded. He spent little time at his place nowadays, but Lorraine would still check, as if she expected him to refuse.

'We should go out on Friday,' he said, surprising himself.

'Really?'

'Yeah. We can go for dinner and drinks. Make a night of it.'

Lorraine's smile widened.

'I'd like that.'

'Good,' said Natty. He hoped going out with Lorraine would take his mind off his feelings.

––––––

As ARRANGED, they went out on Friday, with Lorraine's mum babysitting. Lorraine chose Italian food, the evening carefree, and the conversation fast-paced. Natty felt better about his issues, happy that he was at least doing this right. He wanted to be a man Lorraine could be proud of, which meant making major changes.

After eating, they stopped in a bar, then Lorraine dragged him to one of her favourite clubs. It wasn't Natty's scene anymore, but this was Lorraine's night, and he wanted her to be happy. They danced to numerous tracks, their drinks spilling as they moved. Noticing, Lorraine pointed to her glass and pouted. Smirking and shaking his head, Natty turned on the spot and set off to the bar to get them more drinks.

On his way back, he noted a man crowding Lorraine's space. Natty's jaw tensed. It reminded him of the moves he used to make on women — whether or not they were taken. Standing by Lorraine's side, he handed her the drink.

'Thanks,' she said, smiling at him.

The man turned his attention to Natty, and they sized one another up. He was light-skinned, his hair trimmed with a low fade. He was around Natty's size, and equally well-built.

'I was just chatting to Lorraine,' he said, smirking. 'I haven't seen her in a while.'

'He knows my friend Poppy,' said Lorraine, eyes darting between the men.

'Yeah, Poppy is cool. Anyway, do you wanna come and chill with me and my people? We're heading to a private spot soon. It's gonna be a big night.'

'No thanks,' said Lorraine politely. 'I'm out with my man.'

The man's eyes narrowed, his smirk vanishing. He tried to give Natty a dismissive look, but Natty snorted.

'You're trying too hard, bro,' he said. 'Leave with at least a little dignity.'

'Are you serious? Don't run your mouth,' the man snapped. Natty stepped forward, but Lorraine stopped him.

'Please, Nat. Just leave it,' she pleaded.

Every cell in Natty's body wanted to fight. It was a familiar feeling, that all-encompassing anger. He didn't have to think too hard about it. It would be the easiest thing in the world to break the man's face, and his friends' faces too, if they got involved.

Lorraine was more important, though. Nodding, he stepped back.

'Please go. I think you've done enough,' Lorraine said to the man. For a moment, Natty thought he would resist, but the man sneered and stalked away. Natty breathed deeply, clenching his fists. Lorraine squeezed his hand, and the gesture relaxed him.

'Thank you,' she said. Natty nodded, not ready to speak yet. He could see the man talking with his friends, but when he motioned in Natty's direction, one of the men's eyes widened, and he turned away and began whispering to the others. Natty was sure the man recognised him, despite the two having never met. Natty smirked as the faces in the group converged and departed, shooting him fearful glances.

They left the club shortly after, enjoying older R&B music in another venue. Natty didn't say anything, but the incident with the man had ignited something important.

The *almost conflict* had made him feel more alive, and more like his old self.

CHAPTER TWO

THE NEXT DAY, Natty went for a run, needing to burn off some excess energy. Last year, he'd started to let himself go, physically. He'd got himself back into shape, running daily when he could manage it throughout the winter, and quitting smoking.

Pounding the pavement, his mind wandered to the night before. He was shocked that he'd kept his temper around the man, wondering what it meant.

Natty paused, doubling over to catch his breath, then randomly chuckling. Lorraine could be his guardian angel for all he knew. She seemed skilled at getting him out of trouble that he'd caused. At least when he gave her a chance to. His mind wandered to his altercation with Raider. Natty hadn't spoken to her before he went after him, almost destroying their relationship.

Natty wouldn't take that chance again. He would figure out what was going on in his head, and as he started running again, he knew Spence was the man to help with it.

———

SPENCE HUNCHED OVER HIS BREAKFAST, enjoying the piping hot cornmeal porridge. He was in Dutch Pot on Chapeltown Road, savouring the meal that would set him up for the long day ahead.

It had been an interesting few months for Spence. When Natty turned down his promotion, Spence was next in line, stepping up when it was offered. Now, he was earning more money than he'd ever dreamed possible.

Unlike his contemporaries, Spence always had a long-term plan, and had made the most of the money he'd earned previously, investing it and refusing to waste it on the same trappings that many in the game did; clothes, jewellery, cars and women. With the boost in funds, he'd bolstered his investments and savings, and was able to take more risks, knowing he was financially secure.

Despite this, Spence was under no illusions about the added responsibility. There was no room for mistakes at this level. Messing up would likely mean his death, but Spence was ready for the challenge, especially when it kept his mind from going to places he didn't want it to. He'd been through a lot recently, and what he had lost felt immeasurable at the time. Bit by bit, he was coming to terms with it, and forging ahead.

Spence's phone rang. It was a PGP device given to him by Mitch, totally untraceable. Wiping his mouth, he answered.

'Hello?'

'It's Clarke. I'm outside.'

Clarke hung up. Spence shovelled the last few spoonfuls of porridge down his throat, downed the orange juice he'd ordered, then thanked the cook before stepping outside.

Clarke idled by the curb in the passenger seat of a new-model Nissan 4x4. He was a thick-necked older man with piercing eyes, and a large nose. His balding hair and neat beard were peppered with grey. Spence climbed in the back, and the vehicle rumbled away.

The crew drove out to Moortown, parking outside Mitch's home, and immediately heading to the garage. Mitch waited, on his feet, circling a heavy bag. His head darting side-to-side, he threw out the occasional shot, each blow awkwardly folding the bag. The chains rattled as they strained to hold it in position. Spence had been here once before, and it had surprised him just how old and well-used some of the equipment was. Mitch hit the bag several times, then unwrapped his hands, nodding at Spence. Clarke waited by the door.

Spence had yet to get used to being around Mitch, whether in a personal or business setting. It was surreal.

Mitch was a Hood legend who had always been in the shadows, his reputation growing as the years passed. He and Natty's father, Tyrone Dunn, had founded the crew. Mitch had steered them through tough times after Tyrone's murder nineteen years ago. He was brown-skinned, with hard eyes, a gaunt face and a shaven head, with little facial hair. As always, he was casually dressed, wearing a plain grey tracksuit. Despite this, power resonated with Mitch, overwhelming whoever was around him.

Mitch seemed to like him, but Spence believed he was simply a placeholder until someone else came along to run the crew. He didn't mind either way, as long as they prospered.

'How are you?' Mitch asked.

'Everything's good,' replied Spence, sure Mitch was more concerned with business than his personal life. Mitch nodded.

'How's your pops?'

'He's doing alright,' replied Spence, surprised that Mitch had brought up his dad. 'Still working.'

'He never liked me. When I used to see him around Del back in the day, he always used to give me dirty looks. Despite that, I think he respected me, and the feeling was mutual,' said Mitch, eyes still locked onto Spence's. 'I respect the move he made. Many have tried going legit, but not many stick with it.'

Spence wasn't surprised his dad had left the game behind. Something had changed in his dad after Spence's mum died. It made him wonder how well Mitch knew his dad, and whether he was referring to him at all . . .

'In general, how are things going?'

Spence continued meeting Mitch's eyes. Even though he had bad news to give, he wasn't going to back away from doing so.

'The takings are down from last month in Chapeltown.'

Mitch said nothing, silently imploring Spence to continue.

'We've taken in a quarter mill from our dealers, less than the four hundred grand we took the month before.'

Mitch nodded. 'I heard the same thing. What have you done about it?'

It was a direct question that would have crumbled most and sent them stuttering and stammering for an answer, but Spence took it in his stride.

'I've conducted an investigation. None of our dealers are living beyond their means or flashing silly cash.'

'That's a start. Tell me, what do you think is going on?'

Spence was sharp, immediately understanding what was going on. This was a test.

He took his time, mulling it over.

'It sounds like we have some competition.' He noted the gleam of approval in Mitch's eyes. 'I'm all over it, though. I'll find them.'

Mitch nodded. 'Whoever it is, it won't be long before we get our hands on them. Keep talking to Clarke. He'll keep me updated.'

Spence turned to leave, believing the meeting was over.

'Spence?'

He turned.

'How's Natty?'

Again, Spence mulled this over. Natty seemed happy with Lorraine. Spence had been in the background, waiting for them to stop being stubborn and admit how they felt about each other. Despite all the drama that had transpired, Natty and Lorraine seemed to be doing well.

Despite that, Natty seemed on edge. Spence couldn't put his finger on why, but there was something almost haunting in his eyes the last time Spence had seen him.

Mitch was still awaiting an answer, and Spence gave him one.

'He's fine. Still figuring things out.'

Mitch smiled for a moment.

'I'll reach out to him; see if it's anything I can help with.'

Spence left, climbing back into the car, Clarke following. He wasn't stupid. Mitch wanted Natty back in the fold, and would likely stop at nothing to achieve this.

LORRAINE YAWNED, saving her progress on the snippet of code she was querying. Her courses were kicking her arse, but she enjoyed the challenge. Things had ramped up for her in the past few months in her marketing day job. She'd begun querying customer data to help formulate new marketing campaigns. The extra work she had done was paying off.

Jaden was at a friend's house. Natty had been out all day. Lorraine made herself a drink, thinking about the confrontation in the club. It wasn't the first time she had seen it happen. On more than one occasion, Natty had lost his temper around people and fought. He was vicious and usually got his point across. He was also a huge flirt, and it was strange to see him on the other end, watching someone flirt with his woman.

Despite this, he'd stopped. For her. It was startling, especially with how much Natty wanted it to happen. Lorraine remembered her simple gesture, disarming the hand that had been balled into a fist.

Would he always have that edge to him?

A memory of Raider's assault flickered in Lorraine's mind. Instinctively, she grabbed at her rib. She took a deep breath, steadying herself. Sometimes she was okay. Other times, she felt helpless, just wanting to curl up in a ball.

Sipping a cool glass of water, she considered the request from Raider's auntie. She wasn't sure it was a good idea for Raider to be around Jaden, yet at the same time, she didn't want to stop them from having a relationship. Especially if that would *fix* Raider, and turn him from the destructive lifestyle he seemed to crave.

She wondered if Natty's beating had changed him.

Lorraine double-checked she'd saved her progress, finished her drink, then went for a short walk to clear her head. By the time she returned home, she had her phone to her ear, waiting for Rosie to answer.

'Hey, Lo. Everything okay?'

'Yeah. I'm trying to distract myself. Figured that was a great time to ring my best friend.'

Rosie giggled.

'Natty must be unavailable. I'm near your place. I'll see you soon.'

Rosie wasn't exaggerating. Within two minutes, she was at the house. They made drinks and sat in the kitchen.

'Right, speak,' said Rosie, stirring her drink.

'It's Raider,' said Lorraine, noting Rosie's face immediately darkening. 'Well, not him specifically, but his family. His Auntie Rita keeps requesting to see Jaden. She wants him to visit Raider.'

'Do his family know what Raider did?'

Lorraine shook her head.

'You need to fix that. They should know exactly what kind of man he is and the lengths he's willing to go to.'

Again, Lorraine shook her head.

'I can't do that, Rosie. When it gets like that, it's always the kids that get hurt. Jaden doesn't need to know that about his dad.'

'Kids grow up quicker around the Hood. Jaden is a good boy, and he should know the truth. What's Natty saying about it?'

'He agrees with you, of course,' Lorraine dryly replied.

'That should tell you something, babe. Speaking of Natty, how is Jaden about you two?'

'I don't think he understands, if I'm honest. We're not blatant with it around him, but he enjoys having Natty around all the time.'

Rosie beamed. Lorraine knew she was fond of Natty, and was pleased they had finally entered into a relationship.

'How's Natty doing, anyway? I haven't seen him in ages, and Spence hasn't brought him up.'

'He's restless, but he seems happy to be around me. We haven't argued or anything. Something happened yesterday, though.'

Rosie signalled for Lorraine to continue.

'We went out for some food, and ended up stopping by a club near Briggate. I can't remember the name, but it's really small and easy to overlook. Anyway, we're inside, and Natty goes to get me a drink, and this guy comes over to chat to me.'

Rosie chuckled.

'Bet Natty loved that.'

'He came back over and was quite calm about it at first. The guy was being a prick, so Natty just switched.'

'Of course he did. Natty loves to scrap around you.'

'Don't you think that's wild? I was his only backup, Ro. The guy was in the club with all his friends, and Natty didn't care.'

'Why would he? Once again, this is Natty we're talking about. He's your bloody alpha,' said Rosie.

Lorraine smiled for a moment, amused by Rosie's antics. Her friend always knew just what to do to bring her out of a funk — even one Lorraine hadn't realised she was in.

'I'm worried about him. Like I said, he seems really restless, and at times, it's like he's just shuffling around, waiting for something to happen.'

'Maybe he is,' said Rosie. 'Or, maybe it will just take time. I mean, he did his thing in the streets for years. I can't imagine the transition to being a civilian is easy. Just keep being there for him, and get him talking. You two are strongest when you're on the same page.'

Lorraine felt better after speaking with Rosie. Maybe the situation with Natty wasn't as bad as she thought. They just needed to communicate, and she needed to be there for him.

———

NATTY FOUND Spence at a spot in the Hood, near Francis Street. Several goons were posted around, greeting Natty with smiles, nods, and hand slaps. It was something he'd noticed when he was around certain circles. Despite things being kept low-key with Rudy and Elijah, certain faces in the streets knew what Natty had done. It had enhanced his reputation, and meant people looked at him a certain way.

Just as he had wanted for the longest time.

Natty entered the spot, finding Spence on the phone in the main hangout room. There were several other people dotted around, one pacing the room, and two on the sofa talking in quiet voices. Natty didn't recognise any of them, and they gave him only a cursory glance. Their demeanours were stiff, suggesting something big was going down.

Despite this, Spence appeared unflappable. He shot Natty a grin, finishing his conversation and sliding to his feet. The pair shared a quick hug. It had been a few weeks since they'd seen one another, but they had texted and stayed in communication.

'Come, let's get drinks,' he said, leading Natty to the kitchen.

'You look . . . mostly well,' he added, as he looked Natty up and down, taking a sip of his drink. Natty chuckled. He could never get much past Spence, and he was glad his friend had realised. It would save him having to work it into conversation.

Despite their closeness, Natty still held onto some guilt where his friend was concerned, namely regarding his role in the end of Spence's last relationship. He was glad Spence seemed to have taken it in his stride and bounced back. For years, people had assumed Spence was the weakest of the trio. Natty and Cameron were more aggressive, always willing to throw hands, and Spence was calmer, never rushing into anything.

Now, Natty saw this was a rare skill, and it made him further respect Spence.

'What's going on around here?' He ignored Spence. 'Looks like people are preparing for a war.' He laughed, expecting Spence to laugh too, but Spence shrugged.

'It could be the case, Nat. The takings are down lately.'

'Down by how much?'

'One hundred and fifty bags lighter than last month.'

'How is that possible?' Natty's eyes narrowed, darting around the room, surveying those in attendance. 'Have you—'

'Checked to see if anyone is holding out? Yep, I have. I checked everyone in and around the crew. I suspect there's another crew out there.'

Natty sipped his drink.

'People playing in the big leagues are usually difficult to hide,' he pointed out.

Spence leaned inward.

'Whoever it is, they're doing well so far. I'm asking around, but no one has anything to say about it.'

'It could be nothing. Maybe it's just a bad month,' said Natty.

'I hope you're right, fam. I spoke with your uncle today.'

'What's he saying?' Natty asked. He'd seen little of his uncle since he turned down his offer. It struck him just how unbothered he was by that. Similar to his reputation amongst people in the street, Natty had spent years trying to get his uncle's attention, wanting adulation and more responsibility.

It didn't seem to mean the same now.

'He sent his best wishes. I'm guessing he'll contact you soon.'

'I doubt it,' Natty said, drinking more of his drink and setting the cup on the table. Spence's phone rang. He checked the number, answered, and told the person to call back later.

'I can leave if you need me to. I just wanted to check on you,' Natty added.

'No, you wanted to tell me what's going on,' said Spence. 'Business can wait; if they're important enough, they'll know who to ring next.'

Natty was touched Spence was putting him before the business, and allowed himself a small smile.

'I don't really know what's going on. I feel lost. Can't really explain it.'

'Everything good with Lorraine?'

Natty nodded. 'She's smashing it. She's doing some software development courses, and she's focused. Jaden's doing well too. He's enjoying the school year, and he's getting better at football. It feels like everyone is doing something other than me. I feel like something is calling me, but I don't know what, or what direction it's coming from. I nearly got into some shit yesterday.'

'Tell me,' said Spence. Natty filled him in on the incident in the club. Spence listened as he finished his drink. A man bounded into the kitchen, looked at the pair, then headed back out, closing the door behind them.

'You've got these lot shook,' said Natty, impressed. Spence winked.

'I learned from the best. You always told me to make sure I asserted myself. Anyway, that's not important. It sounds like you made the right decision. There's nothing wrong with growing up, and you don't have to punch your way out of every situation.' He smirked. 'I must say . . . it's hilarious that someone flirted with your girl in front of you . . . that's basically your go-to-move.'

Both men laughed. It was precisely the sort of thing Natty used to do.

'What do you want to do, Nat?' Spence asked, once they'd calmed down. 'You turned down your uncle, right?'

Natty nodded.

'Why?'

'What do you mean?'

'Why did you turn him down? He basically offered you what you always wanted, so did you *plan* to turn him down, or was it a spur-of-the-moment thing?'

'I didn't know he was going to ask me,' admitted Natty. 'I figured when things died down, he'd want to speak with me, maybe let me in on what was going on, but I didn't expect to get offered the top job. As for why I turned it down, I wanted to try something different. I needed to be away from it, to kinda . . . find myself.'

Spence nodded now.

'That's what you need to do then. That's what your mind is telling you, and it's why you're so restless. You've got to do something different.'

'What am I supposed to do?'

Spence shrugged, grabbing their cups and putting them in the kitchen sink.

'You should do whatever makes you happy. You're good with people; maybe you could do something involving club promotion?' Spence chuckled. 'Everyone loves podcasts. You could do one of those. Either way, try, and see how that makes you feel.'

'A fucking podcast?' Natty was incredulous. 'Who's going to want to listen to me? And what am I gonna talk about; the life? Might as well put the handcuffs on myself.'

The pair chuckled together.

'Maybe not a podcast then,' Spence replied, 'but there's a lot of opportunity out there, Nat. You just have to find out what's right for you.'

'What if I fuck it up? What if the only thing I'm suited to is the streets?'

Again, Spence shrugged. 'Then you fuck it up. So what? If you don't try, you'll never know what else gets you going; what else you can put your time and energy into. You should at least give it a go.'

Natty still felt uneasy, but couldn't deny it was good advice.

'Thank you, bro. Even just speaking about this for a little bit has made me feel better.'

Spence smiled.

'I forgot to tell you,' Natty went on. 'I went to visit my dad. Haven't been for a while, so I got some things off my chest. What you were saying brought it back for me. My dad used to tell me that the streets were relentless; that you had to be all-in to survive.'

'I'm not sure I believe that's true. There's a few different ways to benefit from the game we play, but I do believe you get what you put into it.'

Both men fell silent. Natty ran his finger along the rough wooden table. Spence's words made sense, but ran contrary to what his dad had taught him. He moved past it, something else coming to his mind.

'His birthday is coming up.'

Spence's face fell. He didn't even have to ask who Natty was referring to.

Cameron had been their friend. The trio had worked well for years, before Cameron's greed got the better of him. He'd betrayed the crew and his friends. The last Natty had seen of him, Cameron was detained by Mitch's men, and no one had heard anything since. There were plenty of rumours, but no facts, and it was a mystery as to how he met his end. Anyone who knew wasn't talking.

'I miss him sometimes,' admitted Spence. 'I'm not making excuses for what he did, but . . .'

'I know, fam. I feel the same way,' said Natty. 'We should do something to celebrate the man we remember . . . not the one he turned out to be.'

'That sounds good,' agreed Spence. 'We can have a few drinks and tell some war stories.'

'I'll set it up and get back to you.' Natty slid to his feet. Spence did the same.

'Have you spoken to your mum lately?'

Natty's shoulders slumped without warning. He sighed.

'I've tried, bro. She barely speaks to me.'

'Keep trying, Nat. I know how you are and what you and your mum are like, but don't take her for granted. No matter how difficult you think she is at times.'

It was food for thought, and Natty nodded, agreeing to consider it. Spence was speaking more for himself than Natty, and they both knew it. Spence had worshipped his mum, and missed her terribly. She'd died many years ago — before Natty had become friends with him, but that pain had never gone away.

In his own way, Natty could relate. He still felt the hurt of learning his dad was dead, hoping it had been a cruel joke, or his dad using his skills to evade the enemies of the streets, but it wasn't; that reality hit him when he stood over his dad's headstone.

It struck him just how many people he knew, who had grown up in single-parent households, or with no parent at all. He wondered if that was why people were how they were in the streets, whether any of them had a chance.

That made Natty think of Jaden, and his fists clenched.

Natty would make sure Jaden would have that chance; the chance to achieve anything he set his mind to, without fear or the lure of the streets. He would do anything he wanted, just as Natty's dad had wanted for him. Natty recalled conversations about football, and talks about the streets, and what it took to make it.

Whatever happened, he vowed not to let Jaden get caught up in the street life.

DEEDS
TO THE
CITY

RICKY BLACK

CHAPTER ONE

FEBRUARY 2021

NATHANIEL 'NATTY DEEDS' Dunn stood in front of his dad's grave. It had been a while since he had visited, the area around the headstone unkempt, bereft of flowers or care.

Tyrone Dunn
June 10, 1965 - August 2, 2002
Loving Father and Husband

Around Natty, the chilly wind rippled his coat, and he jammed his hands deeper into his pockets, unable to tear his eyes away.

Looking around, he noted the cemetery was empty, and cleared his throat.

'Sorry I haven't been to see you in a while, dad,' he mumbled. Again, he cleared his throat and continued, 'don't really have an excuse, but I've missed you more lately. I always do, but shit's different now, and I wish you were here to tell me what to do. Nowadays, I feel like I understand what you went through when you were alive, but I don't know how you coped. You were loved and respected. I'm not even sure what I am now. I'm a little lost, dad. I wish I could speak to you. I wish you could put your hand on my shoulder like you used to and set me straight. You'd know what to do . . . I know you would.'

Natty continued to stare at the headstone, not knowing what he had expected to happen. He shook off his embarrassment, needing to say more.

'I guess I've been wondering lately how you felt about the things you had to do. For the game we're all playing in the Hood. Whether you enjoyed it or did it because you had to. I'm at a point where I don't know whether I'm coming or going. It feels like I'm looking for a sign . . . something to tell me what to do next. I guess that's why I'm here.'

Natty stopped speaking, wiping his eyes. His dad was thirty-seven when he died. Natty was almost as old as he was, yet life had been different. He'd worked for his uncle, Mitch Dunn, his entire adult life. Starting as a runner, he became a crew chief, languishing in that position for years. A few months ago, circumstances changed when Natty unearthed a plot to bring down his uncle.

The memories overwhelmed Natty as he stood there. What he needed above all else was to talk to somebody. To make sense of what had happened, and why things had turned out as they did.

But who?

With those closest to him central to the plot against his uncle, Natty didn't know who to trust anymore. Spence and Lorraine were probably sick of listening to him, he reasoned, as he scratched his chin.

Natty's phone rang. He glanced at the screen, noting Lorraine was calling.

'Hey,' he said.

'Hey, Nat. Where are you?'

'I'm just out,' he replied. 'Is everything okay?'

'Jaden was asking if you're stopping by. I'm about to start dinner, so I thought I would check.'

'Yeah, I'll be there in twenty minutes,' said Natty.

'Okay. See you then.'

Natty hung up, again staring at the headstone. He frowned, noting some cobwebs at the top of the stone, which he crouched down to wipe away, vowing to come more often. It was clear nobody else visited. *His mum certainly didn't.* Natty couldn't recall the last time they had been together. He tensed. His mum was yet another situation he needed to resolve.

Straightening, he wiped his hands on his trousers. Finally, he whispered goodbye to his dad, leaving the cemetery.

———

'Natty!'

Jaden ran at Natty as soon as he entered the house. Natty hugged him, ruffling his head.

'Yes, J! Have you been looking after your mum?'

Jaden nodded, and Natty grinned at him. Jaden was ten-years-old and favoured his mum, looks-wise. He had her eyes and colouring, but his nose was similar to his dad's. Natty and Jaden had always got along, but Natty wondered how things would change once Jaden realised Natty was in a relationship with his mum. So far, Jaden hadn't commented on the fact Natty seemed to be spending more time at the house, instead revelling in the extra attention.

'Come on, Natty. Let's play on the computer.' Jaden took Natty's hand, leading him into the living room.

'Get everything set up, little man. Let me speak to your mum for a few minutes.'

Jaden nodded, and Natty headed to the kitchen, where Lorraine sipped a cup of tea, her eyes lighting up when she saw him. The pair shared a hug and a kiss.

'Wow, you brought the cold in with you,' said Lorraine, shivering.

'Sorry about that. I'm glad it's warm in here, though,' Natty said. He released her, and made himself a drink, the mug warming his hands.

'Are you helping me with dinner?' Lorraine asked. 'Or has my son monopolised your time again?'

'I don't mind helping,' said Natty. Lorraine shook her head.

'I was just teasing. Go and play with Jaden. I'll call you if I need you.'

'Make sure you do,' said Natty. He again kissed her, this one lasting longer than the first. They broke away only when Jaden called for Natty, stating he had everything ready.

'Duty calls,' Natty said with a wink. Still holding his cup, he went to Jaden, Lorraine smiling after him.

———

THAT EVENING, Lorraine and Natty snuggled on the sofa. Jaden had gone to bed an hour ago, and the pair were watching an action film they'd stumbled across on TV.

'Where were you earlier?' Lorraine asked, pressed firmly against him.

'I went to visit my dad,' he said, keeping his voice neutral, hoping a big deal wouldn't be made. This was dashed when Lorraine immediately muted the TV.

'You did?'

Natty nodded, his cheeks warming slightly as his embarrassment at the cemetery returned to him.

'You should have told me. I would have gone with you,' she said, pouting.

'It's fine,' he replied, appreciating the fact she'd offered.

'What made you go?'

Natty sighed.

'I really don't know. I just feel . . . lost. I needed some guidance, and lately, I've been thinking about some things my dad taught me when I was younger, and how much I enjoyed being able to turn to him when I needed help.'

'Can I ask you something?' Lorraine said.

'Course you can.'

'Are you happy?'

'Yes,' Natty instantly replied. 'This thing, whatever it is . . . it's not about being sad. I feel adrift, like I want to do more, but I don't know how.'

Lorraine didn't immediately respond, but Natty didn't rush her. He had been guilty of doing it in the past, but he was learning to read the signs, and knew Lorraine liked to mull things before she spoke. It was why he wasn't surprised she'd waited so long to ask where he had been earlier.

'You were doing what you did on the streets for a long time. It's bound to take some time to switch off.'

'If I ever can,' Natty murmured.

'Have you spoken to Spence about any of this?' Lorraine asked.

'No. Haven't had the chance.'

'He's your friend, Nat. If you tell him what's going on, he could help you.'

'He's dealing with his promotion. That and whatever is going on with Rosie. I don't wanna overwhelm him with my shit too.'

'Don't be silly. That's what friends are for.'

Lorraine snuggled closer against him. Natty closed his eyes, enjoying the feeling, hoping he could get things in line.

'Mich—Raider's auntie contacted me today. She's been reaching out for a while,' Lorraine said, after a few minutes.

Natty went still. 'What does she want?'

'She wants me to bring Jaden to see Raider.'

A wave of annoyance rose in Natty. Raider was Jaden's dad, and the pair had never got on. This was taken to a new level last year when Raider severely beat Lorraine in a drunken rage. Natty retaliated, fracturing Raider's skull and landing him in hospital. He'd heard through the grapevine that Raider was out of the hospital, now recovering at home.

'Do his family know what he did to you?' He said.

'No. I never told them.'

'Why not?'

'Because I didn't want them to know,' said Lorraine. She shifted away from Natty, playing with her fingers.

'They should know what sort of man he is, and what he did,' said Natty.

'I just want to forget about it, Nat. I don't want to think about Raider or any of that. I'd rather focus on us,' she said, smiling softly. 'Are you spending the night?'

Natty nodded. He spent little time at his place nowadays, but Lorraine would still check, as if she expected him to refuse.

'We should go out on Friday,' he said, surprising himself.

'Really?'

'Yeah. We can go for dinner and drinks. Make a night of it.'

Lorraine's smile widened.

'I'd like that.'

'Good,' said Natty. He hoped going out with Lorraine would take his mind off his feelings.

———

As ARRANGED, they went out on Friday, with Lorraine's mum babysitting. Lorraine chose Italian food, the evening carefree, and the conversation fast-paced. Natty felt better about his issues, happy that he was at least doing this right. He wanted to be a man Lorraine could be proud of, which meant making major changes.

After eating, they stopped in a bar, then Lorraine dragged him to one of her favourite clubs. It wasn't Natty's scene anymore, but this was Lorraine's night, and he wanted her to be happy. They danced to numerous tracks, their drinks spilling as they moved. Noticing, Lorraine pointed to her glass and pouted. Smirking and shaking his head, Natty turned on the spot and set off to the bar to get them more drinks.

On his way back, he noted a man crowding Lorraine's space. Natty's jaw tensed. It reminded him of the moves he used to make on women — whether or not they were taken. Standing by Lorraine's side, he handed her the drink.

'Thanks,' she said, smiling at him.

The man turned his attention to Natty, and they sized one another up. He was light-skinned, his hair trimmed with a low fade. He was around Natty's size, and equally well-built.

'I was just chatting to Lorraine,' he said, smirking. 'I haven't seen her in a while.'

'He knows my friend Poppy,' said Lorraine, eyes darting between the men.

'Yeah, Poppy is cool. Anyway, do you wanna come and chill with me and my people? We're heading to a private spot soon. It's gonna be a big night.'

'No thanks,' said Lorraine politely. 'I'm out with my man.'

The man's eyes narrowed, his smirk vanishing. He tried to give Natty a dismissive look, but Natty snorted.

'You're trying too hard, bro,' he said. 'Leave with at least a little dignity.'

'Are you serious? Don't run your mouth,' the man snapped. Natty stepped forward, but Lorraine stopped him.

'Please, Nat. Just leave it,' she pleaded.

Every cell in Natty's body wanted to fight. It was a familiar feeling, that all-encompassing anger. He didn't have to think too hard about it. It would be the easiest thing in the world to break the man's face, and his friends' faces too, if they got involved.

Lorraine was more important, though. Nodding, he stepped back.

'Please go. I think you've done enough,' Lorraine said to the man. For a moment, Natty thought he would resist, but the man sneered and stalked away. Natty breathed deeply, clenching his fists. Lorraine squeezed his hand, and the gesture relaxed him.

'Thank you,' she said. Natty nodded, not ready to speak yet. He could see the man talking with his friends, but when he motioned in Natty's direction, one of the men's eyes widened, and he turned away and began whispering to the others. Natty was sure the man recognised him, despite the two having never met. Natty smirked as the faces in the group converged and departed, shooting him fearful glances.

They left the club shortly after, enjoying older R&B music in another venue. Natty didn't say anything, but the incident with the man had ignited something important.

The *almost conflict* had made him feel more alive, and more like his old self.

CHAPTER TWO

THE NEXT DAY, Natty went for a run, needing to burn off some excess energy. Last year, he'd started to let himself go, physically. He'd got himself back into shape, running daily when he could manage it throughout the winter, and quitting smoking.

Pounding the pavement, his mind wandered to the night before. He was shocked that he'd kept his temper around the man, wondering what it meant.

Natty paused, doubling over to catch his breath, then randomly chuckling. Lorraine could be his guardian angel for all he knew. She seemed skilled at getting him out of trouble that he'd caused. At least when he gave her a chance to. His mind wandered to his altercation with Raider. Natty hadn't spoken to her before he went after him, almost destroying their relationship.

Natty wouldn't take that chance again. He would figure out what was going on in his head, and as he started running again, he knew Spence was the man to help with it.

———

SPENCE HUNCHED OVER HIS BREAKFAST, enjoying the piping hot cornmeal porridge. He was in Dutch Pot on Chapeltown Road, savouring the meal that would set him up for the long day ahead.

It had been an interesting few months for Spence. When Natty turned down his promotion, Spence was next in line, stepping up when it was offered. Now, he was earning more money than he'd ever dreamed possible.

Unlike his contemporaries, Spence always had a long-term plan, and had made the most of the money he'd earned previously, investing it and refusing to waste it on the same trappings that many in the game did; clothes, jewellery, cars and women. With the boost in funds, he'd bolstered his investments and savings, and was able to take more risks, knowing he was financially secure.

Despite this, Spence was under no illusions about the added responsibility. There was no room for mistakes at this level. Messing up would likely mean his death, but Spence was ready for the challenge, especially when it kept his mind from going to places he didn't want it to. He'd been through a lot recently, and what he had lost felt immeasurable at the time. Bit by bit, he was coming to terms with it, and forging ahead.

Spence's phone rang. It was a PGP device given to him by Mitch, totally untraceable. Wiping his mouth, he answered.

'Hello?'

'It's Clarke. I'm outside.'

Clarke hung up. Spence shovelled the last few spoonfuls of porridge down his throat, downed the orange juice he'd ordered, then thanked the cook before stepping outside.

Clarke idled by the curb in the passenger seat of a new-model Nissan 4x4. He was a thick-necked older man with piercing eyes, and a large nose. His balding hair and neat beard were peppered with grey. Spence climbed in the back, and the vehicle rumbled away.

The crew drove out to Moortown, parking outside Mitch's home, and immediately heading to the garage. Mitch waited, on his feet, circling a heavy bag. His head darting side-to-side, he threw out the occasional shot, each blow awkwardly folding the bag. The chains rattled as they strained to hold it in position. Spence had been here once before, and it had surprised him just how old and well-used some of the equipment was. Mitch hit the bag several times, then unwrapped his hands, nodding at Spence. Clarke waited by the door.

Spence had yet to get used to being around Mitch, whether in a personal or business setting. It was surreal.

Mitch was a Hood legend who had always been in the shadows, his reputation growing as the years passed. He and Natty's father, Tyrone Dunn, had founded the crew. Mitch had steered them through tough times after Tyrone's murder nineteen years ago. He was brown-skinned, with hard eyes, a gaunt face and a shaven head, with little facial hair. As always, he was casually dressed, wearing a plain grey tracksuit. Despite this, power resonated with Mitch, overwhelming whoever was around him.

Mitch seemed to like him, but Spence believed he was simply a placeholder until someone else came along to run the crew. He didn't mind either way, as long as they prospered.

'How are you?' Mitch asked.

'Everything's good,' replied Spence, sure Mitch was more concerned with business than his personal life. Mitch nodded.

'How's your pops?'

'He's doing alright,' replied Spence, surprised that Mitch had brought up his dad. 'Still working.'

'He never liked me. When I used to see him around Del back in the day, he always used to give me dirty looks. Despite that, I think he respected me, and the feeling was mutual,' said Mitch, eyes still locked onto Spence's. 'I respect the move he made. Many have tried going legit, but not many stick with it.'

Spence wasn't surprised his dad had left the game behind. Something had changed in his dad after Spence's mum died. It made him wonder how well Mitch knew his dad, and whether he was referring to him at all . . .

'In general, how are things going?'

Spence continued meeting Mitch's eyes. Even though he had bad news to give, he wasn't going to back away from doing so.

'The takings are down from last month in Chapeltown.'

Mitch said nothing, silently imploring Spence to continue.

'We've taken in a quarter mill from our dealers, less than the four hundred grand we took the month before.'

Mitch nodded. 'I heard the same thing. What have you done about it?'

It was a direct question that would have crumbled most and sent them stuttering and stammering for an answer, but Spence took it in his stride.

'I've conducted an investigation. None of our dealers are living beyond their means or flashing silly cash.'

'That's a start. Tell me, what do you think is going on?'

Spence was sharp, immediately understanding what was going on. This was a test.

He took his time, mulling it over.

'It sounds like we have some competition.' He noted the gleam of approval in Mitch's eyes. 'I'm all over it, though. I'll find them.'

Mitch nodded. 'Whoever it is, it won't be long before we get our hands on them. Keep talking to Clarke. He'll keep me updated.'

Spence turned to leave, believing the meeting was over.

'Spence?'

He turned.

'How's Natty?'

Again, Spence mulled this over. Natty seemed happy with Lorraine. Spence had been in the background, waiting for them to stop being stubborn and admit how they felt about each other. Despite all the drama that had transpired, Natty and Lorraine seemed to be doing well.

Despite that, Natty seemed on edge. Spence couldn't put his finger on why, but there was something almost haunting in his eyes the last time Spence had seen him.

Mitch was still awaiting an answer, and Spence gave him one.

'He's fine. Still figuring things out.'

Mitch smiled for a moment.

'I'll reach out to him; see if it's anything I can help with.'

Spence left, climbing back into the car, Clarke following. He wasn't stupid. Mitch wanted Natty back in the fold, and would likely stop at nothing to achieve this.

LORRAINE YAWNED, saving her progress on the snippet of code she was querying. Her courses were kicking her arse, but she enjoyed the challenge. Things had ramped up for her in the past few months in her marketing day job. She'd begun querying customer data to help formulate new marketing campaigns. The extra work she had done was paying off.

Jaden was at a friend's house. Natty had been out all day. Lorraine made herself a drink, thinking about the confrontation in the club. It wasn't the first time she had seen it happen. On more than one occasion, Natty had lost his temper around people and fought. He was vicious and usually got his point across. He was also a huge flirt, and it was strange to see him on the other end, watching someone flirt with his woman.

Despite this, he'd stopped. For her. It was startling, especially with how much Natty wanted it to happen. Lorraine remembered her simple gesture, disarming the hand that had been balled into a fist.

Would he always have that edge to him?

A memory of Raider's assault flickered in Lorraine's mind. Instinctively, she grabbed at her rib. She took a deep breath, steadying herself. Sometimes she was okay. Other times, she felt helpless, just wanting to curl up in a ball.

Sipping a cool glass of water, she considered the request from Raider's auntie. She wasn't sure it was a good idea for Raider to be around Jaden, yet at the same time, she didn't want to stop them from having a relationship. Especially if that would *fix* Raider, and turn him from the destructive lifestyle he seemed to crave.

She wondered if Natty's beating had changed him.

Lorraine double-checked she'd saved her progress, finished her drink, then went for a short walk to clear her head. By the time she returned home, she had her phone to her ear, waiting for Rosie to answer.

'Hey, Lo. Everything okay?'

'Yeah. I'm trying to distract myself. Figured that was a great time to ring my best friend.'

Rosie giggled.

'Natty must be unavailable. I'm near your place. I'll see you soon.'

Rosie wasn't exaggerating. Within two minutes, she was at the house. They made drinks and sat in the kitchen.

'Right, speak,' said Rosie, stirring her drink.

'It's Raider,' said Lorraine, noting Rosie's face immediately darkening. 'Well, not him specifically, but his family. His Auntie Rita keeps requesting to see Jaden. She wants him to visit Raider.'

'Do his family know what Raider did?'

Lorraine shook her head.

'You need to fix that. They should know exactly what kind of man he is and the lengths he's willing to go to.'

Again, Lorraine shook her head.

'I can't do that, Rosie. When it gets like that, it's always the kids that get hurt. Jaden doesn't need to know that about his dad.'

'Kids grow up quicker around the Hood. Jaden is a good boy, and he should know the truth. What's Natty saying about it?'

'He agrees with you, of course,' Lorraine dryly replied.

'That should tell you something, babe. Speaking of Natty, how is Jaden about you two?'

'I don't think he understands, if I'm honest. We're not blatant with it around him, but he enjoys having Natty around all the time.'

Rosie beamed. Lorraine knew she was fond of Natty, and was pleased they had finally entered into a relationship.

'How's Natty doing, anyway? I haven't seen him in ages, and Spence hasn't brought him up.'

'He's restless, but he seems happy to be around me. We haven't argued or anything. Something happened yesterday, though.'

Rosie signalled for Lorraine to continue.

'We went out for some food, and ended up stopping by a club near Briggate. I can't remember the name, but it's really small and easy to overlook. Anyway, we're inside, and Natty goes to get me a drink, and this guy comes over to chat to me.'

Rosie chuckled.

'Bet Natty loved that.'

'He came back over and was quite calm about it at first. The guy was being a prick, so Natty just switched.'

'Of course he did. Natty loves to scrap around you.'

'Don't you think that's wild? I was his only backup, Ro. The guy was in the club with all his friends, and Natty didn't care.'

'Why would he? Once again, this is Natty we're talking about. He's your bloody alpha,' said Rosie.

Lorraine smiled for a moment, amused by Rosie's antics. Her friend always knew just what to do to bring her out of a funk — even one Lorraine hadn't realised she was in.

'I'm worried about him. Like I said, he seems really restless, and at times, it's like he's just shuffling around, waiting for something to happen.'

'Maybe he is,' said Rosie. 'Or, maybe it will just take time. I mean, he did his thing in the streets for years. I can't imagine the transition to being a civilian is easy. Just keep being there for him, and get him talking. You two are strongest when you're on the same page.'

Lorraine felt better after speaking with Rosie. Maybe the situation with Natty wasn't as bad as she thought. They just needed to communicate, and she needed to be there for him.

———

NATTY FOUND Spence at a spot in the Hood, near Francis Street. Several goons were posted around, greeting Natty with smiles, nods, and hand slaps. It was something he'd noticed when he was around certain circles. Despite things being kept low-key with Rudy and Elijah, certain faces in the streets knew what Natty had done. It had enhanced his reputation, and meant people looked at him a certain way.

Just as he had wanted for the longest time.

Natty entered the spot, finding Spence on the phone in the main hangout room. There were several other people dotted around, one pacing the room, and two on the sofa talking in quiet voices. Natty didn't recognise any of them, and they gave him only a cursory glance. Their demeanours were stiff, suggesting something big was going down.

Despite this, Spence appeared unflappable. He shot Natty a grin, finishing his conversation and sliding to his feet. The pair shared a quick hug. It had been a few weeks since they'd seen one another, but they had texted and stayed in communication.

'Come, let's get drinks,' he said, leading Natty to the kitchen.

'You look . . . mostly well,' he added, as he looked Natty up and down, taking a sip of his drink. Natty chuckled. He could never get much past Spence, and he was glad his friend had realised. It would save him having to work it into conversation.

Despite their closeness, Natty still held onto some guilt where his friend was concerned, namely regarding his role in the end of Spence's last relationship. He was glad Spence seemed to have taken it in his stride and bounced back. For years, people had assumed Spence was the weakest of the trio. Natty and Cameron were more aggressive, always willing to throw hands, and Spence was calmer, never rushing into anything.

Now, Natty saw this was a rare skill, and it made him further respect Spence.

'What's going on around here?' He ignored Spence. 'Looks like people are preparing for a war.' He laughed, expecting Spence to laugh too, but Spence shrugged.

'It could be the case, Nat. The takings are down lately.'

'Down by how much?'

'One hundred and fifty bags lighter than last month.'

'How is that possible?' Natty's eyes narrowed, darting around the room, surveying those in attendance. 'Have you—'

'Checked to see if anyone is holding out? Yep, I have. I checked everyone in and around the crew. I suspect there's another crew out there.'

Natty sipped his drink.

'People playing in the big leagues are usually difficult to hide,' he pointed out.

Spence leaned inward.

'Whoever it is, they're doing well so far. I'm asking around, but no one has anything to say about it.'

'It could be nothing. Maybe it's just a bad month,' said Natty.

'I hope you're right, fam. I spoke with your uncle today.'

'What's he saying?' Natty asked. He'd seen little of his uncle since he turned down his offer. It struck him just how unbothered he was by that. Similar to his reputation amongst people in the street, Natty had spent years trying to get his uncle's attention, wanting adulation and more responsibility.

It didn't seem to mean the same now.

'He sent his best wishes. I'm guessing he'll contact you soon.'

'I doubt it,' Natty said, drinking more of his drink and setting the cup on the table. Spence's phone rang. He checked the number, answered, and told the person to call back later.

'I can leave if you need me to. I just wanted to check on you,' Natty added.

'No, you wanted to tell me what's going on,' said Spence. 'Business can wait; if they're important enough, they'll know who to ring next.'

Natty was touched Spence was putting him before the business, and allowed himself a small smile.

'I don't really know what's going on. I feel lost. Can't really explain it.'

'Everything good with Lorraine?'

Natty nodded. 'She's smashing it. She's doing some software development courses, and she's focused. Jaden's doing well too. He's enjoying the school year, and he's getting better at football. It feels like everyone is doing something other than me. I feel like something is calling me, but I don't know what, or what direction it's coming from. I nearly got into some shit yesterday.'

'Tell me,' said Spence. Natty filled him in on the incident in the club. Spence listened as he finished his drink. A man bounded into the kitchen, looked at the pair, then headed back out, closing the door behind them.

'You've got these lot shook,' said Natty, impressed. Spence winked.

'I learned from the best. You always told me to make sure I asserted myself. Anyway, that's not important. It sounds like you made the right decision. There's nothing wrong with growing up, and you don't have to punch your way out of every situation.' He smirked. 'I must say . . . it's hilarious that someone flirted with your girl in front of you . . . that's basically your go-to-move.'

Both men laughed. It was precisely the sort of thing Natty used to do.

'What do you want to do, Nat?' Spence asked, once they'd calmed down. 'You turned down your uncle, right?'

Natty nodded.

'Why?'

'What do you mean?'

'Why did you turn him down? He basically offered you what you always wanted, so did you *plan* to turn him down, or was it a spur-of-the-moment thing?'

'I didn't know he was going to ask me,' admitted Natty. 'I figured when things died down, he'd want to speak with me, maybe let me in on what was going on, but I didn't expect to get offered the top job. As for why I turned it down, I wanted to try something different. I needed to be away from it, to kinda . . . find myself.'

Spence nodded now.

'That's what you need to do then. That's what your mind is telling you, and it's why you're so restless. You've got to do something different.'

'What am I supposed to do?'

Spence shrugged, grabbing their cups and putting them in the kitchen sink.

'You should do whatever makes you happy. You're good with people; maybe you could do something involving club promotion?' Spence chuckled. 'Everyone loves podcasts. You could do one of those. Either way, try, and see how that makes you feel.'

'A fucking podcast?' Natty was incredulous. 'Who's going to want to listen to me? And what am I gonna talk about; the life? Might as well put the handcuffs on myself.'

The pair chuckled together.

'Maybe not a podcast then,' Spence replied, 'but there's a lot of opportunity out there, Nat. You just have to find out what's right for you.'

'What if I fuck it up? What if the only thing I'm suited to is the streets?'

Again, Spence shrugged. 'Then you fuck it up. So what? If you don't try, you'll never know what else gets you going; what else you can put your time and energy into. You should at least give it a go.'

Natty still felt uneasy, but couldn't deny it was good advice.

'Thank you, bro. Even just speaking about this for a little bit has made me feel better.'

Spence smiled.

'I forgot to tell you,' Natty went on. 'I went to visit my dad. Haven't been for a while, so I got some things off my chest. What you were saying brought it back for me. My dad used to tell me that the streets were relentless; that you had to be all-in to survive.'

'I'm not sure I believe that's true. There's a few different ways to benefit from the game we play, but I do believe you get what you put into it.'

Both men fell silent. Natty ran his finger along the rough wooden table. Spence's words made sense, but ran contrary to what his dad had taught him. He moved past it, something else coming to his mind.

'His birthday is coming up.'

Spence's face fell. He didn't even have to ask who Natty was referring to.

Cameron had been their friend. The trio had worked well for years, before Cameron's greed got the better of him. He'd betrayed the crew and his friends. The last Natty had seen of him, Cameron was detained by Mitch's men, and no one had heard anything since. There were plenty of rumours, but no facts, and it was a mystery as to how he met his end. Anyone who knew wasn't talking.

'I miss him sometimes,' admitted Spence. 'I'm not making excuses for what he did, but . . .'

'I know, fam. I feel the same way,' said Natty. 'We should do something to celebrate the man we remember . . . not the one he turned out to be.'

'That sounds good,' agreed Spence. 'We can have a few drinks and tell some war stories.'

'I'll set it up and get back to you.' Natty slid to his feet. Spence did the same.

'Have you spoken to your mum lately?'

Natty's shoulders slumped without warning. He sighed.

'I've tried, bro. She barely speaks to me.'

'Keep trying, Nat. I know how you are and what you and your mum are like, but don't take her for granted. No matter how difficult you think she is at times.'

It was food for thought, and Natty nodded, agreeing to consider it. Spence was speaking more for himself than Natty, and they both knew it. Spence had worshipped his mum, and missed her terribly. She'd died many years ago — before Natty had become friends with him, but that pain had never gone away.

In his own way, Natty could relate. He still felt the hurt of learning his dad was dead, hoping it had been a cruel joke, or his dad using his skills to evade the enemies of the streets, but it wasn't; that reality hit him when he stood over his dad's headstone.

It struck him just how many people he knew, who had grown up in single-parent households, or with no parent at all. He wondered if that was why people were how they were in the streets, whether any of them had a chance.

That made Natty think of Jaden, and his fists clenched.

Natty would make sure Jaden would have that chance; the chance to achieve anything he set his mind to, without fear or the lure of the streets. He would do anything he wanted, just as Natty's dad had wanted for him. Natty recalled conversations about football, and talks about the streets, and what it took to make it.

Whatever happened, he vowed not to let Jaden get caught up in the street life.

CHAPTER THREE

NATTY HAD A QUIET EVENING, glad he'd gone to speak to Spence. It amazed him how well Spence seemed to be doing in his role. The game was tough at all levels, but there was zero room for mistakes at the level Spence was on. Rudy's murder was proof of that. He'd been down with Natty's uncle for over twenty years, but it didn't matter. Once he'd made his mistake, he was dead.

However, Spence seemed to take it in his stride, just as he always did. Natty wasn't sure if this was down to Spence's upbringing, or if it was a natural skill he had, but it was impressive nonetheless.

———

THE FOLLOWING DAY, Natty decided to go and see his mum, recalling Spence's words at the end of their conversation. After breakfast and some exercise, he drove to Hares Avenue, parked, knocked, and walked into the house.

His mum was in the kitchen, in the middle of cleaning, playing *Lauryn Hill*. He smiled warmly as he watched her, reminded of his youth. Back then, she often sang at the top of her voice, dancing while cleaning or preparing food. Natty's dad would tease her as she did, but she would smile back and carry on. Sometimes she would pull her husband up, and they would start dancing together, lost in the moment.

Natty's smile widened at the memory.

His mum straightened, scowling as she turned off the music. This wasn't a surprise. Things between the pair had been tense since Rudy's death. As he'd grown older, Natty had realised she wasn't always the best at managing her emotions — he couldn't recall her mourning, even after his dad was killed.

It had been the same with Rudy, and Natty believed she was hiding from herself. Their last few meetings had been argumentative throughout, causing him to stay away.

'How are you, mum?' He said, approaching and kissing her cheek.

'I'm fine,' she stiffly replied.

'Good. I just wanted to stop by and make sure. What have you been up to lately?'

'We don't need to do this,' she said.

'Do what?'

'This silly little small talk. I don't need you doddering around me like I'm an invalid.'

Natty sighed. It hurt to look at his mum at times. She'd retained her looks, but she seemed diminished, and had for a long time. He still remembered the beauty of her younger days, and how passionate and dynamic she had appeared. Now, he wondered if he'd seen what he expected to see; whether he'd imagined his mum being happy.

'Do you need any help cleaning?' He tried to move on.

'I said I'm fine, Nat. I don't need help.'

Glancing around the room, Natty saw no issue with the statement. The place looked flawless. She had likely been cleaning out of habit or distraction rather than necessity.

'Are you still unemployed?' She suddenly asked.

'Yep. I'm still figuring some things out,' replied Natty.

'You're too old to be *figuring things out*, Nat. You need a job, especially if you're going to be looking after your ready-made family.'

Ignoring the barb about Jaden and Lorraine, Natty pushed on.

'I'll be fine, mum. I have enough money to tide me over for a while.

You taught me how to save,' he said, watching her preen over his words for a moment. 'I went to visit dad's grave the other day. When was the last time you went?'

'You look more like him the older you get,' she replied, ignoring the question. 'You've got his size and his way of talking, but beyond that, you have something different to you.'

'Something like what?' Natty asked, intrigued, finally taking a seat. His mum had spoken of his dad to him a lot, but she had never said this before.

'I don't know what it is. It's just something I feel.'

A moment passed, the pair staring at one another. Natty snapped out of it.

'I'll make us some drinks,' he said, cutting her off when she went to speak. 'Don't worry; I'll wash them afterwards.'

Natty made his mum a cup of tea, and himself a cup of coffee. She washed her hands, putting her equipment to one side, sitting at the table with him. For a time, they sat in comfortable silence. Natty was glad he had done this. They seemed in a better place than in previous meetings.

'Do you plan on visiting Rudy's grave?' The words sounded casual, but Natty knew she'd been planning them since he'd mentioned his dad.

'No.'

'Why?' His mum asked, eyes flashing.

'It's just a personal choice,' Natty replied, not wanting to go into detail. His mum's stare burned into him, and Natty strained to meet her gaze. When he finally blinked, the image of him squeezing the trigger invaded his thoughts. Natty concealed a deep breath, before reopening his eyes.

He didn't need her making a big deal out of this. He'd avoided mentioning Rudy since he and his mum had argued about his refusal to attend Rudy's funeral.

'I don't believe that, Nat. You two always got along, even if you got a bit moody with him sometimes. I don't think what you're saying is tied to your dad, but there's something you're not telling me.'

Natty sipped his drink, surprised at his mum's perceptiveness.

'We just fell out, that's all. It's not that deep.'

'He did a lot for you, Nat.'

'And Unc did a lot for him. He was an employee, and it served him well to keep me on his side,' Natty retorted. 'Not to mention my dad, who *also* did a lot for him.'

Natty's mum's face slackened, replaced by a neutral expression moments later.

'I'm glad you stepped away from your uncle.'

Natty hadn't known what to expect, but her words still stunned him. He shot his mum a sceptical look. She and his uncle always seemed to have a good relationship. As Rudy had pointed out numerous times, she was the only person Mitch seemed to listen to. Natty assumed it was out of respect for his dead brother. Her husband.

His mum had always been rather vocal about Natty standing on his own two feet, and had never told him he shouldn't sell drugs. She'd liked him working with his uncle, and the idea he was living up to his dad's image.

Or so he had thought.

'Why?'

His mum held her cup firmly with both hands, eyes fixed on the brown liquid sloshing around at the bottom of her cup. Raising the cup to her mouth, she drained the last dregs of her tea, before her eyes finally met her son's.

'Your uncle is a user, Natty. He used your dad, and he used Rudy the same way.'

'How?' Natty leaned forward, eager to learn more. His mum shook her head.

'Mitch had them dancing on strings, just like he does everyone . . . you included. He twists family loyalty, but the only thing he's concerned about is himself.'

'Just say what's on your mind. You're obviously trying to tell me something,' said Natty. She shook her head.

'I've said my piece, Nat. Ask your uncle. See if he'll tell you, but remember this: blood can be used against you.' She stood, grabbing both their cups.

'Mum?'

'Just go, Nat,' she said tiredly. 'You're getting in the way of my cleaning.'

Filled with more questions than answers, Natty left.

———

SPENCE WAS at the main spot in the Hood. He often floated between locations throughout the day, ensuring things ran smoothly.

At present, he was checking his investments online, again thankful for the increase in earnings. The volatile markets he'd invested in were paying off short-term, and he needed to plan his next move carefully. Not wanting to get carried away, he wanted to research new companies and move effectively.

'Spence? You good?'

Spence nodded at Carlton. He'd worked under Natty last year, and when Spence stepped up, he'd picked Carlton out to run the Little London area. Carlton was sharp, and had a knack for picking things up that Spence appreciated, believing he was destined for big things if he stayed on point. He was a short, slight young man, with a patchy beard, neatly trimmed hair, and a bulbous nose.

'Yeah, I was just sorting out some stuff. Did you learn anything?'

Carlton remained standing, rubbing his hands together.

'Something is definitely going on. I've been digging around, like you said. Months back, there were several smaller gangs aligning. We thought it might be a sign they were getting ready to make a move against us.'

Spence nodded, remembering similar conversations just before Natty moved into Little London. Things had gone dark after Elijah and Rudy were murdered, and he'd given the matter no thought since.

'What's the relevance?'

'The gangs have completely pulled back. I've been checking, and there's no sign. Other gangs have been selling closer to the Hood, though. They're wholesaling and offering good prices.'

Spence wiped his face, controlling his irritation. Mitch wholesaled drugs to several customers, meaning he distributed drugs to them in bulk for a reasonable price, and they were responsible for cutting and breaking down the drugs into smaller packages and selling them. Unless they paid extra, they didn't receive protection, nor were they considered part of the crew.

Another gang wholesaling and offering better prices would be a massive blow to their organisation.

'We need to know who's doing this. Do you have any names?'

Carlton rubbed his eyebrow. 'The only name I'm hearing is the name Ro—'

Before Carlton could finish his sentence, they heard the screech of tyres as gunfire ensued. Both men hit the ground as the windows exploded, the rat-tat sound of the guns overwhelming them.

Spence was stunned, unable to comprehend what was happening. He shifted behind the sofa, not expecting it to shield him from bullets, but still wanting cover. Heavy footsteps thundered above him.

'Spence?' He heard one shout. 'We've got you covered, don't worry. Stay down.'

He recognised the voice of one of the goons that guarded the spot. Daring to raise his head, he saw several of them shooting out at the assailants, who'd yet to stop firing. Spence's stomach lurched when one of the men was hit, falling with a strangled yell. More footsteps came from behind.

'Come on!' Clarke hissed, his eyes wild. He dragged Spence and Carlton to their feet, and they hurried out of the back and away from the action.

'What the hell was that about?' Carlton stammered, as he finally caught his breath.

'This isn't the time. We've got backup coming, but we need to get you lot out of here,' said Clarke, bundling the pair into the back of a 4x4, which motored away at speed.

Spence couldn't believe what had happened. One minute he was going about his day, mid-conversation with Carlton. The next, he was in a battle for his life. Someone had tried to kill him. If there was ever a moment that told Spence he was truly in the game, it was this one. He leaned back, closing his eyes, trying to clear his thoughts.

CHAPTER FOUR

NATTY WAS AT LORRAINE'S, chilling on the sofa, watching Jaden play on the PlayStation. Jaden had tried getting him to play, but Natty had too much on his mind. Keen not to disappoint Jaden, Natty told him he was happy watching and learning, *seeing as Jaden beat him so often these days.*

Natty and his mum had shared numerous conversations, but he had never heard her speak disparagingly about his uncle. In fact, it was the opposite. She'd sung his praises, holding up him and Natty's dad as examples to follow.

Now, he couldn't help wondering what had changed, and how it connected to Rudy. His mum knew Rudy had been murdered, but there was no way she could know of his involvement.

Did she suspect his uncle?

'Nat?'

Natty blinked. Lorraine stood over him, concern in her eyes.

'Everything okay?' he asked, sitting up in the chair.

'I was going to ask you the same thing. Where were you just then?'

Natty wanted to tell her it was nothing, but couldn't bring himself to do it.

'I was thinking about my mum. I went to see her earlier, and she was being awkward.'

'About what?' Lorraine sat next to him. Instinctively, she almost hugged him but froze, glancing over at Jaden, still absorbed in his game.

'Just in general,' he said, not wanting to explain his theory. 'Ever since Rudy died, she's just a bit . . . adrift? Don't get me wrong, conversation never flows with us; it hasn't for a while, but something's off.'

'I'm sorry it's not going so well with her. You have to keep trying, though. When it's family, you never really stop.' Lorraine's eyes flitted to the back of her son's head, her mind wandering for a moment.

'You're right,' said Natty, looking down at his phone, flashing and vibrating in his hand. Rejecting the call, Natty waited a beat before moving to place the phone in his pocket, but as he did, it rang again.

'You're not hiding women from me, are you?' Lorraine joked, her eyebrow raised at the same time.

'Not at all,' said Natty. He looked at the number, then answered.

'Sanjay, what's happening?'

'Nat. There was a shooting in the Hood. Your boy was on the scene.'

Natty leapt to his feet.

'Is he okay?'

'Can't get close enough to find out, and I haven't seen him since. Thought you'd want to know.'

'Safe, Sanjay. I'm gonna see what I can find out.'

Natty hung up, heart racing. Both Jaden and Lorraine were staring. He cleared his throat.

'There's . . . been an accident with Spence. I need to go to him.'

Jaden returned to his game, but Lorraine went after Natty as he put his trainers on and hurriedly tugged on a hooded top.

'Is Spence okay? What's happened?'

'I don't know, Lo. There was a shooting.' Dread twisted Natty's insides. He pushed past it.

'Someone was shot? Are you going to be safe?' Lorraine looked horrified. Natty pulled her into a tight hug.

'I'll be fine. No one is going to touch me. I'll text you later to let you know where I am.'

After a quick kiss, Natty headed out to his car. His heart smashed against his ribs, and he had to take a moment before he started the engine. Sanjay was a solid contact. He was reliable and well-liked, but Natty had learned how fleeting trust was. Forcing thoughts of his old friend from his mind, he took a deep breath and called Spence, startled when his friend answered on the first ring.

'Hey, Nat.'

'Spence, what the hell is going on? Where are you?'

'Remember the Harehills spot?'

'Yeah,' replied Natty. Rudy had previously taken him there.

'We're there.'

'I'm on route,' said Natty, relieved that his friend was okay. He drove away, ready to get more answers.

———

As NATTY ARRIVED at the Harehills spot, there was a tinted car parked at the end of the street. Natty imagined there would be a car at both ends, just in case. Spence was taking no chances.

Natty knocked on the door and stepped back. Moments later, the door opened slightly, the chain preventing it from swinging all the way. A pair of dark brown eyes stared out at Natty, sizing him up.

'I'm here to see Spence,' Natty said.

After a moment, the door closed, opening again immediately when the chain was removed. The man behind the door stepped into the light, pointing an Uzi at Natty. He was hard-faced, and Natty knew he'd have no trouble pulling the trigger if given cause. He signalled for someone to frisk Natty, stepping aside when he got the nod from his colleagues.

As Natty entered, he noted the increased noise in the safe house, several loud voices coming from the living room. He followed the noise, opening the door.

Spence sat in the corner of the room, clearly deep in thought, listening to the others argue. There were half a dozen people, and

Natty recognised several of them, though his attention quickly went to the person he didn't. The woman looked younger than him, and was slender, with Mediterranean features and alluring eyes. She noticed Natty's attention and stared right back, her intense gaze cutting through him.

'Good to see you, Nat,' said Clarke. Natty shook his hand, smiling at the older man. Clarke was highly ranked, but Natty had only met him recently, his team responsible for taking down Rudy's after his attempted coup.

'You too, Clarke,' Natty replied. The atmosphere in the room had changed. Those who recognised Natty, were assessing their opinion of him based on Clarke's demeanour. He wasn't someone who spoke or moved when he didn't need to, and the fact he had crossed the room to personally greet Natty, spoke volumes.

'I'm glad you're finally taking your place,' said Clarke. 'We need you on our side.'

Natty shook his head.

'I'm just here to make sure my friend is okay,' he replied. Clarke snorted, but didn't reply. Spence looked up, smiling.

'I think you know pretty much everyone here, Nat,' he said. 'I don't think you've met Lisa, though. Lisa, this is Natty Deeds.'

Lisa held out her hand at an awkward angle, her palm facing the floor. Natty placed his hand in hers, squeezing softly and brushing the top of her hand with his thumb before realising what he was doing.

'Nice to meet you,' he mumbled, trying to save face.

'You too, Natty Deeds,' replied Lisa, her voice soft.

Natty nodded, then focused on Spence, taking a step back.

'What happened?'

'*Roman* happened,' said Spence. The rest of the room shared dark looks. Furiously blinking, Natty weighed up the name.

'The only Roman I can think of that's on any level, is the one that went to prison years back. Are we talking about the same guy?'

'He's back with a bang,' said Clarke, entering the conversation. 'He got out a while ago, but kept to himself.'

'He used that time to plan then,' said Natty. A coffee table was in the middle of the room, laden with drinks. He fixed himself a shot of vodka. Along with the drinks, there were various snacks and the remnants of some food ordered earlier. He sipped the drink, savouring the harsh taste of the strong Russian liquor.

'Who's Roman working for? Unless he had serious backup, he wouldn't be dumb enough to try u—you guys.' He caught himself at the last moment, but Spence's quick smirk told him his slip-of-the-tongue had been noted.

'We're digging into him now. He got caught up during that big sweep in 2015. He had links to the old regime, but we don't know how deep they go.'

'I'm guessing extremely deep,' said Natty. Several in the room nodded at his words, and he continued, 'moving against my Unc is audacious, and definitely costly, especially if he's consolidating gangs.'

'Either way, we have to handle him,' said Spence. He glanced around. 'Give us a minute, please, everyone. I need to talk to Natty.'

To Natty's surprise, no one protested, not even Clarke. Everyone piled from the room. Lisa was the last, and she gave Natty another look before she closed the door.

'You're in a relationship, mate.'

Natty whirled to face Spence, who had another smirk on his face.

'You what?'

'What the fuck was that?'

'What the fuck was what?'

'You know what! Cam had it right all along, *Prince Charming*. I thought you were going to kiss the top of her hand.'

'Fuck off. Nice to know you can still smile with a crisis like this going on,' retorted Natty. Spence laughed.

'Sometimes all you can do is laugh.'

'That's rubbish. You'll smash Roman and whoever he's got backing him. It's just a matter of time,' said Natty.

Spence sighed, deflating for a moment, allowing Natty to see the fatigue that plagued him. He understood why Spence had asked for the room. He and Natty had seen one another at their worst before, and there would be no judgement.

'Who's the girl?' Natty continued, unable to shake his curiosity. She looked like she belonged on a catwalk, not in a room full of killers and goons, talking about warfare.

'Lisa, like I said. I don't know much about her, but she came with Clarke, and she has something about her.'

'You mean other than looks?'

'Of course. If you weren't too busy staring into her eyes, you might have realised that.'

'Fuck off. I was just startled . . . wasn't expecting to run into someone like her. What was it you saw that I don't?'

'She has a function. I don't think she's a hustler, and we know what Clarke does.'

'You think she's a killer?' Natty asked, startled, remembering her soft hands.

Spence nodded.

'We've always heard your uncle's killers come in all shapes and sizes. I think she's proof.'

Natty shrugged. It was a strong theory, but it wasn't one that mattered right now.

'What's my uncle saying, anyway? I'm guessing you've told him.'

Spence chuckled darkly.

'Not yet.'

Natty frowned.

'You're kidding. He hasn't reached out?'

Spence shook his head. 'Me and Clarke are running point, and we need to contain the situation as quickly as possible.'

Neither man spoke for a few seconds. Natty rubbed his face with his free hand, then made another drink. *This would be his last one,* he thought. He didn't intend to get drunk when he had to drive back home.

'I'm with you, for as long as you need me.'

'Are you sure?' The grateful look on Spence's face nearly winded Natty; if he hadn't been sure before that moment, it would have swayed him.

'You're my brother, Spence.'

'I am, and that wouldn't change. You got away from the game. You don't need to come back.'

Natty waved his hand, aware he was risking all the work he'd done to break free of the street life.

'You're my brother,' he repeated. 'I'm not letting you go into the unknown alone. I've got your back, like you always have mine.'

Spence smiled, taking a deep breath, looking more like his unflappable self. 'I appreciate it, Nat. What are you going to say to Lorraine, though? You can't keep this from her.'

Natty sighed, downing his drink.

'I know I can't. I'm just going to tell her the truth. She'll understand.'

'What if she doesn't?'

Natty opened his mouth, closed it, and then held up his hands, not knowing what to say.

———

LORRAINE WAS STILL UP by the time Natty got back, worry etched into her expression. Natty made them both drinks, and they curled up on the sofa.

'Is he okay?' Lorraine asked. 'I spoke with Rosie, but she hadn't heard anything.'

Natty almost grinned despite the situation. Spence and Rosie were an interesting conundrum. They both liked one another, and Spence had claimed he needed time after Anika left him, yet he and Rosie remained close and spent a lot of time together.

'I'm guessing Spence will be getting an angry phone call from Rosie then.'

'You're going to get a slap if you don't start talking. What's going on, Nat? Is Spence in danger?'

'There was a shooting, and someone got hit, but it wasn't Spence. He's fine. I took so long because we were talking.'

'Who the hell would shoot at Spence?' Lorraine's voice was disbelieving.

'He's in the game. They were trying to take him out so they could move in. But they missed.'

'What does that mean?'

Natty sighed. He trusted Lorraine, and she knew a lot about the things he had once done, but he didn't want to talk to her in too much detail about the crime life.

'I can't go into that, but I have to support my friend. I have to back Spence.'

Natty expected Lorraine to panic, or to glare and get angry with him, but instead, she shook her head in exasperation.

'I knew that when you left, Nat. You're not the sort to leave your friend.'

Natty smiled. He wasn't. The circumstances were irrelevant. He would always be there for his friend.

'I'm worried about you, though,' she added.

'I'm worried too, but I'm gonna be okay. Me and Spence work together, Lo. I'm gonna help him sort the problem, and that's it.'

Lorraine sipped her drink, then put the cup on the table, seemingly deflating for a moment.

'We've had a really good few months, Nat. My main worry is that you might regress. You've been trying to get out there and find yourself, and decide what you're supposed to be doing. But, how can you do that if you're going right back into the world you escaped from?'

'I get what you're saying, but I can't leave him to handle this. This is a real threat . . . different to anything we've ever seen before. Once the problem is done, I'll walk away. Simple as that,' Natty replied.

Lorraine gave him a tight smile, kissing him on the cheek.

'There will always be a problem to solve,' she softly said. 'There will always be a reason to go backwards instead of forwards. Situation with Spence aside, I just hope you realise how much risk you're taking with your development. I'll see you when you come upstairs,' she finished, leaving the room.

Natty stared after her. Lorraine hadn't told him not to get involved, but she seemed upset by the thought of him regressing, and Natty understood. He was glad he hadn't hidden anything from her, though.

Lorraine didn't understand the life, however. She didn't understand his obligations to his friend; the street code they'd lived by, in good times and bad. If the roles were reversed, Spence wouldn't abandon Natty.

As he thought this, Lisa flitted into his mind. If what Spence said was close to the mark, she was deep in the game. He wouldn't have to explain something like that to her. She would just get it.

There had been a moment between them that made Natty wonder what might have happened had he been single. He loved Lorraine, but she struggled to understand his world.

How easy would it be if the person he loved was part of his world?

Rubbing his hand, he focused.

It wasn't the time to be thinking about women. He had business to handle, and he would need to get to the bottom of what Roman was cooking up. The starting point would be learning more about him, and understanding his reasons for the attack.

Then, they would crush him. All of Natty's old instincts were returning. He'd always had a knack for handling business on the streets.

Now, he was right back in the thick of it, and there was no going back.

CHAPTER FIVE

ROMAN'S JAW clenched as he drove through Chapeltown. Between his legs, his phone rang, but he ignored it, remaining focused on the road ahead, his dark brown eyes cold. Before long, he turned onto Leopold Street and parked. Leaving the car, he crossed the road and hurried into a nondescript terraced house with a dull white door.

In the living room, Keith waited. He was leant back in his chair, a hazy, unfocused grin on his fleshy face. On the coffee table in front of him was a bottle of Wray and Nephew white rum, along with two glasses. In the background, the TV played an action film Roman didn't know the name of. The layout was basic, with a grey carpet and a simple coffee table.

A slender Chinese girl sat on the sofa, staring at her phone. She didn't even look up when Roman entered.

'How are you doing?' Keith asked. He was dark-skinned and broad, with fathomless dark eyes. His time behind bars had further enhanced his physique.

'How the hell do you think I'm doing?' Roman snapped. He looked to the woman, then to Keith.

'I don't know. That's why I'm asking. You seem stressed.' Keith glanced at the woman. 'Oi, darling. Go and wait upstairs.'

The woman left the room. Roman's glare deepened.

'Maybe I'm stressed because we *did* agree to slow play the situation with the Dunns, right?'

Keith didn't respond, an obstinate expression on his face.

'So, how did we go from slow play, to *let's shoot up a street*?' Roman continued.

Keith sat up. 'We did. We've been sitting around for months, letting those tossers get rich. How long are we supposed to wait to set it off?'

Roman shook his head. It was classic Keith, and he should have known better than to expect differently.

'What's next then? What's the next step in this grand plan of yours, now that you've let the Dunns know that we're out here? They're gonna come for us.'

'Good. We'll take them out when they do. Spence is leading them, and he's a talker. We'll run right through them.'

Roman sat on a sofa near Keith, resisting the urge to snap at him.

'It's still Mitch's crew. He's been around longer than any of us. He's not gonna back down.'

'I don't care.' Keith folded his arms. 'We did our time, bro. Years, spent behind bars, waiting out that stretch. This is it. This is our time. We've got the streets behind us, man. People are ready for a change.'

Roman opened and closed his mouth. Keith hadn't given the situation proper thought. He had charged in half-cocked, and shone a light on what they were up to. They had lost their advantage.

Roman forced down the urge to strike him. It didn't matter now. It was done, and he would have to support Keith. They'd always been up against it, always united, battling all the odds. This was just the latest situation.

Without a word, Keith poured white rum into the second glass, sliding it across to Roman. Roman picked up the glass and downed the potent liquor, nodding at his partner.

———

NATTY SIPPED A CAN OF *NURISHMENT*, watching Jaden attempting to do press-ups. He had woken up early and declared a desire to be bigger, so Natty was taking it easy with him. He'd keep him doing a few exercises, but wouldn't introduce him to bigger weights until he turned thirteen. He was glad Jaden was taking his health seriously.

As he worked with Jaden, he went over things in his head — namely, his mum's comments about his uncle. The attempt on Spence's life had distracted him, but he wondered if it was something to take up with his uncle. *Would he even know what his mum was talking about, though?* It was possible he was overthinking things, and that his mum just wanted to get in his head.

It wouldn't be the first time.

'Take a little rest. Do another five after you've rested for a minute,' Natty said, seeing Jaden looking out of breath.

'But, I don't need the rest, Nat. I'm fine,' Jaden huffed.

'You said you'd do as I say,' Natty reminded him. Grumbling, Jaden stood and did as he was told. Natty's smile faded as he thought about Roman. The attack had been well coordinated, and he'd later learned it hadn't been the only one. They had targeted several, well-entrenched spots that no one else would think of touching, firing shots, engaging the security, then disappearing.

Natty was under no illusions. The attack was a message; it was Roman and his people saying they could get them whenever they wanted.

The message had been sent. The Dunns would need to hit back appropriately, or risk being labelled *weak* by the streets.

'Right, let's get back to it.'

————

LORRAINE ROOTED in her bag for her keys. She had left early to run some errands and clear her head.

When she entered, she stood in the doorway to the living room. Jaden was doing press-ups, and Natty stood over him, ensuring his form was correct. Jaden had his top off, and every now and then, he would flex in a way she had seen Natty do. Lorraine put her hand to her mouth to stop the giggles.

'I think that'll do for today,' Natty said.

'When can I start lifting weights like you?'

'Not for a while yet. You're still growing, little man. You don't want to stunt your body. There's plenty of time.'

Jaden scrunched up his face, but didn't argue. Lorraine loved watching the pair from a distance. They had such a good dynamic, and she adored the fact Natty wasn't just going through the motions. He genuinely cared for her son. Even when things had been murky between them, it hadn't stopped how Natty viewed Jaden.

'Can I ask you something, Nat?'

'Course you can.'

'Are you and my mummy good friends?'

Lorraine's heart leapt into her throat as she waited for Natty to answer. It didn't take long.

'No, little man. We're *best* friends.'

Lorraine smiled, already planning to reward Natty for that perfect answer later. Jaden wasn't finished.

'I thought Spence was your best friend?'

'It's . . . a different type of friendship,' replied Natty, and Lorraine didn't have to strain to hear the mirth in his voice.

'Different how?'

'Well . . . me and your mum like to talk about different things, and we have different interests. I do different things with her than I do with Spence.'

Despite her smile, Lorraine wondered how Natty was really doing. The news of impending war was already doing the rounds on social media. She didn't know how people had found out so quickly, but that was the way of the world. The fact people knew about the shootings, but weren't naming those responsible, was frightening. Lorraine didn't know who was after Natty, only adding to her worry.

Lorraine had always known things about the streets. They were hard to avoid growing up in Chapeltown; her brother was active in the life, and had been to prison. Lorraine was used to being around hustlers. From a young age, she could recall police routinely searching their family home, looking for her brother.

She knew all along what Natty was, what he did, and for a while, she had thought she wouldn't be able to see past that, or rather, that he wouldn't. She knew Natty wanted to be like his dad, and that he loved the life. She thought that would be it for Natty.

He'd surprised her, though. Things between them seemed to change and deepen.

Eventually, he'd told her he planned to walk away from the streets. Lorraine hadn't known precisely what factored into his decision, but she was pleased, and they'd had a good few months since.

Lorraine's phone chirped, interrupting her thoughts. Seeing it was Rita, Raider's Aunt, she glanced behind her, then went outside to answer.

'Hello,' she said politely.

'Good afternoon, Lorraine. It's Rita. I'm hoping you've thought some more about what we spoke about?'

'I haven't had the chance. I've been busy,' lied Lorraine.

'Even so, Jaden's dad wants to see him. We all do. I know things are difficult, but you're forgetting he has two sides of his family. He should know both of them.'

'I'm not saying he shouldn't, but things aren't as easy as you're making them sound,' said Lorraine, gritting her teeth. She recalled Rosie's words about telling Raider's family what kind of man he was, and what he had done to her, but couldn't bring herself to do it.

'You have to get over the fact things didn't work out with you and Michael. That's life. Things happen . . . people fall in and out of love with one another. You can't let that stand in the way.'

'Things not working out is an understatement,' snarked Lorraine, growing more annoyed as the conversation continued. She thought it was telling that Raider wasn't speaking to her himself, but instead putting pressure on her through his family. 'What you're forgetting, Rita, is that Michael never cared about getting to know his son, and that you and the rest of his family went along with his nonsense about me trying to trap him.'

'Was that not the case? It didn't work out, and now it's time to grow up and do the right thing,' Rita replied.

'Do the right thing?' Lorraine repeated. 'Go to hell,' she snapped, hanging up. Breathing hard, she cursed herself for allowing Raider to get under her skin. After everything he had done, Lorraine couldn't believe she was being presented as the problem.

Taking another deep breath and stowing her phone, she headed to find her *boys*, her problems subsiding when she found them huddled side-by-side, deep in conversation.

————

NATTY LEFT the house in the evening, still in a good mood. Jaden was on his mind. He liked the fact they were growing closer. He was touched by the fact Jaden wanted to train to be like him, and hoped he was having a positive effect on the young man.

Lorraine had seemed in a strange mood before he left, but Natty didn't want to ask her about it in front of Jaden, so he'd left her to it, intending to bring it up again later.

Nothing had transpired since the night before. The streets were holding their breath, waiting for something to happen. Natty knew the play. Some guys would be going out of town until things died down, and others would do their best to stay out of the mix.

Natty didn't have that luxury. He would be in it as deep as Spence and his family were.

Arriving at Spence's, Natty knocked and walked in. Spence and Rosie were in the kitchen, eating. Rosie grinned when she saw Natty, and he gave her a quick hug, then slapped hands with Spence, before helping himself to some hardo bread, slathering it with peanut butter. He didn't speak until he had wolfed down his makeshift sandwich and washed it down with some water.

'Hey Natty, how are you?' Rosie asked.

'I'm good. I just need to borrow your hubby for a bit,' Natty said to Rosie. She made a face.

'He's not my hubby yet.'

Natty didn't know what to say. He glanced at Spence, who looked away. Rosie awkwardly laughed, which only seemed to make the moment worse. She stood up.

'I'm . . . going to go and see Lorraine,' she said in a false, cheery tone. She approached Spence, then stopped, simply nodding and leaving after a flimsy wave.

Natty let out a breath after he heard the front door closing.

'Sorry, bro. I didn't mean to make it weird.'

Spence shook his head.

'You didn't know, bro. It's... a conversation we need to have. Probably sooner rather than later.'

'I'm guessing you haven't told her what's going down?' Natty moved on.

'Not in great detail,' Spence replied. 'I won't be able to keep it from her, especially when it heats up, and we're moving between safe houses.'

'I know what you mean. I told Lorraine a few bits, but I don't think she knows how deep it will get,' said Natty.

'I think she might,' said Spence. 'It's all over socials. I don't know who spoke, but people know quite a bit about what's happening.'

'It could be people on Roman's side. They might want to spread disinformation and keep people worried.'

'If they do, it's working. I've picked up a few bits since we last spoke. Roman and Keith have been seen around the Hood.'

'Anything we can work with?' Natty leaned forward, but Spence shook his head.

'They've been spotted twice in different cars, and with different people. Nothing big so far.'

'What do you remember about them from back in the day?' Natty asked, wanting to build a picture.

'I remember they used to have their own crew, and people knew them, but they weren't big. They allied with Teflon's people after that, back when all that stuff was going on with the wars. That elevated their status, and from what I heard, they were getting real money and had people like Shorty and K-Bar schooling them,' said Spence.

Natty nodded. He remembered the conversations around that time; the paranoia about being out on the streets and potentially being mistaken for a rival gang member. It was a tense time, and Natty knew they would likely be inflicting the same pain and anxiety on the community now.

'They got locked up after that.'

It was Spence's turn to nod.

'Sounds like they made the most of that time inside. They kept their mouths shut, which always impresses certain people on the outside.' He rubbed his eyes, no longer interested in his drink. 'What do we do now?'

'We need to know more about their intentions,' said Natty as he mulled it over. 'Best way to do that is to reach out, ask for a meeting.'

Spence's eyes widened.

'Are you sure you'd be able to stay calm if we did that?'

'Course I can. I stayed calm at the one with Crazy Warren that time. These streets are ours . . . well, they're yours, anyway. We have to show people we're not the victims here, which means getting a handle on it, and hitting them hard. If a meeting stops everything, I say go for it.'

'If Roman and Keith are basically fresh out of prison, police might be watching them,' Spence pointed out.

'You're right. That means whatever we do, we have to make sure we're watching our backs.'

Both men sat in silence for a moment. Spence tilted his head, assessing Natty.

'How are you feeling?'

'About what?'

'About things. About doing this.'

'I'll be fine, Spence. I wouldn't have offered to help if I didn't feel I could handle it,' said Natty.

Spence agreed. He was pleased Natty had stepped up, but figured he might be a bit rusty after being away for a few months. To his surprise, it was as if Natty had never been away. He was alert and focused, and it was hard for many to stand up against Natty when he was in that state of mind. He had evolved over the past year — only an immature streak and a silly temper had prevented him from elevating earlier. Spence wondered what the long-term plan would be, and whether it was a good thing.

'Handling it or not, it doesn't mean this is the best place for you to be,' he said.

'I'm here,' replied Natty. 'This is where I have to be, and we need to win. That's all you need to think about.'

Spence didn't reply, but he hoped Natty was right. He recalled what Natty had done before he walked away. In the same circumstances, Spence wondered if he could have pulled a trigger and taken a life.

Reaching for his drink again, he attempted to quash the lousy feeling bubbling within.

———

ROMAN CHECKED HIS WATCH, hiding his smirk as Wonder was shown to him. He was leant against his rented BMW, the street deserted, several soldiers dotted around, just in case.

Roman recalled Wonder from back in the day. He'd hung around with whoever would show him the most attention, and hadn't been particularly well respected. The fact he was now seen as someone with status was telling to Roman; a sign that standards had slipped in the new world. Regardless, he had intended to eventually reach out to him. Keith's actions had simply sped up his timeline.

Wonder looked wary, and his eyes kept flitting to the men around him as he got closer. Just as Roman remembered, Wonder was styled, and had on an expensive-looking watch and chain. He didn't know why, or who he was trying to impress, but that wasn't important.

'Don't worry, I'm not going to hurt you,' he said, his smile almost reptilian. He wasn't surprised when Wonder looked even more nervous. He wanted him to feel off-guard.

'I'm not sure that's true, especially after what your people have been running around doing,' admitted Wonder.

'Keith is the one that does the hitting. As you can see, he's not here. You're a smart guy, Wonder. You wouldn't have come if you thought you would get attacked.'

'You're acting like I had a choice.'

'Everyone does,' replied Roman. 'You're working for the Dunns now . . .'

'So what?' Wonder's eyes narrowed.

'Why?'

'They pay well.' Wonder rubbed his stupidly expensive watch, as if making some profound point.

'I bet Elijah paid well, too,' said Roman, watching Wonder's expression tighten. 'I remember him from before I went away. Even back then, he was outspoken against the Dunns, and you were right there with him.'

'Things change,' said Wonder, but his voice lacked bite. Roman stared him down for a few more seconds.

'Who killed him?'

Wonder glanced away for a moment, looking from the soldiers back to Roman.

'I don't know.'

Roman scowled. 'I don't believe you. Let me break it down for you: I want us to work together, which means trusting each other. The alternative is that *you* become our main target.'

'Who do you have with you?' Wonder asked. 'I know Keith is always down with you. Who else have you got?'

'That's not something for you to worry about, fam. I'm giving you a chance, but now I'm starting to think it's not worth it.'

Again, Wonder looked to the men Roman had brought with him, his jaw clenching.

'You don't need to threaten me. I'm not your enemy.'

Roman shrugged. 'Maybe not. You're an outsider, though. Outsiders often turn into enemies. I guess it's about ensuring you're on the right side.'

Wonder blew out a breath.

'I can't prove it, but I think it was Natty Deeds,' he said.

'What makes you think that?'

'Rudy and Elijah both died the same night. We were at Rudy's spot, plotting. The plan was to drop Mitch Dunn.'

'You lot thought you could take out Mitch?' Roman nearly laughed at the absurdity of it. It was Wonder's turn to scowl.

'We had a solid plan in place, and Rudy was on the inside. He knew Mitch; the people surrounding him. We almost had all the pieces in place, but that night, Natty overheard us. We tried to kill him, but he got away. When we finally caught up with him, Mitch's men scooped us up.

'Next thing I knew, I was in charge of Elijah's old team. Even now, I'm giving up most of the profit, but me and the remaining crew are still earning. Everyone said it was Natty that killed Rudy and Elijah, though, and he got offered a promotion after it all went down.'

Roman listened to Wonder talk, stunned by his good fortune. Wonder working with the Dunns had intrigued him enough to reach out, but he hadn't expected so much. He knew of Mitch's nephew, Natty Deeds, and his solid reputation. Roman knew him as a hothead, so he was surprised Natty was able to get away with murdering two people.

When Wonder finished, Roman waited a moment.

'I want us to work together. You're gonna feed me intel, and I'm gonna make your problems go away.'

'Go away, how?'

'I'll kill the people you're working for now, and get you out of that arrangement.'

Wonder's eyes narrowed.

'How are you going to do that? I mean, yeah, you've attacked a few spots, but you didn't take out anyone important. To the streets, it just looks like you missed your shot. How can you be so sure that you're going to win?'

'Because I have the best team backing me, and I know what I'm doing. We've been planning this for a long time, so it's up to you if you wanna come on board with it. If you don't . . . we won't speak of it again.'

Something in the way Roman finished his sentence worried Wonder, but he pushed past it.

'I'm in. Those fuckers killed my old boss and ruined our plans. Just let me know what I need to do.'

———

'DO YOU WANT A DRINK?'

Spence shook his head. He'd been at Rosie's for the past hour, still thinking about Natty's words earlier. He wondered what winning would entail, and how much they would lose in the meantime.

'Spence?' Rosie appeared in the doorway, her brow furrowed.

'Sorry, I forgot you couldn't see me through the wall when I responded,' he said, shooting her a strained smile.

'What's wrong?' she asked.

'Just some street stuff. The stuff I was talking to Natty about earlier. It's nothing important.'

Rosie's eyes flickered to the floor, then back up to Spence.

'I thought you might have been thinking about what happened earlier.'

Spence put the phone he had been holding onto the coffee table, and signalled for Rosie to sit next to him. He shook away his nerves, or at least he attempted to. Rosie had always affected him, though. She was beautiful, sharp and direct, and when she looked intently at him, as she was now, it jarred his thoughts and put him on the back foot.

'I figured we'd get around to discussing it eventually. What's on your mind?'

Rosie shook her head. 'Technically, I started it earlier. I shouldn't have reacted how I did, but when Natty called you my hubby, it just came out.'

Spence carefully gathered his words.

'I know things haven't been easy with us. You deserve more than that.'

Rosie waited, but when it was clear Spence wasn't speaking, she stepped in.

'What do you want, Spence? From us, I mean. I've given you time, plus space when needed, but I want to know if we're going anywhere.'

'I like you, Rosie. I've always liked you, and I think we can be good together, but I can't help how I'm feeling.'

'How is it that you're feeling?'

'Broken,' Spence admitted, feeling weak for doing so. 'It's been months, and I'm still constantly having to push down how I felt about Anika. She tore me apart when she left, and I'm still trying to pick up the pieces.'

'I get that. I know what she did to you, and I'm willing to be patient, but what do you think will happen next with us?'

Spence didn't know. He didn't want to hurt Rosie, and he liked her company, but he'd avoided having this conversation for a reason. He didn't want to use her, but he also didn't want to rush into another relationship and risk getting hurt again.

'I don't know,' he replied, watching Rosie's expression crumple.

'I've been messed around a lot in the past, Spence. You know that. I know you're not the type to mess girls around, but please, if you don't think this is going somewhere, just say. I'd rather know now than later. Don't feel like you need to spare my feelings.'

'Rosie, I—' Spence reached out to touch her, but froze when Rosie flinched and instinctively moved back. He frowned at the reaction, before he caught on. 'I'm sorry,' he said. 'I didn't think. I shouldn't have moved like that.'

Rosie shook her head.

'It's fine. You don't need to apologise. I just . . .' she trailed off. Spence understood perfectly, though. He wasn't the only one who had scars. Rosie had been in an abusive relationship with her ex, Kyle, who hadn't kept his hands to himself. It made him feel sick that he might have reminded her of that, even for a second.

'I'm sorry,' Spence said again, slowly pulling Rosie in for a hug, gratified when she allowed it.

They still had some talking to do, but he would take this for now.

CHAPTER SIX

NATTY AND SPENCE were in the city centre. They hit a bar near Greek street, ready to get drunk and celebrate Cameron's birthday. Both were aware of the situation, but willing to risk it.

In the bar, Natty ordered them brandy and cokes — Cameron's favourite drink — and they clinked their glasses and drank. Both were dressed for the occasion, Natty wearing a black shirt and trousers, Spence wearing similar — though, his shirt was grey.

As Natty savoured his drink, he scanned the crowds. Noticing the clientele were mostly younger, he wondered when he had started to feel so old. He didn't feel like he belonged here anymore, yet the club scene had been his saving grace for a long time. He wondered how long he'd ignored the signs, and how ridiculous he'd looked chasing after young women in these very spots.

'What's on your mind?' Spence asked, clutching his drink.

'Probably the wrong stuff,' Natty admitted. 'I'm starting to think I might have outgrown the scene around here.'

'You're probably right. I suppose if Cam was still around, you might still be here. He was always good at getting you to do things.'

Natty nodded, conceding that. 'We had a way of egging each other on to do stuff. You were always the sensible one, keeping us from killing ourselves.'

'We had some moments, didn't we?'

Natty laughed. 'So many times we went out for a quiet one, and ended up fighting over something stupid. I remember one time he was working on this woman, but she wasn't having any of it. She must have seen someone she knew, and went to speak to them. Cam lost his shit and was ready to fight the guy — the guy was connected too. I had to jump in there and squash it before he got killed, and then me and Cam nearly ended up fighting. It was nuts.'

Spence chuckled. 'I remember that. I used to think you two had a death wish, the way you used to go on.'

'Were we that bad?' Natty laughed.

'You were. You both had so much to prove, and it got worse the more you were around each other.'

'What made you stick with us then?'

Spence looked surprised. 'You're my brothers. I wasn't going to leave you in the lurch.'

Both men smiled. Natty was glad he still had Spence in his life, knowing things would likely be worse if he didn't. They finished their drinks and ordered more, ignoring the mostly terrible music in the spot.

'I hated his shit coffee,' Natty was saying. 'I think he used to buy the worst stuff in the world on purpose, to piss me off. He bought terrible coffee, and he handled his liquor like a kid.'

Spence sniggered, the liquor definitely having an effect.

'You were always getting at him about his coffee. He definitely kept buying it to spite you.'

Both men shared a look, several drinks in. All the reminiscent energy seemed to deflate. Spence sighed, lowering his head for a moment.

'Do you think he was always against us?'

Natty considered this. Cameron had turned against them and aligned himself with Rudy and Elijah. He resented Spence and Natty, but Natty still got the impression that he wasn't fully against them.

'I don't think so. We both know Cam. His heart was in the right place, but he was street poisoned. He wanted to be the main man by any means necessary, and I think he was envious of the moves we made. I guess it all just got the better of him.'

Spence took another second to pick his words.

'What if you'd chosen Cam to run our crew instead of me? Would we all still be friends?'

Natty mulled over the questions, his eyes on a passing group of people.

'You know . . . If we'd given him that, he would have wanted something else. Cam wanted to be the top guy. As much as it hurts to say, he'd have killed us to get it.'

Spence wiped his eye, nodding. 'You know what . . . I even miss the teasing sometimes; calling me *whipped* for smiling at a woman, starting arguments over the smallest thing.' He sighed again. 'I want to hate him for what he did. I've tried, but I can't.' Spence's eyes were wet as he surveyed Natty. 'We were brothers.'

Natty swallowed down the lump in his throat, wishing he had suggested drinking at home. He didn't want to show weakness around strangers. Cameron had been annoying and overbearing at times, but he was their brother, and nothing would change that.

He gripped Spence's shoulder, then the pair raised their glasses again.

'To Cam.'

'To Cam.'

Natty and Spence had a few more drinks, and told some funnier stories, trying to save the mood. Natty was about to go to the bar for another round, when Spence pointed someone out.

'What is she doing here?'

Natty glanced to where Spence was pointing, eyes widening when he saw Lisa sashaying toward them. Natty hadn't seen her since the meeting at Spence's, but he'd thought about her from time to time, wondering what her game was. She seemed to glide, wearing a form-fitting grey dress with heels, her hair framing her face.

Natty was immediately struck dumb by her beauty. She had several friends with her, all attractive, but Natty's instincts still kicked in.

There was an edge to the group, which suggested they shouldn't be underestimated.

'Hey, Lisa,' said Spence, straightening in place, trying to look less drunk. Natty, by contrast, felt sober. He'd drank as much as Spence, but his tolerance was better, and his system screamed at him to sharpen up. He needed to be on point right now.

'Nice to see you, Spence. I didn't think this was your scene,' said Lisa. Despite her soft voice, the pair didn't miss a single word. Her eyes quickly went to Natty, taking him in. 'I guessed it was yours.'

'Maybe once upon a time,' said Natty. 'Not anymore.'

'You're still here now.'

'I guess you could call it a guest appearance,' said Natty. Lisa shifted on the spot. Natty assumed it was a signal, because her friends moved closer to Spence, engaging him in conversation, leading him a few steps away. Natty blinked, wondering if he was drunker than he thought. It was such a subtle move, and he couldn't believe it had worked so well.

'What the hell was that?'

'What was what?' replied Lisa.

'Did your friends just lead Spence away so you could speak to me?'

'Of course. I bet you would do the same for your friends.'

Natty smirked. 'You've got me there. You look amazing, by the way.'

Lisa's eyes sparkled. 'You think?'

'You're owning the room. I'm assuming that was your intention. I can't see you getting all dressed up otherwise.'

'Do you think I need to be dressed up to command a room?' Lisa's eyebrow arched.

'Dressed up or dressed down, this room is yours. Regardless, you're dressed up now for that reason.'

'Can you really say that? You know nothing about me other than my name.'

'I'm good with people,' Natty fired back.

'Once, maybe. You were out of the game for a while. The game doesn't hang around for anyone. It moves on.'

'I'm adaptable,' said Natty, liking the back and forth. The strange energy was back between them. He'd noticed it when they met, and even now, it seemed more potent than ever.

'I'm sure you are. So . . . why do you think I got dressed up then?'

'I think you wanted to be noticed. You wanted men to want you.'

'Is it working, Natty? Do you want me?'

They locked eyes, Natty quickly drawn to her exotic features and full lips. He blinked, then glanced to Spence, still in conversation with Lisa's group.

'What I want isn't relevant.'

'I disagree. I think it's incredibly relevant.' Lisa took a step closer, stalking her prey. Natty's skin prickled, but it wasn't unpleasant. If anything, it was the tingling opposite, and that was dangerous.

'You seem to know a lot about me,' he said. Lisa tilted her head.

'I'd like to think I know a fair amount.'

'So, you know I have a girlfriend then . . .'

Lisa smirked, which wasn't the reaction Natty expected.

'Maybe I wouldn't mind playing with your girlfriend either . . .'

Natty maintained his composure, but Lisa's words had surprised him, which he imagined was the intention. She continued surveying him.

'I'll see you another time, Natty Deeds. Enjoy your night.'

Natty couldn't take his eyes off Lisa as she walked away. He wasn't sure how else the situation could have gone, but he didn't regret it. He was in a relationship, and he was happy. The last thing he needed were more complications.

Laughter from behind made him turn. Spence had a massive smile on his face.

'Well . . . never thought I'd see the day,' he said.

'Did you hear what was said?'

'No. I was able to gather most of it just from the body language. I don't know what it is with you, but there's a connection there.'

'Even if there is, I—'

Spence's grin widened. 'I know, Nat. It's funny to me because you're the *whipped* one now. I know you were putting Lorraine first and not succumbing to temptation. That tickles me. Maybe it's the night we're having, and the fact we both know if Cam was here he would call you out for what happened, but I just find it funnier.'

Natty laughed with him. Spence was right. They had made fun of Spence for being loyal to his woman, yet Natty was in a situation where he was doing the same. He had no intention of hurting Lorraine, but he still thought about Lisa. Not necessarily her looks, which were stunning, but her demeanour. She had pursued him here, knowing exactly where to find him.

Was he under surveillance? Was that how she knew about Lorraine?

It wasn't hugely important, but if she could track him, Roman's people could easily do it, and that was something Natty needed to be wary about. Word would have spread by now about him getting involved in the conflict, and that made him a target.

'What made you turn her down?'

Natty blinked. Spence hadn't stopped watching him.

'I didn't exactly turn her down. It didn't come up. She didn't put it on me like that. I just told her that I had a partner, which she already seemed to know.'

'I remember speaking to you about Rosie, and you said in my position, you would have cheated.'

'I remember,' replied Natty. 'Your ex was a bitch. I'd have gladly cheated on her.'

Spence shook his head. Natty's feelings on his ex were clearer than they had been when he was with her. He didn't know why Natty had never shared his feelings about her, but equally, he wasn't sure how he would have reacted if he had.

'I was right then. When you're with someone you care about, you don't think about other women. I think that means the next round is on you.'

'I bought the last round. You can't handle your drink, anyway. Quit while you're ahead.'

'Slow and steady wins the race, Nathaniel.'

'Ergh, you sound like Rudy.' Natty's face contorted in disgust. 'Spence?'

Spence stopped smiling, surprised by Natty's sudden seriousness.

'Yeah?'

'Do you think Lisa came here specifically to see me?'

'Of course.'

Natty's mouth fell open. Spence hadn't hesitated to respond.

'Fair enough.'

'Doesn't that worry you?' Spence hadn't expected that reaction from Natty.

'No, do you think it should?'

Spence shrugged. 'Kind of. You've changed in certain ways, Nat. The fact we're even having this conversation is proof of that. I don't worry about her pursuing you, because you won't do anything you don't want to do. You care about Lorraine. You always have, and you love her. Most importantly, you know how it feels not having her and Jaden in your life. I can't see you doing anything to jeopardise that. That being said . . . Lisa is definitely one to watch. She's not normal.'

Natty didn't respond. All his thoughts about Lisa had brought him to this conclusion without him knowing it. She was a paradox; somebody who, on the surface, didn't look like she belonged in their world. And yet, she did belong. Comfortable amongst the upper ranks. Comfortable in her own skin and with those differences between herself and the rest. It was what made her an asset to the organisation.

The more Natty spoke to her, the clearer it was that she belonged.

Sipping brandy and coke, Natty pushed out the thoughts, ready to enjoy the relaxing night with his best friend.

CHAPTER SEVEN

ROMAN AND KEITH climbed from their car. The driver, Dolja, remained seated, his eyes already on the people they'd come to meet. Roman had met Dolja just before he got locked up. When he was released, he quickly ascertained that Dolja was still in the game. Snatching him up, he introduced him to a whole new level of money-making, earning his loyalty.

Roman spotted people working in different clusters, talking in little groups, and felt nervous for a moment. They were heavily outnumbered.

The bonded warehouse was enormous; the largest Roman had ever seen. He didn't know they had such buildings in Leeds, and that made him thoughtful. There was a lot someone could do with these sorts of locations.

Ahmed waited, a bland look on his face as he surveyed the pair. He was heavyset, with an especially flabby face and dark eyes. The last time Roman had met with the connect, Keith had waited in the car, and it had been Mustafir he'd dealt with. Roman had met Ahmed once before and found him off-putting, but this was business. He put his personal feelings aside. Approaching, he shook Ahmed's hand.

'Nice to see you again,' he said.

'You too. I hope the drive wasn't too taxing?' Ahmed shook Keith's hand, then Keith stepped back, signalling Roman to do the talking.

'No, it was fine. No problems.'

Ahmed nodded.

'Good. I know you've mainly spoken to Mustafir, but he had to leave the country. He should be back in a few weeks, but I'm more than equipped to deal with you and your subordinates this time.'

'I'm surprised we still have a relationship with you lot. I heard it ended badly with you and Teflon's people,' said Roman. It was true. He'd heard little bits in prison, namely among the truly connected people, but everything pointed to a split between the black and Asian organisations, and certainly one that hadn't been repaired.

It was a shock to Roman when he got out of prison. There had been a message left to meet with Mustafir, who was immediately ready to work with them. Roman's card had been marked. They were fully aware of his situation, giving him the push he needed to get back into the game. With competitive prices and unrivalled quality, making his mark was a formality.

For their own reasons, Ahmed and Mustafir's bosses kept the prices the same for him, despite the street price increasing. This meant more profit for Roman and his crew.

'We're able to do business without ego, unlike others,' said Ahmed. Roman was ready to skip the comment, but Keith bristled, stepping forward.

'What do you mean by that?'

'I wasn't trying to offend.' Ahmed shot him an icy look.

'It's fine,' said Roman, jumping in. 'Let's just move on.'

Keith shook his head.

'Fuck that. I wanna know what he meant. Making little backhanded comments,' Keith pressed. He stopped forward, but Roman pushed him back.

'Go and wait outside,' he said to Keith. Unlike Keith, he'd noticed the people in the background intently staring at them, waiting for the word to step in. Breathing hard, Keith stormed out.

Ahmed's eyes followed him, before he turned back to Roman.

'These are tense times for you. You've initiated a situation on the streets with a rival organisation. This is a big risk to undertake.'

'Nothing we can't handle,' replied Roman, inwardly cursing Keith again for his undoing of their cautious planning.

'We hope so. It will not be easy for you. But, to business. We want to extend the line of credit. Whatever drugs you need, we can get you, in whatever quantities you think you can handle.'

Roman's eyes narrowed. It sounded too good to be true. Roman's people had worked with smaller gangs, but Mitch's influence was far-reaching, and even with the work they had done, Roman and the others still didn't have the foothold they once had in and around Chapeltown. This forced them to open new markets outside of Leeds.

'For now, we've got the money to buy,' said Roman. 'I'll take twenty boxes. I trust you lot can arrange transport?'

Ahmed nodded. 'This won't be a problem. I presume you have someone on hand who will supervise the delivery?'

'My driver out there.' Roman pointed to the car. 'He's called *Dolja*. He'll pick up the stuff from your guys.'

Nodding, Ahmed shook hands with him.

'Before you leave, we should talk about your partner,' he said.

'He gets stressed sometimes, but he's cool,' said Roman.

'You have potential, but your partner will hold you back. If he cannot keep his composure during a single meeting, how can you trust him to keep his composure under any other circumstances?'

'He'll be fine,' said Roman. 'I'll deal with him, and you deal with me.'

Ahmed smiled, but his eyes remained cold. 'We'll keep it that way then.'

'Dolja,' Roman said, when the driver had pulled away from the warehouse. 'I need you on hand to supervise the delivery. We're getting twenty boxes to work with, so you'll need to move them quickly to make sure they get into position. Cool?'

'Yeah, boss. I'm all over it,' replied Dolja. Roman nodded, satisfied.

Keith hadn't spoken since leaving the meeting. Roman turned to him in the backseat.

'What is your problem? You're starting trouble with the people giving us drugs now?'

Keith scowled, waving a hand.

'Are you serious? They look down on you, and I'm not gonna let them make their little comments. Besides, there are other suppliers if they talk shit.'

'Their supply is the best, though. We have excellent credit with them. Why jeopardise that over some little comments?'

Keith snorted, but didn't respond.

'I got a message while you lot were talking,' said Dolja. 'Did you hear about Natty Deeds?'

'What about him?' Roman asked.

'Word is that he's back working with his crew.'

'Does that worry you?' Roman understood why it might. Natty was a solid hustler with charisma and good street instincts.

'A little bit.'

'Natty's got a good reputation, and he comes from good stock. What do you think about the rumours he's got bodies?' Roman continued.

'I think they're true. He's meant to have whacked some pretty high-up guys too. I don't know all the circumstances, but he's not a pretender,' said Dolja.

'I should take him out,' Keith interjected.

Roman smiled. Despite his frustrations with how Keith handled his business, he appreciated his willingness to throw himself at their cause. Roman respected that Keith could cut past all the nonsense and get straight to the action, but there was a time and a place for that.

'We don't need to do that yet. A lot is going on, and even more is going to happen. Wonder can keep us posted for now,' he suggested.

Whether he agreed or not, Keith nodded, and the drive continued in silence.

———

THE NEXT DAY, Natty was playing on the PlayStation with Jaden, but his mind was elsewhere. He'd offered to play with Jaden to try to distract himself, but it hadn't worked. Lisa and the comments she'd made were on his mind, and he couldn't shake them. He couldn't work her out; *was it just her personality, or was she coming onto him?*

As the final whistle blew on the football game he had been playing, he resolved to speak to Clarke about her.

'Natty, who do you want to play as next?' Jaden asked as he set up another game. Natty didn't reply, staring into space. Jaden nudged him, shaking Natty from his thoughts.

'Sorry, little man. What's up?' Natty asked.

'Who do you want to play as next?'

Natty scratched his nose. He needed to get out of the house.

'Do you wanna go to the Wreck? I fancy some fresh air.'

Grinning, Jaden nodded.

'Yeah. I'll grab my ball.'

When Jaden was ready, they made their way to the park. Sliding through the barrier, Natty stopped when he realised Jaden was no longer at his side. Turning, his eyebrows contracting, Natty's eyes fixed on Jaden, legs parted, standing over the ball.

'Don't you dare,' Natty said, a smile on his face. Jaden scraped his right foot on the grass, like a bull ready to charge. Running at the ball, he swung his leg back and struck it, sending it fizzing past Natty's ear. Wiping his nose with his hand and smirking, Jaden looked at Natty.

'Go get it then,' he said.

As he ran after the ball, Natty was glad he'd worked to get back into shape.

The pair played for a while, practising passing, dribbling and taking turns in goal. Striking the ball with his laces, Natty was pleased with Jaden's ball control as he cushioned the pass and brought it down. It reminded him of his days of wanting to be a footballer when he was younger. Natty had been a decent player, bigger than many of the kids in his playgroup, with strength, aggression and a powerful shot. He was better than his friends and always did well at school.

At the age of ten, though, Natty tried out for a team, and it didn't go well. Some of the kids were better than him, and had better footballing brains, even at a young age. He recalled his dad speaking with him about it, and telling him shortly before he died that he would need to pick between football and the streets, as he couldn't do both.

At the time, Natty hadn't realised it, but his dad was imparting serious wisdom. Natty had chosen to focus on the streets, especially after his dad died, but he'd wondered over the years how life would have played out if he had picked the football route.

Ultimately, it had left him adrift; even now, he remained unsure where he truly fit in.

'Nat?'

Natty looked up. The ball was at his feet, and Jaden was staring at him, waiting for him to do something. Apologising, Natty kicked the ball, and the game resumed. Eventually, it turned into him guarding the goal, and Jaden attempting to score past him. He took it seriously, and before long, he wasn't thinking about Lisa, the streets, or the future. He was in the moment, trying his hardest to stop the ball from going into the net.

Soon, Natty was too tired to continue, and they headed home. As they did, Natty noted a car following them as they walked from the park. His pulse throbbed, hands instinctively balling into fists as he stopped, facing the car. He placed a hand in front of Jaden, stopping him. Looking at the car before turning to face Jaden, Natty crouched in front of him, ensuring he shielded Jaden's body.

'Nat?' Jaden asked, startled by Natty's sudden seriousness. Before either could do anything, the grey Astra with tinted windows drove away. Natty stared after the car for a moment.

'Nat? Are you okay?'

Natty blinked, then smiled at Jaden.

'Sorry, little man. I just got distracted.'

Jaden frowned, almost as if he knew there was more to it.

'Who was in that car you were looking at?'

'I recognised the car, so I thought it might be a friend of mine,' he lied. Jaden nodded, running on ahead and dribbling his football.

'Watch the road,' Natty called out, already planning what he would do that evening.

———

NATTY LEFT his spot that night. Despite not spending much time at his place — preferring to stay at Lorraine's — he worried he might be putting them in danger. He planned to be more careful from now on, vowing nothing would happen to Lorraine and Jaden on his watch.

He drove to Jukie's gambling spot in the heart of the Hood, parking across the street. Usually, there were people hanging around outside smoking, but the pathway was clear as he entered the house, immediately overwhelmed by music, the buzz of steady chatter, and the slamming of dominoes on table tops.

Natty spoke with a few people, then headed to the bar, where he ordered a beer. He noticed that people were watching him. Not aggressively, but there was definitely some curiosity — unsurprising considering the current situation with Roman.

'Tell Jamie that Natty Deeds is here to see him,' he said to the bartender, who nodded. Jamie stepped out of the backroom a few minutes later, grinning when he saw Natty.

'Yes, Nat! How long's it been?'

'Too long. Business is doing good,' he pointed out. Not that it was a surprise. Jamie was the nephew of Jukie, who owned numerous gambling spots in and around Chapeltown. Natty had met people here before, and they were known to be neutral spots where you could hang out, or discreetly do business. People rarely, if, ever, caused trouble on the premises.

Jamie was a few years older than Natty, though they looked the same age. He had dark brown skin, bushy eyebrows and a muscular build, wearing a heavy gold chain around his neck. Like many in the Hood, he took his look seriously, and Natty understood it. Jamie oversaw the gambling spot for his uncle; for some reason, his looking the part inspired confidence. It clearly worked, as the place was packed every time Natty came in.

'Yeah, you know how it is. We've been lucky.'

'Hard work, you mean, not luck. I know how hard you lot hustle,' said Natty. 'Look, I'm here on business. I need your help.'

'Okay, step into the back.'

Natty followed Jamie to the backroom. A slim blonde sat there, staring at her phone. She glanced at the two men, her eyes lingering on Natty, who gave her a polite smile.

'Nice to meet you,' he said.

'You too,' she replied, smiling back.

'Kel, wait out there,' said Jamie. 'We need to talk business.'

Kelly didn't argue, sashaying from the room and closing the door behind her. Jamie locked it, shaking his head, grinning.

'Please don't bang my girl. I'm trying to keep her around for a bit.'

Natty chuckled.

'I'm in a committed relationship, mate.'

'So I heard. You and Lorraine finally stopped fucking around.'

'You're not the first one to say that,' said Natty. He and Lorraine having feelings for one another was the worst-kept secret in the Hood. Natty had downplayed their situation for a long time, and knew Lorraine had too.

'Better late than never, or whatever they say. What did you wanna talk about, anyway?'

'You know what's going on in the Hood, right?'

Jamie nodded. 'Course. It's all people have been talking about.'

'I know you don't get involved in the politics, and I'm not asking you to get anyone in trouble. I want to know two things.'

Jamie sighed. 'We go way back, Nat. I'm glad you recognise my position. If I can help you, I will.'

'Cool. What's Roman's deal?'

'Okay. What's the second thing you wanna know?' Jamie asked.

'Can you arrange a meet?'

Jamie rubbed his forehead, an uneasy expression on his face. Natty realised he wasn't putting him in the best position, but if he could help, it was worth pushing it. Jamie grabbed two glasses from a tabletop in the corner of the office, and poured both men a glass of vodka.

Natty sipped his, waiting Jamie out. He would have to play it this way, needing Jamie to be as comfortable as possible to work with him.

'Nat, you know what you're asking me is tough, right? Might even be looked at as me taking sides, which I'm not doing.'

'I wouldn't ever put you in a dangerous position, bro. Your family is well known. Everyone trusts them, and I give you my word nothing will happen that's gonna get you in trouble. I need to speak to the other side, and ask them some things.'

Jamie sipped his drink, nodding and going over Natty's words.

'I'll see what I can do for you, but Roman is driven, bro. People look at him the same way they do you. You're both sharp, engaged, and well-backed.'

'I can't see Shorty and them coming out of retirement to back Roman,' Natty idly replied.

'I agree, but he's got a tough team around him, regardless. Keith, for one. He's deadly. They've got a knock-around guy too; Dolja. They trust him, though, and keep him close.'

'What does Roman want?' Natty pressed.

'The streets. They want to take over, and you guys are in the way.'

Natty mulled this over. They'd worked that out for themselves. He'd wondered if there was more to the move, but that didn't seem to be the case.

'Arrange the meeting, Jamie. Please. If we can get a quick resolution, it benefits everyone.'

After a long moment, Jamie nodded.

'Keep an eye on your phone.'

'Jamie, I appreciate this. I promise your name will be kept out of it.'

Jamie shot him a wry grin.

'Those nosey pricks out there probably saw you come into my office, so I'm sure word will spread. I appreciate it, though.'

Natty drained his drink and slid to his feet, placing some notes on the desk. Jamie shook his head.

'Your money is no good here, Nat. I didn't give you much, anyway.

'You took the time when you didn't need to,' said Natty. 'Buy your girl something nice.'

'Speaking of girls, tell Lorraine I said hi when you speak to her.'

Natty didn't stay long after leaving the office. He had another drink, then left the spot, feeling eyes burning into him as he did. Jamie was right, he reasoned. He wondered how many people would be reporting back to Roman right now, and how Spence and the others had been so blind to the power growing under their noses.

CHAPTER EIGHT

LORRAINE AND ROSIE sat in a coffee shop. They'd had a coffee, attempting to make small talk as they looked around expectantly. Lorraine had given it a lot of thought over the last few days, and despite Rosie's misgivings, she had made up her mind. Rosie squeezed her hand, shooting Lorraine a reassuring look when she glanced up.

'It'll be fine, Lo. I'm here for you.'

Lorraine gave her friend a thin smile, tensing as someone approached their table.

Raider looked more diminished than she remembered; thinner, with some scarring on his face. He awkwardly stood for a moment, then gestured to the chair in front of him. Swallowing, Lorraine nodded.

'Hey,' he said to her.

'Hey,' Lorraine replied. Raider faced Rosie.

'How are you doing, Rosie?'

Rosie sniffed and ignored Raider. He seemed to take it in his stride, shooting Lorraine a small smile. She couldn't believe he had the gall to smile at her like that, after what he had done to her.

'Thank you for agreeing to see me,' he said.

'Why have you been getting onto your family about me?' Lorraine asked testily.

Raider sighed.

'I'm sorry about my auntie. She's stubborn, and she got it into her head that she wanted to see Jaden, so she reached out. I didn't have anything to do with it.'

'Course you didn't . . .' Rosie mumbled. Raider again looked at her, then focused back on Lorraine.

'I've been meaning to reach out, and I wanted to apologise for what I did to you. I'd been drinking, but there's no excuse for it. I was deep in the streets, and doing a lot of drugs.' He rubbed his forehead. 'I was doing a lot of things I shouldn't have been doing.'

Rosie spoke before Lorraine could.

'Funny that you just said there was no excuse, then tried to make a bunch of excuses. What you're saying isn't going to fly.'

'Why are you getting involved?' Raider cut his eyes to her, glaring. Rosie was equal to the look.

'You put your hands on my friend. You're lucky she's even here talking to you. She's always been better than you, and you know it.'

Raider's eyes flashed, and Lorraine gripped the table without thinking. Her skin prickled, and she trembled, glad she was in public. She felt furious for reacting. Raider took a deep breath.

'I don't expect to be forgiven, but I just wanna see my son. I'll do that any way you want; we can even go through my family rather than communicate directly.'

Lorraine didn't immediately respond, not knowing what to say.

'I'll think about it,' she finally said, expecting Raider to protest. Instead, he nodded.

'That's fine. Like I said, I appreciate you even considering it, given what happened. You two enjoy your day, and hopefully, I'll see you soon.'

Lorraine watched him walk away. Rosie's nostrils flared, but she said nothing, fingering the empty coffee cup in front of her.

'What are you thinking?' Lorraine asked.

'You don't owe that abuser a thing,' said Rosie.

'I have Jaden to think about — he deserves to have a relationship with his dad.'

'Not if he's a man like Raider, he doesn't. Raider could have had all of that; he could have had a relationship with his ten-year-old son at any point, but he wasn't interested. Despite that, you still allowed him to, and he repaid you by putting you in the hospital and nearly breaking your ribs. You can't trust a man like that around your son.'

Lorraine's stomach churned, the memory of being helpless and in pain as Raider loomed over her returning to the surface. She never wanted to feel that way again. She took another deep breath. Rosie was angry, and she understood it, recalling the abuse her friend had suffered in her past relationship. It was undoubtedly a sore spot, but she appreciated Rosie being there for her, and wasn't sure how things would have gone if she had been alone.

'Are you going to tell Natty?' Rosie asked after a while. They'd ordered another coffee, and the old mugs had been replaced. Lorraine's insides twisted. She hadn't thought about what Natty would think, remembering his thoughts the last time the subject was brought up.

'I'm not sure. Nat's got a lot on his mind with what's happened with Spence. The last thing he needs is another distraction.'

Rosie shook her head. 'Lo, your relationship with Natty was nearly destroyed because of Raider. I don't want it to seem like I'm telling you what to do, but just seriously think about things. There's a lot going on, and I don't want you to get hurt.'

Lorraine smiled at her friend. She wasn't wrong. Natty had gone after Raider when he heard about the beating, and Raider still wore the results of that assault. She wondered how he felt about that. Raider took himself seriously and often bragged to Lorraine about how tough he was; that no one could take him on. To get beaten badly enough to get his skull fractured must have been a massive blow to his ego.

Lorraine recalled the scarring on Raider's face, and the skin discolouration in certain places. Natty had done major damage to him, making her consider what else he could be capable of.

'I know. I really do appreciate it, but I'm trying not to think about myself. If Jaden wants a relationship with his dad, he should have that chance. Too many mums use their personal issues with their exes to prevent them from having relationships with their children. I'm not going to be like that.'

'This is one time you might want to consider being like that. There's a lot on the line, so be careful,' said Rosie.

'I will,' Lorraine assured her. 'Has Spence said anything to you about what's going on?'

Rosie shook her head. 'Everything I've heard has come up in general. There's definitely a lot going on in the Hood, but people are saying Natty will handle it.'

Lorraine frowned. 'What do you mean? I know Natty is well known, but you're acting like he's instrumental in what's going on.'

Rosie sighed. 'I don't know what to tell you, Lo. Natty has a reputation, and people are scared of him on the streets. Him helping Spence is a big deal, and people are seeing it that way.'

Lorraine felt nauseous. 'Are you saying Natty is going to hurt people?' The thoughts of what else Natty might be capable of flittered back to the surface. If his reputation on the street was as big as Rosie implied, he would likely be fully involved in whatever was going on.

'I don't know, but I wouldn't rule it out. We don't know how bad things are going to be, but Natty is going to be right in the middle of it. I don't want to worry you, but that's the truth.'

Lorraine didn't know what to say. Along with the situation with Raider, she now had to worry even more about Natty being in the streets. She clutched her mug, trying to stay calm.

———

NATTY STOOD OUTSIDE HIS HOUSE, looking around, waiting for Clarke. He'd called him earlier, saying he was picking him up.

A few minutes later, Clarke pulled up in a grey Ford Explorer. He nodded at Natty as he climbed in.

'Hope you weren't waiting long,' he said.

Eventually, they pulled up outside a semi-detached house, a dark blue Ford Mondeo in the drive. A man walking his dog smiled at the pair as they left the car. Both men returned the gesture.

Natty burned with curiosity. He hadn't spent much time with Clarke, and certainly hadn't expected to go on a trip with him. His immediate thoughts were that it was connected to his uncle. He hadn't checked in with Mitch yet, but knew it was an inevitability if he was going to be helping the team.

Clarke had a key, and he unlocked the front door.

'That you, Pete?' A female voice called.

'Yes. I've brought a friend with me. We're going to have a chat in the kitchen,' said Clarke. Natty heard the thundering sounds of kids afoot, and nudged Clarke.

'I didn't know you had kids . . .'

'It's a long story,' said Clarke. They walked through the hallway and into the kitchen.

'Drink?' Clarke asked.

'I'm good, thanks,' replied Natty. He sat on a spindly black chair, scared to lean on the table in case he broke it. As Clarke busied himself making a drink, a woman entered the room, the one who had called out earlier. She was on the plump side, and was short, with brown hair flecked with grey, and blue eyes. Despite her plain appearance, she had a friendly smile and beamed when she saw Natty.

'Hello. My name's Paula. It's nice to meet you.'

Natty stood, shaking her hand.

'Call me Natty. It's great to meet you too.'

'Natty's Mitch's nephew,' said Clarke. 'We're just gonna talk a bit of business.' He gave Paula a hug and a kiss, squeezing her tightly.

'That's fine. Would you like me to make you any food?'

'Nah, you don't need to go to any trouble,' said Clarke.

When Paula had left, he slid into a seat opposite Natty. Natty had taken the time to check out the kitchen. It was small, and the collection of kitchenware looked well-used, a slight smell of garlic hanging in the air. It wasn't overpowering, so he didn't mind. Something about the room relaxed him.

'Are you much of a cook?' He asked Clarke.

'I know my way around, but I'm no expert. I'm not much of a food-ie,' said Clarke.

'Fair enough. You let Paula do most of the cooking then?'

'We take turns, but she's definitely more comfortable in here than I am. We can talk about her later. I know you're wondering what you're doing here.'

'You knew I would be.'

'True. How have you been doing after the Rudy situation?'

'Why?' Natty's eyes narrowed, but it had no effect on Clarke.

'I was right there with you, remember? I'm curious.'

Natty blew out a breath.

'It was tough at first. Had a few sleepless nights, and did a bit of soul-searching, but I'm feeling better now.'

Clarke took a sip of his drink. 'Good. You'll need to be, going forward. You need to be front and centre in this conflict.'

'I don't know everything about my uncle's business, but I'm guessing he's got more than enough soldiers,' Natty pointed out.

'You're far more than a soldier, Natty. You got your uncle's attention when you turned down the top job. Word spread after that, and it enhanced your reputation in the streets. This makes you an active target to the other side, so it's my job to ensure you stay alive.'

'I know how to look after myself,' said Natty.

'I'm sure you do, but this is different to smacking around some prick in a bar. You were incredibly lucky the night Rudy died. It could have easily been you that was killed.'

'I survived, didn't I?'

Clarke nodded. 'You did. You've got solid instincts, but you need more skills.'

Paula opened the door, apologising to the pair, as she looked in a drawer, removed what she was looking for, then left again. The noises from upstairs seemed to grow louder. Natty glanced at the ceiling, his worry growing.

'Don't worry about them. They play rough, but they know not to go too far.'

'Sounds like there's a whole football team up there.'

'There are three kids. All boys.'

Natty waited for Clarke to elaborate, but instead, Clarke drank some more of his drink.

'We'll get back to the skills bit in a second. Did my uncle ever suspect Rudy was up to no good?'

Clarke chuckled.

'I'll say this: if you're ever plotting, keep it small and contained. Otherwise, it's more likely the people you're plotting against will find out what you're doing.'

Natty smiled, but he still had more questions. *If Mitch had known what Rudy might try, why hadn't he shut him down earlier?* It irked Natty that there were so many pieces to the mystery, and he had no idea about any of them.

'Can I ask another?'

'Not right now. Like I said before, I know you're curious, but we need to stick to the matter at hand. That means beginning your training.'

'*Training?* What training? Who are you? Fucking batman or something?'

'Maybe,' Clarke replied in a low, gruff voice. The pair laughed, and Clarke continued. 'Let's just say you'll be able to more than hold your own when I'm done with you.'

Natty mulled this over for a second, scratching his chin as he considered Clarke's words.

'Fine. When do we start.'

Clarke drained his drink and stood.

'Right now.'

———

LEAVING THE HOUSE, they drove to an old hangout spot on Spencer Place. Natty knew it was frequented by members of the crew, but he'd not been in a while. They went to the cellar, and Natty's mouth fell open. It was larger than he'd imagined, and had several paper targets. In the corner of the room was a shelf, with various weapons. There were pairs of headphones nearby, and the fading smell of gunpowder lingered in the air. Clarke approached, picking up a gun, keeping it pointed at the ground.

'The first step is to get you used to holding and shooting a gun. You did your thing last time, but the circumstances won't always be like that.'

Clarke walked Natty through some basic gun safety, then he shot at paper targets for over an hour. Natty enjoyed it. His accuracy wasn't as bad as he imagined, and he took to the instruction well.

'Remember, in a situation, never hesitate,' said Clarke. 'Even a split second can make the difference when both sides have guns. Always think about your positioning, and watch the angles.'

'What does that mean?' Natty asked, taking a break, rubbing his wrists.

'If you're shooting, try and make your body less of a target. Keep to cover where possible.'

They spoke for a while longer about positioning, then Natty did some more shooting before they left.

'How often do people use that cellar?' Natty asked.

'We have other spots, but that's usually the first one we take people to. We're going to get into more complicated stuff soon, Nat. I hope you're ready,' said Clarke, as they climbed into the Explorer.

———

THAT NIGHT, Lorraine, Natty and Jaden ate, then sat down to watch a film together. Lorraine's heart melted when she saw Jaden pressed against Natty, and she wished she was stealthy enough to take a picture.

As he watched, Natty's jaw was tense. He seemed distracted, and Lorraine wondered what was going through his mind, and what street business he'd brought into the house. Despite obviously being distracted, Natty had still spent time with Jaden, helping him with homework and kicking a ball around with him in the garden. Lorraine stopped watching him, trying to focus on the film. She didn't want to overthink things. This was meant to be relaxation time, and she wanted to make the most of it.

Natty put Jaden to bed, stifling a yawn and collapsing on the sofa when he returned.

'He must have been tired. He was asleep the minute his head hit the pillow.'

'Bless him. He's had a busy day . . . You seem really tired too. Are you okay?'

Natty nodded. 'I'll be fine. There's just a lot going on, that's all.'

'I can imagine. Is there anything you want to talk about?'

Natty shook his head. 'Nothing to say right now. Still trying to get a clearer picture.'

'How's Spence doing?'

'He's handling things well. He's always had that inner strength, though. He probably should have led my crew all along; he's definitely better at it than I was.'

'Don't sell yourself short, Nat. You're a great leader, and the fact you see areas you can improve is a good thing. Spence wanted your help for a reason; don't forget that.'

Natty chuckled.

'Never thought you'd be giving me pep talks,' he admitted.

'Trust me, neither did I,' said Lorraine.

'Forget about me for now. How has your day gone?'

Lorraine closed her eyes for a moment. The meeting earlier, followed by the subsequent conversation with Rosie, had her emotions all over the place. The fear Raider had instilled in her crept to the surface, before she took a deep breath. She was speaking to Natty, not Raider. He loved her.

She decided to go for it.

'I . . . spoke with Raider.'

Instantly, Natty tensed, all traces of happiness leaving his face.

'I thought . . . we . . . okay.'

Lorraine shook her head.

'Don't do that, Nat. Please, don't just shut me out. Say what's on your mind.'

'Fine. Why did you talk to him?' Natty coldly asked.

'I told you that his family had been contacting me. Well, Raider contacted me to apologise.'

'What else?' Natty saw right through Lorraine's attempts to down-play the situation.

'He wants to see Jaden. He apologised and said he wants to have a relationship with him.'

Natty shook his head now.

'Lo, the man beat you up. He didn't care that Jaden was in the house. He wasn't thinking about his son. When he did that, he lost any right to be around Jaden.'

'I get what you're saying, but it's just like I said before. I don't want Jaden to miss out on his dad because of issues I'm having with him.'

'He's not a good man. That's the whole point, Lo. He doesn't *deserve* to see Jaden. There's more to being a dad than just making a child, and he failed every damn time. I can't even believe you're entertaining him, or thinking of trusting him around your son.'

Despite knowing Natty was talking sense, Lorraine's annoyance grew.

'What the hell is the difference between you and him? You both hurt people, and you both throw your weight around. Should I stop you from seeing Jaden too?'

Silence followed Lorraine's words — words she regretted instantly. All the light seemed to leave Natty's eyes, and he physically recoiled when she reached out to him.

'Nat, I didn't mean what I said. I got annoyed, but—'

Natty shook his head. 'Don't worry about it. I thought you knew why I was different from Raider, but I guess I was fooling myself.' He stood, wiping his trousers.

'Where are you going?' Lorraine was upset. She'd lashed out, and desperately wished she could take the words back.

'I'm going to go home. Probably best I'm by myself for a bit, so I don't *hurt anyone.*'

'You're taking this the wrong way. Like I said, I got annoyed, but—'

'But what? I've done dirt, Lo. I've never hidden what I did, or who I am, but I would never put my hands on you or any other woman. You may not condone what I did, but I promise you, the only thing I regret about what happened to Raider is that I didn't speak to you about it first. He hurt you. He put your life at risk, and I hurt him right back. That's the difference between us. I thought you knew that, but obviously, I was wrong.'

Natty headed for the door, with Lorraine following.

'I didn't mean what I said, Natty. I promise I didn't.'

'Don't worry about it, like I said. You said your piece, and now I'm gonna leave you alone. Probably best for everyone.'

When he'd got his things together, Natty left. Lorraine flopped back down on the sofa, angrily wiping the tears from her eyes. She couldn't believe what she'd done, and didn't blame Natty for how he'd reacted. Taking a deep breath, she closed her eyes.

———

NATTY SLAMMED the door behind him when he arrived home, still furious. He'd tried his hardest not to flip out on Lorraine, mainly because he didn't want to wake up Jaden. Heading to the kitchen, he grabbed a beer and stood in the middle of the room, draining it.

Raider had some nerve. He'd ignored his son for years, put Lorraine in hospital, but still had the audacity to come back around and try to see his son.

For a moment, he wished he had killed Raider. If he had, he would never have had to deal with the man again. Natty loved Lorraine, and cared about Jaden. He'd killed people in the past on the orders of others. Killing to protect the people he loved would have been easy in comparison. He hated the idea of Raider spending time around them. More than that, Natty hated the fact that he had no input in the decisions regarding Jaden. Jaden was as good as his son, but there was still a gulf between them.

He didn't even know Natty was in a relationship with his mum.

Holding his beer, Natty remained in the middle of the room, regretting storming out of Lorraine's. He couldn't stand that she thought he was like Raider, though.

Natty stewed as he considered the hold Raider had over Jaden. Natty had been there for him his whole life, but Jaden having the same blood as Raider apparently cancelled that out.

Natty slammed his hand down on the kitchen table, pain shooting through him. He wondered if that was the key; if having his own child would give him the right to input on the critical decisions in their life.

What kind of dad would he be?

Natty considered his own. His dad had loved him, but Natty often wondered if he'd regretted having a family. He never showed it openly, but there were times around Natty and his mum when he seemed restless. Natty hadn't understood as a child, but he did now. His dad was out in the streets, working with Natty's uncle, playing the game.

Natty couldn't imagine how he could do that, and then switch off and come home to chill with his family.

But, he was doing a similar thing . . .

Natty was confused. He wasn't sure what was going on, nor was he sure of his role in the matter. He wiped his eyes, shocked that he still felt hurt over what Lorraine had said. He'd hoped he would shake it off by now.

That was what relationships did to people, he reasoned. Shoulders slumping, Natty left the beer bottle on the table and headed upstairs. He needed some rest. Between his altercation with Lorraine and the planned meeting with Roman and Keith, he wondered how much sleep he would get. *He needed a break,* he thought, as his head hit the pillow.

CHAPTER NINE

NATTY SIPPED HIS DRINK, keeping his eyes on the people in front of him. Natty and Spence represented the Dunns, whilst Roman and Keith sat opposite them. A third man had accompanied them, but swiftly left.

The meeting was being held in a private room in a restaurant in the city centre. It had a large, well-varnished table encompassing most of the space, surrounded by numerous comfortable leather chairs. In the middle of the table was a tray of drinks.

No one spoke at first. Roman had a relaxed air about him, whereas Keith appeared on edge. He reminded Natty of Warren, and he instantly resolved to keep an eye on him. It had taken a while to set up the meeting, but Jamie had eventually pulled through.

'I'll start then,' said Spence, his tone calm. Roman nodded. 'We do business, and we do it well. We have no issues with anyone, because we understand our boundaries and where we operate. I'm not sure the same can be said for you.' Spence let the statement hang for a moment before continuing. 'I guess a starting point would be understanding why you thought it necessary to attack directly, having already indirectly attacked our profits.'

Roman ignored Spence, locking eyes with Natty.

'How come he's doing the talking instead of you?'

Natty scowled at Roman. He didn't like his friend being disrespected.

'We're on the same team. It doesn't matter which of us you're talking to, so answer the question,' he said.

Keith leaned in, eyes narrowing.

'You're in the way, and we didn't think you would step aside, so we took a different approach,' said Roman.

'I would've thought you'd know better than making such a rash move, considering who you used to work for, but that's not important, I guess. What is it you want?'

'We want the streets,' said Roman, as if it was obvious.

'There's enough real estate in Leeds for two large gangs to co-exist. I think you know that. So, why *did* you attack us?' Spence replied.

Roman shook his head.

'I've heard good things about you, Spence, but you're in over your head. We're not sharing the streets, because they're *ours*. You had them while we were away, but we're back, and we're not respecting old arrangements. Me and Keith fought to get to the top, and it was taken away from us, so we're gonna fight to get it back.'

'It's not that simple,' said Spence.

'No, it *is* that simple. We're out now, and you guys are the biggest team out there. That makes you competition, and we take out competition.'

Spence kept his eyes firmly on Roman, but Natty noted his friend's demeanour was starting to shift, and was unsure how much longer he could keep his mouth shut.

'Just to clarify then . . . you're saying there's no deal to be made?'

'If you leave Chapeltown without a fuss, you can settle in Harehills, or wherever you like. Chapeltown and Little London will belong to us, but the rest of Leeds is fair game,' replied Roman.

Natty glanced at Keith, who was already glaring at him. Natty matched the look, and Keith's scowl deepened.

'Take that bad look off your face,' Keith warned.

'Make me,' replied Natty, seeing Keith as the perfect outlet for his frustration. Both men shot to their feet. Natty rounded the table and grabbed Keith, but Roman and Spence got between the men, pushing them apart.

'Keith, this isn't the time,' said Roman. Natty didn't resist Spence, but kept his eyes firmly on Keith. Spence turned to the others.

'No deal,' he said to Roman. 'I'm sorry we couldn't come to an arrangement, but you had your only free shot. Now, you're all going down.'

Natty and Spence left the restaurant, heading towards their car, bodyguard's falling in line around them. They had taken three men, as had Roman and Keith, but it was a formality. Jamie's connections had set up the meeting, guaranteeing everyone's safety to ensure everyone came to the table.

'What's going on?' Spence said, noting Natty was still furious. 'I know you. You wouldn't get triggered over a dirty look. Talk to me.'

Natty didn't speak until they were in the car and driving out of the car park.

'Lorraine.'

'What about her?'

Natty filled in Spence on his conversation and subsequent argument with Lorraine. Spence shook his head when he was done.

'I don't think she meant it the way it sounds,' was the first thing he said.

'It doesn't matter. She still said it. I've done everything to care for her and Jaden, and it's like it doesn't mean anything.'

'Of course it does. You love her, and she loves you. Jaden does too.'

'Jaden likes having someone he can play his PlayStation games with. I'm like a friend, or a big brother to him. We can't even tell him we're a couple, but Raider can slide back onto the scene after trying to break Lorraine?'

'I know you're pissed, but you're not going to get anywhere by avoiding her, Nat. We've all this stuff going on that we definitely need to talk about. The last thing you need are things going on in your personal life too.'

'She made her decision, Spence. I don't know what else there is to say. Maybe the relationship just isn't meant to be.'

Spence glanced at Natty as they pulled up at some traffic lights.

'You don't mean that.'

'Course I fucking mean it,' snapped Natty. 'I'm just kinda there. I don't have any say, and if Lorraine thinks I'm just like Raider, then she doesn't know me, and all of this is pointless.'

Spence knew Natty was mad, but hoped he would calm down and make peace with Lorraine. Despite Natty's attempts to downplay it, the situation was clearly hurting him. It was a sign of how much Natty had grown. The old Natty would have wanted to go after Raider again, whereas now he was keeping his distance.

He wondered if it was worth speaking to Rosie, or seeking out Lorraine himself to talk to her. Spence felt the issue could easily be resolved, if both sides just spoke to each other.

His face tensed as his mind refocused on what had just gone down. Roman and his people would not be appeased. They had already shown they were willing to kill to get what they wanted. He needed to arrange a meeting with the whole team, and they needed to devise a suitable plan to rectify things. Sooner, rather than later.

————

SPENCE AND NATTY drove to a safe house, where Clarke and several others waited. Natty shelved his frustration, knowing he needed to keep focused on business.

Clarke, Lisa and several other faces waited in the living room. Drinks were poured, and Clarke signalled for the pair to speak.

'Roman isn't interested in any sort of truce,' said Spence. Clarke frowned.

'What does that mean?'

'He made a shit offer for us to give up Chapeltown and Little London, but it didn't sound proper. I think he wants it all.'

'There's something we're missing then,' said Clarke. 'Roman is good, but they must have big support to be thinking they can take out Mitch.'

'He only wants Little London because it's all built up,' said Carlton. 'We've made it relevant, and definitely more profitable.'

Natty's eyes scoured the room as the others talked. Lisa had her eyes on him, shooting him a small smile, which to his surprise, he returned. Straightening, he attempted to focus.

'If there's no room for compromise, then the gloves are off, and we get right to it. What's the plan?' asked Spence.

'We go after Dolja,' said Natty, speaking for the first time. Everyone faced him, but Natty didn't even flinch.

'Dolja?'

'He's a joke, but he has direct access to Roman and Keith. We snatch him. We make him talk.'

Clarke shrugged. 'It's a start. We've put everyone on alert to have eyes in the back of their heads, but the sooner we start identifying more of their crew, the better.'

'It's risky going on the offensive without knowing much more about their structure,' said Spence.

'We still have to, though,' added Natty. 'We can't hang back at this stage and allow them to get too much momentum. Look at what happened in Little London before. We tried to bargain with that prick Warren. We sat back and hoped he would come to the table. He didn't, and we took hits for it.'

'Ahh, Warren. What a joy,' said Lisa, staring off into the distance. Natty looked across at her, confusion etched on his face.

'Nat, Lisa, Spence, stay. Everyone else, give us the room,' said Clarke.

Everyone left, leaving Spence, Clarke, Natty, and Lisa.

'Clarke,' said Natty, before he could speak. Clarke glanced at him.

'What's up?'

'I think this would be a good time for us to be more open with each other.' He motioned to Lisa. 'You could start by properly introducing us to Lisa and explaining her role.'

Clarke grinned. Lisa stood, giving a mock bow.

'Fair enough. Lisa specialises in wet work.'

Natty glanced at Spence, then back to Lisa and Clarke. 'You mean she's a—'

'Lisa, Natty here . . . he was acquainted with Warren. I believe that's something you have in common.'

Natty rubbed his eyebrow, putting it together in an instant. Lisa had been responsible for Warren's death.

'That's how you managed it . . .' he said to Lisa, still stunned by the revelation. She smirked, moving closer.

'You'll have to be more specific,' Lisa replied, standing directly in front of him.

'I wondered how someone could get so close to Warren . . . close enough to take out him and his bodyguards. I'm guessing you were his girl?'

'He thought I was.' Lisa's finger trailed down Natty's chest. 'Were you impressed?'

Natty grinned, forgetting himself for a moment. He leaned in closer to Lisa.

'I'm sure you have a lot of impressive skills.'

'We do what we can, with the gifts we have,' said Lisa silkily.

Natty came to his senses and blinked, moving back. He'd almost forgotten himself and slipped back into his old ways. That person was gone, though, and he wasn't coming back.

'I'm guessing Warren wasn't the first one you handled,' he said, having got himself back in line. If Lisa noticed, she didn't comment.

'I do what is needed, but to answer your question, no. Warren wasn't my first. I understand it's an area you have experience in.'

Natty instinctively almost clammed up, but remembered where they were. Speaking openly was necessary here, and so he went for it.

'How long did it take for you to become comfortable with what you did . . . what you do?'

Lisa stared at him for a few seconds, and Natty wondered if he'd asked an inappropriate question.

'I'm not sure it ever gets to be comfortable.' For a moment, she almost looked vulnerable. 'It's them or us. That's how I choose to look at it. It stops me from going crazy,' she admitted.

The pair shared another long look, and Natty felt, without saying it, that she could relate to the feelings that he often felt. For the first time, Natty was fully aware he was his dad's son. He remembered when he would see a moment of intensity, or sadness on his dad's face that was quickly covered. Now, he was sure that those moments were his dad getting to grips with the things he had done.

'Everything okay, Nat?'

Natty blinked. Spence and Clarke were both looking at him. There was a knowing look in Clarke's eyes that Natty didn't like.

'Yeah, we're just talking,' he said.

'We're gonna have to speak to Mitch, and let him know what's going on.'

'I'll come with you,' said Natty. It would give him a chance to feel out his uncle, and see what the vibe was.

Clarke nodded. 'Lisa. Stand down for now. Rest while you can, because you'll be in the mix soon enough.'

Lisa smiled.

'Not a problem. Speak to you later.' She paused at the door again, and locked eyes with Natty before leaving.

'Are you still trying to tell me nothing is going on?' said Spence, mirth in his voice. Natty flipped a finger at him.

'We were just talking.'

'I've gotta say, I've never seen Lisa talk like that with anyone. Usually, she just sits in the corner and stares at people. You must have something special,' said Clarke, shooting Natty a furtive look.

'Of course I do. Looks and charisma. Don't be jealous, gents.'

Natty and Spence laughed, before Clarke spoke again.

'Seriously, just watch yourself. Lisa is a nice girl, but she doesn't like not getting what she wants. If you're not . . . available, you never know how she might react. You might wake up to her about to slit your throat.'

'Doesn't matter, because that's not going to happen,' said Natty. 'We were just talking, and she knows my situation.'

'That's good enough for me,' said Clarke. 'Let's get to business.'

CHAPTER TEN

NATTY LED the way as the trio of himself, Spence and Clarke entered another house in the Hood. It was the same spot Natty had met his uncle in six months ago. The distinction wasn't lost on him. Unlike last time, there was no party taking place. Instead, there were numerous unsmiling men dotted around, a not-so-subtle sign that Mitch was taking the war seriously.

Mitch waited for them in the back. He looked as inscrutable as ever, his eyes studying each man, pausing on Natty. He smiled, his eyes almost sparkling. Natty couldn't remember ever seeing such emotion from his mostly stoic uncle.

'Good to see you, Nat. You look well.'

'You too, unc.'

Mitch nodded, returning to Spence and Clarke. The pair stood a fair distance apart, with similar demeanours, ready for the conversation. Natty was pleased he was surrounded by people who knew what they were doing. Again, Lisa flitted to his mind, but he pushed her out. He didn't need to be thinking about her right now.

Maybe ever.

'What's the latest?'

'We sat down with Roman and Keith to discuss terms,' said Spence.

'How did that go?'

'Roman thinks he's owed something. He was affiliated with Teflon's team, got caught up, and did five years. Guess he thinks the streets would be his if he hadn't.'

Mitch scratched his chin. 'I see. I've had people digging into the background of their collective. They are well-funded, and their supply is impeccable. It comes from a group of Asian men I've done business with. Have any of you heard the name *Jakkar*?'

Natty and Spence shook their heads. Clarke folded his arms.

'I thought not. These men work in the background, focusing purely on business, not politics. They tend to stay out of the way, but they are massively influential. With their support, Roman will be formidable.'

Natty hid his smile, unsurprised his uncle had gone out of his way to find information. It was the kind of thing Natty's dad would have done, and how Natty liked to operate.

'What would happen if we took out his supplier?' Natty asked. Mitch's eyes surveyed him for another moment. What was going through his mind, Natty couldn't say, but he didn't look away.

'They're too powerful for us to do that. It would lead to a cross-continent war that we wouldn't win.'

'How can we go against Roman if he has a war chest, then?' Natty continued. Spence and Clarke had stepped back, letting him handle the conversation.

'As I said, they don't play politics. Don't directly attack the connect, and there will be no issues. Roman and the others are fair game.'

Natty nodded.

'We'll start with Dolja, and then I'd advise going after Keith. He's tough, but he's a hothead. He'll send a solid message.'

Mitch scratched his chin. 'Lisa will do well there. Send her after them.'

'Can she handle that?'

Mitch smirked. 'Lisa is built for what she does.'

'What about the old guard? Are they likely to be involved?'

'I've lost track of what they're doing. To my knowledge, they haven't stayed abreast of the streets.'

Natty mulled over this. He didn't want to tangle with Teflon,

Shorty, or anyone else that left the game behind. He assumed Roman had been looked after when he'd been released from prison, and had likely gained access to the supplier that way.

'Clarke,' said Mitch. 'What's going through your head?'

'I'm thinking how stupid it was of Roman to make the move he made. He could have been more decisive with it, but doing it this way will cost him,' Clarke replied.

'I agree,' said Natty. 'He's ruined the element of surprise he could have had.'

Spence hid a smile as he watched Natty talking with Mitch. His friend had come a long way, and it was clear to see. He recalled the older days, when Natty had been frustrated with his uncle, constantly scheming ways to get his attention. Now, he seemed more his own person. He had his own inner steel and confidence, and his uncle's eyes shone with approval.

Spence glanced at Clarke, seeing that he'd noticed the same thing.

'You seem surprisingly calm about all this, unc,' Natty continued.

'It's not the first time I've been to war, nephew. Me and your dad did this a few times, and I learnt back then that every now and again, you have to put someone down. Nothing stays the same forever.'

Natty smiled at the mention of his dad. Mitch glanced at the others in the room.

'Leave the room for a moment, please. I want to speak with my nephew.'

Clarke and Spence didn't hesitate. Immediately, they closed the door behind them. Natty and his uncle sized each other up. Despite the months since seeing one another, there was a comfort that hadn't been there previously.

'How have you been, Nathaniel? Seriously.'

'I've been fine. I've kinda struggled to get something popping since I walked away. I'm still trying to work out what I want.'

'You're young. You have plenty of time to do that. Why are you here?'

'I'm here to help Spence.'

Mitch's eyes bore into Natty's. 'Is that the only reason?'

'It's the main reason. I don't want anything to happen to my boy, and I don't want anything to happen to the crew, either. I grew up around it. I spent my adult life in it, and it needs to continue.'

'Why?'

Natty frowned. 'Don't you want it to continue? You built it.'

Mitch smiled.

'I'm just trying to understand what makes you tick, nephew. Is it love? You changed a lot when you got with that woman of yours. Does she influence you to be better?'

Natty forced himself not to scowl, thinking about Lorraine and the conversation they'd had.

'Most of the time. I think it was bigger than her. I just wanted to fully understand what I was doing, and why. She and Jaden tied into that, and I wanted to do something more than be on the block, for the sake of being on the block.'

'That was your dream when you were younger.'

Natty shook his head, chuckling. 'I wanted to be a footballer. I told my dad, and I thought he might tell me I couldn't do it. But, he didn't. He said I'd have to pick between the streets and the footy pitch, and I did, eventually.'

Mitch smiled. 'My brother had his moments. He could be a hothead, but when he was on form, his brain was like nothing else. He just seemed to get it; saw all the angles, and operated on a different level.'

'He still got killed.'

Mitch's eyes saddened. 'Everyone dies, Nathaniel. Your dad loved you, and he wanted to provide. He would do absolutely anything to achieve that. So, make that your focus, and don't worry about the other things.'

Natty smiled. 'I will, unc. Have you spoken to my mum lately?'

'Not since Rudy died. I've called her and popped by a few times, but she doesn't answer. She still has a lot of anger toward me.'

'You and me both. I don't know what's wrong with her sometimes.'

Mitch sighed. 'She's unhappy, Nathaniel. She's been unhappy for a long time. When I first knew your mum, she was bright and happy and smart, and she and your dad together were special.'

Natty could remember when his mum used to work, and had a social life. Sometimes she'd even have her friends come by the house, and they would drink and listen to music, and watch films. Somewhere down the line, she stopped all of that, isolating herself. He even remembered the times he would sneak downstairs and see his mum curled against his dad, proud he had two parents that loved one another.

He didn't know when it changed.

'What am I supposed to do about her?' He asked. Mitch sipped a drink he'd poured earlier.

'All you can do is be there for her. We'll talk about your mum another time. I want you to come back to work for me properly.'

'Spence is doing a good job,' said Natty.

'He is, but he also knows it was never going to be permanent.'

'Why not?'

'Because I was waiting for my nephew to assume his position.'

———

'WHAT DO we think is being said in there?'

Spence and Clarke had been sitting outside the office for a few minutes before Clarke spoke.

'Family stuff,' said Spence, taking a guess. He knew Natty and his uncle didn't talk often, so it would be good for them to catch up.

'Do you think he's giving him your spot?'

Spence hadn't considered it until Clarke mentioned it. Now that he had, he wasn't sure what his feelings were. The money he made was brilliant, and he liked the added responsibility. At the same time, he couldn't deny that he enjoyed having Natty back in the fold.

Natty had an inner strength and something that made people around him take notice. Spence felt they needed that more than ever right now. Natty had stood up to Roman and Keith, showing them that he wasn't to be taken lightly. Spence wondered how it would have gone if Natty hadn't been there.

'You know Mitch better than I do,' he finally said. Clarke shook his head.

'You've done well, Spence. You're respected, and everyone is making money.'

'It's appreciated, Clarke. We all knew I was only the temporary option, though.'

'How do you feel about that?' Clarke was looking at Spence shrewdly.

'I won't lie and say I don't like the increased responsibility, but I just want to thrive.'

Clarke grinned. 'I don't know where you get your personality from.'

'What do you mean?' Spence asked.

'I knew your pops back in the day. We weren't friends, but we spoke, and he was a beast.'

'I've heard stories about how he used to move. He changed after my mum died.'

'He was scientific with it, and Delroy used him well. We didn't have all that many specialists in the Hood at that point, but your pops really gave life to the *enforcer* title. Wasn't as big on the slanging, but he was smart enough to get people to do it for him.'

It was always strange for Spence when he heard people talking about his dad. He remembered flashes from the old days. His dad had been proactive with him, similar to Natty's relationship with his own dad. He supposed this was one of the main reasons they got along so well.

Both had been bred for the streets, but the more Spence considered it, the more he realised their fathers had expected more from them. Spence wasn't destined to be a grunt that hung around on the street corners. He was taught to cook drugs; how to move in certain circles, and he still retained those lessons.

Spence wondered if that was the main difference between them and Cameron. Cameron had grown up without a father figure. He had to grow up fast to survive in their harsh world.

Clarke was still assessing Spence. He cleared his throat and spoke.

'You're fine, though. That was the point I was getting at. You've got your own reputation, and whatever happens, it won't be a demotion.'

Before Spence could respond, the door opened, and Natty signalled them back in.

Mitch remained impassive, but there was a slight sparkle in his eyes that made Spence believe it had been a positive conversation between the pair.

'Thanks for waiting,' said Mitch. 'If it wasn't made clear before, I'll do it now to ensure we're all on the same page. Roman and his crew need to go. If it's quick and quiet, then great. If not, everyone in this room knows how to move. Keep things off the radar where we can. I'll probably have to reach out to my people in the police force, and see what I can do.

'Clarke, make sure Lisa's fully briefed.' Mitch glanced at Natty, then at Spence. 'I don't mind which of you captains this shit. I know you're close, so run it as you see fit. Any major changes, keep me in the loop. Other than that, you all have the access you need; safehouses, straps, product . . .' Mitch didn't need to say anymore.

Everyone filed out of the office, and Clarke drove them back to the safe house. He fixed them drinks, and they toasted the potential success of the battle plan.

After Spence left, Clarke drained his drink.

'We have some more work to do.'

Natty grinned. He'd enjoyed the sessions he'd had with Clarke. They focused mainly on shooting, but there had been some hand-to-hand work too. Natty had relaxed into the session, expecting to concentrate on technique. But, the examination was far more practical than he'd expected, and he paid for not anticipating it. Clarke had taken him down with ease, leaving a bitter admiration surging through Natty. He vowed he wouldn't be caught off guard again.

Before then, Natty had never realised how seriously Clarke's people took their training. They worked like they were always on the edge of a war, and it paid off massively. Their bodies were always in shape, and their minds always sharp. They knew how to track enemies and take them down. Seeing them made Natty hungry to improve himself and step up.

It also helped that concentrating on learning new skills meant less time thinking about Lorraine, and that messy situation.

'We'll do some more shooting practice. I told Paula I'd get in early tonight,' said Clarke.

'What's the deal with you two?' Natty's curiosity was piqued. He'd seen Paula once more since the first time, and other than the fact she had several children, he knew nothing else about her.

'She's a good woman,' said Clarke. 'She got a raw deal in the men department, but she never let it defeat her.'

'The kids aren't yours, then?'

Clarke shook his head. 'I still care about them. I'm sure you can relate.'

Natty nodded, his stomach twisting when he thought of Lorraine and Jaden.

'You've known her a long time, I'm guessing.'

'Over fifteen years. We've helped one another a lot. I'll always look out for her.'

Natty mulled this over. He liked getting insight into Clarke, and found he liked the man's character. To Natty, this was how Rudy used to be, before things grew tense between them. An older man, with wisdom to bestow and stories to share.

'You worked with my dad, right?'

'I worked for your uncle. That means I worked for your dad as well.'

'Can you tell me about him?'

Clarke smirked. 'Yes. Not now, though. We have work to do.'

'Let's go then,' said Natty, sliding to his feet, ready to work.

CHAPTER ELEVEN

NATTY SHIFTED IN HIS SEAT. He and Clarke were staking out one of the new spots Roman and Keith had set up. It was a brilliantly impressive setup; a nondescript property in an inconspicuous area. Finding it was a real coup.

Two tense weeks had passed, with both sides waiting for the other to strike.

Outside of his training with Clarke, Natty and the others had been learning more about Roman's infrastructure. Similar to the property they were surveying, he'd done well in a short amount of time.

A man stood outside, talking into a phone as he puffed on a cigarette.

'I don't think that's a spotter,' said Clarke. 'Looks like he's just making a private call.'

'Do you recognise him?' Natty asked. The man looked younger, and Natty placed him in his early twenties. He was hard-eyed and looked like he could handle himself, but that didn't bother Natty.

'No. He'll be good for sending a message, though.'

'What do you want to do?'

Clarke grinned.

'Let's see how you do, son. You've been out of practice for a few months. What do you think we should do?'

Natty had considered it before Clarke asked. He had a few ideas, but decided to go for the simplest.

'Pull your gun. I'm gonna approach, so cover me. I'll signal if I need you to move.'

Still smiling, Clarke drew his gun. Natty put up his hood and climbed from the car. He ignored the biting wind as he headed towards the man, keeping his head low. The man was engaged in his conversation but paused when he saw Natty coming closer.

'Who the hell are you?' He snapped. Natty ignored him. The man moved forward, ending his call. 'Did you hear what I said, dickhead?'

He was close enough, and Natty acted, swinging. His aim was true, and the man crumpled from the force of the blow. Natty searched him, finding no gun. Taking the man's phone, he smashed it on the floor, then left the barely-conscious goon in a heap. Signalling for Clarke, they advanced on the house.

They heard a commotion of noise once they opened the door. Music played, mixed with the loud sounds of a video game coming from one of the rooms.

Natty had his gun out. Clarke had given it to him earlier, and he gripped it, ready to use it if necessary. Quietly, they padded up the stairs, checking each room, but found no one. Both men moved well together, seeming to know how to act without being told. Natty let Clarke take point as they burst into the living room, startling the men.

'On the floor, now,' said Clarke. No one moved, so he fired a shot, and the group jumped. There were four in total, all around the same age as the man Natty had knocked out. 'Check the other rooms,' he said to Natty. Natty left the room, still moving cautiously. He nudged open the kitchen and found a girl cowering in the corner. A smashed cup was on the floor next to her, and Natty assumed she had dropped it when she heard the gunshot.

'Come with me,' said Natty, signalling her to get up. She didn't move, frozen with fear. 'I'm only gonna hurt you if you don't do what I say,' he snapped, scaring her into action. He led her into the living room, keeping her in front of him.

'Right then, now that we've got everyone. We're here for the stash. Don't try to bullshit us. We know it's here.'

'We don't know what stash you're talking about,' one of the youngsters moaned. 'We're just chilling. That's it.'

Clarke chuckled.

'Are we doing this the hard way then?'

'We wouldn't be here if we didn't know what you had,' said Natty. 'Help yourselves; tell us where it is. Roman isn't worth dying for.'

No one moved, but the girl Natty had accosted spoke up after looking at the others.

'I'll show you where it is,' she said.

'Oi, sit the fuck down, Rachel!' One of the men snapped. Natty kicked him in the ribs, making him cry out in pain.

'I'll take her. You cover them.'

Natty followed Rachel upstairs, and she headed to the main bedroom where Natty had looked earlier. He hadn't seen anyone, but she seemed to know the place well, heading to a wardrobe and digging within a bag. She removed several blocks of what Natty assumed was cocaine.

'Find something to put them in,' said Natty. Rachel did as she was told, handing Natty the bag. He aimed the gun at her, and she whimpered.

'I helped you,' she pleaded.

'How old are you?'

Rachel hesitated.

'Sixteen,' she mumbled.

'Why are you here?' Natty asked, shaking his head and lowering the gun.

'What do you mean?'

'You seem like a nice girl. What are you doing here with these clowns.'

The girl shrugged, and Natty kicked himself. He didn't know why he had questioned her. It was irrelevant in the grand scheme of things. She had made her choice just like the others.

'You better watch it being around here in future. We might come back, and I don't think your little friends down there have your best interests at heart.'

Rachel just looked at him, and he didn't bother continuing.

'Get on the bed and lie face-down.'

Trembling, Rachel did as she was told. Clutching the bag with the drugs, Natty left the room and headed downstairs just as the man he'd hit earlier stumbled into the house. Moving quickly, Natty hit him in the head with his gun, then dragged him into the living room with his free hand.

'Did we get what we needed?' Clarke asked, not turning away from the downed men.

'Yeah. These clowns had four boxes of white. Roman and his little crew aren't gonna be happy with them.'

Clarke laughed again, clearly having fun with the assignment.

'Listen up; tell Roman what happened, and tell him that he wanted it this way. Be thankful we're leaving you alive, too. We could have done a madness in here and killed you all, but we won't. Next time we see any of you, though . . .'

Clarke left the room first, then Natty did the same after taking the phones of each man, then locking the front door and flinging the key into the garden. He and Clarke hurried down the street and into the car, where they drove away.

'You did well in there, Nat. Still, we should have killed at least one of them. They got one of ours when they missed Spence.'

'People will go in time, but robbery is fine for now. We have some extra boxes we can put to work. Should help to offset what we've lost since the drama started,' said Natty.

'Sounds good. Drop me off at the safe house. I'll speak to Spence and see where he wants them to go.'

'Cool.'

After Natty dropped off Clarke, he dumped the car, walking down Roundhay Road until he found the Vauxhall Vectra he'd stashed earlier. He drove home, having left his weapon with Clarke. His phone buzzed as he was about to take a shower, but when Natty saw it was Lorraine, his mouth tightened, and he ignored the call.

In the shower, he went over the night. It had gone well. They'd sat on the spot for a while, and decided it would make an easy target with very little protection. The fact that it had multiple kilos of product, but no real security was telling, and Natty wondered if that was a sign that Roman hadn't tightened up his organisation.

If his supplier was as solid as Mitch believed, he would likely have more product than competent people to handle.

Natty thought about what they knew so far. Roman and Keith were the main guys. Then there was Dolja, and Natty had heard rumours through the grapevine that Manson was involved with the pair. Natty had seen Manson around a few times, and wondered if it was worth reaching out to him to see exactly how deep he was. It was as good a plan as any.

———

'THEY'RE DEAD. We need to kill them all!'

Roman watched Keith trashing the living room of the safe house they were in. He'd yanked the television off the wall, slammed it on the floor, kicked over the coffee table, and was now standing in the middle of the shabby room, bristling. Dolja stood near the door, warily watching Keith, his eyes occasionally flicking to Roman.

'I'm serious,' Keith growled. 'I'm gonna shoot the lot of them.'

'You tried that,' said Roman. 'We need to play it carefully.'

'We fired at some spots, made a fuss, and then fell back. They've hit several of our spots, and we've done nothing about it. How the hell is that a war?'

Roman scratched his ear.

'Keith, we need to move carefully. Trust me when I say, they want us to attack them now. They want to lure us in, but we're not going to do that.'

'Gimme something then,' demanded Keith. 'Prove to me that there's at least some sort of damn plan, because right now, we just look soft.'

'And whose fault is that?' Roman snapped. 'You shot at them, and you couldn't even hit Spence while doing it. You're the one that got us into a situation that you hadn't planned, and I'm the one picking up the fucking pieces, and making it work.'

Keith glared at Roman, who met his gaze. Dolja held his breath, waiting for the explosion, knowing that if Keith went nuclear, he would have to try to stop him.

Another moment passed, then Keith snorted, shaking his head.

'Fine. We're not gonna fall apart over this shit. I'm with you, fam.'

Roman smiled at him.

'Trust me, Keith. They won't see it coming.'

———

THE FOLLOWING AFTERNOON, Natty left a safe house after making some calls, and drove to Chapel Allerton. Lorraine had tried calling twice more, and had sent several messages, but he'd replied to one telling her that he wasn't ready to talk, then ignored her. He didn't feel good about doing it, but he needed to focus on the task at hand, and he had no idea what to do about the situation.

If Raider was going to be involved in her life, he didn't know where he stood in that equation, and it hurt him.

Natty shook away the thoughts. It wasn't the time for them. He had to stay in the moment.

Pulling up outside a house on Dominion Avenue, he knocked on a door, which was opened by a tall, brown-skinned girl. Her dark eyes widened when she recognised Natty, and he gave her a grin.

'What are you doing here?'

'Let me in, and I'll tell you. I know you don't want to talk business outside.'

The girl weighed up her options, then let him in. Natty kicked off his shoes, following her into the living room. She sat on the sofa, but he remained standing.

'What do you want, Natty? I haven't seen you in years.'

'The years have been good to you, Marie.'

Natty had known Marie for over ten years. They'd had a fling back in 2010 after meeting in a club. It was never serious, but they were on and off for years, before things fizzled out.

He hadn't seen her in at least two years.

Marie shook her head, though a small smile escaped. 'Don't try to charm me. I know you're not here for that. You'd have come at night if you were.'

'I would have sweet-talked you on the phone too,' agreed Natty. 'I'm here about Manson.'

'What about him?' Marie cleared her throat, biting her lip.

'I heard you were checking him before he got banged up. Stands to reason he might look you up now that he's out.'

'What does that have to do with anything?'

'I need to talk to him,' said Natty.

'What about? Are you gonna tell him about us?'

'There hasn't been an *us* for years, Marie, but I always knew that you two had a thing. That doesn't bother me. I need to talk business with him, so I'm gonna leave you my number, and you're gonna tell him Natty Deeds wants to speak to him.'

Marie sagged. 'I don't want to be involved.'

'That's tough, because you already are.' Natty smiled disarmingly. 'Look, I don't want to be a prick, Marie, but I need to speak to him. It's important, and you know I wouldn't ask if it wasn't. Can you help me out on this one? Please?'

Marie blew out a breath. She didn't know what business Natty and Manson might have, but she didn't want any of her secrets coming out. She had been involved with both Natty and Manson, and the pair had often overlapped, and she'd thought neither was aware. The fact Natty was revealing he knew this now was significant. Despite his apparent warmth, there was something cold and calculating in that move. She vowed to be careful around him in future.

'Fine. I'll tell him, okay? Can you leave me alone now? I have things to do.'

Natty's smile widened, his eyes glittering. 'Lighten up, Marie. Smile. You probably owe me one, anyway. I'll let myself out, but don't keep me waiting too long.'

———

'WHAT DO you know about it then?'

Spence swallowed the mouthful of food before he responded to Rosie. He had visited her house and decided to cook for her, but she had been in a strange mood the whole time he had been there. At first, he'd put it down to the fact they'd not spoken again about their future, but evidently, he was wrong.

'I only know that they argued about Raider.'

'Don't you think it's a little childish for Natty to be ignoring Lorraine? She's trying to sort out the situation.'

Spence hadn't known Natty still wasn't talking to Lorraine, the streets taking priority for both men. He knew Natty and Clarke had successfully robbed a few of Roman's spots, which had been their primary focus. Roman was keeping the robberies quiet for now, but Spence shuddered at the money they must have cost him.

'She shouldn't have said what she said to him. Comparing Natty to Raider is the worst thing she could have done,' he said, again trying to eat his food while it was still warm.

'She didn't mean it the way he's taking it. She meant they were both in the game and had solid reps.'

'Rosie, I'm not trying to take sides, but maybe Lorraine should have worded it better. What were you thinking, meeting up with Raider, anyway?'

'We were in public, so what do you think he was going to do? Kidnap us?' said Rosie sarcastically.

'It's happened before. Raider is dangerous. You remember what he did to your friend, right?'

'I do, but you need to realise I can take care of myself. I was there supporting my friend, just like you're supporting Natty right now.'

'You think her letting Jaden see Raider is a good idea?'

Rosie shook her head. 'No, I think it's a terrible idea, but I see where she's coming from. She just wants her son to have a relationship with his dad if there's one to be had.'

'And the fact that Raider has never been there for Jaden before, whereas Natty has?'

Rosie's eyes narrowed. 'I don't like how you're coming at me, Spence. Don't bring any of that street crap to my house, please. I'm not involved like that, and I'm not one of your *opps*. There's no easy way to fix this situation; that's all I'm saying.'

'Of course there is. Jaden doesn't need a dad that's just going to abandon him again. That's not going to benefit him in any way,' snapped Spence.

'That's not our choice to make. It's Lorraine's, and to be honest, she doesn't need your approval, Spence. If you want to take it one step further, she doesn't even need Natty's.'

Spence pushed his plate aside, resigned to the fact he wouldn't be finishing his meal. He glared at Rosie, and she gave him the same look right back.

'Natty has been more of a dad to Jaden than Raider ever has. All Lorraine has done is show Raider that the beating he gave her doesn't matter. Where are the fucking consequences for what he's done?'

Rosie took a moment to respond, and her look hadn't diminished in the slightest.

'Firstly, stop swearing. Watch your tone when you're speaking to me, and I'll talk to you in the same fashion. Secondly, the consequences for Raider were deep, and I'm saying this as someone that isn't a fan of his.'

'What do you mean?'

'He nearly died.'

'He deserved it,' said Spence. Rosie shook her head.

'That's not the point. The point is that he beat up Lorraine, which he should not have done, and then Natty put him in hospital, and even now, months later, he's still wearing the beating. That's a pretty big consequence for what he did.'

Spence's nostrils flared, and he tried to control his annoyance. He hadn't seen the conversation coming, and hadn't expected Rosie to come at him about Natty's actions. He wondered what else Lorraine was saying, and what would happen next.

'That doesn't mean he should suddenly get to see his son again.'

'Either way . . . like I said, it's not your problem, Spence. What is your problem—'

'Hang on,' Spence interjected. 'You made it my problem. I wanted to eat my food, and you baited me into this conversation. Why did you ask for my opinion if it's not my problem? If you just want someone to agree with you, you're speaking to the wrong person.'

'Fine,' Rosie conceded. 'I accept that. But, let's focus on how your best friend is acting. I like Natty and always have, but ignoring your woman because you had an argument isn't the way to handle things. He needs to talk to her like a man, or he needs to move on.'

Spence's eyes bore into Rosie's. 'Is that Lorraine talking, or you?'

'Spence, talk to your friend. That's all I'm saying to you.'

'Talk to *your* friend. This is her problem. She can't do something Natty is against, call him out when he's done nothing wrong, and then expect him to run to her and apologise.'

Rosie eyed him harshly. 'You're sounding foolish right now, which isn't like you. The fact you and Natty are friends is blinding you to what you know is the right way to handle this situation.'

'And you're saying it's any different for you? Lorraine shouldn't have said what she said.'

'I'm not saying that she should, but she's never going to get the opportunity to explain herself if he keeps blanking her calls.'

Spence didn't respond, believing anything he said would be twisted against him. He had to give Rosie props. She was a tiger when it came to making a point.

That being said, he wasn't pleased with how Lorraine had handled things, especially with her knowing that he was involved in the Roman situation. Natty being his friend aside, he wanted him on point, and didn't want him making mistakes that could get him, or anyone around him, killed.

'You're just not going to say anything then?' Rosie wasn't done with him.

'I don't have anything else to say about it. You've made your position clear, and you know mine.'

Rosie's face softened. 'I don't want to argue with you. Really, I don't. I want to fix things before they go too far to be fixed.'

'What if they already have?' Spence poured a glass of red wine from a nearby bottle.

Rosie didn't reply.

CHAPTER TWELVE

CLARKE LOOKED up as Lisa entered the living room of the safe house. She wore a casual outfit; a hooded top, leggings, and grey Converse. She took her hood down as she sat, and watched Clarke, waiting for him to speak. He smirked, used to her quirks.

When he'd first met her, he had his doubts. He wasn't convinced she would be able to keep up with the pace and demands of their work, but she shocked him by not just keeping up, but excelling. Since then, she'd yet to fail a job she'd been assigned, never leaving a trail. She was like a ghost. There were rumours about her skill set and how she operated, but nothing concrete. Lisa's discretion became her calling card, never leaving evidence or ties that bind.

'You look thin,' he said to her, his voice softer than usual. 'Are you eating?'

'I'm fine, Clarke.'

'Make sure you're taking care of yourself,' he cautioned. 'I know how you get.'

'We don't need to do this. Seriously,' said Lisa. Clarke found it hard to look at her sometimes. Despite the swagger and bravado, it was hard not to see the broken little girl he'd rescued during a raid all those years ago. Young, mistreated by the people she lived with, Clarke

551

couldn't bear to leave her there. So, he took her, helping to raise her and ensuring nobody would ever treat her that way again.

In doing so, he'd poured himself into her. All of him. The grit and steel of the street life. The cunning and deceit. The result was a beautiful viper. Lethal, unflinching when it came to her duty.

'This is serious, Lis. You haven't had any work in a while, and you can't fuck this one up. There's too much on the line.'

'I understand, Clarke. I always understand. Can you please get to the point?'

'In a minute. First, what about Natty?' Clarke expected a reaction, but Lisa's expression remained blank.

'What about him?'

'I saw you eye-fucking him, Lis. In fact, I've seen it a few times.'

'So?'

'So, I don't want anything messing up the business. More importantly, *Mitch* doesn't want anyone messing up the business. I don't want to end up on the missing list, and you don't either, so watch what you're doing.'

'I always do, but I don't see why it's a concern of yours, or Mitch's. Natty and I are grown-ups.'

Clarke sighed. He couldn't help caring about her, even when she was being stubborn.

'It's a concern because he's Mitch's nephew, and Mitch wants his nephew back in the fold. He doesn't need him being distracted by you.'

Lisa smirked, and Clarke didn't bother reacting. He knew Lisa too well to expect any other sort of reaction. He'd had a word and tried to clear things up. Whatever happened next was up to her.

'I guess we'll stick to business. You know who we're after and what we need to do.'

'Which one am I going after?'

'Keith and Roman haven't been seen properly, not without people around them. It might be best to work your way up, starting with Dolja. Natty's heard through conversations with people that he's someone that Keith and Roman keep close, so that's your starting point. Get in good with him, and see where that leads you.'

'What do we know about him? I've heard the name, but no real details.'

'He's single, but he likes women, so you're in luck there. Keeps different ones on his arm, but doesn't seem to have one he's kept around. Likes to party, but he's not out every week. He hangs around the Hood a lot, and doesn't seem to have much of a routine.'

'We don't seem to have much to go on,' said Lisa, her voice not concealing her distaste. The more information she had when taking on a job, the easier it tended to be.

'As soon as we know more, we'll let you know,' said Clarke.

Lisa nodded, her expression softening for a moment.

'I'll stop in and see Paula soon,' she said. 'It's been a while.'

'She'll like that,' Clarke replied. 'She worries about you.'

Lisa left soon after, and Clarke rubbed his forehead. Lisa could be hard work at times. Once she was on the job, she was flawless, but everything else about her was hard to handle. Clarke worried he might have made Natty even more of a target by declaring him off-limits. He knew how Lisa could get when she saw something as a challenge, and he wondered if it was worth having a word with Natty directly.

Despite his worry, Spence seemed to be okay with it, believing Natty would be okay, so Clarke was possibly overreacting. He poured himself another drink as he got an alert from Mitch, wanting a conversation. Finishing the drink, he got to his feet and left the safe house, knowing better than to keep Mitch waiting.

———

MITCH WAS in the back garden when Clarke arrived. Several of his men remained posted around the spot. He smirked, impressed with their discipline.

Mitch stared up at the sky, giving no indication he'd heard Clarke. Rather than wait for him to pay attention, Clarke cleared his throat.

'Everything good, Mitch?'

'That's what I'm hoping you're going to tell me. I've heard we've been on a robbing spree. How much do we have?'

'Ten, fifteen boxes. Mostly white, but a fair bit of dark mixed in there. Not much money, but we've got maybe fifty grand.'

'How have they retaliated?'

'They've driven by a few spots, but we're well-guarded. They won't catch us slipping again.'

'They shouldn't have caught us slipping in the first place.'

Clarke stayed quiet. It wasn't his time to speak, and he suspected Mitch had been building up to this for a while.

'We're supposed to be on point at all times. That's why we've been around so long. When every other crew crumbled, we kept going, because we didn't let our guard down. A relative newcomer like Roman shouldn't have been able to catch us unawares.'

'All due respect, but Roman isn't exactly new. He was around back in the day and has solid connections.'

'That's not the point. Answer me honestly; how do you think Spence is doing?'

Clarke's eyes narrowed, recognising Mitch's angle. It also irked him that Mitch had asked him to be honest, when he never lied. He wasn't scared of anyone, and never held back with what was on his mind.

'I think he's doing very well. People respect him, and before this shit, he was making good money for us.'

'Is he built for wartime?'

'He was there alongside your nephew when their friend switched on them that night. We saw it when we broke into the room; he had his gun raised, ready to shoot if he needed to. You know his pops, like you told him. He's from good stock. He was taught well, and he's one of the best we've got.'

'He's not Natty, though.'

'No, he isn't, but they complement one another. Spence thinks a little more than your nephew does, and if it wasn't for Spence, I doubt your nephew would be in any position to help us. He'd probably be in prison.'

Mitch didn't respond. Clarke waited for him to speak. He had known Mitch a long time, and it wasn't the first occasion they'd had a conversation like this. He'd learned long ago that Mitch gravitated toward people who spoke their minds, rather than telling him what he wanted to hear. Of course, there was a limit, and if you went too far, you could find yourself in trouble, but Clarke was aware of that line.

'I want you to evaluate Spence. If he looks like he's going to crack, make him take a step back. My nephew can take the lead.'

'You've got it, Mitch.'

Mitch glanced up at the night sky again. The chill didn't seem to bother him, but Clarke was glad he'd worn his fleece top. He wasn't a fan of cold weather. It was a sign he should consider going abroad once the war had finished. He hadn't been on holiday in a few years, and he had cousins that were annoying him about coming to see them.

'Are you using Lisa?'

'I've given her a mission, yeah,' said Clarke.

'Good. She's another one that knows what she's supposed to do. Keep up the pressure on Roman. Everyone is watching on this one, and I don't intend to lose.'

————

SEVERAL NIGHTS LATER, Lisa checked her appearance in the mirror before she headed out. She'd heard about a party in the Hood to celebrate someone's birthday, and the person she'd sent to scout the party had reported that Dolja was there. Apparently, he was close friends with the party host, which was enough for Lisa to go on. She'd done a bit of checking into Dolja, and wasn't impressed. He'd been affiliated with a few crews, but there was nothing special about him. Nothing made him stand out.

Not like Natty.

Lisa took a taxi to the party. It was already dark as she climbed from the Uber, ignoring the driver's request for a good rating. The thumping bass from the House music made the ground tremble. Lisa put on her game face, approaching the spot, ignoring the few people milled around, heading inside to look for her contact. Each room of the house was packed with people. Lisa nodded and smiled at a few, but kept it moving, not wanting to talk, or to be a part of any group photos. No one present knew what she did, but she didn't want to tempt fate.

Finally, she found Clara in the corner, drink in hand, standing with a man. He was talking a mile a minute, Clara nodding along, but Lisa knew she was simply entertaining him. With that in mind, she stepped into the conversation.

'Can you give us some space, please?' She said to the man. 'I need to talk to my friend.'

'We were just . . .' the man started, but faltered when she narrowed her eyes. He towered over her and outweighed her significantly, but something in her demeanour made him wary. Coughing to excuse his embarrassment, he turned to talk to another woman.

'How do you do that?' Clara asked in awe.

'Magic,' Lisa dryly replied. 'Is our friend still here?'

Clara nodded. She was uncommonly pretty, with dark brown hair, greyish-blue eyes, and round cheeks.

'He's in the corner over there,' she said. Lisa subtly angled her body so she could see without drawing attention. She recognised Dolja immediately. He was a big man, wearing a warmup tracksuit and a thick chain. He seemed to be staring into space as the group around him, consisting of several men and a few scantily clad ladies, spoke.

'Are any of the women with him?'

'No. His friends brought them over. What's the play?'

'I'm going to get his attention. Hang back, and ring my phone if I need to be alert.'

'Got it.'

'No flirting, Clara. You can do what you want when I go, but I need you on point until then. No more drinking either.'

'Yes, boss,' said Clara sarcastically. 'You'd better get over there before one of them steals him.'

Lisa winked, then moved through the crowds. Near Dolja, there was a table laden with various drinks. Lisa made herself a glass of vodka, lightly clutching the plastic cup. Moving within range of Dolja, she saw him glance her way, but she ignored him, complimenting the dress of one of the nearby groupies. It worked like a charm, and soon the girls were excitedly complimenting her blouse and asking her where she got it. Lisa kept up the pretence, able to see Dolja in her peripheral as she finished her drink. He approached, a smile on his face.

'What's everyone drinking?' He asked, standing next to Lisa. When they'd given their orders, he signalled for one of his men to go and get them, the others engaging the remaining women in conversation again. Despite herself, Lisa was impressed. It was a similar move to one she used with her own friends, cutting off her prey. She was forced to slightly re-evaluate her low opinion of Dolja. If anything, he had presence, plus people willing to listen to him.

'I haven't seen you around any of these parties before,' he said.

'I've seen you,' Lisa responded.

Dolja scratched his chin, his jewellery catching the light. Lisa resisted the urge to roll her eyes. She wasn't the sort of person to be impressed by a few bits of bling, and hoped he had more in his arsenal than that.

'I think I'd have remembered a girl like you.'

'Why's that?' Lisa kept playing along.

'You're stunning, that's why. I always notice the really sexy ones.'

Lisa gave him a bland smile.

'You're making up for it now,' she told him. Their drinks arrived, and Lisa sipped hers. It would be her last drink of the night. She could perform under the influence, but didn't plan on doing that tonight.

'I suppose I am. Do you know my name, seeing as you know who I am?'

'Something with a *D*,' she replied, again almost rolling her eyes when she saw the smirk on his face.

'The D stands for Dolja. I'll let you off for not knowing it, as long as you promise to remember it from now on.'

'I'll remember,' she said, smiling sweetly. One of Dolja's men came over to talk to him. His tone was urgent, but he spoke too low for her to hear any words other than *Keith*. Whatever else was said, Dolja's whole demeanour changed. He gave Lisa a sad look.

'Summat's come up, babe. I've got to go and handle it.'

'That's too bad,' said Lisa. 'Guess I'll find someone else to talk to.'

Dolja's eyes narrowed. He surveyed the room briefly, taking in the scene. Numerous guys were staring hungrily in Lisa's direction. Dolja was active with the women in the Hood. The fact he didn't recognise this young beauty was a good sign. She was untapped and unspoilt. He was going to make her his, and wouldn't let anyone else muscle in.

'Take my number. I'm gonna call you tomorrow, and we're going to do something.'

'Are we?' Lisa's eyebrow arched. She was impressed by his confidence. Were he more her type, she'd likely be receptive, even if he wasn't just a job.

'We are. I want to get to know you some more.' He pulled out his phone. 'Put your number in there.'

Lisa didn't immediately move, nearly laughing when she saw the worry in his eyes. She finally put him out of his misery and added her number.

Dolja stowed his phone and gave her a satisfied smile.

'Good. I'm definitely gonna check you, babe.'

He hugged her, and she let him, knowing he was marking his territory, as if it would put off any of the guys at the party. After that, Dolja and his men hurried from the party, leaving the girls behind, who looked stunned at the sudden departure. Lisa conversed with them for a few moments, then headed back to Clara, now talking with another guy. This time, she moved away from him and toward Lisa.

'How did it go?' She asked, planting a ditzy smile on her face in case anyone was watching.

'It's a good start. He left in a hurry, and it sounded like it was for business, but I can't be sure.'

'What are we doing now then?' Clara asked.

'I'm leaving. I did what I needed to do. You can stay if you want, but I'll likely ring you early tomorrow, so I'd be careful about being here all night. Okay?'

'Got it.'

Lisa left the house, walking down the street. When she was a distance away, she called Clarke.

'It's me,' she started. 'Make sure everyone is on alert, just in case. Something could be going down.'

DOLJA CLIMBED FROM HIS CAR, Keith waiting. He noticed Roman wasn't in attendance, and felt his good mood evaporating. He wished he could have stayed at the party and spoken to the beauty. He hadn't even gotten her name, and she hadn't saved it when she'd given him her number, but he had called it in the car on the way over, and she'd answered. Dolja wouldn't have been pleased if she had given him a fake number.

She was interesting, he mused. She was comfortable around crowds in the Hood, but he hadn't seen her before, and wondered how she had stayed under the radar. Shelving it for now, he decided to find out the next time he saw her.

'Keith, what's happening, bro?'

Keith smiled, which made Dolja more nervous. When Roman and Keith were released, they'd put Dolja down to work with them. The money was excellent, and he'd agreed without hesitation. For a few months, they were stacking, and everything was great.

Then Keith attacked the Dunns.

Dolja knew the pair were ambitious and wanted to make waves, but he hadn't expected such an audacious move. Keith had forced him to be the driver, and they had been lucky to get away once the Dunns mobilised. Since then, Dolja had waited on tenterhooks for the next move. The Dunns had clapped back by robbing several spots, affecting Dolja's money, but that was just the beginning. He was sure of it. Keith wouldn't have demanded his presence if more wasn't going on.

'Don't you think it's a bit risky to be out partying when we're up to our necks in drama?' Keith stared at Dolja. It was an unnerving habit of his, making Dolja think he could see right through him sometimes. Dolja looked away after a few seconds.

'I was just having a few drinks,' he said. 'I had people watching out for me, just in case it popped off.'

'If Dunn sent his best people at you, do you think you'd even see them coming? Focus on business instead of trying to get laid. We've got a lot on the line here.'

'Okay, Keith, I get you. I'll be careful like I always am. What's going down?'

'I need you to meet with Tobey. He's gonna give you a bag of straps and some other little bits. Hold them until I come for you.'

'You want me to hold a bag of straps? I'll get years if I get caught.'

'Don't get caught then,' said Keith bluntly.

'Does Roman know about this?'

Again, Dolja was victim to Keith's stare.

'Let's say he didn't. Would you be planning to tell him?'

'N-No, course not,' said Dolja. 'I was just asking. Sorry.'

Keith nodded.

'They're not gonna get away with disrespecting us and taking out our spots. If we ride out on them, I want you with us. Understand?'

Dolja wasn't going to argue.

'Okay, bro.'

'Good. Come, let's go get a drink. You look a little too nervous for my liking,' chuckled Keith. Dolja held his breath, and Keith led him to his car. Climbing in, he resolved to pick up his ride later.

CHAPTER THIRTEEN

SPENCE SAT IN A SAFE HOUSE, lost in thoughts over his issues. It had been weeks since his disagreement with Rosie, but regardless of the time that had elapsed, he couldn't shake his musings. He cared about Rosie. She had been there for him during a troubling time. She'd understood the situation, his pain, and his need to heal. She wanted to be with Spence, but had to settle for a supporting role when it became clear the timing wasn't right.

Anika had deeply hurt Spence, and he struggled to get past it. Shaking off the insecurities that plagued him was easier said than done. Not knowing what he and Rosie were to each other hadn't been an issue to begin with, but it seemed to be becoming one recently. They hadn't spoken properly since their argument about Natty and Lorraine, and Spence winced whenever his mind slipped to the image of her flinching before him. He knew better than most what scars the past could leave, and still, he hated that he'd dragged up such a painful memory in Rosie.

Spence blew out a breath. With everything happening on the streets, he needed to be on point, especially with Clarke and Natty leading the charge on the front line. That only worked if they could rely on Spence to co-ordinate and ensure nothing slipped through the cracks.

He was determined not to fail.

Clarke entered the spot. It was one of many, but this particular place was Spence's favourite, especially after they'd abandoned the last one after the shootout. It was located in Chapeltown, at the bottom of Louis Street, with a small patch of grass masquerading as a field in front of it. A while back, it had been converted into three flats. The Dunns occupied all of them, and Spence had taken a liking to the middle flat.

'How are you doing?' Clarke asked, warmly greeting Spence.

'I'm good,' Spence replied. Clarke's eyebrow rose.

'Wanna try that again?'

Spence smirked.

'Woman trouble. Nothing I can't handle.'

Clarke laughed, taking a seat on a squashy brown sofa near Spence.

'Whatever it is, just say you're sorry and move on,' he said.

Spence glanced at him. 'I don't think it'll be that easy.'

'Depends how badly you want to make up.' Clarke shrugged. 'Pride gets in the way, but apologising is often the best way, youngster.'

'I'll keep that in mind,' said Spence. He meant it, too.

'Good. Keep your head up. Our people dropped three boxes on Carlton. He's got things on lock.'

'Carlton's a good one,' Spence agreed.

'He kept his head when bullets were popping off too. Could be one to keep an eye on.'

'That's why we gave him Little London to run, ' said Spence. 'I saw the potential a while back. Natty always liked him as well.'

'Natty's good at spotting talent. He's even better after his time away.'

Spence's mind flitted back to him and Natty in the club, *speaking about Cameron; wondering whether Natty should have promoted Cameron over Spence.* He recalled Natty saying he deserved it. Clarke was right. Natty was good at spotting talent. In Spence's case, he'd always pushed and supported him.

It was the same with Carlton.

'Why didn't Mitch fight to keep Natty?'

Clarke thought it over for a few seconds, before again shrugging.

'I don't know.'

'Give it your best guess then.'

'You're learning,' said Clarke with a grin. He cleared his throat. 'Mitch has survived all this time by knowing when and how to move. Natty . . . he's his dad's son. Strong-willed, hard to push and pull. At the time, maybe Mitch thought he didn't have it in him anymore.'

Spence almost brought up what Natty had done to Rudy and Elijah. He remembered seeing Natty a few days later, and how serious his friend had seemed. They'd never spoken in detail about that night. He wondered if they ever would.

'Natty is a force,' Clarke went on. 'He'll be our best if he carries on how he's going.'

Spence held his tongue for the second time in the last few minutes. Natty wasn't planning on hanging around. When his obligation was complete, he would return to his own life, whatever that entailed.

Clarke left a while later. Spence made a few calls, then left the spot, driving to his dad's house, wanting a change of scenery. His dad lived around the corner from Chapel Allerton Primary School. When Spence pulled up, he noticed his dad's car wasn't there. Calling him, he received no answer. He'd made up his mind to leave, just as his dad showed up.

'What are you doing here?' he asked, grinning at his son when he'd parked. Heading to the boot, he began unloading several shopping bags.

'Just thought I'd come and see how you were doing.' Spence grabbed the bags as his dad led the way to the house and unlocked the front door.

'I don't need you to carry the bags like I'm an invalid,' his dad grumbled, closing the door and following Spence to the kitchen.

'I noticed you only said that *after* I carried them inside,' said Spence, as he began to put the shopping away.

'Coincidence,' his dad replied, and they both laughed. As Spence put the shopping away, his dad made them both cups of coffee.

'You haven't said much about what's going on out there,' his dad said after a while. Spence had been waiting for the conversation, surprised it had taken so long.

'There's not much to say.'

'Isn't there? A bunch of bandits try to kill you, go after your spots, and you don't think there's much to say?'

'All part of the game, dad. You taught me that.'

As Spence had mused earlier, he had his role, and was content to play it.

Mitch had been quiet, which Spence assumed meant he was speaking to the others and dealing with Spence less. Whilst that irked him, it wasn't a hill to die on, and he'd focused on the task at hand.

'You need to get your name out there on this one, son. Could be a chance for you to get your hands dirty, and get a body,' his dad said.

Spence paused for a moment before responding. Very little his dad said shocked Spence these days. Between the lessons he taught his son and the stories Spence heard on the streets, it was clear how deep his dad went.

'I don't need to do that.' He shook his head.

'You might get left behind if you don't. Men are made in war, and you need to protect your position.' His dad took a long sip of his coffee. 'Remember, you're the one who decided to join up with the Dunns, against my wishes.'

'Who else was I meant to join?' Spence resisted the urge to roll his eyes. The conversation had been done to death.

'No one. You could have started your own crew and got people to join you. You're a natural leader; you shouldn't be answering to anyone.'

'Even you?' Spence liked to push his dad's buttons. It was the only way to stop him from overwhelming him.

His dad snorted.

'You don't listen to me, anyway. You'd be in a better position if you did.'

Spence drank his coffee, taking pleasure in making his dad wait.

'Let's talk about positions. I joined the crew, and I started working with my friends. You didn't like it. I kept doing it. Saved my money.

Made connections and kept plodding along. I ran the crew for a bit, stood tall during a crucial situation, then received a promotion, making me one of the top people in an organisation that has been around for well over twenty years. I'm still here, doing better than ever, but you're determined to look for the bad in what I'm doing.'

His dad shook his head. 'You can't be half in, half out. Being a gangster doesn't work like that.'

'I'm not a gangster. I'm a hustler,' Spence replied.

Finishing his drink, Spence's dad put his cup in the sink and filled it with water.

'I wish you'd listen to what I'm saying.'

'And I wish you'd stop trying to mould me. I don't need it. I appreciate your advice, dad. You set me on my way, but you have to let me be a man and make my own decisions.'

The pair locked eyes. After nearly a minute, his dad nodded.

'I will, Spence . . . I'll try, anyway. You're a good son, and a good man. I just want you to always be solid.'

'I will be, dad. I promise.' Spence clutched his cup, no longer thirsty. 'Do you know anything about Roman's lot? I know you still have connections in the streets.'

'They came along after my time, but they're to be taken seriously. They impressed Teflon's crew, and that's not easy to do.'

'I heard a little about that. They joined forces during that last war, right?' Spence settled in to listen to his dad.

'Yeah. They had a mutual problem, but it was just Teflon's lot being sneaky. They needed more forces, so they co-opted the little dudes to come and work for them.'

'What do you mean?'

'Lennox Thompson. You might not remember, but he was always a dangerous sod. Always had a look in his eyes that suggested he was up to something. He went at Delroy, and then he went at Teflon. I'm guessing you've heard the story before . . .'

'I've heard a little bit. I think there's a lot that goes unsaid about that era.'

'Makes sense. It wasn't easy for everyone. Delroy had to admit he wasn't the toughest guy out there anymore. His time had come, and he didn't want to accept that. What Teflon did with that Roman dude and Keith, Delroy tried to do with Teflon. Offered him a million quid to fight his war.'

'A million?' Spence's eyes bulged. He'd heard about the power and wealth of Teflon's organisation, but he didn't know they were worthy of such fees.

'Is that how Teflon got involved?'

Spence's dad shook his head.

'Nah. He turned him down. More money than sense, if you ask me. What kind of idiot turns down that sort of money?'

'I guess someone who either has enough money, or cares about other things more,' replied Spence sagely.

'No such thing,' his dad scoffed. 'Whoever says money isn't everything, obviously has never had any. Money makes the world go round.'

'Let's get back to Roman. What would you suggest?'

'If you're actually going to listen to me, you need to figure out how to make yourself indispensable. Get your hands dirty and show them you're a force to be reckoned with.'

'You really think that's important?'

'I do. I want you to be the best at whatever you choose to do, and this is your moment. If you're in the game, and you're lucky . . . you get that one shot where you need to step up or step off. This is your moment. They went after you, and you can't let them think that's a smart option. You'll be watching your back the whole time if you do.'

Spence mulled over what his dad had said, and couldn't deny there was some truth. Keith had come for him. He'd essentially toyed with Spence. If he'd known he was in the spot, he could have come for him directly, or taken him out when he left. It was possible he and Roman hadn't seen Spence as an actual threat. He wondered if they would have gone after Natty if he had been there.

Spence had never considered having to kill. When he'd pulled a gun at Cameron's house the night he'd betrayed them, he had been willing to use it, but had been relieved that he hadn't had to. He wondered what it would be like to take a life, and how Natty felt about it. Despite knowing what Natty had done that night, and who he had taken out, Spence had never spoken to him about it. He filed the thought away for future consideration.

'I can see you thinking yourself into a coma, son. You don't need to. Don't bother overthinking this stuff. You think too much; that's your problem.'

'Somebody needs to,' said Spence. 'My team relies on me for it. Someone has to watch over things while everyone else charges in. Can I ask you something?' He said to his dad.

'I'm listening.'

'Why didn't you back Delroy during the Lennox Thompson situation? I'm guessing he reached out to you.'

His dad looked down, then glanced at his son, who was shocked by the hurt in his eyes.

'I didn't have anything to offer him. You're right. He reached out, but I was a broken-down old man, and I didn't have it in me to go after those younger men. They were ruthless and out for blood. What they did to Delroy's family . . .' The sadness in his eyes was palpable. 'That goes against the rules, and we *did* have rules, son. They went too far, and I didn't know how I could go against that sort of aggression. Not anymore.'

Spence could see how hard it was for his dad to talk about it. There was clearly a lot his dad regretted, and Spence wondered whether that shaped the advice he was giving him. There were times when he felt his dad was trying to live through him, but now he wondered if he was trying to stop him from making the same mistakes that he had, and from accruing the same regrets that clearly still plagued him.

The problem was that Spence and his dad were not the same. In fact, their approaches to the game were polar opposites; brain vs brawn. Spence wondered if his dad thought he just needed to toughen up.

Pushing this to one side, Spence smiled across at his dad.

'Let's have a drink, dad. We can eat something before I go, if you're hungry.'

ROMAN SIPPED A DRINK, staring out the window into the darkness, deep in thought.

The crew had suffered numerous recent setbacks, and the cost was stacking up.

It was an uncomfortable feeling not being in control, and one he wasn't used to.

Before they aligned with Teflon, their operation was small-scale, but expertly run. With Keith's ferocity and Roman's sharpness, they kept their people on point and things running smoothly.

Lately, Roman had begun wondering whether Keith had lost his touch. The ferocity was still there, but there was no sense to it. It was like a boiling pot, liable to spill over at any point. He struggled to see his friend as the asset he once was, which posed a significant problem. Between strategising how to beat the Dunns and placating those closest to him who wanted blood, he was spreading himself too thin.

Massaging his temples, he blew out a breath.

Chapeltown wasn't just his desire; Roman believed it was his right. When Teflon left the streets behind, Roman and Keith seemed like natural successors. They were young, hungry, experienced and ready to make their move. When fate conspired against them, and they were arrested, their claim to the streets was seemingly cast in doubt. But not in Roman's mind. As far as he was concerned, Chapeltown belonged to him and Keith.

He wished the Dunns had taken their offer and moved out, but he understood why they didn't. In the streets, maintaining pride was as important as making money. In their position, he would have done the same.

The main problem was that they weren't bargaining from a position of strength. Keith had surrendered the element of surprise, and it had left them on the back foot. Since their meeting, multiple spots had been robbed. The stolen drugs gouged mercilessly into their profits, and morale was rapidly disintegrating. Roman wasn't sure where the Dunns procured their information from, but it was impressive. There seemed to be very few spots unknown to them, and, given their limited firepower, it left them uncomfortably exposed.

Roman reached into his pocket, retrieving a slip of paper that he unfolded and flattened on the coffee table. Reaching into his other pocket, he pulled out a pen, clicking it and exposing the ballpoint. On the paper were various addresses and dates. Roman moved his pen over them as he read, shaking his head as he read *Spencer Mount x2.*

Arriving at the bottom of the list, he added three more addresses.

Leopold Street
Hamilton Terrace
Hillcrest Avenue

After a moment, Roman circled two of them, clicking the pen closed, refolding the paper and placing it back in his pocket. Grabbing his drink, he drained it in one, analysing the empty glass with a sinister smile. Putting the glass on the table and picking up his phone, he dialled a number and called it.

'We need to talk,' he said, when the person answered.

CHAPTER FOURTEEN

DOLJA SHUFFLED DOWNSTAIRS, yawning and immediately going to make coffee. He, Keith and several others had spent multiple nights driving around, meeting different people, looking for any sign of important members of the Dunn clique. Keith's manic energy puzzled Dolja. He wondered if Keith and Roman coming back into the fold was a good thing.

The money was better, but they were under a spotlight, and Dolja was moving around with guards like he was the president, paranoid he would be attacked. It seemed like Keith and Roman had different agendas for the most part, which worried him. In doing as Keith said, he feared he was doing the opposite of what Roman would want.

Dolja's mind drifted to other things as he prepared his coffee, ignoring the constant ringing of his phone. He thought about the woman he'd met at the party a while back, before Keith had taken him away. He hadn't planned to go out that night but had been persuaded. The same old faces had surrounded him, plus a few groupies trying to get him to take them home, and then he had seen her.

Looks-wise, she'd outshone everyone. It was more than just attraction, though. There was something about the girl that suggested she was worth his time. She carried herself a certain way, and Dolja dug it.

When he'd initially spoken to her, she'd distinguished herself, able to banter and keep him on the back foot. If she was aware of his status, she didn't care. She spoke to him like a normal person, and while that prickled his ego, part of him liked it.

They'd exchanged texts and spoken a few times since, but she kept playing hard to get when he suggested a meeting.

Determined to see her, he took out his phone and called her.

'Hello there,' she said, her voice as soulful as ever. Dolja found himself smiling widely.

'I'm glad you picked up for me. What are you saying?'

'Just enjoying the morning. How about you?'

'Me too. When can I see you? I've had loads of stuff to handle, but we still have some talking to do.'

'Oh, you think so, do you?'

Dolja closed his eyes and tilted his head back, smiling to himself. Goosebumps rose on his arms as her voice drifted into his ears and surged through his veins. She knew what she was doing, and it only made him more determined to have her.

'We do. Last time we spoke, you said you were out with your girls. Did you meet any guys?' Dolja didn't care, but he wanted to ensure she wasn't seeing anyone.

'Me and my friends had a few drinks, but no . . . I didn't meet any guys,' she said.

'Good, that's cool. But let's get back to the point. When can I see you? I want it to be just the two of us.'

She paused, and he felt his stomach plummet.

'I don't know you that well. How do I know I'll be safe one-on-one?'

'Ask around about *Dolja*, babe. People will tell you I'm official. Nothing is gonna happen to you around me, and I'm not gonna hurt you. I promise.'

Again, she paused, but her voice seemed less anxious when she spoke.

'If I do say yes — and I'm not saying I will — then what do you have in mind?'

'Whatever you like. We can do dinner, drinks, or we can chill. I don't mind, as long as I get to see you. I think there's more we can discover about each other,' he said smoothly.

'Maybe. I'll message you later, and we'll see. Enjoy the rest of your day, Dolja . . . make sure you think about me.' Blowing him a kiss, she was gone.

Dolja stared at the phone, smirking. She was playing hard to get, but he didn't mind. He was sure she was worth it. It crossed his mind that he still didn't know her name, but that was part of the appeal. There were layers to the mystery girl, and he was determined to peel back each of them, sure the reward would be worth it.

———

LISA GRINNED as she hung up on Dolja. She had him wide open, and her teasing demeanour had driven him crazy. She'd enjoyed keeping him on the string, flirting and then pulling away. Lisa had used his eagerness against him, pretending to be uneasy about meeting up with him, which only made him more determined.

The next step would be crucial, and she was fully aware of that fact. If she moved incorrectly, everything would explode. She was a natural when it came to this step, though. She had done it many times before, most recently with Warren.

Lisa would need to play it totally differently with Dolja, but that was fine. This was what she did, and she did it better than anyone else.

Sliding from the table, she grabbed her secure phone and called Clarke.

'I think we're on for a meeting,' she said.

'Are you sure?'

'He's open, but I won't push too hard. I'll let him do all of the work.'

'Good. I trust your judgement, so do whatever you need to make it happen.'

'I will,' she replied. 'Is there anything new that I need to know about?'

'We're handling everything else.'

'Does *we* include Natty?'

Lisa almost rolled her eyes when Clarke chortled.

'I knew you were sweet on him.'

'I don't get sweet on anyone. I was just asking a question.'

'Don't get huffy with me. I know how delicate you are deep down, Lis. I already told you. Be careful. Mitch has plans for his nephew. He won't want you getting in the way.'

'I don't plan to, but at the same time, Mitch has no say in my personal life. I work for him, and that's where his influence over me stops.'

'You're not stupid enough to believe that, Lis,' said Clarke. 'Don't get hurt going after something you can't have.'

'Maybe I can't, but I wouldn't want to hurt anyone who got in my way either,' she replied.

Clarke laughed. 'Keep me posted on your situation. Let me know if you need anything.'

With that, he was gone. Lisa shook her head, smiling. Despite his demeanour, she knew Clarke cared about her, and she felt the same way.

She wondered about the plans Mitch had for Natty, and how Natty would feel about them, wondering if it was worth a conversation.

———

NATTY PULLED his car to a stop, taking a gun from his stash spot. It was a risky move, but he didn't want to be caught unawares. Clarke knew where he was, and had people ready to intervene if it got too bad, but Natty didn't think it would. Not yet, anyway.

He was pleased with how things were going at the moment. He and Clarke had run roughshod over Roman's forces, snatching drugs and product, smacking around runners and soldiers alike, with little resistance.

Marie had finally contacted him, saying Manson had agreed to speak with him. He didn't know what had taken her so long, nor did he ask. With everything that had transpired since, it hadn't seemed as important.

The meeting spot was arranged, and Natty had someone watching the site for hours, ensuring he wasn't walking into an ambush.

Manson waited in the middle of *The Wreck*. Natty and Jaden often played football here, and he'd wondered if it was Manson's way of sending him a message.

Nearby, several men were working out, some doing press-ups on the grass, while others performed pull-ups, struggling to get higher. In the nearby park, kids played on the swings in the playground, laughing and joking. It made Natty think of Jaden, and he tensed. He missed him more than he had expected.

In no time at all, Lorraine and Jaden had become the central part of his world, and it seemed unnatural not to be around them. He knew he still had to talk to Lorraine, but he couldn't help how he felt. Natty didn't want to speak to Lorraine until he had the right words.

He'd settled for the occasional text message, saying he needed more time.

Manson didn't move, despite knowing Natty had seen him. He cut an impressive figure, dressed all in black. His closely cropped hair had a smattering of grey throughout, his age beginning to show. Manson was an old-school legend. He and his crime partner, Maka, were well respected and had links to the old regime. Things had moved on since then, but he retained his formidable presence. Chapeltown had seen its fair share of tough guys, and Manson was most definitely cut from that same cloth.

He gave Natty a sharp nod, and as Natty came closer, the pair touched fists and started walking.

The wreck had an attached football pitch, and a dusty, concrete perimeter that many locals used as a walking path. They walked along it, keeping up appearances in case anyone suspect was watching.

Manson's face was closed, and Natty knew he'd have to talk first.

'How long have you been out?'

'A year,' Manson replied in his gravelly voice.

Natty raised his eyebrows.

'A whole year, huh . . . you must have done your best to stay low. We never realised.'

'We're not friends, Deeds. Why did you want to meet me?'

'I think you know why,' replied Natty. 'I'll play along, though.

What does Maka think about everything that's happening?'

Manson's face hardened for a moment. Natty happened to be glancing at him and caught it.

'Maka is chilling. He's doing his own thing.'

'Makes sense,' replied Natty. 'I'm guessing he built a nice life while you were locked down for years.'

'What the fuck are you getting at?' snapped Manson.

'It doesn't matter,' said Natty. 'Roman and Keith. They're your people too, right?'

'What about them?'

'They're out here starting shit, as you probably already know. Where do you stand in it.'

'It's nothing to do with me. Why did you reach out to Marie?'

'I knew she could get a message to you.'

Manson stopped, glaring at Natty.

'How do you know her?'

It was an intense look; one Natty had no doubt Manson could back up. Even if he hadn't been training with Clarke, Natty still wouldn't have been worried. Manson had been a big deal in his day, but Natty was no slouch, and he knew how to fight.

After all, Raider had been bigger than Manson.

'You know exactly how I know her.'

Manson's glare deepened.

'What the fuck do you want from me?'

'I want you to speak to your people. Money's the name of our game. I tried talking to Roman and Keith, but they made a bullshit offer. Everything that happened after, is down to them. Some of their boxes went missing . . . we're keeping them as restitution, but we can end it there, and they can take their business to another city with no hard feelings.'

Manson's face remained blank.

'I'm not involved. I don't know shit about shit.'

Natty shot him a sceptical look.

'Pass it on. If you happen to run into either of them on your travels. On that note, I'm gonna dip. Give Marie my love.' Natty paused, smirking. 'Actually, I can do that myself.'

With that, Natty left Manson, feeling his eyes burning into him.

He wondered if Manson was telling the truth, but quickly shook it off, doubting Manson would have met him if he wasn't aware of the conflict.

Starting the engine, Natty put the thoughts out of his mind. He had someone else he wanted to see.

———

KEITH GLARED at Wonder as one of his men showed him into the room. The man nodded at Keith, signalling that Wonder had been searched. Keith motioned for him to sit.

'What's going on? We haven't heard from you.'

'I've been busy,' Wonder replied. Keith frowned, not liking Wonder's tone.

'Busy? Busy ain't an excuse.'

'Why am I here? Where's Roman?' Wonder asked.

Keith's nostrils flared as he slid to his feet.

'Are you serious right now? Who the fuck are you talking to?'

Wonder back-pedalled, before realising his way out was blocked by Keith's people. Audibly swallowing, his eyes widened.

'Me and Roman are cool, I—'

Keith backhanded Wonder, the sound ricocheting around the room. Wonder staggered backwards, dazed.

'I don't care how cool you think you are with Roman. You're nothing, and he's not gonna lift a finger to save you from me.' Keith gripped Wonder by the scruff of his jacket, pulling him close. 'If it's not us, I promise your own people will finish you. I'll see to that; I'll spread the word about you telling tales myself, you little bitch.' He shoved Wonder into the nearby wall.

'I'm sorry,' Wonder moaned, all the fight leaving him.

'You're sorry, alright.' Keith cocked back his fist, just as the door opened, and Roman walked in. Instantly taking in the scene, he shook his head.

'What are you up to now?' He asked Keith, paying no attention to Wonder.

'This little prick ran his mouth.'

'Let him go.'

Snorting, Keith released Wonder, who remained where he was.

'What do you have for us then?' Roman asked.

'I . . . nothing. No one's saying anything around me,' Wonder mumbled, his face still smarting.

'What use are you then?' Roman asked, his eyes narrowing. 'You're meant to be helping us, and you haven't done anything.'

'I'm trying, I—'

'Not good enough,' said Roman. 'Keith, we can use Wonder to set up Spence. Get him out in public, then you can finish him.' He turned to Wonder. 'You do that . . . we'll know you're really down with us. If you don't . . . Keith will deal with you.'

In the background, Keith evilly grinned, folding his arms. Wonder blanched, his lip trembling.

'How the hell am I supposed to do that?' He asked. Roman shrugged.

'How you do it is up to you. Let us know, so we can have people in place.'

WONDER SAT IN HIS CAR, trembling after his meeting with Roman. There was no denying he was in an unwinnable situation. Wonder had stood with Elijah and Rudy, fully on board with their plan to take out Mitch Dunn.

Natty ruined it. He'd cost Wonder everything.

Wonder had agreed to work for the Dunns, allowed to keep earning, giving up most of the money his crew earned. Even being left to his own devices hadn't quashed his resentment. When Roman and his team had sent shots at the Dunns, Wonder had been giddy, and when Roman reached out, he'd signed up.

The aftermath stalled him. He wasn't sure they could win, and Natty and the crew seemed to be carving through them at an alarming rate. It was the thought of Natty Deeds that infuriated Wonder the most. His reputation had gone through the roof. He wasn't even in the game anymore, but people still bent over backwards to accommodate and show him love. It made Wonder sick.

None of that mattered anymore. Wonder had been given a task, and he didn't have a choice about carrying it out. He had to survive, no matter what. He cursed himself for not blowing the whistle when Roman had reached out to him.

Before he started his engine, he called a number.

'Yes?' Spence answered in his usual clipped tones. Not that Wonder minded. Out of the Dunn crew, he was probably the coolest. He'd always had that demeanour, and he treated Wonder fairly. Wonder regretted that Rudy had co-opted Cameron instead of him last year. Had Spence been on their team, Wonder had no doubt their side would have won.

'I need to get with you,' said Roman, trying to keep his voice level.

'About what?'

'It's about what's going on with Roman and them. I've got some news, and this is a face-to-face thing, trust me.'

For a moment, Spence didn't speak. Wonder's heart hammered against his chest. If this didn't work, he didn't know what he would do.

'When?'

Wonder felt the relief surge through his body. Spence trusted him, and he would use it to his advantage.

'As soon as we can. I don't want shit to go left. You know how quickly things move around here.'

'Okay. I'm in the middle of something now, but how about tomorrow, around midday?'

'You can't do any sooner?' Wonder pressed, instantly regretting it. He didn't want to spook Spence.

'I wish I could, but it's crazy right now. Tomorrow is the earliest. Will that work?'

'Yeah, bro. Meet me at the bottom of Francis Street, just off Frankland Avenue.'

'Got it—tomorrow at 12. I'll be there,' Spence replied. He hung up.

Beaming, Wonder immediately called Roman to give him the good news.

CHAPTER FIFTEEN

LORRAINE WAS HAVING breakfast with Jaden, unable to stop staring at her phone. It had been over four weeks since she had seen Natty. She missed him, feeling sick with guilt over what had happened. She had let things get out of control when they were talking, but she hadn't meant what she said, at least not in that way.

Lorraine had known both Natty and Raider for a long time, and had always felt like there were similarities between the pair. They were both big men with fearsome reputations, and they did illegal things in Chapeltown.

At the same time, there were a lot of differences. Natty had a kind side that Raider didn't possess, and he seemed to have rid himself of the selfishness she had once found off-putting. She understood why he was mad at her, but she hoped he didn't stay away for too long.

Lorraine's dad had split from her mum when she was little, staying away for a long time. Her mum fought tooth and nail for him to stay away, and the rare times he had got in touch, he had been rebuffed.

Lorraine didn't want that for Jaden. She was determined he would have more of a choice than she did.

'Mummy?'

'Yes, baby?' She replied, turning to her son, smiling at the jam all over his face.

'Where's Natty? I miss him?'

Lorraine's stomach plummeted, and she had to fight to put a smile on her face.

'Natty's been busy, baby. That's why he hasn't been around.'

'Oh.' When she saw Jaden's face fall, she inwardly cursed Natty, along with herself. She had never wanted to see such a look on her son's face, but it happened far too often, usually when Raider had broken a promise.

Ironically, Natty was now causing that same disappointment in him.

'I'm sure he'll be back to spend time with us soon. In the meantime, I want to talk to you about something, so hurry up and eat your breakfast.'

Jaden nodded and returned to his toast. When he'd finished and drank his orange juice, Lorraine spoke to him.

'Your dad has been in touch, and he wants to see you.'

Jaden frowned, a thoughtful look on his face.

'I haven't spoken to him in ages. Where has he been?'

'He . . . had an accident,' said Lorraine, quickly thinking of a story. 'He was in the hospital, because he needed to get better.'

'Just like you went to the hospital when you hurt yourself that time?'

'That's right, baby,' she said, unhappy about lying to her son.

Jaden didn't say anything for a moment. He stared into space, and Lorraine waited, part of her hoping he didn't want to see his dad.

'I want to see him, mummy. Can I?'

Sadly, Lorraine nodded.

'I'll send him a message, and we can arrange something. Now, you need to hurry and get ready for school. Straight in the shower, okay?'

'Yes, mummy.' Jaden bounded from his seat and hurried upstairs. Lorraine sighed. This wasn't going to make things easier, but it was the right decision, and her son had made it. Rosie wouldn't be happy, nor would her family, and it wouldn't make things any easier with Natty, but it was still the right thing to do.

———

SPENCE SAT IN A CAR, down the road from the spot Wonder had asked him to meet. He'd been there for half an hour. The people he'd sent to scout the area had reported seeing a car full of people they didn't recognise, along with a white van that wasn't normally in the area. Spence had positioned himself behind the men, and hadn't left his car.

He'd gone with his instincts, contacting Clarke, ensuring they had people in place. They'd been watching the roads in shifts ever since. Spence didn't trust Wonder, but he didn't see the man's angle. He was earning with the Dunns, likely just as much as he'd earned from his association with Elijah.

'It's almost time,' his driver said. Nodding, Spence took out his phone and dialled Wonder.

'Hey bro,' he said, making his voice sound anxious. 'I'm here. Where are you?'

'I'm just coming outside,' said Wonder. 'What car are you in?'

'I'm in a grey Yaris,' said Spence, looking at a nearby car.

'Say nothing. I'll be there in a sec.'

Minutes later, the van in front of Spence accelerated, blocking off part of the street. At the same time, the car of shooters that Spence's men had seen earlier ran out and began spraying the Yaris.

Spence and his men kept their heads down, waiting for the carnage to end. He dialled a number on his phone and allowed it to ring once before ending the call. Suddenly, his men popped up, firing on the shooters, hitting one before the others fled. The van that had served as a blocker was shot at too, and the driver sped away in a panic, side-swiping several parked cars.

Spence didn't hang around, signalling his own driver to leave the spot. They had another car parked nearby, so he wasn't concerned about potential witnesses seeing the license plate.

———

WONDER HASTILY FLUNG clothes into a travel bag. News of the hit going wrong had reached him, and he knew Roman and Keith would be after him. There was a chance Spence and Natty would be too.

Luckily, Wonder had been cautious about where he lay his head, and made sure no one in the crew knew, having moved a month ago. He had a few grand he could get hold of. That would be enough to tide him over when he landed in another spot, especially if he sold his jewellery too.

He couldn't believe the hit had gone wrong. Spence had said he was in place, sounding like his usual cautious self. Wonder hadn't seen anything amiss, but ultimately, one of Roman's lot was dead, and the streets were buzzing about the situation. Everyone knew the dead man was affiliated with Roman's camp, and that would lead to more problems. Wonder was a problem they would need to silence, so he would need to stay low-key for a while. He planned to stay in Manchester, before looking for somewhere permanent.

Once he'd finished packing his things, he hurried to the door, wrenching it open and locking it behind him. He'd taken all the necessities, but wished he could have taken more.

Wonder approached his car, frantically scrambling around his pockets for his keys. His hand shook as he pulled them out of his pocket and thumbed at the button to unlock the car.

Reaching for the door handle, he dropped his keys, stooping down to pick them up. By the time he returned to his feet, the colour had drained from his face. Before he could react, the knife slid beneath his ribs, and was twisted. Wonder opened his mouth to scream, but nothing but a gurgle came out, blood seeping from both his mouth and the wound. He slid to the floor, shaking, his eyes wide as he went into shock.

A man stood over him, a grim expression on his face. Again, Wonder tried speaking, but more blood came out. His last plea as he died was one for more time, something that would not be granted.

Roman looked down at Wonder, watching him bleed out. He couldn't believe the man had been foolish enough to return to his spot. He'd waited for him, and when he saw Wonder hurry inside, he allowed him to leave, before finishing the job.

Wonder had outlived his usefulness. If his own team didn't trust him, there was nothing more he could offer them. He was useless; a loose end that needed tying up. Roman didn't enjoy wet work, but it was sometimes necessary. At this stage, leaving it up to Keith didn't feel like an option he had. He figured it would get messy and that the cleanup would be complicated. It was far better he did the job himself.

Once he was sure Wonder was dead, Roman turned and walked the way he'd come from, seeing no need to hurry. People who did those things were more likely to be caught. Wonder had been taken care of, but he had some work to do to eliminate the Dunns. Taking out Wonder was barely a retaliation. If anything, he'd done them a favour, as they would have killed Wonder once they'd found he was dirty.

———

NATTY WAS EATING dinner at a Caribbean restaurant in the Hood. It was a fairly cramped location, with several tables near the entrance, and had a red and green theme, with a mural on the main wall depicting numerous black leaders. In the background, Natty heard cooks talking loudly as they worked, the pungent smell of food lingering in the air.

Lost in thought, the vibration of his phone startled him. Wiping his mouth, he answered.

'What's happening?'

'Did you hear about Wonder?' It was Spence.

'Yeah. It's all over the place,' replied Natty. 'Was that us?'

'No. It was going to be, though. He was working for the other side.'

Natty scratched his bottom lip.

'Doesn't surprise me. I never did like him. They probably finished the job then. If they couldn't use him to spy, obviously they had no use,' he said.

'I know. I had a feeling he was up to something,' said Spence. 'He tried setting me up, but we flipped it. Be careful when you're moving. Don't let them catch you slipping.'

'Got you,' said Natty. 'We'll chat later, and plan the next move face to face. Business aside, have you sorted that shit with Rosie yet? You said she was switching on you.'

Spence sighed, and Natty had his answer. Spence had mentioned that Rosie was annoyed due to Natty falling out with Lorraine.

'We're up and down. Don't worry about it, though. It's not your problem, fam. Have you spoken with Lorraine yet?'

'No,' admitted Natty, frowning.

'Maybe you should. You both have more things you need to say to one another. If that ends badly, or you go your separate ways after that, then fine, but you should still talk.'

Natty listened to Spence, smiling at the cook, as she came over to clear away his plate. He signalled for her to bring him a can of Rio, and to put it on his tab.

'Okay.'

'Sooner the better, bro. Why don't you speak to her tonight?' Spence asked.

'Can't tonight,' Natty bluntly replied.

'Why not?'

'I'm following a lead. Nothing confirmed yet, but it seems legit. I'll speak to her, though, bro, I promise.'

'Bet. I'll check you later, bro.'

Spence hung up. Natty rubbed his forehead, more nervous about speaking to Lorraine than he was about dealing with street politics. However, Spence was right in what he was saying, and Natty knew it. Avoiding Lorraine forever would solve nothing. He needed to be mature about the situation and talk to her.

Standing, Natty wiped some crumbs from his clothes, then approached the counter, handing the cook a twenty-pound note and smiling.

'Keep the change,' he told her.

'You're too generous, Nathaniel, child,' the old woman said, beaming at him.

'Guess that's why they call me *Deeds*,' he said, with a wink, before leaving. Outside, his eyes flitted in all directions as he headed for his car. It would be brazen for a shootout to take place on Chapeltown Road, but it wouldn't be the first time. In fact, Natty recalled, a man had been shot near where he stood. It had taken place the day Trinidad's barber shop had gone up in flames. The man had been shot at point-blank range, dying soon after.

Shaking away those thoughts, Natty climbed into his car and drove away. There was a lot to do.

––––––

'WE KNOW what we're doing here, right?'

Everyone nodded at Keith's words. He'd gathered a group of his best soldiers for this mission. Wonder had failed to set up Spence, meaning their team had lost face again on the streets. Now, they would give the Dunns a taste of their own medicine.

Keith and the three-man crew jumped out of the car, guns hidden by the darkness. The spot they were at was on Grange View in the heart of the Hood. They'd watched it for a few days, and it was perfect for their needs.

Keith hung back as one of his goons approached the door, kicking it in as they flooded inside. They heard yells and shouts as they bounded from room to room, smacking up the men they found there, and restraining them on the ground.

Keith ran into the kitchen, dodging a jerky knife thrust, disarming the youngster who'd tried to stab him, then flinging him to the ground. The youngster tried to crawl to the knife, but Keith brought his foot down hard on the youngster's hand, beaming as the kid screamed out in pain. Lifting his foot again, Keith brought it down once more on the youngster's back, then dragged him to his feet by his hair. Flinging him across the room, he watched with relish as the youth crashed against an array of cupboards at the back of the room. They held against his weight, but shuddered.

Keith stalked toward the boy.

'You're a brave little shit,' he muttered.

'Please, man, I'm sorry . . . I'm just a kid,' the youth gasped, but Keith shook his head.

'You're old enough to be in the streets. That means you're old enough to deal with the consequences.' He punched the kid in the stomach, smiling as he went to his knees, retching. 'Get up.' He dragged the kid into the main room, where five others had been secured, their hands tied behind their backs.

Keith stood on the sofa so they could see him, giving them a sinister grin. He hadn't bothered with a mask, and was fine with them seeing his face.

'Where's the stash?'

No one spoke.

'I'm gonna start making examples of people if you don't tell me,' he warned. 'Your boy there knows how I get down. He tried shanking me in the kitchen.' Keith's eyes went to the boy in question, and he whimpered where he lay. Keith pulled his gun and shot the same boy in the leg. He screamed in pain, and everyone else flinched, startled by the sound of the gunshot, and the coldness of the act.

'Anyone wanna speak yet? I didn't come here intending to kill, but you best believe I will if I don't get what I want.'

Finally, one of the men spoke up, after Keith aimed his gun at him.

'I'll show you where it is.'

Keith signalled for one of his men to go, and he returned downstairs minutes later with two hold-alls.

'You lot have been busy,' said Keith. 'Guess you can afford to be after all the product your people stole from us. We're gonna go, and we're gonna leave you all alive, but make sure you tell them exactly what happened here.' Signalling to his men, they all began shooting, the men screaming as they were each shot in the left leg.

Laughing, Keith led the team out, leaving the unfortunate crew members to bleed. Jumping in the car, they sped away, leaving a buzzing street in their wake.

———

THE NEXT DAY, Roman sat in a safe house, lighting a spliff and putting it to his lips. Keith was alongside him, along with a third man, who leant against the wall, arms folded as he surveyed the pair.

'Is there any response to your attack yet?' Roman asked Keith. Keith shrugged.

'I haven't heard anything. Doesn't matter, anyway. They have to take it on the chin,' he said.

Roman nodded. It was the best he was getting out of Keith for now. His eyes flitted to the other man.

'Natty reached out to you since?' Roman asked.

Manson shook his head, his eyes hard.

'Not since he said he's keeping the boxes they took. And that bit about you lot leaving town. Like I said, he was feeling me out, but I doubt he'll get in touch again.'

'Fuck him. We shouldn't even be entertaining him. Besides, we're getting back at them now. Look at what we took from their spot the other day. That will sting,' said Keith, taking the joint from Roman, inhaling, then exhaling, closing his eyes.

'Maybe we need to switch up and go after him,' Manson suggested.

'Spence is the soft one. We'll get him eventually,' said Keith.

'Manson might be right,' said Roman. 'We've gone at Spence twice and failed. They might expect a third attempt, so going at Natty could be the smart play.'

Keith grinned.

'Good. Let me get at him then. I still owe him for trying to mug me off at that meeting.'

Roman shook his head.

'Hold fire for now.'

'Again?' Keith exploded to his feet, glaring down at Roman. 'What the fuck is wrong with you? Why are we still pussyfooting around?'

'Relax. I need you to trust me on this,' Roman replied, unfazed. 'Going gun for gun isn't the first option. It's the last. I have a plan to get at them. When everything unfolds, you'll see.'

THAT NIGHT, Natty was posted near another of Roman's drug spots. He'd learned of this one through an informant desperate to curry favour with the Dunns. He hoped that the time since the last robbery would have made them paranoid, but would take his time regardless.

He'd heard about Keith and the others attacking one of their teams. Hopefully, his quick response would deter them from striking again.

Safe from his vantage point, Natty watched as a man left the spot, carrying a bag. He had a split-second to decide what to do. Going with his instincts, he followed him, starting his engine as the man climbed into a black Nissan Qashqai.

Natty trailed the driver, keeping his distance, reminded of the time he'd followed Spence's ex when he'd suspected her of cheating. The thought made him shake his head as he focused. Soon, the driver turned onto a street in Scott Hall. As Natty parked nearby, he called Clarke, not taking his eyes from the driver, watching them walk into a house.

'What's going on?' Clarke asked.

'I'm at a spot on Scott Hall Avenue,' said Natty, giving him the address. 'Tailed a package. I'm gonna pick it up.'

'You sure you should be doing that alone?' Clarke replied.

'I'll be fine. If you don't hear from me. You know where to start.'

'Got it,' said Clarke, before hanging up. Natty smiled to himself, pleased with Clarke's trust. Climbing from the car, he steadily headed to the house, walking right in. Immediately, he heard loud voices, and headed in their direction, his gun out. Opening the door, he pointed the gun, freezing the three men present. The man he'd trailed was stood over a table, still holding the duffle bag he'd carried earlier. He appeared to be the oldest in the room, with a fleshy face, thinning hair, and a patchy beard. Two younger men were sat on a faded green sofa, mouths wide open at the sight of Natty.

'Drop the bag,' Natty said to the older man. He hesitated, and Natty tightened his finger around the gun. 'Trust me . . . don't make me ask again.'

Cursing under his breath, the man dropped the package.

'Kick it over here toward me.' Natty stepped into the room, keeping his back to the wall, preventing any potential ambush. Clarke had taught him well about positioning, and the correct ways to enter a spot.

Once the courier had complied, Natty knelt to pick up the bag, not taking his eyes off the trio. He straightened, still studying them.

'When you have to explain to your bosses what happened . . . remind them that they wanted it this way,' he said, before shooting a cocky smile and leaving.

CHAPTER SIXTEEN

NATTY'S PHONE woke him up in the early hours of the morning. After dropping off the drugs he'd taken, he'd pottered around the house for a while, before going to bed. Grumbling, he sleepily groped around for his phone.

' . . . Yeah?'

'Nat, it's me,' said Spence, his voice panicked. 'I'm outside. I need you to let me in.'

Natty had already sat up once he heard Spence's tone. Spence wasn't one for hysteria. If he sounded upset, it meant something significant had happened. Sliding from bed, Natty shrugged into a rumpled grey t-shirt and padded down the stairs. Spence had a serious look on his face, his posture loose. Natty let him in, locking the door behind them.

'What's happened?' He asked, when they'd sat down.

'We got stung,' said Spence. 'Three of our cooks are dead. A fourth is in hospital.'

'What? How did that happen?' Natty asked, jerking his head back.

'They sampled some dodgy drugs. It's not the normal way they do it. They'll test them before they cut and weigh them, but they never dip into the stash. They did, though . . . and it fucked them.'

'Fuck.' Natty's mouth fell open. With mounting horror, he realised they'd sampled the drugs that he'd dropped off on them.

'I can't believe it,' he continued. 'They fucked us. Roman and them. They knew what we'd do.'

Spence rubbed his eyes. 'I'm not one of the CSI guys, but there was enough fentanyl in those drugs to wipe out a footy team. I don't know if they wanted to take out the testers, or if they thought we'd just punt the gear to our customers, but they got us.'

Neither man spoke for a moment, weighing up the ramifications.

'It's probably best you speak to my unc, and let him know what's happened.'

Spence nodded. 'I will, bro. We should pay out the families too. Give them money for funeral costs . . . whatever else they need. I know at least one of them has a kid.'

Natty rubbed the back of his neck, already rethinking his future strategy. Hitting the stash spots held a more considerable risk now. It was an audacious move by Roman, and one he hadn't seen coming.

'Make sure we're testing any drugs we get too. Thoroughly.'

Grimly, Spence agreed.

———

HOURS LATER, Roman and Keith left a gym in Harehills, flanked by a guard. Roman was in good spirits. Word had reached him about a flurry of overdoses on the Dunn's side. His risk had paid off. Spiking the drugs had been a calculated move that could have backfired, but they had taken out several testers, and likely rattled their opposition.

'It was a good move,' Keith said as they climbed into their ride. 'I'm more of a straight-up hitter, but you got them good.'

'It doesn't end there,' said Roman. 'The next step is to put the word out about their quality. It won't ruin them, but hopefully, it'll have an effect on their customers.'

'I'll deal with that,' Keith offered. 'I'll speak to Dolja. He'll get the word out quickly.'

'Sounds good,' said Roman, grinning. 'Let's go and get some food. I'm starving.'

MANSON TAPPED HIS FOOT, deep in thought as his driver pulled to a stop outside a house in Moor Allerton. He climbed from the car after telling the driver to wait. He headed up the drive and knocked on the door. As he waited, he surveyed the area. He liked the quiet neighbourhood; it was peaceful and inviting. A woman answered, giving him a polite smile. She was brown-skinned, with warm, dark eyes, slender and nicely dressed in a pair of jeans and a floral blouse.

'Hello? Can I help you?' She asked. Behind her, Manson heard the sounds of a child playing.

'I . . . was looking for an old friend. I heard he lived here, but I think I've got the wrong place. Sorry for bothering you.' He turned to walk away.

'You don't have the wrong place, bro.'

Manson turned, grinning when he saw his old crime partner smiling back at him. The pair shared a hug.

'Babe, this is Manson. I've told you about him. He's my oldest friend, and I haven't seen him in years.'

'Invite him in then,' the woman said.

Manson was taken on a quick tour of the house, his head whirring. He knew Maka would have moved on, but he wasn't expecting this. His friend was married, and had two young children. It was a jarring reminder for Manson of how different their lives were.

Since leaving prison, Manson had been in two minds about reaching out to Maka, but the current situation with the Dunns had him on edge. Bringing Maka into the fold had seemed like a good idea that would bolster their ranks.

Now, he wasn't sure.

'Come on, bro. Let's go and talk in the garden,' Maka said. Both men had beers, and Manson sipped his as they walked. Everything had changed. Maka seemed at peace. He wasn't tense, or looking all around to ensure they weren't being overheard. He was casually dressed in a t-shirt and tracksuit bottoms, with sliders on his feet. Manson wondered when he'd last held a weapon.

'How have you been, Manson?' Maka asked, after they'd stood in the garden for a few minutes. There was a child-sized football net at the back of the garden, various footballs, and a bike left on its side.

'I've kept my head down since I got out,' he said. 'I had to come and look for you, though; see what's what.'

'I'm glad you did. I wasn't sure when you were getting out, and you never mentioned anything in the letters.'

Manson didn't say anything. Maka continued.

'I'm sorry I stopped coming to see you. I didn't plan to. Life just happened, and everything started moving at a thousand miles per hour, with the wife, and the kids and everything.'

'It's cool, bro. I'm glad you're doing well. You keep up with things on the street?'

Maka shook his head. 'Not really. When I got out, I got out. I did at first, and I had a few people wanting me to get involved, so they could work through me, but I turned it all down.'

'What about now?'

Maka's brow furrowed. 'What do you mean?'

'I mean that it's me coming to you. You know me. You know what I'm about.'

Maka wet his lips, frowning at his oldest friend.

'You're still in the game?'

Manson shrugged, feeling strangely defensive all of a sudden.

'What else am I supposed to do?'

'You can do anything you want. I know you had some money put down, and you said yourself that the Feds didn't get it. Teflon took care of you too, so why be in the streets?'

'Because I don't have a wife, or kids, or anything like that,' Manson snapped. He took a moment to calm down. 'We're out there; I'm working with Keith and Roman, and they're taking over the streets. We're gonna be right back where we were, but bigger.'

'Manson, we're practically old men. We don't need to do that stuff anymore.' He looked around. 'Why don't we sit down and think about potential career paths or investments for you? You can live off the interest, and not get back involved in the life.'

Manson snorted, turning away. He was regretting visiting Maka, and had expected a much easier sale. It didn't sit right that Maka had adjusted to life after the streets, when he couldn't even imagine how that would work.

'It's easy for you to say. You didn't get locked down for five years. I kept my mouth shut and stood tall so you could have the happy life. What kind of shit is that?'

Maka's eyes flashed with anger. 'I can't believe you fucking said that. Are you serious? Either of us could have been locked down, and I'm sorry it was you, I really am. Don't think you're gonna stand in my house and guilt trip me, just because I don't want to put my family on the line and go back in the streets with you.'

Manson's fists clenched, nostrils flaring as he breathed deep.

'We've got the plug, Maka,' he tried again. 'The Asians that used to deal with Teflon are dealing with us. Dirt cheap prices, better product than anyone else. Roman and Keith are good. They need people to keep them on track, and that's what I do. What *we* can do.'

Again, Maka shook his head.

'That's not me anymore, Manson. If it's what you need to do, then I guess you've gotta do it, but I'm not going back to the streets. Not now. Not ever.'

———

LISA RECLINED ON THE SOFA, watching Dolja fix their drinks. After chasing for a while, Lisa had finally agreed to meet him. She had expected him to rush to see her, but he had taken his time, explaining that things had kicked off, limiting his free time. Now, though, he was definitely trying to create a mood; a vanilla candle burned on the coffee table, and *Jodeci* played from his Alexa.

Dolja had shaved, and the shirt and jeans he wore looked pristine. He was trying to pull out all the stops, which Lisa found cute. Dolja wasn't bad looking, and he was soft-spoken. She supposed he likely did alright with women, except when he was going for the ones out of his league.

That being said, he hadn't done anything to make her feel uncomfortable. On the contrary, he had been quite attentive.

'Here, Amaretto and Cranberry, just like you wanted,' he said, handing her a drink. She thanked him, taking a sip. She didn't plan on getting drunk, but she could handle her job even if she did. She'd done it before.

Dolja slid next to her on the sofa, eyes flicking to her legs for a moment, before smiling at her. He had a nice spot. He lived on Newton Lodge Garth, just off Chapeltown Road, in a semi-detached house that Lisa was surprised he could afford. Seemingly, he didn't spend all his money on drinks and women, which impressed her.

The living room was spacious, with a large burgundy corner sofa they were currently sitting on, a nearby armchair, a reddish brown coffee table, and a large television and entertainment centre. There were several family photos and paintings dotted around.

Lisa took in the photo of a young child, wondering if it was Dolja's. Not that it mattered.

'I'm glad you decided to give me a chance,' he spoke again.

'I'm glad you're glad,' replied Lisa.

'You don't talk much, do you? You're one of those prestige chicks, aren't you . . . you look good, but you don't have much to say.'

'What I have to say depends on the conversation, and who I'm having it with.'

Dolja sipped his drink. Lisa followed suit, enjoying the way he'd mixed it. It wasn't something most people were good at, in her experience. They either made the drinks too strong, or too weak, and Lisa was very particular.

'I'm happy to talk about anything you want,' Dolja said to her.

'What do you usually talk about in these situations?'

'You think I do this a lot?'

Lisa nodded. 'You're smooth enough that I could see a few women being taken in by what you're saying.'

'Are you including yourself in that?' Dolja asked. He'd figured she would be tricky after their previous conversations, but she was giving him nothing to work with.

Lisa smiled. 'The night is still young.'

'It is,' said Dolja. Finishing his drink, he made another. 'What's your name?'

'You haven't earned the right to know that yet.'

Dolja's grip tightened around his glass, and his face contorted into a frown.

'Are you taking the piss?'

'I'm known for that, but in this case, I'm not. You have to earn everything you get from me, so it's up to you whether you're up to that.'

Dolja's frown deepened for a moment, then he chuckled.

'I knew you were high-maintenance the moment I saw you,' he admitted.

'Knowing that, does it make you more or less likely to try harder?'

'I guess we'll see,' said Dolja.

They had a few more drinks, and Lisa relaxed. The music kept playing in the background, and the conversation continued, with the woman giving him little bits, and Dolja telling her about himself, namely about his family; what school he'd gone to, and what he liked to do for fun.

Eventually, he made his move, elated when she didn't pull away. He pulled her closer, Lisa allowing him to deepen the kiss for a few minutes, before backing away.

'What's up?' Dolja asked, trying not to pant. He was aroused and wanted to close the deal.

'I just need to use the toilet. Get yourself ready for me, and I'll be right back.'

Grinning, Dolja downed his fourth drink, enjoying the buzz. He was lost in his thoughts, going over what would happen next, when he felt a sharp prick in the back of his neck.

'What the hell?' He gasped, whirling around, seeing the woman standing there, clutching a large hypodermic needle. 'What . . . did . . . you . . . do . . . to me?'

'Lisa,' she replied as he crashed to the floor, the room steadily darkening. 'My name . . . is Lisa.'

A SLAP to the face jolted Dolja. Blinking, he tried to focus. He found himself unable to move his arms, and had been tied to a chair in a room he didn't recognise. The floor was covered in plastic; besides the chair, there was nothing else in the room.

Lisa was in the corner, playing with her nails. She glanced in Dolja's direction, her expression blank. A man loomed over Dolja. An uncontrollable shudder swept through his body when he realised who it was.

'How was your nap, Dolja?'

'What the hell do you want?' Dolja mumbled, struggling not to show his fear. Natty Deeds grinned down at him.

'I want to know everything you know about Roman and Keith.'

'Who?'

Natty burst into laughter, shaking his head. Behind him, Lisa smiled.

'That's cute. I needed that, Dolja. It's been a stressful time of late, but it's good to know that I can still laugh from time to time. Now, let's stop messing around, before I have to start hurting you.'

Dolja forced himself not to tremble. This was the worst possible situation to be in. He knew of Natty Deeds, and the reputation he'd earned. Dolja was loyal to his team, but he didn't want to die, trussed up in the middle of nowhere. Lisa met his eyes, and his fear dissipated, replaced with rage.

'You treacherous bitch. You better hope I don't get loose,' he warned.

'You can't see it, but I'm trembling on the inside,' she said dryly.

Before Dolja could speak again, a fist slammed into his chest. His head lolled, his body held in place by the restraints as he struggled to breathe.

'I know that hurt. Don't make me do it again. Keep messing me around, and it's gonna get messy for you,' said Natty.

'What if I don't know anything?' Dolja said desperately, when he'd caught his breath.

'I'd probably still have to check . . . it wouldn't end well for you. Best thing for you to do is to give me what I'm after.'

Dolja hung his head, defeated.

'Look, they move around a lot. I—'

'—Don't even try to hustle me. I want the spots of theirs that you know about. Give me them all.'

Taking a deep breath, resigned, Dolja told Natty everything he knew. He was right, there wasn't much. Several of the addresses he gave were locations that were no longer in use.

'What about the tainted drugs?'

'What tainted drugs?' Dolja asked.

'Don't play dumb. I warned you once. I won't do it again.'

Dolja sighed.

'It wasn't my idea. I swear.'

'I don't care. How do your people differentiate them from other packages?'

'They don't. It was a one-time thing. Roman considered doing it repeatedly, but he thought once would be enough to stop you lot,' said Dolja.

Natty wasn't sure if he was telling the truth, but he'd been suffi-ciently cowed. There was a lot to think about, but he would handle his current situation first.

'Is there anything else you want to tell me?'

Dolja shook his head.

'I just wanna go, bro. I didn't even want to be involved. You lot have run things for years, but I was still eating. Now, these lot are out, and they just took over. I had to go along with it.'

Natty smiled.

'That's horrible, mate. Must have been tough for you to go along with it all. If I did let you go, though . . . how could I be sure you'll stay quiet?'

Dolja's lips trembled. He stared at Natty, unsure if he was being serious or not.

'I don't want anything to do with this shit. That's why I helped you,' Dolja spluttered.

'That's the thing, though,' Natty started, as he slid out his gun, attaching a silencer. 'How do I know you're telling the truth.'

'I am, Natty! I swear, you've gotta believe me.'

Natty shook his head. 'I don't buy that. I'll tell you this, though. If you've missed something out, I might have to take it out on your family.'

'I haven't,' said Dolja.

Natty's expression hardened.

'Good. There's something else I know about you. You haven't admitted to it, which isn't surprising, but I know you fancied yourself a proper gangster. A while ago, you even rode out on my friend, Spence. If you know me, you know him. He's my brother, and you lot tried to kill him. I know you were there. I know you were popping off shots, and if you'd killed him . . . my brother . . . you'd probably have celebrated, right?'

'I . . . How do you . . .?' Dolja's eyes widened. He'd rode out with Keith when he'd shot at Spence, but he hadn't had a choice.

'Doesn't matter how I know,' said Natty, 'but it's why I'm doing this. You tried to kill my bro, so now you go.' He raised the gun.

'Wait, no—' Dolja tried to protest, but the gun fired, and the bullet slammed Dolja's head back, red mist and brain matter splattering everywhere.

Natty stared at Dolja's body for a moment as he toppled to the floor. To be sure, he put another bullet in his head, and one in his body. When he was sure Dolja was dead, he placed the gun on the ground.

'Took you long enough,' said Lisa, stifling a yawn. 'I thought you were going to let him go for a moment.'

'I told you what I was going to do,' said Natty, staring at Dolja's body. The third life he'd taken.

'You did well. Didn't even flinch.'

Natty didn't know what to say to that, so he didn't respond.

'Get out of here,' Lisa said. 'I'll go back to Dolja's and make sure the cleanup is complete. We're done with this spot, so no need to bother moving him.'

'Fine,' Natty replied. 'I'll check in tomorrow.' Not knowing what else to say, he left, giving Dolja's body one last look.

CHAPTER SEVENTEEN

LISA GLANCED around before climbing into the black Range Rover on the corner of Frankland Avenue. Clarke sat in the back, giving her a small smile.

'We good?'

Lisa nodded, relaxing against the plush seats. She knew the driver, but couldn't remember his name. He was staring ahead, giving no sign he was listening to their conversation.

'Dolja's gone. We searched his place. Didn't find much. He gave up a few spots, but Natty didn't look impressed with the information.'

'Good work. How did Natty do?'

Lisa smirked. 'He did well. He's very impressive. Good under pressure. Has presence . . . You've done well with him.'

Clarke gave her a look, then sighed.

'Lis . . . we've been through this. Do you remember what I said?'

'I do. I was answering your question. If we're done here, I'm going to go home and get a bath,' said Lisa.

'Do you need a ride?'

She shook her head.

'I've got a car nearby.'

'Take care of yourself, Lis. Stay low, and I'll be in touch.'

————

ROMAN HUNG UP, his shoulders slumping.

'Well? What is it?' Keith demanded. He, Roman and Manson were sat at Roman's place. His main spot was an apartment in the city centre. He'd only moved in a few weeks ago.

Consequently, he'd been too busy to decorate, and furniture had been left by the previous tenant. The walls were white, contrasting well with the darker furnishings. Keith and Roman sat slumped on the well-worn brown leather sofa. Roman shuffled, attempting to get comfortable. Once they'd handled their problems, he planned to dedicate time to working on the place.

Keith was still waiting for a response, as was Manson.

'Dolja's dead. He missed a drop-off this morning. Someone went to check on him, and he was missing. Someone called it in. They found him in an abandoned house in Harehills, shot up.'

'Fuck!' Keith roared. Manson closed his eyes, shaking his head.

'We should have known they'd get to him. He was too accessible, out and about partying,' he said.

Roman didn't reply. He was hurt by Dolja's death, and not just because he had been an asset. Dolja had been a good friend, loyal and dependable. He hadn't deserved to die.

'Anyway,' Manson continued, sighing, 'I'll step up for him. At least until you decide who'll take his spot.'

'Forget that. What are we doing next?' We need to ride out,' said Keith, jumping to his feet.

'We will, but we're gonna do it properly,' said Roman.

'Enough planning! We just go out there and take care of it. I'm tired of all the pussyfooting around. We've got soldiers and guns. Let's go and get them all . . . even Mitch, the old prick,' said Keith.

'We won't get close to Mitch, not yet. I keep telling you, Keith. This isn't the time to start spazzing out. We're gonna get Natty. And Spence. And that other one . . . the one in Little London . . .'

'Carlton,' said Keith, nostrils flaring.

'Yeah. Him. No messing around. We'll get them, Keith. Stick with me, and it will be done.'

———————

'HAVE you and Rosie sorted it out yet?'

Natty and Spence drove through the Hood the next day. As was their habit nowadays, they'd switched cars, not wanting anyone keeping an eye on them to get too used to their vehicles.

Spence leant back in the passenger seat, his eyes sweeping the roads as they cruised by.

'I've been avoiding it. No change since I spoke to you on the phone that time. I mean, we've spent time together, but it's like we're waiting for one another to make the first move. I'm not sure how we get there. What about you and Lorraine?'

Natty's face tensed. 'I haven't spoken to her yet. You were right last time. I don't want to lose her, and I can't ignore the conversation forever.' He smiled. 'Or, maybe I can. Maybe this is fate's way of telling us we both need to be single.'

Spence chuckled. 'I don't think either of us wants that right now. Like you said, you can't avoid it any more than I can.' He sighed. 'I think I'm ready to leave the past behind me.'

'Good,' Natty joked. 'I don't want you running after Anika and begging for her to come back.'

'I'll try not to.' Spence laughed again, before his expression changed. 'Can I ask you something?'

'Course you can.'

'Dolja.'

'What about him?' It surprised Natty how little he'd thought about the man he'd killed. The nausea that had racked him last time was nonexistent. If the shoe was on the other foot, Dolja wouldn't have hesitated to do the same. He hoped it convinced Roman and Keith not to try them, but suspected it wouldn't be that easy.

'How did it feel to . . . you know . . .'

'I didn't feel anything,' said Natty. 'It's like . . . I cleared my mind; like I was looking right through him, and then I just did it.' He glanced at Spence as he stopped at a red light on Roundhay Road. 'Why do you ask?'

'I was just curious,' said Spence, downplaying it. 'Listen, are you in a hurry? I was gonna stop by my dad's.'

'Nah, I'm good. Let's go,' said Natty.

———

WHEN THEY ARRIVED, Spence led them into the house. Spence's dad was slouched on the sofa, watching a western and smoking a cigarette. His eyes went from Spence to Natty.

'Nathaniel,' he said coolly.

'How are you doing, Wayne?' Natty replied, his tone politer.

'Same old. Spence, crack the Wray and Nephew if you lot are staying.'

'We're fine, dad,' said Spence. 'I just wanted to stop by and make sure you were okay.'

'I'm not an invalid. I'm fine.' Wayne again looked at Natty. 'How's your uncle doing?'

'Same as ever.'

'Spence told me you lot are having an issue with another crew.' His expression turned sly. 'You getting your hands dirty yet?'

'Dad . . .' Spence started. Natty cut him off.

'We all play our roles. Did Delroy ever get his hands dirty in your beefs?'

Spence looked from his dad to Natty, aware of the mounting tension. He considered speaking up again, but didn't. Natty could more than take care of himself.

'The thing about your uncle is that he always had your old man around,' said Wayne, ignoring Natty's question. 'Tyrone wasn't one to play. He took out anyone who crossed him. Are you living up to his reputation?'

Natty just nodded, not knowing how to respond. He and Wayne had sniped at one another before, but he'd rarely mentioned his dad. Natty wondered what had changed.

They stayed a while longer. Wayne ended up warming up some food for them, despite Spence's protests. The conversation became a little lighter, with Wayne having a glass of white rum, again trying to offer it to the pair.

'We'll party after you lot win your little war,' he said.

When they left, Spence wore a bemused expression.

'I don't know what the hell that was about,' he admitted. Natty chuckled. He still didn't know why Wayne had brought up his dad, but put it to one side.

'I guess we'll ask him when we go back to party,' he replied with a wink. Spence laughed as they climbed into the car and drove away.

———

NATTY'S CONVERSATION with Spence remained on his mind the following day. He needed to do something about Lorraine. As angry as he'd been about Raider, he didn't want to lose her from his life. With that in mind, he sent her a text message.

———

LORRAINE HUGGED JADEN, fussing over him and ensuring he had everything he needed. Raider was due to pick him up, and he was already a few minutes late. Lorraine had contacted him several days ago, and they agreed on him taking Jaden out for the day. She still had her reservations, but counselled herself that she was doing the right thing.

Raider had stopped by the house to see Jaden a few times, never staying long, but always on his best behaviour. Jaden seemed to enjoy seeing him, which made Lorraine feel better.

'If you're not happy at any time, you can tell your dad you want to come home, okay?'

'Okay, mummy. It'll be okay.'

Smiling, Lorraine kissed him on the cheek.

Ten minutes later, Raider knocked at the door. When Lorraine answered, he gave her a small smile, then beamed at his son.

'Look at you! Every time I see you, you look bigger,' he said, hugging Jaden, who had a massive smile on his face. Lorraine stood back and watched them. Despite everything she had gone through, the moments when Raider and Jaden were happy around one another always moved her. When Raider finished speaking to Jaden, he straightened, looking to Lorraine.

'Sorry I'm late. I got caught up.'

Lorraine nodded. 'Where are you taking him?'

'I thought we'd do some shopping, and go and see my family. After that, we might go kick a ball around or something. It's up to him.'

'Okay. We're going to my mum's tomorrow, so please don't keep him out late,' said Lorraine.

'I won't. C'mon, J. We've got a lot to do.'

They said their goodbyes, and Lorraine closed the door behind them, pressed against it, taking deep breaths. She kept telling herself it would be okay; for all his faults, Raider had never physically hurt Jaden, and she didn't think he would start now.

Emotional abuse was another story.

Finally moving, Lorraine headed to the kitchen to make a hot drink. While the kettle was boiling, she called Natty, pleased when he picked up.

'Natty? Can we talk now?'

―――――

NATTY REMAINED on high alert as he drove to Lorraine's. He wanted to resolve the situation, but the streets didn't stop for his personal life, and he was fully aware of that. Going around armed was a way of life now, and he had to keep switching up his cars to stay off the radar of the police.

Dolja's death had caused some ripples. Roman and Keith had yet to retaliate, but Natty remained vigilant.

Pulling up outside Lorraine's, he scanned the street, took a deep breath, then knocked at the door.

When Lorraine answered, the pair stared at one another. It had been over a month, and she still looked as beautiful and intense as ever. Natty felt his fingers tingling, the feeling spreading throughout his body. He opened his mouth, not knowing what he would say.

'Come in. It's cold outside,' Lorraine spoke first. He nodded, stepping in and closing the door behind him. He removed his shoes and coat without thinking about it, and sat in the living room. Lorraine sat next to him.

'Where's Jaden?' He asked.

'He's out,' said Lorraine delicately, not wanting to mention he was with Raider. It had been two hours, and she remained antsy, hoping everything was okay.

'How have you been?'

'You mean in the past month or so that I haven't seen you?' Lorraine's tone was sharper than she anticipated.

'I do.'

'I've been fine, Nat. Things have been tough from time to time, but what else am I supposed to do?'

'I get that.' Natty forced his eyes to Lorraine, pushing past the anger he saw in her face. 'I'm sorry I went off like that, and I'm sorry I didn't stay in contact.'

'Do you think sorry is going to cut it?' Lorraine asked, still giving Natty her full attention. The room seemed smaller, Lorraine's presence filling the space around them.

'That's up to you,' replied Natty. 'I'm sorry for how I handled things, but you know why I was annoyed. How dare you compare me to that piece-of-shit baby father of yours. What the hell were you thinking?'

Lorraine took a deep breath. 'I was thinking that you both came up in the streets, and that you both have reputations for hitting first, and thinking afterwards,' she admitted.

'That's where you're wrong then. Maybe you should have spent this time apart speaking to people in the streets, and asking them about me, because that's not my rep. It wasn't my rep when I stood on your doorstep and told you I loved you. I'm not that person anymore. I changed, and you were a big part of that change.'

'Nat . . .' Lorraine's mouth fell open, but he held up his hand.

'He beat you up, Lo. He came into this house, attacked you, and left you for your son to find. I would never do that, and when you insinuate I'm the same as him, that hurts. I don't ever want you to think that.'

Lorraine wet her lips, emotional after Natty's outburst, but determined to fight it.

'I'm sorry, Nat. I didn't mean it as it sounded, and I shouldn't have said it. I regretted it the moment it came out. You two couldn't be more different when it comes down to it, and I recognise that. I was stressed about the situation, and I just reacted. It wasn't the right thing to do, and I'm sorry I hurt you.'

'I get it. I shouldn't have been speaking on Jaden like that.'

Lorraine shook her head. 'Nat, you've more than earned the right to speak about Jaden. You've been there for him repeatedly, and you've gone above and beyond to spend time with him and make him happy. As I said to you before, it wasn't about forgiving Raider for what he did, but I can't deny him a relationship with his son if he's serious about having one. That wouldn't be fair to Jaden.'

'I get that,' said Natty through gritted teeth. Lorraine squeezed his hand.

'I want you to feel you can share your opinion, Nat. Please, just respect mine too.'

'I think I can do that,' said Natty. Their lips met, and a feeling of complete fullness cascaded over him. As the kiss deepened, and he savoured the taste of the green tea she'd had earlier, he wasn't sure how he had managed to last without seeing her. The streets and everything else drifted away, leaving only Lorraine, and this moment.

Finally, they pulled apart, both breathing hard.

'I think we needed that,' said Lorraine, wiping her mouth, eyes dancing.

'I think the proof is in the pudding,' said Natty, smirking. 'Why don't I make us some drinks, and you can give me the lowdown on how you're getting on with your training?'

———

NATTY SPENT the afternoon catching up with Lorraine, pleased they were back on an even footing. He regretted the fact he'd ignored her, but it had led to a conversation they needed to have about where the other stood.

He was in the kitchen washing up, having made a quick call to Spence to check in, when he heard the door, and murmuring voices. Not recognising them, he wiped his hands, then hurried out to the hallway. The door had already closed, but Lorraine stood with Jaden.

'Hey, little man,' he said to Jaden, waiting for the boy's face to light up. Instead, Jaden glared at him.

Natty frowned. He had seen Jaden throw tantrums and get angry, but he'd never had it directed at him.

He cleared his throat.

'I'm sorry I haven't been around, but how have you been? Still playing footy?'

'I know what you did,' Jaden said, his voice colder than Natty had ever heard.

'What do you mean?'

Lorraine stopped short, her eyes darting between Jaden and Natty.

'What's happened?' She asked.

'I don't know,' said Natty. 'J, what is it I'm supposed to have done?'

'You hurt my dad.'

Of all the things Natty had expected Jaden to say, that hadn't made the list. He looked to Lorraine, whose eyes were wide, then back to Jaden.

'. . . Who told you that?' He asked. Jaden shook his head.

'Is it true? Did you hurt my dad? Is that why he couldn't see me?'

'Jaden . . .' Lorraine started, but Jaden ignored her, still glaring at Natty.

'I hate you,' he said, then ran upstairs.

'Jaden!' Lorraine ran after him, leaving Natty rooted to the spot, horrified. He couldn't believe what Jaden had said to him; the raw emotion in the child's voice. Never had he spoken to Natty in such a way. Eventually, the words filtered through, jolting Natty.

Raider.

Raider had told Jaden, meaning Jaden had seen him. Heading back to the kitchen, Natty sat at the table, rubbing his forehead and taking deep breaths.

'Natty.'

He looked up. Lorraine stood in the doorway, eyes full of concern.

'I'm sorry about that,' she said.

Natty stared back at her, but remained silent. He didn't know what words would escape if he opened his mouth.

'Nat, seriously, he didn't mean that. I'm sorry.'

'He saw Raider then?' Natty's voice was colder than he had ever heard it. Lorraine paused, then nodded.

'He wanted to. I spoke to him, explained that Raider wanted to see him, and he wanted to see his dad.'

Natty shook his head, unsure how long he would be able to control his anger. He'd known Raider would try something, but even he was surprised at how quickly it had transpired.

'He doesn't *know* his dad, does he? I said this to you before. He doesn't know who Raider is, and after one day, he's already getting in Jaden's ear, spitting his poison. He's stirring it, and you're falling for it.'

Lorraine's mouth opened and closed. This wasn't the first time Jaden had seen his dad, but she didn't think telling Natty that would help.

'No I'm not! How dare you say that to me.' Her voice rose. Even knowing she was fighting a losing battle, she couldn't back down.

'Course you are. Did you mention to Jaden that his dad might have an agenda? That he might twist the truth? That he put you in hospital, and to be careful about what he says and does?'

'Of course I didn't. I'm not going to say that about his dad.'

'It's the truth, Lorraine!' Natty roared, startling her. 'I would never tell you how to parent your son, but I'm involved in his life, and I care about him. I always have. You've always prepared him for life; encouraged him to do the right thing . . . until now. You sent him out unprepared, with a dangerous man. He could have done anything to use him against you, and he's already started.'

'Nat . . .' Lorraine was aghast, but Natty wasn't done.

'We have something, Lo. We're in a relationship, and I appreciate that we need to take our time with telling Jaden, but I wish you would listen and take on board what I'm saying.'

'You mean that you want me to do what you say. That's not the same thing.' Lorraine stood her ground.

'That's not what I want. I want us to communicate and make the right decisions. Allowing Jaden to see Raider, without him truly understanding who Raider is, is bad.'

'He's ten!' Lorraine fired back.

'And I was fucking eleven when my dad was murdered. I understand it. I understand it's tough, and shit, and the world is cold, but I'm glad I knew, and that it wasn't hidden from me. You should have prepared him, and now Raider is already using him against you.'

Lorraine sighed, trying to calm down.

'I'll speak to Raider and let him know that what he did wasn't on.'

'What is that going to do? He knows what he's doing, and he'll do it again, because you've given him a way in. You're falling for his crap.'

Lorraine shook her head. 'Let's just leave it for now.'

Natty's mouth fell open, furious she wasn't taking this seriously.

'Do you even care?'

'What?' Lorraine frowned.

'About your son hating me. About the fact Raider is turning him against me . . . against us. If Jaden hates me, how can we possibly work?'

'Of course I care. None of this is easy, though. I just need some time to get things right, Natty.' Lorraine blew out a breath.

Nodding, Natty turned to leave.

'Nat, please don't leave again. We've only just made up.'

Natty faced down Lorraine. 'J told me he hated me, because you let him meet Raider, and then you didn't even tell me about it. I don't see how you expected things to turn out.' He rubbed his eyes. 'I . . . I can be a dad to him, Lo. I've looked after him more than Raider has. I know what you're saying about him having access to his dad, but he hurt you. If he hurt you, he can hurt Jaden. I wish you saw that.'

Lorraine stared at him, but didn't say anything. With a grunt, Natty nodded and left without another word.

Lorraine stared at the door, wanting to go after Natty. She wiped away a tear. They'd come so close to moving on, then fate had intervened, throwing a spanner in the works. After a few moments, she went upstairs to Jaden's room. He was sat on the bed, scowling at the wall. Lorraine noted he was wearing a t-shirt and jeans that Natty had bought him, something that hadn't stood out to her when she had ironed them in the morning.

After a moment, Jaden fixed his attention on her, and she shook her head.

'You shouldn't have spoken to Natty how you did, Jaden. It was extremely disrespectful. I raised you better than that.'

Jaden looked at the floor, but didn't respond.

'*Jaden.*'

Recognising that she meant business by her tone, Jaden again looked at her, his scowl dissipating.

'Is it true?' He asked.

'Is what true, darling?'

'Did Natty hurt my dad?'

Lorraine sighed. It wasn't a conversation she wanted to have with Jaden, just as she had told Rosie a while back.

'There's a lot of things you don't know, but I love you, J. Natty cares about you a lot. He cares about both of us.' Jaden didn't say anything, so she went on. 'When you're finished sulking, you're grounded for a week.'

Jaden opened his mouth to protest, but Lorraine shook her head.

'I told you. You were disrespectful. You're not to spend time with your friends after school, no playing football, and you're not playing any of your computer games either.'

'That's not fair,' Jaden moaned. 'Natty hurt my dad. I don't want him to come here anymore.'

Lorraine's eyes narrowed.

'That isn't your choice. You'll do as you're told, and the next time your dad says anything to you, you need to speak to me first.' Lorraine went to leave the room, then stopped and turned, looking back at Jaden. 'Natty would never hurt either of us.'

CHAPTER EIGHTEEN

NATTY BROODED, watching one of Roman's spots. He'd seen several people come and go, mostly small-timers he didn't recognise. Lorraine was on his mind.

Natty remained furious that she had let Raider get access to Jaden. Hearing a little boy he cared about tell him that he hated him, had jarred Natty. He loved Lorraine, but it was getting harder now, and he wasn't sure they were meant to be. The recent events proved it. He was practically a side-man. There was nothing he could say or do. His opinion counted for nothing in this situation.

A police car drove by, but didn't notice the car. It didn't matter to Natty if they did. He wasn't armed, and he wasn't rushing the spot. He was only watching.

After Roman's trick with the tainted drugs, they had become wary of direct robberies. Consequently, their focus switched to information gathering after Dolja's murder. They had hoped it would raise the stakes and cause their opposition to crumble, but they seemed as tight as ever.

From what they had gathered, they believed Roman dealt primarily with strategy. Keith was less tactical, holding things down on the streets. Keith being more visible than Roman made him a more accessible target, but to cut the head off the snake, they would need to take them both out.

So, they took turns watching the spots Dolja had given them. As expected, most of them had been rotated out — possibly due to Dolja's murder — whereas others were mainly staffed by small-timers.

Natty was utilising an old strategy, having their people pay the locals in exchange for information, but Roman and Keith had better reputations than Warren had, so the locals were less inclined to work against them.

'Are you going to tell me what's wrong?'

Natty glanced at Lisa. He'd been surprised when she had offered to watch the spot with him, but hadn't argued. He'd expected her to flirt and be all over him, but she had remained quiet, speaking only when she noticed something or someone relating to their mission. It had been a relaxing surveillance, enabling him to sink into his thoughts.

'Nothing,' he said.

Lisa nodded.

'If you tell me it's nothing, and that you don't want to talk about it, I'll leave it alone. If you tell me you do, I'll give you my honest opinion. Sometimes it's better to talk about it, rather than keep it in.'

Natty mulled that over. Lisa was removed from the situation, and Spence was busy. Maybe getting it off his chest would help.

'Relationship stuff,' he mumbled. Lisa grinned, not hiding her pleasure at hearing this. Natty chuckled, despite himself. 'You're shameless.'

'Whatever you say. What's the problem?'

Natty told her about the arguments with Lorraine, and Raider's attempts to get back into her life. Lisa listened, not speaking until he'd finished.

'You're not looking at it from her point of view,' she said bluntly.

'Are you silly? Did you even hear what I said?' Natty snapped. Lisa shrugged.

'I told you I would be honest. I'm not saying you're wrong, and I'm not even saying she's making the right decisions, but you can't fault her for putting her child first. She's a mum, and that's not something you can understand.'

'Miss me with that shit. I can fault her if her decision puts her and Jaden at risk.'

'You don't know they're really at risk. Again, I'm not saying you're wrong, but Raider could want to make up for lost time.'

'Bullshit. He's dangerous. He wants Lorraine to *want* him, and her not submitting puts her in danger. Why can't she see that?'

'Open your eyes, Natty. All we know is that she's making what she sees as the right decision, based on the facts as she knows them,' said Lisa.

'Bullshit. She's wrong. Nothing you say changes that.' Natty huffed.

Lisa chuckled. 'Ultimately, Natty, you're at fault for this.'

'How the hell do you figure that out?'

Lisa's smirk made Natty's nostrils flare, but she appeared indifferent to it. She glanced out of the window. The house had been quiet for the past thirty minutes, with no arrivals, departures or noise.

'I know what happened between you and Raider. I know what he did to your girlfriend, and I know how you handled it. You made the wrong call.'

'You're saying I should have let him go?'

Lisa looked at him again, and there was no emotion.

'You should have killed him.'

Natty opened his mouth, then closed it. She'd caught him flat-footed. He hadn't expected Lisa to say that. It took him right back to their fight in Raider's living room. They'd destroyed the room, trying to take the other out. Raider had almost gotten the better of him, and Natty suspected he wasn't planning to let him live.

So, why had he hesitated? Was Lisa right?

'I . . .'

'You used a half-measure. You hospitalised him, and you battered his ego. A man like Raider won't take that lying down. He doesn't know how to. And if he knows he can't beat you physically? What's his next move?' Natty stared across at Lisa, dumbstruck by her words. 'Next time, you won't use a half-measure if you really have a problem,' she concluded.

Lisa said nothing more, leaving Natty deep in thought, wondering if she was right about what she had said. There was no doubt that if he had killed Raider, he wouldn't have these problems now. Raider wouldn't be politicking behind his back, turning Jaden against him. He wouldn't be having as many issues with Lorraine.

Would Lorraine have forgiven him if he had killed Raider, though? The beating he'd given him had almost driven Lorraine away for good.

Regardless, Lisa had given him food for thought, which was surprising. It was apparent she had a thing for him, and they had chemistry. Lisa had ultimately agreed with Lorraine's motives, but she at least understood Natty's perspective. He wasn't sure if she was playing a game, or how she would use this to her advantage if she was.

If there was one thing Natty was tired of, it was games.

———

THE NEXT DAY, Natty linked up with Carlton, driving around Little London. Other than a minor blip after Natty's firing the year prior, the area had continued to thrive, bringing their crew large amounts of money daily.

'You've done well around here,' Natty said to Carlton, leaning back in the passenger seat as Carlton nodded along to the *Blade Brown* mixtape playing through the aux cable. 'I can see you've put the work in. We all can. Everyone is singing your praises.'

As always, Carlton took it in his stride. He had incredible poise for a young man, always managing to keep his composure, similar to Spence. His hair was styled in a low fade buzzcut, he had dark brown skin, minimal facial hair, and light brown eyes. At present, he was attired in a black hooded top and matching bottoms.

'You did the hard work, fam,' he replied. 'You set up the network around here, and it's paid off. Everyone around here is on our side. A few of Roman's people tried doing the rounds, but they didn't get anywhere.'

Natty grinned, enjoying Blade's delivery for a few moments.

'Still, I'm proud of how you've stepped up. Keep going, and the sky's the limit for you. I mean that,' he finally said.

'I appreciate that, fam.'

Natty meant what he'd said. Carlton was the future of the crew. With him and Spence directing the crew, and the buzz they'd have after they eliminated Roman and Keith, they would go to the next level. As long as he was around, Natty would support Carlton more positively than Rudy had ever done for him.

As they were pulling up by Natty's car, his phone rang. He frowned, not recognising the number.

'Yeah?'

'Deeds.'

Natty stepped away from Carlton.

'Manson.'

'I've been mulling things over since our chat.'

'That was ages ago.'

'I don't rush into anything. If you know my rep, you'll know that. We need another meet, to hash some things out.'

Natty considered this. His last encounter with Manson had been fruitless, but they'd kept a close eye on Roman and Keith's people, and there was no indication Manson was aligned with them. Even Dolja hadn't said he was.

'Fine. We'll meet at the Wreck tonight.'

After setting a time, Natty hung up, ignoring the feeling in the pit of his stomach telling him he was doing the wrong thing.

After leaving Carlton, Natty went to see Clarke. They stood outside Paula's, Clarke looking more casual than Natty had ever seen him, in a baggy hooded top and a pair of faded tracksuit bottoms.

'Manson wanting to meet out of nowhere is suspicious,' said Clarke, after Natty had told him the situation. 'Is it worth it?'

'If Manson knows something, it's definitely worth the risk,' Natty said. 'I'm ready for all of this to be over.'

Clarke wordlessly surveyed him for a few seconds.

'If you've considered the implications, then make sure you're prepared. Most importantly—'

'Get there early,' Natty interjected, making Clarke chuckle.

'You're learning.'

———

'HE TOOK THE BAIT.'

Manson was with Keith, sitting in the back garden of a safe house. Several of the crew were inside, but Roman wasn't among them. He'd gone to meet Ahmed and Mustafir. After Keith's previous argument with Ahmed, the decision had been made to leave him behind, one that still smarted for Keith.

'Good,' Keith said, rubbing his hands together. 'I'll wait for him at the Wreck. One of Dunn's people was pillow-talking to one of our girls. He mentioned Spence has this girl that he's sweet on. Can't remember her name, but apparently, it's on her social media that she's going to dinner later. I'm gonna have people watching, ready to hit Spence if he's slipping.'

'Make sure it's done right,' said Manson. 'You thought you had the drop on Spence last time, and someone died. Don't engage either of them until you're sure they're in place. Take some backup for Natty too.'

'Are you dumb? I don't need backup,' said Keith, as animated as ever.

'Don't be stupid, Keith. That pride will get you killed. Natty's a harder target than Spence, and we need to take him out. Doesn't matter who gets the credit, as long as we knock him off the board.'

Keith's nostrils flared, but he finally nodded. It was a good plan, and the fact Manson had enough skill to sucker Natty into a meeting was a win. He didn't care what happened, as long as he took out both men.

'Fine.'

———

SPENCE CUT INTO HIS STEAK, the tender meat separating effortlessly. It had been cooked to perfection, and he savoured the succulent flavours. Miller and Carter was one of his favourite spots. He enjoyed the dark fixtures, the mood lighting, and the relaxed feel of the place.

Across from him, Rosie was eating her food with gusto — one of the things Spence liked about her. She took pleasure in everything, and she loved food and trying different things.

Spence had contacted Rosie earlier and suggested they go out for dinner, booking the restaurant when she said she was up for it. He hoped it would help fix things between them. They'd spoken a little about their days, and Rosie had talked about a project she was leading at work, yet things still seemed stilted.

With that in mind, he finished his mouthful, wiped around his mouth, and then spoke.

'I'm sorry.'

Rosie blinked, puzzled.

'Why are you sorry.'

'Things haven't been easy with us for a while, and I'm sorry.' Spence gathered his words. 'I care about you, Rosie. Really, I do. I want us to properly communicate, and work through our issues. When we argued that time, and you flinched . . . it jarred me. I don't ever want to make you fear for your safety like your ex did.'

Rosie's expression softened, her eyes watery. She dabbed at them with her napkin, letting out a breath.

'I . . . put on a brave face a lot of the time, but sometimes I slip into that old mindset from time to time.'

Spence nodded. 'I get it. Anika . . . she broke me, Rosie. I gave her everything, and tried to be the person who was right for her, only to have it thrown back in my face.' He sighed. 'It's not fair to you. You deserve better, and that's important to me. I know you're a better person than she is, but I'm just worried that next time, I might not recover from another betrayal.'

Rosie reached out and squeezed his hand, smiling at him.

'I appreciate you sharing that with me, Spence. I know it wasn't easy. You were too good for Anika, and she probably realised that, which is why she did what she did. I just want to know we're going somewhere. It doesn't matter how long we take to get there.'

Spence smiled now too.

'We're definitely going somewhere, Rosie. I want you in my life, and I want to be in yours.'

Both smiles only grew wider. They sipped their wine, pleased they'd spoken openly about their issues.

'I spoke with Lorraine,' Rosie said a few minutes later, surprising Spence.

'What was said?' Spence wasn't sure what was going on. Natty was spending a lot of time with Lisa and Clarke, and handling business. That was something Spence still wondered about. Lisa and Natty had chemistry, and despite Natty's change, Spence wondered if he would revert to his old ways. He didn't know much about Lisa, and she was only known in certain circles, meaning he wasn't sure about her intentions for Natty.

Rosie sighed, sipping her wine.

'She let Raider see Jaden.'

Spence shook his head.

'I bet Natty loved that.'

'Raider took Jaden out, and told him Natty was responsible for his beating, so now Jaden isn't talking to Natty.'

Spence scowled. 'Please tell me you're joking.'

'I'm not done yet. I spoke with Lorraine earlier. She had another argument with Natty — two minutes after they'd made up, and now they're not talking again. Lorraine was telling me that Jaden doesn't want to see Natty anymore . . . because he's dangerous.'

Spence blew out a breath, stunned by what he'd heard. 'How the hell could Raider have done so much damage in such a short time?'

Rosie ate some more of her meal before she replied.

'I don't know.'

'She must have known something like this could happen. Natty said she couldn't trust Raider,' said Spence, his scowl returning.

'I'm not saying I agree with everything Lorraine has done, but she's my friend and only doing what she thinks is right.'

Spence agreed, for the most part. He liked Lorraine and thought she was good for Natty, but this was a sign that there was more to consider than just the pair of them. Spence wasn't sure how that would work out in the long run — especially as Jaden grew older.

'I asked you this before, and I didn't get an answer: do you think it's too late for them?'

Rosie took her time to reply.

'I wasn't sure last time you asked, and I'm even less sure now. There seems to be a lot riding against them, and it's only growing. What do you think?'

'I'm not sure. That Jaden bit has shaken me,' Spence admitted. 'It'll be tough for them to work their way through it . . . unless Jaden truly knows who should be feared, and who can be trusted.'

They finished their meal, leaving the heavy drama that was Lorraine and Natty's relationship behind them. The bill came, Spence paid it on his card, and the pair left the restaurant, walking through the city centre.

Spence loved the city centre at night. He loved the bright lights, and the calm nature of people walking around. He was lost in his thoughts, walking towards the car park, when he saw a man walking toward him. He didn't recognise him, but the angry expression on his face got Spence's attention, and he tensed when the man seemed to hesitate. He wore a black jacket, black jeans and strangely, grey trainers, along with black gloves. Heart racing, Spence squeezed Rosie's hand.

'Listen, Rosie, I need you to go on without me.' He handed her his car keys.

'What do you mean?'

'Something is about to go down, and I need you to listen to me,' he hissed, not taking his eyes from the man, still heading in his direction.

Rosie didn't get a chance to move, as the man drew a knife from the folds of his jacket, and lunged at Spence. He pushed Rosie aside, ignoring her shriek, managing to avoid the sloppy thrust. Spence kicked out, catching his attacker's thigh, knocking him off balance, before smacking his hand and knocking the knife to the ground. The man paused, but Spence didn't, his fist crashing against the attacker's cheek, folding him. Spence kicked him in the ribs, and the man groaned in pain, rolling further away from the knife.

'Spence!'

Spence didn't get the chance to learn why Rosie was screaming, as a shot rang out.

NATTY HAD AGAIN SWITCHED CARS, driving a Toyota Auris to the meeting spot. Heeding the warning Clarke had provided, he decided to take a gun, driving carefully, keen to avoid unwanted attention. Natty pulled up on the road alongside the park. He hoped any attempt at an ambush would be easy to spot, intending to position himself to ensure the entire park was in view.

Looking out across the park, things seemed normal. Natty paused a moment, watching a mum walking by with her son, their faces alight, smiles wide. Natty's face softened as he observed them. After a moment, he thought about Jaden. His soft smile fell, and he averted his gaze. Adjusting his rearview mirror, he saw a car pull in behind him. Slowly, he dropped his hands, placing his left hand on the wheel, and his right on the key in the ignition.

Before he could do anything else, a large bang jolted him as his rear window shattered.

BEFORE HE COULD THINK, Spence dove at Rosie, taking her to the floor. People all around began screaming and running. Spence jumped back to his feet, looking for the gunman, but he couldn't see anything. The man he'd attacked had disappeared too.

'Spence.' Rosie flung herself against him, sobbing. Spence held her tightly, heart smashing against his chest. It was the second shootout he had been in, and he wasn't sure how they had tracked him down. He'd told no one he was going to the restaurant that evening, so it couldn't have been an inside job.

'Are you okay?' He asked Rosie. She nodded, wincing.

'I hurt my knee, but I'm fine. What the hell was that?'

'We'll talk about it later. For now, we need to move.'

Before they could, police raced onto the scene, almost blinding Spence with the flashing lights.

NATTY DUCKED DOWN. More gunfire quickly ensued, panic rising within him as he realised he'd been set up. Worse, the enemy had pre-empted him arriving early. Natty had no idea of the numbers he was facing, his fear growing as he fumbled for the gun. Finally, he took a deep breath and rose up in the car, firing three shots. He heard a yell, then was forced to move as return fire nearly hit him.

Saying a prayer, Natty started the engine, gratified when it worked. He floored it as the car took two more shots. Speeding across Chapeltown Road, Natty drove up Louis Street, calling Clarke simultaneously.

'They tried it,' he said, still catching his breath. 'They tried to hit me.'

────────

'FUCK!' Keith howled, paying little attention to his driver, whose brains were currently leaking over the steering wheel. He had been so close to getting Natty, but he'd gotten carried away, and started shooting early. Now, Natty had escaped, and he needed to get out of there. His people had already driven away after the hit went awry. After shoving the dead driver onto the pavement, Keith followed suit, barely closing the driver's door as he rocketed off.

────────

NATTY PACED THE SAFE HOUSE, staring at his phone, surrounded by Clarke's soldiers. When it finally rang, he saw Spence's number and breathed a sigh of relief.

'Spence, what the hell happened?' He said. 'Everyone's saying you got shot in town.'

'It's been a long night,' Spence replied, and Natty could hear how tired his friend sounded. 'I've been dealing with the police all night, and trying to get Rosie sorted out. I'll get with you tomorrow, and we can hash it all out.'

'Cool, bro. Do you need anything?' Natty decided against mentioning his own ambush. It could wait.

'I'm good. I need to get some rest, then we can meet up.'

'I'll have someone sitting outside your spot, just in case,' said Natty.

'Nat, you don't need to do that—'

'It's done. Get your head down, and we'll talk.' Natty hung up, relieved that Spence was okay.

It felt like déjà vu.

After calling Clarke and getting someone positioned to watch Spence's house, Natty made a drink, standing in the kitchen, looking out at the night sky.

Manson had played him.

Natty had ignored his instincts, and gone along with it anyway. He was in league with Roman and Keith, and now he would be treated the same as them.

Police would likely be on the scene, canvassing for witnesses, investigating the shooting. Natty had definitely hit someone. There was a chance he had killed them. He'd left no trace, yet he was still worried he could be implicated.

All it took was one mistake . . .

Draining his drink, Natty placed his cup in the sink, gripping the sides of the counter, taking a deep breath. Everything was getting to him, and he didn't know how to control it. For months, he'd been relaxed, out of the mix, and now he was on the frontline, dodging bullets, unsure of how to relieve his mounting stress. Yawning, he closed his eyes.

He'd had Lorraine during those months away from the streets, he mused. When he was overwrought, or anxious, she had been there, her presence calming him. It was a luxury he didn't have anymore.

Some things still needed to be said, and Natty wasn't ready to say or hear them.

With a sigh, he scrolled through his phone one last time, then trundled to bed.

———

THE NEXT DAY, Natty entered the safe house. They'd moved to another spot on the corner of Hamilton Avenue in the Hood. It had a red door, large hedges that prevented people from seeing into the garden, and a large metal gate.

Spence was already inside, drinking coffee. Clarke was alongside him. The safe house had dark brown armchairs and a black stool in the corner of the room. Natty greeted them both, then plopped down on the stool.

'When were you going to tell me that they tried to kill you?' Spence said, still clutching his cup.

'Today,' admitted Natty. 'They fucked up either way, and I'll handle it. What happened with you?'

'I was out with Rosie. A dude tried to knife me, but he was weak. I took him down, then someone started shooting. I hit the ground, and when I got up, they were gone,' said Spence.

'Brazen move. Hitting at you in the middle of town, cameras all around. Seems like a sloppy way of doing things,' said Natty.

'Maybe so, but they nearly did it. They knew where I was too. I never told anyone I was going out, so they had someone watching me.'

'Did you put anything on socials saying where you were going?'

'No,' said Spence. 'I don't need the world knowing everything I do.'

'Either way, it's a sign you need to fall back.'

'Fall back how?' said Spence, rubbing his face.

'Stay indoors. Work the teams, then go home. People can watch your back, out of the mix,' said Natty.

'Do you think that's the best move? I mean, they shot at you too,' said Spence, sensing the shift in dynamics. On paper, Spence was still running the streets. Despite his belief that he was a caretaker for the role, it was still his role. Natty had essentially given him an order, but the pair were supposed to be working together.

'I think it's the only move.'

Clarke nodded in agreement. 'He's right, Spence. You're too valuable to be out there, so accessible. Natty's got more experience in gunplay.'

Spence didn't respond immediately, weighing up his thoughts.

Natty and Clarke were both in agreement, and while he felt he was being coddled, from a practical standpoint, he knew it was the smartest move for the time being.

'I figured something like this would happen. I'll play along. Other than that, what do we do?'

'We wait,' said Natty. 'We don't rush out and get crazy.'

'Watch for the ripples,' added Clarke. 'Someone out there is gonna talk about this. This isn't like when they shot up the spot. If they wanted you both dead, then that means someone messed up.'

Sighing, Spence nodded, hanging his head. 'I know. For now, I'll hang back. I'll speak with Carlton and tell him to watch out too.'

'We all need eyes in the back of our heads from now on,' said Natty, the others in the room nodding.

Clarke left the spot. Recalling his thoughts the previous night, Spence cleared his throat.

'Spence, I need you to promise me something.'

'What is it?' Spence straightened, noting how serious Natty looked.

'If shit goes left, promise me you'll take care of Lorraine and Jaden.'

Spence frowned. 'What do you think is going to happen?'

'Don't worry about that. Just in case, I need you to promise me, okay?'

Spence tilted his head, staring at Natty before finally nodding.

'Okay. I promise.'

CHAPTER NINETEEN

'ARE YOU FUCKING SERIOUS?'

For once, it was Roman pacing the room. Having learned of the attempts against Natty and Spence, he was beside himself with rage.

'We had an opportunity, and we took it,' said Keith, folding his arms, still stewing over the missed attempt.

'You got one of ours killed. Again. You had people firing shots in the middle of the city centre. There are fucking cameras everywhere. How the hell did you think that would work out?'

'You wouldn't be getting so aggy if we'd got them,' said Keith. 'They were there. We had them both out in the open, and we weren't gonna miss the chance to finish it.'

Frustrated by Keith's responses, Roman almost lunged at his friend, stopping at the last minute. Clenching and unclenching his fists, he glared at him.

'You and Manson should have spoken to me, but I'll deal with him when I see him. All you've done is made things harder. Police are out there, looking to solve this. The victim is affiliated with us. I'm not going back to prison over some nonsense.'

Keith shook his head. His jaw had tensed when Roman practically lunged at him, but he didn't comment on the action.

'It's calm, Roman. Don't get so stressed. We'll lay low for a bit, let them get comfy, then finish them for real. Remember, if we can't move, they can't either,' he finished.

Roman didn't bother replying. Ahmed had mentioned previously that Keith would hold him back, and Roman had dismissed it at first. But, the more he thought about it, the more what Ahmed had said made sense.

Keith seemed determined to demonstrate what a liability to their cause he was.

———

LORRAINE FINISHED her cup of tea, getting ready to head out to work. Jaden had been driven to school by his friend's mum, so she hadn't needed to take him. Sticking the cup in the kitchen sink, she called Raider.

'Lo, what's happening?' he said, sounding sleepy.

'Sorry If I woke you. Can you stop by later? We need to talk.'

'Of course. What time?'

'Nine would be good, if that's okay.'

'I'm looking forward to it. Talk to you then.' Raider hung up, sounding happy. Lorraine frowned, hoping he didn't get the wrong idea. That made her think of Natty. She hadn't spoken to him since he'd walked out, which seemed to be becoming a common occurrence for them. They seemed to go one step forward, two steps backwards. Lorraine missed him, and wanted to work things out. Hopefully, speaking to Raider and laying down the law would be a start.

———

NATTY ROSE TO HIS FEET, having completed a round of press-ups. Since the incident, he'd been distracting himself from his thoughts by training harder, heading to the cellar to shoot for hours on end, trying to make sense of things.

He kept thinking about the recent attempt on his life, comparing it to the last time people had tried to kill him. Since the prior year, his reactions had improved. He could defend himself, shoot back, and escape without injury.

He couldn't help wondering how badly things could have gone, though. It had been stupid to trust Manson, and more foolish to meet him in the current climate. In future, he would be better prepared.

As Lisa had said, no more half-measures.

Natty's thoughts shifted to Lorraine and Jaden. It was impossible to separate them from Raider, which irked Natty. Raider sliding back into their lives caused a wave of anger in Natty that he struggled to suppress. His fists clenched, and he took a deep breath. Leaving the room, he went to wash his face, then changed his clothes. As he continued to simmer, he sought a distraction. Making his mind up on the spot, he picked up his car keys, deciding to visit his mum.

He headed to his car and drove to her house, driving past the guard he had watching her place — just in case. As always, he knocked and walked in.

Natty found her lying on the sofa watching television. She glanced up at him, glaring. Neither spoke for a few moments, before his mum broke her gaze and looked back at the TV.

'I haven't seen you in ages,' she reluctantly said.

'It hasn't been that long, ma,' Natty replied, kissing her on the cheek. 'Sorry. I've been busy.'

'Busy doing what?'

'Handling business.'

'You're unemployed. What business could you possibly have been handling, or have you got a new job?'

'I'm working with unc again,' said Natty. His mum shot up, sitting upright.

'What? Why?' Frowning, she frantically shook her head.

'Things happened, and I had to get back involved. I can't get into it.'

She stared at him, her expression slowly returning to normal.

'Of course you can. I was around your dad and uncle when they were talking business, and I know what I'm talking about. Going back to work for your uncle is stupid; all it has done is show him that you're still ripe to be manipulated.'

'You can't be serious,' said Natty, annoyed at his mum's reaction, and the fact that he always seemed to let her get under his skin. 'All my life, you've been taking his money, especially since dad died. Does that mean he's manipulating you too? You're a fucking hypocrite.'

'How many times have I told you not to talk to me in that manner?' His mum shrieked, and Natty unconsciously took a step back. He had seen his mum get angry before, but he had never seen her in such a rage. It was easy to understand how she could have intimidated his dad when he was younger, if this was what he had to contend with. 'You're not a fucking gangster, Natty. You're just a kid. When your dad was your age, he had the world at his feet and the city on its knees. You think you know it all, but you don't. Your uncle is not the man you think he is. I told you this, and you didn't listen. You deserve whatever happens to you. Get out of my house.'

'Mum . . .' Natty started, but she shook her head. Radiating anger, she seemed younger, her rage emitting a youthful vibrancy.

'Don't *mum* me. I've told you and told you. If you can't speak to me respectfully, and if you can't listen to what I'm telling you, then I don't want to see you. Get out.'

Natty sighed. He hadn't meant to swear, but he didn't feel he was wrong in what he'd said. She took money from his uncle even now. *Why would she continue that practice if she felt so strongly about being indebted to him?* Shaking his head, he walked out.

Natty's phone rang, and he picked up without checking the caller.

'Yeah?'

'N-Nat . . .?' a shaky voice said. Natty froze.

'Lorraine?'

'I need you, Nat . . . now,' she gasped. Natty's blood ran cold. She sounded like she could barely speak.

'I'm on my way,' he said, hurrying to his car, starting the engine and driving away as fast as he could.

————

LORRAINE WAS AT HOME, waiting for Raider to arrive. Jaden had already gone to bed, though Lorraine doubted he was asleep. When Raider left, she would go and check to make sure.

At nine pm, there was a knock on the door. Lorraine took a deep breath and let Raider in. He grinned at her, dressed in a black tracksuit. She looked down at his trainers, then back up to his face, raising her eyebrows. Chuckling, Raider kicked off his shoes. It crossed Lorraine's mind that she'd never had to tell Natty to take his shoes off when he entered her house. It was something he had always done, and while it was a small difference, it was telling.

She entered the living room behind Raider, and he zeroed in on the wine on the coffee table, smirking at her.

'Are you trying to create a mood? I'm not sure my girl would like that,' he said. Lorraine shook her head.

'I didn't invite you here to talk about your girl, Michael. I would like it if we were civil, but as I've said before, I need you to understand that we're not friends, companions, or anything other than Jaden's parents.'

'We could be,' said Raider, as he ambled across the room toward the coffee table. Picking up the bottle of red wine, he inhaled the scent, his eyes remaining on Lorraine. 'Jaden is our kid. We could be a family again. Like I said to you last time.'

Lorraine shook her head again.

'I'm not getting into this. Why the hell did you tell Jaden what you did?'

'What are you talking about?' Raider feigned confusion.

'I'm talking about you telling your son what Natty did to you?'

'Why wouldn't I tell him? He deserves to know about the lunatic that his mummy's grinding.'

'Who I'm involved with is of no concern to you, Michael. Are we going to talk properly?'

'I thought we already were?' Raider's brow furrowed.

'We're not, but we're about to. You attacked me.'

Raider turned away, then turned back, rubbing his palms.

'It wasn't like that.'

'Wasn't it? You didn't beat me up in this same living room, with your son upstairs, because I wouldn't sleep with you?'

Raider didn't meet her eyes. 'You pissed me off, and maybe I handled it all wrong, but you pushed my buttons. You always push my buttons.'

'If me rejecting you while you were drunk, and not wanting to have sex with you is *pushing your buttons,* then you're even more deluded than I thought. The fact of the matter is that you said what you said to Jaden to drive a wedge between Natty and me, and you had absolutely no reason to do so.'

'It's not my fault that your man is sensitive. He's lucky I didn't call police on him after what he did,' snapped Raider.

'A *roadman* like you, calling the police on someone?' Lorraine snorted, growing angrier as the conversation went on. 'Doesn't that go against *the code*? Furthermore, I could have done exactly the same thing to you.'

'You didn't, though . . . did you? You fucking told your man what I did, and he attacked me from behind. He could never see me in a one-on-one fight, and we both know it. He's a pussy.' Raider's voice trailed off as he spoke, his eyes darting between Lorraine and the ground.

Lorraine watched Raider for a moment, eyes wide and mouth open. She blew out a breath and threw her hands up.

'This doesn't matter. If you're going to see Jaden, I don't want you filling his head with rubbish. Whether I agree with what Natty did to you, we both know it wasn't unprovoked. Just do what you said you wanted to do, and build a relationship with your son.'

Raider's nostrils flared as he scowled at Lorraine, both still on their feet in the living room. He grabbed the bottle of wine, took a swig, and made a face.

'That stuff's crap,' he said.

Standing in silence and shaking her head, Lorraine impaled Raider with a glare. Turning and heading for the door, she stopped beside Raider's shoes, kicking them in his direction.

'I guess we're done here,' she said. 'I hope you think about what I'm saying, Michael. If you want to be a good dad, you can be. If your intentions are positive, then I promise I'll never stand in the way of you being in Jaden's life. That's all I ask for.'

'That's all you ask for?' Raider's voice rose. He made his way toward Lorraine, deliberately stepping over the shoes she had kicked at him. 'What about what I want, huh? When do we talk about me?'

'We've been talking about you the whole time, Michael. What else do you want me to say?'

Raider's mouth tightened, and the danger sign came a shade too late for Lorraine. His palm connected with her cheek, the power jerking her head back. Before she could react, Raider grabbed her by the throat, pulling her close.

'I think you've done enough talking,' he muttered, eyes hard. 'I am sick and tired of your mouth.' Lorraine struggled in his grip, but it was futile. 'You're gonna listen to me now. What did I tell you last time? I told you that you belonged to me.' Raider slammed his fist into Lorraine's stomach, driving all the breath from her body, then punched her in the face, letting her fall to the floor.

Lorraine couldn't move as she gasped for air. Her face felt like it was on fire. Raider stood over her, bristling as he scowled with disgust. He reached down for Lorraine, snorting when she flinched.

'Understand, this is all your fault. Because of you, I suffered through months of recovery . . . you and your little fancy man, who thinks he can step into my shoes . . . thinking he can be a dad to my son.'

Raider grabbed Lorraine, hauled her to her feet, and flung her across the room. Lorraine crashed against the coffee table, sending the bottle of wine and other contents tumbling to the ground.

'I'm gonna sort you out once and for all,' vowed Raider. He grabbed Lorraine by the hair, pain shooting through her as he yanked her up. Her hand grasped the corkscrew, and as Raider went to hit her again, Lorraine jabbed it into his throat. Raider's arms released her, but she stabbed the makeshift weapon back into the same spot, now covered in his blood, as Raider tried to yell.

They tumbled back to the ground, and Lorraine's hands wrapped around his throat as she grunted. They stared into each other's eyes for a long moment, Lorraine watching as Raider jerked beneath her, the light leaving his eyes as he went perfectly still.

Tears spilled down Lorraine's cheeks. She heard a noise behind her, instantly reacting.

'Jaden, don't come in here!'

Jaden's feet stilled.

'Mummy?'

'Mummy cut herself, and there's lots of glass on the floor . . .' she said, trying to keep her voice calm, her body racked with pain.

'But—'

'Please, Jaden, go back upstairs,' she said, breathing a sigh of relief when Jaden hurried back to his room. Shakily, she stood, sobbing at the sight in front of her.

Raider lay there, unmoving in a pool of blood. Bile rose in her throat, but she forced it back down. She didn't want to get close enough to confirm, but it was clear Raider was dead. Lorraine looked at her hands, covered in the dark liquid. She took several deep breaths, her panic growing.

Scrambling to the kitchen, Lorraine washed the blood from her hands, grabbing for her phone, trembling. She froze, seconds away from calling an ambulance. More seconds passed, before she dialled a number, sniffing as the person picked up.

'Nat . . .?' Her voice broke. 'I need you, Nat . . . now.'

CHAPTER TWENTY

THE TYRES SQUEALED as Natty drove to Lorraine's, burning rubber, going as quickly as he could. He'd tried calling her back, and she hadn't answered.

Natty tried controlling his panic. He wondered what could have shaken her up like that.

Was she in trouble? Was he walking into a trap?

Finally, he arrived on Lorraine's street, jumping from the car and hurrying into the house. The door was open, and his heart was in his throat as he charged into the living room, before stopping short.

'Lo . . .' he gasped.

Raider was laid out on the living room floor. The room looked like a bomb site. Lorraine sat in the corner, phone in hand, looking at Raider's body. Natty was sure she wasn't even aware he was in the room.

'Lorraine . . . what happened?'

It was a stupid question. Raider was clearly dead, but Natty still cautiously moved toward his body. He saw a corkscrew next to his head, covered with blood, and various marks around his neck. Taking a deep breath, Natty turned to Lorraine, sitting next to her, but keeping his movements soft, not wanting to startle her.

'Are you okay?'

As if a switch had been flicked, Lorraine's face crumpled, and she burst into tears. Instinctively, Natty put his arms around her, not caring that she was covered in blood, no longer concerned with their issues . . . issues that concerned the man lying dead on the living room floor. Their eyes met as Natty inspected the bruising on her face.

'I'm sorry . . . I'm so, so, sorry,' she said, babbling nonsense words, until Natty pulled her closer. His mind whirred, trying to figure a way out of the situation. He'd put the pieces together, but needed Lorraine to confirm.

Raider had tried attacking Lorraine again, and she had fought back to defend herself in the struggle.

Self-defence or not, she had killed someone. There would be an investigation, and he couldn't see it ending without her serving time, and ruining her career, the career she was working so hard toward.

He made up his mind.

'Lorraine, listen to me,' he said sternly, his change in tone startling her. 'I need you to go upstairs, and I need you to shower. Take off your clothes, and leave them here.'

Lorraine's eyes widened, but she didn't argue, standing and pulling off her clothes as quickly as possible, her eyes flitting back to Raider.

'Good,' Natty said when she'd stripped. 'Go upstairs and shower.'

'What about . . .' Again, Lorraine glanced at Raider.

'Don't worry. Go upstairs, straight in the bathroom, and clean up.'

Lorraine left the room. Sighing, Natty rubbed his forehead. This level of clean-up was beyond him. He would need professional help to resolve this.

He considered calling his uncle, but didn't think that would go down well. Instead, he settled for Clarke.

'Nat, what's up?' Clarke sounded alert as ever.

'I need your help. There's been an incident.'

'Don't say anymore. Give me an address.'

Natty gave him Lorraine's address, then hung up. He stared at Raider, not feeling any sorrow for him. He was a horrible man, and had caused pain and misery to Lorraine. The world wouldn't miss him.

His family could, though.

Natty wondered if they had known he was going to see Lorraine. Rummaging through Raider's pockets, he grabbed his phone, gratified that it wasn't password-protected. He scanned his text messages and call log, but found nothing out of the ordinary.

A sudden wave of anger overtook him. Raider hadn't learned his lesson. He had attacked Lorraine again, and it was a pity Natty couldn't finish him personally. Lisa's words came back to him, about the half-measure he'd taken against Raider last year. He had severely beaten him, but he should have killed him.

If he had done that, Raider wouldn't have hurt Lorraine for the second time.

CLARKE ARRIVED IN RECORD TIME. He entered the living room, not even blinking at the sight of Raider's body.

'Did you do this?' He asked. Natty considered saying he had, but shook his head.

'He attacked my girl. She defended herself.'

Clarke nodded. 'Good. Not a fan of dudes that beat women. Looks like she got him good. Big mess, though.'

'That's why I called you,' said Natty. 'I know you've got connections with cleaners that can handle this. He has to disappear, and she can't be involved.'

'I do, but they answer to your unc. I can't use them without his approval.' Clarke glanced away.

Natty tensed, smart enough to read between the lines and understand what Clarke was telling him.

Still, he pushed against it.

'I have money, bro. Cost isn't a problem for the clean-up. Put me in touch with them, and I'll negotiate myself, throw you a nice chunk for the hook-up.'

Clarke shook his head. 'That's not going to work, and you know it. I can't go against your unc, and he doesn't want your money.'

The penny dropped for Natty.

'He knows, doesn't he?'

'That your missus dropped a body? No, he's not that good. I told him you had an emergency before I came over.'

'Why?' Natty asked another stupid question, surprised when Clarke's shoulders slumped.

'Because . . . look, this is my job. I take chain of command seriously. I like you, Nat. You're one hell of a soldier, and you have excellent instincts.' Clarke's lips pursed. 'Like I said, though, I'm loyal.' He sighed. 'I have to be.'

Natty scratched his cheek.

'Do I need to speak to him?'

'Eventually, but not right now. The cleaners are a phone call away, but he needs your word. Loyalty gets you full access.'

Natty blew out a breath. As hollow as he felt, it was a necessary sacrifice. Lorraine didn't deserve to be punished, and if he handled the scene himself, there was a chance he'd mess it up, and make it worse.

Until now, he'd seen his helping Spence and the crew as a temporary measure, intending to leave again once the conflict ended.

This changed that.

'I'll return full-time to the crew, if he helps me out, and protects Lorraine from prosecution.'

Clarke's eyes were full of pity, but he took out his phone, made a call, and gave the cleaners the address.

'Get your missus and take her out of here. I'll let you know when to bring her back.'

'Thanks,' mumbled Natty, leaving the room and heading upstairs, his thoughts jumbled, remembering his mum's words about his uncle. Sensing he was in trouble, Mitch had forced him to permanently commit his time to the crew. He had been manipulated for his uncle's gain.

Shaking the thoughts, Natty waited until Lorraine left the shower. She gave a start when she saw him sitting on her bed.

'What's going on?'

'I'm handling it,' said Natty. 'We need to go. You need to wake up Jaden, and pack some things. We'll stay at my place for a while.'

'Nat, I can't . . . my face . . . I can't let him see me like this.' She pointed out the bruising around her mouth and cheek. Seeing her beautiful skin marred by Raider's fists, Natty felt a fresh wave of anger.

'I'll wake him up and speak to him. I might need your help to get him to cooperate. Stay out of the light, and things should be fine. You can give him a story in the morning.' He headed for Jaden's room, hoping Jaden didn't think Natty had attacked her. Lorraine's voice stopped him.

'I . . . his dad, Nat . . . what am I supposed to tell him?'

Natty sighed.

'One problem at a time, Lo,' he replied, then went to wake Jaden.

'Natty?' Jaden mumbled, rolling over and opening his eyes after hearing Natty enter his room. Natty gazed at him for a moment, feeling a surge of affection for Jaden, even after everything that had happened.

'J, I need you to get up and get some stuff together.'

'Why? What's going on?'

'There's been a gas leak. It's not safe for you lot to stay here,' said Natty, watching Jaden shuffle to his feet and wipe his eyes. Natty helped him gather clothes and other essentials, which went into a sports bag.

'Thank you, J. For not making a fuss,' Natty praised.

'I heard banging before . . .' Jaden said, stifling a yawn. 'Mummy told me to go back to bed.'

'She's waiting for us downstairs,' replied Natty, avoiding the topic. 'We're gonna go to my place for a bit.'

Lorraine waited at the bottom of the stairs, turning away so Jaden couldn't see her face.

'J, what games are you playing at the moment?' Natty said, noting Jaden about to open his mouth to speak to Lorraine. Thankfully, Jaden responded, telling Natty about a first-person shooter he was enjoying. They headed to the car, driving to Natty's place on King George Avenue in Chapel Allerton.

Natty led them inside, switching on the hallway light.

'Mummy?' Jaden gasped, noting her bruised face. Before Lorraine could speak, he angrily whirled on Natty. 'What did you do to her?'

'I didn't do anything, J,' Natty insisted, shaking his head.

'First, you hurt my dad, now you're hurting my mum—'

'Jaden, that's enough! Natty didn't do anything. Now, I want you to go to sleep, and we can talk about things tomorrow.'

Jaden shot Natty a hard look, then glanced at his mum, then back to Natty. Lorraine took his hand, leading him to the stairs.

'He can sleep in the second room on the left,' said Natty, finding his voice. 'No one uses it.'

Lorraine was about to lead Jaden upstairs, when Natty spoke again.

'J?'

Jaden looked at Natty, his expression showing his conflict.

'I would never hurt you or your mum. I need you to know that.'

Jaden didn't respond as they headed to bed. Sighing, Natty went to make a drink, feeling wiped out after the night's events.

———

LORRAINE WAS on the sofa at Natty's the next day, numb, unable to forget what had transpired. She saw how foolish it had been to fall for Raider's mess again, and to have him in the house without Natty or a third party around. She wasn't sure if Raider's intention had been to harm her the whole time, but it was an adequate guess.

Natty had taken Jaden to school. Apart from the initial frostiness, Jaden had been fine. He chatted happily to Natty as he ate his breakfast, not knowing that his dad was dead, and that he would never see him again.

Getting to her feet, Lorraine went to wash her face and change her clothes. She found herself analysing Natty's place as she did. She had never been here before. Natty spent all of his time at her house, but she liked his layout. He had light brown walls and cream ceilings, a corner sofa, a few chairs and rugs dotted around, and an entertainment system Jaden had used in the morning, his video game console already hooked up. The other rooms were nice, the kitchen smaller than hers, but laced with new gadgets.

Lorraine hadn't expected such an investment from Natty into his home, especially when he didn't spend much time there anymore, but that didn't matter.

Lorraine was starting to get restless, but leaving the house made her feel nervous. It felt like people would see right through her when they looked at her. She couldn't stay inside forever, though. Natty had told her the problem was handled. She needed her friend more than anything.

Taking her phone out, she called Rosie.

'Lo, are you okay? I thought you'd be at work.'

'I called in sick,' said Lorraine, her voice low. Unsurprisingly, Rosie saw right through it.

'What's happened? Is it Natty? Are you two fighting?'

'Can I come and see you?' Lorraine asked, fighting to keep it together.

'Of course you can. You don't need to ask,' said Rosie.

'I'll be there soon. I promise you, I'll tell you everything then.'

———

NATTY WAS WITH SPENCE. The pair sat in the kitchen of a local safe house. He had just told Spence what had transpired, and now his friend was in shock, unable to process it.

'She killed him?'

'He beat the shit out of her, Spence. Again. She did what she had to do.' Natty's nostrils flared, his anger closer to the surface than ever.

Spence held up his hands. 'I get that. I'm not saying she did the wrong thing, but how are you going to handle it?'

'I rang Clarke. He had a clean-up crew at the house, sorting things out.'

'For free?'

Spence's question didn't surprise Natty. He'd been running the crew for long enough to understand the higher levels of power in the organisation.

Natty shook his head.

'The cost?'

'I'm back in. Properly. No way out this time,' he replied.

Spence mulled that over.

'How do you feel about that?'

'I'm not sure,' Natty honestly replied. 'Right now, all I can think about is Lorraine and Raider. I mean, I warned her about him, and she still decided to have him at the house alone?' He shrugged. 'I'm not sure what the fuck she was thinking, but it backfired.'

'I'm sure she realises that,' said Spence delicately.

'I wish he was still alive,' said Natty, glaring at his friend. 'I wish he was alive, so I could do it myself. I wish I'd killed him. Should have done it last year, when I had the chance.'

'It's not good thinking like that, Nat. I'm sorry it happened this way, but it's done.'

Natty's phone rang, disturbing the room's tense quiet. He saw the withheld number and answered.

'Yeah?'

'It's sorted. Go back anytime. I'll be in touch.'

The line went dead. Natty dropped the phone on the table, a low noise leaving his throat.

'Clarke?' asked Spence. Natty nodded.

———

LORRAINE KEPT it together during the Uber ride to Rosie's. She ignored the driver's babble, tapping her fingers on her leg, unable to remain still. Mumbling thanks when they arrived, she hurried up the path and knocked at the door. When Rosie let her in, Lorraine barged past her, hurrying for the bathroom and doubling over the toilet, where she threw up. Before long, Rosie held back her hair as she hurled, not saying a word until Lorraine was finished.

'Lo . . . I knew something was wrong on the phone,' she said, hurrying to get Lorraine some water. Gingerly, Lorraine took a few sips, breathing deeply, slightly dizzy. Rosie helped her to the bedroom, sitting Lorraine on her bed.

'Please, tell me. It was Raider, right? He hurt you again.'

Lorraine opened her mouth to speak, then started crying. Rosie laid her down on the bed, and sat next to her, holding her friend as she cried. Before long, she'd cried herself to sleep.

Rosie left her on the bed, staring at her friend with concern. She wasn't sure what had happened, but suspected it had something to do with Raider. Lorraine's face was marked, and she didn't think Natty would ever hit her. Despite his reputation, she knew how much he cared about Lorraine, recalling what he had done to Raider last time.

Silently leaving the room, she went downstairs to make a drink. She would contact Spence later, and make him tell her the whole story.

CHAPTER TWENTY-ONE

AS HE ENTERED Mitch's home, flanked by Spence and Clarke, Natty didn't know what to expect. Mitch waited, sipping a drink and reading a newspaper. He folded it and pushed it to one side as the men entered, his eyes lingering on Natty.

'Drinks?' He asked. Everyone shook their heads. Mitch took another sip of his own drink, steepling his hands. Natty took a seat, as did Spence. Clarke remained standing. Mitch's eyes flitted from Spence to Natty, neither man reacting, both waiting for him to speak.

'How are we doing?' He finally said. Spence glanced at Natty, who met his uncle's eyes.

'We're stalemating at the moment, but they're getting desperate. After we took out Dolja, they've been reckless. They failed on Spence in the middle of town, and they failed on me,' said Natty.

'Yeah . . . explain yourself, nephew. Why did you put yourself in that position?' Mitch's eyes surveyed Natty, waiting for an answer.

'We've been working on intel for a while now, since the robberies went awry. Nothing we found suggested Manson was in league with Roman and Keith. My gut told me something might be up when he contacted me, but it seemed worth the risk.' Natty held his uncle's stare for a long moment.

'And what do you think about this move, Clarke?' Mitch responded, keeping his eyes on Natty.

Clarke scratched his chin, taking a moment before responding.

'He took all the necessary precautions. He got out alive, and my sources tell me he took out one of theirs in the process. It was messy, sure, but we gained a lot of info from it.'

'Good,' Mitch said after contemplating Clarke's words. 'Well done, Nathaniel.' He took a drink from his glass before continuing, 'so what's next?'

'I think they're a little stuck. They're getting careless. Or stupid. If Manson hadn't tried to stitch me up, I think they'd be reaching out for another meeting to see if there's a deal to be made,' Natty responded.

Mitch nodded.

'Keep working on them. Put pressure on certain people in their team, and they'll fold,' he said.

'Any ideas which people we should start with?' Natty asked. Mitch didn't reply straight away.

'I couldn't say. It's about money at the end of the day. Look for the greedy people that think they deserve more. Every crew has them. Your old man was a natural when it came to sniffing them out. They can make or break the war when it's a hit-and-run situation.'

Natty absorbed the story about his dad, deciding to mull it over when he was alone.

'For now, I want to address the leadership situation. Natty, you are now in charge. Spence, you've done well. I want you to remain in an elevated position, working alongside Natty. What do you think about that?'

All eyes were on Spence, and he gave a small smile.

'I'm fine with that. It's the best thing to do.'

'I'm glad you said that,' said Mitch. 'Nat, how's your woman?'

Natty was surprised Mitch had brought up Lorraine. He hadn't expected it.

'She did what she needed to do. She's shaken up, and it'll probably take a while to get used to it. All I can do is support her,' he finished.

Mitch nodded. 'It's a bad bit of business. I never liked the guys that went around beating up women. It's good he's out of the way.'

Natty too nodded, thinking about Lorraine's reaction, and the scene he had walked in on. His stomach lurched, imagining how much worse it could have been if she hadn't done what she had.

'Have you thought any more about the supplier?' He asked, changing the subject. 'We know who he is, and if we get to him, we could apply a lot of pressure.'

'It's a no-go, Nat. Jakkar and the people he keeps around him are top-tier. If you move against his distributors, more will take their place, and we'll enter their crosshairs. As I've said previously, it would bring a level of opposition we couldn't handle.'

Natty didn't push the matter further. Nothing his uncle said was worth disputing, and he knew far more about the upper echelons of the crime world than Natty did. Once everything was squared away, he decided he would spend some time with his uncle, and learn the proper lay of the land.

The group spoke about other matters for a while. When they were making moves to leave, Natty asked his uncle if he could talk to him in private. Spence and Clarke waited outside for him. This time when Mitch motioned to the bottle of brandy, Natty agreed to have a glass.

'What did you want to speak about?'

'I wanted to ask you about my dad,' said Natty. If Mitch was surprised, he hid it well.

'What about him?'

'Was there anything about him that I don't know . . .? Things he was doing in the game, or things that might have just got him killed?'

Mitch tilted his head. 'Where's this coming from?'

'I've just been thinking lately,' replied Natty. 'I didn't know much about him, and now I'm in the game at a high level. I want to know what I don't already know.'

Mitch leant back in his chair, taking a deep breath.

'I get that, nephew. You were young when your dad died. Too young to properly understand it. Your dad was a force. Anyone from the old days will tell you that for free. He didn't back down, and he wasn't afraid to go that extra mile to put someone down. Trust me, that's a skill that not many have.' Mitch took a sip of brandy. 'He was flawed; sometimes he went a little too far, and sometimes you need to have a little bit of fear for things around you, to keep you sharp; keep you making good decisions.'

'Are you saying his decisions got him killed?'

'I'm saying that he always had something to prove. Above all else, this is the only thing you need to truly remember about your dad; he loved you more than anything. He would be proud of the man you've become, Nathaniel.'

———

MITCH'S WORDS stayed with Natty as Clarke drove him and Spence back to the safe house. They sat outside, out of earshot of a man standing guard nearby.

'Are you sure you don't mind stepping aside?' Natty asked. To his surprise, Spence smiled.

'I was keeping the seat warm, Nat. The question is, how do you feel? You kinda got the position under duress, but is it actually what you want?'

Natty rubbed his hands together, tempted to put them in his pockets.

'So much has happened that I'm not really sure. If it's not the game, it's Lorraine and everything going on there. Seems like just yesterday my biggest concern was buying some new clothes so I could go out and grab some women. Now, we're in the mix, playing for keeps.' He shrugged. 'Maybe this is just what I'm destined to do.'

'Your destiny is whatever you make it, Nat. No one can take that from you, whether it's your uncle, or the streets.'

'Easier said than done.' Natty looked at his friend, who nodded in agreement.

'Maybe so. Still, just do what you want to do, and never feel that you don't have options.'

———

NATTY SLEPT EARLY THAT NIGHT, exhausted after the past few days. He'd checked in with Lorraine, and while she still seemed shaky, he planned to spend some time with her, after he ensured things were set up within the team.

When he woke up and got ready, he went shopping, planning to stock up on some essentials. Leaving Tesco's and heading for his car, he stopped short when he saw a man standing by his ride, smiling at him. Natty searched his mental *street database*, but didn't recognise him. He was a few inches shorter than Natty, wearing slim-fit jeans, a t-shirt and a black jacket with boots. He had dark brown skin, with copious facial hair and light brown eyes. Natty cautiously approached, eyes narrowed.

'Can I help you?' He asked, wondering if he'd been caught slipping by Roman's people.

The man's smile widened.

'I hope so, Natty. I've been waiting to speak with you. When I heard you were doing the big shop, I figured this was the chance.'

'Who are you?' Natty bluntly cut across the posturing. If this bothered the man, he didn't even flinch. Reaching into his pocket, he showed Natty his identification, and Natty's stomach sank.

'Detective Brown, but you can call me Brown. Can I call you Natty Deeds, or do you prefer *Nathaniel*?'

'No comment,' said Natty, pressing a button and opening his boot. To his surprise, Brown reached for a bag, but Natty stopped him. 'I don't need your help. Just fuck off.'

'We're friends, Deeds. At least, I want us to be.'

'I don't have any friends that are pigs, so you're wasting your time.'

Brown shook his head.

'Trust me, I'm the best friend you could have. The streets have been talking a lot about you and your promotion. It's your lucky day. You have the best detective in the city watching your back.'

'Are you planning on getting to a point anytime soon? I don't know what you're talking about.' Natty grabbed the shopping bags from the trolley.

Brown gave him a suspicious look.

'I could have gone to Roman and his mates, bro. Instead, I picked you, and I hope you realise that importance.'

'Pretend I don't,' said Natty, placing the bags in the boot. He would give Brown nothing, but would ensure he got the rest out of him.

'Raider,' said Brown, his smile almost joker-like.

'Who?' Natty closed the boot, but didn't move to get in the car.

'He was a friend of mine, for years now. He gave me titbits, mostly little bits about which crews were moving and where . . . until some sod put him in the hospital last year. Now, he's dead, and I know you're involved.'

Natty's stomach turned to ice. He didn't know how Brown had linked him to Raider, and whether Raider had mentioned him to Brown, but he couldn't fall apart now. The only good thing was that Brown hadn't mentioned Lorraine.

'Are you going somewhere with this?'

Brown laughed. 'I heard you were a little more patient than this, Deeds. I know what you've got going on, and I respect it. I want us to be friends, and I want us to be partners.'

'I still don't know what you're talking about,' said Natty. Brown's laughter vanished in an instant, and Natty's eyebrows rose.

'Don't make me show you my bad side, Deeds. You've got a lot to lose; your livelihood, Raider's bitch and his son. If you want to keep providing, and if you don't want the whole thing brought down on you and your team, get with the program.'

Natty's thoughts were all over the place. Brown had played this perfectly. He had approached Natty in public, and lured him in under a veneer of friendliness. Now, he was showing his teeth.

Natty had encountered various law officers during his time in the streets. He'd learned well and granted them little time or attention. They'd tried breaking him in his younger days, wanting him to snitch, threatening him with various punishments. Natty had stood tall, and knowing they had nothing on him, the police had backed off.

Now, he had Brown on his tail.

Brown took out his phone.

'Take my number, Deeds. If you're serious, get in touch, and we'll talk numbers.' He stepped away from Natty's car. 'Don't keep me waiting too long, though. Who knows what I'll end up doing if you do.'

CHAPTER TWENTY-TWO

NATTY KEPT things low-key after Brown's impromptu ambush. The visit from the detective had rattled him, making him second-guess his movements. He had Carlton handle his running around, namely returning calls to contacts Natty had attempted to pump for information on Roman and Keith. Besides this, he spent several hours with Spence, learning more about the organisation; things he hadn't previously known.

In doing so, he realised just how much power his uncle had.

On the streets, they had over one hundred dealers, then numerous distributors, along with dozens of distribution spots and safe houses, carefully curated over the years. They had sites that were generally known about, along with others that were intricately hidden from the majority. They dealt with people all over Leeds, but Mitch had made Chapeltown his stronghold over the past six years, and it was the seat of the team's power.

All in all, the organisation brought in over a million pounds a month. Once overhead was factored in, along with all the other running costs, the profits were still out of this world.

Even Spence, who ran the team for a short while, had made tremendous money. He received numerous bonuses and percentage-based targets initially, though the rise of Roman's crew had dipped into his profits slightly toward the end.

To Natty, this explained Brown's desire to get his hooks into him. If he had any indication of the money being made by the Dunns, he would do whatever he needed to get a piece of that.

Natty hadn't decided what to do about the officer. He'd done a bit of digging into the name, and found he was linked to numerous seizures and arrests across Yorkshire and the surrounding areas, and had run his own drug squad for a while, with significant results. With what Natty knew about him, those results were likely based on his sway with local gangs and organisations, and he knew paid informants would often give information on other people to continue plying their trade.

It surprised Natty that Raider had been one of them. While he had little respect for Raider as a man, he'd always had the impression he was the sort who would rather do time than cooperate with the police. Now, that was tarnished, but it wasn't the most critical factor. Doing something about Brown, and keeping him away from Lorraine, was.

Natty had been too busy to spend real time with her, but she was on his to-do list, along with his mum, whom he drove to see after making some calls. Her reaction to him working for his uncle again had stuck in his mind. It seemed overblown then, but since then, Natty had been practically forced to commit himself to Mitch's crew.

There was something his mum wasn't telling him, and it irked Natty. He planned to give his mum his full attention. Spence was holding down the fort and would tell him if anything else came up.

Hopefully, he would catch her in a better mood this time.

SPENCE UNLOCKED his door and entered the house. As he entered the living room, Rosie rushed from her seat to greet him, flinging her arms around him.

'I was worried about you,' she murmured. Spence held her tightly. She'd been like this ever since the shooting attempt. Constantly worrying about him, sending him texts to see where he was, and what time he would be finished.

'You've been more concerned for my welfare lately,' he pointed out.

'Is that a bad thing?' Rosie looked up at him. Spence shook his head.

'I guess not. You don't need to worry about me, though. Me and Natty were sorting some stuff.'

'That doesn't sound as reassuring as you think it does,' said Rosie. 'People tried killing you both.'

'I get that,' said Spence gently. 'Nothing like that will ever happen again, though.'

'You can't be sure about that.'

Spence sighed. They were rehashing things they'd said previously. He was trying to remain positive; they'd had dinner before the shooting, getting things out in the open, ready to move forward, but then the attempted assassination happened, putting a dampener on their situation.

'We've been through this,' he started. Rosie shook her head.

'I know. I can't shake it. I know what you're into, but it never really hit me until I saw it first-hand.' Rosie took a deep breath. 'All of this is so real. Lorraine got beaten up . . . in her own house, and it wasn't even the first time. She — people are dying. It's all just too much.'

All Spence could do was hug Rosie. He understood her concerns, but overthinking things would only make them worse for her.

'Rosie, please listen to me when I say there is nothing to worry about. I will protect you. Nothing is going to happen, and I promise that I'm going to be safe.' He brushed his lips against hers. 'Okay?'

Slowly, Rosie nodded, and Spence inwardly breathed a sigh of relief. He had enough things in the streets to handle, without worrying about Rosie too.

———

BEFORE STOPPING by his mum's, Natty ordered her some food, knowing that she had a particular penchant for ox-tail, along with rice and peas, and salad. Picking himself up the same, and a bottle of Guinness

Punch, he knocked and walked into his mum's house, finding her on the sofa, wrapped in a blanket.

'Are you okay, mum?' He asked, kissing her on the cheek. 'I bought you some food from Dutch Pot.'

'I'm not hungry,' she replied. 'I'm on painkillers for my stomach, and I don't have much of an appetite.'

Natty put his mum's food in the kitchen, then sat in the living room next to her to eat his.

'What's wrong with your stomach?' He asked. She made a face.

'You never listen to me. I told you before that I was having issues. I've tried different tablets, but they don't seem to work.'

Natty frowned. He couldn't recall his mum mentioning anything about her *condition*.

'Do we need to go to the doctors? Have you had an x-ray or anything?'

His mum waved him off. 'I'll be fine. I just need to rest.'

Natty finished his food, thinking about how things were with his mum lately. He didn't know how to get them back on a positive footing. If he was honest, he couldn't remember the last time they had been. Natty had been deep in the streets for years, but he tried to look after his mum. He spent time with her, cooked for her, and tried to maintain an interest in things she wanted to talk about, regardless of whether Rudy had been around.

That said, he'd never questioned her decline, and why she just seemed to stop living. It was hard comparing her to the energetic, outgoing woman he remembered from childhood.

'Why do we argue so much?' He found himself asking. His mum shifted, brow furrowing as she paid attention to her son.

'What?'

'Me and you. Why do we argue so much?'

'Nat, what are you talking about?' His mum looked even more confused.

'I'm interested. I just want to know,' Natty replied.

'I don't know what you mean.'

Natty tried another angle.

'Do you love me?' She opened her mouth to reply, but Natty spoke again before she could. 'Do you even like me?'

'Where is this coming from?' She asked. Natty hadn't seen her so off-guard before.

Natty rubbed his arm, then finished the rest of his drink, leaving the can on the table with the remains of his food.

'I've just been thinking. I mean, we clash constantly. I love you, ma. You've always been there for me, but you're always angry, and I don't know why.'

His mum sat up, her expression thunderous.

'I don't have to listen to this crap, Nathaniel. I told you I was sick. I don't know why you've come around, looking to provoke me, but I don't like it.' Her voice rose. 'You don't have a clue about anything. You don't know what my life has been like. How dare you?'

Natty shook his head, controlling the conversation, refusing to be baited.

'That's why I'm asking,' he replied. 'I want to find out. I want to understand, but I know there's more to it than that. My life is hard too. You wouldn't believe the things I've been dealing with lately.' Natty's thoughts flitted to his enemies, then to Lorraine on the living room floor, covered in blood, barely able to communicate. Nostrils flaring, he tensed.

'You're my son,' she finally replied, her voice devoid of energy. Natty didn't understand the sudden switch, but he felt like he was onto something, and kept pushing.

'That's not an answer, ma. Or . . . maybe it is. Maybe the fact you can't say it is the answer. I never had to worry about whether my dad loved me.'

Natty wasn't sure what reaction he would get, but when he saw the fiery anger in his mum's eyes, he knew he had overreached.

'What the hell do you mean by that? You think you know it all, Nat, but you know nothing. You don't know a thing about your dad. You were a kid when he died.'

'He was flawed, I know that. Aggressive, hard to deal with at times; a bit of a hothead. I can relate to all of that. Regardless, I know he cared about his family. I always knew that he loved me,' Natty shouted, unsure why he was suddenly so furious with his mum, putting it down to her avoidance of the question.

'Family?' His mum shrieked. 'He was a cheating bastard, that's what he was. Slept with whatever woman he could, while I was at home, cooking, cleaning, working, looking after his son. You have absolutely no idea about anything, Nathaniel. Your dad was a terrible husband, and that's why I did the same thing back to him.'

'What are you talking about?' Natty's voice wavered, head reeling with his mum's emotional outburst. He noted she'd said *his son* . . . realising this was likely why his mum had never been affectionate toward him. *She'd chosen not to nurture him; he'd been thrust upon her by his absent dad . . .*

'I'm talking about Rudy, what else? I was seeing him for years behind your dad's back. While your dad was with his women, Rudy took care of me. Like a real man.'

Natty's mouth fell open, his throat dry. He tried to find the words; tried controlling the building emotion. He knew about his mum and Rudy before they'd announced their relationship, having caught them kissing, but the idea that they'd carried on an affair behind his dad's back was a revelation he hadn't expected.

'You cheated on my dad, with Rudy?' He said in a low voice. His mum sneered.

'Why is it one rule for him, and another rule for me?' Her expression changed, becoming more calculating. 'Did you kill Rudy?'

Natty and his mum locked eyes, and he fought to show no emotion as he responded.

'No.'

She continued to stare. To Natty, it was like looking into the past. His mum's words seemed to give her energy, and she looked more alive than she had in years.

'You're just the latest in a line,' she finally said.

'What the fuck are you talking about?' Natty lost his temper, uncaring of the ramifications. He was tired of snide remarks and half-answers. Whatever state his mum was in, at least she was giving him actual responses he could work with.

She shook her head, chuckling.

'I'm talking about your dad that you love so much. His death.' She was trembling; Natty didn't know if that was from rage or excitement. 'It was planned.'

'You don't . . .' Natty started.

'*You don't*, you mean. I already said, you don't have a clue, Nathaniel. They pinned it on the yardies. You were young, but back then, they were shooting and stabbing everything in sight. They didn't want to, but your dad . . . he was out of control.' She bit her lip, shaking her head. Natty went completely still, brain roaring, trying to make sense of the monumental information he was being hammered with.

'You're lying.'

Again, his mum shook her head, sounding more alive, yet flatter than ever.

'I loved Tyrone Dunn for a long time, but he was damaged.' She wiped her eyes. 'I couldn't fix him.'

'You couldn't . . . fix him?'

'No one could. He was killing people, not listening to reason . . . not thinking about the consequences.' His mum took a deep breath. 'That's why he had to die.'

Natty couldn't speak. His throat completely closed up as the magnitude of his mum's words truly hit him. His eyes were wet, but he did nothing to stem the tears rolling down his face.

His mum nodded, seemingly understanding why he hadn't responded.

'It was death or jail, Nathaniel. Death was better.' She sighed. 'Rudy told me about it a few months after he'd been killed.'

Now, Natty found his words.

'You stayed with the man that killed your husband . . . for years?' His cold, deadly tone sounded foreign; connected to the out-of-body experience he was enduring. His mum didn't flinch, totally unrepentant about what she had just admitted.

'I'll ask you again; did you kill Rudy?' She nodded, sniffing. 'I know you did. Mitch probably put you up to it, just like he did Rudy with your dad. That's what he does. That's what I tried warning you about, before you were stupid enough to get involved with him again. Mitch always keeps his hands clean.'

Natty shot to his feet, his leg catching the coffee table in his haste. The remains of his food clattered to the floor, but he paid it no attention. He couldn't be here any longer. He had to leave.

'Natty? Nathaniel!'

Natty ignored his mum, stumbling for the door, more tears spilling down his cheeks. Hurrying to the car, he jumped in and sped off, giving way to racking sobs in a manner that he hadn't in years. If ever.

His phone buzzed, and Natty wiped the tears away. Carlton was calling, but Natty ignored the call. He needed to go home, and he needed to drink until he could forget what had transpired.

———

CARLTON FROWNED, calling Natty again, surprised when he didn't answer. He'd been trying to reach him for a while. Dropping his phone on his lap, he continued driving from Little London to his spot.

Recently, Carlton had moved to a new house on Grange Crescent. With the extra money and responsibility, he had more than enough to rent the property, and had splurged on some top-notch furniture. Lately, things had been brilliant for him. He had been elevated since his early days as a runner. Natty had always treated him well, and Spence had continued the tradition after Natty's departure.

Still, he was glad Natty was back. As efficient as Spence was, something in Natty's demeanour made Carlton feel more secure about the future. He wasn't worried about Roman or any of the others. As long as they stayed strong, they would be fine.

Carlton turned up the music, rapping along with *Fredo*. His meetings on behalf of Natty had yielded nothing, people still cagey about taking sides in the conflict. He planned to speak with Natty, imagining his mentor would have a plan. As he pulled up outside his house and unlocked the door, his thoughts were on the fat spliff he was going to smoke. Those thoughts were dashed when a gun was pointed at his face.

'Get in the living room,' a voice growled. Carlton froze, unable to believe what was happening, recognising Keith's angry features.

'How did you . . .'

'Shut up,' said Keith. 'Get in there.'

Carlton was dragged into his living room and flung to the floor. Another man waited, also armed. He was tall, strongly built, and looked older than Keith.

Carlton looked at him, then behind to Keith, who closed the living room door, cutting off any avenue of escape.

'Where's Natty, you little bitch?' Keith snarled. Carlton shook his head. Keith's eyes bulged, and he pointed the gun at Carlton. 'I swear, you better tell me, or you're dead.'

'Keith . . .' Manson said, but it was too late.

Carlton didn't immediately realise what had happened. He heard the shot, then there was a split-second before the searing pain, his chest feeling like it had exploded. He didn't even get the chance to scream, before the second shot, followed by darkness.

———

'WHAT HAPPENED TO INTERROGATING HIM?'

'Fuck him.' Keith stepped forward, aiming the gun again, and firing twice more into Carlton's body. 'He's a little messenger. He won't know shit. Let's just get out of here.'

Manson opened his mouth to protest, but changed his mind. Keith wasn't going to listen to reason. He gave Carlton's body one final look, then followed Keith, leaving Carlton in a pool of his own blood.

CHAPTER TWENTY-THREE

SPENCE HUNG BACK, watching Rosie with Lorraine. It was strange seeing her fuss over her friend. In the past, they would laugh, joke and poke fun at each other. That was long gone. Lorraine had begun depending on her friend more and more recently.

With Natty tied up, Rosie was about the only person she could speak to. Even when Natty was free, she didn't get much sense out of him. Talking about the situation made him furious, meaning Lorraine never got the comfort she needed from him.

Raider's death was public news, but nobody had a motive or a reason behind it; no one who wasn't deep in the game, anyway.

'How are you doing?' Rosie asked, as she sat next to Lorraine. She'd made them cups of tea, but Spence had settled for water.

'I don't know,' said Lorraine, her voice quiet, trembling. Rosie put her cup down, putting her arm around Lorraine's shoulder and squeezing her. Taking his cue, Spence moved in and took Lorraine's hand, not speaking. 'I still can't believe what I've done. I keep waiting for it to settle in; to be able to go about my life as normal, but I can't. Not yet. I struggle to eat and sleep. I'm just shuffling along.'

'I know you're hurting,' said Rosie, 'but you have to realise that you did what you needed to do.'

'I killed someone,' Lorraine glumly responded, but Rosie wasn't having that.

'You defended yourself. Raider tried to kill you, and you had yourself and Jaden to think about. You should be proud, Lo. I mean that.'

'She's right,' Spence gently added. 'Raider was out to get you. What was the alternative? Letting him succeed?'

Lorraine sighed, closing her eyes. When she opened them, she looked right at Spence.

'Why hasn't Natty been around? He hasn't been answering my calls, and when I see him, he doesn't stop by for long.'

Spence shifted in place, not knowing how much Natty had told Lorraine about their business. Things had been frosty between them and despite the aftermath of Raider's death seemingly fixing that, it was taking a while to return to normal.

'He's making sure things are safe,' said Spence, thinking of their meetings with Mitch and Clarke. 'Part of that involves being out in the streets and making things happen. I suppose another part of it could be Jaden.'

'What about him?' Lorraine's eyes narrowed. The last thing Jaden needed was more drama. He didn't know his dad was dead, but knew he was missing.

'Natty thinks he hates him.'

Lorraine shook her head, though she understood how hurt Natty had been by Jaden's comments after he had seen his dad.

'Jaden's a kid. He was excited to see his dad, and Raider manipulated him and took advantage of that. Natty doesn't need to worry.'

Spence was about to reply, when his phone rang. Moving a short distance away from the women, he answered.

'Yes?'

Spence's eyes widened as he listened to the person on the other end.

'I'm on my way. Get everyone there,' he said, turning to the women, who could tell by his tone of voice that something had happened.

'I need to go. I'll be back soon.' He rushed from the house.

Natty's head lolled as he took a deep breath, regretting the amount of white rum he'd drunk. He couldn't stop going over what his mum had said.

As disturbed as she was, Natty didn't doubt she was telling the truth. She had cheated on his dad, with a man Natty had grown up knowing . . . later working for. She had looked him in the eye every day, knowing what Rudy had done, and Natty didn't know how to deal with that fact. His mum had played him for a fool. Rudy had played him for a fool, and for the first time since he'd pulled the trigger on the man, Natty was truly glad he'd done it. Part of him now wished he'd gone further. If he had the chance to go back, he would have tortured Rudy until he begged for mercy.

Natty rubbed his throat, his eyes heavy. His uncle, the man he'd looked up to, had been equally involved in his dad's death. Mitch had killed his own brother, over business. He'd kept that to himself for nearly twenty years, happy to go on filling his pockets and growing richer. Natty had foolishly tied himself to the man. He was working with his uncle, getting deeper into his pocket, while Mitch was probably laughing at him, knowing what he'd done.

Natty's phone rang. He saw Spence's number, but didn't answer. He'd ignored multiple calls from workers and associates. He didn't have anything to say to them. The fact they worked for his uncle was an additional factor. He couldn't trust them. For all he knew, they were spying on him.

Lately, everything seemed to be falling apart. Natty had made the wrong decisions in his personal and professional life. He remembered sitting by himself in a similar position last year after attacking Raider. He'd been professionally cut off, Lorraine wasn't talking to him, and he had fallen out with Spence, yet he had pulled himself up. He didn't see how he could get back this time.

Roman and his people were circling. Lorraine was adrift, and he didn't know how to help her. He had a corrupt police officer on his back. Jaden hated him, and the way things seemed, he had just cut ties with his mum, and his uncle would be next.

Natty thought about his dad, trying to dredge up childhood memories. His dad had been a happy-go-lucky man, and they had spent a lot of time together. They would go to football games, and often hung out at the Caribbean Cricket Club on Scott Hall Road. His dad would even sit and play video games with him, even though it was clear to Natty he didn't want to.

As Natty had grown older, his dad had trained him in the garage, giving him little tips for life — tips Natty had kept close to his heart as he'd grown older. Despite those moments, Natty recalled his dad spending a lot of time out of the house. At the time, he had assumed he was handling business, but now he wondered if he'd been going to see his other women all those times.

It made Natty think about his own path. After his dad died, he'd started selling drugs, and over time, he'd picked up some of his dad's characteristics. He wasn't afraid to fight, never backed down, and, importantly, he liked the ladies, and they liked him.

Still, he had settled down, part of him thinking that when he did, he would be okay; that the right woman would *fix* him.

Lisa flitted across his mind for a moment, but Natty closed his eyes, overwhelmed by his different thoughts. Tears spilt down his face, but this time, Natty wiped them away, breathing hard. He couldn't do this. This wasn't the time for pity. He wouldn't let his mum, or anyone else, ruin his dad's legacy in his eyes.

Whatever his dad had done, Natty held onto one fact above all: his dad had loved him. He was proud to be a Dunn, and that had been instilled in him from a young age. His dad had never made out he was perfect, but he had tried to make the right moves, trying to treat Natty better than he'd been treated. Natty knew his dad had grown up without a father, forcing him to grow too quickly; to hit the streets with a vengeance, because there was no other option.

Despite everything, his dad had never backed down. Natty wouldn't either.

'You can't slip up. The streets are waiting for that, and they'll tear you apart if you're not prepared. Get me?'

Rising to his feet too quickly, Natty squeezed his eyes shut, overcome with dizziness for a second. He went to the bathroom, splashing cold water on his face to freshen up.

'I'm not going to back down,' he mumbled, looking at his bleary expression in the mirror. He wasn't sure what his first move would be, but a knock at the door made his mind up for him.

'Nat? If you're in there, I really need to speak to you,' said Spence. Natty went to let him in, still feeling ropey from the liquor he'd drunk. Spence wrinkled his nose.

'Christ, Natty, you stink. You been having a party for one, instead of answering your phone? I tried you half a dozen times.'

'Sorry,' Natty mumbled. 'I had some stuff going on. What's happening?'

When Natty saw the serious expression on Spence's face, he immediately straightened, bracing himself for the worst.

'It's Carlton,' said Spence, sighing. 'He's dead.'

CHAPTER TWENTY-FOUR

'WHO DO WE GET NEXT?'

Roman and Keith were at *The Wreck*, watching a football match being played. The chilly weather had them well-wrapped up. They didn't think Natty and co would dare attack in public, but had soldiers nearby, just in case.

Roman watched a player delivering a pinpoint pass to a striker, who then lost their composure in front of the goal.

'We should have gone for Natty, or at least Spence again,' he said. Keith sniffed.

'You keep saying that, but we had the drop on Carlton. It opens us up to move in and establish ourselves in Little London too.'

'What if it makes the others go to ground? It's hard enough tracking them as it is. They're gonna be gunning for us even more now.'

'We knew the risks,' said Keith, tired of the back and forth. He didn't know what had happened to Roman in prison, but he seemed to have lost his edge. He was still intelligent and strategic, but his caution was annoying. Keith remembered how they used to be. They would simply devise a plan and act, damn the consequences. He wanted to ride out on Spence, Natty, and anyone else who got in their way. The soft approach they were taking was taxing.

'I know we did, but one big move could have been the way to go. We've exposed ourselves with how we've gone at them,' Roman said, eyes still on the match.

'Don't worry about it. Me and Manson have it all—'

'Fuck Manson,' snapped Roman. Several nearby spectators glanced at them, but turned away when they saw the expression on Roman's face. 'I don't know what's happened with you two, but you're making a lot of moves without informing me.'

Keith cut his eyes to Roman, instantly on edge.

'What are you getting at?'

The two friends locked eyes, Keith's frown deepening. Roman spoke a moment later.

'I want to be involved, and not after the fact.'

Keith nodded.

'Fine. We'll get the rest of them. Don't worry.'

Roman relaxed. As he watched the match, he wondered how Natty and the others would react to the loss of one of their people.

———

NATTY SAT with the crew chiefs and higher-ups. Half a dozen people were squashed in the room, waiting for him to speak. He noticed Lisa standing at the back of the room near Clarke, but turned away when her eyes locked onto his. Natty hadn't yet spoken with Mitch about Carlton or anything else. The things his mum had told him were still percolating, but for now, he had more than enough to focus on.

'Everyone knows what went down,' he started. 'Carlton was real, all the way to the end.' Natty scanned the room. 'He started from the bottom . . . like most of us. He hustled, kept his head down for years, always did his job . . . represented the crew to the fullest. They shouldn't have gotten near him, but they did, and now they need to go . . . that means no more messing around, hitting and running. We're gonna make a plan, execute it, and eliminate them for good. Spence,' Natty faced his friend, who waited, alert, 'smother the hood. I want to know where they're hiding. Put fifty bags on their heads . . . whoever gets them, gets the money.'

Spence nodded, and there were several murmurs and small smiles. Fifty thousand pounds was a tremendous amount of money, and they were sure it would put the Hood on notice.

'That's all I have to say for now. Get out there to our people, make sure they toe the line, and we'll have this sorted, then we can go back to doing what we do best: making money, and running the blocks.'

The chiefs made their way from the room. Lisa didn't move. Spence and Clarke hesitated by the door, looking from Lisa, to Natty. Natty nodded, and Spence left the room. Lisa did the same to Clarke, who closed the door behind him.

'That was a surprise,' Natty started. It had been a while since he had been alone with Lisa, and whilst he was still aware of the chemistry between them, his newfound focus seemed to keep it at bay.

Natty had three priorities: the war, Lorraine, and Jaden. Lisa could positively contribute to one of them, but do harm to the other two. He planned on having a conversation with Lorraine, and making sure she was okay. Part of him wanted to confide in her about what his mum had said, but he didn't want to pressure her, given what she had been through. He hadn't even said anything to Spence, unsure where to start.

'What was?' Lisa asked.

'You dismissing Clarke. I know you two are tight, but he seems to only answer to you and Mitch.'

'We understand one another,' said Lisa. 'We've been working together a long time.'

'How long?' Natty asked, intrigued.

'A long time,' Lisa repeated.

Natty shrugged, moving on.

'While you're here, I know you've been skirting around Roman's crew, but I need you to infiltrate fully. No holding back.'

'Fine,' said Lisa. Natty knew she understood the assignment, but it still left an odd feeling in his stomach.

'Goes without saying, but you'll get the fifty grand if you get either of them, along with double your usual pay,' he added.

'Fine.'

Natty sighed.

'I hate what I'm asking you to do.'

Lisa moved toward him. Natty watched, frozen to the spot.

'Regardless, you asked anyway, didn't you . . . because you're a leader.' She stared, standing directly in front of Natty. 'You do what you have to do . . . just like me.'

Natty's heart hammered against his chest, and when Lisa moved into his arms, he didn't move when their lips met. Rather than immediately pull away, he deepened the kiss, grabbing the small of her back and pulling her closer. Desire surged through him before reality hit, and he pulled away, setting Lisa down and stepping back, panting.

'We shouldn't have done that,' he said, when he'd got himself under control. Eyes glittering, Lisa simply licked her lips and walked away. Natty stared at the closed door, stunned at what had transpired. He wasn't surprised by what Lisa had done, but he was surprised he hadn't pulled away.

Shaking it off, he brushed himself down and left the house, channelling his dad. There was still plenty to sort out, and he didn't have time to stall.

———

Natty hesitated outside Lorraine's. He wiped his mouth. Lisa hadn't worn lipstick, but he still felt paranoid being around Lorraine, knowing what had just happened. Getting himself together, he knocked on the door. Lorraine answered, and let him in without a word.

Jaden was in the living room, watching television. Natty noticed a book on the sofa, along with a blanket, deducing Lorraine had been sitting there. Jaden glanced up, eyes widening when he saw Natty. Natty remained standing by the door, even as Lorraine took her seat on the sofa, giving him a weird look.

'J, I love you,' he said.

Lorraine gasped. Jaden's mouth opened, his brow furrowing, but Natty shook his head, and the child didn't speak.

'I've always loved you. I . . . always wanted to be your dad, but I wasn't good enough. Maybe I never will be, but regardless, I'll always be there for you, even if you hate me.' Natty glanced at Lorraine, who was looking at him in stunned silence, then turned back to Jaden. 'Your dad did a bad thing. He hurt your mum, so I hurt him right back. I would do the same to anyone who tried hurting you or your mum.' Walking to Jaden, Natty rested his hand on his thin shoulder. 'You're a good kid, and I'm proud of you.'

For a moment, no one moved, then Jaden jumped to his feet, hugging Natty around the waist. Natty stroked his hair, tears in his eyes again. This time, he didn't care. They were happy tears, and he was elated that he'd shared what was in his heart. Just then, Lorraine's mum left the kitchen. Natty hadn't even known she was there.

'Come on, Jaden. Let's let your mum and Natty talk,' she said, squeezing Natty's shoulder and giving him a small smile. She led Jaden from the room, leaving him with Lorraine.

For a long moment, they stared at one another. Lorraine's bruises were fading, but remained visible. Despite this, it didn't detract from her beauty.

'How are you?' Natty asked.

'I'm . . . a killer,' replied Lorraine, barely above a whisper. Natty didn't respond, though he wanted to. She had to get it out. 'I've tried dealing with it, but I can't. It consumes me, and I feel dirty. All the time.'

Finally moving, Natty sat next to Lorraine, wrapping his arms around her as she pressed against him.

'That makes two of us, Lo.' Natty paused, letting the words sink in. Lorraine lifted her tear-soaked head, looking directly into Natty's eyes.

'Lo, you're the best person I know,' he continued. 'You protected yourself. Your family. That's the only thing that matters, because that's what good people do. They protect family.'

Lorraine placed her head back on Natty's body. He felt her tears marring his jacket, but didn't move her.

'You and Jaden are my family. I'll always protect you. I need you, both of you. You need me too.'

Lorraine truly broke down then, openly crying.

'I was so scared,' she sobbed. 'We weren't talking, and I thought he was going to kill me, and . . .'

'I know,' murmured Natty. He swallowed down the guilt he felt over what had transpired with Lisa. 'You did what needed to be done. It's okay to be scared. When it gets too much, you can always lean on me.'

CHAPTER TWENTY-FIVE

SEVERAL DAYS LATER, Natty linked up with Spence. He'd kept it close to home, spending time with Lorraine and Jaden, taking him to school, ensuring he was okay and looked after.

The pair met at the main safe house, Spence holding a hot drink as Natty paced the room.

'I spoke with your unc,' Spence said. 'He's up to date on what happened. 'I don't think he's arsed about who replaces Carlton. I doubt he even knows who he is,' said Spence sadly.

Natty just nodded. Nothing surprised him about his uncle anymore. He was a ruthless man who didn't seem to have real feelings for anyone.

'Don't let my uncle fool you,' replied Natty. 'He knows more than you think.'

Spence shot Natty a quizzical look. 'What do you mean by that?'

Natty shook his head. 'Nothing, bro. I'm just saying . . . he's on top for a reason. He doesn't miss a trick. Forget it. Do you have someone in mind to replace Carlton?'

'There's a dude called Jermaine. He runs a few spots for us near Spencer Place.'

'Is he tidy?'

Spence nodded. 'He's doing well around there. We can try him temporarily, and think about other people to do it permanently if it doesn't work out.'

'Sounds good,' said Natty.

Spence rubbed his knuckle, glancing around the room and lowering his voice before he spoke again.

'Lisa reached out to me,' he said.

Natty ignored the jolt in his stomach at the mention of her name.

'Why are you whispering? We're the only ones in the room,' he pointed out.

'Don't worry about it,' replied Spence, speaking normally again. 'She's been working on getting close to Keith. Apparently, he's got this Chinese girl that he's sweet on. She's called Danielle or something. She's an escort . . . been around the Hood apparently, too. Anyway, they had a falling out, and she cursed him out to her friends.'

'How did it get back to Lisa?' Natty asked.

'Word got around to one of her girls, and she passed it on to me. They're already back together. You know what those social media arguments are like. It's all for attention.'

'That's our way in then,' said Natty.

Spence tilted his head, smirking.

'What's going on with you two?'

'Who?'

Clearly exasperated, Spence sighed.

'You and Lisa. I saw your face when she got brought up. What's happening?'

'Nothing is happening.'

Spence sipped his drink. 'You don't need to lie to me, Natty. If you don't want to tell me, then don't, but I know you. I know your body language, and there have been more than a few close calls between you two.'

Natty began pacing again, sighing.

'We kissed.'

After hearing nothing from Spence, he turned to face his friend.

'And?'

'And nothing. We kissed, and I pulled away.'

'Are you going to do anything about it?' Spence had a calculating look on his face.

'No,' said Natty. 'It shouldn't have happened. It won't happen again.'

'Just like that?'

'Just like that,' affirmed Natty. 'Let's focus on business. Get an address for this Danielle chick, and we can tail her . . . see if she leads us to Keith.'

———

KEITH INHALED as he lifted the heavy dumbbells, exhaling as he lowered them. Living from spot to spot made it challenging to hit the gym, meaning he was forced to train with basic weights wherever possible. He finished his set and made a protein shake, staring out the kitchen window, deep in thought. He and Roman were staying at separate spots now. The Dunns had made things difficult by putting money on their heads, which limited their ability to move around further.

Keith wasn't sure who to trust, meaning he kept fewer men around him, not that he thought he needed them.

As was typical, he thought over the conflict with the Dunns. Slowly, the money was drying up, and even the fact their drugs were more potent wasn't swaying people. Keith had expected people to flock to them. They were linked to the last true kingpins of Leeds. They'd stood tall, rather than snitch, yet they were seen as troublemakers who had broken the peace and prevented numerous teams from making real money.

Keith didn't like that things were so strained between him and Roman. They had been friends for a long time, but the situation with the Dunns had tested them, and the cracks were forming. Roman was smart, and he was driven, but he'd softened over the years, and Keith knew one thing above all else; there was no room in their world for being soft. He couldn't let Roman hold him back.

When they'd taken out the Dunns, he would need to think hard about the next move.

Regardless, he thought to himself, Manson would be on his side.

He shared the same opinion of Roman, and Keith was already thinking of the heights they could ascend to.

One thing at a time, though, he cautioned himself. There was still plenty to do.

Grabbing his phone, he sent a text message to Danielle, telling her to come and keep him company.

Keith had met Danielle after he got out of prison. She'd told him what she did for a living, and he hadn't minded, only wanting sex from her. He didn't mind paying for it, and didn't care what she did when she wasn't around him. After giving her the usual instructions, he went to take a shower and get ready.

———

SPENCE SIGHED as he put the phone down. Natty was also talking on his phone, his voice low and urgent. Spence waited for him to finish.

'We've got a lead on this Danielle girl's house. I'm gonna take some people, head over there, and follow her, see where she goes,' said Natty. He finally noticed the tense expression on Spence's face. 'What's wrong?'

'Nothing,' said Spence. 'Just Rosie doing my head in. Sometimes, she's okay; the next, she's paranoid I'm gonna die.'

'It's sweet that she cares about you. I get it in the neck from Lorraine every time I see her. You just have to allow it, bro.'

'I know,' said Spence. Natty patted him on the shoulder, then went to leave the room. 'Nat, wait a sec.'

'What's up?' Natty paused.

'I want to come.'

Natty's mouth fell open as he stared at Spence.

'You what?'

'I want to come with you. If Keith or any of them are around, I want to be there.'

'Spence . . .' Natty started.

'No, Nat. I can't explain it, but I need to be there . . . this is something I need to prove to myself.'

'You don't need to prove anything,' said Natty. 'I know what you're all about, Spence.'

Spence folded his arms, his jaw tight.

'I'm not trying to prove anything for anyone else. I said it's for me, and I mean that. I'm coming.'

Neither man spoke for a moment. Natty blew out a breath.

'You really think you need to be there?'

Spence nodded. 'I know I do.'

'Fine. Hurry up and let's go. We'll strap up on the way.'

'SHE LOOKS DRESSED UP, doesn't she?'

'She does,' agreed Natty, as their driver followed Danielle's Uber. She was a thin woman, with silky black hair in a ponytail, honey-shaded skin and haughty features. She didn't look familiar to Natty, but that didn't matter.

'I hope that means she's going to see him,' Spence continued. Besides him and Natty, two of Clarke's best shooters were in the car with them, one behind the wheel.

'Even if it doesn't, we'll keep on her. She's our best chance at finding Keith,' said Natty.

They drove to a house in Wortley. When Danielle entered the house, they pulled up. Natty, Spence and one of Clarke's men climbed from the car, the driver keeping the engine running. They had on balaclavas, just in case, each man armed. The soldier led the way, Spence following, Natty bringing up the rear.

Carelessly, Danielle had left the front door unlocked, making it easy for the trio to enter the house. Treading carefully over the floorboards, Natty signalled for Clarke's soldier to go upstairs. Spence opened the living room door, then shots rang out.

KEITH HAD SENT Danielle to the kitchen to get them some drinks. He had some cocaine and a few pills for them to take, placing them on the coffee table. He thought he heard the door open, and paused. Thinking he was being paranoid, he ignored it, but when he heard the creak of the floorboards outside the living room door, he reacted instantly, going for the gun he'd placed on the table. The door opened, and he fired, grinning as he caught a masked man in the shoulder, sending them back with a piercing shriek. Before he could do anything else, he heard a yell, then a searing pain toppled him.

Dizzy and bleeding, Keith held his stomach as the man who'd shot him stepped into the room. He tried lifting his gun, ignoring Danielle's screams, but his arm felt too heavy. The man aimed the gun at him again.

———

NATTY HAD INSTINCTIVELY REACTED. He'd heard the gunshot, seeing Spence fall in slow motion. Seeing red, he fired, hitting Keith in the stomach. He stepped over Spence, approaching his downed foe, who was bleeding from the mouth, trying to lift his gun. Natty ignored Danielle's scream, aiming the gun at Keith's head. For a second, he hesitated, then taking a deep breath, he fired, the bullet slamming Keith's head back. He fired twice more, into the body this time, then aimed the gun at Danielle, who was frozen in the doorway to the kitchen.

'Shut your fucking mouth. Stop screaming and lie on the floor on your stomach.'

Danielle hurried to comply. Natty rushed to Spence's side. He was sat up now, breathing hard and hissing in pain.

'Are you okay?'

'I'm fine,' said Spence, shakily getting to his feet. 'Check on the other dude.'

Natty nodded, hurrying upstairs.

'It's me,' he called, gun raised, just in case the soldier didn't know it was him. He checked each room, finding no one until he saw the soldier — Tony — in the bathroom, standing over a downed man. He turned to Natty, nodding.

'He never saw me coming. I just knocked him out. I heard shots downstairs. Did you get him?'

Natty lifted the downed man to see his face. When he didn't recognise him, he dropped him back down.

'Yeah,' he said. 'Keith is down. Spence took a shot to the shoulder. We'll get out of here, get him some help, then hit the other spots we know about. Maybe we'll get lucky and find Roman.'

Tony nodded, and they hurried back downstairs. Natty put the gun to Danielle's head, not enjoying her terrified whimpers.

'You saw nothing. You heard nothing. We know who you are, *Danielle* . . . don't make us have to come for you,' he warned. Danielle nodded, still whimpering.

Natty helped Spence from the house, bundling him into the car, which drove away.

———

ONCE NATTY HAD SITUATED Spence at a safe house on Rigton Drive in LS9, they called a doctor on payroll to stitch him up. Natty's adrenaline hadn't abated. He'd felt nothing when he killed Keith, wondering if that was how it would be for him from now on. He found he didn't mind, willing to do whatever it took to protect his people. It was still surprising compared to his reactions after killing Rudy and Elijah, but he had changed since then. He'd left that part of him behind, understanding why he'd done it.

If push came to shove, he would do it again.

'Everything is in place,' said Tony. It had been less than an hour since they'd killed Keith. Natty didn't know if the word would have spread yet, but they would need to move quickly, while they still had the element of surprise.

'Let's go,' said Natty, grabbing his 9mm. 'Tell everyone to move in.'

———

THE CREW WAS IN PLACE. Over a dozen men, Natty included, attacked three spots held by Roman. The plan was to raid the spots, and take out anyone inside.

Natty checked his gun as one of his men kicked open the door to a spot on Hillcrest Avenue. He charged through the house, straight into a room, dropping to the floor as shots went off above him. His quick action saved him, but not his comrade, who took a shot to the head and toppled backwards. The shooter turned his gun on Natty, who was quicker, two shots slamming into the man's neck and jaw. Springing to his feet, he charged into another room, a large man getting to his feet.

Natty recognised Manson, seeing the surprise in the man's eyes as he recognised him too. Manson's eyes narrowed, but he was too slow on the draw, and Natty shot him in the leg. With a grunt of pain, Manson crumpled to the ground, holding his left thigh, gritting his teeth. He looked up at Natty, his eyes a question.

'You lot started this,' said Natty, firing again.

EPILOGUE

MAY 2021

NATTY SAT in his car on a street in Little London, tapping his fingers on the wheel. He had the engine off, but a gun within reach, just in case.

Two days had passed, and the ramifications of the move Natty had made were in full swing. Roman's crew were on the back foot, with few showing their faces after what had transpired.

The streets were talking about the moves, shocked by the quick murders of Manson and Keith. With Roman in the wind, all the momentum was with the Dunns, with many crowning them the winners of the conflict.

The weather had improved over the past two days, the sun shining in the sky. Despite that, Natty still wore a hooded top with an insulated hood, along with a pair of woolly gloves.

Natty tensed as a car pulled up nearby. Detective Brown pulled up, sliding from the car. Schooling his face, Natty mirrored the action, leaving the gun.

'You've been a busy boy, haven't you?' said Brown, smirking. He was dressed similar to Natty, wearing a hooded top, a jacket over it, and Gore-tex boots.

'Am I supposed to know what you're talking about?' said Natty.

'You've made a lot of my colleagues very interested, Deeds. You pulled some big moves, and your name is ringing out.' His smile widened. 'Don't worry. I'll protect you, fam.'

'You're not my family,' said Natty coldly. He reached into the folds of his hooded top, handing Brown a stack of notes. 'Count if you want. Two bags, as we agreed.'

Brown counted the money, nodding in approval.

'It's a start, Deeds. I'll be in touch,' he finished, walking away. Natty glared after him, but decided he was a problem for another time. Climbing back in the car, he drove to see Spence.

When he entered the house, Natty noted Spence resting on the sofa, watching television, his left arm in a sling. He smiled when he saw Natty.

'How are you doing? I wasn't sure if you needed anything,' said Natty.

'I've got everything I need,' said Spence. 'It'll be a while before I recover, so I guess I've got time to regroup, mentally check myself.'

'I have no idea what that means, but I'm glad you're good,' said Natty.

'Don't worry about me. What do you have going on? You know Roman's still out there, right? He's gonna come for us.'

'I know,' said Natty.

'You took out Manson. He's old school, Natty. He has friends.'

'I know he does, Spence. He had his gun on me. It was kill or be killed.'

'I get that, but just keep watching your back. I'm sorry I can't do it properly for now.'

'You've done more than enough, Spence. You took a bullet in the line of duty. Now, you can hang back, keep an eye on things and stay out of the mix.'

'I could have done more,' said Spence, sounding chastened.

'Oi,' said Natty, raising his voice, startling Spence. 'You did enough. Keith was faster. That's it. I was slightly faster than he was, but it could have easily gone the other way. There's no point thinking about it any other way.'

Spence nodded, but didn't look fully convinced.

'I mean it, Spence. You're my brother. I don't want you feeling bad over anything that happened.'

'Okay, bro. I won't,' replied Spence, smiling.

Spence's dad came out of the kitchen, nodding at Natty when he noticed him.

'How are you doing, Wayne?' Natty asked, surprised to see him there.

'I'm good. Took the day off to care for my little boy here,' Wayne replied. Natty laughed, and even Spence gave a good-natured chuckle.

'It's good he's got you looking out for him then,' said Natty. Wayne surveyed him for a moment.

'He told me what you did for him. You got the guy that tried to end his life . . .' Wayne bowed his head for a moment, Natty able to feel his pain at the thought of losing his son. 'Thank you, Nathaniel.'

'He's my brother, Wayne. I wasn't going to let him go out like that.'

Wayne rubbed the top of Spence's head, then stepped away. When he looked at Natty, his eyes were hard, and Natty could see the man Wayne had once been when he was deep in the streets.

'I don't know all of it, but they're gonna come for you. You need to be ready, Nathaniel. You all do.'

———

MITCH DUNN RECLINED in his home office, watching as Clarke made himself comfortable. He'd already poured glasses of premium brandy for them both. The room had cream walls, with dark furniture, and several books dotted around. He tended to divide his time between this room and his makeshift gym in the garage, but enjoyed sitting back with a drink and contemplating the life he'd created for himself.

'Talk me through it,' he said to Clarke, who took a deep sip of his drink before speaking.

'They got Keith. He was one of the main troublemakers. Fresh out of prison, with a reputation for being able to handle himself. Natty got him, and he got Manson too. You remember him from back in the day, I'm guessing.'

Mitch nodded, smiling. 'My nephew's killer instinct is growing. If he's half as good as you've been saying, he's gonna be the best out of everyone.'

'We still need to get to Roman. Everyone had him pegged as the brains of the operation,' said Clarke.

'We're in a solid position to do so. Keep up the pressure, and make sure everyone remains on high alert.'

Clarke nodded, knowing the drill. He took another sip of his drink, then cleared his throat.

'One thing I don't get . . . why did we need to bring Natty back full time? He was already helping us regardless.'

Mitch grinned at his subordinate.

'Natty was born to do what we do, Clarke. He's an investment; a long-term one, that is finally paying off. More importantly, he's family . . . the last real family I have. I want to keep him close to me.'

Clarke rubbed his chin. 'When was the last time you spoke to him? He seems a little tense lately.'

Mitch shrugged. 'He's always been emotional. His dad was the same way.' His piercing eyes locked onto Clarke's. 'Something else for you to work on with him.'

Clarke nodded and savoured his drink. He had his marching orders.

———

ROMAN SMOKED HIS CIGARETTE, his thoughts clouded. He stood in the middle of a room, thinking about the last few days, and all that had transpired. The Dunns had struck cleanly and efficiently, proving once again that they were an enemy to be taken seriously. Keith . . . his oldest friend . . . was dead. Roman had cried, and he had ranted, and now he wasn't sure what to feel.

Toward Manson, Roman felt apathy. He seemed to be the catalyst for Keith's change. In the end, he suspected they were scheming together, conspiring against him. It backfired, and Roman tried hard to remember Keith for the man he was before Manson poisoned him.

Now, Roman was the sole voice in charge. He was at war, and ready to go all the way.

'You've hidden yourself away well,' Ahmed remarked as he entered the room. He wore a grey overcoat, trousers and a shirt, looking surprisingly groomed. 'I'm sorry about your associates' deaths.'

'Thank you,' replied Roman.

'I'm sure you have considered this, but you could likely arrange another sit-down, now that your partner is out of the way.'

Roman shook his head.

'There's no going back,' he said.

Ahmed beamed.

———

SPENCE TURNED FROM THE TELEVISION, glancing at Rosie, who sat at his side with a face like thunder. She had been like this ever since she'd learned of his injury, and he understood why. He had promised her he wouldn't get hurt, and then he'd gotten shot.

It was humiliating, but he was trying to push past it. Natty had been forced to rescue him, after he'd insisted on being part of the team. He knew Natty had been right in what he'd said, though. It could have easily been the other way around, and that was a sobering thought.

'Rosie, I really am sorry,' he said.

'If you were, you wouldn't have gotten shot,' she said, still staring at the television. 'You promised me.'

'I know I did, and I'm sorry, I truly am. It couldn't be helped.'

'It could have been helped, Spence! Don't act like everyone is out there getting shot.' Now, she looked his way.

'I'm not, but you have to understand that you're with a man who takes his responsibilities seriously. You know that. I won't throw myself in danger. I want us to have a long and happy life together, but this is what I am. This is what I do, and I need you to support me.'

Rosie sighed, snuggling against him, taking care not to touch his injured arm.

'It'll take some time, Spence, but I'll be okay. Just please, be careful.'

'I will,' said Spence. 'Fancy coming out for some fresh air? I've been inside all day.'

Rosie shook her head. 'You go, babe. I'm going to get in the bath. You don't mind me staying the night, do you?'

Spence laughed. 'Even if I said no, you'd stay anyway.'

'You know me so well.' Rosie stuck out her tongue as she headed upstairs. Still smiling, Spence went outside, breathing deeply. He planned to take a few more days off, then he would go back to work. He was in two minds about speaking to Natty about specialised training. Even though Natty had only been training with Clarke a short time, he'd seen an overall improvement. Spence had noted he seemed more alert, and stronger in a way. More solid. If Spence was going to be alongside him, he was determined not to let the side down. Feeling his phone vibrating, he grabbed it, frowning at the number, not recognising the caller.

'Hello?'

'Spence?' a familiar voice said. Spence's legs buckled for a moment, his skin tingling with discomfort.

'Anika?'

———

LATER, Natty, Lorraine and Jaden approached Tyrone Dunn's gravesite. Natty and Lorraine held hands, Jaden running slightly ahead of them. Natty smiled as he looked at the gravestone, absorbing the words as he always did, pleased he hadn't left it so long this time. It felt like a lifetime since he had visited, but in reality, was just over three months. He couldn't count on both hands the number of things that had happened since.

'This is your dad then?' asked Jaden. Natty nodded.

'That's right. *Tyrone Dunn* . . . my old man.'

'You told me you were young when he died, right?' Jaden asked, looking to Natty for his reaction. Next to him, Lorraine squeezed his hand, but let her men talk.

'I was eleven, only a bit older than you. He was my world, and it was never the same after he died. He was a good man, J. I never had to doubt his love for me. He showed it every day, and he taught me to be strong; to stand on my own two feet, and to never back down.'

Jaden smiled, but Natty wasn't sure if he actually understood what he was saying.

'Do you think I'll be strong when I'm older, Natty?'

'Come here,' said Natty. Jaden walked over, and Natty pulled him against him, hugging both Lorraine and Jaden.

'You're strong now, J. As you get older, that will only grow. You just need to keep working, on your body *and* your mind. You'll be absolutely fine.'

The hug between the trio continued. Natty tuned out, his thoughts returning to the issues still ahead. There was still plenty to do. Brown remained a potential problem. Roman was still out there, biding his time. There was also Lisa. He hadn't spoken to her since their kiss at the safe house . . . a kiss he couldn't stop thinking about, despite his guilt.

Above all, his uncle, Mitch Dunn, was still at large, and he and Natty had unfinished business. Whether Natty ever forgave his mum, Mitch Dunn would receive no reprieve.

At his dad's gravesite, the man his uncle Mitch had betrayed, Natty inwardly vowed to kill him.

Even if it destroyed the entire Dunn organisation.

ALSO BY RICKY BLACK

ABOUT RICKY BLACK

Ricky Black was born and raised in Chapeltown, Leeds.

In 2016, he published the first of his crime series, Target, and has published ten more books since.

Visit https://rickyblackbooks.com for information regarding new releases and special offers, and promotions.